The Music of an *Unequal* Love

\- A Venture in Romance –

Gigi Stybr

The Music of an *Unequal* Love

Liebe Sibylle ~
Dieses Buch ist ein Geschenk
von Dorothee aus Stuttgart.
Ich hoffe, Sie werden es
mit Freude u. Spannung
lesen.

Herzliche Grüsse,
Gigi Stybr

Okt. 2011

- A Venture in Romance -

Gigi Stybr

Gigi Stybr

The Music of an *Unequal* Love

- A Venture in Romance –

Gigi Stybr

Gigi Stybr

Published by G and P Stybr Press
P.O. Box 3834
Mission Viejo, CA 92690
U.S.A.

Library of Congress Cataloging-in-Publication Data

Stybr, Gigi
The Music of an Unequal Love
ISBN-13 9780615391106
ISBN-10 0615391109

Cover design by Alixandra Mullins: http://alixandramullins.com

For my husband Purcell
who shows me the true
meaning of love.

The Music of an Unequal Love

The power of music,
The power of love,
Their gifts of joy, their wings of grace,
Their sparks of blessings and surprises,
As a glimpse of the divine,
Filling the vast space of life...

And with a single spark
Setting afire our trembling hearts
To make us recognize the do-ability
Of the assumed impossible:
To rise above the prison of duality:
Fighting or taking flight from one's opponent.

On the wings of love and music
We trust to lift off into the unknown,
With grace, and unburdened of weight,
To listen to the silent song
Of tenderness, forgiveness, letting-go
And moving on.

This song is written in a much higher key,
Beyond the staff-lines of a human composition,
To be heard only in the bell-like overtones
Of an angel's voice within.

Gigi Stybr
June 2010

Acknowledgements

My thanks go out to everyone who inspired me to write this novel: musicians, singers, soloists, orchestra conductors, record producers, editors and sound engineers. I appreciate their kindness in sharing their day-to-day reality and the practical aspects of music making. I am grateful for their insights into creating and conducting a performance and their knowledge of music history.

I would like to thank my friend, Dr. Herta Fechner, who is no longer with us, for her constructive criticism and her humor.

My sincere thanks go out to Richard Andrew King who inspired me to make a new start with his valuable advice as a Master Numerologist. Richard is also helping me to surmount the technical hurdles of uploading this book to the internet. Without him, my manuscript would still just be a word document on my computer. My heartfelt gratitude, Richard!
www.richardking.net

I would like to thank my dear friend, Rosemary Serafin, (also called *Honeybunch*), for volunteering to read the first draft of the revised version of this book. I gladly followed her suggestion to add a musical and culinary glossary at the end of the book. Big thanks, *Honeybunch,* for your patience, editing and (surprising) comments.

I consider myself very lucky to have found Alixandra Mullins for the cover design. Thank you, Alix, for your patience, reliability and creativity. My book *loves* your cover! http://alixandramullins.com.

My thanks go out to Chyanna Davis for creating my web site, www.gigistybr.com, which is like a calling-card for this book. Chyanna, your ideas, creativity and ingenuity are highly appreciated. www.powerfulsitedesign.com.

Most of all, I'm grateful to my husband Purcell who helped me with saintly patience as my editor, advisor, linguist and cheer leader, and without whose encouragement this book would have remained unwritten.

Last but not least I feel a deep and sincere gratitude for all the gifted composers of the past, and especially for those who became part of my story – Beethoven, Brahms, Mozart, Schubert, Verdi, Berlioz, Mahler and Corelli. Without their genius, vision and relentless creativity we would live in an unimaginably emptier world, a world without the splendor of their music.

Introduction

In a Manhattan coffee shop the renowned orchestra conductor, Orson Mahler, explains to a young woman from Austria: *Isabella, conducting is merely making love to music. No detail should be left unattended to bring out the best in music... or in a woman. If a piece of music is worth performing and a woman is worth making love to, it's worth giving it your best.*

Isabella's recollections of the maestro go back to her native Austria where her mother was once a fan of Mahler. Isabella now lives in the U.S. and is happily married to James, who loves her deeply. In the elevator of her office building she meets Beverly, a member of Orson Mahler's chorus. When Isabella and the maestro meet, she is disappointed by his looks and lack of warmth. But soon she becomes captivated by the magnificence of his music and his enigmatic personality.

Isabella enters Mahler's entourage as an unwelcome outsider. Joan, the manager of Mahler's chorus, openly claims the maestro's heart, and Paula Mahler stands firmly by her husband. Beverly turns into Isabella's greatest rival. It seems that her only friend and ally is Matthew, a young pianist.

For Isabella the music, the maestro and the man become one and she struggles with an impossible attraction. Gradually, Mahler draws Isabella into his world of splendor, secrecy and surprises. James is unaware that his wife has become entrapped in a web of forbidden romance and the shadows of the past…

The Music of an Unequal Love takes us into the heart of 1986 New York City, its busy streets, office buildings, art galleries, rehearsal venues, recording studios, Lincoln Center, Carnegie Hall and Central Park.

We also visit the beautiful, clear mountain lake in Austria that Isabella left behind.

For many years Gigi Stybr worked for a major classical music label in New York, where she became acquainted with all aspects of music-making. She attended rehearsals, concerts, recording sessions, and also sang in a chorus. She feels honored to have met some of the finest musicians, singers, soloists and orchestra conductors of our time who generously shared their insight and love for the music they created.

It is Gigi Stybr's heartfelt wish to convey the joy and excitement that this timeless music can bring to our lives. She would like you to accept Maestro Mahler's invitation to *Just sit back and let the music wash over you.*

All characters are fictional.

To order copies or learn more
about the creation of the book,
please visit:

www.gigistybr.com

The Music of an Unequal Love

Table of Contents

Part One

- Allegro –

(Enchantment, Desire)

There is nothing good or bad,
but thinking makes it so.

William Shakespeare

Prologue

I caught my first glimpse of Orson Mahler when he was not wearing his dark glasses. I had expected him to have them on, because Beverly had warned me that he never went outside with his eyes uncovered. She said he wore dark glasses to protect his private person from his public face, and that he felt his public image was a barrier between him and other people, that his fame prevented him from being free.

Familiar to music lovers all over the world, Maestro Mahler's much-photographed face was on records, posters, programs and, sometimes in gossip columns.

On this day in May 1986, he was standing at the corner of Madison Avenue and Forty-Ninth Street, wearing a light-gray suit and carrying a briefcase. He had just reached the top step of a platform leading to the small restaurant where Beverly and I were to meet him for lunch.

He stood there, very still, looking out over the midday traffic, the traffic that prevented me from joining him from across the street. It was odd to think that this famous man was waiting for me.

Under the protection of the faceless crowd, I felt free to look at him, because we had never met and he was used to being stared at. But I also missed a feeling that I had expected to experience but didn't. To be awe-struck. It was a sobering sensation to see someone so well-known in the reality of flesh and blood and find nothing about him that would make me turn around and look again.

Still waiting for a break in the never-ending yellow stream of cabs, I found myself thinking, He is quite ordinary looking, with his gray, thinning hair and disappointing shortness of stature, in contrast to the impression projected by his presence on the podium.

Does fame automatically glamorize a person in our minds and raise our expectations above reality? If I were a celebrity, that thought would bother me and probably make me wear dark glasses too, as Orson Mahler usually did. To see, but not to be seen. To keep others at a distance. He wore them, though, he told me later, only to block out the bright daylight, because he was a night-owl and preferred darkness to the glaring sun.

And now, although the lights had turned to red, a policeman in the middle of the intersection kept the traffic moving, making it impossible to cross the street.

I changed the strap of my purse to my right shoulder and looked at him again. His eyes caught mine and held them in a brief grip of quiet power. Even now his face bespoke nothing of the awe of the world's greatest concert halls or the splendor of the music he conducted. He exuded none of the grandeur of the Beethoven symphonies or the fire of a Verdi aria. His face was like a fine-boned mask, immobile, uninvolved and pale.

How on earth was it possible that my mother could have had a crush on this man for two decades or more? But I realized I was thinking with my mind, not hers.

My recollection of Orson Mahler as an orchestra conductor went back to my childhood and adolescent years in Austria, where I grew up. My mother loved Orson Mahler's recordings of the Brahms and Beethoven symphonies, and in time the symphonies became synonymous with the maestro's features on the record jackets. As a teenager listening to Beethoven's *Ode to Joy*, I used to linger over pictures showing Orson Mahler in his tails, smiling, standing on the podium, waving his baton or drinking hot chocolate during a rehearsal. Over the years Maestro Mahler's face grew older and his pictures turned from black-and-white to color. They were much more interesting and lively than another picture I lingered over, that of my father.

My father's black-and-white portrait stood in a silver frame on one of our bookshelves. Unlike the Mahler pictures, it showed no arms or legs, and the man on it never got any older. Both of these men had in common the fact that they were far away, across the Atlantic, unreachable and unrelated to my mother's life and mine. Both men were the same age.

Sometimes I thought I knew more about the conductor than about my father. I knew that Orson Mahler had gray eyes, but I had forgotten the color of my father's and never dared to ask my mother. Sometimes when she was not there I would look at the silver-framed face and say his name: Franz, although I had never called him anything but *Papa*.

My mother never talked about him, and I respected her wish to remain silent, because I could guess all too well the things she didn't say. You, Franz, who vowed to be my husband, you left me with this delicate, dreamy daughter, this big house and garden to take care of and all the bills to pay. Why are you not here sharing your life with me? Don't you know that your money is no substitute for our marriage? Why have you deserted me? I'll never forgive you for that.

During those years the silent approach in her eyes seemed justified, but weighed like a heavy burden on my young, growing mind. As she and I sat on the large Oriental rug in our living room, listening to Brahms, the big stack of Orson Mahler records leaned against the new hi-fi equipment like a shield against her sadness. Years later, when I was twenty-three and had married James and moved with him to the U.S., I recognized the same silent reproach in her eyes. Isabella, why are you deserting me? You too. Everybody does.

After I had left, her love for books and music remained with her as a reliable companion, and her records became a squadron of bodyguards against loneliness and fear. I was never certain, though, whether her love was for the music of Beethoven or Brahms or for the music conducted by her favorite maestro. I remember her looking over the gold rim of her glasses, counting the stitches of her needle-work, as she explained to me that orchestra conductors have a magic of their own.

A man like Orson Mahler, she said, is caught in the spotlight of the podium and becomes the focal point of the performance, the mastermind of music-making, shaping the sounds and leading the orchestra as a bridge to the public and a messenger between the players and the composer's intentions.

My mother changed the color of the thread she was working with. In a voice that was part lecturing, part love-struck, she told me that a conductor should serve only the composition but never himself. Watching him should provide an insight into the music, but if he draws too much attention to himself, rather than communicating the inner content of the work, he fails the music.

My mother gave a little sigh and resumed her needlework. I sensed that, besides her conductor-cult attraction to Orson Mahler, the musician, there was also an unquenched curiosity for Orson Mahler, the man. She always wanted to hear him speak, because the maestro was widely known as "the man with the velvet voice." He was supposed to have a commanding voice that persuaded, soothed and stroked. It was said to have the feel of velvet. He was also known to have a small birthmark on his upper left lip, a little black pearl that he could have easily hidden by growing a mustache, but then, a Maestro Mahler with a mustache was unthinkable.

My mother collected newspaper clippings and photos in her correspondence folder. I never looked at them, not out of respect for privacy, but simply lack of interest. She said the press depicted him as a man who worked at a high level of intensity with his singers and musicians and was often seen with them away from the studio or stage. He didn't seem to mind being photographed with them in public. In those pictures he never wore a wedding band.

Was he married? If so, his wife had not accompanied him on the concert tour through Europe, the only time my mother had actually met her idol face to face. It was some twenty years ago that she had attended his concert at the *Musikverein* in Vienna and had gone backstage to ask for his autograph.

And there he was, wearing black tails and a magic smile, she later told me breathlessly. She had heard that some of his fans had given him the middle name of Magic. Orson *Magic* Mahler. How appropriate. How well she knew him without knowing him at all.

Because she had spent so much time listening to his records, she had developed her own intimate relationship with him and was surprised to find that, except for an impersonal smile, she received nothing from him in return. Without looking at her or asking for her name, he had hastily scribbled his signature on the back of her program. In this pushing back-stage crowd she had not even heard "the man with the velvet voice" say "hello" or "good-bye." She had wanted to ask him how he liked Vienna, the city of so many composers, but his aloofness and the abundance of his female fans had discouraged her. She didn't even have a chance to take a look at his birthmark, his black pearl, let alone ask him how he liked his stay in Vienna. She felt that she had splurged on *Eau de Joy* for nothing. My mother had finally got Mahler's autograph, but had lost her illusions.

Coming home to our house on the lake, she simply said, "It's his music. That's his gift. It's the only gift he is capable of giving." And then she paused a little and opened a window with the view on the lake and inhaled the fresh air. "Maybe Orson Mahler can inspire dreams, but then he leaves them with you to dream for yourself. Orson Mahler can supply dreams, but not share them. At least I got that feeling about him." She smiled to herself and caught the curtains in the blowing wind.

And now, twenty years later, I tried to imagine my mother's face as she would read my letter. Last week I had been to a concert at Avery Fisher Hall where Maestro Mahler had conducted Beethoven, and today I would be having lunch with him. The invitation to the concert had come from my friend Julia, and the suggestion for today's lunch had come from Beverly, whom I had met in the elevator of my office building.

The sound of sirens forced me back into the present. At last the traffic light showed "Walk" but three ear-splitting fire engines forced their way down Forty-Ninth Street and turned right into Madison. They held me back but didn't block my view of Maestro Mahler, or his of me. The directness of his stare made me wish he had his dark glasses on, or I mine. I tried to stop the power of his gaze as though I were a red light, but in the asphalt jungle of Manhattan a red light didn't mean a thing.

The blast of the sirens subsided, and the traffic light showed "Don't Walk" again. I played with the dangling belt of my raincoat. Why wasn't Beverly here yet? I wished I had left the office five minutes later and taken the time to make another cappuccino for Mr. Stringer. What if Beverly didn't show up and left me alone with the world-renowned maestro? It didn't make sense that she asked me to join them in the first place, especially since she wanted to go over his portfolio with him. What was Beverly's reason to ask me along? In the elevator I had expressed a certain curiosity about meeting Mr. Mahler, but who wouldn't? He would hardly be interested in meeting still another female fan who would ask him for an autograph for her mother.

I looked up again. He was standing in the same spot as before, at the top of the steps leading to the restaurant. His face was immobile, but there was an underlying expression in his eyes, exuding that irritating self-assurance of someone who was used to getting his way too fast. I felt his eyes on me, like lights, trying to expose my every thought in public.

The long chain of cars and cabs still hadn't broken up, postponing from instant to instant my crossing the line from innocence to knowing. It occurred to me that there was still time to turn around and leave. I could offer the pretense of a meeting at the office or an upset stomach. I could call Beverly later and apologize for not being able to come. Orson Mahler, never having met me, could not complain of my absence. I wasn't even sure that Beverly had told him my name. Yes, I could still walk away and undo everything that was about to happen.

I stepped from the sidewalk, hesitating, holding on to my purse and the belt of my coat. Across the street, Orson Mahler's eyes touched me from head to toe. I sensed their lure, their invitation. They seemed to whisper. *Look at me. I'm here. I'm not going anyway. I'm waiting. I'm ready for you. Whenever you are, I am. Come.*

Suddenly all the cabs and cars had disappeared and the street was free to cross. On the other side, this ordinary-looking man stood, controlled and cool, like a stranger in an ominous dream from which I could no longer escape. I had to cross the street before the weakness in my knees got worse. I would walk up to him and be factual and friendly. I'd say, "I'm Isabella Barton. I'm supposed to meet you and Beverly. I'm honored to meet you, Maestro Mahler."

1

Beverly and I worked in the same office building on Park Avenue. It was one of those all-glass, all-steel monstrosities with sixteen elevators, forty-five floors, a corps of uniformed security guards and a building staff that had just ended a strike.

Ever since I had started working there five months before, it was Beverly's face in the ever-changing crowd that I noticed again and again, because it was impossible not to notice her. There was something in the pride with which she refused to acknowledge anyone else, or with which she shook her mane of red curls, that seemed to stimulate the air around her. Her high forehead and her olive eyes behind thick, horn-rimmed glassed suggested her ability to think, and a galaxy of funny-looking freckles was sprinkled like stars across her face. But Beverly was more than the sum of her red hair, olive eyes or funny-looking freckles, her overall allure was an overture to fun and flirting.

When she crossed the lobby in her four-inch heels the place started to revolve around her. Every man's head turned in her direction, but she only cast a long, arching look above all of them, knowing that a head that turned was like a knee that bent. Lawyers, lobby guards and CEO's would mentally fluff their peacock tails in shared awareness of her presence.

One morning she and I found ourselves in the same elevator. I had picked up a copy of the *New York Times* for Mr. Stringer and pushed the button for thirty-four. She stepped in behind me and pushed thirty. It was after the morning rush-hour and no one else followed. The doors closed. Suddenly alone with her, I pretended to read the inspection certificate on the wall, fearing that she might have seen me staring at her on previous occasions.

There is no escape route in an elevator, though, and the energy of her presence behind me made me turn around. Through her thick glasses her eyes seemed strangely magnified. She gave me a scrutinizing look. What did she think of me? In an elevator going up thirty-four floors, what would anyone think of a tall, blond woman in a yellow suit and a white blouse, carrying a copy of the *New York Times*? Would anyone think that her nose was too large or her breasts too small? Would anyone guess that she didn't like her boss, that she loved to collect paperweights or that her husband was out of work?

Suddenly the elevator slowed down, stopped, started to descend and shuddered to a stop between the nineteenth and twentieth floors. My stomach danced like a yo-yo.

"We're stuck," she said. Her voice was high-pitched.

"I'm afraid so." I grasped the handrail.

We looked at each other.

"No need to worry." She laughed and made a dismissive gesture with her hands. She carried no purse.

"Should we push the alarm button?" I wanted her approval.

At precisely that moment an alarm went off somewhere in the building.

"I don't think it's necessary," she said, "The whole elevator system is messed up. They'll find us... and uh... if you don't mind, could I borrow your paper for a sccond?" She snatched the paper out of my hands before I had a chance to hand it to her. "I'm looking for an article that's supposed to appear today." She flipped the pages with incredible speed. "It's the concert review of Orson Mahler's performance at Avery Fisher Hall last Friday. I was singing in the chorus."

"What a coincidence," I said, "I was at that concert with my friend Julia."

"Small word, isn't it?" She didn't seem to be impressed and ran her pink nail down the page to the review. "Here it is. Since you were there, do you want me to read it to you?"

She didn't wait for my reply. Being trapped in an elevator obviously quickened her reflexes but slowed mine.

In Friday's performance of Beethoven's Ninth Symphony, Orson Mahler led his chorus and the New York Philharmonic to heights of brilliance and delicate shades of tone color. Although some tempos almost seemed willfully languid, Mahler's mark is grandeur. His hands are overwhelmingly expressive and were unfailingly in command throughout the whole work, which he conducted from memory. In the choral movement he maintained a beautiful balance among soloists, chorus and orchestra.....

As she read I watched her freckled skin stretched economically across her face, just enough to cover every bone. I also noticed her small nose and large breasts.

She went on, *...the Orson Mahler Oratorio Chorus was at its best and put its finely blended sound to the service of elucidating the splendor of Beethoven. The orchestra responded alertly to Mahler's cues and phrasing indications, which leads one to think that the musicians might actually enjoy performing for him. The maestro left no doubt about his solid internalization of this masterpiece. Beethoven himself would have felt honored.*

She had scarcely paused for breath so I jumped in quickly. "It's a good review."

She closed the paper. "Good? Are you kidding? It's an incredible review. He couldn't buy a review as good as this."

I drew a deep breath and took the paper from her. After all, it *was* for Mr. Stringer. She smiled, as if congratulating herself on an achievement. For a moment her unspoiled ease erased the frightening feeling of being trapped.

She said, "I hope he's seen it. I'll call him as soon as I get upstairs."

"Who, Maestro Orson Mahler?"

"Of course, Orson Mahler. I've been a member of his chorus for ten years. I sing soprano. I'm also his investment broker. I tell him where to put his money."

I wanted to add, "How interesting," but she was faster.

"You have a cute accent. Where are you from?"

"From Austria. I was born and raised there."

She pushed her glasses up on her nose. "My husband and I took a tour of Vienna, Innsbruck and Salzburg three years ago. Orson was conducting in Salzburg at the festival. He had given us tickets for all his concerts but we sold them on the black market for three times their value. Rudy doesn't care for symphonic music that much. And from the profit we could afford to stay a few days longer."

She took a quick look at my wedding ring and I knew she'd ask about James.

"Is your husband Austrian too?"

"He's American, but we met in Pörtschach, my home town, twelve years ago."

"Oh," she said, "that sounds so romantic." But then she immediately talked about Orson Mahler's love for Austrian *Sachertorte* and *Mozartkugeln.* I was glad she hadn't asked me the usual question women ask about other women's husbands. What does he do? What company does he work for? I'd have been proud to say that James had a Ph.D. in chemistry and an MBA, but I wouldn't have had an answer for the second part.

Meanwhile she was saying, "... and imagine, on the hottest day in July we went up all the way to the Salzburg castle on foot..," but her words hardly registered with me and my thoughts stayed with James, suddenly full of love and tenderness. The feeling of being trapped made me remember the most precious moments of my life with him.

James and I had met in August 1974 at the Davis Cup tennis tournament in Pörtschach. After the last match of the day he had come up to me along the courts at the entrance of the complex where I was handing out flyers for the tourist office. His face was turned towards the setting sun, and in his eyes was the golden glow reflected from the surface of the lake.

He smiled at me and squinted. "I'm glad you're still here. I was afraid I'd lose you in the crowd. I hope you don't think I'm being pushy. I've been thinking about you all afternoon, ever since you handed me this flyer when I came in. Could I ask you… uh, I mean, would you be free to have dinner with me tonight?"

It was some moment. During the few seconds before I answered with a simple "yes," the warmth of his eyes connecting with mine had opened the combination lock of our hearts.

The elevator shook, fell a few inches and stalled again, but this amazing woman next to me continued to list her itinerary through half a dozen Austrian cities.

"... oh, yes, and then I bought myself a *Dirndl* in Innsbruck and we passed through Mürzzuschlag, where Brahms wrote his *Fourth Symphony*... uh… and Budapest isn't part of Austria, is it?"

The close, airless space of the cabin intensified my rising irritation at her never-ending stream of secondary issues. Was her boisterous cordiality her way of reacting to the scare we were experiencing? When would we get out of here?

At last there was a rattling of elevator cables and banging noises in the shaft.

"I guess they're working on us..." She tossed her head back and her long, red curls danced above us in the mirrored ceiling. I was aware of the warm film of moisture on my palms when the elevator started up.

She gave me a quick look. "Are you all right? You look terribly pale."

"Yes, thanks, I'm fine."

Her hand reached out. "My name is Beverly. Beverly Honeycup."

I took her hand. It was cool and dry. "I'm Isabella. Isabella Barton."

We were traveling at normal speed now. She smiled at me. The tension was gone. "Since we work in the same building, would you like to have lunch some day?'

"Sure." I smiled back.

The doors opened at the thirtieth floor. She stopped in front of the light beams and I wrote down my office phone number on a used movie-ticket from my pocket.

She took it. "Good. What about tomorrow? It's the only day I'm free this week."

"Sounds fine," I said, knowing that I didn't have to check my calendar. I wasn't that busy.

Beverly's hand suddenly flew to her jaw and she sucked in her breath sharply.

"What's wrong?" I asked.

"I just had a sharp pain in my tooth, but it's O.K. now." She forced a smile but for a change had no further comment.

Our adventure was over. She had done all the talking but seemed adequately pleased that I had done none, or very little. We exchanged a final glance. An odd feeling had grown between us, more curiosity than caring, an underlying knowledge that we had something to give to each other, or take away. And there was only one way to find out which it would be.

Back at my desk a few dabs of *Eau de Joy* behind my ears helped me recover from the recent shock of being trapped. I started to sort through Mr. Stringer's mail and wrote down my date with Beverly in ink, permanently inscribed on fate as well as on the page of my appointment book.

Beverly called just after Mr. Stringer had dropped a pile of expense reports in the in-box by my computer. My first thought was that she would call to cancel.

"Hi, it's me again, Beverly."

"Is lunch still on?"

"Sure it is. Only I'm bringing someone else along."

"Fine," I said politely, assuming it would be a co-worker.

Her voice sounded important. "I thought you might enjoy meeting Mr. Mahler."

"Who?"

"The maestro himself, Orson Mahler," she repeated solemnly as if by pronouncing his name she momentarily shared his spotlight.

"Wait until you meet him..," her voice was high and shrill now. "You know they call him 'the man with the velvet voice'..."

I meant to say, "I've heard that somewhere," but she went on.

"Only, if you don't mind, I have to take a moment to go over some of his portfolio with him. He's so conservative. He wants his money in all the wrong places. But it'll only take a minute."

"But are you sure he won't mind my being there?"

"Don't worry. I already told him about you. He enjoys meeting new people, and he has a special love for Austria. He says he has very fond memories of Vienna. But he refuses to tell anyone how 'fond' they were.... uh, uh...," she giggled grotesquely, as if she had said more than she wanted. And in a more sober tone, "He'll love your accent. You can tell him you were at his concert."

A bit overwhelmed by all her news, I put the phone into the crook of my neck so I could use both hands to sign for an office-supply delivery.

Beverly went on to explain, "Orson doesn't like big lunches because he gets up late. And he always orders turkey sandwiches. He's definitely not a salad person. I mean, it's not like we're going to the *Four Seasons* for a five-course meal. Orson doesn't like to be seen in trendy places, because no matter whom he's with it'll be in the papers the next day. He says experience has taught him that a noisy coffee shop is the safest place to hide from gossip-hungry journalists. That's why he always wears dark glasses. He'll have them on tomorrow too. You'll see."

It seemed to me that she had spoken in one single breath. I handed the receipt back to the delivery man and said to Beverly, "You seem to know him very well."

"Well, yes..." she stopped her words in mid-air as if to convince herself of their truth, "... we are very close."

There was a pause. I wondered how close "very close" was.

I said, "Thanks for asking me along."

"How about 12 o'clock at *Charlie's* across the street?" Her voice became softer. "I wonder what your reaction to him will be."

Funny, I thought. I was wondering much more about James' reaction when I would tell him tonight that I was going to have lunch with Orson Mahler.

2

All around me spring was making its statement. There was muted music in the awakening of bulbs and blossoms, but it could only be heard if everything else was silent. Nature was infallible as it combined colors, and unlike man, nature never did anything in poor taste. I was glad I lived in Montclair and not in Manhattan. Every night when I stepped off the bus I took a deep breath and marveled at the pinks, whites and yellows. The suburban air of New Jersey and the azaleas and magnolias on the front lawns were as different from the city as my life at home was different from my life at work.

As I passed the forsythia bushes of my neighbors, I thought that, in another two weeks, maybe three, the rhododendrons would come out again and then, in another two weeks, maybe three, James would be working again. Maybe even earlier, I caught myself hoping. Maybe there was good news today. Maybe the fertilizer manufacturer he had interviewed with would make him an offer. In the nine months since James had lost his job, I had not yet learned that sometimes the only way to handle a problem is not to think about it. As the days grew longer, so did the waiting.

Before entering the house I glimpsed James' car through the garage door window. It was nice, in a way, to have him waiting for me at the end of the day instead of having to wait for him. In his former position as Director of Science and Technology at a pharmaceutical company, I had often waited up for him after meetings or business dinners, and when he traveled there had only been his calls to wait for.

I clicked the brass lock shut from inside and inhaled the air of our house. I liked its smell, because it was the smell of our life. Today it came with the mouth-watering aroma of spaghetti sauce that got stronger as I climbed the stairs to the kitchen. Two pots were simmering on the stove and in the sink was a strainer with rinsed lettuce. The kitchen counter was spotless. James possessed the rare ability to clean up after himself as he cooked.

The sound of the shower from upstairs stopped, and I knew James would be down any minute. In the living room I scanned through the mail on the glass table by the window, the usual junk mail and the phone bill. Except for the bill I threw everything in the wastepaper basket next to the woodpile by the fireplace. And then I spotted another letter on the bottom of the wastepaper basket. I picked it up. It was from the fertilizer manufacturer.

My hands shook slightly as I read it. They were impressed by James' expertise and background and expressed their best wishes for future success, but regretted having chosen another candidate over him. My stomach turned. Back to square one. I had reached my limit for accepting rejection letters gracefully. And what about James? It looked as if he hadn't planned on showing it to me.

The same thing had happened three months before, when he was turned down for the position of VP for Business Development by a drug company and didn't tell me about it. When the reimbursement check for his travel expenses arrived, one day after Valentine's Day, I had flung his heart-shaped card into the fireplace. In tears I told him that if I didn't have his trust, I didn't want his card either.

But maybe under the umbrella of protecting my feelings he was really protecting his own. Maybe being rejected for a job was no longer the only rejection he feared. My nagging impatience may have turned into just as large a problem for him.

Right. I shouldn't be an additional burden for him. I would pretend not to have seen the letter. If he chose to handle it this way, so be it. Today I'd do my best to pretend everything was fine, or at the very least was going to be fine soon.

With a feeling of impotence I grasped the mantelpiece with both hands as if by trying to move it I could move the heavens. And here my eyes were caught by something that always seemed like a small part of heaven to me, my paperweight collection. I would never cease to marvel at the perfectly shaped domes, the tiny millefiori canes, the lampworks or ribbon twists creating abstract dreams caught under glass. At one point, when the mantelpiece wasn't long enough anymore, I had begun to put them on the window sills, and after running out of windows, I had started using the bookshelves in front of the books. Now the late afternoon sun was just at the right angle to spread its light across the back yard onto the mantelpiece and bring out the sparkle of my colorful and endlessly varied crystal balls.

James had never shared my passion for these funny-looking *objets d'art*, but tolerated their taking up more and more space, along with their appearance on our credit card statements.

Since the beginning of James' unemployment I had given up paperweights, the cleaning lady and our trip to Hawaii. Instead I had taken up collecting coupons but always forgot to use them. James had given up tennis, the country club and our trip to Hawaii too.

Instead he had taken up exercises for his hurting back, but refused to see a doctor.

On Saturdays, when we vacuumed and did the laundry, I felt that we had never before grown so close in our duties, if apart in our dreams. James seemed to be on temporary hold for a better future. I seemed to be on permanent hold for a bleak life of having to work for an impossible boss to provide a living for both of us.

A creaking sound announced James' footsteps on the stairs. The first thing I saw were his sneakers, and then his jeans, his hand on the banister and his white T-shirt. I took a few steps towards him and we stopped, face to face, except that his was three inches above mine.

"How was your day, Beautiful?" It was his normal greeting. His eyes winked at me and he began to whistle a tune, exhibiting an air of contentment with himself and the world around him.

I managed a smile. "I'm glad the day is over."

Noticing a strain in my voice, he stopped whistling and held out his arms.

I leaned my head against his shoulder and inhaled the aroma of soap on his skin. His embrace was like a ticket home, and I felt that this was the best moment the day had thus far to offer. He held me tightly, as if trying to absorb my exhaustion and exchange it for new energy that would turn my fatigue into lightness.

James ran his finger down my nose and kissed my forehead. Looking deeply into his dark brown eyes was like looking into the core of his soul, which seemed to have an in-born device for rejecting worry. His smile accentuated the twin creases running from the corners of his mouth.

He asked tenderly, "Why the long face, Beautiful? Come on, let's have a smile. I'm trying out a new recipe for spaghetti sauce and I'm starved. You're a little late, aren't you? I suppose Stringer kept you busy."

"I muddled through his travel receipts in five different currencies, but I'm up to date now due to the fact that I skipped lunch. I'm starved too."

"I'll put on the water for the pasta and we're ready to eat."

"Anything new today?"

"Actually," James moved towards the kitchen, "I cleaned out the storage shelves in the garage. I think I'll buy some paint tomorrow. They'd look much better in white."

"Good idea." I followed him, wishing that all I had to worry about was the color of the shelves in the garage.

At the stove, James lifted the lid off a pot and stirred the spaghetti sauce with a long wooden spoon.

I inhaled. "It smells good. Let's have a glass of wine with it.

James checked on the boiling water for the pasta and licked the wooden spoon, delighted by his culinary creation.

"Mmm... great. Guess what I put in it. Zucchini, mushrooms, onions, thyme and garlic."

I took out the place mats and napkins and smiled at James' passion for spaghetti. He loved the same things about making spaghetti as about making love. The taste, the touch, the heat, the satisfaction.

"*Prost!*" I handed him a glass of Chianti and our glasses clinked. "To the world's greatest pasta chef!"

"To us!" And in a voice that was much more serious, "I'm convinced there's nothing you and I can't do."

For a moment I wondered whether he would mention the rejection letter after all. But he didn't.

"I know," I whispered and swallowed hard. "I remember you said the same words before. There's nothing you and I can't do, and I believe you, James." I looked straight into his kind brown eyes, proud of myself for being such a perfect liar.

The first time I had heard him say these words was under much happier circumstances. It was the day of our wedding in Austria, in my little home town of Pörtschach. The second time he said them to me things were less happy. It was the day when the pharmaceutical company we both worked for had let twenty percent of its employees go, and James and I had been among them. That night James had ceaselessly dried my tears and I had since ceaselessly marveled at his strength and invulnerability in the face of adversity. "There's nothing you and I can't do..." was the expression of James' determination to overcome obstacles.

I took my shoes off and kicked them in front of the pantry door, wishing I'd never have to wear them again.

James said, "Your new shoes look very elegant. I'll bet you got some admiring glances from your boss."

"I couldn't care less about Mr. Stringer's glances, if only the leather weren't still so stiff."

"Just give them another day or two and you'll have them broken in. If not, leave them with me and I'll find a way to stretch them for you."

This was typical of James. His gift for taking a day at a time, his belief in perseverance and, above all, in his ability to make things right. He chose to handle any kind of hurt, including that of the stiffness of my shoes or his back, or even his rejection letter, *like a man,* afraid that released feelings would too easily get out of hand.

We sat down at the table and started to eat the lettuce. James lit the candles in the silver candlesticks that my mother had given us for our wedding

I cut the lettuce into smaller pieces.

"Do we have any French bread?"

"Oh yeah, I forgot...." James got up and unwrapped the long loaf that he had put in a wicker basket on a lower shelf. As he bent down, a shock of hair fell onto his forehead. Occasionally his wavy brown hair got a bit too long between trips to the barber.

I thought, I should get up and help him, but he obviously enjoyed puttering around with pots and pans as much as pondering his chemical formulas. Mindlessly, I rubbed some dirt off my sleeve. Yellow always showed the slightest stain.

Absorbed in adding a squeeze of lemon to the spaghetti sauce, James started whistling again. Maybe it was a nervous reaction, maybe he was thinking of the rejection letter after all. And maybe he was not. How could he be so cheerful after such a blow?

I began rolling pasta around my fork and tasted the sauce.

"How is it?"

"You did a great job," I smiled and thought for the hundredth time that everything was going to be all right.

James reached behind him and dimmed the lamp over the table. He said, "I spent most of the day reading. Being at home gives me the chance to read books I never had time for. It's something I always dreamed of doing, spending a whole day with Tolstoy."

My "Uh-huh" came out like a burp. I fixed my eyes on my plate in order to avoid looking at him. This was not what I wanted to hear. Did he think he could avoid facing reality by taking refuge in a novel?

His eyes took on a far-away glow as he scratched some hot candle wax off the table with his thumb.

"I think Anna Karenina died for nothing." Unaware of my rising irritation he went on. "I mean, she didn't have to throw herself under that train. There must have been a way to work things out, either with her husband or her lover. Of course, tragic endings are very effective. If somebody is killed or kills himself it makes a nice, neat plot and it's very compelling for the reader and convenient for the writer."

He looked into a dreamy distance at the cookbooks on the shelf. "In modern life no one should die of a broken heart any more. I mean, whatever problem we have to face, including being out of work, life has to go on and we have to find solutions..."

I put down my fork. I needed all my willpower to stay silent. To hell with his book. Why didn't he tell me what I wanted to hear? Had he sent out any more resumés or called any more headhunters? After a long day at the office and the goddamn rejection letter, I didn't care if society had judged Anna Karenina cruelly or that she had been unable to find her own courage.

James looked at me surprised. "Finished already?'

I sighed, "I think so." I leaned back in my chair and closed my eyes. Instead of allowing my frustration to escalate, shouldn't I try to contribute to our conversation? Didn't I have anything interesting to say? The image of Beverly's red curls dancing in the mirrored ceiling of the elevator revived under my eye-lids. I wanted to tell James about her, but he was still engrossed in Tolstoy.

"Honestly, Isabella, this notion of ending a life to solve a problem sounds brave and romantic, but I think those people are giving up too fast. We all have to accept difficult times, when everything that seemed safe and established is falling apart. But our problems are exactly as big as we allow them to be and these times are temporary. The stage of life keeps turning, and ... uh...," he took a sip of Chianti, "nobody is allowed to jump off the platform except cowards. With patience and a healthy fighting spirit everything will fall into place again. We have to give time some time."

I said, "I agree," and thought, Thanks for the sermon.

Time. Time. Wasn't nine months time enough to find a new job? And yet I wronged him by being so bitter. This was his way of expressing our problems without inviting contempt in his mind, but inspiring comfort in mine.

James reached to the chair on his left and picked up the paper. He held it at a distance in front of him and squinted.

"After all this reading today my eyes feel tired. I might need reading glasses soon."

"At forty-three? Isn't that a little early?" I picked at the last lettuce from the wooden bowl that Julia and I had once bought in Chinatown.

"The truth is," James frowned, "I'm still trying to figure out whether my eyes have got weaker or whether my arms just aren't long enough anymore."

I laughed.

His eyes shone happily. "It's good to see you laugh, Isabella. You know, you're absolutely beautiful when you laugh."

How could I not be flattered by his words? Maybe I didn't try hard enough to understand his carefree disposition. Maybe I should see it as a conscious choice to act successful at all times, even if he wasn't. Imagine us both worriers. That would never work. Patience. Yes, I should be more patient.

I leaned over and my lips brushed his cheeks.

"Let me return the compliment. You don't look too bad yourself. My mother warned me against marrying a good-looking man. She said good-looking men were no good and I'd be sorry one day."

"And are you?"

"Are you asking me if I'm sorry I married you?"

"Don't avoid the question."

I smiled. "No, James, I'm not sorry. I'd marry you again."

"I'm glad." He smiled. "You know, when you toss your head in that defiant manner, you look exactly like your mother."

I mumbled, "I guess I look a lot like her without tossing my head."

I got up and stretched to ease my perpetual stiffness from too much sitting, on the job, in the bus and at the table.

James put his napkin down and got up.

"I'll clean up. You relax."

I yawned, "I'm going to take a shower. I can't wait to get out of my clothes."

James opened the dishwasher. "Good," he said, "I never liked you in that suit. Yellow is not a good color for you, Isabella."

In one second the card-house of my patience and composure collapsed. I grasped the back of my chair and felt the pressure in my chest exploding.

"Today I finished seventeen weeks of expense reports, I got stuck in the elevator, and my new shoes were killing me all day. And now I'm trying very hard not to get upset over a color that I happen to like and you don't."

Without looking at him, I stormed out of the kitchen, up the stairs into my bathroom.

My bathroom was a place where no harm could reach me and nothing bad could happen. Nothing is expected of anyone in a bathroom, no one has to keep smiling or hold back questions or tears. And finally, under the warm spray of the shower, I allowed myself to cry over another day of wasted hope.

I am not strong enough for this, I thought. But if James is, why can't I be the same way? At which point had I stopped sharing his trust in life? Or had I stopped trusting him? Was nine months enough to lose your trust in the most important person in your life? Was he really trying hard enough at networking or was he enjoying himself too much reading novels? As a good-looking and well-educated man he had always been used to having doors opened for him by other people. Did he expect the same thing to happen now? Or was it possible that my mother was right with her warning about marrying a good-looking man? She claimed that because of their good looks they never learned to try hard enough at anything. And yet, wasn't it wonderful to have the most handsome husband in the world, a husband whose smile could stop the world?

As the water cascaded down my body I thought of that first smile James had given me at the entrance to the tennis complex back in Pörtschach. He had smiled at me with a mixture of animal magnetism and gentleness, and our eyes had clicked like a key in the right lock. From that first night, when after dinner we had walked along the shore and got caught in a storm with no umbrella, our love had been like a force of nature. To this day that force had never ceased to exist.

I liked the bathroom full of steam, the illusion of being in a cloud or on a planet of moisture and warmth. When I opened the shower door, James was standing there, holding my big yellow towel. His smile stopped the world.

"Instead of a flag of truce, can I just hold up a yellow towel?"

"James..," I rubbed my face and stepped out of the cabin.

"This is your friendly neighborhood towel-service. Come into my arms, you gorgeous man-trap." His voice was begging.

My heart quickened. I attempted a gesture of protest, but James enveloped me in the towel, turned me around and kissed my ears from behind. He rubbed me dry with a care suitable for a royal baby, cupping my breasts as if they were his own most valuable parts and rocking me to and fro in front of the steam-covered mirror.

I looked at him and smiled. He was standing there in nothing but his T-shirt.

He hugged me tightly, and beneath the soft cotton of his shirt I felt a muscular, hard body that was making its demands known. He traced the outline of my lips with his fingers and wrapped the towel tightly around my body. Suddenly he bent his knees and swung me over his shoulder and carried me into the bedroom.

"*Pass auf, James*!" I tried to struggle free. "Your back!"

"Don't worry, I'm a healthy man," he put me down on the bed with a grin, "and I can't wait to show you how healthy I really am."

The fire in his eyes was claiming its territory and his kisses were like an aromatic wine, warm and racy, causing a drunkenness that brought back the joy of living in me. The signal of his lips on my neck, my shoulders and the space between my breasts was the prologue to a wonderful moment, the initiation of desire and the knowledge that it would be quenched.

There was no need to close the door or draw the curtains. We had entered our own orbit inside the outer world. James held me possessively, nuzzling my hair and running his hands across my stomach, and farther down, giving answers to my body without my having to ask questions.

His kisses deepened and I felt his strong thighs against mine. A smile formed on my face and I knew there couldn't be any other place in the whole wide world where I would rather be. To be in this room, in this bed with this man, where our skin was no longer our limitation, was being at the homestead of my heart, my body. I wasn't Isabella anymore, I was part of James and he was part of me.

In the slow, seamless dance of our bodies, we suppressed our urgency in order to prolong the trip. It was a drifting without the need to define the destination, a flight on weightless wings. But suddenly our flight turned into a reckless fury. I sensed James' desperate need to drown in the ocean of my femaleness, and with him I felt the need to drown myself, to surrender to the moment of delirious pain following desire.

And then, surrounded by a deep peace, we lay still, very still. With my head resting on his shoulder and my nose touching his chin, we breathed to the same beat, as one person, breathing happiness, as if curled up in the corner of each other's heart.

All at once I remembered something. I opened my eyes and was wide awake.

"James?" I whispered. "Are you asleep yet?"

"Mmmmh..?"

"There is something I meant to tell you all evening."

"Wha..?" he muttered.

"Tomorrow I'm going to have lunch with Orson Mahler."

Under the blankets James pulled me even closer to him and growled. “Huuu..?”

“Did you hear me?”

I nudged him slightly, but despite his firm grip around my shoulders, he was fast asleep.

3

The next morning five people were waiting behind me to get on the seven-thirty bus to New York. The clasp of my purse was stuck, and in my struggle to open it to get out my ticket for the driver, I broke one of my freshly done nails. Dammit, I thought, while looking for a seat, this has to happen to me today of all days when I'm going to have lunch with Beverly and Orson Mahler.

When leaving the house, I had found myself looking forward to the event from my mother's perspective. She would have given her grandmother's engagement ring for a lunch with Orson Mahler, and I could easily relate to the naive excitement of a female fan who was about to meet her idol.

With my head against the window, riding east, my eyes followed the sun along its hide-and-seek path through the trees and clouds. In contrast to some people I didn't consider commuting a waste, but a gift of time during which I could think, dream and analyze. Only lately I was analyzing my life too much instead of living it. Life seemed more burden than bliss, more silence than music. When had I last been truly excited about the sheer fact of existence? Tired of doubt and worry, I suddenly longed for the bliss and the music.

Music...

The man sitting next to me coughed and his head appeared briefly from behind his *Wall Street Journal*. He said, "Never a dull moment in the stock market..." He gave me a fleeting smile that was factual and friendly. I thought, This is how I would be with Orson Mahler, factual and friendly.

Music... Maybe music was the key. I've always loved music and maybe I should spend more time with it. And what better day could I have picked to start?

My eyes landed on my broken nail and I decided to hide it under the table from Beverly and Orson Mahler. I wondered what the conversation would be like with him. What does one talk about with a conductor? I should think up some questions, such as which of the twenty-seven Mozart piano concertos he liked best or why Beethoven had written only one opera?

And there it was again, the old fear of not having anything to say, or not being able to speak fluently enough. Very often I found it more interesting to listen than to talk, to observe than to participate. With English as my second language, my thoughts frequently came to me first *auf deutsch* and I feared that my slowness to articulate was seen as doubts about my ability to think.

However at thirty-three I was past the age where I had to practice flirting or try to be someone I was not. Somehow, and despite Beverly's seamless eloquence, I would find a moment to ask Mr. Mahler how he liked Vienna, the music capital of Europe, a question my mother had meant to ask him twenty years ago.

The traffic on Route 3 was running unusually fast. Up ahead, across the Hudson, the skyline of Manhattan stretched like a parade of giant exclamation marks. Only a few more minutes and the bus would enter the Lincoln Tunnel. Only a few more hours and I'd be having lunch with the famous maestro.

Today I would go out for lunch even if Mr. Stringer had to wait for his cappuccino or his reservation on the Concord. Today I would go out even if I found Mr. Stringer unconscious on his polished mahogany desk.

And I did. I mean, I did actually go out.

4

I caught my first glimpse of Orson Mahler when he was not wearing his dark glasses. He was standing at the top of the stairs leading up to the restaurant. My eyes searched the bustling lunch-hour crowd for Beverly. Why wasn't she here yet? The never-ending yellow stream of cabs made crossing the street impossible. But I didn't need to rush. I was on time. It was noon.

Across the street the man in the gray suit was still standing in the same place. It was odd to think that he was waiting for me. I felt disappointed by his small stature in contrast to the impression projected by his presence on the podium. His hair was gray and thinning and his face lacked the inspiration captured in so many of his pictures.

With the immunity of a stranger I felt free to stare at him, though in a little while I would renounce that freedom for the privilege of meeting him.

But why was he looking at me? His eyes held me in a grip of quiet power, as if touching me from head to foot. If only Beverly would get here. What if she didn't show up at all? I should have made another cup of cappuccino for Mr. Stringer.

Three fire engines with ear-splitting sirens rushed by. I told myself to remember to hide my broken nail under the table, but all I could think of was the lure of this stranger's eyes resting on me. They seemed to whisper, *Look at me. I'm here. I'm not going anywhere. I'm waiting. Whenever you are ready, I am. Come.*

I would walk up to him and be factual and friendly. I'd say, "I'm Isabella Barton. I'm supposed to meet you and Beverly. I'm honored to meet you, Maestro Mahler."

There was a clutch, fear's little tickle under my ribs, as I crossed the street and walked up the steps. He took a step in my direction. We stopped face to face, only his was three inches below mine. I was struck by the extraordinary whiteness of his skin and the message in his eyes, as if he had always known me.

He bowed slightly and said, "You must be Isabella Barton."

"Yes." My mind went blank. What else had I planned to say?

"You look exactly as Beverly described you. I immediately picked you out in the crowd. I've been watching you for a while. I like to watch beautiful women. I even made a little bet with myself that *you* would be... *you*." He gave a musical laugh and added, "And I won."

I forced a smile, still unable to speak.

He checked his watch and grinned. "You are a little early. It's exactly thirty-three seconds before noon. Technically you don't have to talk to me for half a minute."

He motioned towards the revolving door of *Charlie's* Restaurant and let me pass. I summarized my first impressions. He was not someone I felt spontaneously comfortable with, much less attracted to. His face remained expressionless even when he talked, but his voice was everything I had expected. It had the dark texture of velvet.

Once inside I turned to him. "It's such an honor to meet you, Maestro Mahler," but my voice was drowned by the sound of the pop music from the speakers above.

Mr. Mahler made a face and said to the hostess, "I can't stand this music. Can you turn it off, please?"

We were seated at a corner table at the far end of the room and the music miraculously stopped. He gestured at the speakers in the ceiling. "God, such awful noise! This kind of music is an insult to my aural nerve-endings."

The black birthmark on his upper lip moved in perfect synchronicity with the rhythm of his speech. He put down his briefcase on the bench next to him and it was obvious that it must have seen better days, since it was rather old and beaten.

I repeated, "It's such an honor to meet you, Maestro Mahler."

"Please don't...," he shook his head and his smile was in his eyes rather than on his lips. "I detest being called *Maestro.* It's Orson, please."

The waitress took our drink order and I decided not to address him by his name at all. I said, "I'd like an orange juice."

He said, "Three orange juices, please," and to me, "I'm sure Beverly will be here any moment. She told me about your adventure in the elevator yesterday. Well, as a result you made a friend."

His teasing tone made me wonder whether he was referring to Beverly or to himself. He made a little tent with his hands and his gray eyes took in every inch of my face. At this moment nothing was more disturbing than to be with this man, separated only by a patch of tablecloth. Where was Beverly?

He said, "You haven't said much yet, Isabella, but Beverly was right. You have a charming accent."

For the first time I managed a smile. "You haven't said too much either, but they don't call you 'the man with the velvet voice' for nothing."

He smiled and shook his head. "You know, they call me many things..."

The waitress put the drinks and the menus on the table. I scanned the salads. I sensed that Orson was waiting for me to decide not only on the food but also on the course of our conversation.

I looked straight into his gray-metallic eyes.

"I attended your concert of Beethoven's *Ninth Symphony* with my friend last Friday. It was wonderful."

"And what do you especially remember about it that was so wonderful? Maybe I can learn something from you that I don't know yet."

He looked at me expectantly and I was startled.

"Frankly, I wasn't able to concentrate too well. Julia had a headache and asked me to get some aspirin for her. And in the intermission she spilled her coffee all over my skirt."

I could hardly believe my words. What was I saying? Unable to look at him, I hastened to add, "But the music was very moving..." and my eyes fell on the bandage around his left pinkie.

His velvet voice was full of warmth. "I know exactly what you mean. If you don't have a good day, you sit in the audience and worry about your income taxes and wonder how they ever got the light bulbs high up into the ceiling."

I broke out in a nervous laugh, relieved that the tension was broken.

Beverly was zigzagging between the tables towards us. Her bouncy step always made her seem in a hurry, exuding the enviable fascination of being hard to catch. Like a living frame, her red curls moved around her freckled face. She waved elaborately.

"Hi, Bella! Hi Orson!" She bent down to offer him her cheek. Before I could tell her that I prefer to use my full name, Orson said, "You look lovely, Beverly," which bothered me a tiny bit.

She smiled grandly and with a tilt of her hips sat down next to him. "I won't be able to stay for lunch. I had a terrible toothache last night. It felt as if my tooth was singing an aria. I'm glad my dentist could give me an appointment at twelve-thirty."

I said, "I'm so sorry," and didn't mean it.

Orson said, "So am I, indeed," and it sounded sincere.

Beverly shrugged. "It'll be all right," and unzipped the briefcase on her lap.

"I brought these papers for you to sign, Orson." She placed several documents in front of him and pointed with her impeccable pink nail to the lines marked with an "x." I remembered to hide my broken nail under the table.

Orson took out a small silver pen and signed his name at the bottom of half a dozen pages. In a gesture of helplessness he shook his head and turned to me. "I trust this woman completely," and to her, "How can I be sure you're not ruining me?"

Beverly put down her glass ringed with lip-stick. “How often have I tried to explain your investments to you? You don’t even listen. You are not in the least interested.”

He looked up from his papers. “You’re right. And you’ll never get me to read all this Wall Street junk you keep sending me in the mail.”

“In that case, you’ll just have to trust me.”

He grinned sourly. “It seems I have no choice.”

Beverly adopted a more motherly voice. “Orson, don’t you see that I want only the best for you, like so many other people in your life.”

He picked up his silver pen again and started drawing doodles on the margins of his papers.

“That’s not the impression I get most of the time. If that were so, the chorus would do a better job of articulating their consonants, and the orchestra would shape my *crescendos* gradually, and no one would complain about occasional rehearsal overtime.”

Beverly pushed her glasses up on her nose and her diamond ring sparkled in the glow from a spotlight.

“Well, Orson, nobody can spare you that kind of occupational frustration, but there are a lot of people who are dying to help you with all the nitty-gritty that’s necessary to get you up on the podium where you belong.”

“I suppose I can’t complain.” He was still doodling.

“No, you can’t. And don’t complain to me, because I’m too busy running around doing things for you.”

She rolled up the sleeves of her beige suit.

“Speaking of which, I got a good deal for the new chorus scores for the fall season. It’s thirty percent off the store price if we order a hundred and fifty. I also meant to tell you I heard rumors that the rent for the rehearsal hall is going up, and I’m sure Joan mentioned the new application forms for the chorus. They’re designed to record a personal profile of each member.”

Beverly had spoken in one breath, compressing a maximum of information into a minimum of time. In order to say something, Orson had to lift his hand in a conductorly fashion. He turned to me.

"Isabella, Joan is the manager of my chorus. She's been an invaluable help to me for uh... more than twenty years."

Beverly's olive eyes became slits. "I hate the woman, and Orson knows it."

To my surprise, some blood rushed to Orson's face and I was glad to see that he was human. There was an awkward little silence, but Beverly jumped in fast, careful not to let his attention go astray.

"One of my clients has a printing business. He agreed to print our new forms for free, as a contribution to the arts, so to speak."

Orson nodded. "Please thank him in my name and make sure he gets a pair of free tickets for our concert on Sunday."

Beverly checked her watch. "I'll take care of it. But now I really have to go."

She stood up and gave Orson a wistful smile that seemed just a little too long for an investment broker and her client or a chorus member and her maestro. Fiddling with her scarf she said, "I'll call you tonight," and it was clear that she was not talking to me. Orson's look held a tinge of embarrassment. Secretly, I blessed her hurting tooth.

After she had gone, our silence didn't feel uncomfortable as it had before. Orson smiled, as if something was pleasing him and I reminded him of it. "I like the defiant way you toss your head. I once knew someone with the same mannerism."

"Are you ready to order now?" The waitress sounded politely impatient.

Orson opened the menu. "No, not yet. I'm still trying to figure out which page the food is on."

I said, "I'll have a spinach salad."

"Make that two."

"Beverly said you are not a salad person."

"I am now. Beverly was wrong."

"Beverly is obviously a very competent person."

"Yes, she has lots of connections in the city. But she can be wrong too, and as an investment broker she's far too conservative. I'm afraid she has my money in all the wrong places. But what can I do? I don't have the time to deal with these things."

The salads arrived almost immediately.

Orson said to the waitress, "What took you so long?"

I laughed, "You have the same talent as my husband for one-liners."

"Oh. You're married?"

"Yes."

He looked at me differently and for the first time smiled his magic smile, and it was more than I imagined it could be. One by one his features registered in my mind, his gray-metallic eyes, his finely-boned face and high forehead, etched from decades of listening and thinking.

He picked on his spinach and said quietly, "I want to hear more about you."

"I'm not sure..," I felt my throat closing, "I never talk much about myself."

He smiled encouragingly. "You don't have to tell me anything you don't want to, but I'd like to know what's behind those blue eyes of yours. Just start anywhere."

My napkin was sliding from my lap to the floor, but I didn't bother to pick it up.

"I'm from Austria. I was born and raised in a small town called Pörtschach. Johannes Brahms wrote his *Second Symphony* there during a summer vacation."

Orson nodded. "It's a wonderful piece. I've conducted it many times, but I don't want to hear about Brahms now." He kept looking at me.

"The house I grew up in has a wonderful view of the lake, and my mother used to grow roses and tomatoes in the garden. I could swim almost before I could walk and I enjoyed swimming in any kind of weather, but I hated my piano lessons. After my *Matura,* I went to Innsbruck to study French and English and then returned home and got a job as translator for the local tourist office. At twenty-one I was engaged to a young man called Hans."

"Tell me about Hans."

"Thinking back, he was more my mother's choice than mine. When I met James, my husband, I gave Hans his ring back. He went on with his life, but my mother never forgave me. She loved Hans. She said I had broken my promise to him."

I took a quick sip and continued. "My mother has been a great fan of yours for many years. She once met you after a concert in Vienna some years ago. She was so excited to get your autograph, and she played your records all the time. I feel I've known you all my life from the pictures on the covers."

Orson put down his fork and I could tell that he was not a salad person.

He asked, "What is your mother's name?"

"Elisabeth."

"*Eli-sa-beth.*" His German pronunciation was impeccable and by the way he caressed the syllables he could have fooled me into believing that he knew her.

"Please tell your mother that I thank her for doing such a wonderful job."

"Of what?"

"Of producing you." A broad grin crossed his face.

I blushed and thought, If she could see me now.

Orson kept grinning. "You look charming when you blush."

The spinach leaves were swelling on my tongue. Orson seemed to wait for me to lead the conversation, giving me a feeling of importance and that the rest of the world was shut out at this moment. He had stopped being a conductor and was just a human being.

He said, "I also heard from Beverly that you started a new job in January. Tell me about it." His voice had a soothing sensuality that overpowered the visual impressions of his thinning hair and pale complexion.

I sighed. "I'm not happy with my job."

"Why not?"

I looked down at his long, sensitive hands, thinking of the review Beverly had read to me. *His hands are overwhelmingly expressive and were unfailingly in command throughout the work...* I realized he wasn't wearing a wedding ring.

His voice brought me back. "Go on."

"I can't stand my boss."

"Why is that?"

"He talks down to his employees, he thinks he is the best-looking man who ever graced the planet and he believes every woman shares his opinion."

"What else?"

I hesitated. Why would a man like Orson be interested in listening to my complaints? Didn't he get enough of this from his players, his chorus and his critics? Yet his eyes said, *I'm here. I'm listening to you. Go on.* So I stopped wondering whether he was sincere or just doing a good imitation.

"Mr. Stringer is unable to give clear directions and refuses to be asked any questions. He'd say, 'Find out for yourself,' which makes working for him very hard."

Orson pushed his unfinished plate out of his way.

"What's his job?"

"He's the president of a German bank here in New York."

"What's your job?"

"I was hired to do German and French translations, but there aren't enough translations to keep me busy, so the job has developed into a sort of personal assistant. I deal with his realtor and his daughters' teachers, and I order all his golf equipment."

Orson gave an amused laugh and his velvet voice was all encouragement. "Don't stop now..."

The feel of his eyes on me made the room blur.

"I detest the way my boss blows his cigar smoke over my head when he's standing in front of my desk. I hate him for embarrassing his wife in front of everyone in the office, and I hate him for looking at me like... uh... when I'm alone with him."

Orson rattled the ice cubes of his orange juice. I thought that this was all wrong, having him listen to my life like this. My common sense was doing back flips. Hadn't I planned to ask him about the Mozart piano concertos or Beethoven's only opera?

Orson asked, "Can't you change jobs?"

An embarrassing tear was forming in my eye and the expression on this face told me he had seen it. I moved a little bit away from him and straightened up. "Talking about this is like removing the bandage from an unhealed wound."

He said firmly, "Try," and suddenly took my hand across the table. It was the hand with the broken nail, but that was no longer important. Under his touch the colors of the room drained into shades of whites. I whispered, "I have to keep this job. It pays well and my husband is out of work."

Orson nodded, "I see," and tightened his grip.

I didn't know what was more confusing now, talking or his touch.

"James and I were laid off from the same pharmaceutical company we both worked for, along with two hundred others. That was nine months ago. It was easier for me to find a position that needed translations than one looking for a Ph.D. in chemistry. James is still unemployed."

Orson continued to hold my hand and took a deep breath.

"I understand exactly how you feel. Living in a society where the profession defines the individual, you become vocationally naked when you lose your job."

"The funny thing is…James is not the problem. I am. I'm afraid he'll never find another job, whereas he takes everything with such irritating ease."

Orson said, "He's obviously a man who believes in himself."

"James says life doesn't always work out the way we want it to. He spends his time reading nineteenth-century novels and painting the shelves in the garage. He thinks difficult times are just a test we have to pass, and everything will work out just fine."

Orson was still holding my hand, while I was falling through a room of white clouds. And I kept falling.

He said calmly, "I share your husband's view, and so should you. Life doesn't always spoil us. There were times, when I was in my late twenties, when I thought I'd never get to stand on a podium again."

I swallowed hard. "I was never spoiled when I grew up, yet I had everything I ever needed. But in my book, waiting for an unemployment check means reaching the verge of poverty."

"I used to wait for an unemployment check in the mail myself. And in order to pay my rent I waited on tables in a nightclub. But things never stay the same. Never."

He caught his breath and I felt that he had revealed more about himself than he was comfortable with.

"Isabella, you have to understand that if you are willing to handle the lessons a crisis is trying to teach you, you will also become strong enough to see it through."

The strange thing was that the way he said it made me begin to understand. If Orson had come out on top and be the man he is now, James would come out on top too.

Orson's eyes looked at me with a soft steadfastness while he still didn't let go of my hand. I could have pulled it away under the pretense of having to blow my nose. But I didn't have to blow my nose. I hardly breathed under his touch, and yet it felt like a fire without warmth, a gesture without passion and an implication without meaning.

Very slowly I said, "I think I see what you mean," as if under the grip of Orson's hand the past had lost its grip on me and I was free to let it go and take charge of my happiness.

He explained, "There was a time in my life when I seriously considered taking up chemistry. Does your husband enjoy what he is doing?"

"James is fascinated by chemistry. He can go on about it forever. Unfortunately, he can never keep his audience, because nobody cares to hear about amino acids or long-chain molecules for very long."

Orson laughed his musical laugh.

"Tell me more about him."

I joined in his cheerfulness. "Well... James is in favor of atomic energy, women's right to choose and... uh... garter belts."

"He seems to be a very nice man."

"He is."

"Do you love him?"

"Completely."

Orson's hand was still covering mine. The energy generated by his hand flowed through my whole body.

I asked, "But tell me, what made you decide on conducting? Music was obviously the right choice."

His eyes moved far into the distance, too far to notice the busy waitress clearing away our plates.

"Isabella, deep down in the core of music lies something that's beyond the notes. It's like a promise, a light, a ray of hope that touches us and carries us away. Music is a power that words or formulas can never match, and although I've lost a lot of my initial illusions, I learned to give them to other people. That's my reward."

I nodded silently and realized that I had missed the moment when he let go of my hand. Without his touch the room became real again, the rattling of the dishes louder and the voices from the other tables clearer.

Orson said, "I know you understand. I can see it in your eyes." And then in a different tone, "I'm sorry. I didn't even ask you whether you wanted coffee or dessert. Normally I'm crazy about hot chocolate, but I'm afraid I have to leave."

I checked the time. It was past my regular lunch time. In an hour and a half my world had changed.

I shook my head. "Thank you, I can't eat any more. But I wanted to ask you one more thing. I'm aware that you have written a book about music that for months was on the *New York Times* bestseller list." I hesitated, embarrassed that I couldn't remember the title. "I'd love to read it". Secretly I thought that by asking for his book, I might have a chance to see him again.

To my surprise he looked at me but said nothing. He paid the check and mumbled, "I'm late for an audition in Alice Tully Hall."

Outside the restaurant our eyes engaged in a short, confusing struggle. I sensed that we were keeping ourselves on guard, trying to protect our identities from the silent pull between us. He opened his beaten briefcase and put on his dark glasses.

I said, "Thank you for lunch. It was wonderful meeting you, uh... Orson."

He said, "It was wonderful meeting you too, Isabella. I'll see to it that you get a copy of my book," and the birthmark on his upper lip hardly moved.

He bowed stiffly, as if welcoming the mention of his book as the closing subject for our meeting. But how could I expect him to ever want to see me again, with the prospect of having to listen to a variation of my insecurities and fears? Right from the beginning I had ruined my chance for an intelligent conversation. Silly me. What about Beethoven and Mozart? I didn't even know what to tell James about this lunch or what to write about it to my mother. How could I explain to anybody that, like a catalyst, he had changed me, while remaining unchanged himself.

Watching him as he got into a cab, a bitter-sweet feeling was washing over me, of having touched someone who was moving on without me.

5

"Fortunately it was only a loose filling. But I was so sorry I could keep you company for only such a short time." Beverly's silvery soprano mixed with the rhythm of our combined four heels clicking away on Fifth Avenue.

"I'm glad your tooth was caught in time," I said and thought, This was typical of me. I couldn't even get up the courage to ask her whether it had been her idea or Orson's to invite me as a guest listener to a rehearsal of the Orson Mahler Oratorio Chorus.

It was the day following my lunch with Orson, and here I was, walking with Beverly past St. Patrick's, hardly believing my luck at being able to see him again so soon. Never mind that my new shoes were still far from comfortable.

After Beverly had called me in the morning I treated myself to the rare luxury of having my nails done during lunch. At the sight of their turning red and shiny, I fantasized about tonight's rehearsal. Would I have a chance to talk to Orson? What would I say? What would he say? Considering the multitude of people he dealt with on a daily basis he might have forgotten me already, and considering all the fears and feelings I had so innocently revealed to him, part of me wished he *had* actually forgotten me. But the other part of me bargained with the first one for any small detail he might still remember, including holding my hand.

Eager to prevent Beverly from inquiring about my lunch with Orson, I decided to be the one who inquired. "You say you've been a member of the chorus for ten years? That sounds like a very long time."

She shook her red curls. "Not really, considering the fact that Orson founded the chorus about thirty years ago. I always tell him that he's about two hundred and fifty choral performances ahead of me since I joined the chorus, and I'll never be able to catch up. But seriously, he has led the chorus to an outstanding reputation. We're all amateurs, but everyone has to pass a rather strict audition to be accepted. We perform at Carnegie Hall, Avery Fisher Hall, Newark Symphony Hall and Kennedy Center in Washington. Five years ago the chorus recorded a series called 'Great Oratorios with Orson Mahler.' It sold very well and Orson's record company is going to re-issue it on CD next spring."

A young kid on roller-skaters darted past us at neck-breaking speed.

I said, "I'm so excited that you asked me to come along."

"Orson is very open to the general public. He *loves* meeting fans. He says it's good for his ego. But it's really never more than a one-time thing."

Was she trying to tell me she didn't consider me worthy of Orson's further attention? She smiled a smile of superiority, a smile of power. But maybe she wasn't even smiling at me. Beverly smiled at passing strangers in an effortless mobile flirtation. When her eyes met those of passing men, a message was exchanged, an affirmation of availability whose short-lived thrill swept her like a wave to the next block. How much fun she had by being so carefree, so openly sexy. The bright late-afternoon light wasn't flattering to her freckled face, and yet walking next to her nullified my chances of even being noticed. Why couldn't I get myself to believe James, who said I had a great figure with great legs, beautiful hair and lovely eyes?

Obviously Beverly understood something that I didn't, that being sexy was a state of mind and not of body, a state of mind that could manifest itself in as small a detail as her tiny red purse swinging playfully from her shoulder.

In her other hand she carried a tote bag with a thermos bottle sticking out of it. She saw my perplexed look and explained with a laugh, "I always bring hot chocolate to the rehearsals. Orson insists he can't go a day without it. Paula packs brownies for him."

I meant to ask, who's Paula? But she laughed again. She was always laughing. "We all spoil him. He's irresistible." Her skirt swayed from side to side. "But he's so impractical. Except for his music, he always needs someone to tell him where to go and what to do. He's so conservative about money and clothes, except for... uh... his colored underwear, and he looks adorable in it, especially in red."

Her face showed no trace of blushing and I hoped mine didn't either. What the heck did she mean to imply with this piece of information? Why would she have any business knowing the color of the maestro's underwear?

Beverly pushed her glasses up on her nose.

"Orson moves within a very small circle of friends. With a chorus of over a hundred and an orchestra of the same size, it stands to reason that he can't be friends with everyone. Some accuse him of favoritism, but there's never enough time in his schedule of rehearsals, auditions, music committees and concerts, let alone his tours. So, Bella," she glanced at me importantly, "if he doesn't talk to you tonight, don't take it personally. But be assured you're welcome as a visitor."

I swallowed and thought, I would ask her another time not to call me Bella. I just said, "That's fine with me," trying to conceal my growing resistance at being patronized.

"Even I can't always talk to him when I want to, and on some days I drive Paula crazy when I call him three or four times. But then, Paula and I exchange recipes for brownies, and I help Paula on the computer with her mail-merging for the chorus newsletters."

Paula is probably his secretary or personal assistant, I thought, and started to ask. But Beverly beat me again. "Paula has twelve different recipes for brownies. With almonds, caramel, carrots, cinnamon, cloves, ginger, hazelnuts, pumpkin, raisin, vanilla, walnut and whole-grain. It's a standing joke between us to recite the list alphabetically by heart. Orson is crazy about brownies and says that because of Paula's brownies their marriage is still intact after almost 35 years."

"Oh, Paula is his wife?"

"Yes, and they make a perfect couple. They're the same age, the same height, they have the same gray eyes... but not exactly the same weight any more, as 35 years ago. All those brownies left their mark on Paula, not on Orson. The two of them met in their doctor's waiting room, and Orson jokes about the fact that their doctor, a certain Louise Schumann, has long since retired, but that their marriage continues to last. Well, Paula is completely devoted to him, and Paula and I are *very* close friends. Even though the Mahlers entertain rarely, Rudy and I recently spent a Saturday night with them when Orson didn't have a concert. Orson and Paula have a very nice apartment on Park Avenue and that night Orson even played the piano for us. We talked and listened to music until two o'clock in the morning and ended up sleeping in their guest room." She was bursting with pride.

Perhaps this was the explanation for her knowledge about the color of Orson's underwear. She had probably run into him in the bathroom.

Our passing reflections moved across the windows of Gucci's and mingled with the lifeless, uninvolved faces of their mannequins. Involvement, I thought, involvement was the key to feeling alive. Beverly had it, involvement and enthusiasm. But despite her lively nature, my impression was that she didn't live her own life, but only watched someone else live. I began to think that Orson was her entire repository of identity and self-esteem.

Her hair was caught in the breeze and flamed like liquid bronze in the Fifth Avenue rush hour crowd.

"For years," she went on, "before we could finally talk Orson into using professional artist-management, Paula served as his manager, treasurer and director of development. She used to negotiate his Carnegie Hall contracts and kept in touch with his overseas-agents in Paris, London and Vienna for his international concert tours. She went over all the orchestral parts and corrected any discrepancies against his conductor's score. Orson always knew he could rely on her."

"He must appreciate her very much."

"Not enough, maybe, or not always..." Her silvery soprano escalated. "You know, Paula has endured some pretty hard times with Orson, but she withstood every storm with the shrewdness of a sailor who knows when to let the sails down."

Her straightforwardness made me curious. "What kind of storms?"

"Well," she luxuriated in every syllable, "besides brownies and hot chocolate, Orson loves the company of women with... uh... big breasts. He says, he can resist anything but brownies and... uh... breasts."

Her steps sounded louder, like a threat.

Considering my own anatomy, I hardly qualified to cause him much excitement. My breasts were firm and visible enough but gave no reason to turn heads. As much as I appreciated James' comforting comment that "some things are much more beautiful by being less obvious," I would rather have done without the need for his tactful choice of vocabulary.

Unaware of my self-absorption, Beverly sighed meaningfully. *What* was she saying now? Her voice was drowned by the growling of a jackhammer. Was this woman telling me blithely that Maestro Mahler had affairs? My alertness returned.

"... I mean, it's remarkable," she shouted to make herself understood, "but poor Paula never tired of believing that he would never leave her, and he never did. He stayed with her and her brownies for all these years."

We wound our way around a man pushing a hot dog cart. By now it was clear to me that Beverly would never talk about anything else but Orson Mahler. Whether it was loyalty or obsession was too early to say.

"Paula's a very poised woman, with the reputation that no crisis can ruffle her. She opens his mail, answers his calls and takes his tails to the cleaners. She and I are Orson's *only* confidantes."

She squared her shoulders and began to walk a lot faster, detouring around a group of tourists who pressed their noses flat against the windows of the Tiffany displays.

I said, "Could we walk a little slower? My feet are hurting."

She said, "I'm sorry, Bella. We're almost there. We rehearse at CAMI Hall, right here on Fifty-Seventh Street. Orson's artists' management company, Columbia Artists, is in the same building." And then, jumping to the next topic, she said, "Orson is worried about the box-office sales for his upcoming concert of the *Verdi Requiem* on Sunday."

We were walking up Fifty-Seventh Street now and I thought, Tomorrow I'm going to have a blister on each heel and I finally should tell her that I don't like to be called Bella.

Beverly continued. "Tonight should be a great rehearsal, Bella. It's the last one before the dress rehearsal on Sunday with the orchestra. I hope you and your husband will come to the concert."

"I'll order tickets first thing in the morning as a surprise for James," I said and thought, We haven't gone out since November and now it's May.

"You can buy them at a preferred member price tonight. Joan Hunter, our chorus manager, always keeps some in her desk.

"Joan? Oh, yes, I remember Orson mentioning her name yesterday. Didn't you say that you didn't like her?"

Behind her glasses, Beverly's olive eyes narrowed.

"Correct. Watch out, Bella, she's a bitch. She's shrewd and manipulative. Paula and I don't exchange anything with her but chilled glances. She's a good administrator, though. The chorus has been under her dictatorial thumb for twenty years, but she aspires to a much too important place in Orson's life. After all, she's only his employee, but she's convinced he's helplessly in love with her."

"And, is he?" My pulse quickened a little.

"Far from it. The nerve of that woman. She's fifty, but makes every effort to look thirty-five. Admittedly, with her drop-dead size six body and her figure-hugging outfits, she could even fool me."

Before crossing Sixth Avenue, Beverly made sure the top of the thermos bottle in her tote bag was properly closed.

"We have plenty of time before the rehearsal," she pointed at *Wolfe's Coffee Shop* on the corner. "Do you want to have a sandwich?"

"Anything that enables me to take off my shoes."

Inside the restaurant we were seated at a table by the window. On the windowsill, an array of colorful glasses with red and yellow peppers softened the view of the ever-busy mid-town traffic.

Standing or sitting, Beverly talked seamlessly. Her compulsion to communicate needed a congregation, not a contributor. She sought an adoring audience for her relationship with Orson, which seemed to be the driving force of her existence. Knowledge of Orson's portfolio, the color of his underwear and his preferences for brownies and large breasts elevated her self-worth to a level she could not attain without him. To share part of his life lifted her to the stars, where she sparkled in the eyes of anyone who listened. The reason she had chosen me as a companion was for my ability to listen and my ineptitude for small talk. In a way, we made each other whole.

Beverly put a pinch of salt in her black coffee. She said that the taste reminded her of the sea and male skin. In the same breath she also told me that her breasts had recently been *enhanced,* basking in my subsequent stare at the outcome of her elective surgery.

"Orson was quite impressed. He sent me a very funny card, saying ... uh..." She paused with elaborate mystery. "Well, never mind... we had such a good laugh."

And suddenly, waving her knife as if to threaten me, she smiled, "Just don't ever call him *Maestro*. He's allergic to the word."

"It's too late. I already did," I said, mentally staggered from all her information.

I looked into her eyes and forced a smile, and the longer I smiled, the happier my smile became. The invigoration of a sip of hot coffee seemed to free me from her verbal strangulation. No matter how much Beverly counted on Orson's indebtedness for her devotion, no matter how much she was convinced that the ties of time cemented their relationship forever. All this was only *her* side of the story. What if she knew that he had held *my* hand for a solid hour?

6

My first sight upon entering the rehearsal hall was of Orson standing on the podium wearing a black polo shirt and a broad smile. The reason for his smile was that a young woman was kissing him while trying to wrap her short, heavy body around him like a boa constrictor.

"That's Daisy," Beverly laughed.

A flock of sopranos and altos clustered around the podium, all eager to exchange places with Daisy, but she held her ground firmly.

Beverly said, "Even if she couldn't hold a note, she'd come here every Wednesday night to kiss Orson hello and good-bye. But wait until you hear her sing. She's the section leader of the altos and a member of the jury at the auditions. Daisy is the only one in the chorus with absolute pitch."

Trying to ignore the sight of Daisy clinging to Orson, I let my eyes travel around the hall. This room apparently also served as a performance hall, with a small stage and long, Romanesque windows, hung with thick red drapes. About a hundred choristers of both sexes and all ages were milling around. Some were busy arranging the rows of chairs, others already sitting down. By now Daisy had to share Orson with other chorus members circling around the podium. He was enjoying himself, exchanging smiles, jokes and hugs.

Beverly, next to me, flashed him a brilliant smile across the room and he returned it, as if he had known she'd be here at exactly this second. Or did he merely associate her arrival with that of his eagerly awaited hot chocolate? My stomach gave a little flip. He hadn't noticed me at all. Unlike yesterday, he was completely distant, out of reach. Here he was everybody else's property, and I didn't have the slightest share.

Fragmented melodies drifted from the grand piano to the left of the podium.

"There's Joan." Beverly pointed to the petite woman at the desk to the right. With her chestnut hair pulled back into a chignon, her dramatic eye make-up and her picture-book cheekbones, she looked like a Russian ballerina. Her beige knit dress fit tightly, it was as if it were painted on her body.

Beverly guided me in her direction. "She'll give you a score and then you'll be on your own. Enjoy yourself."

Joan, having seen me in Beverly's company, gave me a look without a smile. She tapped her long, sand-colored nails on the wooden desk.

"Are you the aspiring singer who left a message earlier, asking for a private audition? Maestro Mahler doesn't see anyone without a referral or appointment. I make his appointments."

I shook my head. "No, I came with Beverly. I'm a guest listener. My name is Isabella. Beverly told me you could lend me a score."

Her face softened just a little bit. "Okay, here you are, Isabella, but be sure to return it. You can take a seat here, next to my desk. You are required to be absolutely quiet during the rehearsal. Non-members are not permitted to sing along."

I looked at her hands. A dozen bracelets clattered on each wrist.

I said, "Thank you," and my eyes searched for Beverly. But she was already mingling with other singers, bear-hugging half a dozen tenors and artfully pecking some sopranos without transferring lipstick. Apparently she was very popular.

Joan handed out flyers for the concert and an announcement memo for the fall season. Most of the singers were seated now and were flipping through the pages of their scores, some highlighting their parts with yellow markers.

Next to the podium, Beverly handed Orson a cup of hot chocolate. He inhaled the steam and granted her his magic smile. His birthmark twitched. She smiled proudly. By supplying hot chocolate, she assured incontestable access to the maestro's immediate attention.

Sitting on my assigned chair between Joan's desk and the coat rack, I rested my hands on the score in my lap and thought, He doesn't even know I'm here.

At seven-thirty Orson opened his score on the music stand in front of him. The last singers were taking their seats and the buzz of voices diminished to a few scattered whispers. Orson crossed his arms and let his gaze come to rest on the group.

"Good morning, ladies and gentlemen, I hope you're all up and awake..."

Laughter greeted his words.

"I also hope you realize that this is our last rehearsal before Sunday. We've got a lot of material to cover and I'd like to suggest that we don't take an intermission today. If you have not yet signed up with Joan to sing on Sunday, you have to do so tonight after the rehearsal. If you don't, you won't have a stage line-up number for the concert and you will not be allowed on stage. I assume you are all in possession of a red cover for your music and the proper concert attire. You are all welcome to attend our party at Café Carnegie after the performance. Any questions, ask Joan."

His metallic eyes smiled in her direction, but no one else turned to look at her. Her ballerina face showed no emotion, but her nails kept tapping the surface of her desk.

In the first row of the soprano-section Beverly crossed her legs elaborately, showing off several inches above her knees, while exchanging smiles with a bass. Was there any man she could leave dispassionate? Daisy was seated in the first row of the alto-section. Her legs were hardly long enough to reach the floor and her plump body seemed to flow over the edges of the chair. Her jovial smile rendered her face the pleasant roundness of a Botticelli angel. With bangs that long, how could she see anything at all? Yet through her blond, wavy mane, her eyes were glued to Orson's every move.

Orson lifted his baton and looked at the young man behind the grand piano. The pianist nodded.

Orson said, "Let's start right at the beginning... *Andante* in four." He gave the upbeat and after a few opening bars from the piano the tenors and basses entered, followed two bars later by the sopranos and altos.

I opened my borrowed score and read. *Requiem Mass by Guiseppe Verdi (1813 - 1901). Requiem aeternam, dona eis Domine, et lux perpetua -luceat eis (Eternal rest give to them, O Lord, and let perpetual light shine upon them...)*

The singers seemed sure of their parts and produced a sound that was magnificent. Their voices floated through the hall and up to its rounded ceiling as if to blast open the gates of heaven. For a long moment the glory of Verdi's music made me forget that Orson had not noticed me.

Orson stopped the chorus suddenly. "No, no! Ladies and Gentlemen, don't shout! How often do I have to tell you? Get the sound by excitement and not volume. Let it float! It should be nothing more than an aura of tone. And please roll the 'R' of 'Requiem'... and *please* don't drop the music... From the beginning again."

His authority filled the room. It was a force that propelled the chorus by exuding fellowship, not fear. Having experienced him only as a listener, I now experienced him as a leader and a creator.

Watching him, I was mesmerized by the expression of his hands, whose touch had only yesterday caused me such confusion. The same hands now turned into symbols of power, shaping, even caressing the music according to his vision. His movements drew lines and figures in the air and left no doubt about their implications. He loved what he was doing and instilled his love in his singers and his audience.

In the next movement, the *Dies irae*, he explained, "Ladies and Gentlemen, this is *not* a maypole dance. This is *Verdi.* Here the music is sheer drama. So get as mad as you can. Don't be afraid to give it your all! I hope you realize that I try to be as economical as possible in my movements, so that when the real climaxes come, it's something special."

From behind her desk Joan never took her eyes off Orson. She had eyes that were dark and possessive, the mark of a devoted friend or a dangerous enemy. God forbid she'd ever have to make that choice about me.

Orson turned to the *Salva Me* and explained, "Here I want you to produce the same tonal-texture as in the first movement. Imagine yourself gasping, begging for salvation... Let's start at bar three-twenty-two, and please put the accent on the 'e' of 'me,' or else you're going to need salvation yourself."

There was some laughter and after a second of silence the chorus followed his lead, as if their voices were connected to his hands by a silver thread. I thought, This is beautiful. If I never talk to him again, this is so beautiful that I want to be part of it myself. I want to become a member of this chorus and I can't wait to tell James or Julia about it. I can't wait for the concert on Sunday. I hope she can come along with James and me.

Orson shouted over the music, "*Yes,* that's what we want… gasp, whisper, keep the excitement! Follow me!"

A hundred pairs of eyes watched the maestro alertly. He became the spirit of the piece itself, the messenger of the composer. From my removed observation point, I caught myself wondering just for a second about the color of his underwear.

At the conclusion of the *Sanctus*, Orson rested his arms on the music stand. "Could you see me grinning? It was beautiful. Don't touch it. Do it exactly this way on Sunday. You kept a nice steady tone and no one started pumping, and I liked your *fortissimo* in bar sixty-two. Bravo."

A collective smile formed on the singers' faces. In the first row Daisy's ample bosom heaved happily and Beverly's lips pursed coyly as if to throw Orson a kiss. The woman next to her yawned.

Orson put his baton on the music stand and said, "The last time I conducted this piece was five years ago in Italy, in Padova in the Basilica di San Antonio. It was a beautiful performance, although the acoustics of the church were less than ideal. In many churches there's a problem with too much echo, and in this case it forced me to slow down the tempo. But that's certainly not a problem in Carnegie Hall, and I hope you'll do me the honor of outdoing my previous experience with this piece."

Orson launched into the rest of the rehearsal, leaving no doubt in the chorus's mind that he possessed unlimited energy to achieve, even enforce, his musical ideas.

He stopped half-way through the *Agnus Dei*, screaming. "Don't slow down in the middle of a phrase because of a page turn...," and went on with a sigh, "You know you can't wear me down, so you'd better give in, or else I'll have Joan lock the door until we get it right."

Two sopranos giggled into each other's ears.

To ease the tension Orson smiled encouragingly. "If you sing, *sing!* At that moment singing becomes the most important thing in your life."

And I thought again, I want to be a member of this group, I want to be a part of all this energy.

Next to me, Joan shuffled noisily through some papers on her desk, inviting an irritated glance from Orson. For a second I seemed to feel his eyes on me. Had he recognized me? He seemed to acknowledge my face as if it rang a bell but had no reference in time.

The singing continued and the young pianist, playing the reduction of the orchestral score, was beating the living daylights out of the Steinway. His job was to simulate a full orchestra and to be heard over a hundred singers in full volume. I considered him the unsung hero of the group.

At three minutes after ten Orson ended the rehearsal.

"It was a good rehearsal. Do you know why? Because I'm perspiring. Thank you for giving me three minutes and eight seconds overtime. See you all on Sunday."

He stepped from the podium and within five seconds Beverly handed him another cup of hot chocolate. He nodded appreciatively and her triumphant face made it clear that the maestro was hers, at least for now.

I returned my score to Joan. She took it without looking at me.

I tried to be polite. "I had a wonderful time, thank you Joan."

To my surprise she looked up. "We welcome visitors," and the trace of a smile flushed across her joyless face.

Most of the singers left or gathered at Joan's desk. Several women clustered around Orson, headed by Beverly and Daisy. In order to say good-bye to him I would have to use my elbows through a fence of female flesh. Considering that this was the last practice of the season I *had* to see him now unless I wanted to wait until the rehearsals started again in the fall. I had no choice but to take up battle with the competition, even if I had to peel Daisy off his shirt.

I wound my way through rows of empty chairs and suddenly heard Orson's voice addressing the young pianist.

"Matthew, just a moment please, before you leave…"

Matthew had just locked up the Steinway and was packing up his music. He looked up. "Yes?"

Orson gestured for him to come over.

Matthew and I joined the group surrounding Orson at the same moment. Orson absent-mindedly handed his empty cup to Beverly and gestured to me. "Matthew, could you give this young lady a lift home? I believe she lives in Montclair."

All heads turned in my direction.

I looked at Orson. "How did you know I live in Montclair?"

"Beverly mentioned it to me."

Matthew turned to me. "I live there too. It'll be a pleasure taking you."

We shook hands.

"I'm Isabella Barton."

"I'm Matthew Hunter."

His smile was warm. We liked each other instantly. I turned to Orson. There was no more need to fight my way to him. By granting me his attention, he had caused everyone to step aside, including Beverly and Daisy.

I said, "Thank you for arranging a ride for me. It's very thoughtful of you. And thank you for inviting me tonight. The music was heavenly."

He said, "I'm happy to hear it, but don't thank me. Thank the composer, Guiseppe Verdi," and as in a dream, he took my right hand with his left and held it.

For a split second I thought of my immaculate red nails and felt the texture of the bandage covering his pinkie against my fingers. Each second that Orson continued holding my hand was registered by a dozen alarmed female eyes, and I was frightened by feeling so impossibly close to him. But Orson seemed totally at ease and smiled at me as if all the others had already gone home.

The touch of my hand seemed to cure him of the loneliness I sensed deep down hidden in his heart.

He said, "I'm glad Matthew is taking you. I'll sleep better tonight knowing you got home safely."

At long last he let go of my hand and bowed somewhat stiffly. There was a collective sigh from the women around us, who had been holding their breath for the duration of this unusual scene.

I looked at Orson and said nothing, because, as so often, I couldn't think of anything to say.

7

As we left the building Matthew said with an apologetic frown, "I saw you talking to my mother before the rehearsal. I'm afraid she wasn't all too friendly, but you have to understand that before concerts she's always overworked, and having to deal with Orson's entourage can be a pretty tough job."

I said, "Joan's your mother?"

He pulled up the zipper of his leather jacket and giggled. "Yes, she's my mother. I'm sorry. Of course you couldn't know."

He stepped ahead to open the door for me. I judged Matthew to be in his mid twenties, though his refreshing giggle made him seem like a teenager. The large, soulful eyes that I now saw that he had inherited from his mother gave him the appearance of wisdom.

A few blocks down the street, his Volkswagen beetle looked as battered as Orson's briefcase, and while he searched his pockets for the keys he pointed through the window.

"I hope you don't mind that we have another passenger. I'm taking Allegro back home. My friend Tom and I were away over the weekend so my mother took care of him."

He opened the door and removed a wooden travel birdcage from the passenger seat. Inside, a little green and yellow parakeet flapped its wings excitedly.

Matthew beamed and held the cage up to eye-level.

"He's so happy to see me. Isn't he pretty?"

"He's adorable." I peeked through the bars at the exotic little creature who was uttering strange guttural sounds.

I felt Matthew's large, dark eyes searching mine.

"Would you mind ... uh... holding the cage on our way home?"

"I'd be thrilled," I laughed, and Matthew was relieved.

With Allegro's cage safely positioned on my lap, Matthew negotiated the Manhattan potholes as if he were test-driving a Porsche. The noise from the exhaust system could have frightened Superman, much less little Allegro, who, clinging to his perch, nervously stretched his neck in every direction. At first, he had to struggle for his balance, but after a few moments he seemed fine and reveled in fluffing his green and yellow feathers.

A little later, under the flickering light-patterns of the Lincoln Tunnel, Matthew's eyes traveled adoringly to Allegro's cage.

"Tom and I have had him for four years. Tom gave him to me when we moved in together. He's been a real source of joy for us."

Allegro opened his rounded beak and gave a bored yawn.

I studied Matthew's features from the side. There was something in his evenly sculptured face, under the mop of curly hair, that reminded me of someone other than Joan, but I couldn't put my finger on it. There was also something in the shape of his long, sensitive hands, hands ideal for the piano keyboard, and now curled around the steering wheel, that resembled someone else's, someone I might have met in a dream.

I said, "You are a wonderful pianist. I loved listening to you tonight."

Matthew gave me a side-ways glance that was too long for safety's sake.

"I appreciate the compliment. When you play every day for a living, it becomes so routine that you sometimes forget that you're dealing with an art."

The car in front of us swerved alarmingly close.

I shut my eyes. "Watch out!"

Matthew stepped on the brake and Allegro chirped. *Allegro ma non troppo... non troppo... troppo...!*

My nerves recovered but I couldn't believe my ears.

"Allegro's talking! He's amazing!"

Matthew giggled. "Isn't he? He's a real cutie..."

I asked, "But where do you play?"

He kept his eyes straight ahead this time.

"I do all kinds of free-lance jobs. I accompany and coach singers and ballet dancers at the Met, I do voice training and I'm the staff accompanist at Montclair State College. Running around from one job to another like this keeps me as much behind the wheel as behind the piano."

"Wouldn't you like to become a concert pianist, tour the world and make recordings?"

He shrugged and shifted gears, and Allegro scooted along his perch in perfect synchronicity.

"I love to play, but I recognized early in life that I'm not a candidate for stardom. It's a tough business out there. The rosters of the record companies are stretched with waiting-lists, and in any good orchestra there's only room for one pianist. If I were a violinist... well, a good violinist should always be able to land a position with an ensemble... but anyway, Orson always tells me that the most important thing is to be able to enjoy what I'm doing.

From the cage came, *Allegro molto, Allegro molto.... moltooo...moltooooo...*

I was laughing so hard the cage was jumping up and down on my lap. This little bird gave me the feeling of having wings myself.

After a moment I said, "I really enjoyed myself tonight at the rehearsal."

Matthew smiled. "I'm glad." And I noticed a tiny golden earring in his right earlobe.

Coming out of the tunnel, Matthew took the uphill curve to Route 3 as if he were practicing for the Indianapolis 500. Some of his cassette tapes between the seats fell down.

"Damn it," he mumbled, glancing at the spilled tapes and then asked, "Have you done a lot of singing?"

"Not really, except as a member of the school choir. My most vigorous attempts at singing were as a child, when I went strawberry-picking with my mother in the woods."

"How's that?" He looked at me again, and I was glad the road was straight now."

"My mother always made me sing, so she would know where I was and also so I didn't put too many strawberries in my mouth instead of the basket."

We both giggled, Allegro twittered, and the two of them made me feel marvelously young.

A question had been on my mind since we left CAMI Hall.

"Matthew, how difficult is the audition to become a member of the chorus?"

He shrugged. "It's not a big deal. You have to be able to carry a tune and sight-read. But you don't have to be a Marilyn Horne or a Roberta Peters. You just need a voice that blends well."

"I used to take piano lessons, but I played deplorably, and I could never sight-read."

"I know, that's the problem with a lot of singers who might have good voices. But sight-reading is only a skill. You can learn it. If you're serious about it, I can help you."

He changed lanes, shifted gears and had the gas pedal down the floor.

"That would be wonderful, Matthew, but how?"

"Which part do you sing?"

"Alto, I suppose."

"I thought so too, from listening to your voice. I can make you a tape with the alto part of the piece we're singing in the fall, the *Brahms Requiem*. That way you can listen to your own part while you study the score over the summer. The auditions will be based on the Requiem."

"You're an angel, Matthew. I *am* serious about this, you know. Very serious. How can I thank you?"

"I'm glad I can help. It'll be wonderful to have you in the chorus." His thoughts seemed to drift away and he giggled again.

".... you know, once at a chorus party, Allegro escaped from his cage and someone let him sip some champagne. You should have seen him. He acted like a lunatic, snatching olives from the bar, landing on everyone's shoulder, and later... ," he giggled even harder, "he pooed on Orson's tails..."

Picturing the scene, Matthew and I roared with laughter.

Finally he said, "But tell me, how did you hear about the chorus?"

"I came as Beverly's guest. We work in the same building on Park Avenue."

Matthew grimaced. "Beverly, our flamboyant redhead?"

"Yes, that's right. What about her?"

"Uhhh.... are you good friends with her?"

"No, not particularly." I felt surprised at my assessment of our brief relationship and added, "I don't think we're made to be bosom buddies."

Matthew sneered. "That woman sets my teeth on edge."

My curiosity was sparked. "You don't like her? Men seem to go wild over her."

On my lap Allegro hopped from one perch to another.

Matthew shook his head. "Not me. She thinks she owns Orson. Nobody is allowed to get close to him without her approval. She forms a tight team with Daisy, and the two of them act like self-appointed bodyguards."

He reached into the pocket of his jacket and produced a roll of lemon drops.

"Do you want one?"

"Thanks." I took one, hoping he'd tell me more.

He chewed his drop noisily and went on. "God forbid that Orson would dare to talk to my mother an instant longer than Beverly deems appropriate. If it weren't for Orson's diplomacy, they would probably throw kitchen knives at each other."

From the cage came, *Allegro serioso, seriosoo....seriosooo... oooo...*

"Why is that?" I asked, delighted by Allegro's aria, but burning to hear Beverly's story from Matthew's perspective.

"Well, there's something else..." Matthew hesitated and his neck stiffened under his mop of curly hair.

"What's that?" I said softly, hoping to inspire confidence.

"Uh...," he moved uncomfortably. "I hope you don't think I'm gossiping, but I feel more comfortable talking to you than with anyone in the chorus."

"Why?"

"Because you obviously have no personal interest in Orson. Or do you, Isabella?"

"No, no," I hastily assured him.

"Good. Everybody else seems to be hung up on him in some way."

"That's incredible," I cleared my throat, hoping to keep the conversation going.

He swallowed his lemon-drop. Allegro mumbled something in bird language.

I said, "What about Beverly? Why don't you like her?"

His face hardened. "Beverly tries to make herself indispensable by taking care of all kinds of jobs for Orson, and very often she steps into my mother's territory as manager of the chorus. If Beverly would just behave like any other chorus member, show up at Wednesday nights, sing and pay her annual fee, I could tolerate her. But she gets involved in every administrative issue and considers herself the unofficial president. She should stick to her stocks and bonds and leave the chorus and Orson to my mother."

He was on a roll and about to say something else, but along with a battery of wing flaps, our feathered friend shouted excitedly, *Allegro vivace e furioso... furriosoooo...*

Matthew nodded to the cage on my lap.

"He loves to ride in the car."

I said, "That's a difficult situation for your mother to be in."

Matthew frowned. "But that's not the end of it. Last week Beverly outdid herself. She wrote an open letter to the chorus board, suggesting they eliminate my mother's position."

"No! Did she really?"

"She certainly did. She said that by dividing up my mother's duties into a team of volunteers, the management of the chorus would be balanced much better. And the chorus budget would benefit by eliminating my mother's salary. And Orson could spend more money for P.R. and advertising." He sighed.

"*Unmöglich!* How can Beverly justify her behavior?"

Matthew shrugged. "She simply doesn't. Needless to say, she thinks the maestro is hopelessly in love with her."

"And is he?" I held my breath.

"Who knows....? On a couple of occasions he's said that she can be too much and tries to keep her at arm's length. But on the other hand, he enjoys her attention."

His answer was not as clear-cut as I would have liked it to be.

To our right, the Meadowlands sports complex flew by. Allegro was diligently gnawing on one of the wooden poles of his cage.

Eager to stay on the subject, I said, "If you ask me, anyone who serves Orson hot chocolate seems to qualify for his attention."

"Right," he giggled. "That and brownies."

"Beverly told me that Orson's wife has a dozen different recipes for brownies."

Matthew said, "That's right," and started chewing on another lemon-drop.

By now Allegro seemed to have some reason to complain. He chirped angrily, *Ma non troppo, ma non, non, non... troooooo.*

I decided to take the bull by the horns. "Why would Beverly tell me that Orson wears red underwear?"

Matthew didn't seem surprised.

"Oh, she bragged about that to you too, did she?"

"She certainly did."

"Well, apparently a week ago or so Beverly and her husband Rudy were invited to the Mahlers' for dinner and the two of them ended up sleeping in the guestroom. Beverly made sure the whole chorus knew about it. Apparently, early in the morning, Orson got up to get himself a glass of juice from the refrigerator. For some reason Beverly heard Orson swearing at the top of his voice from the kitchen. He had spilled the juice. She found him on his hands and knees on the floor, and yes, *in his underwear,* his pinkie caught in a mousetrap. That's why he's still wearing a bandage."

I took a deep breath and thought, That explains it.

Looking at Matthew I laughed lightheartedly and meant to say, "That's a funny story," but Allegro, who had been busying himself with the lock of the cage, let out a triumphant cry as the small door opened and he escaped.

"*O mein Gott!*" I shouted.

Matthew's giggle turned into an explosive laugh.

"That little rascal. He's done it again... I'll catch him later. It's O.K. as long as the windows are shut."

Allegro flew in elegant circles around our heads.

Matthew assured me, "Don't worry. I'll catch him."

Having explored enough of his freedom, Allegro landed expertly on the steering wheel between Matthew's hands, eyes ahead on the road.

Matthew winked at me.

"He's got the best seat in the house, hasn't he?"

I laughed, enchanted by the company of my new friends. Encouraged by Matthew's kindness, I decided to ask him another question.

"I heard that Beverly does a lot of office work for Paula, Orson's wife, and that they are very close chums."

He shrugged vaguely. "Maybe, maybe not. Let's just say, they worked out a system for exchanging services." Allegro was still sitting on the steering wheel. "If you ask me, Paula's an odd sort. She's a complete homebody. Except for her husband's concerts, she hardly ever leaves the apartment. She never attends a rehearsal. I suppose it's partly because of her natural inertia, partly because of her ever-painful ankles. But considering the weight she has to carry around, that's hardly a surprise."

Matthew adjusted the rear-view mirror and we passed two other cars at eighty miles an hour, causing my pulse to accelerate to the same speed.

"I said, "So by making herself indispensable and keeping herself in Paula's good graces, Beverly assures herself a safe place in Orson's life."

"That makes sense," he said, "but there's something else..."

He turned the vent on full blast.

"Yes?" I buttoned my jacket to diminish the impact of the draft. Allegro's feathers fluffed up like a bag of colored cotton balls.

Matthew beamed, "He loves the draft, you see?" and then in a more serious tone, "Beverly is Paula's second pair of eyes, especially at rehearsals. Paula is a very jealous woman and my mother is her prime target. Beverly serves as her spy. Everything that happens on Wednesday nights is reported back to Paula."

Matthew's words were like the multiple curtains of a theater play that opened one by one, each revealing more surprises. A driver honked his horn at us, but Matthew didn't bat an eye.

For a moment I recalled Orson's words: *I'm glad Matthew is taking you home. I'll sleep better tonight, knowing you got home safely.*

I wondered if Orson had ever been in a car with Matthew.

Allegro left his observation post and hopped onto Matthew's shoulder, from where he announced, *Allegro a tempo, a tempo...*

The next moment he vigorously pulled at Matthew's earring.

"Ouch..." Matthew shook his head and moved his shoulder. The bird's claws slipped on Matthew's leather jacket, and he decided to move to a safer landing place, this time on the padded shoulder of my jacket. I shuddered a little. Allegro immediately dug his beak into my hair, aiming for my ear, but was disappointed at not finding another earring. Still, he held his position and became suspiciously quiet.

With my hands still on the bars of the empty cage, I said, "After so many years of working together, your mother and Orson must be like... uh... like family."

Matthew's dark eyes seemed to be lost somewhere past the horizon. Then he went on as if he had skipped a thought. ".... but things will always be the same. My mother's miserable with him and without him."

He relaxed a little, as if deciding against saying more.

"I think I understand what you mean," I assured him and held onto the door-handle as we careened up the ramp onto the exit from Route 3.

Still on my shoulder, Allegro softly serenaded into my ear. *Allegro con amore, con amore... amore...* His romantic declaration almost brought tears to my eyes.

I said to Matthew, "I live on Valley Road. I hope it doesn't take you too far out of your way."

"Not at all. Tom and I live farther down, at Hawthorne Place." And without my asking he volunteered further, "Tom and I are kind of an odd couple..." He stopped in mid-sentence, uncertain how to continue. "He's a corporate pilot. Flying his boss around in a corporate jet is much more lucrative than accompanying singers on the piano."

Now safely on residential streets, I heaved a sigh.

"You're quite a driver, Matthew."

He giggled again. "When you become a member of the chorus, I'd like to apply for the job of your regular Wednesday night chauffeur."

"That's an offer I can hardly turn down." I tried to appear enthusiastic, weighing the convenience and companionship against the potential hazard.

Matthew said, "Then we have a deal. I'm looking forward to your company, Isabella. And here we are on Valley Road. Tell me where I should let you off."

In front of my house, he reached over to my shoulder and with the speed and dexterity of a pianist, caught the feathered adventurer and put him back in his cage.

"We've been through this on more than one occasion, haven't we, Allegro?" And then to me, "I'll remember to drop that voice-tape off for you."

I said, "Are you sure the tape isn't too much trouble?"

"Don't worry. With the end of the chorus season I won't be so busy over the summer. No concerts, no rehearsals. Of course, Orson will have other conducting commitments."

I climbed out of the car and put the cage back on the seat. From inside, Allegro sang ardently, *Con amore... amooore...*

I smiled at my new friends. "It was such a pleasure." I was sad to leave them.

But I also thought, sadly, of Orson. When would I get to see him again? Maybe not before the fall. Never before in my life had I wished the summer away.

In the headlights of Matthew's car as he turned, the yellow forsythia bushes stood aflame against the blackness of the night. From the sidewalk I could see that the lights were on in our kitchen.

Before I could find the key, James opened the door from the inside. The lights from the hallway shone on his freshly blow-dried hair. His eyes shone warmly.

"Hi, there, Beautiful. I heard a car and saw you get out. You seem all excited. Who brought you home?"

"The pianist from the chorus offered me a ride. His name is Matthew. He's a nice young man, but I can assure you he's not interested in women... But you should hear him. He plays like a stuntman and drives the same way… and..." I paused to take a breath and stepped inside.

"And?" James closed the door behind me.

"He has this adorable bird who can talk. He escaped from his cage and sat on my shoulder. Believe it or not, he told me the most amazing things, *in Italian!*"

James grinned broadly. “Isabella, I’m sorry to tell you this, but I’m afraid you’re full of it...”

“No! It’s absolutely true!”

James turned me around in front of the Venetian mirror next to the coat hooks. “Oh, I believe you. I meant the bird did a number all over the back of your jacket.”

We looked at each other and doubled over laughing.

8

Would I keep my promise to myself? I had no choice. Regardless of my restless imagination, I would have to adhere to reason. Since my ride with Matthew two days ago, I had committed myself to a step-by-step plan for the summer. I would wait to receive Matthew's tape, study my voice part of the *Brahms Requiem*. At the beginning of September I'd try to pass the audition and maybe see Orson again. In the meantime I wouldn't expect any miracles, such as the lighting of the tree at Rockefeller Center in the middle of May or accidentally running into Orson Mahler at *Saks Fifth Avenue* during my lunch hour. I was counting on the rewards of patience, and if need be, I would wait. I would wait for the fall and get ready, and apart from singing, I wasn't even sure what it was that I was getting ready for.

For now, I was busy with my daily duties at the office. I refilled the paper supply in the feeder before making thirty-five copies of the April Performance Analysis. By doing a routine-check I noticed that, of the document's eighteen pages, page eleven was missing. Where was it? It was not on Mr. Stringer's desk, nor in the controller's office, and to everyone's consternation, the financial analyst who had created it on his computer, had accidentally deleted the entire file.

Mr. Stringer was fuming. He needed the report for his meeting at the Plaza Hotel in twenty minutes. He stood in front of my desk and blew cigar smoke over my head.

"Isabella, as soon as the missing page turns up, take a taxi and bring it to me at the meeting."

He fretfully played with my pencil holder and then said in an equally fretful voice, "And make sure you send out my party invitations today. I want you to address them by hand. The list is in my out-box. I think there are sixty-five."

"Yes sir." I avoided looking at him.

The receptionist put her head around the door.

"Isabella, the architects are here with the color samples for the new cubicles."

I said, "I'll be out in a minute."

Mr. Stringer remained rooted in front of my desk like a potted plant.

He said, "Call the people at the Plaza and tell them I'll be ten minutes late. And cancel the appointment for my haircut."

"Sure," I nodded, wishing for five o'clock, or at least for one little light from the tree at Rockefeller Center to brighten up my day.

Sandy Maxwell, our V.P., stormed out of her office, and her long black mane, artfully styled in a two-hundred-dollar perm, moved around her tiny face like a dark swarm.

"Isabella, I need a limo immediately to go to that merger meeting at the World Trade Center."

I speed-dialed the limousine company and they put me on hold, politely but seemingly perpetually, to wait for the confirmation number for Sandy's car. Meanwhile, I tried to reach the Plaza Hotel on my personal line, but couldn't get a dial-tone because yet another call was coming in.

I said, "Isabella Barton, please hold."

The other voice said commandingly, "But I don't want to hold," and it sounded alarmingly familiar.

I said uncertainly, "How can I help you?"

Now the voice was all velvet. "I just wanted to make sure you got home safely the other night."

I whispered, "Orson..," and my head began to swim.

Sandy frowned impatiently and Mr. Stringer was puffing faster on his cigar.

Orson said with leisurely warmth, "It's nice to hear your voice. How are you?"

"Fine... uh…" My mind was as empty as a soap bubble.

"I'm glad. I haven't forgotten that you were interested in reading my book. I dug out one of my copies and I'd like to give it to you."

The "on-hold" light from the limo company stopped blinking. Sandy let out a desperate sigh and Mr. Stringer cleared his throat impatiently.

I said to Orson, "How will I be able to get it?"

He assumed a matter-of-fact tone. "I'd like to give it to you personally. If you're free, I have some time on Monday around three. I suggest we meet in the lounge of the Omni Berkshire Hotel."

"Uh-huh..," I mumbled, completely taken by surprise and immediately aware of how difficult it would be to leave the office at three.

Orson said, "It's this coming Monday, May twelfth, the day after my concert at Carnegie Hall. Will you be there?"

Not sure whether he was referring to the concert or our meeting, I said, "Yes, I'll be happy to come," covering both options.

Orson asked, "Do you know where it is?"

"Carnegie Hall?"

"No, no, I mean the Berkshire, of course. I picked it because it's close to your office."

"I think I know where it is."

"It's between Madison and Park, on Fifty-Second Street."

"I know."

Sandy and Mr. Stringer were still hovering.

Orson elaborated, "It's on the north side of the street."

"I'm sure I'll find it."

He continued unwaveringly. "The lounge is past the reception desk in the back."

“Very well.” I was starting to recover from the surprise of his call and added, “I enjoyed watching you conduct at the rehearsal. You must get a lot out of it.”

He said dryly, “Do you know what I get out of it? A chance to vent my spleen...” And then he laughed heart-warmingly. “All right then, Isabella. See you Monday at three.”

“See you,” I replied. But he had already hung up.

All at once the office seemed awesomely altered. Everything was warm and lovely, as though bathed in a celestial light. Sandy and Mr. Stringer had become adorable little cherubs who seemed confused, like actors in the wrong play.

Sandy’s voice took on an angelic tone. “Isabella, I’m still waiting for the confirmation number of my limo.”

Mr. Stringer said helplessly, “What about my call to the Plaza?”

I smiled at both of them.

“Would you believe they could light the tree in Rockefeller Center in the middle of May?”

Mr. Stringer gave me a baffled look through his cigar smoke.

Sandy said, somewhat concerned, “Isabella, are you feeling all right? You look all flushed and I’m not sure what you mean.”

“But I’m absolutely sure. They lit the tree at Rockefeller Center just now. Isn’t it lovely?”

9

Yes, my world had become lovely, as if seen through a multi-colored lens. Even the rain against the windows of the bus during my commute home, creating patterns of intertwining droplets, looked lovely and inspiring. Strangely, though, the closer I got to home, the more the perspective changed from inspiring to disturbing, just as the thought of seeing Orson again.

Why did he want to see me? Why had I agreed to see him? I had no truthful answer and dismissed the question the moment I realized that James wasn't home. He was normally always home on a Friday night when I returned from work. His car wasn't in the garage and the kitchen smelled of popcorn and salt. James' favorite red bowl sat upside down in the sink.

There was no message on the table and it occurred to me that I hadn't been alone in the house for several months. Without the reassuring feeling of James' presence, I was more alert, as if returning from a long absence and now questioned the familiarity taken so long for granted. To ease my disquietude about his absence, I decided to put on some Mozart. I chose one of the early symphonies, conducted by Orson Mahler, and its youthful sound soon filled the house. As I began to water my plants, I explained to them that Mozart was barely ten years old when he wrote this delightful, sparkling work. Their leaves seemed to open up like hundreds of tiny ears.

James and I loved the simplicity of our house. We agreed that a living room should have enough open space to practice a *Wiener Walzer* without having to move the furniture. Yet our furniture's functionality was counterbalanced by a few selected objects, milestones of memories, each recalling a special occasion. There were a large Tiffany bowl, a dozen silver framed photographs and my cherished paperweights.

Carefully balancing the watering can above the beige carpet, my eyes swept around the living room as if I were a first-time visitor to my home. When had I last stopped to contemplate the row of gold-framed paintings above the couch?

The six portraits of Austrian royalty were painted on ivory. My mother had given them to me the day I left Austria.

The monarchs usually exuded a stark, stalwart air, as though stiffened by the burdens of their crowns or from too many hours of modeling for the artist. But today the Empress Maria Theresia seemed to wink at me, and it was as if their Highnesses were whispering among themselves. *Monday at three. Monday at three.* The gilded frames appeared to move slightly from suppressed chuckles beneath their painted dignity.

With the watering can refilled I moved on to the small adjoining room that now served as our office and had formerly been part of a porch. It contained my old roll-top desk and swivel-chair, a well-worn rocker from James' family home in St. Louis and three Kentia palms.

On the desk was a printed invitation. I put down the watering can to read it. On the first Sunday in June, Angela and Barry were having their annual party, promising lots of food and fun for their wide circle of friends. The last two years, since they had lived together, James and I had happily attended.

And there was an air-mail letter from my mother. James had already opened it. My mother's small, bouncy handwriting in pale blue ink reminded me of the color of her eyes and the rhythm of her steps on the wooden floors. She hoped I could visit her in the summer. Wasn't I always complaining that New York was unbearable in August? By that time she would have the shutters painted green, matching the flower-boxes outside each window. I could stay in my old room, swim in the lake, she would bake *Apfelstrudel,* and we could go to the courtyard concerts at *Schloss Leonstain.* Wouldn't it be nice?

Yes, I thought, it would. Yes, I would go to see my mother, enjoy the party with Angela and Barry and meet Orson on Monday at three. Whether James was working or not, the future didn't look so bleak anymore. Suddenly I couldn't understand why I had allowed myself to be so listless during the last few months. Didn't I realize it was a mockery of all the good things that life afforded?

I looked at my old desk with its antique inkwell and its modern electric pencil sharpener, connecting the past with the present. All at once I wondered if, after all these years, my mother had kept her collection of Orson Mahler's pictures and clippings. When I saw her in August, what would there be that I could tell her… or keep from her?

I opened the drawer of my desk and it seemed to contain a reflection of my whole existence. Why did I keep all these things? Was there any reason to hang on to old *Stagebills,* brochures from the Bronx Zoo or my shell necklace from Bermuda? Out they went, straight into the waste paper basket next to one of the Kentia palms.

There was also an old city map of Vienna, restaurant matchbooks and an unfocused snapshot that Julia had taken of James and me on Liberty Island. They went too. So did the calorie-counter, a seed catalogue and several cards that I had received for my birthday in November.

For a moment I sat with my elbows on my knees and looked at my new shoes. They would never be comfortable. So I took them off and threw them out too. With every discarded item I sensed I was shedding a layer of old skin.

James' voice caught me off guard. "If you keep throwing things out like this, I'd better hold on to the furniture."

"Why?" I swung around, startled.

"Because," he said, cocking his head in amusement, "you might want to throw me out too."

James seemed in high spirits and looked strikingly different.

I said, "You got a haircut."

"Very observant, Beautiful." He bent down to kiss my forehead.

"It was about time you went to the barber," I chuckled, eager to divert his attention from the fact that he had seen me throw away my shoes.

"How does it look?" He ran his hand through his hair, unable to hide his amazement at how little he had left.

"Not bad." I got up and walked around him, shoeless. "It looks neat, to say the least. Very neat."

"Good." He seemed glad to hear this and made himself comfortable in the rocker between two Kentia palms. He started rocking and his smile broadened.

"I dropped off three suits at the dry-cleaners."

"What's the occasion? Sensing something else up his sleeve, I sat down again in front of the desk.

The twin creases running from the sides of his mouth deepened into a triumphant grin. "I've got three interviews lined up for next week. The first is on Monday at three. The others are on Tuesday and Thursday morning. What do you say, Beautiful?"

The first thing that registered with me was Monday at three. I looked at him in confusion. "Are you serious, James?"

"Of course, I'm serious. Didn't you think I'd ever get another interview? I haven't been sitting around doing nothing, regardless of what you might think." He got up from his chair, visibly irritated.

After a few seconds, the message sunk in and I jumped up and threw my arms around him. "That's great! Just great! Congratulations..."

He softened quickly.

"That's my Isabella." He held me tightly, rubbing my back. "Don't you know me by now? I never stopped believing that our future would be fine." He let go of me and smiled, staunchly confident.

My toes curled excitedly into the carpet.

"Oh, James you have to tell me..."

He paced to the window and back. "This morning I got a call from Harold Gladley, one of the headhunters. He has three companies lined up to see me, one of them in Philadelphia and one in Connecticut."

I blurted out, "Would it mean we'd have to move?"

"For the right job, we'd have to consider it."

I sank back on my chair in silent horror. *Move*? Not now, now that I planned on joining Orson Mahler's chorus... The Mozart symphony had ended, but James' voice hardly reached me any longer.

"But the best news is," he continued, "he also got a call from the company that turned me down three months ago. Remember? That was the job I really wanted most of all. They put me through three interviews and then decided on another guy. Well, for some reason the man they hired tried to pull a fast one on them. Something went wrong with his background check. So now they want to talk to me again..."

Back in control, I clapped my hands together.

James scratched his newly styled head. "... and that's Monday at three."

Through all this I heard another voice from far away, making me blush. *The lounge is past the reception desk in the back.* I hoped that James would attribute my glow to the excitement of the moment.

I said, "You'll have to tell me about the other two companies."

James picked a long blonde hair from the back of my blouse and dropped it in the wastepaper basket on top of my new shoes.

He said, "Why don't we celebrate a little? Let's go out for dinner and I'll give you all the details." He didn't mention my shoes.

I said, "I'd like that," and thought, Maybe I should try to wear them one more time.

James made the face of a martyr. "Besides, I'm starved. I haven't eaten at all today, except for some popcorn. I have to make one more phone call and change my clothes."

I smiled. "I'll freshen up too."

At the door he turned around, his eyes sweeping my desk.

"What kind of a mess have you made here?"

".... uh, just creating space for a new beginning...," I explained teasingly, unsure which beginning I had in mind.

He shook his head and left the room. Eager to clean things up, my fingers ran through the remaining pile of papers. Because of my agitation I was almost tempted to discard the whole pile at once. But the waste basket was full and my mind was not yet fully made up about my shoes.

And then, between a stack of coupons and business cards from caterers and carpet cleaners, another *Stagebill* emerged. It was the one from last Friday's concert, where Orson had conducted Beethoven's *Ninth Symphony.* On that day, when Julia had dumped her coffee on my skirt, I felt somewhat upset and I had not read the program.

Involuntarily, I sat down again and leafed through the booklet, forgetting dinner with James and the unresolved question of my shoes. On the *Meet the Artist* page was a small photo of Orson and next to it his biography. I started reading, fascinated.

Orson Mahler is one of the rare conductors who was born in New York City and, despite tempting offers for prestigious conducting tenures all over the world, has remained faithful to his native city and made it the center of his career. After much soul-searching whether to settle for chemistry or conducting, he chose the latter and earned his Master's Degree in Music at Yale and his Doctorate at Columbia University.

Because of a lack of conducting opportunities with established ensembles, he founded his own organization, the renowned Orson Mahler Oratorio Chorus and Orchestra, and he has led both groups in outstanding performances for almost three decades. Maestro Mahler has often appeared as guest conductor with the New York Philharmonic, the Philadelphia Orchestra, the Boston Symphony, the London Symphony Orchestra and the Vienna Philharmonic. He is always enthusiastically received at festivals such as Salzburg, Tanglewood, Aspen, Florence, Bregenz and Verona, and he has led his orchestra on tours throughout the United States, virtually every European country, Canada, South America and Japan.

The recipient of four awards for adventuresome programming from the American Society of Composers, Mr. Mahler has demonstrated a commitment to performing the music of our time. He has recorded exclusively for RCA for almost 30 years and, in addition to 26 Grammy Awards, his recordings have won such prestigious prizes as the Grand Prix du Disc and the Diapason d'Or. His extensive discography contains cycles by Beethoven, Brahms, Schubert, Elgar, Rachmaninoff...

"I thought you wanted to freshen up." James' voice startled me for the second time.

My head shot up. "I...uh, I'm sorry...," I pushed the booklet into the now empty drawer, surprised about feeling guilty.

"Come on. Let's go." James sneezed, got hold of a tissue, and motioned me to get moving.

"*Gesundheit...*" I closed the drawer and got up.

"Do you want to try that new French restaurant down the street?"

I nodded enthusiastically, but couldn't figure out why James followed me upstairs. Maybe he just wanted to make sure that I would actually get ready without being side-tracked again.

Halfway up the stairs I turned around.

"Did you see the invitation from Angela and Barry?"

"Yes, Barry mentioned it to me on the phone. I told him we'd be there."

"And, James... my mother wants me to visit her in August. I'd really like to go."

"I saw the letter. I think you should go too. After all, you haven't seen her in two years."

We had come to the top of the stairs. James reached up to remove a burned-out light bulb from the chandelier above our heads.

"And also, James..."

"Uh-hu?" He tried to read the wattage on the bulb in his hand.

"I really wanted to tell you something else."

"What's that?" He looked at me and put the bulb on the corner of the banister.

"I want to join the Orson Mahler Oratorio Chorus in the fall. I had such a wonderful time at the rehearsal the other night."

James seemed unimpressed and searched his pockets for a handkerchief. But before he could find one, he sneezed again.

"Damned allergies," he grumbled.

"You know," I added keenly, "it's the same chorus we're going to hear at the concert on Sunday night. Just imagine, James, one day I could be singing on the stage of Carnegie Hall."

James blew his nose and one hand moved to his lower back. I wondered if his old pain was bothering him. I was about to ask him, but he straightened up and smiled cheerfully.

"Good idea. Singing would keep you busy. And it would certainly keep you out of trouble."

10

On the stage the musicians finished tuning their instruments. In our box in Carnegie Hall, Julia leaned over to me and her voice was well above a whisper.

"I want to write that bestseller more than anything else in the world. I want it even more than I want to have Phil back, but my mind is as dry as a desert."

Several heads turned.

"Shhhhh..," I hissed, annoyed at her insensitivity to the rising tension in the hall. Hadn't I heard it all before? Her face darkened and she shifted in her chair, high-strung like a cat in a cage. Wasn't she aware that this was one of the most exciting moments of a concert, when the lights dim and the audience waits for the soloists and the conductor to appear?

From the brightly-lit stage the members of the orchestra and the chorus looked out into the undefined darkness of the auditorium, and three thousand pairs of eyes from the auditorium were expectantly glued to the door on the left.

My eyes drifted worriedly to the door of our box. Where was James? Fifteen minutes ago he had deposited Julia and me in front of Carnegie Hall and had driven off to park the car. I feared that once the performance started they wouldn't let him in.

The next minute the hall thundered with applause as the four soloists emerged, the two young women in flowing gowns of black and green, the two men in tuxedos. They bowed and took their seats facing the audience. Now only Orson and James were missing, both delayed for unknown reasons. The applause continued but got thinner by the second. How long is an audience willing to cheer for an invisible conductor?

After several suspenseful moments Orson appeared and strode briskly towards the podium, like a New Yorker trying to catch the cross-town bus on Forty-Second Street. In his tails he looked devastatingly elegant. He leaped onto the podium as if reaching a safe island in a storm. His smile seemed to say, "I'm glad you didn't start without me," and he bowed to the waves of applause, obviously loving his audience and loved by them in return.

I clapped my hands and thought, *Tomorrow at three.* Tomorrow at three I would have him all to myself.

The applause subsided. Orson lifted his baton, and the musicians and singers held their breath in concentrated apprehension. The strings started with a few somber bars before the chorus came in, almost eerily gasping.

Requiem aeternam... It was the same music that I had witnessed taking shape at the rehearsal, and now it sparkled as a finished performance.

Suddenly James was sitting in the chair next to Julia. I hadn't noticed his arrival. He winked at me past Julia's face and I could see by the set of his jaw that he was aggravated at the hassle of getting here so late. Earlier, when we had picked Julia up, she had kept us waiting in the car for twenty minutes, explaining miserably that she had been looking for her second earring. James, who was always on time, couldn't stand her recurring lateness. I sighed. Since her divorce Julia was sensitive and skittery and she seemed to have lost her sense of time. Without Phil, she was indeed as miserable as a solitary earring.

But I couldn't allow my concern for Julia to interfere with this special moment. Orson was leading his orchestra and chorus through the turbulent *Dies Irae*, as exciting as any crowd scene in an opera. In the *New York Times* Orson had labeled this Requiem as

Verdi's finest opera, and it was easy to see why. Under his baton the music ran the gamut from spine-chilling whispers to overwhelming climaxes. His gestures were precise and more restrained than at the rehearsal. I wondered why, and then I remembered the comment he had made that night, shortly before Matthew had taken me home. "In a concert I prefer the economy of movement and the simplicity of the beat. I can't stand conductors who are too dramatic during the performance. Usually it means they haven't done their homework in rehearsal."

And now, with a minimum of input he got maximum results, effortlessly conveying the meaning of the music through the rise and fall of tempo and dynamics.

The chorus, dressed in black and white, stood on five rows of risers behind the orchestra. In the middle of the soprano section Beverly's curls shone under the spotlights like red gold. Without her heavy horn-rimmed glasses her face seemed fragile, and no doubt the only focal point her squinting eyes could recognize was Orson. Across the stage from her, Daisy stood in the first row of the altos. Her Botticelli features bespoke unflagging good humor, her plump body heaved with the intensity of her breathing. Would I ever qualify to stand there on the stage with them? And what about the remaining hundred singers? Did they all aspire to a special spot in the maestro's heart?

I decided to ignore all my rivals, real or imagined, and make use of my own resources. Tomorrow at three Orson would be out of reach of Beverly's and Daisy's webs.

Tomorrow at three James would have his first interview. I gave him a brief side-ways glance and was glad to see the relaxed expression on his face.

Julia, between us, looked perfect and unreal. With her even features and straight blonde hair, she resembled the statue of a saint in a cathedral. And with her brown eyes contrasting my blue ones and her tiny nose compared to my... uh… much larger one, I found it hard to believe that some people took us for sisters. When she smiled, surprising dimples appeared in both her cheeks. But she seldom smiled now. Lately, there were rings under her eyes from too many aspirins and too much worrying instead of writing. Julia had published two successful novels and had burned a third in the fireplace. At thirty-seven, she was at the height of her beauty and the depth of her expectations.

Her two biggest goals, to find a way to get her husband back and to write a bestseller, seemed as unattainable as Orson's podium. But how could I allow my thoughts to wander in the midst of Verdi's haunting *Lacrymosa* that was as moving as an operatic love duet? To focus more fully, I closed my eyes, but after a few more bars the music stopped. When I looked up again, the musicians were bowing to roaring applause before the intermission.

James got up and stretched.

"What a piece! The chorus sounded superb."

Julia played with the clasp of her Chanel bag and yawned.

"I found it either too loud or too soft."

Her nothing-in-this-world-can-please-me attitude finally got to me. "Julia, this is not a maypole dance. This is *Verdi.* His music requires a sharp contrast in dynamics."

James ran his hand through his short hair and nodded his head in favor of my answer. "From now on we have to accept Isabella as our music expert."

But Julia didn't understand and looked at James blankly. Immersed in her own world, she had given no sign of interest when I had told her about the rehearsal, and I hadn't decided yet if I could trust her with my thoughts about Orson Mahler.

James smiled superficially and tossed his *Stagebill* on his chair. I knew he would come up with a reason to avoid Julia's company during the intermission.

"Uh... I saw Angela and Barry in one of the Second Tier boxes. I'll try to find them. How about we all meet for a drink afterwards..."

I said, "Tell them to meet us at Café Carnegie. The chorus is having a party and guests are welcome."

"If you think so," he said, not fully convinced.

"Yes, I think it would be great." I looked after him over my shoulder and a glint of hope appeared in my mind. I would even see Orson tonight.

Julia leafed through the *Stagebill* and spoke without looking up. "Who are Angela and Barry? Have I met them?"

"I don't think you have. Barry Schumann is our family doctor. James used to play tennis with him, but stopped since his back has been bothering him."

She asked, "Have they been married for long?"

I stuffed my *Stagebill* into my purse as reading material for tomorrow on the bus.

"They're not married. Angela and Barry have lived together for two years. She's originally from Italy, that's where they first met. In Rome, at the train station."

Julia looked down from our box at the milling New York concert crowd returning to their seats, giving the impression of not listening to me at all. Still, I went on.

"Angela says she'd marry Barry any day, but that doesn't keep her from flirting with James. Sometimes it's just a bit too much for my taste," and counting on Julia's support, I added, "one day I'll scratch out her pretty eyes."

With no comment for the confession of my jealousy Julia moved her chair back from the velvet-covered railing and studied her ankles. "When Phil sends me my monthly check he doesn't even include a personal note anymore..."

Her words flowed like blood from an open wound, and if I hadn't heard them a million times before I would have been more sympathetic. But today my sympathy reversed in speaking my truth.

"Julia, everything is always about you, you are the most self-centered woman I've ever known."

Her eyes turned to almond-like slits, I expected her to blow up. But she didn't. I almost felt sorry for her again.

"Julia, listen, how will you ever write a book again if you have such little regard for other people's lives? That's where the real stories are. They're everywhere. But you have to find them and shape them."

She made a monstrous attempt to smile without meaning it. My intuition warned me against ever telling her about Orson.

The sound of James' voice broke the taut atmosphere between us. "So, ladies, we're all set. We'll meet Angela and Barry downstairs at Café Carnegie."

I welcomed the reappearance of the musicians and the continuation of the concert. At the sight of Orson reappearing on the stage I told myself not to waste another thought on Julia.

Orson. Tomorrow at three. Would he ask my opinion of the concert? What did I think of the soloists and the orchestra? What on earth would I say? I didn't know how to prepare an answer in advance, much less come up with one spontaneously. Would he take my hand? What else would happen?

And then I realized with a jolt that my meeting with the maestro was absurd and inappropriate. The man down there on the podium directing two hundred people could not be reconciled with the man who had taken on such disproportionate dimensions in my imagination. What did I expect? Did I expect to go down in history as Maestro Mahler's fateful passion, ruining his reputation and his blood pressure? What kind of a mess was I trying to get into? Come on, Mrs. Barton, I reminded myself, be reasonable.

And reason returned. It returned with the next entrance of the chorus, when I became aware that I was merely moved by the music and no longer by the man who conducted it. My emotions for Orson were paralyzed, as in a sleep with my eyes open, a peaceful, cleansing sleep. It was a feeling of such relief that I instantly forgave Julia, resolving to show my sweetest side to Angela and planning to seduce James the minute we got home.

Verdi's powerful fugue, *Libera me*, sung by chorus and soprano solo, ended the performance, and its words befitted the regained balance in my soul. I had liberated myself from Orson. As he bowed to the enthralled crowd, accepting their standing ovation, he was simply a conductor, an older version of the pictures on my mother's record jackets.

Minutes later, James navigated me by the elbow through the streams of people leaving the hall. I assumed Julia was right behind us, but James didn't care. It was unlike him to rush ahead so carelessly, as if the bar would run out of drinks.

On the curved stairs leading down to Café Carnegie I recognized Joan and Matthew coming towards us. I motioned with my head. "James, that's the chorus manager and her son, the pianist. You know, the young man who took me home."

Their heads disappeared behind other heads and with the flow of people separating us, and I didn't think either of them had seen me. Joan, in a simple black dress, was covered with faux pearls and layers of paint. Matthew bent down to her ear and for the first time I saw her laugh. Laughing became Joan.

Café Carnegie was aswirl with chorus members, their spouses, relatives and friends. The small room was dimly lit, noisy and jammed to the rafters. Julia had caught up with us, and I pulled her between us, like a child, afraid to lose her in the crowd. Behind us, masses of people were still pressing in.

James grimaced. "Look at the line at the bar. It'll take forever to get a drink."

"You like-a sip of mine, *Giacomo*?" A voice cooed behind us. Angela insisted on calling my husband *Giacomo,* the Italian equivalent of James .

James swung around and laughed. "Hey, Angela," and to the man next to her, "How the dickens did you two manage to make it down here before us?"

Barry gave me a big smile. "Hi, Isabella. Nice dress..."

I performed my compulsory kiss on Barry's cheek, trying to avoid his beard. Beards had always appalled me, an issue Julia and I could not agree on.

"You sucha big-a gorgeous man, *Giacomo*." Angela rubbed against James like a kitten. I forced a humorless smile and thought, Here she goes again.

Obviously Barry felt the same. A mock-frown formed between his bushy eyebrows as he looked at his Roman beauty languidly clinging to James' neck. Her strapless purple dress was easily held up by a generous gift from nature.

I said, "This is my friend Julia," suddenly proud of her quiet beauty, her erect carriage and her mysterious aloofness.

Julia and Angela exchanged quick, appraising glances and Barry seemed uncomfortably intrigued as Julia offered him her outstretched hand. For a long moment they didn't move, surprised by a spell, and when he took it, she lowered her eyes and suddenly withdrew.

"Excuse me for a moment. I need to freshen up."

The next moment she disappeared into the crowd, leaving Barry's blue eyes wide open. "I've never seen anyone disappear so fast, or was she only an apparition?"

James said drily, "I wish she were. Because then we wouldn't have to take her along on our way home tonight."

"Jaaames..." I gave him an elbow and explained. "Julia lives in Montclair too. We came together in the car. She and I are very good friends. "

More people were trying to get into the cafe, and our group was forced to move farther back towards the bar.

James quipped, "Isabella, you always have an excuse for Julia. I just think she's a spoiled brat. She's always late or depressed or feeling sick. And the only reason she's still alive is because her ex-husband knew it was against the law to strangle her."

Angela let out a dark, guttural laugh. She knew how to laugh without wrinkling her face.

I tried one more time to defend Julia. "James, she's going through a very difficult time after her divorce." But now James was pushing his way through to the bar.

Barry asked with the quiet, professional tone of a physician, "How long have you known her?"

I said, "We met four years ago at the check-out counter in King's Supermarket. Her husband is a wealthy investment broker.

He was fooling around and wanted his freedom back. Julia had no choice but to agree to a divorce."

Barry clung to every word. Quite unlike him, he bent over to me and whispered with dreamy innocence, "I think she is an exceptionally beautiful woman."

There was no doubt that Angela had heard him. Her vivacious face ran as scarlet. Blissfully oblivious to her reaction, Barry took Angela's arm. "Isn't it funny that we've never run into Julia before? After all, Montclair is a small town. Why don't we invite her to our party?"

I said, "I can give you her address," but read in Angela's eyes that she had no intention to mail an invitation. Instead, she suddenly rose on her toes and waved at someone over Barry's shoulder.

"Hey, there's you-a Mamma."

Barry turned around.

A small, gray-haired woman in a navy blue suit and with vibrant eyes was having her champagne glass refilled.

"Mother!" Barry exclaimed, circling around a group of people in order to reach her. Barry put his arm around her shoulders.

"Mother, my gosh, I had no idea you were coming tonight."

Angela bent down to kiss her cheek. "Louisa, *cara mia*, why don't-a you tell us you comin'...? You look-a beautiful. *Molto bella.*"

The older lady smiled benevolently, causing her face to show a hundred wrinkles.

"First of all, I don't need a baby-sitter. Secondly, I'm here to admire the conducting skills of my former patient."

"*What?*" Barry's voice rose. "Orson Mahler was your patient?"

She took a sip of champagne. "He was my patient for about twenty-five years, until I retired. And he still tells me he hasn't found another doctor with whom he's equally comfortable."

Barry couldn't believe it. "But mother, you never mentioned him to me."

There was wit and wisdom in her eyes. "My boy, I always knew how to guard my professional secrets. And I'm glad you're the same way. I've never heard you speak of any of your patients either."

Now I remembered the story Beverly had told me during our walk to the rehearsal a few days ago.

I turned to Barry's mother. "Is it true that Orson Mahler met his wife in your waiting room some thirty-five years ago?"

"That's right." And without ado she offered me her hand and smiled. "I'm Louise Schumann."

Barry said, "Excuse me, Mom, I haven't introduced you. This is our friend, Isabella Barton."

"... and this is her husband, James." James's voice came from behind me, and he took her hand. He handed me a glass of wine and for a brief, spellbound moment we looked at each other. I was incredibly proud of my handsome husband.

Louise looked from James to me and back again.

"You two make a beautiful couple."

I took a gulp of wine and felt the exhilarating tingle of a blush. Yes, James and I were beautiful together. Who needed a gray, aging man like Maestro Mahler?

I explained to James, "This is Barry's mother, Dr. Louise Schumann. Imagine, Orson Mahler was Dr. Schumann's patient for twenty-five years."

Louise gestured with her hand for us to draw in closer.

"Unfortunately, I didn't see him often enough. He's always been as healthy as a horse and still is. I'm sure he owes his exceptional constitution to the fact that he's always doing what he liked to do. He loves making music and he loves life, and..." She looked up and handed her empty glass to Barry, "... there he is in person..."

A sigh went through the room. In two seconds the noisy crowd was as still as a well-behaved school class, and then there was thunderous applause. The maestro had made his entrance. To his left was Beverly, immediately followed by Daisy, like a second lieutenant, next in line for Orson's favor. On his right side was a silver-haired woman who looked a little like a fire-engine. Her bright red gown was artfully draped around her massive grandeur.

Louise said, "That's Paula, his wife."

I couldn't take my eyes off her. Paula gave the impression of a kind, well-balanced person, whose shape confirmed her love for brownies. Paula's silver hair was short and modernly styled, and I imagined her keeping Orson warm in the winter and shaded in the summer.

The applause wore on despite Orson's attempt to stop it. Eventually it became clear that it was all for Paula, not for Orson, and that indeed Paula was stealing her husband's show. I had no idea why. Friends, chorus members and orchestra players formed a wide circle around her and literally stood in line to hug her. She accepted each well-wisher warmheartedly, accumulated presents and cards and displayed an amazing memory for everyone's name. Orson, flanked by Beverly and Daisy, merely stood as an onlooker in a scene of clicking glasses, laughter and kisses.

Suddenly there was the sound of a pitch-pipe and the room began to sing.

Happy birthday to you... happy birthday, dear Paula...

The volume of the chorus threatened to blast the walls of the narrow room, and after another round of applause Orson raised his arms, commanding a moment of silence. The birthmark on his lip twitched and he smiled a delighted smile.

"Believe me, Ladies and Gentlemen, I just wish I had a chorus like this to work with," and after the laughter had died down, "Thank you, everyone, for a wonderful concert. It was truly magnificent. I'll see you all after the summer."

Angela smiled raptly. "*Mamma mia,* I never hear him-a speak-a before. I can't believe he sound-a so sexy at hees age. Is-a no wonder they call him the man wida velvet voice."

In a motherly gesture Louise took her hand. "My dear, I thought so many times myself. The power of a conductor is so complex. In the best possible case it's a mixture of musical proficiency and personal myth, and Orson has both."

As Louise and Angela stood side by side, enchanted by the same object, I thought of my mother and me. Was there any woman he left unmoved?

Not in the least affected by sentimental scenarios of this kind, James grunted impatiently. "Let's go Isabella. I don't want to get home too late."

My eyes searched in every direction.

"Julia hasn't come back yet."

"Well, where is she?" James's voice grew testy. "I can't believe the woman is making us wait again."

I tried to gain time. "Maybe she ran into a friend."

"Dammit, she's been gone for thirty minutes..."

Barry said, "If you want to leave and she lives in Montclair, we'd be happy to take her home."

Angela took a deep breath. She said nothing but would doubtlessly make up for it later.

James gave Barry a friendly slap on the arm. "Would you? That'd be great. I'd really appreciate it, buddy."

Barry made no effort to conceal his satisfaction.

"Sure, don't worry. We'll watch out for her."

We waved good-bye. I wanted to say that I wasn't comfortable abandoning Julia like this, but James took my arm and steered me through the crowd.

I said, "I hope Julia is all right."

He said, "I have to get out of here, otherwise I'm the one who's not going to be all right. I'm sorry, Isabella, but with all the details for my interview tomorrow going through my head, I don't seem to be able to breathe in here any longer."

We squeezed our way between two groups of singers.

I said, "I know what you mean, about tomorrow," and freed myself from his grasp, but in the next moment I took his arm in mine and navigated him single-mindedly towards Orson's group.

I whispered, "The woman with the red curls, that's Beverly."

Her eyes brushed me briefly but she gave no sign of recognition. She either didn't see me because she wasn't wearing her glasses or because in the maestro's presence no one else counted. Her silvery soprano rang out against the voices around her. She proclaimed, stretching every syllable, "One day I want to write his memoirs."

There was no doubt whose memoirs she had in mind.

Paula, still to Orson's right, chatted with the alto soloist. I caught a fragment of her deep, throaty voice. "... in restaurants my Orson and I always hold hands."

James and I were just passing Orson, who was shaking hands with the two male soloists, thanking them for their performance. And then, in the middle of this cheerful, pushing, glass-clicking and eager-to-catch-a-glimpse-of-the-maestro-obsessed crowd, Orson turned his head. His eyes met mine and sent an arrow in my heart.

They said, *Tomorrow at three.*

James, next to me, let out a short, surprised laugh. "Hey, that's amazing. Did you see that? He remembered you."

All the excitement was back.

11

On Monday at three I was less comfortable facing Orson than I had imagined. *The New York Times* had lost no time reviewing last night's concert and had panned it completely.

Before I left the office, under the pretext of a doctor's appointment, I scanned it one more time. The printed words seemed to scream out at me:

... *Mahler's own orchestra and chorus, usually known for solid workmanship, failed in last night's performance under its leader. Mahler's tempi were drawn out in sheer self-indulgence, but worse, he retarded the music's flow with showy dynamic contrasts and labored cadences...*

After reading this, it wasn't hard to guess the mood the esteemed maestro would be in. I turned the corner of Park Avenue and Fifty-Second Street and thought that this might not be the most favorable day for him to act on any gallant impulse that had caused him to call me in the first place. A minute later I caught a glimpse of myself mirrored in the heavy glass doors of the Omni Berkshire, and I was surprised by my outer expression of ease. The person I saw did not correspond with the nervous one I felt inside. I was nervous because I expected something without knowing what it was. A uniformed doorman held the door open, and my reflection passed through it like Alice through the mirror into Wonderland.

In the skylit lounge past the reception area, Orson was sitting in one of the armchairs against the wall. He was wearing a light gray suit but no tie. As his eyes revealed a stir of recognition he uncrossed his legs and got up. But he didn't move forward to meet me. As he stood there, waiting, watching, his spontaneity seemed subordinated to a mental discipline, holding him back.

I seemed to fly towards him with my shoes hardly touching the carpet and stopped at arm's length away. I said, as poised as my pounding heart permitted, "I'm so pleased to see you again."

He smiled like a man sure of his power to make others happy.

"I'm pleased you could make the time to see me." He motioned me to sit down.

Our table was next to a harp, but no one was playing. A waiter bowed.

Orson said, "Would you care to share some hot chocolate with me?"

I nodded. I was so glad to be here, I would have shared a glass of vinegar with him. But Orson seemed detached. The innocent directness of our first meeting had turned into something more deliberate, disturbing. Or maybe he was simply disturbed by his bad review.

I opened the conversation. "I saw your review. I'm outraged, and you must be too."

Orson shrugged and his birthmark twitched.

"I'm not surprised. It happens all the time and you get used to it. Many times when I felt a concert went exceptionally well, the critics seemed to think otherwise. I know this particular gentleman personally, and I wouldn't expect anything else from him. I once voted against his participation as judge in a music committee, and today I know I was absolutely right."

I crossed my legs and folded my nervous hands across my knees. "But still, it's not fair."

Orson waved dismissively. "It's not important. I hope it won't penetrate the foreign press, but my New Yorkers will have forgotten about it by tomorrow."

Our hot chocolates arrived. Orson drank the first cup like a boy after a day of ice skating.

I looked around. The colors of the lounge in beige, green and pink were like an oasis in the hustle of Manhattan. And flowers! A huge arrangement towered majestically in the center of the room and was reflected a hundred times over in the mosaic mirrors on the walls.

Orson leaned forward and his gray-metallic eyes met mine.

"I caught a glimpse of you at Café Carnegie last night. Was that your husband?" Barely waiting for my affirmation, he smiled gently, "He's a very handsome man. You must be crazy about him."

I whispered, "Yes, he is. And yes, I am," and took a sip of hot chocolate to hide my confusion.

I could have told Orson about James' interview now, but it didn't feel appropriate. He had undoubtedly forgotten the details I had revealed to him a week ago. Today there was something dignified and distant about him that made it impossible for me to call him by his first name. It seemed as if I had talked too much the first time and now talking created a strain.

But he didn't say anything either. I could almost hear my thoughts, and they sounded like a traffic jam in Times Square.

Finally I came up with, "We met Dr. Louise Schumann last night. Her son Barry happens to be our friend and family doctor."

Orson laughed. "Good old Louise. She and I always used to kid each other because we each share last names with two famous composers. And that's right, her son Barry has a private practice in Montclair. I remember his pictures on her desk. Small world."

His voice was so impersonal that I couldn't imagine he once held my hand and that I had unloaded my sorrows on his patient ears. To my surprise, he took out a small silver pen of the inner pocket of his jacket and started drawing doodles on a piece of paper next to the silver tray holding our cups.

From another table a woman with unruly blonde hair stared at him. While doodling, Orson ordered more hot chocolate and asked the waiter, "Would you have any brownies?" The waiter shook his head and the woman continued to stare.

I uncrossed my legs and for a second closed my eyes. I felt sure I was doing something wrong but didn't know what.

He looked up from doodling. "You know, this was my last concert in Carnegie Hall for a long time. The hall will close at the end of the week for a seven-month renovation, and a few days after its scheduled re-opening in December, I'm going to conduct the *Brahms Requiem* with my chorus. I just hope with all their remodeling they won't mess up the acoustics."

I thought of my plan to join the chorus. I could possibly be part of that concert myself. For a moment I considered mentioning it to Orson, but I didn't. What would he have said?

I looked down at the pink table cloth. Apart from commenting on James' good looks, did he intend to say anything personal at all? How about *my* looks? Was he going to give me his book? It was impossible to say if he was relaxed or bored to death. He was still doodling.

I studied his finely-boned face under his pale skin. Except for his forehead, none of his features were outstanding. He was like the creation of a sculptor who worked without a model or had not yet made up his mind about the finished piece. Much of Orson's expression was in the eye of the beholder and leaving a wide range for painting one's own feelings on it. To remind him of my presence I noisily stirred my drink.

"I always wanted to ask you something..."

"Yes?" He stopped doodling.

"Are you in any way related to Gustav Mahler, the composer?"

"No, no relation."

I explained. "The house where I grew up is just across the lake from where Gustav Mahler had his summer residence at the beginning of the century, when he was director of the Vienna State Opera."

His eyes lit up with curiosity. "Have you visited the house?"

"It's not open to the public, but my grandmother still remembers Alma Mahler. They say she was a stunning lady, irresistible to everyone who met her. As Gustav Mahler's wife, she is still very much alive in the minds of the local people. They say it was really she who orchestrated all his symphonies."

Orson said, "To think that Gustav Mahler wrote all those masterpieces merely as a summer composer..."

I thought, my God, this was not what I had imagined we would talk about. Our conversation sounded like a song in the wrong key. We weren't even looking at each other. I moved my hand to an accessible spot on the armrest of my chair and thought, *Why* isn't he taking it? Was he suddenly afraid to transgress decency in a public place? But then I didn't consider him the type of man who would deprive himself of something he wanted.

Wishing for the sensation of his touch, the world stood still around us. I wished someone would start playing the harp or that a waiter would drop a tray, anything to move the air. Maybe I was taking too much of his time and his thoughts were wandering. And yet I was oddly happy in his presence.

He emptied his third cup of hot chocolate and looked at me. His magic smile broke across his face. "... sorry, I was just thinking of a title. Maybe you can help me. I've been commissioned to write a series of program notes for *Stagebill* on music appreciation for the layman. I'm quite enthusiastic about the project and I want them to be easy reading, educational and yet entertaining. I want them to cause a nod of understanding on the reader's face, maybe even a smile of pleasure, a little bit like having received an unexpected gift, a mental gift..." He hesitated and his smile was in his eyes rather than on his lips. He added, whispering, "In my own way I want to make love to the reader's mind by way of music, but I'm still looking for an appropriate title, a title that can express what I just explained in a few words."

His gray- metallic eyes looked at me expectantly.

The wheels of my mind were spinning in overdrive. His arm moved and for one second his hand touched mine on the armrest. Only for one second.

He said, "There's no rush. I have six months to write the essays and come up with a title."

I laughed, elated, because of the one second that had made a difference. "What about *Musical Trifles* or *Music, Nota Bene...*"

He shook his head. "No, no... that's not it," and assumed the same aloofness as before. I tried to make sense of the chaotic lines of his doodling and realized I didn't know the private man behind the public person.

Orson finished his fourth cup of hot chocolate. I finished my first one and asked, "Did you remember to bring your book?"

He gave a musical laugh. "I almost forgot. That was the reason for our meeting, wasn't it?"

His beaten briefcase stood next to his chair. He opened it on his lap and handed me the book.

I read the title. *BE SILENT AND LISTEN.*

As I opened the cover, today's review of yesterday's concert fell out. I reached down to pick it up. Orson leaned forward, resting his elbows on his knees while holding the book. "I don't need it back. The book is yours to keep."

"Oh, thank you, thank you very much..." I still didn't call him by his first name.

Orson paid the check and I wondered whether I should have him sign the book. But I was warned by a thought, a signal, and I let the moment go by.

He checked his watch.

"I promised a friend of mine, a lady who teaches voice at Juilliard School, to listen to one of her outstanding students."

We got up. The flowing feeling of a warm friendship had turned into polite formality. There was no indication that my company had turned his day into a joyful one. Had I failed my audition for some kind of affinity?

On the street I said, "I had a wonderful time."

He put on his dark glasses and bowed somewhat stiffly.

"I had a wonderful time too," but it merely sounded like an echo of my words. Except for that one second, we hadn't touched and we hadn't called each other by name. I was sure he didn't remember mine.

On my way back to the office my legs were steady, but my head was a ship in a storm.

12

I had Orson's book now, a reflection of his mind, a part of him. It would enable me to penetrate the thinking of a man regarded as an eminence in music but hooked on brownies and hot chocolate.

The two principal words in the title *BE SILENT AND LISTEN* consisted of exactly the same letters in a different sequence, but related in their meaning, one asking for the balance of the other.

Inside the cover a picture showed a younger Orson, along with a brief biography and his date of birth. I was struck with a personal emotion. He was born in the same year, even the same month, December, as my father, which made them both fifty-nine.

Growing up, I never knew what it felt like to have a father after the age of six, when he left. It was very unsettling to have a father and yet not to have one, not to know where he was, whether he was miserable or well, alive or dead. After he left, I would often look out of my bedroom window during sleepless nights and wondered if he was looking at the same moon and the same stars and maybe wondering about me.

I recalled our walks through the woods and along the shoreline of the lake. Papa showed me how to skip stones across the water and we invented stories that involved the birds, the fish and the trees. Our walks bonded us in the complicity of two friends who couldn't bloom in the presence of my mother, and it was not until we returned home and the lock of the garden gate had clicked behind us, that we resumed our old roles as Elisabeth Berger's husband and daughter.

My mother greeted us at the door, wearing one of her starched, embroidered aprons, and a frown. I could never tell whether her blue, clear eyes were just squinting against the light or spelling out guilt for something Papa and I had done wrong. Only then we became aware that our feet had sunk into spongy earth, our best leather shoes had become muddy. Only then did I notice that my fingernails were black and that I had torn a hole in the sweater she had knitted. Had Papa gone out again without wearing his watch? He was setting a bad example by not keeping track of time. Coffee and cake were waiting on the table, and he had forgotten to call cousin Christa for her birthday. Papa lowered his eyes to the rose bushes, which were so much like my mother: beautiful, upright and thorny.

From inside the house came the sounds of Mozart's *Concerto for Flute and Harp*. Papa went into the living room and, as an excuse to avoid talking to my mother, he turned up the volume. He pretended to be absorbed in the record jacket and the photograph of an American conductor who sported a funny-looking black birthmark on his lip and was considered the rising star of his generation.

My mother felt neglected and knew how to articulate her complaints. How could he not talk to her, not eat her cake, not even defend himself against her accusations? Didn't she earn his attention through duty and loyalty, like dividends on capital? But she never understood the cruel law of love, that the one who makes emotional demands is the one without power.

Gradually, she lost more and more of this power over him, a power she seemed to crave more as time went by. How could he refuse to do what she asked of him? Wasn't she full of good intentions and didn't she always know what was best for him and me? Wasn't she the one who canned strawberries for the winter, knitted sweaters and ironed his shirts, while my father and I spent too many hours outdoors or in his library?

On rainy Sundays we would stand in front of his large globe, watching the green continents rotate under his pointer, which, as I now came to think of it, resembled the baton of a conductor. At a very early age I learned about the Leaning Tower, the Blue Mosque, and the Great Wall of China and, westward across the Atlantic, of the skyline of Manhattan. I admired my father for the journeys of his mind, but didn't realize that his only access to the world was the printed page, and that he dreamed of turning the trips of his imagination into real ones.

I remembered standing at his desk in front of a large window overlooking the lake. He was writing and I asked, "What are you doing, Papa?"

He looked up from his papers and quietly spoke his truth.

"I'm filling out immigration forms for Canada, *kleiner Spatz.* I'm going to leave soon."

I turned my head away, unable to bear the sad determination in his eyes.

His hand touched my face. "I'm sorry. I know you don't understand, but I hope you will one day."

He was wrong. Deep down inside I understood his longing. Children possess an unconscious capacity for accepting their parents' truth if it's an honest emotion.

Not so, understandably, my mother. Seeing his papers, she laughed sarcastically and derided his daydreams, his eccentric ideas and his attraction to Hilde, a young woman who worked in the bookshop we owned.

But Papa hadn't joked about his plans. A month later, Papa left with Hilde, two suitcases and the smell of freedom. Apparently they meant more to him than everything he left behind: his wife, his daughter, his house, his store and enough money that my mother never had to worry. That was twenty-seven years ago. One day divorce papers arrived for my mother to sign, and no one had heard from him since.

I remembered how the house and my heart felt empty without him and how I missed his voice when he called me *kleiner Spatz,* my little sparrow. His absence was a subject that my mother's pride would not allow to be discussed. All his things went into the garbage, except one black-and-white photo in a silver frame. The living room began to fill up with records of Orson Mahler. Dreaming about him granted my mother unlimited powers of imagination and manipulation. But then, why shouldn't she enjoy her dreams, to balance the burden of responsibility that she had to shoulder as the remaining parent?

Who was ultimately to blame for my father's leaving? It was a question I could never permit myself to answer. It was difficult to be angry with someone I missed. Absence, as well as death, has a transforming effect on the memory of a parent.

Over the years I taught myself not to think about him anymore. And yet, a passing look at his framed photo always reminded me of something that could have been but never was. It would have been nice to say, "This is my father, and I am proud of him," or to listen to his voice saying, "This is my daughter Isabella, and I am proud of her."

But there was no voice for me to listen to, just silence. The thought stirred me from my memories and back to Orson Mahler's book. *BE SILENT AND LISTEN.*

I began to devour it as if in search of a secret that promised to be hidden somewhere between the lines. In the ears of my mind the printed words became colored by the sound of Orson's voice, as if he were reading them to me.

All great music asks for moments of silence between the listening. These are not empty moments, but pauses containing the full meaning of the music, just as the moments between lightning and thunder carry the full impact of the storm...

I read on the bus, in bed, in the bathroom and during lunch-hour, finishing all 378 pages in one week. I reached for the last page of the book like a swimmer trying to reach the other shore, in competition only with myself and time. But why was I rushing? Did I remember how Bach came to write the *Goldberg-Variations* or how Brahms and Tchaikovsky once met and couldn't agree on anything but a certain kind of local dumpling? Could I remember the structure of the Sonata-Form or how the piano-forte developed into the well-known keyboard instrument of modern times? Could I remember anything at all? I wanted to be able to say to Orson, "I enjoyed reading your book," but I was afraid that he might not remember me if I let too much time go by.

A week after we had met in the lounge at the Omni-Berkshire, I looked up Orson's number in the phone book. I had no idea that there were so many Mahlers in the Borough of Manhattan. A whole column. My finger ran down the alphabet of first names and stopped at "O". There was one Orson Mahler with a Park Avenue address. So he *was* listed.

Before losing heart, I dialed from my desk at work. It rang four times and my pulse began its ascent.

Orson's recorded voice confirmed the dialed number, asking for a message after the tone. I was almost relieved that I didn't have to speak to him directly. I hesitated for a second. There was still time to hang up. Then I heard myself speak in a clear voice.

"This is Isabella Barton..."

There was a click in the line and Orson's real voice said, "Hello?"

"Hello? This is Isabella," I repeated warily, not sure if I was speaking to him.

"Yes, Isabella?"

"Oh, is it really you?"

"Yes, I screen my calls. How are you?" His tone was hurried but friendly.

"Uh... fine... I finished reading your book. I would like to ask you to sign it for me."

"All right... Do you have it with you today?"

"No, it's at home."

"I see...," he took a moment to think.

"What about lunch tomorrow?"

I made no effort to hide the buoyancy in my voice when I agreed to meet him.

13

There was an instant foreshadow of bad news from the sound of Orson's voice when he called me the following morning at work. His words fell like a tree across the road. A repertoire meeting with the board of his orchestra had come up and then a late rehearsal at Avery Fisher Hall that would last until five-thirty. He didn't even say he was sorry about having to cancel our lunch.

The text on my computer screen blurred into a film of moisture. Having to fight tears over a canceled lunch made me feel downright ridiculous. Yet it occurred to me that to risk ridicule wasn't always weakness but sometimes courage. Making fools of ourselves could sometimes lead to triumph, and a crazy idea took shape. The rehearsal, he had said, would end at five-thirty...

At five-twenty-five I crossed Broadway and approached Avery Fisher Hall, thrilled with myself. I still wasn't sure what I would say to Orson. Why was I ambushing him? After all, he should have been the one to suggest we meet after the rehearsal, and not I.

At five-thirty sharp I peeked through the glass windows of the stage entrance of Avery Fisher Hall on Sixty-Fifth Street. During the next ten minutes my courage deflated while a stream of musicians, carrying their instrument cases, passed through the door. I moved further away to the left, assuring myself a safe distance if things shouldn't look good. And they didn't.

When Orson came out, he was not alone. The surprise element next to him talked seamlessly under her red curls and carried a tote bag with a thermos bottle sticking out. My heart sank. How could I explain my presence in front of Beverly?

To my immense relief they turned right and walked up Sixty-Fifth Street to Broadway. Beverly's silvery soprano chimed amid a mixture of flamboyant gestures. Her excitement about walking next to Orson seemed to punch the spring air, spelling flirtation.

I bit my lip. So, Beverly had attended the rehearsal. Was *she* the meeting for which Orson had canceled our lunch? I decided to follow the two of them at a safe distance.

Unexpectedly, at the traffic light at Broadway and Amsterdam Avenue, they separated. Orson nodded briefly, but Beverly kept waving and shouted something I couldn't understand. She continued south and Orson crossed Broadway, heading east.

By the time I reached the intersection, the light signaled "Don't Walk," leaving me with the choice of losing him or risking my life before the on-coming traffic. I raced across the street and reached the other side with a pounding heart and a broken heel.

Shortly before catching up with Orson, he involuntarily turned his head and looked at me. But he didn't stop. "Ah... there you are."

His voice betrayed no surprise at seeing me. Was he aware all along that I had been following him?

"Hi! Perfect timing," I grinned and swallowed a rising sense of discomfort.

At last he stopped and looked down.

"What happened to your foot?"

"I just broke my heel running after you."

He gave a musical laugh and for the first time I sensed a warm gleam through his dark glasses. He said, "I'm sorry it happened. Are you able to walk?"

"Sure, if you don't mind being seen with a semi-invalid?"

"Never mind," he waved dismissively, and the ice was broken.

I couldn't believe my luck. Broken heel or not, here I was with Orson Mahler and I had him all to myself.

He asked, "Can you join me? I have to go cross-town. We could walk through Central Park."

"Sounds good," I smiled abstractly at a street vendor selling imitation watches.

Something about my face seemed to ring a bell in Orson's mind. He finally looked at me as a person he had known before, and I wondered if he remembered my handsome husband or my nervous hand in his. I considered telling him about seeing him with Beverly, but dropped the idea. After all, she was gone.

We passed the brick buildings on Sixty-Fifth Street and I tried to hide my limp.

I said, "Your rehearsal ended right on time."

He answered grimly. "Rehearsals always do. The damned unions have us over a barrel. God forbid you keep the players five minutes overtime or they go on strike. The unions in this country have managed to price themselves out of the market. The recording companies can't afford to make large-orchestra recordings in the U.S. anymore, because it's too expensive to pay the musicians their hourly rates. For most of my big orchestral recordings, except for pieces with small ensembles or chamber music, I have to go to England or Germany."

He sighed. In the long shadows of the afternoon his face looked strained and, as usual, extremely pale. His gray turtle-neck sweater and gray pants didn't help to brighten his complexion, either. But I was tired myself, and I felt a tremor of solidarity with him, lowering him in my mind from the glory of the podium to the level of a working man after a long day at the job.

We crossed Central Park West and entered the park on a footpath. On a playground to our right some children were engaged in a wild hit-and-run game, enjoying every moment, without worrying about the outcome. In the same way, I walked next to Orson.

He explained, calmer now, "You see, Isabella (*Isabella? Ah, he remembered my name!),* part of the art of conducting is to know what *not* to rehearse.

I considered his statement. "I don't quite understand."

"To save money you should never rehearse the parts that go well and save your time for the difficult things."

I nodded, wishing he'd slow down. We passed a sign that read "Quiet Zone." To our left, people were sun-bathing on the grass, enjoying the spring sun after work.

"There was a time," Orson said, "when I used to walk here every day instead of taking the cross-town bus, but nowadays there seems to be less and less time in the day."

Several joggers passed us, and I asked, "Did you ever jog?"

"Never. I never exercise, but I enjoy a brisk walk. And I don't have a house in the Hamptons or a chalet in Aspen. Central Park provides me with all the nature I ever need."

I said, "What you call a brisk walk, others might call training for the marathon. I'm sorry but I can't walk that fast with my broken heel."

He stopped and said, "I apologize, Isabella, I should be more considerate."

"It's okay." I felt embarrassed. He was almost twice my age and I was the one out of breath. As we stood looking at each other, I felt his eyes smiling through his dark glasses, conveying a message that was whispered, making it even more powerful by its silence. His smile brought a disturbing sweetness to my heart, like a perfume to the lungs of an asthmatic.

To escape the feeling, I saved myself with an academic question. "What do you consider the main task of conducting?"

Surprisingly he let out a laugh and mused in a non-academic tone. "First of all, it helps to get everyone started and stopped at the same time and to keep them together in between. Come to think of it, Isabella, what do you remember about the chapter in my book that I dedicated to conducting?"

Was he mocking me? He obviously enjoyed himself.

"Frankly, I can't remember much because I was reading it too fast."

"Why did you read it too fast?"

I couldn't believe he was pressing the point.

I said, "I wanted you to sign the book and was afraid you wouldn't remember me if I let too much time go by."

"Good thinking," he laughed, and I had a mind to kick him in the shins, but realized that I was the one to blame for the patronizing turn our talk had taken.

A couple of foreign tourists with cameras and maps asked us for directions to Lincoln Center, the American Mecca of the Arts, as they put it. Obviously music lovers, they recognized the maestro and asked permission to take his picture. Orson agreed charmingly. I ended up taking the shot with Orson in the middle, balancing on my good heel. Finally everyone was happy and they moved on.

Orson and I crossed the East Drive. On the asphalt my broken heel made similar noises to the clicking hooves of two horse carriages going by. I thought how much fun it would be to take a ride together, and it would temporarily eliminate the predicament of my limping. What, if I mentioned it to Orson?

Instead I said, "Of course I remember what I read in your book. Conducting is a matter of body language. Anything is good that gets the message across. The tempo has to be established, the dynamics, the phrasing, the balance between the instruments..."

"Good, good, "Orson interrupted. "I'm glad to see you did your homework."

He pointed to a pavilion on the hill, the Chess and Checkers House. "I realize it's hard for you to walk. Would you like to sit down for a while?"

I nodded gratefully. The sun was behind his head and suddenly he smiled. A spark was born that seemed to change the air around us. I followed him up the stairs and a squirrel emerged from some dead leaves, crossing in front of us. On the platform, several people were sitting on benches, playing chess on stone tables or reading. We sat down at a table, facing each other. Being with Orson was a little like being with one of the invisible fantasy-friends my father and I used to create. Like a fable creature, Orson didn't seem real, and I wondered if he ever would. He didn't fit into my reality, and if he ever did, would it rob him of his magic?

I opened my purse and put Orson's book on the table.

I hoped to sound convincing. "Your book taught me to listen to music in a different way, maybe more intellectually."

Orson moved from his position in the sun into the shade. "That's good, but let me warn you. Don't intellectualize too much." he smiled a lazy, languid smile.

I sensed his eyes on me and I moved from my spot in the shade into the sun.

"Isabella, do you know how I listen to music? I listen with my gut, my heart, my ears, and with my mind, and exactly in that order. And I'm telling you, Isabella, if it doesn't get me in the gut," and here he pointed at it... "it will probably not get me in the mind either. Don't think too much of the technical aspect of music. It's the composer's job to get you excited. Unless a piece of music truly moves me, I'm not interested in performing it, because then it becomes nothing but problem solving."

I listened in awe. He had a very calm way of sitting there, barely moving, keeping me prisoner with eyes that were hidden behind dark glasses.

"Isabella, when you listen to music, sit back, relax, let it wash over you and say, *take me, here I am, try to excite me."*

In a surprise gesture he stretched his legs out in front of him and opened his long arms, as if trying to embrace someone. Who? The world? *Me?*

I said, "I envy you. You are a happy man. You get so much pleasure from what you are doing."

"I want to make sure you get this right. Pleasure is the most important part about music. It's the emotional part. It's what counts. In music, theory without pleasure is worthless, but if you combine the emotional with the intellectual, it's like a big bang, an explosion in your mind, and in your heart, and a new dimension opens up."

I leaned forward and openly studied the birthmark on his lip.

"And, Orson," I was finally comfortable enough to call him by his first name, "what is your greatest pleasure in all of this?"

He replied without hesitation. "It's the freedom to create my own vision within stylistic boundaries."

I had opened Orson's book and the wind blew through the pages, pushing it to the rim of the table.

He added as an afterthought, "... isn't it pleasure we live for?"

Pleasure. The word stuck in my mind.

Now he leaned forward too. Across the table, our faces drew closer.

"I'd like to show you how to listen to music. But don't ever let anyone, not even me, tell you what to *feel* in music. What you feel is between you and Mozart or you and Beethoven and Brahms. Music sounds as emotions feel, and I'm telling you, Isabella, *feel* it, feel it... feel the music, feel life, even at the risk of messing it up."

A cool breeze blew my hair across my cheeks, but I didn't move. Orson's face was still close to mine. He said everything with such ease, yet enjoying my bewilderment.

I whispered, "What do you mean by 'messing it up?' Are you talking about risk-taking or being sorry?"

He let out a funny little laugh and sat back. "There are no guarantees, Isabella."

An uncertain silence settled between us.

I pushed his book across the table. "Would you sign it for me?"

"All right." He opened his beaten briefcase and took out his small silver pen.

What would he write? I envisioned the line of a well-known aria or some staff lines with one of his favorite musical themes. But no, watching him scribble, I was disappointed at the result. After the first line that said, *For Isabella,* he left three inches of empty space under which he put his name, followed by the date. Not very original.

But he seemed to be pleased and pushed the book back in my direction. "It's the best offer I can think of making you."

I stared at his impersonal autograph. "Why?"

"Because you have my permission to fill in the blank space with whatever you wish. Notice... I signed my name to it. I put myself completely in your hands." He smiled his magic smile.

I said, "Aren't you afraid of having signed a promise or ... uh... a curse?"

He sat up regally. "There are very few things I'm afraid of."

"It sounds so simple when you say it."

"Why?"

I didn't instantly reply, but he insisted. "Isabella, what are you afraid of?"

I coughed. Our cautious conversation seemed to be on hold, as if waiting for a page to turn. My first impulse was to mention my fear of spiders, but then I said, "Actually, I'm afraid of the New York subway. So many people get mugged down there, and I'm afraid it could happen to me too."

I knew my fear was not so much about spiders or the subway, but rather the confused state of my emotions.

Orson giggled blissfully. "I think that's funny. I love to ride the subway. Unless you hire a helicopter or a horse, it's the fastest way to beat the traffic. In fact, some of my best musical ideas came to me on the subway. Seriously, Isabella, for the New Yorker it's a daily part of life."

Almost abruptly he made a nervous move to check his watch.

"I promised Paula to take her to her favorite Italian restaurant and then to the movies. She loves Fettuccini Alfredo and Robert De Niro, and I think she should get what she wants."

He picked up his beaten briefcase. "I have to go."

I wished he hadn't talked about Paula. The mention of her name was like snow on the first flowers of spring.

Already he was up, prepared to move on.

I picked up his book and said, "Now I have no reason to call you."

He replied quickly. "You don't need a reason to call me."

He hurried down the stairs, but stopped and turned around.

"I'll call *you*."

At that moment Orson was no longer a fantasy-friend from my childhood days. Suddenly Orson was real, frighteningly real. And the magic was still there.

I watched as he got into a cab on the East Drive. A horse carriage pulled up next to the cab, blocking my view of the window from which Orson might have waved good-bye. As the cab passed, I caught a glimpse of his dark glasses looking straight ahead.

My thoughts raced in curious directions. It occurred to me that Orson was a person ruled by opposites. Aloofness smothered his warmth and led him to take refuge in facts, just as his dark glasses covered the emotions in his eyes. I felt now that I understood the riddle of his nature. He was a virtuoso of happiness and hurt.

14

On my way home on the bus I weighed the pros and cons of showing Orson's autographed book to James. In all the years of our marriage nothing like this would have qualified as a reason for secrecy. But today was different. Something else was at stake. Was I setting a trap or running into one? At a time when James was still out of work and without a response from his interviews, Orson's company served as an escape that instilled vitality in me and dissipated worry.

I pictured myself saying to James, "Orson Mahler signed his book for me at the Chess and Checkers House. He suggested we sit down because I had trouble walking with my broken heel... you see, I had broken it running after him, after Beverly had finally left and I had him all to myself..."

Not a good idea. Any way I tried to describe the situation, my words would come out wrong and I could hardly expect James' approval.

Yet approval came my way. To my surprise a token of love was waiting for me on the kitchen table. A dozen pink roses immediately took my mind off the autographed book and its author. The small card between the blossoms read: *For my beautiful wife Isabella, with love and appreciation for all your support and patience, James.*

What was all this for? I thought I'd seen James' car through the garage-door window, but where was he? Upstairs? Still absorbed in James' regal handwriting, I heard the sound of the shower, together with his voice singing at full volume. I rushed to the bottom of the stairs to listen more closely.

... kiss today good bye,
The sweetness and the sorrow,
Wish me luck, the same to you...

James had a nice tenor, and compared to my skimpy alto, he would never have to worry about being auditioned for Orson's chorus or even a Broadway show.

What was happening? The roses, the card, and now he was singing his heart out..."

...but I can't regret what I did for love.
What I did for love..."

I ran upstairs. In his bathroom, thick steam frosted the mirror like a coat of sugar. James liked to boil under the shower.

"Isabella..." James stopped singing. "Where were you?" He gesticulated through the glass door. "I've got news for you... Come here, Beautiful. Come in here with me..." He chuckled as if he had emptied a bottle of bourbon.

This was new. We never took a shower together because we couldn't agree on the temperature. Years of swimming in an Austrian mountain lake from May through September had stretched my tolerance for cold water beyond James' limits. What I considered refreshing would freeze the blood in his veins. Conversely, I seemed to suffocate in a shower that James found snugly warm. As a result, we enjoyed sharing spaghetti and sex, but not showers.

James turned his face into the spray of water and hurled, "Hurry up... or I'll come and get you while you're still dressed."

He meant business. Was he drunk after all? I dropped my clothes in a pile on the bathroom scale and pushed the glass door open. He instantly pulled me to him, and before I could plead for a compromise in temperature, he encircled my body with his arms and we exchanged the most elementary form of bio-chemistry, as he called it, a sweet and soulful kiss. I struggled free, eager for an explanation.

He straightened up proudly, mindless of the water running down his face. "How did you like kissing the new Business Development Vice President of Technicon Corporation?"

"Jaaames..!" I screamed and swallowed water. *"Ehrlich?... Vice-President?"*

"They called me just two hours ago. I tried to get you at the office, but you had already left. Where were you?"

My foot slipped on a piece of soap that had slid out of James' hands. I staggered but he caught me and pulled me close again.

"... ooops," he laughed, forgetting his question. "And guess when I start?" His voice was triumphant. "*Tomorrow!* I'll have a staff of four engineers and a secretary."

Under the cascading water we clung to each other, laughing, like survivors after a storm. I planted several kisses on his slippery cheeks. "Oh, James, I'm so proud of you."

"That's what I wanted to hear, as much as I wanted to get the job."

He gave the kind of sigh that follows success after a hard struggle.

"First," James put his hands on my hips, "I'll have to visit all the manufacturing locations to get acquainted with operations and management at the division level. That will mean a lot of travel, and just imagine, some of it will be in the corporate jet."

He didn't check for my reaction to his prospective absences. In this hot steam he was completely at ease and at long last in control of his life. Nothing could stop him any longer. Now, at forty-three, he had the job that he had dreamed of and the woman he loved. But did he realize that she was about to faint from the heat?

Yet along with the physical discomfort, the stream of hot water on my body seemed to burn off all the doubts and fears I had been harboring.

James was ecstatic. "I report directly to the President. He seems to be a very competent guy, and he told me he has high hopes for me as a problem solver..."

All this could wait until later. I put my wet finger on James' lips and then my hands on his long torso, in the soft space where the ribs end just above the waist, and drew him close to me again. I just wanted to put my head on his shoulder and close my mascara-smeared eyes in a moment of blissful gratitude.

We didn't remain still for long. Through the spray of water, I listened to the message James' body was communicating to me. With a moan of longing, he signaled his desire and, except for the scalding water, I felt outrageously happy.

I pleaded, "James, I'm so hot."

James mumbled into my ear, "I know. I like you that way."

I struggled free of him. "*No!* I mean it's *boiling* in here," and groped behind him for the faucets. I got the hot water turned off, but not the cold, and we got hit in the bone-chilling spray.

James roared, "*Oh, dammit!*" He turned the water off and let out an exasperated sigh.

I drew back against the glass door and noticed that his desire had not withstood the cold shock. He glanced down, shivering and miserable. But today nothing could be miserable. We collapsed with laughter, and as James reached for the beach towel that hung over the edge of the shower stall, I felt the overwhelming need to sing, to make this moment last, to sing and greet the future.

Kiss today good-bye...
And point me t'ward tomorrow...

James wrapped the towel around both of us and joined me at the top of his voice.

Won't forget...
Can't regret
What I did for love...

Under the towel my hand ventured to the spot of James' misery, determined to reverse the condition that the shock of the cold spray had caused. He gave a luxurious sigh.

I said, "You don't seem to mind what I'm doing."

James let go of the towel and his hands splashed out in innocent surrender.

He smirked broadly. "That's the way I am. You know me. I rape easily."

15

The subway was oppressive, dark and smelly. No one but Orson Mahler could have made me go down there, to what seemed more like a coal mine than the public transportation system of a civilized society. But here I was, at the Lexington Avenue and Fifty-First Street station, following Orson's instructions.

He had called my office earlier in the day. "Hello, Miss Austria. I remember you were afraid of something. May I take you for a ride on the New York subway?"

In the flow of the rush-hour crowd, I descended the stairs. From a distance came the passing thunder of heavy metal. The change booths. The gates. People rushing like ants. Only one person was not moving. Orson was standing on the other side of the turnstile. Through his dark glasses he looked at me with a quiet stare.

As I rushed toward him he seemed amused by my disorientation. Still separated by the turnstile, I said, "I'm glad you're here already."

He bowed with mock humility. "It's nice to be wanted."

Our eyes met, and for a single second a dream-like veil separated us from the crowd.

He handed me a token, grinning. "A token of my esteem."

The moment I pushed through the barrier a train approached.

Orson pointed at it. "This is the Lexington Line. It will take us to Grand Central."

The doors hissed open and the surging crowd carried us inside. Standing, we strap-hung side by side in the press of people.

With the collar of his raincoat turned up and his dark glasses, Orson blended inconspicuously with the rest of the commuters.

The train started with a jolt. Somewhat uncomfortable, I read the ads above the window. *Milk, New York's Health Kick... Pregnant? We can help... Foot Pain...?* Not today, I thought, blessing my comfortable pumps.

Orson smiled invitingly. I leaned forward and felt the warmth of his breath brushing my ear. "In the subway I like to pick out attractive, well-dressed women and take my time to look at them."

Not very diplomatic, maestro. What about *my* outfit? Following the elation of James' new job I had treated myself to a beige spring suit with an incredibly slim skirt and a long slit in the back to reveal my legs. I showed him a forced grin. Outside the train signs were flying by. Grand Central Station… Grand Central Station…

Orson said, "From here we'll take the shuttle to Times Square."

Back on the platform his long strides caused me to lose him in the crowd.

I shouted after him, "Orson... wait for me!"

He stopped, sizing me up. "Did you break your heel again?"

I shrugged helplessly. "No, my heels are fine, but my skirt is too tight. I can't take such long steps."

He shook his head. "Why are you wearing a skirt like that in the first place?" and in a softer tone, "Come on... let me take your arm."

But taking my arm didn't mean he was slowing down. I felt like a poodle that had to make two steps to keep up with one of his.

I said defensively, "Do you always walk this fast?"

"Always," he chuckled to himself, "That's why I've never been accosted by a prostitute."

In this oppressive, noisy place where Orson seemed at home, I saw an unsettling side of him that I hadn't seen before. But I had to give him credit for knowing his way around in this labyrinth of tunnels, stairs and escalators.

In the crowded Times Square shuttle we stood as close as we could without touching. In the dense air I tried to read behind the many faces that were staring, thinking, feeling tired, anticipating dinner, the family, TV, maybe sex.

At the screech of the wheels before the train stopped, I fell against Orson. He caught me expertly with his arm around my waist, resting his hand on my hipbone for a moment longer than I needed to regain my balance.

His velvet voice said, "This is a nice curve, if you don't mind my saying so."

What should I have said? A decade of fidelity to James had made me inexperienced at flirting. The idea that Orson was thinking of my body filled me with an odd mixture of defiance and delight. Wishing for Beverly's eloquence, I longed to come up with a remark that would shock or humor him. Instead, I felt myself tensing up. Was it just the subway, or was it the sensation of Orson's hand on my hip?

On the platform again, we kept a discreet distance and Orson explained the network of the subway lines on the wall map.

"See the number one train all the way down to the south tip of Manhattan? We'll take that now."

I said, "You had the whole trip figured out in advance."

He nodded. "I hope you're getting used to it by now. I want to free you from an unreasonable fear. I always feel that riding the subway gives me time to think. I've conducted all of Beethoven's symphonies in my head down here."

As he spoke, the magic that he exuded from the podium returned, his eyes seemed to shine through his dark glasses, and I thought of his hand resting on my hip.

On the crowded platform a man played an amplified guitar, invading every corner with the noise.

Orson shuddered. "What an imposition..."

From the tunnel, a light approached.

Orson pointed up. "See the lovely reflection on the curved ceiling?"

This train was less crowded and I slid onto the bench next to Orson, positioning my purse between us like a cushion. I didn't know if it was intent or indecision. Anyway, I chose not to correct it.

We passed Thirty-Fourth, Twenty-Eighth, Twenty-Third and Eighteenth Streets. Orson dug his hands into the pockets of his raincoat. I told myself to snap out of my self-inflicted tension. Everything was almost perfect, wasn't it? Naturally, I would have preferred riding with Orson in a carriage through Central Park, but riding the subway was obviously the maestro's preference. I thought of my mother. She would have gone parachuting with him.

Orson pointed to a sign above the doors. *No littering, spitting or smoking.*

He said without turning his head, "There's this old joke, that when you spit on the subway you get a twenty-five dollar fine, but if you vomit you get away with nothing."

He finally made me laugh.

"Good...," his head turned, "it's nice to see you lighten up."

Suddenly I felt the need to tell him about James' new position and I gave him the whole story about my husband traveling around the country and consolidating six divisions.

Orson took a deep breath of relief. "I'm so glad for you, for both of you."

He smiled and made a move to reach over with his hand. But my purse was blocking his way and forced him to withdraw.

While thinking of his hand, I continued telling him about hermetic sealing materials, electrolytes, substances for bonding enzymes, and polishing compounds for metallographic processes.

Orson was impressed. "All this sounds so interesting. I'd love to hear more about it one day. Sometimes I still wonder what my life would have been like if I had become a chemist." He stood up, then leaned down and said softly, "Maybe I wouldn't have had the chance to meet you."

The train stopped at South Ferry and my heart almost stopped along with it.

Orson motioned with his head. “We have to get off. It’s the end of the line.”

I was glad. I needed air. Outside, at the top of the stairs, the bright sun felt good. The wind was like an infusion of fresh energy. We walked through Battery Park towards the waterfront. What a sight, the Statue of Liberty, the Lady of the Harbor. Her fascination never failed to lift my spirits.

But Orson made a face and squinted through his dark glasses.

“Orson, why do you always wear those dark glasses?”

“Why do I wear them? Because I’m a night-owl and I hate the bright sunlight. You haven’t seen me awake yet. I come to life at midnight and when I sleep I hang upside down from the rafters and wear a black sleeping mask.”

A shiver crept along my spine. But looking at his uncomfortable face against the sun, I couldn’t argue with his assessment. Why was I spending my time with such a strange man?

Then all at once the sight of Lady Liberty reappearing from behind the trees enticed my thoughts into the past. For how many people had she symbolized the promise of a new life? Not only did those people bring their hopes to a new country, but their traditions, heritage, humor and beliefs. And I was one of them. And Orson? He was born here and had never lived anywhere but in Manhattan. I was the stranger in his life, not he in mine.

I looked at the crowd surrounding us. Tourists taking pictures, children playing, mothers pushing baby carriages. Colored balloons. Hot pretzels. A postcard stand offered thirty sights waiting to be sent around the globe. Should I write one to my mother? *With love, Isabella and Orson Mahler...* Imagine her face.

A bus pulled up and disgorged a giggling flock of young Swedish girls. An open street map of Manhattan fluttered on the pavement.

Orson, now used to the bright light, walked single-mindedly past the hot dog cart to the ice-cream wagon. “How about some ice-cream? I love chocolate chip.”

I nodded. “Fine.” But as he handed me the double-dip cone I felt a secret craving for a hot dog.

In a sudden breeze, a flurry of colored summer skirts from the Swedish tourists swirled in the air. Orson openly relished the sight of their legs as he picked each chocolate chip separately with his teeth. But his pleasure seemed to stem from yet another source. He signaled with his hand toward the postcard stand.

“For a moment I thought the red-haired woman was Beverly.” He chuckled to himself. “It wouldn’t surprise me. She somehow always knows where to find me.”

I bit hard on a chocolate chip, slightly irritated.

“I see who you mean. But it’s not her,” I said, hoping to close the subject.

But he went on. “I’m glad that you and Beverly have become such good friends. She speaks so highly of you.”

I wasn’t so sure about the “such-good-friends” part and forced a smile. “I feel the same.”

“You know, Beverly is wonderful.” There was an intense thrill in his voice. “I wouldn’t know what to do without her. She’s clever, attractive and extremely helpful.”

I gave him a cool look. “Don’t forget your supply of hot chocolate.”

He didn’t catch my sarcasm, but continued licking his ice-cream. “You’re right. I nearly forgot about that. She always takes care of me.”

Now I was gritting my teeth. “Yes, Beverly is invaluable,” I said grimly.

“And not only that,” he added with a spirited smile, “the woman certainly knows how to dress.” He gave a musical laugh.

What about my new outfit? Annoyed, I threw my unfinished ice-cream cone in a wide arc into a nearby garbage can and snapped, “If you think Beverly is so goddamn wonderful, then why aren’t you here with her instead of me?”

Orson's birthmark twitched. His eyes traveled with trance-like slowness from me to the garbage-bin and back. Then he exploded with laughter.

"Hah... I *love* it! You're jealous!"

Still holding his ice-cream cone with his right hand, he clutched his heart with his left and in a theatrical gesture went down on one knee. He smiled his magic smile.

"Isabella, will you marry me?"

Very funny. This was probably a trick he used with women to get out of a sticky situation. Yet for a touch of time my world was spellbound.

I laughed nervously. "I'm flattered. Your proposal makes me feel like Juliet on the balcony, but right now I'm dying for a hot dog with a lot of mustard."

The crowd grew thicker around us. Behind my back a camera clicked. Orson got up and gave me a lost look.

I was still laughing. But he wasn't.

16

When Julia arrived at my house, late again as usual, it was due to Ludwig, her Dover Terrier, who had got hold of her Godiva chocolates and made a mess on her pink satin sheets. I laughed, picturing the scene, and decided not to say anything about her perpetual excuses.

At last, Julia settled next to me in the passenger seat and I started the car. We set out for our long-planned Sunday picnic. From the back seat, Ludwig alertly watched her pull her long blonde hair back into a pony-tail. Our picnic basket was safely tucked away in the trunk. With the windows down and our hair blowing, I navigated along the winding road leading through the forest to Eagle Rock Reservation, south of Montclair. Through the budding branches the sky offered a spotless blue. It was one of those days in late May when the serenity of spring turned into the promise of summer.

Ludwig, fully aware of the unattainable picnic basket behind him in the trunk, made playful attempts to lick Julia's ears. His beige fur had become a little too shaggy and gave him the appearance of a sheep that needed to be shorn. Four years ago Julia had received Ludwig as a birthday present from her now ex-husband. Phil had given him the first name of his favorite composer: Beethoven. And now, without Phil, Ludwig had become her emotional life-saver and her security system, a comprehensive task that this funny, fluffy creature performed with awesome dedication.

I remembered the time after Julia's divorce, when she would crawl up in a ball on her couch, crying, even brushing away my comforting hand. All I could get out of her was her wish not to be born, when along came Ludwig, softly punching her shoulder with his muzzle, and she would turn to him and smile.

But living by herself had not yet become natural for her. It was still a condition that made her linger in the shadows of resignation, where she was always searching the blue sky for clouds. And this, I feared, was exactly what she would do again today. My willingness to lend her an ear was running thin.

Before starting off, I bluntly told her that I would not share my home-made shrimp salad with her if she mentioned Phil again. I figured that for the trouble of peeling and cooking shrimp, chopping avocados, olives, scallions, chives and mushrooms, I deserved to be spared the repetitive tale of how expertly he had handled her body but hurt her pride.

My shrimp salad turned out to be the culinary treat I'd hoped for. Following our Sunday breakfast, James had watched me take it out of the fridge and transfer it into a plastic container. I couldn't believe how much I had made. In passing, James snatched a shrimp with his fingers and laughed. "Did you invite the marines?"

He was right. Back went half of it into the fridge, and James went off to join Barry at the club. It was good to see James with a new tennis racket and a new impetus to competition. Today, after putting in a week of ten-hour days at his new office, he seemed more energetic than ever and, as if afraid to lose his momentum, he was too restless to spend another Sunday with a Tolstoy novel.

Julia had been truly happy to hear about James' good news. She agreed not to think or talk about Phil, albeit with some indignation over my straightforwardness. When the road permitted, I gave her a quick sideways glance and smiled to myself, at peace with the world.

In her white jeans and blue sweater Julia looked like a wind-up doll of a princess, perfectly mannered and fully expecting life's best treatment. But in her unguarded moments she was like daddy's spoiled little girl, biting her nails and upset when she didn't get her every wish.

With James' employment situation resolved, my life was ideally straightened out in her mind, and it was selfish of me not to allow her to talk about her heavy heart. But today I was determined to make her listen to me instead of me always offering my patient ear to her.

What would she say if I told her that my good spirits could only partially be attributed to James' new position? What if I told her that Maestro Mahler, whom we had cheered together in a sold-out Carnegie Hall, had kneeled and proposed to me in the middle of a crowd of tourists?

With practically no traffic on the road, we reached the top level of the reservation and parked the car. The lawn still sparkled with dew, and we seemed to have the place to ourselves. In the dusty distance to the east, the towers of Manhattan looked like a miniature architectural model. I opened the trunk and handed Julia the blanket, taking the basket myself. Ludwig raced across the grass, and Julia, clutching the blanket, ran after him, her white clogs flopping with each step.

I always liked to watch Julia, who was spreading the blanket on the grass, because her outward appearance mirrored so much of what I felt was part of my inner self. Behind the armor of dignity lay a fragile and ever-searching mind. Since we had first met at a supermarket check-out counter, where we had exchanged some superficial thoughts about rising strawberry prices, our subsequent talks were effortless and mutually supportive. Unlike those with Beverly, our conversations were not contests in cleverness, but a sharing of ideas that flowed naturally between us.

As I emptied the picnic basket, setting out napkins and plates, Julia sat with her arms wrapped around her knees. Ludwig circled us and expectantly eyed the food containers.

I cut the bread and handed Julia a plate of shrimp salad. Ludwig put his head on Julia's knee and barked soft sounds of pleasure. She praised my culinary efforts, trying hard to sound lighthearted.

"You know, Isabella, this morning I put a new message on my answering machine."

"What does it say now...?" I looked at her across my first forkful of shrimp.

"Listen to this," she giggled and added in a stilted voice, "Please call me later, I'm still sleeping..."

"That fits you to a tee," I said, swallowing, and we both laughed.

Sitting or kneeling, my jeans felt too tight, and in search of a more comfortable position, I emptied the rest of the basket: grapes, apples, cheese and crackers.

Ludwig moved restlessly around us, and my mind searched equally restlessly for an appropriate entry to tell Julia about Orson Mahler.

It wasn't quite as easy as I had imagined. After some consideration I had chosen Julia as my confidante for an objective opinion on the puzzling newcomer in my life. Maybe I should merely mention that I planned to audition for his chorus. It would also be safe to say that Matthew had made a tape of the *Brahms Requiem* for me, which I was already listening to. But all this had nothing to do with my ambush of Orson at Avery Fisher Hall or his invitation to the subway that had led to a rather icy atmosphere following his mock proposal. What had he imagined my reaction would be? That I would fall right into his arms? What would Julia have done?

Had I confided in her from the beginning, starting with the point when he had taken my hand during our first lunch, it would be natural to follow up. But too much had happened in the meantime.

Still, no time would ever be as perfect as the present, with Ludwig racing back and forth, sniffing at trees, and with Julia surprisingly serene and enjoying my food.

Julia didn't notice that I was only half-listening as she told me about her older sister, Hanna, who was moving into a new house on Hilton Head Island with her husband, Steve, and three teenage kids. As the minutes passed and my shrimp salad disappeared, I noticed how hard it was to put my complicated story into simple words.

For a short, peaceful moment we both lifted our faces to the sun, our eyes closed, dreaming of summer. The birds seemed to hold their breath in anticipation of a revelation.

I re-opened my eyes to the brightness around me and saw the top of the Chrysler Building glistening in the distance. Julia's eyes squinted, watching Ludwig pee on a shrub.

"Oh, something funny I wanted to show you," she said, pausing to sip soda through a straw. "There was a picture of you and Orson Mahler in the *New York Post* this morning."

My blood froze.

"What?" I whispered as unperturbed as I could manage.

"Wait a minute... Where is it?" Unhurried, she combed her ponytail with her fingers. "I saved the page for you... but where did I put it?"

After what seemed an eternity, she produced a crumpled piece of newspaper from her pocket and unfolded it with maddening slowness as Ludwig merrily chased an insect.

"Look here." She dropped the wrinkled page in my lap and finished her Camembert, more interested in the food than the photo.

My throat tightened up. *O mein Gott!* Here I was in my beige suit, seen from behind. The picture was postcard-size. Orson knelt in front of me, holding his ice-cream cone in one hand and clutching his heart with the other. The subtext read, *Spring Fever can affect anyone, including Maestro Orson Mahler in Battery Park.*

I blurted out, "That's not me..."

Julia wiped her mouth. "But it looks exactly like you from the back."

"Maybe," I gasped for air, "but I don't have a suit like that."

"Never mind," she shrugged, "I just thought I'd show it to you. I mean, you could fool anyone by saying it's you."

I blurted, "Mr. Mahler probably pulled a prank on one of his chorus members."

She took the page from me and studied it again. “He’s probably quite a clown. At least that’s what it looks like here. Probably a ladies’ man too. I wonder if he’s seen the picture.”

Meanwhile Ludwig was rolling on his back, offering his stomach for Julia’s strokes, which he accepted unashamedly. Recognizing my narrow escape, I knew I could never wear my beige suit when I was with her.

Now I was filled with remorse about declining Julia’s need to talk about Phil. Anything but this ridiculous picture. I should also ask her if Angela and Barry had invited her to their party next week. Or even better, I could broach the subject of her new book project and ask if she had come up with any good ideas. I was ready to listen to anything if she would just let me off the hook with Orson.

The photo seemingly forgotten, Julia trailed her fingers through the grass and suddenly asked, “Isabella, did you ever cheat on James?”

My mouth went dry. Never before had she asked such a personal question. But I had nothing to conceal.

“No, never...” And it came with honesty and a feeling of relief that I didn’t have to lie.

She raised her head and her brown eyes focused on me openly. “I’m glad. James is the best husband any woman could wish for.”

“I know.” I played with the lid of the basket, and it was clear to me that I could never tell her anything about Orson. Admitting my impossible attraction would be like a hot iron burning a hole into the white linen of our friendship.

17

I shouldn't have talked Orson into this, a ride through Central Park in a horse carriage. What a face he made. It was obvious that he was not in a good mood.

Through his dark glasses his eyes seemed to say, *Doesn't she have the decency to remember that I hate the bright daylight?*

As we climbed into one of the colorful carriages lining Central Park South, Orson seemed intent on hiding his face from the coachman. His open display of discomfort smothered my enjoyment. But it was too late now.

The coachman tipped his hat and the horse pulled away from the curb and into the park. Orson awkwardly clutched his beaten briefcase on his lap and then put it on the seat next to him. He wasn't sitting next to me, as I had hoped, but opposite, eyes towards the rear.

Seeing him framed by the old-fashioned street lights and the pink wax flowers on both sides of the carriage, it was clear that he looked out of place, like an aging suitor in an operetta.

He ran his fingers through his gray, windblown hair.

"So this is what you want."

I gave him my sweetest smile. "Isn't it romantic?"

Orson laughed condescendingly, chasing a wasp that darted in erratic circles around our heads. "You call this romantic?"

"Yes..." I was still smiling, though with some effort.

Orson leaned back as if I had the measles. He gave a humorless little snort. "I feel ridiculous."

Odors of questionable origin rose from the bucket dangling under the carriage. I was overcome by the conviction that this was the last time we would meet. Our little game was over and I wasn't quite sure which rule I had broken.

I was on the verge of apologizing when Orson spoke in a dry, even tone. "I consider myself an incurable romantic, Isabella, but riding in a horse-drawn carriage is not my idea of the picture. To me, true romanticism means surrender to pleasure. It is to hold and behold a woman in the natural flow of love-making."

I shivered. It took me a moment to digest this. *... to hold and behold a woman in the natural flow of love-making.* His words trailed in my ears as the horse trotted along wearily under the low branches of some old, majestic trees.

Orson and I were silent.

The sky stretched like a yellow, leaden roof over the park. As the horse rounded another bend, the coachman looked back over his shoulder, sporting a shining moustache. I suspected pomade.

I should have been enjoying every minute of this, but instead the moments crept with torturous slowness. Orson's eyes met mine. Our knees could easily have touched, but we were careful that they didn't. What did Orson expect of me?

I was aware of every breath I took. The knowledge of his discomfort burst the bubble of my fantasy, in which some sort of magic would keep us captive in the carriage and we would spend the rest of our lives riding through Central Park.

I didn't dare mention the photo in the *New York Post*. Was it possible that he had not seen it? Or that Beverly or Joan or *anybody* in the chorus had not seen it? But then Orson was used to the indelicacies of the press, and time had taught him that the only way to survive gossip was to ignore it.

Our carriage passed a girl walking seven dogs. Three of them pulled to the right and four to the left, causing the leashes to twist around her body like a whirlwind of human passions. How would she untangle them? How would I untangle mine?

The skyscrapers surrounding the park seemed to belong to a different world. In our world, Orson was like a live illusion that I was trying to carry into the ordinary business of daily existence. Some minutes went by. I smiled and leaned closer to him.

Orson smiled too and said, "Oh, I wanted to tell you, I just had a meeting with Joan. She picked out some amazing new artwork for the fall chorus brochure. What a jewel of a woman! Sometimes I wonder where she gets her ideas. Besides that, she came up with the preliminary budget for the chorus and the orchestra and has even managed to balance it."

He sighed and then, to my surprise, beamed broadly.

"Frankly, Isabella, this woman has me in the palm of her hand..."

I began to feel resentment, but he was not finished.

"You know, Isabella, after Paula, my wife *(as if I didn't know),* Joan is probably the most important woman in my life. She's bright, efficient and," he chuckled meaningfully, "so naturally feminine."

Insensitive monster! Why did he always have to tell me how he felt about other women, be it Beverly or Joan, but never mentioned anything nice about me? I had a mind to jump off the carriage. Obviously, I merely represented a non-threatening entity with a pair of patient ears. Orson was comfortable with strong, ambitious women who took care of the practicalities of his daily life. He needed them in order to be free for his art.

But what was I doing here with him? And what about his proposal, even though it was made in jest? Up to now he hadn't made the slightest attempt to move closer, yet he talked about *holding and beholding a woman...* I wondered what Sigmund Freud would have made of his enigmatic conduct.

Our silence was accompanied by the soft creaking of the wooden wheels and the clopping of the horse's hooves on the asphalt.

"Listen to those sounds!" Orson whispered alertly and adjusted his dark glasses. "Two rhythmic patterns that occur simultaneously. This is the concept of polyrhythm in music. It's that simple. Isabella, I would like you to open your ears to all kinds of sounds. I once made a tape recording of two water faucets dripping at different intervals. The result was surprisingly interesting."

I nodded, taking in the fresh air and feeling better. Orson seemed suddenly elated, but I couldn't imagine why. From one moment to the next, the mood had changed between us, like the color of the sky, now showing a friendly blue. Or had I only imagined the oppressive clouds in the first place?

I tried to see Orson's eyes through his dark glasses.

"Orson, why do you spend any time with me?"

The seconds he took to answer stretched into a suspenseful interval. In front of us the coachman sneezed.

At last Orson broke into a heart-stopping smile.

"Maybe it's because I like the way you toss your head." And he added reflectively, "You're like a lost song. And now that I've found it again, it's even more beautiful than I remembered."

"I don't know what you mean."

His voice was barely audible. "I'm not sure I want you to know. But why do you spend time with me?"

A terrible sweetness rose in me.

I whispered, "I'm happy in your company."

"Good. I'm glad."

He continued to smile. So did I, and squinted against the sun. The ensuing silence was no longer a silence of our hearts.

I thought, Of course, we'll meet again...

18

At our arrival the party spirit was already soaring. Glasses, long and short-stemmed, wide and fluted, were being filled for about thirty guests. James handed me the bottled gift for our hosts and straightened his tie.

Three years ago to the day, Barry and Angela had first met in Rome, and this sunny afternoon in June was perfect to celebrate their anniversary. Barry greeted us at the door with Angela in tow. He hadn't bothered to dress up for the occasion and his white shirt couldn't make up for his worn jeans.

Angela, all radiant hostess, wore a snug, flower-laden crêpe-de-chine dress. Her long, dark hair was set in artful waves, framing her Italian features. As expected, she had no intention of keeping her crush on James to herself.

"Ah, *Giacomo...*," she opened her bare arms and flung herself at him, a routine that had become embarrassingly repetitive.

Over her shoulder James winked at me, basking in his imposed helplessness. He was not romantically interested in Angela, but he enjoyed his ability to bring out heat in another woman.

Barry and I exchanged patient smiles.

Inside the house dozens of red and yellow tulips in several vases brightened the decor like designed flames. Before we joined the living room crowd James tucked in the label at the back of my dress. His attention was immediately diverted by our neighbor who wanted to discuss the re-paving of our driveways. The two men aimed for the only empty spot, between the baby grand piano and a rack holding at least a hundred bottles of wine.

Looking around, I first felt "in" with the crowd and then, as the moments passed, I realized, I wasn't. I wandered around, avoiding groups rather than joining them, fearful of having to face the chore of casual chit-chat. Sometimes a crowd of people made me lonely. I seemed to walk through them, and they through me, as if with each new move I had the ability to blend with the colors of the room and become invisible.

After my first exploratory round of distant nods and smiles I decided to head for the kitchen, hoping to find Angela or Barry. In the hall at the bottom of the stairs a big porcelain rabbit grinned at me with cheerful malice. Everything looked different. Since Angela had discovered her affinity for Victorian decor, the house had been taken over by ruffled curtains, lace pillows and velvet ribbons. Hadn't Barry always liked contemporary?

I sneaked into the kitchen. It was filled with appliances and shiny copper pans, carefully polished like the perfect surface of their lives. Angela was taking two more bottles of champagne from the fridge. Her dark eyes shone at me warmly.

"Isabella, I love the red of-a you dress."

I said, "I'm afraid it's a bit too low in front, but James loves it."

"Mamma mia, you-a woman. Don't be afraid to look-a like one..." She frowned, holding a bottle with a kitchen napkin, and then popped it expertly. As she picked up a carton of orange juice from the floor her cleavage was remarkable. Sometimes I wondered if she ever regretted having abandoned her career in the fashion industry in Italy for her life with Barry in New Jersey.

The doorbell rang. A moment later half a dozen hors d'oevres platters, artfully prepared by the local deli, were placed on the counter. The draft between the door and the open window blew an empty pretzel bag into the sink, but Angela's mousse-styled hair didn't move an inch.

Barry poked his head around the door, puffing his pipe.

"Oh, have the caterers finally come?"

Angela hissed between her white teeth, "You mean it wasn't you who let'm in?"

I found a pair of scissors in a drawer and cut the ribbons on the plastic wraps. With her burgundy nails Angela pointed from plate to plate as Barry checked each item against the bill: Bay scallops in a shell, beef tartar on rye-rounds, tuna on cucumber rounds, skewers of roasted vegetables, and a pot of steaming oysters Rockefeller.

Barry handed a tip to the delivery man.

At the sight of all the food my mouth started watering. "Mmmm," I reached for a cucumber round. "I'm really hungry."

"Good." Barry's blue eyes sparkled at me. "I like hungry women." He plopped a hot oyster in my mouth and I felt his eyes running down the neck-line of my dress. Secretly I wondered if he could guess that I was wearing a push-up bra.

"Looks great...," he raised his bushy eyebrows, his eyes fixed at the same spot.

I snorted with my mouth full, "I can't say the same about your shabby jeans."

He waved his pipe in mock-despair. "You don't like my jeans?"

Angela intervened. "Enough." She made a face at him and pushed him out of the kitchen.

I picked up a magnet that had fallen off the refrigerator.

"I'm sorry, Angela, I didn't mean to offend..."

She emptied her glass of champagne in one desperate gulp. "You're right to tell him, Isabella. I mean, this is our anniversary party, and he think his-a blue-eyed charm, his pipe and his beard is enough to make him irresistible. Ha! I think he over-estimating his charm and he under-estimating some people's aversion against-a pipe smoke.

".... and some people don't care for beards, either," I giggled softly.

"But no... Madonna! I love his-a beard..," Angela rushed to his defense. "You know, Isabella, it's a little bit like having a fuzzy pet on his-a face..." We reveled in our girlish laughter and in the fine line that separates the act of respecting from ridiculing a man.

Chewing on a beef tartar round, I thought of Julia. Had Angela invited her? She probably had, I assumed, and Julia was just late, as usual.

I wiped my hands on a towel. "Let's take the food in."

In the living room everyone was engaged in congenial cocktail conversation. I filled my plate with lots of cucumber rounds and oysters Rockefeller and settled on the couch before the fireplace, where James was discussing the NBA with Rob, from the club. Would the Knicks ever beat the Celtics in Boston again? Frankly, I couldn't care less.

One by one, James snatched all the oysters from my plate, each time placing a playful kiss on my cheek and then returning his attention to sports.

Nancy, a pretty red-haired woman, introduced herself to me as Angela's interior designer. She was now working on the bedroom and carefully chose every trim and ribbon to create a perfect space. Her elaboration stretched into a taxing monologue.

"How fascinating," I lied, and got up to fill my plate again.

Someone raised the question of another space shuttle after the disaster earlier in the year. I turned my head and saw Dr. Louise Schumann, Barry's mother. For a second her small, lively eyes met mine as I felt someone tap my shoulder.

Barry held a tray and asked, "Wine or champagne?"

"Wine please," I cooed sweetly, hoping to make up for my previous "I-don't-like-your-jeans" remark.

But Barry beamed at me with undiminished glee. I took a glass from him and tried to move in Louise's direction. I was fully aware that my interest in her was less because she was Barry's mother, but rather Orson Mahler's former doctor. Yet I cautioned myself not to expect her to reveal any secrets about her famous patient.

Not far to Louise's left, Angela and James sat on the piano bench and laughed about something that Angela dramatized with a gesture of her hands.

The crowd was now exchanging views about tennis, specifically the pleasures and perils of mixed doubles, when for some couples the tennis court threatens to turn into a divorce court. I ran my finger around the edge of my glass and caught myself looking forward to going home already. I thought dreamingly how Orson's company made me feel alive, whereas here I seemed to moon-walk among strangers.

And then I saw Louise again. She was sitting in an armchair by the window, joyfully raising her glass of champagne. Through the murmur of voices I could make out fragments of her conversation.

"... I always felt suspicious about the bourgeois notion of normality. It's a very limited concept."

"Hi, Beautiful! Having fun?" James brushed my ear from behind. His plate was stacked with vegetable skewers and scallops.

I cheered his appetite. "The food is good, isn't it?"

He nodded with his mouth full and smiled. "Not as tasty as you...," and ran his free hand down my back.

"No flirting with-a you own wife..." Angela raised her glass in a mock-warning. From the sound of her voice she should have switched to Perrier some time ago. But the same was true for me, because two glasses of wine were already too much for my weak bladder.

"Excuse me," I grimaced at James, who understood where I was headed.

Down the hall the bathroom was locked from the inside. I waited. When the door opened, Louise came out. The older woman smiled Barry's blue-eyed smile. She took both of my hands and spoke without introduction. "My dear, I'm so glad you and Orson get along so well."

"*What...?*" I stuttered, shocked beyond words.

Her lively eyes looked at me with wit and wisdom. Her hair was somewhat unkempt and revealed many shades of gray. She was a head shorter than I, but there was a greatness of personality about her that made me feel small in her presence.

Louise didn't blink. "I'm Orson's confidante, and he speaks to me quite openly about you." Her smile spread a hundred wrinkles on her face.

I was still speechless.

"Isabella, love," she finally let go of my hands, "I fully approve of you. You are good for him. Very good for him. They say he's less grumpy lately."

At that moment another woman joined us. Louise noticed that she had left her purse inside the bathroom and went back to retrieve it. The shock from her words had paralyzed my bladder. I no longer needed to go where I was originally headed, so I re-joined the party, profoundly baffled.

Had Orson actually spoken about *me?* He, who never said anything personal? Why would he discuss me with Louise? Or did he speak to her in the same manner as he spoke to me about Beverly and Joan?

Absentmindedly, I picked some grapes from a crystal bowl on the credenza and studied a painting without really seeing it. A frightening feeling was creeping up my spine. It would be difficult to keep my meetings with Orson secret. First the photo in the *New York Post* and now Louise. What would be next?

I thought of Julia and the question she had asked me. Had I ever cheated on James? The room felt hot. And where was Julia? I remembered Barry's smitten look when he had seen her at Café Carnegie after the concert. Obviously, Angela had conveniently forgotten to invite her.

Angela and Barry were collecting dirty plates from the side tables and the piano. Among the voices behind me, a familiar name was mentioned. Its sound rang clearly through the room. I turned around from looking at the painting and felt my pulse-rate rising. *Orson Mahler.* Had Louise spoken? I looked for her, but she was gone.

A woman in a purple blouse tugged at James' sleeve and said in a brassy tone, "Don't they call him the 'man with the velvet voice'?"

An elderly woman with lots of shiny gold chains rose elaborately from the couch. "Years ago the maestro had a reputation for having quite a temper, but his professional successes and the passage of time have softened him."

The group of listeners grew. I was oddly touched to see that Orson's name was known to everyone present.

Angela, now standing in the middle of the circle, remarked casually between two sips of champagne, "Don't-a forget his-a success with the opposite sex."

From the fireplace James gave her a bemused look. Aware of the rising attention she was getting, she bubbled like the liquid in her glass.

"Well, it was-a no secret. The story even made the tabloids in Roma... The rumors connect him to some Italiana flute player with the New York Philharmonic. One day she come on-a stage and along with her instrument, she gotta glass-a water in her hand..."

I sensed something embarrassing coming up.

Amazingly armed with all the facts, Angela went on. "Right in-a middle of-a the concert, she wind her way through the other players and head-a straight for the podium, and she splash-a the water right in Mahler's face..."

The room seemed to hold its breath, as undoubtedly everyone in the orchestra had done at the time. I imagined the musicians frozen with their instruments in place. On stage, the silence following the music must have been as tense as the silence in this room. How could Angela smear Orson with gossip, especially since he was not here to defend himself? I guessed, though, that this story was only part of a much bigger war. What had Orson done to that woman? He was clearly not the sort to impose himself on a woman against her will.

Certain of Orson's innocence, I stepped into the middle of the circle.

"It's not fair," I heard myself say in a self-assured voice that hid the trembling of my heart, "to dig out old gossip. After all, Orson Mahler is one of our foremost conductors, and we have every reason to be proud of him. He is an outstanding musician and a very distinguished gentleman. I am proud to know him personally."

Having captured every eye and ear, I shivered as if standing there naked. Again I was seized by fear, that old feeling of not being able to speak well when put on the spot. But I concluded. "A public act of poor taste was committed by that woman, and not Mr. Mahler."

A woman said, "Well, you never know what goes on behind the scenes."

Angela, who had been leaning against the baby grand, took over once more. "Anyway, after that," she added tipsily, "This woman was asked to resign from-a the orchestra." She rolled her dark eyes suggestively.

My cheeks were burning. Had I gone too far to protect Orson's reputation? I gripped the backrest of a chair and looked around the room. James' eyes were rooted on me in surprise and I knew that the color of my dress was not the only thing red about me.

The general conversation resumed *sotto voce* and everyone was glad to change the sour subject of Orson Mahler's story to something sweet: Dessert was here.

Our hosts appeared carrying four large silver platters. A display of delight, but a disaster in indulgence. My eyes searched the crowd, trying to locate Louise.

"Where is your mother?" I asked Barry who set a tray of nougat treats on the piano.

"She had a ride back to Manhattan. She left a while ago."

"I didn't even have a chance to talk to her."

"I know," he shrugged. "I didn't either. She's a very popular party-girl."

"How old is she?"

"Seventy-nine this August."

"An amazing lady," I said, watching Angela cut a luscious green lime pie.

Playfully, Barry put a chocolate covered strawberry in my mouth and offered me a small plate with Petit Fours. At the credenza, James filled his plate with cream puffs and glazed orange slices and then balanced everything skillfully on three fingers as he moved like a restless tiger from group to group.

I checked my watch. It was almost eleven, quite late for a Sunday night, when most people had to get up in the morning.

A distinguished-looking gentleman put down his brandy snifter. “I can’t stay up this late,” he said in a stiff-upper-lipish tone. “Fortunes are earned before noon.” He left without dwelling on his clue.

I was ready to leave too.

James’ hand brushed some chocolate crumbs from my dress.

“All set to go?”

I placed my unfinished plate next to a vase of yellow tulips and nodded. Already I was suffering the overeater’s penalty, where the brain loses the fight for blood, that feeling of fullness and fatigue when no place seems to be more desirable than bed.

In the hall we thanked our hosts for their hospitality. Barry leaned over and his beard tickled my face like a cactus.

“Thanks for coming, and... I really like that red on you, Isabella.”

James folded his arm possessively around my waist. I sensed the old familiar animal attraction that was suddenly alive between us and gave him a little peck on the cheek. Nothing could be better now than to rest my party-drained body in the familiarity of James’ touch and warmth.

Angela, still holding her glass of champagne, said in a surprisingly sober tone, “You two still so cute with each other. I always see you kiss. It’s amazing, after all these-a years together.”

I was touched by the sweetness of her words. It seemed like a sad awareness of something that was missing in her life with Barry. I thought, Poor Angela, and the two of us performed the implication of a hug.

As James and I walked to the car the wind played a high-pitched melody with the leaves of the huge oak tree. Its branches tried to invade the upper windows of the house.

I huddled against James. He pointed upwards.

"Barry mentioned that he's planning to have that monster of a tree cut down."

"Mmm...," I yawned, too tired to look up once more.

James tightened his grip around my shoulder. In the dark, the flagstones were hardly visible against the lawn.

"And uh..," James made something like a burp, "... what I wanted to say is, holy mackerel... that guy Mahler must have made quite an impression on you that one time when you and Beverly had lunch with him. Honestly, I've never heard you make a speech like that."

Though alarmed, I managed to say calmly, "Yes, I liked him."

James grinned, "Do you have a crush on him?"

Wide awake now, I heard my laugh, oddly out of place, drift through the night.

"Are you jealous of a gray, fifty-nine-year-old man who is almost a head shorter than I am?"

For a moment our laughter was much too unruly and loud. In a sudden chilly breeze, James hurriedly rummaged through his pockets for the key.

19

A breeze blew ripples across the surface of the lake. The oars dragged idly alongside the boat. I picked up a pebble from the wooden planks and tossed it into the water, watching the circles widen, remembering my native lake in Austria. *Wie schön!* Here was a small taste of my lost paradise.

I looked around and thought that the scenery corresponded exactly with the description of the brochure.

Tucked away on the top of the Shawagunk Mountain Ridge is Lake Mohonk, a forty-foot deep freshwater lake where a sprawling Victorian castle stands guard. This is one of the last of the great mountain resorts from the nineteenth century: Mohonk Mountain House.

James had surprised me with this weekend trip on the second Friday in July when I returned home after work. He fully expected me to pack my things in ten minutes, a skill that two decades of business travel had bestowed on him as second nature. I doubted that I could ever master the trick. James' luggage was already in the car while I still rummaged through my closet. What would I wear for dinner? I quickly took a white cotton dress off the hanger, but before I snapped the suitcase shut, I added one more garment: a black silk nightgown I had bought as a surprise for James, and as an invitation to desire.

On the New York Thruway, I read the booklet on Mohonk to James, since neither of us had been there before: *Just 90 minutes from the nerve-jangling heart of New York City there exists an idyllic world, an escape to a more peaceful time and place. With huge masses of rock tumbling in wild confusion, concentrated with rich forests, distant views of mountain ranges, smiling valleys and a clear lake reflecting at your feet, Mohonk Mountain House stands on a magnificent twenty-four thousand acre resort...*

"Sounds promising," James said as he pulled into a gas station.

I tossed the brochure on the back seat, surprised to see James' tennis racket.

He lowered the window and spoke to the attendant and in the same breath turned to me. "Barry and Angela are joining us for the weekend. Barry and I thought we could take advantage of the tennis facilities and hit a few balls..."

Hit a few balls! I thought, pushing the selection button of a soft-drink machine while waiting for the tank to be filled. After all the recent business travel James had done, I had hoped to spend some time alone with him rather than in the company of another couple. I gulped down a few sips of soda, throwing my fantasies to the wind. I had imagined us hiking, rowing and maybe taking a passion-powered nap before dinner.

But with Barry there, the two men wouldn't waste a moment getting on the red clay and *staying there.* And Angela? I would be stuck with her company and her habit of spending long and costly hours at a beauty parlor. I had no desire to waste my weekend trying out the latest make-up colors.

Back in the car, I drew a deep breath and told James in a calm but determined voice that I would have preferred spending the weekend alone with him instead of witnessing his aspirations to greatness on the tennis court. Didn't he realize that since he had started his job we had hardly spent any time together? And I thought to myself, There hasn't even been time for intimacy.

James was dumbfounded. "I didn't think you would mind," he said, looking tense.

I could hear him think, *Doesn't she know how much I like to play?*

"Well, it's O.K." I put my hand on his arm. "I know since your back problems you've been worrying about your game. It means so much to you."

He gave me a soft pat on my left thigh, and I realized that I was behaving like a possessive brat who couldn't share the object of her love, not even with a tennis racket.

We didn't talk much for the rest of the ride. But beneath our silence, we were still communicating at the most basic level, trying to see the other person's viewpoint. Secretly, I was looking forward to his reaction to my new nightgown. But for the time being if felt safe to share silence with James.

When we arrived at the hotel, the clerk at the reception desk told us that Mr. and Mrs. Schumann had just arrived ahead of us. We checked into a room adjoining theirs on the fifth floor, with a breathtaking view of the lake.

On Saturday, things developed exactly as I had expected. I found myself rowing alone on the lake, before and after lunch. Across the water the wind carried the rhythmic sound of tennis balls striking the courts. I pictured James and Barry running, panting and cursing, their socks the color of the clay. I also pictured Angela in a beautician's chair, her face covered with mud, abandoned to the promise of beauty.

But being by myself in a boat in this place of natural poetry wasn't so bad. I trailed my hand in the dark, green water. Then, starting to row again, I studied the shorefront curving around the forest with its luscious trees. A family of ducks swam by, most probably in search of supper. My magazine lay unread at the bottom of the boat. This place inspired a glorious laziness.

My thoughts drifted back in time to Orson. Back in time, because I hadn't heard from him since our ride through Central Park, and that had been six weeks ago. His voice seemed to rise from the waves clapping against the boat. *You're like a lost song. And now that I've found it again, it's even more beautiful than I remembered.*

Six suspenseful, silent weeks. The first two weeks I didn't think much about it. And then when he still didn't call, I experienced a certain sadness, remembering our meetings as dreamlike experiences, transcendental moments that pierced my heart with excitement, joy... and jealousy.

Yes, jealously. I had felt it when I ran into Beverly in the lobby of my office-building. Without hesitation, she produced a postcard from her purse and pointed to the Norwegian stamp, as if to a trophy. I instantly recognized the meticulous handwriting. Orson had actually written to *her!*

Dear Beverly,
After Italy, the Maggio Musicale Fiorentino, where we attended a wonderful concert at the Teatro della Pergola conducted by our good friend Zubin Mehta, we are now in Bergen and about to start on our cruise through the fjords. The sun never seems to go down, and I don't have to tell you how I hate all this light surrounding me. Thanks to your ingenious gift I'm able to get a little sleep...
Paula says hello,

Warmly, Orson.

"What kind of a gift?" I asked, returning the card without looking at the picture.

"A big, black sleeping mask, of course." She tossed back her red curls, smiling with supreme satisfaction. "You know, Paula nagged Orson about a cruise for years and finally got her way. It happened to fit into his schedule, because afterwards they're flying from Oslo back to New York, and he'll go straight to Tanglewood to start rehearsals with the Boston Symphony and Evgeny Kissin... uh, a young pianist from Russia," she explained, not trusting my knowledge of classical virtuosos.

I said, "His name is familiar," and noticed how Beverly artfully covered her freckles with ivory foundation.

"The performance will be Saturday afternoon on July twelfth." She waved flirtatiously at a group of men passing by. "Of course, Rudy and I get complimentary tickets from Orson."

With a start, I realized that today was July twelfth, and that at this very moment, as I was rowing across the lake, Orson was conducting a concert only a hundred miles to the north. The shadow of a cloud moved across the lake and reflected in my mind. During all these weeks, had Orson ever thought of me? What if I wrote him a postcard from here?

Dear Orson,
I wish you could see the confused architecture of this complex, as if it had been built without concept and in haste, adding rooms, floors, wings and corridors in every manner, reflecting too many stylistic opinions.
With kind regards from Mohonk Mountain House,

Isabella.

But no, I lacked the courage.

The noise of a small plane overhead frightened a flock of bluebirds from a tree, and they rose against the sun. What would it take for me to trade my safety for the lure of flying, to have the courage to live life against convention?

Along the shore, six horseback riders were returning home. The sound of their hooves on the wooden bridge snapped me back to reality. I checked my watch. Where had all the hours gone? The sun's golden glow danced low on the water, only moments before being swallowed by the ridge of the mountain. My skin stretched tight and warm across my face. Suddenly I looked forward to company, to sharing a table with James, Angela and Barry, to wine, laughter and a four-course dinner.

An hour later, James and I stood in front of the large dining room. It conveyed an overwhelming sense of wood, and entering it was like stepping back in time to the beginning of the century.

"Remember," I touched the sleeve of James' dinner jacket, "the brochure mentioned that some of these high-backed chairs are still the same as in the photograph taken in 1910."

"Uh-huh... and I think some of the waitresses are the same too," he mumbled, but the smile breaking across his face wasn't directed at me. Barry and Angela were approaching from the end of the long corridor.

Even from the distance I noticed that James and Barry wore identical ties. Angela looked eye-catching in a pink silk dress, and it seemed a waste to hide her shoes, with matching rhinestone bows, under the table. In comparison my white cotton dress was clearly too bland.

With a sweeping movement of her arms Angela gave James an enfolding embrace. "*Ah, Giacomo!*"

Tonight I got the impression that Angela was doing this less to compliment James than to make Barry jealous. But if it bothered Barry, he concealed it well.

My suspicion seemed confirmed when Angela fluted audibly into James' ear, "I watch-a you guys play tennis... and I no take-a my eyes off your body..."

Poor James. How defenseless he became in the face of flattery. To get our group moving, I took Barry's arm and we followed the hostess to our table, passing a small bandstand on which musicians were setting up their instruments. Behind my back I could hear Angela's subdued laughter and the clicking of her pink heels on the parquet.

Even after we were seated and the four of us had settled on the same choice of food, Lamb Provençale, Angela continued to monopolize James' attention, reaching across the table to examine his cuff-links or to take a sip of his aperitif.

"I love your tie, *Giacomo.* You pick it out yourself?"

I said drily, "If you care to take a look at Barry's, they're identical."

The men grinned boyishly. Barry spoke through a cloud of pipe-smoke. "Remember, James, we picked them out together in that little shop in Upper Montclair?"

James tugged at his tie in mock-embarrassment.

"Gee, Barry, I'm glad we rehearsed this earlier over the phone."

But Angela was far from giving up and rolled her big eyes at him. "You dance with me later, eh, *Giacomo*?" Her voice was more challenge than question, and glancing at Barry she decided, "We stay for the after-dinner dance, eh?"

Visualizing James and Angela dancing cheek to cheek through the evening hours made me put down my spoon with an intended clatter. "There hasn't been a vote yet. What does everybody want to do?"

Barry looked hesitant and knocked out his pipe in the ashtray.

James stretched and yawned. "To tell the truth, I'm tired. You girls didn't play tennis all day."

Barry rushed to his support. "That makes two of us."

For a second Angela lowered her eyes to the pink nails that matched her dress. When she looked up, her voice was pleading.

"Dance with me, *Giacomo*. I promise to tell you a secret."

James forced a patient smile.

"Angela, I wouldn't know what to do with a secret."

Barry let out a tortured sigh. Was she that innocent or that conceited? Somebody should set her straight, but nobody spoke. From my perspective, Angela's face was framed by a huge palm whose leaves moved in the draft of an overhead vent.

After our cream of broccoli soup, the conversation split into duets. Barry and James fled into the safe topic of their tennis match. Earlier, when they had returned from the court, toweling themselves off, I had seen in James' face that he had not been the winner, and now it turned out that they had played to a tie. James was not a good loser. Behind his casual front lay an iron will to beat the pants off Barry in the future.

Bored by Angela's mind-deadening details about her facial, I lifted my head and spotted the arrivals of our racks of lamb.

Some pent-up tension drove me to say bluntly, "Angela, right now, I am *not* interested in discussing facial creams, be it with vitamins or herbs..."

Her nostrils flared. "Well, Isabella, you no need to watch-a you looks. You are a married woman."

"And what does this have to do with my looks?"

"All you need is a wedding band and you think you-a perfect."

Despite telling myself not to rise to her bait, I exploded. "Angela, if you count on receiving a wedding band from Barry, I suggest you stop flirting with James."

It was out. *Finally.* And it felt good.

Angela's face froze.

"Ladies...." James sawed away on his lamb, deliberately detached. Barry poured some mint sauce across his meat and then squinted under his bushy eyebrows into some unfocused distance. He refused to be part of this.

The air was cold with estrangement.

I would have given the rest of my delicious meal for an appropriate joke or a clever line to save the situation, for which I felt partly responsible. And, miraculously, one of James' recent jokes popped up into my mind.

I cleared my throat meaningfully into the silence.

"Hey, listen, everybody...did you hear the latest story about James Bond and his brother Municipal...?"

Barry chuckled, he had to put down his fork and knife.

James grinned, "Isabella, you're getting very witty in your old age."

But Angela thought otherwise. "Why-a change the subject, Isabella? It's-a so easy to make a joke." Across the rim of her glass she gave Barry a measured glance.

Composed again, Barry looked at her. "And what *is* the subject?"

The glistening of her eyes was no longer due to the reflection of the candle on the table. "The subject that you no wanna hear, Barry Schumann, is the subject of commitment."

She had gone for his Achilles heel and it hurt him.

He nodded too quickly, "You're right on the money, my dear."

With a quick, flurried gesture she tossed her napkin on the table and ran towards the exit. James and I exchanged helpless glances. With no apparent discomfort, Barry continued to soak his bread in gravy. "She'll come back."

With the three of us stunned into silence, the clatter of dishes and the scraping of chairs surrounding us seemed to rise in volume.

"I'll look after her." I rose, propelled by a need to help.

James nodded. Barry shrugged, exasperated.

When Angela saw me in the ladies' lounge mirror, she gave a brittle laugh. Her hand shook as she powdered her face. Usually headstrong and spirited, Angela had never before allowed herself to lapse into a state of vulnerability in public, and seeing her like this was infinitely touching.

"Angela, I'm sorry ..." I took her arm. Our eyes met in the mirror.

Her voice sounded strangled. "We live-a such approximate lives, where all is-a fine on the surface, but underneath..."

She blew her nose in a lace-edged handkerchief. I knew that in all this I couldn't be a solver. If anything, at most a soother. I put my arms around her bare shoulders and we remained silent for a long, loaded moment.

I thought, thankfully, that James and I had never had a commitment problem. We had fallen in love and acted on it. A wave of tenderness for my sometimes self-absorbed husband rushed through me.

At last Angela screwed her lipstick shut and made a brave attempt at cheerfulness. "Is all right, Isabella. Is all right. Who need one more damn paper, eh? But you, you a good friend..."

During the years that we had known each other I had never felt closer to her than during the few moments when we walked back to the table, whispering conspiratorially.

Under the apprehensive looks of James and Barry, we took our time sitting down and graciously accepting their courteous gestures of holding our chairs for us. Angela and I announced that we didn't care to stay for the after-dinner dance and would be perfectly content to go to bed early. The men looked puzzled.

Barry coughed sourly. "Well, I suppose women have been called 'whimsical' before."

"Barry, let me correct you," I said regally, "not 'whimsical,' just wise enough to compromise."

The men frowned solemnly at each other. Across the table Barry reached for Angela's hand, eager to make things right. A warm glow returned to Angela's face and she smiled at him forgivingly.

Suddenly, a tray with four servings of hot apple pie, topped with a large scoop of vanilla ice cream, materialized before our eyes. Glad that the storm was over, our quartet of voices bubbled with playful exaggeration.

"Too much."

"I can't eat any more."

"Mamma-mia..."

"Take it back."

The poor, confused waitress hovered at our table, not knowing what to do.

At last James winked at her and said, "Just put it down, and don't worry. If we don't like it, we'll feed it to the ducks for breakfast."

Over dessert James kept us listening to the challenges of his new job. But his enthusiastic elaborations seemed to cause proportional mental exhaustion in the rest of us. Or was it the effect of our third bottle of wine?

Anyway, to get some after-dinner exercise the four of us decided not to use the elevator to get back to our rooms on the fifth floor, but climbed the carved wooden staircases leading to other wings and hallways, and they in turn to other doors and stairs.

James and I led the way, and Angela and Barry followed us arm in arm like a pair of lambs.

James toyed with our room-key and turned around.

"In this maze of architecture you need to attach a thread of your underwear to your doorknob so you can trace the way back to your room." He was still wound up and didn't realize that Angela and Barry only had eyes for each other and no more ears for his explanations of why Technicon saw the lack of their inter-divisional communications as a threat to corporate growth.

Even in bed he kept talking about how he envisioned maximizing the efficiency of his company's technologies and how its divisions could benefit from them to solve operational problems.

I thought wearily, Couldn't he have explained all this to me in the car on the way here?

I gave a hinting yawn and cuddled close. James failed to catch my hint and turned to the topic of tennis and how glad he was to have regained the full strength of his back.

Before falling asleep he rocked me briefly in his arms and I could hear his heart singing for a dozen reasons, none of which included *me.*

In the silvery shadows of the room I could see his tennis racket leaning against the chest of drawers. It seemed like an ambitious mistress, laughing at the drop of bitterness poisoning my heart.

Through the open balcony door the moon flickered behind moving clouds, making the walls seem to recede and draw closer at uneven intervals. They threw back echoes of masked voices.

Dance with-a-me, Giacomo. I promise to tell you a secret.

Isabella, you're getting very witty in your old age.

Orson, why do you spend your time with me?

You're like a lost song... and even more beautiful than I remembered.

Gigi Stybr

My body stirred, wide awake under the cool silk of my new nightgown that had gone unnoticed. Despite the warm summer air I shivered and pulled the covers tighter, trying to adjust to James' even breathing.

From the open bathroom door a faucet was dripping. Its rhythm irritated me, but an abstract weight seemed to hold my body down, preventing me from getting up. There were other sounds too. From the room above, footsteps were pacing up and down, causing the wooden floor to creak. Somebody else was unable to sleep, a ghost without a face, like the steps of time caught in a cage.

20

Suddenly Orson was back. It was on a Tuesday afternoon, when Mr. Stringer had his weekly manicure in the office, and I remembered riding down in the elevator with the manicurist after work.

I couldn't believe my eyes. Orson was leaning against one of the big concrete flower pots at the Park Avenue entrance of my office building, reading a small book, his beaten briefcase braced between his legs. I knew I would never again be able to look at these flower pots without picturing him standing there.

First I was overjoyed at the thought that he was here because of me, but then I realized that he was probably waiting for Beverly. After all, I hadn't heard from him in seven weeks. But despite the possible arrival of my competition, my feet aimed in his direction as if attracted by a magnet. Orson continued to read, and because of his dark glasses, I couldn't tell where his eyes were focused. I stopped three feet away from him.

He lifted his head and smiled his magic smile.

"I didn't need to look up. I recognized the rhythm of your footsteps. How are you, Isabella?"

"Orson... I can't believe it's... it's you," I stuttered.

He dropped his book into the pocket of his jacket and unexpectedly opened his long arms to enfold me in a hug. As I moved closer, I clumsily stepped on his foot. "I'm so sorry," I said as our cheeks touched.

He laughed warmly. "I'm so glad to see you again."

I felt a rush of happiness, but I needed to be sure about something.

"Are you waiting for Beverly or for me?"

"Beverly?" He seemed surprised. "No, I've been waiting for *you.*"

I was tempted to cavil about his long silence, but I realized I had no claim to him. I asked instead, "How did you know that I would come out at exactly this time?"

Orson made a reflective little pout. "That was the risk I took. I wanted to surprise you. I simply imagined you coming out this door... and," he smiled victoriously, "you *did!*"

I pushed my point a little further. "What if Beverly had come out before me?"

He ran his hand through his gray thinning hair and gave a musical laugh. "In that case, I'd ask her to come along too..."

"What?" I drew a deep breath and added in a cooler voice, "To go where?"

Orson picked up his beaten briefcase and adopted a tone of carefree merriment. "We're going to meet Louise in an art gallery in Soho. She offered to help me pick out a present for Paula. It's our 35th wedding anniversary next week, and Paula's crazy about this Czech artist Milan Bèlohlàvek... or whatever his name is. Louise tracked down an art dealer who has some of his paintings. I don't understand the first thing about this stuff, and I thought you and Louise could help me make a choice."

"But why me? I don't know a lot about art either," I tried to hide my mixed feelings.

"I just thought it would be nice to have you along."

So he wasn't there only because of me. He needed an extra pair of eyes to pick out an anniversary gift for his wife. Would I ask him along to buy a tennis racket for James? I couldn't believe he was married to this woman for thirty-five years and didn't know her taste in art. It diminished my elation at seeing him again, though I tried to find a grain of humor in his unconventional request. But apparently things would never be conventional with Orson, and the thought that he had chosen me over Beverly gave my pride a little lift.

Orson flagged down a cab. As I slid into the back seat he shot a long, luxurious glance at my legs. He gave the driver a Soho address and the meter started to tick. On this day in late July the car was like an oven, and through my skirt the vinyl seat felt hot against my thighs.

I asked, “How was the midnight sun in Norway?”

Not in the least impressed by my inside information, he snorted, “The midnight sun is a damned nuisance. I never got more than three hours of sleep a night. But do you know whom we met on the boat?”

“No.”

“Nancy and Henry Kissinger,” he chuckled as if he thought this was funny.

“And what happened further?”

“Well, Paula took a picture with me and them ...” He said this as if there was more to come, but fell silent. In the rush hour our cab inched through the traffic until we finally made a turn onto Fifth Avenue. After two blocks the meter was already at $5.25. This trip was going to last forever.

Orson fiddled with the handle of his briefcase. “You know what Henry Kissinger told me? That he had bought my new recording of the *Mozart Requiem* and that on the back of the cover my record company had managed to list my name as the soprano...”

“That’s hilarious!” I gave a heart-felt laugh. “Hadn’t anyone noticed it before?”

“No, of course not,” he said sourly. “Did you?”

“I’ve never seen the release.”

“Mmm...” he mumbled, “I’d like you to have a copy. I’ll give you one next time I see you.”

I thought, Does this mean I was good for one more time before he disappeared for another seven weeks? We passed the

Empire State Building on our right. Cars stretched bumper to bumper on Fifth Avenue as far as I could see. I assumed that the wrinkles on Orson's forehead were most likely due to the rock music from the driver's radio.

Suddenly he cleared his throat and looked at me. "You look absolutely beautiful today, Isabella."

"Thanks." I showed him an uncertain smile. God knows what the humidity was doing to my hair. Yet I felt more comfortable now in his presence, as if this were a recurring dream that became less confusing with time. A happy dream, really.

But I was somewhat worried about meeting Louise in Orson's company. God forbid she would mention anything to Barry and he would pass it on to James.

For a short moment Orson took off his dark glasses and started to rub the corners of his eyes. My elbow brushed against his arm. He looked at me and I discovered a fiery sparkle in his gray-metallic eyes.

"Honestly, Isabella, it's wonderful to see you again." His voice sounded as if he had found a long-lost score of a piece by Mozart.

"It's wonderful to see you too," I echoed, eager to see what followed.

Our cab rattled over a pothole but Orson remained silent. The vinyl seats squeaked as I moved a little closer.

I said, "I thought of you sometimes when you didn't call all these weeks."

But Orson didn't react. If he was so pleased to see me, couldn't he quite simply hold my hand or steal a kiss? Bolder things have happened in the back seat of a cab. I sensed that, under the shell of his dark glasses and his detached manner, Orson was a man who internalized his feelings… or didn't have any.

At Fourteenth Street our car got stuck in a soup of exhaust fumes. A demonstration was going on in Washington Square and nothing moved. The heat was stifling. The meter kept ticking and was now at $22.50.

I asked, "How is your recording schedule going?"

He straightened up. "As a matter of fact I finished a recording yesterday at the Manhattan Recording Center. The Sibelius Violin Concerto."

"How did it go?"

"Ah, a wonderful piece... lush, romantic melodies with a rich, complex orchestration." He hesitated and suddenly reached over and took my hand. My pulse rate jumped so high that I prayed he couldn't feel it.

Orson continued, "But I'm becoming very concerned about the musical integrity of some of the world's so-called best artists..."

"Why?" I whispered, not truly interested, at least not now. I prayed to prevent my palm from sweating. Despite the heat, Orson's hand was dry.

He said, "Well, you see, Isabella, nowadays some soloists are so much in demand that their travel schedules don't leave them time for practicing. They show up at recording sessions unrehearsed and rely on the skill of the producer and the sound engineers to fix their mistakes. By cutting the takes and splicing them together, in the end the technicians make everything sound like a perfect, continuous performance."

He sighed and squeezed my hand. I didn't have anything to say about the problems in the studio, because I was thinking too much about my hand in his. I smiled softly, drawn between feelings of fire and fear. The meter was at $24.75 now, but I wished we could go all the way to Florida like this. Orson's fingers moved across my knuckles.

He explained further, "Now this violinist yesterday, I won't tell you his name, but the *Washington Post* singled him out only recently as an *artist of incontestable genius*. This man needed twenty-seven cuts for the cadenza alone... the cadenza! It's meant to be the show-off section of the whole work, where the soloist can prove his virtuosity! I'm sorry to say that it's not unusual when a finished recording is patched together from several hundred different takes."

"Several hundred!" I exclaimed and almost accidentally withdrew my hand. "I had no idea."

"I remember in the old times of the LP's, we just recorded a single movement until it was acceptable. In a recording session it was always my philosophy to maintain as much of a spontaneous feeling as possible. If you over-edit, you risk losing that feeling. A musical experience has to have the human element, so it's bound to have flaws. As long as the flaws are small and don't distract from the music, I think they should be left in." He took a deep breath.

I squinted against the light and let the colors of the narrow streets of Soho blur together. Orson's fingertips drew a slow circle in my palm.

Without looking at him I said, "So modern recordings are perfect, but in a way, sterile."

"Exactly," he nodded and let go of my hand.

By now I had lost my orientation. The quaint cafés and galleries all seemed to look the same. The streets were full of people, many of whom probably came here after work. One more turn and the cab stopped in a cobbled side street. Orson paid the driver and checked the address against a piece of paper.

"This must be it," he said, and got out.

Still in the car, I caught a glimpse of a small unimpressive shop. A moment later as we pushed through the glass door, I said, "I wonder if Louise is here," and welcomed the cool air inside.

In the dim light our eyes adjusted slowly. The only lighting in the dark room were the spotlights on the paintings. Even here, Orson didn't take off his glasses. I doubted that he could see much at all. A handful of people were browsing. I picked up a brochure from the reception table.

"Orsoooon....!" I heard Louise's voice. She approached from the back of the shop with a dark, Oriental man in tow who was wearing a turban.

"Louise!" Orson and I called in unison.

The mere presence of this small, older woman seemed to turn up the lights in the room, making it a friendlier place. The straps of her slip showed through her beige short-sleeved blouse.

She took my hands. "Isabella, love, I'm so glad to see you."

Then she threw her flabby arms around Orson, just short of strangling him. She had been Orson's physician for decades and the image of her giving him an injection in the rear forced me to suppress a laugh. Orson gently untangled her arms from his neck.

"This is Mr. Bala," Louise smiled, and a hundred wrinkles formed on her cheeks. "Mr. Bala is kind enough to give us a private tour."

Orson gestured to me. "Mr. Bala, this is Miss Austria."

The dark-looking man bowed and revealed a row of perfect teeth. "I'm honored to meet you, Maestro. And you, uh... Miss Austria."

He led the way and we stopped in front of a two-foot square canvas showing several female figures painfully confined in geometric cubes. In the next painting a naked woman had wings instead of arms that were spread wide open, as were her legs. Her tortured expression originated from painted cigarette burns scattered like confetti across her skin.

Louise tugged at my arm. "The artist is obviously not sympathetic to the female creation."

Orson blurted out, "Louise, are you sure we came to the right place?"

Mr. Bala found a reason to excuse himself.

It was difficult to come up with an enthusiastic remark and I turned to the brochure for intellectual support. I read aloud. *Milan Bèlohlàvek's oeuvre is composed of all the fears and fear-generating hostility that the masculine mind projects onto the unknown female force of threat and thrill, attraction and danger.*

The three of us looked at each other in confusion. Was this what Paula wanted? Did this woman, who had twelve recipes for brownies, identify in some dark way with this degenerated vision?

"At least," I broke the silence, "the colors are vibrant, like flowers on a tropical island."

Louise passed a hand over her unruly gray hair.

She explained, "The pictures have no individual titles but are numbered under the collective subject of *Seduction.*"

Orson shook his head. "I'm glad I'm in the music business."

We passed other paintings with shapes of female bodies shown stretching, sprawling and suggestive in their sexuality. As we moved on, an embarrassing silence swelled between us.

I picked out another line from the brochure. .... *I want to create my own art, exceeding the lines of expressionism into experimentalism...*

"Into *horrorism..*," Orson exclaimed in full voice and everyone in the room turned towards him. He gestured for us to move closer. "Ladies, I'm a worshiper of the female body. I love its beauty above all other beauties. And frankly, nothing else, not even music, is able to fulfill me as completely, or render me completely mad." He paused meaningfully and looked at me. "But this is beyond my comprehension. Why would anyone degrade nature's most beautiful gift in such an awful way?"

Was he sending me a message? I remembered his words during our ride through Central Park ... *to hold and behold a woman in the natural flow of love-making.*

Orson gave Louise a helpless look.

"Paula left no doubt about this, did she?"

Louise dropped heavily on a chair next to a display desk.

"No, she didn't. I'm amazed you still have so many secrets from each other." The shrewd expression on her face turned into a spitting image of her son Barry.

I felt Orson wanted to get this over as quickly as possible.

He said, "Paula should get whatever she wants," and turned around to look for Mr. Bala. At the reception desk Mr. Bala clicked out a ball-point pen and jotted down a few numbers for Orson.

I stayed with Louise and whispered in her ear, "Louise, you won't mention any of this to Barry, will you?"

She waved her hand dismissively. "My dear, you think too much instead of enjoying yourself. You are the best thing that has happened to Orson in a long time. Since he's known you, he has more patience with Paula and he needs to take fewer sleeping pills."

"But Louise," I said in a strangled voice, "he never tells me that he ... uh... likes me."

"But he tells *me,* my dear." She placidly folded her hands in her lap.

"W*hat* does he tell you?" My whisper exploded.

She smiled secretively. "Orson is absolutely in love with you, my dear. But you never seem to give him any encouragement. He thinks you have a charming naïveté about you that makes you untouchable like a piece of fine glass. And he's afraid to break it..."

What? ... a charming naïveté? I wanted to kick the chair out from under her, but realized that she was only the messenger of this ridiculous revelation. I couldn't have felt more insulted, belittled... or *delighted.*

Suddenly my knees felt weak, but there was no other chair to sit on. Louise waved flirtatiously at Orson across the room. His face bespoke frustration while listening to Mr. Bala's sales pitch.

I said to Louise, "Excuse me, I can't stay around these pictures anymore," and walked to the back of the room to an adjoining atelier with rows of empty chairs. There were no paintings on the walls. I sat down on a folding chair and tried to make sense of the voices in my head. *Orson is absolutely in love with you... you have such a charming naïveté about you... and he's afraid to break it.*

Was this a conspiracy between them? Was Orson aware that Louise would tell me this? The white, unused canvases stacked against the wall stared back at me like unwritten pages of the future.

"Are you okay, Isabella?" Orson's voice was behind me. He pulled up a chair to face mine and removed his dark glasses.

I said, "I'm sorry, I haven't been much help to you."

Orson rested his elbows on his knees and his metallic eyes looked straight in mine. "With me, you never need to say 'I'm sorry' for anything."

I asked, "Where's Louise?"

"She left. She and I picked out a painting, the one we disliked the least. Paula can exchange it if she wants."

"I found them quite unsettling."

Orson smiled bitterly. "Odd, really, that they should be called *Seduction.*"

"I assume you don't agree with their statement?"

"Absolutely not."

Unwilling to let him guess my discomfort, I had to ask him something fast, or I would never ask at all.

"Orson," I whispered, "is it easy to seduce women?"

He leaned back, walking his thoughts through his life experiences and said calmly, "I never liked the idea of seduction. It either happens by itself or not at all. But *if* it happens... yes, then it's easy. Very easy."

His eyes were filled with dreams. Neither of us moved.

I swallowed. "So you consider women *easy*?"

He leaned forward. "As a man, you just have to be there, ready to catch them, and they will fall right into your arms."

His voice, sure of victory, irritated me.

I said defensively, "And it's your pleasure to… uh... catch them."

"Indeed...," he beamed at me, "remember, Isabella, just as in music, it's pleasure that's the most important part of a relationship."

It was out. He had pronounced the word. *Relationship.* My mind searched for a synonym. Acquaintance? Affair? Had we come to the dead-end of friendship?

Orson said, "Whenever you are with me, Isabella, I want you to float freely. I want you to dance and to swirl about and never be afraid to hit anything that's in your way. Because there isn't. I want you to feel that kind of freedom."

Slowly he reached out to touch my face, but Mr. Bala's voice sounded from the door. "Sir? Excuse me... uh, Maestro, but we have to set up this room for a private showing."

Orson said impatiently, "We'll be out of here in a minute."

He checked his watch. “Dammit, Isabella, I promised Paula to help her interview a new housekeeper. In fact, I have to call her right now.”

He got up and left, but I remained seated for another moment. Under the spell of his words, my heart was a flame in a storm lamp. Only the glass had just begun to break. I finally knew what to do.

21

That night James' flight from Chicago was delayed and when he finally came home he wanted to go to bed without dinner. As James' electric toothbrush buzzed through the bathroom door, I took off my robe and looked at my naked body in our bedroom mirror.

It was a comfortable body to be in. Except for my height of five feet nine, it was a body with moderate dimensions, where nothing was large or opulent enough to be called sensational or might cause heads to turn. James adored my long legs and narrow waist and politely dismissed my wish for larger breasts or smaller hips. But could I measure up in the kind of femininity that lay beyond mere inches?

Would any man ever say about me, Look at her, she's a sexy woman? Or did I just possess a charming naïveté and covered my insecurities under the safe blanket of marriage?

The sight of my mother's features in my own face did not come as a surprise to me. I was also aware that I sometimes tossed my head in her defiant manner. My mother had told me that a woman's sexual disadvantage was inevitable. Her guidelines for developing into a self-assured, seductive woman were far from encouraging.

Before I got married I asked her, "Do you enjoy being a woman?" She answered, "No. Next time around I'm going to be a man."

And she meant it. Men had all the power in this world. That was her lesson to me. Instinctively I was angry at her statement and wanted to prove her wrong. While looking at myself, I fought a battle with my mother. I didn't want to live a copy of her life, finding security in the lifelong passivity of compromising and complaining. Yet I agreed with her, that in matters of courtship the man should always be the initiator. Sure of her impeccable good taste, she had taught me to select the best in literature, music and wines. For my dowry she had lovingly embroidered a dozen white linen sheets and aprons.

I smiled at my reflection in the mirror. It revealed a secretive smile born of the seeds of forbidden possibilities. Today I was ready to discard my mother's apron and dirty my dress.

I recalled my moments with Orson as dreams, illusions, invitations. The Garden of Eden. The Apple Tree. The Serpent. To take the risk or not. What was at stake? Disobedience or exploration? How could I already feel remorse for something that was just a vision? Yet nothing counted but the act of daring. The image of Orson accepting the fruit out of my hand was without color or sound. It just *was.*

I was still looking at myself in the mirror when James joined me in the bedroom. He looked over my shoulder and let out an admiring whistle. I turned around and held him as tightly as a frightened child, clutching all my anxieties in his arms and the warmth of his body.

"Isabella, hey... is something wrong?"

"Nothing, honestly."

Not believing me, he said, "You know, I love you."

I couldn't look at him and closed my eyes to the music of his words. I was filled with an odd sadness that was sweet and scary. It was a queasy feeling, like leaving the dock in the fog, heading for an unknown shore. But finally, the familiarity of the room mitigated my emotions of confusion, fear and desire.

22

I closed the leather menu and pushed the ashtray to the far end of the white tablecloth. I had come to a decision, but it was not a selection from the menu that was on my mind right now, especially since Orson had called me so soon again, only three days after our visit to the art gallery.

Across the table, Orson pushed back the sleeve of his jacket and checked the date on his watch.

“This means you’re leaving in four days...”

“That’s right.”

I had just given him the flight details for my trip to Austria, my departure from JFK, my arrival in Vienna and my connection to Klagenfurt, from where I would take a cab to my native Pörtschach. I didn’t think he really cared, but rather liked to give the impression of a caring man.

The air-conditioned interior of *Fontana di Trevi*, an Italian restaurant across from Carnegie Hall, was a refuge from the heat and humidity outside. It was early for dinner and most of the tables were still empty.

“Would you like to share a Caesar’s Salad?” Orson asked, looking distracted, as if his meetings with Carnegie Hall management were still on his mind.

“No, thank you.” My throat tightened at the thought of what I really wanted to discuss with him. “But I would like a glass of *Brusco Barbi*,” I added, hoping it would boost my confidence.

Orson gestured to one of the waiters in red jackets. He bowed and addressed Orson respectfully with *Maestro.* Orson placed our order.

A moment later he reached inside his jacket, took out a piece of paper and his silver pen, and started to draw doodles. He started to tell me about his two nieces in Connecticut, a subject I found tedious, at least today. I was also annoyed at his irritating compulsion to draw, though the speed of his hand and the variety of his designs amazed me. I reached over and took the pen out of his hand.

He looked up. "You don't like my doodles?"

"*Nein, nicht besonders.*"

"Mmm, that's funny." He shrugged. "Some women frame them."

Some women! I took a swift breath, tore his doodles into little pieces and dropped them in the ashtray. Orson smiled a patient smile.

The restaurant was filling up. Our food arrived. And the wine. My eyes traveled to the oval bronze plaque above our table. It was Bacchus, the god of wine, harvesting the grapes. I thought, How is this year's vintage, Bacchus, son of Zeus and Semele?

But yes, the nieces. Orson loved to talk about them. One had just had her appendix taken out and the other was going back to college at the age of thirty-four. Paula tried to be of help as much as possible.

I sighed and sneezed. The room was freezing. I sneezed again.

"*Gesundheit,*" I heard Orson's voice as though from far away.

I shuddered. "Orson, I am cold."

"Would you like my jacket?"

I nodded. He got up and put it caringly around my shoulders. It was heavy, its weight could stun an ox. What did he carry in it besides keys, pens and papers? *Rocks?*

I asked between two sips of wine, "How did Paula like her painting?"

Orson, busy with knife and fork, mumbled dismissively, "They'll deliver it tomorrow." Then he looked up. "How is your Filetto di Bue?"

"Fantastico, mille grazie," I smiled, "and how is your Cotoletta alla Milanese?"

"Delicious, thank you." He looked more relaxed. The rustic atmosphere of the restaurant, resembling an Italian grotto with its white stucco walls, removed us from the world outside. But there was something else I wanted to talk about. I could simply start out and say, "It's wonderful to be with you, as always," but I put it off, like a difficult phone call that would change the course of history.

Orson put a lump of sugar in his hot chocolate with a splash, and his velvet voice whispered, "Like this one, some moments are close to being perfect."

His gray-metallic eyes shone in the glow of the round iron chandeliers from above. There was a new intensity about him that said life is sometimes only for the moment.

I remembered my reflection in the mirror. *What was at stake? Disobedience or exploration? Nothing counted but the act of daring.* The chandeliers started spinning.

"Orson, I've been meaning to ask you a question."

"Yes?" He put down his cup.

"Do you think it's right for two people to have an affair?"

"Well, young lady..." His voice lacked the surprise I had expected. "Let's look at it from all sides." His matter-of-fact tone made things easy, at least for now. He didn't even care to whisper.

"Having an affair can be a glorious experience, and falling extramaritally in love is like playing hooky from school, only in this case you excuse yourself from the rules of society. But if you do it, Isabella, don't get caught by the teacher. Choose a time when the teacher is sick, your parents are out of town or a friend is covering for you. The questionable thrill of being discovered will only lead to hurt for everyone concerned."

I was amazed at how well prepared he was. Or was this his stock answer?

He stopped to check my reaction, but I could only look at him.

"Isabella, the start of an affair is always exciting. It's like the beginning of a new life. You learn about each other, your moods, your mannerisms. No matter how old you are, you have reached the point most distant from death, because you are truly *alive."*

He looked at me expectantly.

I took a sip of coffee. "That's an interesting lecture."

His voice became less factual. "Why did you ask?"

Now I was afraid of my own demons. Somehow things weren't proceeding as I had planned.

I said, "No special reason. Just an abstract consideration."

Orson mock-frowned, making no attempt to hide his disbelief. "And for this abstract consideration of yours, did you have anyone special in mind?"

I was running out of resolve. Of course I could have said, *you* and got the whole thing over with. But I resented his arrogance in withholding the one thing that I wanted... an old-fashioned, romantic proposition. I looked at him. He was on the verge of balding, shorter than I and obviously an experienced, cold-blooded Don Juan.

"Isabella, I repeat, did you have anyone special in mind?" The gleam of firm intention in his eyes belied his measured voice.

I felt cornered. All I could do was play for time. So I looked him straight in the eye. "I'm not going to make this all that easy for you, Orson Mahler."

"What do you want me to do?" He smiled his magic smile.

"I want you to ask the same question in a different way."

Suddenly I felt hot under his heavy jacket.

"Mmm." He sipped from his hot chocolate.

"Mind if I take a guess?"

"Go ahead."

Now he was like a volcano, still covered with snow but ready for a fiery eruption, and yet I felt a humble hesitancy about him before he asked, "Could it be that you mean ... *me*?"

My "yes" came lightly, without effort.

His face lit up and his words danced like weightless stars.

"I'm delighted, I'm thrilled and, believe me, I am very touched."

A sigh. A breath. How easy it had been. The spark in his eyes was like a gift to me, and his face became the focal point before my eyes as the room around him spun and blurred in fragments of medieval chandeliers, white walls and red jackets.

I was shivering, but worse, I went from cold to hot, sure to run a temperature. I sneezed twice.

Orson said, "There's a handkerchief in the left pocket of my jacket."

"Thanks." I used it noisily. My face burned.

Orson leaned forward. "So you are serious about sharing your body with me?"

"Yes," I whispered, though it didn't feel real.

Orson smiled dreamily. "I feel extremely honored... but why would a beautiful young woman like you choose a man like me? Doesn't it bother you that I'm almost twice your age?"

I sniffled, "It's only an accidental separation of the calendar."

He shook his head. "Consider all the good-looking men on the streets of Manhattan. I assure you, you could have any man you wanted."

"But I don't want any good-looking men off the streets of Manhattan, I want *you.*"

"Why?"

I felt my head getting hotter and my hands turning to ice.

"Orson, I'm afraid, I'm getting the flu."

He asked again, "Why do you want *me,* Isabella?"

I blew my nose. We declined the waiter's offer for dessert.

I had to sneeze again. "I'm sorry about this, Orson."

He stayed firm. "*Why,* Isabella, why me?"

I tried to straighten up and ignore my running nose.

I said, "I want your mind *and* your body. And I think it will be wonderful."

His velvet voice reveled in every word. "It will be, I assure you. I will treat you very tenderly, like a sublime piece of music. It will be my pleasure and my responsibility to see you satisfied and happy."

He took my fingers to his lips and his soft touch led to the unforgettable first taste of desire.

He smiled, "I hope I'll see you again before you leave for Austria."

I spoke through a congested nose. "Orson, you should stay away from me until I get over this flu, or whatever it is."

A bitter little line formed on his lips. "Now of all times... you have the flu and you're going away."

"Only for two weeks."

"I'll be here when you return." And in the same breath he started to whistle a tune.

I had never heard him whistle and would have bet my grandmother's pearls that he was not the whistling type, especially not at such full volume and in public. But Orson carried on his happy tune despite heads turning around us. He even whistled while he paid the bill, oblivious to the puzzlement of the waiter. When he gestured to me to get up I decided to put an end to it and tugged his arm as we passed the bar.

"Orson, *what* are you whistling?"

He stopped and grinned. "It's the *Allegro* movement of Vivaldi's *L'Amoroso,* one of his several hundred violin concertos. The *Siciliano* rhythm gives it a mood that is befitting for its title. It means of course, 'The Lover' or 'The Man in Love'."

He held the glass door open for me to pass. On the street the humidity hit us like an overheated greenhouse. His move to take me in his arms was interrupted by yet another sneeze.

I said, "It's best we don't touch."

I gave him back his jacket.

He bowed and smiled. "I'll never have it cleaned again."

23

At six-thirty the next morning Barry was sitting on the edge of my bed and putting the stethoscope back into his satchel. After I had spent a night of sneezing, James had called Barry, who agreed to stop by before his official office hours.

Barry squinted sleepily while trying to read the thermometer. "Hmm. A hundred and two. We'll have to get that under control before your trip. There's no way you can go to work. A sick body needs rest so it can use all its energy to get well."

He wrote out a prescription and handed it to James, who was selecting a tie from the rack in his walk-in closet.

Barry gave me a pat on the arm. "I'm only a phone call away."

The two men talked. The room was tilting. My aspirin-ridden stomach growled.

James blew a light kiss to my forehead. "You look darling with your eyes and nose all swollen like that."

I pressed my face against the pillow, thinking that maybe true love meant telling a woman she looks darling when she really looks dreadful. Thank God Orson couldn't see me like this.

James returned from the drug store with nasal spray, cold capsules and six boxes of tissues. Before leaving for work he handed me a steaming mug of awful-tasting tea. "Promise me you'll drink some every two hours. I'll call your office at nine."

Yes, yes, I'd do anything to sweat this out. But taking a shower and putting on a fresh nightgown exhausted me completely and, back in bed, I let my spirits fall into the dark, itching realm beneath my eyelids. I knew that the cause of my stuffed sinuses was not only in my head but also in my heart, while my ears drummed. *Orson. Orson.* It was the rising and receding flood of fantasy, teasing me with the touch of our lips that remained untasted.

When the phone on the night table rang, I assumed it was my office.

"Isabella? How are you?" Orson's voice was careful.

"Uh... Orson? Not so good."

"Your voice sounds terrible."

"I know. I have a temperature. Barry was here this morning. He and James are taking care of me."

"I'm glad."

Something was different today. In my condition I found it embarrassing to talk to him. Hearing only his voice, I perceived him as Mahler, the maestro and not Orson, the man. My mind reached for a neutral topic to avoid the mention of our romantic bond.

I sniffled. "Orson, uh...I've been wondering about something..."

"Yes?" He implied a smile as if expecting something intimate.

I said, "I remember you told me about your commission to write a series of essays for *Stagebill.* How is it coming?"

There was beat of silence and a trace of disappointment in his voice, switching from familiar to factual.

"I'll probably miss the deadline, and I still haven't thought of a title yet."

I took a tissue. "What about *Mahler Meditations* or *Maestro Memories*?"

He said, "I'm surprised you still remember. But no, that's not what I had in mind."

I blew my nose.

"It's very sweet of you to think about my essays."

We went on to talk about my trip, but not our promise, until he casually explained, "I've always believed that one makes love to the mind first, and then to the body."

My answer was a gigantic sneeze.

His voice was music when he said, "Get better, Isabella. And that's an order."

After we hung up I thought, I could still get out of this. I could go to Austria and cleanse my mind of Orson, as long as he wasn't under my skin yet. But I realized that it was more complex. He was in my heart.

He called me again the next day, when my fever and the unrest of my mind were pretty much the same. I told him I wasn't going back to work before my trip.

And then his voice took on an insistent, rising tone.

"Are you still sure about our agreement?"

"I'm afraid it'll have to wait."

"But are you still sure about it?"

I sat up and searched for the cold part of my pillow. "Yes, I'm still sure."

He pressed on. "But tell me, Isabella, why didn't you ...uh... approach me earlier?"

Now I was so hot that I had to throw off my covers.

"Orson, I could never bring myself to make the first step. You might have laughed at me."

"Not a chance." He laughed warmly. "That would be like a hungry man with a gourmet meal in front of him who won't eat it."

I almost choked on my cough drop. "Are you a hungry man?"

"*Yes.*" He said it with such ease.

My nightgown was soaked with perspiration.

I said, "But why didn't *you* ask *me* in the first place?

He gave a sigh. "Ah.... you know, Isabella, since our first lunch with Beverly I've had my secret claws around you. I wasn't going to let you escape. Only I had to avoid imposing myself on you. I had to create a vacuum between us that would eventually draw you to me."

My nose was running again. I said, "And it worked."

He beamed, "It worked beautifully!"

Orson was on wings. And I? Was I crossing a sea, unlearning the rules?

He said, "When you come back we'll have a nice fall."

I knew he meant it in more ways than one.

The next day my fever was down and I had to pack. My mind wandered from Orson to my mother, and I realized how little I knew about her. Did she still embroider aprons, wear *Eau de Joy* and listen to Maestro Mahler's records? How would she react if I were bold enough to tell her the truth about him and me? With nobody else to turn to, I considered entrusting my unsettling secret to her. Who would be in a better position to understand how I felt? But would she hate or hail me for living out her own dream? Had she ever gone after a dream of her own?

After my father's departure she always needed the reassurance of a structured and orderly life to save her damaged ego. She obviously thought it best to replace pleasure with sacrifice, for my sake and for the acceptance of society. But what else could she have done? The world had come a long way since the late 1950's, when hiding behind the "rules" was a safe way of soldiering through life in a small Austrian village.

Growing up, I had willingly followed my mother's concept of how her daughter should turn out. Having everything I needed gave me no reason to be unduly imaginative with ideas of my own. Marrying James finally meant choosing the length of my hair and hemline without my mother's censorship. How easily had I crossed the threshold from signing my name as Fräulein Isabella Berger to Mrs. Isabella Barton. The threshold I would now be crossing with Orson would involve more courage. The step to be just *me.*

On the day of my departure Orson called me at the exact moment that the sound of the garage-door opener announced the arrival of James' car.

"Orson, James is here to drive me to the airport. I have to go, but tell me, can I bring you anything from Austria?"

His voice smiled. "No. Just yourself. I'll be waiting for you. Have a safe trip."

Later in the car, James said, "You look a lot better today. In fact, there's a real glow about you."

He was going faster now, and I put my hand on his arm.

"We have plenty of time to get to JFK. There's no need to get a ticket."

He shrugged, "You know me. I like to keep moving if I can."

"Exactly." I pinched his arm."That's why I'm bringing it up."

At the Triboro Bridge toll booth he asked, "Are you happy to be going home?"

Actually, he made me wonder if I was on my way home or leaving home. A visit to my mother always meant saying good-bye to James, and coming back to the U.S. meant saying good-bye to her. Someone was always left behind. Today it was even true for Orson.

I studied James's profile. Would I be able to hide Orson from him? Unwilling to face the question now, I reminded James of a few things. He needed to water the plants, pay the mortgage and have the plumber fix the faucet in my shower. And could he remember that the package for the Salvation Army was in the garage.

With a sobering objectivity I became aware of James' disadvantage when compared to the framework of romance that I shared with Orson. Talking about the plumber, the Salvation Army and the mortgage payment doesn't usually set hearts on fire.

But despite matters of maintenance and money, I whispered, "I'll miss you, James. Who will warm my feet at night?"

"Nobody else, I hope." He gave a lusty little laugh and squeezed my thigh.

For a second, which was as much as the traffic allowed, he turned his face and our eyes connected in a flash of tenderness.

"James, can I bring you anything from Austria?"

He shook his head. "No. Just yourself. I'll be waiting for you. Have a safe trip."

I shuddered. Those were Orson's exact words. Was he already sitting in the car with us? The hot summer air trembled with the chill of my secret.

24

LETTERS AND POSTCARDS FROM AUSTRIA

Pörtschach, August 3, 1986

My dearest James,

Thanks for calling me yesterday when I arrived. Yes, it feels good to be back home. Mother looks great and seems less bitter about life. When we sit together out on the terrace overlooking the lake it feels as if I'd never left. Waking up this morning I heard the same old birds, the same church bells and the same damn trains thundering past as close as ever. I can't understand how mother sleeps though the 5:45 AM "Wörthersee-Express" which seems to be as long as the Great Wall of China. But I remember I used to do it too.

I've re-discovered the pleasure of our huge, old-fashioned bathtub and mother's favorite fragrance, "Eau de Joy," still filling the rooms. She said its scent once gave her so much confidence at a very romantic time in her life. I wonder?

My room is re-papered and new curtains put up. It looks "wunderschön." The house with its thick stone walls and creaking wooden floor never changes. The garden is full of roses. I went swimming in the lake today and practiced my voice part of the Brahms Requiem. You know why...

I'm sorry I'm not going to be there for your birthday! Have a happy one. I already miss you and I love you! Take good care on your business trips, and try not to lose your expensive sun glasses again! Here's a big kiss. Mother also sends one (a kiss).

Isabella

Pörtschach, August 4, 1986

Dear Matthew,

Blessings to your "Brahms-Requiem-Alto-Voice-Part" study tape. My daily walk takes me to the tip of the wooded peninsula, and I practice my part equipped with my walkman, your tape and a lot of leftover breakfast rolls to feed the ducks. Fortunately, the ducks don't mind my singing. Just think, Brahms composed his symphony in D (No.2) right here, also called the "Pörtschach Symphony," in 1877. When he was writing it, he remarked that "in this place the melodies seem to float in the air and one must be careful not to tread on them..." And looking around I feel what he meant: the pastel colors and the soft lights mirrored in the crispness of the lake.

Believe me, I so want to pass the audition in September. Does your offer to drive me home on Wednesday nights still hold? Can I bribe you with a box of "Mozartkugeln?"

Please keep Saturday, August 30, open for a summer party at our house. You and your friend Tom are invited. Love,

Isabella

PS: My mother told me that 7 years ago she had gone to Vienna to attend a performance of the Brahms Requiem. Guess who conducted? Our own maestro, O.M. She says it was glorious.

Pörtschach, August 5, 1986

Dear Angela and Barry,

Thanks again, Barry, for helping to cure my flu. Now that I'm here I realize how much I need to rest. My whole life prior to going to the U.S. comes back to me now and I see what kind of person I was then. To some extent I feel like a stranger in the country where I grew up. People here see me as American and people in the U. S. see me as Austrian. It's so confusing.

I ran into my old boyfriend Hans. He's quite successful in banking, and marriage with him would have been as safe as Fort Knox, and about as boring.

Barry, keep James busy playing tennis, will you? And let him win a few sets occasionally, please! Also, you are both invited to our summer party on August 30. Could you bring a pot of Oysters Rockefeller, which I still remember from your party in June... they were delicious.

Love to both of you,

Isabella

PS: Angela, I told my mother your story about Orson Mahler and the woman flutist who threw a glass of water in his face. Actually, my mother went to see one of his concerts in Vienna 7 years ago, and unlike the disappointing encounter she had had 13 years previously, this time she managed to get an autograph from him...

Pörtschach, August 6, 1986

Dear Beverly,

I'm enjoying a lovely stay with my mother. My days consist of swimming, eating, sleeping and shopping. Sounds like a perfect break for a stressed Manhattan working girl, doesn't it? In the fall I really would ***love*** *to become a member of your fine chorus. I told my mother all about it.*

Incidentally, she had the honor of spending a little time with Mr. Mahler after his concert of the Brahms Requiem in Vienna about seven years ago. As it happened, they even had a drink together. Imagine!

And how are things with you? We haven't run into each other in the elevator for a long time. I hear your company is moving out of the building on Park Avenue. Let me know where you will move to.

I'm looking forward to having a summer party at my house on Saturday, August 30. It would be wonderful if you and your husband could come.

With warm greetings from Austria,

Isabella

PS: Could you also invite Daisy on my behalf? I don't have her address. (I remember you telling me about her absolute pitch and stunning alto voice).

Gigi Stybr

Pörtschach, August 6, 1986

Dear Louise,

I'm happy to be "back home" to re-connect with my roots and to spend time with my mother. Did you know that Brahms wrote his Second Symphony right here at Schloss Leonstain, less than a mile from the house where I grew up? It's a beautiful little renaissance castle (now a hotel), and I'm sure Orson would love to see it.

But what a small world! Just imagine that my mother actually met Orson seven years ago after a performance of the Brahms-Requiem in Vienna... He was staying at the Grand Hotel "Imperial" and invited her to have a drink at the "Maria Theresien Bar." Afterwards they had dinner at the restaurant "Majestät." She tells me that he was just as magical as he could be, but that she also stopped idolizing him. Suddenly he was no longer a myth, but a man of flesh and blood who miraculously freed her of a life-long obsession. Just think, Louise, she waited seven years to tell me all this!

Hope you are well.
A big hug,

Isabella

PS: Please keep Saturday, August 30, open. I would like to invite you to a summer party at our house in Montclair (just five blocks down the street from Barry's).

Pörtschach, August 7, 1986

My dear Julia!

How could I have forgotten the beauty of this place? Growing up here hides miracles from the view of the natives, but after working in Manhattan I see everything with different eyes. No wonder painters and composers have been inspired for decades, even centuries, by the lake and the surrounding woods with its many shades of green, blue and gray.

My mother is well and for her age (54!) looks spectacular. Slim, blonde and blue-eyed as ever, she has a different energy about her and finally admits that Hans (my old boy-friend, remember?) wouldn't have been the right husband for me. He is still a bachelor and has put on about fifty pounds. ... but anyway, the great news is (and I learned this only now, my mother says there was never a good time to tell me before) that she met a man seven years ago in Vienna. Obviously she was completely overwhelmed by his charm. He was staying at the very elegant Hotel "Imperial," where he took her for drinks and then to dinner. This was followed the next morning by breakfast in his suite. He was from out of town and stayed in Vienna for six days, and five of those days she stayed with him. She says those days gave her a new life. It was her happiest time ever. This man, by the magic of his personality, freed her from a deep-rooted bitterness about my father and from her obsessive day-dreaming. He showed her that dreams are meant to be pursued. Since then she has become a member of a poetry club and is now working on her green belt in karate. I'm so proud of her! How is your new book coming along? Or did I just provide you with an idea for one?
Keep open: August 30, for our summer party!

Much love to you and Ludwig,

Isabella

Pörtschach, August 8, 1986

Dear Orson,

It's wonderful to be back in Austria. Of course I don't need to tell you that Brahms wrote his Second Symphony right here at Schloss Leonstain in 1877. The small castle is less than a mile away from the house where I grew up.

Last night my mother and I attended a concert there. I Solisti Veneti played an all-Vivaldi program, including the concerto "L'Amoroso." The small courtyard was packed with people (one woman moved her chair the wrong way and fell into the fountain...) and the nine o'clock train from Venice to Vienna made a considerable racket during "Il Cucù." Those damn railroad tracks have always been a problem for the concerts there. Apparently they already existed in Brahms' time.

With warm regards,

Isabella

PS: I'm sorry to miss your two concerts at the Mostly Mozart Festival in New York.

Pörtschach, August 9, 1986

My dear James,

My first week is over. I'm starting to get a tan and have become divinely lazy. But despite my daily swim I'm afraid that all the delicious Apfelstrudel, Sachertorte and Germknödel mother is feeding me will have an unfavorable effect on my waistline.

I bought a magnificent blue paperweight of Murano Glass. Mother is excited about the idea that I might join Orson Mahler's chorus in September. She's not the same wallflower any more. She is now a member of a poetry club and is practicing for her green belt in karate. Seven years ago she had a romantic affair in Vienna (I now remember, she sent us a postcard from the Hotel Imperial). She says this man completely turned her self-image (and her life) around. But she has never seen him since.

I miss you, you delicious, wild, cuddly animal! I can't wait to be in your arms again. (Did the plumber come yet?)

Tons of love,

Isabella

PS: What do you think of having a little summer party at our house on Saturday, August 30?

25

The dashboard of James' Buick needed a good dusting. As I sat next to him on the Van Wyk Expressway, a flash of nostalgia made me want to turn around and go back to Austria. Why had I ever come to this country with its hot and humid August days? The deplorable scene of JFK's outskirts, with its run-down highways and reckless drivers, James included, had not bothered me on the way *to* the airport, but coming back the scene struck me as a place I didn't want to be in.

James pointed out the abandoned wreck of a car on the shoulder. "He'll have trouble getting that thing started in the morning..."

We laughed. Anyway, I was home, though my lungs were still filled with the aroma of the Austrian forests and my body still remembered the rhythm of swimming in the lake. I felt like a stranger on American soil, with one foot still in my native country. Would I always feel like this?

But despite the humidity, the traffic and the potholes, there it was again, this vast contentment I felt in James' presence. As he ran his fingers through his slightly too-long hair my heart was full of tenderness and a twinge of guilt for a sin not yet committed.

James turned up the air-conditioning, and his brown eyes smiled at me. "That tan looks great, and your hair got lighter too."

I reached over to blow a kiss on his face.

"You've got a nice tan yourself."

Oh yes, he and Barry had been playing tennis, he reported. The faucet was fixed, the Salvation Army had picked up the package and Barry and Angela had taken him out to dinner for his birthday.

I slipped out of my sandals and wiggled my toes.

"James, I'm so sorry, but I couldn't find a birthday present for you. It's so difficult. You don't drink, you don't smoke and you don't eat candy. You hang on to your clothes forever and you go to the library for books. You have drawers full of socks, belts and handkerchiefs..."

He smiled and searched for something in his pocket.

"That's all right, Beautiful. You're back now, and you are my present. Uh... do you have some change for the toll booth?"

"No, why should I? All I have are a few Austrian shillings. A true gentleman never asks a lady for the toll money."

"I guess I'll have to remember that," James said with mock repentance.

We laughed, and a flash of our old familiarity passed between us.

I said, "I bought a gorgeous yellow silk dress with a matching stole. The shops are very chic there, mostly Italian designers. And wait until you see my blue Murano paperweight. I also bought a dozen herbal mud treatments for the face and body."

James made a face. "Mud...? Ugh..!"

Hardly interested in shopping talk or mud, James recounted his first trip in the corporate jet, a Cessna Citation, to Cleveland and back. "What a way to travel!" he raved. "It's like a flying lounge. I'd like you to meet my boss and his wife one day soon, too. The four of us could go to dinner together."

"Nice idea," I nodded, somewhat absentminded.

We took the upper level of the George Washington Bridge. To our left, Manhattan was spread out in a red, oppressive evening glow.

Thirsty and tired, I let my head sink against his shoulder and closed my eyes.

He said, "I'm glad you and your mother had such a good time together. I was kind of surprised at her confession about the affair in Vienna."

My head shot straight up again. Now that I was back, talking about her intimate encounter didn't seem right anymore.

I said, "It's an amazing story. She said it was the most exhilarating experience of her life. She had never known that making love could be... *like that*."

James shrugged philosophically. "Maybe every woman should go through an experience like that once in her life. Look how it changed her. Now she's into poetry and karate. I'm glad for her, though. I always thought she was an attractive woman and I felt it was a shame she lived such an unfulfilled life all these years."

James honked his horn at a van that had started to veer into our lane and asked, "Who was the man she was with?"

"No idea. She wouldn't say," I lied.

I had been holding my breath. I thought about my mother and me sitting wrapped in blankets on the terrace that night, listening to the distant tango of a dance band down by the lake. I had been on the brink of confiding to her about Orson when she stopped rocking in the swing and told me her well-kept secret. She said that opening up to Orson had enabled her to open up to herself and the whole world. At first I was paralyzed with shock and didn't know how to react. My cheeks burned, despite the cool air of the night. Then I gradually relaxed and accepted her right to happiness in whatever form it took. Besides, her story was long over, while mine was just beginning. The fact that we had a common object of desire endeared her to me with a new intimacy, without any feelings of embarrassment or competition.

And oddly enough, she used James' words. "Every woman should go through an experience like that once in her life."

Was it my turn now? I knew that I would never be able to tell her about Orson and me. We had sat for a long time into the night, pulling our blankets tighter. The dance band had taken a break and the leaves rustling around us in the wind seemed to bewail the fragility of dreams.

Valley Road at last, and home. As we turned into the driveway, I saw that James had put on the sprinkler system. A few moments later I was greeted by the familiar low rumble of the garage-door opener and the air-conditioned house.

James unloaded my bags. I walked up the stairs into the living room, feeling the softness of the carpet under my sandals. For a split second everything was new again. My paperweight collection on the mantelpiece, the ivory portraits of Austrian royalty and my plants. But then it sank in. This was *home.*

The phone rang in the kitchen.

I picked up to the sound of a slow, velvet voice.

"May I see your lovely face for lunch on Monday?"

"Orson," I whispered, not prepared for this. "Yes, but..."

"I just wanted to see if you got back safely." His voice sounded content and gathered speed. "You can hang up now and say it was a wrong number."

"Who called?" James asked as he appeared with my bags from the garage.

"Wrong number." To hide my blushing face I reached for a cool drink in the refrigerator.

That night, after making love, I slept securely in James' arms, yet not quite as soundly as I should have after a nine-hour flight and a six-hour time lag.

26

I could hardly move my chair another inch and found it hard to believe that Orson was comfortable in a place with so little elbow room. For our first lunch after my trip I had expected him to take me to a place with dim lights and lots of space between the tables. The coffee shop on Forty-Seventh Street was packed.

Orson smiled at me over the rim of his menu as if he could read my thoughts.

"For me it's the same as in the subway. This density of bodies fills me with a sense of anonymity."

He put his menu on the Formica table and I felt his eyes wandering along the neckline of my blouse. From a speaker above us, a waltz mingled with the sounds of scraping chairs and rattling dishes.

Proud of my knowledge, I said, "It's Tchaikowsky, from the ballet *Swan Lake."*

Orson grimaced. "Ah... these ballet waltzes. They are so superficial."

"Why?" I made sure my purse was safely braced between my feet.

"Because they just go *da-da-da…* there's no substance, no development. Do you know the Berlioz waltz from his *Symphony Fantastique*? Now, *that's* a waltz!"

"But what's the difference?"

"The difference is in the imagination of the composer, how he varies the melody, changes the keys and the rhythm, the richness of the harmonies and orchestration. That's what it takes to produce a masterpiece." He gesticulated dramatically with his hands.

Because of people passing by, the waitress had to press her body against our table and she smiled adoringly at Orson. Without asking me he ordered deluxe hamburgers and hot chocolate for both of us.

He grinned. "It's something I never get tired of."

From other tables I felt eyes staring at us. I didn't dare to look around, but Orson didn't seem to feel any kind of unwelcome exposure.

His eyes rested on me smilingly. But suddenly he frowned, and his voice had a hint of sarcasm. "Isabella, you have a tan."

"Don't you like it?" It was half question, half self-defense. "James and everyone in the office say it looks great."

Orson shook his head. "No. I liked your soft, white skin. It looked like marble, only much more beautiful."

I said, "Sorry, I couldn't avoid getting tanned," and hated myself for being so apologetic.

Our hamburgers arrived, and this time the waitress aimed an even more inviting smile at Orson. It was always this way. In every restaurant they treated him like an aristocrat, and me like air. Orson poured a flood of ketchup on his French fries and grumbled, "Well, then don't ever get a tan again."

I realized he looked as pale as if he had been locked away in a dungeon for a year.

He said, chewing on an onion ring, "Thank you for your postcard. I'm glad you attended a nice concert in Brahms' castle." And then he added dreamingly, "I used to know someone who lived there..."

The wheels of my mind spun backwards. *You're like a lost song... even more beautiful than I remembered.* My mother. I knew I looked a lot like her. Had he recognized me as her daughter right from the beginning? Not now, I thought, not now. The moment wasn't right. I didn't have the nerve to ask, although I was burning to know if he still remembered her.

To forestall any further reveries from the past, I said, "Did you miss me?"

His voice was light. "Now that you're back, I miss you even more... and what about you? Did you have any thoughts of what we talked about before you left?"

"Yes." My whisper was so low that it could hardly reach him.

"And?" The birthmark on his lip twitched.

I took my time to answer. At this point I could still get out. But then, clutching the paper napkin on my lap, I said, "I have not changed my mind. What about you?"

"Certainly not," he said with some relief, "but I don't want you to do anything for my sake. You have to do it because you want to."

My stomach danced.

I said, "I'm doing this for egoistic reasons, just for myself. Not for you. I see it as *a venture in romance*."

Orson's face shone excitedly. "Isabella, I *love* your attitude. This way your egotism reflects back on me as proof that you really want me," and after a little pause, "you know, the art of making love is a skill that has to be acquired by practice, like learning to play an instrument. When I was twenty I might have had a fuller head of hair, but looking back I sometimes wonder what kind of lover I was then."

"You arouse my curiosity."

For a frightening second I had the impression that all motion froze around us and all voices fell silent as everyone listened to what Orson Mahler had to say.

Orson held his hand out to me past the ketchup bottle. I put my hand in his and felt his gentle touch.

He smiled. "I will treat you like a precious jewel that I hold and polish in my hands."

I was filled with wonderment and a sense of farce. I finished my last bite of hamburger and left the fries untouched. I felt half disappointed, half relieved that he hadn't yet suggested a specific time and place.

He leaned forward. "There is no rush. From now on we have all the time in the world. The moment you said *yes* we became lovers. The fact that it hasn't materialized yet is a mere technicality. You are mine and I am yours."

He picked up a French fry from his plate and fed it to me. Then he snatched one of mine and ate it.

A mix of voices buzzed around us. I wondered what sort of things he had said to my mother.

Orson sipped on his hot chocolate with relish. "But tell me, when did it first occur to you that we might become lovers?"

I clamped my hands around my cup.

"In Carnegie Hall, when I watched you conducting the *Verdi Requiem.* I thought, if you make love the same way you conduct, with passion, sensitivity and self-assurance..."

He didn't let me finish. He laughed with delight.

"Isabella, conducting is merely making love to music. No detail should be left unattended to bring out the best in music, or in a woman. If a piece of music is worth performing and a woman is worth making love to, it's worth giving it your best."

He paused. Then he dreamily repeated to himself, "*Making love to Music...* mh... why didn't I think of it before." And after another moment he smiled, "Isabella, from now on this metaphor will always remind me of you."

Under the table our knees touched for the first time.

A curious smile danced on his lips. "And you know, Isabella, I haven't even kissed you yet."

27

First it seemed like a good idea to take Julia on a sailboat cruise around the south tip of Manhattan. With James in Denver and Orson conducting the L.A. Chamber Orchestra in a series of concerts on the West Coast, I wanted to catch up on Julia's life. Sailing had been an important part of my adolescent summers at my native lake, where, after obtaining my sailing permit, I had occasionally helped out as an assistant instructor at the local yacht club. Julia had never been on a sailboat before.

I said, "A fresh breeze under the wide-open sky will do wonders for your nerves."

Yet her unfriendly look at the young, handsome sailor who helped us aboard made me abandon any hope of putting her in a carefree mood. Besides, why was she suddenly blushing like a poppy blossom?

When the sailor warned her, "Don't sit on the cockpit, miss, it's freshly painted," she shot him an spiteful glance and refused to let him take her hand. And that was just for openers.

To make up for her lack of congeniality I showed the sailor a sunny smile.

He grinned. "Somethin' wrong with your sister, miss?"

I shrugged helplessly behind Julia's back, amused at his assumption that we had shared the same playpen.

About a dozen more people came aboard before the *Petrel,* a 70-foot yacht, embarked from Battery Park for a three-hour cruise around New York harbor. Three sailors with flat-topped straw hats raised the sails and soon the yacht was plunging over the steady rhythm of small waves that glimmered with each rise and fall.

Julia and I sat cross-legged on the wooden planks at the bow, and in her immaculate pink sneakers and white jeans she was a model of perfection and discomfort. In the wind her hair had the color of ripe corn.

As the breeze grew stronger and the distance to the shore greater, her eyes narrowed and tensed. My nostalgic wish to share my joy of sailing seemed illusive. Was it really just a week since I had returned to the U.S.? Austria seemed farther than the moon. Julia was complaining again about her lack-of-inspiration syndrome. When would she ever be able to write again? Seeing her like this, with her mind and eyes at half-mast, it was only at matter of minutes before she dug up her old "I-miss-him-so" lament about her ex-husband Phil. She fixed a long piercing stare into the unblemished blue sky, as if searching for horses in the heavens that would take her to her prince and inspire her to write again.

On the water around us a few sails were fluttering like white flags in the wind, and the Statue of Liberty ferry rumbled past us with people waving and clicking their cameras.

The sailor who had helped us aboard came around with a basket and offered sandwiches and sodas.

Julia ruffled her nose and snapped at the poor, blushing guy.

"Didn't your mother ever tell you that white bread isn't good for you?"

I hissed between my teeth, "Julia, this is *not* a cruise on the QE2," and accepted a ham and cheese sandwich.

The sailor tipped his straw hat and turned to me.

"I doubt your Barbie-Doll sister here always follows her mother's advice..."

I tore the plastic wrap off my sandwich and forced a grin.

"Maybe her mother warned her about blond sailors with straw hats and snoopy minds."

The poor guy shrugged his shoulders and continued his rounds.

Julia raised her chin and traced the outline of the mainsail. "Thanks," she said and bit one of her nails.

"Thanks for what?" I swallowed a piece of cheese.

"For getting rid of him."

"He didn't do anything wrong."

She held her hand out against the water splashing off the boat. "I know that guy," she whispered, blushing again. "During the week he works in my divorce lawyer's office. One day when Mr. Walters was held up in court... uh... we sort of started talking... I mean, he ended up inviting me to his place. I don't know what came over me, but I accepted."

A short silence followed in which the news sank in. This was not the cautious, conservative Julia I've always known.

Her voice gathered poise. "Frankly, I'm not sorry about what happened, it just happened," she paused, "and it was good. He made me realize that there was life after Phil and somehow helped me to find myself again."

I thought, *Hallelujah!* and said, "But Julia, why didn't you tell me this before?"

"I felt awkward telling you." A frown formed on her forehead. "But there's more to the story."

"What... tell me."

"A few days later, I paid him a second visit and his girl-friend, who had a key, walked in on us."

Our extended "Oooops…" came out in unison. Her voice trailed off in a forced, brittle laugh and her tucked-in top came out of her jeans and whipped around her torso in the wind.

She took a deep breath. "Now I'm glad I told you."

I said, "So am I," and all further attempts at the subject were drowned by peals of laughter. The whole episode had no more weight than a feather in the wind.

A flock of sea gulls swarmed around the boat, their cries filling the air, their white wings flashing against the blue sky. In this moment of perfect complicity I ached to tell her about Orson, leaning towards the thought that one confession deserved another. But an inner warning made me bite my lip. After all, maestro Mahler was a man with a worldwide reputation and not just a clerk working in a lawyer's office. And looking at the white immensity of the foresail I knew that I wouldn't be able to talk about him until long after everything was over.

Julia shaded her eyes with her hand and scanned the Manhattan skyline. Following the direction of her eyes, I said, "It looks just like a postcard."

People were moving around on the boat now, careful to avoid the painted cockpit, taking pictures and munching on sandwiches. I rolled up my jeans.

Julia had settled into a more comfortable position with her back against the mast. She languidly closed her eyes and said, "It was so intriguing, what you wrote in your letter from Austria, about your mother having this affair in Vienna. What kind of a prince charming was he, anyway?"

With a sudden jerk I hit my elbow on a metal ring that held a line in place. Feeling guilty of betraying my mother's past, all I could do was protect Orson's identity.

"Ouuuch..." I hugged my elbow, which allowed me to avoid an immediate reply.

Unimpressed by my misfortune, Julia ran her hand through her blowing hair and insisted, "How old was your mother then?"

I began carefully. "She was forty-seven." I stared at my water-stained sneakers.

"And what happened?"

"He was in Vienna for just six days, on business. They met at a concert of the Vienna Philharmonic, followed by drinks at his hotel…"

"And?"

I said, "I remember my mother's exact words."

Try to picture the elegance of the hotel, so old-world, with its antiques, silver coffee trays and crystal chandeliers. Being there made me feel like a queen, but in his arms I felt like a goddess. In five days he gave me a new life. Afterwards, I stopped feeling bitter or that I was unjustly treated by fate. He convinced me that I was someone very special, and the ability to think about myself in that way changed the way I lived my life...

Julia's brown eyes grew round, somewhat skeptical. A sudden spray from a big wave hit us and made us squirm.

She lowered her voice, "Isn't it amazing what five days of luxury and pleasure can do to a woman's self esteem…"

I slid closer on the wooden planks. "I think there was true romance to it."

I feared I was doing a poor job of repeating what my mother had told me with such effortless conviction. It was much easier to describe wars and revolutions than another person's flight on the wings of love.

"And afterwards?" Julia asked.

"Afterwards? A new beginning. Poetry and karate instead of needlepoint and scratchy Beethoven recordings that she had played too many times."

Julia looked up. The high-pitched cries of some sea-gulls spying for food sounded shrill and steely. She seemed to be up there with them, high as a kite, filled with a weird sort of elation.

She said, "And this man, whoever he was, never came back to Vienna?"

"Yes, he did, but his wife was with him. Besides, my mother was almost afraid that by seeing him again the memory of their encounter could be spoiled by something less perfect."

"So she never heard from him again?"

"Oh, yes. He called her once or twice from the States, but then their connection just tapered off. My mother says that passions are like plants. They die if left unattended."

I definitively wanted to get off the subject. I had already exposed too much, but Julia pressed on. "So he was American?"

I nodded wearily, warning myself to choose my words with care.

She further asked, "But why did she wait all these years to tell you?"

"I guess some things need the right time and place to be shared. Look at you and what you told me just now about your sailor."

With her eyes closed, Julia spoke as from a world of her own.

"I can see it all…Prince Charming and your mother talk after the concert. He asks her out for drinks, then to dinner... and somewhere along the way they test each other a little, both of them curious. And then he realizes that she's responding to him. She moves closer or he touches her lightly in passing and she reacts by pressing against him, and then, before you know it, he takes her in his arms and kisses her, and she's lost."

"Julia," I exclaimed, unduly loud, "your imagination is running away with you."

"Why are you so emotional? I could make this into a good story." Fearing more questions coming up, I said, "I don't think it would make a good story. Not at all."

"Yes it would. A very good story. It shows that sometimes you have to break the rules in order to find yourself. Take me and my handsome sailor."

I didn't reply. I thought, with discomfort, that I was about to break the rules myself.

Julia smiled blissfully between her dimples, having reached the state of ease I had intended to get her into from the beginning. Only now I was the one who was tense.

The yacht turned around, making us duck our heads as the mainsail swung to the other side. Seen from the opposite direction, the water glittered like silver against the sun, as if a giant hand had sprinkled millions of polished dimes across the surface of the waves. There was a brightness and a sharpness to this vision, a blinding quality that hurt, conveying a mental image of Orson kissing my mother for the first time. I closed my eyes, and in the no-man's land between light and dark I listened to the wind whispering to me. It spoke in a clear, velvet voice.

And you know Isabella, I haven't even kissed you yet.

28

When Orson kissed me for the first time it was far from an earthshaking experience. It happened on a gray, rainy day in the passage that links Fifty-Second and Fifty-Third Streets between Fifth and Madison. It was about 1:30 PM.

Orson had returned from L.A. the night before, and we had just shared a quick omelet in a coffee shop on Fifty-Second Street. Orson anxiously checked the rain and his watch. Neither of us had an umbrella. Every passing cab was taken, which left us with the choice of getting soaked or seeking shelter.

His gray-metallic eyes shone at me warmly, and the first touch of our lips was soft, careful and not unduly long. I wondered if he feared that I was merely enduring his touch or that I might be appalled by the first contact with his birthmark. Then, after a short breath, Orson's lips traveled down my neck until the collar of my raincoat stopped their quest.

He smiled. "I can feel your heartbeat."

I smiled back. "This is very nice," uncertain of what would come next.

Orson took a step back. "I agree. This is a very nice romantic stage."

His voice lacked the indication of enraptured bliss, as if he were adding comparative data to his series of previous liaisons or just biding time until the rain let up. We caught a glimpse of our reflection in the window of a map store. Our physical unlikeness was mirrored against the background of globes and a poster showing the population density of Africa.

Orson gave his thinning hair a worried run-through with his fingers. "Look at us. We don't match at all. What an unequal pair we are. Here's this tall blonde at the height of her beauty and this short, balding man next to her."

"Are you fishing for compliments, maestro?" I asked with forced cheer. "After all, I'm spending my time with you."

He turned up the collar of his jacket. "Well, I'm glad for that, but I just don't understand your reasoning."

"Romance happens outside the rules of reason."

Orson laughed acidly. "Let me explain my reasoning then. I want you to understand that I'll be kind to your body but mean to your mind."

I told myself he wasn't having a good day and gave him a disbelieving look. But deep down I felt the first taste of the bittersweet discomfort that he would expertly inflict on me. Shouldn't I feel delight instead of discomfort? Or would I have to live for some few moments when he would choose to be kind and irresistible?

Orson searched his pockets for a piece of paper and couldn't find it. He mumbled impatiently. "I should call Joan. She promised to messenger me the speech I'm giving tonight at the *Tavern on the Green* for the Juilliard Awards Dinner. Joan is good at writing speeches. She was once a journalist and an editor. The only trouble is, I haven't seen it yet myself, and I'm worried that I don't have enough time to rehearse it."

Unwilling to grant Joan's literary skills further attention, I said miserably, "Orson, my toes are wet and cold. I wish you could warm them."

He looked at me with a quiet naughtiness. "Isabella, I would love to do much more to your toes than just warm them."

After a moment he took my hand and drew it to his lips.

"I'll give you a call soon. I want to be with you, but I don't want to squeeze you in between an audition and a rehearsal. I still feel very honored by your offer."

I felt playfully flirtatious. "Orson, since Joan writes your speeches, that frees your time to write me love-letters. I imagine opening them with burning fingers."

Instantly I was struck by the foolishness of my request.

Orson let go of my hand. "Where did you get an idea like that?"

We started walking the length of the passage. The rain didn't stop. Despite his sarcasm I held my ground.

"I'm sure you write exquisitely. I picture your letters with originality and flair, constantly crossing the line between sincerity and jest, and to protect your identity you could sign your name backwards, as Mozart used to do. *With love, Nosro."*

I had no doubt he thought I'd gone mad and his eyes rested absent-mindedly on the dancing puddles flooding the sidewalk.

He grumbled, "I can honestly say I've never written a love-letter in my life."

I froze. Things weren't exactly proceeding in a poetic manner, or did he intend to kindle my desire by means of deprivation? For now I took an emotional leap away from him.

"Rain or not, Orson, I have to get back to work."

"I should be going too." He looked up at the clouds. "But what the heck, it's only water. I'll walk you back to your office. Maybe we can find a cab on the way... and, Isabella," he smiled self-pleasingly, "I can also honestly say, I've never owned an umbrella in my life."

Before we stepped out into the elements, I asked, "Orson, are you saying that there's a connection between never owning an umbrella and never writing a love-letter?"

His eyes shone mischievously.

"You've just created a connection."

"What do you mean?"

"Now I'm sorry I never got into the habit."

29

I picked up a long black feather from the living room couch. It had come off the feather duster I had just run along the gilded frames of my portraits of Austrian royalty. Their ivory faces stared at me with hollow ignorance. Why couldn't they tell me where James was? My heart had turned into a lump of lead. It served me right, this gripping, irrational fear that something might have happened to my husband.

The images flashing through my mind were three-dimensional and colored, depicting his plane in a crash or his car on fire. Or someone had seen Orson kiss me and told James about it. And now he was in the process of carrying out some kind of revenge.

I knew he was to spend the day with his boss, Randolph Harte, to submit plans for a manufacturing modification. The clock on the kitchen wall showed seven-thirty, and James, who normally called when he was ten minutes late, hadn't given a sign of life.

In his absence the house seemed to hold its breath in order to ward off disaster. Through the silence, the hum of the refrigerator started with a jolt. I called James' office for the third time, and for the third time got only his voice mail. Without feeling hungry I gulped down a handful of walnuts from a jar on the counter.

Then I remembered that Barry had the big oak tree in front of his house cut down this week and had offered James some logs for our fireplace. He and Angela had probably called him to drop by.

Still chewing on some walnuts, I called Barry. No answer. I almost panicked. Maybe this was the punishment for my resolution to embark on the venture of forbidden romance, showing me that betrayal wouldn't sit easily on my shoulders. Suddenly I experienced an awesome humility, where the thought of munching popcorn with James in front of the TV or cutting each other's toenails in the bathtub became a lost ticket to the gates of paradise.

Trapped in a deal with fear and fate, I was ready to strike a bargain with the Angel of Salvation. If James would come back *right now*, I'd never see Orson again.

But James didn't come.

I began pacing up and down in the living room. On the glass table lay one of Orson's old recordings that I had brought back from Austria. I compared its picture against that of his latest release, the *Mozart Requiem* that he had given me on the occasion of our first kiss, just yesterday. The two photos were more than twenty years apart.

Orson had never been a truly handsome man. Now, as then, the little black pearl, his birthmark, sat on his upper lip like a drop of tar. His pale skin, gray eyes and unremarkable features made him almost devoid of personality, like an actor without make-up, ready to slip into any role, from Hamlet to Professor Higgins. Maybe this was his magic and mystique. Every woman could project her fantasies onto him and he would always fit the part.

I climbed the stairs, wondering which role I was trying to attribute to him. Was it merely the attraction of the opposite, or of looking at myself with him as my mirror?

But in the here and now I stood in front of the bathroom mirror. I looked at myself and then read the yellow label on one of the mud body treatments I had brought back from my trip. *...draws toxins from skin, clears blemishes...*

Why not now? So I pulled my hair into a pony tail, got out of my clothes and began applying mud all over my face, throat and shoulders. I wanted to hurry the time along, until everything about James' whereabouts would be explained. But miraculously, the moist, aromatic substance cooled my skin and soothed my mind. If James was in danger I would learn about it soon enough, and if not, I could greet him with a glowing complexion.

This was more fun than I had expected, spreading and smearing mud all over my skin, as if creating a mask for Halloween. Now only two holes for my eyes were left uncovered, and in the underworld of my imagination I joined a group of witches, our voices shrieking, our broomsticks rattling in the storm.

And then there was another kind of rattling. It was the garage door opener announcing James' car. A warm wave of relief flooded through my body. Everything was fine. James was fine. And I loved him dearly.

I wanted to rush down and tell him how I felt, but there was no time to rinse my face. The mud was just starting to harden. I heard his footsteps and, folding a towel around me, I skipped down the stairs, singing, "*Jaaaames, I looove you sooo...*" to a Rossini aria.

On the landing leading to the living room I stopped cold. The first thing that I saw on the beige carpet was a pair of green suede pumps and, a little further up, a matching green purse on a woman's arm. Dressed in an off-white linen dress, she first stared at my bare legs and then worked her eyes upwards, letting out a scream as they reached my face.

Behind her stood James and a man I'd never met.

There was a shiny mist on James' forehead. "*Isabella!*"

I whimpered helplessly, "But... James..."

The couple stood rooted to the spot, but within seconds James' laughter broke the spell. His ease surprised me.

"Mrs. Harte, Mr. Harte, I'd like you to meet my beautiful wife, Isabella."

Oh mein Gott! Now I remembered. Today I was to meet James' boss, Mr. Harte, President of Technicon Corporation, and his wife, Marilyn. And now I had blown it for him. Too preoccupied with Orson, I had forgotten to mark down the date in my calendar.

Securing my towel tightly above my chest, I stepped down the last two stairs and shook their outstretched hands.

I stammered, "I'm very, very sorry about this."

Mr. Harte's smile befitted the perfection of his three-piece suit. He bowed. "It's my special pleasure. James speaks of you quite often."

I said, "I'm so happy to meet you," hardly able to move my facial muscles. The mask had reached a state of dryness that pulled my skin in all directions.

Marilyn Harte smiled unconvincingly and withdrew discreetly to the middle of the room. At the glass table, she shook her auburn hair and said, "I see you are an Orson Mahler fan." She picked up the old record showing the younger Orson. A dreamy look formed on her face.

"In my mind he's the most charismatic conductor of our time."

Mr. Harte, who had drifted to the fireplace, shot his wife a slightly irritated glance.

James stood by the bookshelves and jumped at the idea.

"We like him too. Isabella even had lunch with him once."

Color rushed into Mrs. Harte's face and her eyes showed a gleam of ecstasy. She rushed back to me and grabbed my hand, the one that was not clutching the towel.

"You'll have to tell me all about him. I always felt he had a unique presence." And moving her glossy lips even closer to my mud-covered face, she lowered her voice meaningfully. "I know the *true* secret of his powers."

"What is it?" My face was getting unbearably tight under the mask.

"It's all because of his initials, *O.M.*," she whispered and a saintly expression crossed her face. "I'm practicing meditation and yoga, and every yogi knows that the sound *O...M* symbolizes a mysterious power. These two letters, *O...M* are considered to be *the word* from which all words were made, the root of sound and language."

Out of the corner of my eye I saw James' jaw drop. At last Marilyn let go of my hand and closed her eyes.

"Chanting this magic formula *O...M* empowers and purifies the mind."

James and I exchanged glances. My face threatened to burn away.

Unimpassioned by his wife's elaboration and my inappropriate appearance, Mr. Harte stood perched above my paperweight collection on the mantelpiece.

He mused over the rim of his glasses, "Some nice *Baccarats, Caithnesses* and *Perthshires* you've got here. My father was an avid collector himself, and he always said they were islands of beauty and perfection."

With all the poise I could muster, I said, "Their designs strike my imagination."

He turned around and smiled ingratiatingly, "which is the great end of all art."

Meanwhile James cleared his throat diplomatically. "I'm sure we'll have plenty to talk about over dinner," and with a telling hint in my direction, "Why don't you get dressed while we have a drink?"

I nodded. "Fifteen minutes?"

James checked his watch. "We have a deal. Fifteen minutes."

Upstairs, bent over the sink, I rinsed my face and suddenly felt James' presence behind me. I expected him to blow up and looked remorsefully at him as my face came up in the mirror.

"I'm sorry James. I wanted so much to be a perfect wife for you."

He grinned. "Why? I have no problem with the way you are. I wouldn't want you to be perfect. Think of all the entertainment I'd miss."

Before leaving the bathroom he gave me an upbeat pat on the behind. "You were pretty funny, you know. And you certainly picked an original way to show off your legs. But hurry up now, will you?"

30

Another day at the office. I had just finished creating the name tags for the participants of Mr. Stringer's conference. Amanda, our temp, craned her neck around the door of the conference room where I was helping Gary set up the monthly executive committee meeting. Gary was our corporate waiter and he maneuvered his serving cart around the oval table with considerable clatter.

From the door, Amanda winked at me and her eyes darted to the phone in the middle of the huge table.

"Isabella, there's a call for you. A man. I don't think it's your husband. He didn't give his name, but he sure has the sexiest voice in town."

Heat rushed to my cheeks, but I said coolly, "Put the call through, please."

Amanda frowned. "What's the extension in here?"

"4-5-7-7."

Her head disappeared and Gary lined up bottles of Perrier, Coke and orange juice in the center of the table. I pulled the phone to the edge of the table and sat down in one of the black leather chairs. Gary's white jacket hovered nearby, as he efficiently counted spoons, cups and saucers. I wished he'd go back to the kitchen for napkins. Instead, his flat, pink face exposed a broad grin that made me turn my back to him.

The next moment I had Orson on the line. His velvet voice said without preliminaries, "Isabella? Do you have a pencil ready?"

"Uh... yes..." I reached over to grab a corporate pad from a chair.

"Ready?"

I couldn't believe Orson's business-like tone, as if Paula were standing right behind him.

"Take this down. Thursday, September fourth, at three P.M."

"Where?"

"My apartment."

"Oh." My fingers tightened on the receiver. They still smelled faintly of the egg salad sandwich I had just eaten for lunch.

Orson asked, "Will you be able to come?"

"Yes," I said, thinking that I'd have to pretend another visit to the dentist.

Orson was all fact and no flirtation.

"You *do* know what will happen then?"

"Yes." My voice became less stable.

"Tell me *what* will happen."

The egg salad sandwich was turning over in my stomach.

"Orson," I whispered, "please, not now..."

Across the table Gary was setting out sugar bowls and cream pitchers at exact intervals.

"Isabella...?" I heard Orson's voice after a while.

"Yes?"

"I thought I'd lost you for a moment. Now again, I want to hear why you're coming."

In order to be able to give Orson an answer, I had to wait for Gary to rattle some dishes. I felt like a concertgoer suppressing a cough until she could drown it in the blaring sounds of drums and trumpets. But Gary moved like a snake.

The balm of Orson's voice was gone. He insisted, "Tell me, I *am* waiting."

How dare he pressure me. I was starting to resent the fun he was getting out of this.

I said defensively, "I *am* nervous about this, very nervous."

"Oh, no..." His tone changed from challenge to concern. "That's not how I want to make you feel. I want you to be eager, but not anxious. Do you know the difference? It's often misused in everyday language."

On the verge of irritation, I hissed, "Thank you. I think my command of the English language is adequate."

Gary reached across the phone cable to replace a chipped cup.

There was an empty moment. I was tempted to hang up the phone, but Orson's voice returned softly. "Isabella? I'm sorry, I didn't mean to lecture you."

I adopted his business-like tone. "It's all right. I'll be there."

What he said next had an exuberance that equally touched and troubled me.

"Believe me, Isabella, it's going to be wonderful. Trust me. Who would know better than I? You know, I think of it in bed at night when I'm unable to sleep."

I whispered, "I promise to be eager and not anxious."

"Good." His voice smiled through the line. "I'll see you then."

And he hung up. So suddenly. Now what? Lapse into leisurely passivity? Should I just cross my arms and wait for the remaining days to pass? Today was Friday, which left me six days to get into the spirit.

It's going to be wonderful.

At the door, Gary surveyed the set table, pleased with his work.

He smiled at me, rubbing his palms. "At last, all set to go."

31

Nervous? Was I ever nervous. The impending reality of becoming Maestro Mahler's muse and mistress hardly fueled the zeal to host my long-planned summer party.

From far-away Austria it had seemed such a nice idea to invite my friends, but now the necessity of selecting recipes, compiling lists and shopping for food loomed before me like having to cross the Rockies on foot. I was ready to bless anyone who canceled, but only Matthew and his friend Tom were to receive this secret benediction. They wanted to fly to Halifax for the Labor Day weekend. Unfortunately, no one else had travel plans and they all accepted my invitation with much enthusiasm.

So on Saturday, August 30, I got up at dawn, rolled up my sleeves and turned on the air conditioning. To the blaring sounds of Beethoven's *Choral Symphony*, the bookshelves were converted into a bar and the dinner table into a buffet. Neither Beethoven nor Orson would mind that I divided my attention between their symphony and the pages of my cookbook. But what caused the gradual rising of my spirits even more than Schiller's *Ode to Joy* was the array of promising aromas that rose from the stove. After all, what were four hours of cutting cucumbers and mushrooms, peeling shrimp and marinating beef cubes against the pleasure of feeding my friends?

If I wanted to surprise Orson at the beginning of the fall season by becoming a member of his chorus, I needed every friend I could put my hands on. So far, the only ones within my reach were Beverly and Daisy, who would merrily murder me if they knew what I was up to with their maestro. I put on the old record one more time and returned Orson's smile on the cover. His smile said, *Isabella, conducting is merely making love to music.*

James had left after breakfast with his tennis racket. I had assured him that I could handle everything with a twist of the wrist.

Could I really? I surveyed the living room. Finally everything was in place: flowers, fruit, olives, veggies, crackers, nuts, napkins, silverware and glasses. The kitchen also passed inspection and looked deceivingly untouched, with my mushrooms à la Grècque and skewers of beef and Shrimp Provençal stored away in the refrigerator.

Indeed, after straightening out one last wrinkle in the white tablecloth, I could rest my mind and my body too. When James returned I had just emerged from a bubble bath. He caught me leaning naked against the closet door while uttering the ultimate female line.

"I have nothing to wear."

He dropped his soaked clothes into the hamper, grinning.

"Then don't wear anything. You look great like that."

He banged the shower door shut and sang at the top of his lungs, "*When I fall in love, it will be forever...*"

I slipped into a pink-and-black striped summer dress, listening to James and trying to ignore another voice inside me. *Trust me. It's going to be wonderful.*

An hour later I found it quite wonderful that my guests all arrived at about the same time, their cars parked in the driveway and their arms full of wrapped bottles and flowers. The sun was still above our neighbor's lilac bushes, setting Beverly's red hair aflame like liquid gold. Her purple dress stunningly complimented the features of her body. Behind me, James pushed aside the kitchen curtains to enhance his view.

I said, "There's Angela with a pot of Oysters Rockefeller," as I saw Barry helping his mother out of the car. Louise's short legs landed slowly on the pavement. Her bright smile matched her floral-print suit and her gray hair was as unruly as ever. Suddenly I was afraid that inviting her could turn out to be a mistake. Not that she would purposely divulge what she knew about Orson and me, but I feared that the spirit of champagne might outwit her tongue and make it slip.

On the flagstones leading to the house, Louise was blocking Daisy's way, and instead of moving on, the two introduced themselves elaborately. I hadn't seen her for three months, but Daisy still reminded me of a Botticelli angel. Sweet and full of mischief. Her pleasantly round body bounced uncomfortably on her high heels, as her left hand held a bunch of baby roses and her right Louise's hand. Behind them, a tall thin man carried two bottles and waited patiently for the conclusion of their chat. This could only be Rudy, Beverly's husband. Barry took the pot of oysters from Angela and almost tripped over one of the flagstones with it. Now that she had both hands free, Angela rearranged the spaghetti straps of her skimpy top. I had never seen her in green before.

Beverly's tiny red purse danced around her body as she motioned for the group to move on. Only Julia was late, as always.

Our front door opened to the sight of a smiling group that Norman Rockwell would have been happy to paint. My proud introduction, "This is my husband James," was followed by handshakes and hellos. James and Beverly glanced appraisingly at each other. Beverly blushed. Her heels clicked on the ceramic tiles in the entrance hall and her silvery soprano rose through the house. She was excited about being in New Jersey, which, for a typical New Yorker, was far beyond the culture line, the Hudson River, and so terribly rural.

On the stairs, her husband threw an apologetic glance at me. Rudy's fragile frame and enormous brown eyes conveyed the shyness of a deer. I judged him to be kind, unexciting and comfortable in his wife's shadow.

James immediately attended to his assigned duties as bartender, making vigorous use of a hammer to separate the ice cubes.

Daisy shook her blonde angel's head and looked around the living room. "How beautiful you have it here."

She smelled overwhelmingly of lemon and looked like too much of everything. Too much lipstick, too much jewelry and too much need to please. She gave the impression of a little girl who had borrowed her mother's wardrobe to dispel the boredom of a rainy day. Daisy was the first to inspect the buffet and, with her cute way of wrinkling her nose, accepted a plate from James' hands. Impressed by his good looks, she smiled at him coyly.

"Unfortunately, food seems to weigh more after you've eaten it."

James grinned dryly, guessing at a waist-line under her mu-mu dress. "Whatever the weight, I *adore* food. I wouldn't eat anything else."

She insisted that she was on a diet and was only picking. Then, happily blushing, she began picking herself through enough food to feed the homeless in New York.

James had that effect on women. He made them blush. First Beverly, now Daisy, with Louise next in line.

With a hint of rheumatism, Louise fell heavily into James' armchair by the window. She winked at me meaningfully, as if to refer to our secret. James supplied her with a glass of champagne and his 1000-watt smile.

On my way to the kitchen I passed Barry who leaned leisurely against the doorframe, holding a full plate. I took in his white pants and black silk shirt.

"Barry," I chirped, "how elegant you look."

"You really mean it?" he asked, scratching his beard.

"Of course." I lowered my voice. "And congratulations on winning the tennis match today."

"Did James tell you?"

"No, he didn't. That's how I know."

We snickered conspiratorially and looked at James at the bar mixing drinks. James caught my eye, and the twin creases on either side of his nose deepened his smile. Suddenly I felt as if they all had left and we were alone again. A wave of warmth from his eyes touched my heart and made me fight off the other voice. *I want you to be eager, but not anxious.*

And then, late as usual, Julia came up the stairs, hiding her thin figure under a wide, colorful skirt and an oversized white blouse. She moved as regally as a princess, not in the least intimidated by the eyes turned in her direction.

Barry nearly dropped his plate of Shrimp Provençal. He gazed at her with a kind of animal instinct that was independent of the intellect.

I took my late-comer by the shoulders and turned her around like a mannequin. "This is my dear friend Julia."

Barry fiddled with his fork and said with blissful bluntness, "We met before. At Café Carnegie. You look even prettier today."

Luckily, Angela was out of earshot. Her sudden burst of laughter came from the kitchen, and it reminded me that I had to remove my mushrooms à la Grècque from the refrigerator. James, wearing one of my mother's embroidered aprons, was already attending to that task. Angela's eyes flashed an indignant look at James.

"*Giacomo*! Ah, your idea of humor is disgusting..."

I took the mushrooms from him. "What did you tell her?"

James handed me the serving platter. "We had a discussion about recycling."

"Recycling what?"

He shrugged innocently. "Used toilet paper."

"Jaaames..." I tried to give him a kick, but stumbled instead. James caught me as well as the mushrooms.

Now Angela's turned-up voice resounded from across the living room. "Our host is always-a flirting with his own-a wife."

Her complaint was directed to Rudy, whom she had picked as her next victim. But Rudy, whose suspenders made a red cross on the back of his shirt, didn't fit the part. Slightly hunched, he heard her out politely and then set out on his own to look around the room like a curiosity collector.

To satisfy his interest in my ivory portraits of Austrian royalty, he got me talking like a museum guide. As we advanced from frame to frame, I prayed his inquisitiveness would not outlast the party.

"And yes," I continued to explain, "Ferdinand the First became Emperor after Charles the Fifth, his brother, had retired as a monk."

A glance over my shoulder informed me that Beverly and Angela were on the love-seat, relishing my marinated beef skewers. Turning back to Rudy and the last portrait, I resumed, "And this is Maria-Theresia, Archduchess of Austria and Queen of Hungary. She had sixteen children, most of whom she married off to royal courts all over Europe."

Fortunately, Beverly arrived to collect her husband, whose enormous eyes flooded me with admiration.

At the fireplace, Julia and Barry spoke in low voices, drinking champagne and enjoying something yet undefined between them. There was a suppressed intensity in their look, a longing and a new awakening. I thought with alarm, He is going to kiss her!

Louise, still in the armchair by the window, shot her son an uneasy glance.

At the buffet, James was admiring Daisy's dangling flower earrings and she, in turn, his burgundy tie. Rudy stood dreamily between two potted palms and seemed to be counting the curtain rings. For a moment we shared the spell of separate daydreams. Mine whispered. *You are like a lost song, but much more beautiful than I remembered.*

Restlessly, I settled on the armrest next to Louise. My eyes zig-zagged from guest to guest. Was everybody having a good time? Louise took my hand and patted it. She gestured for me to move closer.

"Orson is right. You are a very special woman, and that doesn't include your talents as a cook."

Meanwhile, Daisy sat by herself on the bottom of the stairs, a full plate on her knees and her fork rising and falling above my shrimp and mushrooms.

I realized I didn't have a drink yet and decided to get a glass of wine. I passed Beverly and Julia, side by side on the couch, and heard them mention Orson. Or rather Beverly was elaborating on her intended writing project, which she would call *Maestro Mahler, Memoirs and Memories.*

She shook her red curls flamboyantly.

"I *love* to meet real-life authors, like you, Julia. They are such interesting people. Maybe one day you could work as my ghost-writer. I'm constantly collecting material and I know him quite intimately... uh... I mean, we are very close friends." Her voice shrieked with pride.

I stopped in my tracks.

Julia's eyes widened and her lips moved, but inaudibly for me. Beverly pushed her glasses up on her nose, flattered by the attention that a professional writer was bestowing on her creative ideas.

Beverly gathered more steam. "If only I could get the names of all the celebrities who've fallen for his charms," she laughed importantly, "I'd have the fire-works for a best seller."

Wrinkles, indicating doubt, appeared on Julia's delicate forehead. It was impossible to read her lips.

Beverly jumped to her feet. "Are you kidding? Most women would poison their husbands for him. He's the most charismatic man alive."

In a spell of dizziness, I had to hold onto the mantelpiece. A nightmarish vision crossed my mind, of Beverly and Julia perched over a manuscript that left nothing unsaid.

Beverly's olive eyes glistened through her glasses.

"Together we could do it!"

Now Julia's voice rose to the point where I could just barely hear her. "...an intriguing idea."

To prevent their talk from becoming more specific, I moved towards them as in a desperate trance. In my mind Orson's voice returned. *The moment you said "yes" we became lovers. The fact that it hasn't materialized yet is a mere technicality. You are mine and I am yours.*

With the instinct of a bloodhound, Louise got up from her chair and joined us. Was it possible that she had been listening to their conversation? Something inside me told me that though she was trying to prevent disaster she would invariably cause it.

Her face broke into a hundred wrinkles of joviality.

"Isabella, did I thank you for your postcard yet? How interesting to hear that your mother had dinner with Orson years ago at the Hotel Imperial in Vienna."

Beverly caught on instantly. "I thought your mother *just* had drinks with him."

Julia's eyes narrowed. She had made the connection.

I froze. How could I get out of this? I had set my own trap by withholding parts of the truth. Three pairs of eyes stared at me for an explanation.

James' voice sounded from behind my back, "Sorry, ladies, but I'd like to borrow my beautiful wife, it's a surprise."

A spoon banging against a glass caught everyone's attention. Barry furrowed his bushy eyebrows, asking for silence. He held up a piece of paper.

"Ladies and Gentlemen," he squinted against the smoke of his pipe, "I'd like to express a few words of thanks to our lovely hostess." He bowed towards me. "And our host." He grinned at James. "I've written a little poem for the occasion and I'd like to read it to you."

Everyone rose and formed a semi-circle. James' reassuring arm around my waist made me want to send them all home and crawl under the covers with him.

Barry spoke with the distinct baritone of a man who was used to giving lectures.

By an Austrian lake that was bright
Lived a Fräulein, a beautiful sight.
And then James one day
Came and took her away
And that's why she's with us tonight.

Isabella's the type to enthrall,
With her cute little accent and all.
And he couldn't resist,
So right after they kissed,
It was destined that James sure would fall.

We never could quite understand
How their love stayed so steady and grand,
Even now in their home,
While reciting this poem,
I can see that he's holding her hand.

I think I'm one lucky fella,
The food and the drinks have been swella.
To the friends we love most,
I propose this short toast:
Here's to James, and to dear Isabella...

In the midst of a chorus of laughter and applause, James and I kissed theatrically. From their gilded frames, the faces of Austrian royalty seemed to nod their approval.

Daisy, alone, stood at the window and studied the old Beethoven record I had played that morning. From the corner of my eye I saw her remove the disc from the cover. She appeared to be looking for something on the label and, after reading it, tossed the record thoughtlessly onto the big armchair. Its color blended inconspicuously with the chair's fabric. Was she always this careless with other people's records? Somebody could sit on it, I thought, and I set out to retrieve it. After all, this was an irreplaceable relic.

But my attention was side-tracked by the sight of James and Barry carrying the dirty dishes in precarious stacks to the kitchen. They were competing, as usual, trying to see who could pile the plates (of my mother's good *Rosenthal* china) higher. Torn by the conflicting impulses of rescuing my dishes or my record, my momentum was lost in the paralysis of indecision. I expected at any second the crash of dishes on the kitchen tiles. But when James emerged with the bowl of chocolate mousse and a big smile, I knew I had overreacted.

"Hi, lovely hostess," Barry's arm wrapped around my shoulder. "Look at you. Always cool and in control."

I said weakly, "Never trust appearances, Barry. But thank you for the poem. It was truly adorable."

A subconscious signal made me look at Angela and Rudy, sipping martinis at the bar. Her face spelled boredom as he offered her a thin-lipped smile and then stared silently into his drink. Clearly, Rudy was not the man to speed up the circulation in Angela's Italian veins.

Instead, Rudy prepared to settle into the armchair with Orson's old record still in place. Should I leap or scream? It was too late. A cracking sound. Poor Rudy was sitting on the fragments of Orson's Beethoven recording. In a miraculous balancing act he had saved his drink from spilling but had ripped the zipper of his pants.

He jumped to his feet. "Oh... shit...!"

Beverly immediately grasped the humor behind the humiliation. "There you go again, Rudy, always tearing your pants open in public." She used her sweetest tone, aware of all the eyes fixed on the spot of her husband's distress.

We all tried very hard not to laugh. James offered to lend him a pair of pants, but Rudy refused all help, preferring to sit the rest of the night with his hands folded in his lap. He made believe that his ruined zipper, like a war wound, had been honorably gained.

It gave him the license to sit with a succession of drinks and assume no further involvement in what went on around him.

He looked at me morosely. "At least I showed good taste."

"How?"

"By sitting on an Orson Mahler record, *that's how.* I can't stand to hear that name anymore. There's too much of him everywhere, and I can't get him out of my life." His voice almost broke. So much was pent up within him.

He went on to explain, "Have you seen Beverly's collection of records, tapes, photos and posters? And now she wants to write about him too. I'd love to shit... er... to sit like this on all of it."

To my consternation his enormous eyes filled with tears.

I leaned forward. "Rudy, it's an innocent form of infidelity."

But gin and jealousy made him even bolder. "Mahler's a vampire sucking the blood of our marriage."

To my relief, Beverly arrived, eternally smiling. She bent over him with benign protectiveness. "Let's go, Rudolph."

His eyes seemed to stare through her and he didn't move. Even when supported by a large quantity of gin, spontaneity was not his forte.

Next to Maria Theresia's portrait, Julia ate her chocolate mousse with apparent pleasure, licking some whipped cream off her fingers. Tentative and tense, Barry stood facing her to say good-bye. Was he lost on a far-away planet without a map? But Julia's smile froze as Louise and Angela tugged from each side at his sleeves.

Daisy was still eating glazed strawberries and wrinkled her nose cheerfully at James. Behind her, Rudy grumbled unhappily at his wife. He was sorry to give up his chair, which had become a symbol of retaliation.

The laughter of the room grew tired and the conversation innocent of thought, and soon they all left. Alone again, James and I exchanged a smile of relief. I felt a wave of fatigue, like heavy clouds rolling in.

I turned to James. "Did everybody have a good time?"

Carrying a tray of used glasses, James glanced over his shoulder. "If nothing else, the food was fabulous. So was the hostess." His smile blew all the clouds away.

I said, "Still, I'm glad it's over."

James switched the spotlights off.

"I'm sorry about that broken record. I know it was a sentimental token of the past."

I shrugged, picking up the last pieces from the carpet.

"The past is not important anymore."

"That's my Isabella," James laughed, "I think you're growing up."

Our eyes met for a teasing, happy moment before I turned away to open the door to the backyard. The air was hot and rich with summer, and the moon hung in the sky like a forgotten lamp after a ball. The crickets formed a huge, invisible orchestra, and although I tried not to listen to their song, I kept hearing the lyrics.

Thursday. This Thursday. Trust me. It's going to be wonderful.

The night was filled with smiles.

32

On Thursday at two-forty I stopped a cab at Park Avenue and gave the driver Orson's address. "It's between Ninety-Third and Ninety-Fourth Street," I explained and moved over on the creaking springs.

The countdown was on, and I made sure my carefully chosen lace bustier was still in place. My alertness rose with each of the forty-four blocks we passed going north. Had I ever noticed before that the traffic lights on Park converge on the horizon like the lights at the end of the Lincoln Tunnel? Would this trip become routine? At least *this* one was unique, a fantasy not yet satisfied by fact.

Orson had called me twice this week. He had sincerely regretted that he couldn't see me before our *date.* There was a press reception at the Carlyle, a photo session and a lunch with the Managing Director of Lincoln Center. His call earlier today had hardly lasted fifteen seconds, like a dentist confirming an appointment.

To make things more complicated, James was on business in Manhattan and wanted to take me to the Four Seasons, which would have meant stretching my lunch hour, in addition to leaving early for my *date.* I had managed to coax James into taking me out for dinner instead, although I was not sure what would be more difficult, facing him *before* or *after*.

It was two-fifty and the countdown was running. Only ten more blocks to Orson. Was this the beginning of a soulful passion or just the thrill of stolen love? Surely I expected nothing less of Orson than a perfectly polished act of love. Would his love-making be perfect, but without love? Would I ever hear the words *I love you* from his lips? Would they come from mine?

The cab stopped at two fifty-five at my destination. The broad entrance of the building was divided into three stone-laced arches behind which I could guess an inner courtyard with trees and a fountain. The grim appearance of an armed guard struck me as grotesque in contrast to the spirit-lifting gothic architecture.

"Who are you visiting, ma'am?"

I gave him Orson's name and apartment number and followed him into a security office with two secretaries, computers and fax machines. They asked me to wait until another guard came to usher me across the courtyard to a private elevator.

I pushed "12" with an unsteady hand and thought, This is it now. How was he going to receive me? *It's going to be wonderful.*

My head collapsed faintly against the elevator wall.

Orson was standing in the doorway. "Come in, Isabella." His gray-metallic eyes smiled as if seeing me was the closest thing to happiness.

To my immense relief, he wore beige pants and a white shirt. Only now did I become aware of my subconscious fear that he might not be correctly dressed.

He shut the door behind me. "I should have warned you about the tight security."

Our eyes met and danced in each other. Did he have a plan of action?

We stepped into an entrance gallery with dozens of framed photographs covering the walls. As I turned to look around, Orson took me gently by the shoulders and wrapped me in his arms.

"Happy, Isabella?"

I could feel his birthmark touching my ear.

I nodded but disengaged myself to examine some of the snapshots reflecting his life. There he was shaking hands with Mayor Koch, Sir George Solti and Placido Domingo. In another photo he was sharing pasta with Jackie O. and Arnold Schwarzenegger. In the next he was reading a score with Jasha Heifetz and then was on the podium kidding around with Jessye Norman. Was this Joan, his chorus manager, with Matthew when he was just a little boy? They were about to attack a big bowl of popcorn. And this had to be Paula, years ago, in Venice. God, was she beautiful. And here was Henry Kissinger on the boat in Norway...

"Isabella... don't you want to come in?"

Orson gestured to a long, silent corridor with doors right and left. I smiled but felt hypnotized into silence. A new feeling. Alone with Orson. For the first time. Really alone. How mindful we were of the space separating us.

"Orson?"

"Yes?" His voice held an eager question.

"Can I use your bathroom?"

"Certainly." He pointed to a door.

"Please don't leave a trace of lipstick anywhere." He gave me the feeling of walking on forbidden ground.

Inside the bathroom the checkerboard design of the tiles was matched by the never-ending black and white pattern of the piano keyboard printed on the bathroom tissue.

"I love your bathroom tissue," I giggled, coming out.

"I hate it. Beverly gave us a dozen boxes for Christmas." Orson was standing in the hall, listening to a tape with phone messages.

There was an odd sense of uncertainty about what to do next. Where was the magic? Orson took a step in my direction and I stiffened like a schoolgirl who had swallowed her ruler.

He instantly withdrew. "I won't force anything. Would you like something to drink, or do you want me to show you around the apartment?"

"Nothing to drink, thanks. But I'd like to see your place."

We walked in an awkward silence. Our steps were muffled by the thick oriental rugs on the waxed wooden floors. The apartment reeked of pine polish, brownies and artistic creativity.

"Excuse the mess." Orson pointed to the grand piano at the window, buried under stacks of sheet music. The sunlight reflected off the metal of the music stand.

He said, "The music profession follows you home. You never get away from it. I hold my auditions here for the soloists I engage."

My own audition for the chorus, which Orson knew nothing about, was scheduled for tomorrow. It loomed ominously in the back of my mind. But tomorrow was an infinity away.

I considered sitting down on one of the burgundy sofas facing each other in front of the fireplace. But Orson had already moved on to the next room. It had high windows and was loaded with statues, objects and vases without flowers. They seemed like forgotten luggage from the past, and I expected them to start talking or to hear their joints groan.

Funny, I had never given a thought to Orson's life outside the concert hall. And now this careless collector mentality and the simplistic functionality of the furniture told me the story of two people who were above any effort to impress. Right. Two people. This was where the esteemed maestro lived with his wife, Paula.

Orson had never discussed his marriage with me. I judged it to be routine, maybe, but far from ruinous. A soothing, secure arrangement to balance his professional and personal ups and downs.

I felt his breath behind my neck, a breath that burned my skin. He was waiting for me to make a move and I for him.

"Would you like to sit down?"

"No, I'm comfortable standing."

"You don't look comfortable," he smiled, pretending to be entirely at ease.

He pointed to another door. "This is my office."

In the dark room, with a desk and two chairs, three walls were covered with file cabinets from floor to ceiling.

He explained with pride, "I'm an archivist at heart and this is the archive of my life. I have a record of every concert, lecture, radio or TV program I ever did and at least one copy of all my recordings."

Then he pointed to a tower of piled up boxes.

"These are my fan letters. I can't throw them away. I'm up to about thirty-eight thousand, and I've read them all."

The oppressiveness of the sight made my chin drop. I wasn't prepared for anything like this. "Do you ever answer them?"

"Unfortunately, life isn't long enough." His face shone with the glow of memories. "Paula used to say that any woman who wanted to take me away from her could have me under one condition..."

"Which is?"

"She would have to take all this stuff along with me. That way Paula ended up keeping me." He grinned with a kind of irritating self-satisfaction.

I said flippantly, "Paula has a point there," while starting to count. There were about forty boxes.

"What do you mean?" Orson asked defensively.

"I mean," still marveling at the vast literary treasures, "the monstrousness of your stuff places a handicap on your romantic market value."

Orson shot me a funny look, but I wasn't sure he was amused. My eyes searched his with a plea for tenderness. I found his eyes, but not the tenderness.

I asked, "What now?"

"Our bedrooms," he aimed past the open kitchen to the end of the hall.

"Rooms?" I repeated, close at his feet. "Why plural?"

"This way," he indicated, and his birthmark twitched. "Paula and I always had separate bedrooms. From the beginning. The secret of why we're still talking to each other after thirty-five years is separate phones, separate bank accounts and separate bedrooms."

"Oh." My voice echoed through the hall. "Don't you think you've missed a lot of cuddling in your life?"

Orson swung around. His velvet voice was dissonant and haughty. "I've had all the cuddling I ever wanted."

His bedroom was dark, the curtains closed and the blinds let down. He switched on the lights and squinted his eyes. If it hadn't been for the queen-size bed with two bedside tables against the windows I'd have thought I was in a music library. Three walls of the large room were covered with dark wooden shelves holding an enormous collection of LP's, CD's, tapes and a complete sound system.

Orson walked to the middle of the Chinese rug and his arms gestured in a circle. "I have every work of the recorded repertoire. Imagine the millions of notes within the four walls of this room."

So, I thought, this was it. This was where he thought of me at night when he was unable to sleep. On a black velvet pillow, a black mask was hardly visible. I remembered what he had told me about his sleeping habits on our subway ride. *At night I wear a black sleeping mask while hanging upside down from the rafters.*

My eyes shot to the ceiling. To my relief there were no rafters.

Orson was standing by the bed, holding the mask. "I think I told you that I can't stand the daylight."

I sighed and tried to imagine what the room would look like with sunlight flooding in. Orson dropped the mask and slowly moved in my direction.

The expression of his eyes softened. A sudden vacuum surrounded us, a moment of utter nothingness, where the Chinese rug seemed to drop out from under our feet. As we stood face to face, his gray-metallic eyes captured mine, not allowing them to wander. He reached out to trace my hairline with his fingers, and then the contours of my face and lips, drawing a straight line down to the hollow of my throat.

For a moment he remained motionless, hardly touching me, but firmly locking my eyes in his. "Let go, Isabella. Just *feel.* I want you to feel naked even before you are."

His voice sounded as if it came from inside a sea-shell, a droning in my head. The room around us fell away, and his lips were mine and mine were his. His arms already knew all about me, sending a current through my skin like a shrill, ringing sound.

It rang again. It was the phone by Orson's bedside.

In the silence between two rings I held my breath. Would he pick up?

He would.

Before answering, he mumbled something to me that was supposed to sound like "sorry." A spark of resentment flared inside me. I turned on my heels and left the room.

Another door stood open. It was Paula's bedroom. Uncertain of what to do next, I hesitated. Fragments of Orson's voice tumbled, low and business-like, into the hall.

Still bewildered by the turn the situation had taken, I entered Paula's room. It was light and pink and pleasantly cluttered. Pink satin curtains flapped in the window. Dozens of perfume and prescription bottles mixed with heavy silver combs and brushes on the dresser. Under its glass top, family pictures were evenly lined up. Ah... here were the nieces in Connecticut whom she was presently visiting. In another shot Paula was holding a kitten and Orson a garden hose.

Glancing at the array of pink and white pillows on her bed, I imagined Paula at night, next to her pink teddy-bear, next door to Orson, brushing her hair or reading. My eyes fell on the book at her bedside. *The Complete Guide to Winning Poker* by Albert Morehead. I opened it and ran my fingers through the well-worn pages with highlighted paragraphs. The thought of Paula playing poker made me smile. I began to see her, as in a Polaroid picture that slowly came to life. I recalled my ride home with Matthew when he had told me about Paula's inertia and her painful ankles.

I read some of the titles on the shelf above her bed: *Specialty Baking, Cajun Cuisine, The Texas Cookbook, Fighting Depression.*

The woman's complex character puzzled me. The room seemed to vibrate with her presence, taking all the power out of Orson's words. *I want you to feel naked even before you are.*

How much pride did she have to swallow for the honor of being Mrs. Orson Mahler?

Orson stood behind me in the doorway, watching me. He seemed to pick up on my thoughts. "Food is Paula's avocation. Food as fashion, as a form of art. Food makes Paula feel secure."

I looked at Orson and disillusion seized me before he could even say the words.

"Sorry, Isabella, I have to leave. Immediately. Such is life. That was the Managing Director of Lincoln Center. The guest-conductor who was supposed to be here from Philadelphia has a personal emergency and the assistant conductor is having his tonsils out today. I have to lead the Philharmonic rehearsal at Avery Fisher Hall. And I have to conduct tomorrow night's concert too."

He checked his watch. "And I have fifteen minutes to get there."

We shared a glimpse of sadness, but it was fleeting. No, my visit had not worked out the way we had imagined. Neither of us said "another time."

Orson rushed along the corridor to his office. I followed him, not knowing why. "What are you going to rehearse?"

Instead of answering he asked, "Do you have time to come along? You're most welcome."

Did he really think I had made alternative plans for the rest of the afternoon?

With the sureness of his organized mind he aimed for the shelves. He reached for a large orchestral score positioned between other scores by Beethoven and Brahms.

"Here, will you hold this for a moment?"

I looked at the cover. *Symphonie Fantastique in C major, Op. 14*, by Hector Berlioz.

His tone was hurried and light-hearted. "I have to get my jacket and my briefcase, my keys and glasses, and uh... I should take a clean shirt, too."

Orson was ready to beat the world. Sex and seduction were forgotten. How true, I thought, when people say that men know only one love, *the world*… and that women knew only one world, *love.*

A minute later, he called building security for a cab and piloted me to the elevator.

33

In the taxi across town, a gentle sadness settled over me. The Berlioz orchestral score was open on his knees and Orson leafed through the pages, reading his markings from previous performances. Central Park flew by outside, and I thought back to my walk there with him in May. I felt like someone on a platform who had just missed the train. Did Orson feel the same way?

He said, "It's been a while since I conducted this work."

A brochure fell from the score and landed at my feet. I picked it up and saw that it was the program from a concert by the Los Angeles Philharmonic in January 1977, with Orson conducting the *Symphonie Fantastique.*

Orson looked at it. "You can read that during the rehearsal. I wrote the program notes, and I wish I could do that for all my concerts. In my mind, it's part of my responsibility to the public to bring out the best in a piece of music, not only by conducting it, but also by pointing out what I consider to be the most important elements to listen for and what one should know about the piece from an historical standpoint."

I studied the finely-boned face behind his dark glasses.

I said, "That's the concept of combining the emotional with the intellectual enjoyment of music."

"That's right. Did I talk to you about this before?"

"Yes," I gestured with my head towards the window, "right here in Central Park."

"Of course, I remember now." He smiled. "We walked up to the Checkers House and you had broken your heel."

Our eyes met. I nodded. "You said, *feel the music, feel life, even at the risk of messing it up.*"

There was a pause in which the vinyl of the seat cracked between us.

Orson's voice was soft and serious. "Isabella, are you sorry about what has happened since then?"

My carefully chosen lace bustier was beginning to scratch me, but I tried to project all the lightness I could muster. "Not yet, Orson. Not yet..."

His broad grin was interrupted by the honking of horns after which the traffic ground to a halt and our cab with it. Suddenly we were surrounded by police cars, blinking sirens, horses and security people.

"Oh, damn!" Orson addressed the driver. "Is there an accident?"

"No sir." He turned his head. "Looks more like a drug bust to me."

We heard a whistle and caught a glimpse of a man being handcuffed.

"Damn! Damn! Damn!" Orson's voice rose in angry arpeggios. "How long are we going to be stuck here?"

The driver shrugged. "No idea, sir," he pointed to the jam of stalled cars ahead of us. "There's nothing I can do."

With an impatient sigh, Orson fell back into the seat and drummed his fingers on the open score.

"Well, Isabella, are you familiar with the *Symphonie Fantastique?*"

"No, not very familiar," I said, meaning not at all.

Orson's dreamy smile indicated that his mind had crossed the border into a different world.

"It's perhaps *the* most romantic symphony ever composed, and what a sensation it must have caused in 1830, when Berlioz wrote it."

He opened the score at the beginning and ran his fingers along the staff lines.

"Look here... the long introduction. It's sprawling, building suspense..." His fingers flew through the pages. "You don't seem to know where it's going... and *finally* you get to the first theme. See here? And notice how long it is. This isn't anything you could whistle in the shower."

His face lit up. "This is a break-away from the classical form as it was observed by Mozart and Haydn. This is *Romanticism,* where the form is less important than the excitement of the instrumental sound. The music becomes a dream-like ebb and flow. Structure is replaced by unpredictability, effect, emotions and tone color. It's not so important anymore *what* is said, but *how* it's said."

The driver started the car.

"At least, we're moving," Orson exhaled with relief and continued, "Berlioz came up with a new kind of sound. He was twenty-seven when he wrote this, living in Paris. He subtitled the work *Episode in the Life of an Artist under the Influence of Opium."*

"Nothing much has changed, has it?" I remarked, looking behind us to where the police were shoving two men into a squad car.

Orson grimaced. "Unfortunately, you're right."

We had left Central Park and were turning into Columbus Avenue.

Orson closed his score. "Do you know the story behind the symphony?"

I shook my head.

"You'd like it," he mused and smiled at me teasingly. "This work was inspired by the Irish actress Harriet Smithson. She came to Paris with a Shakespearean company, and Berlioz fell in love with her when he saw her as Ophelia and Juliet. She refused his advances, wouldn't have anything to do with him, and he handed out flyers all over the city, proclaiming that his symphony was dedicated to her."

I said, "A true Romantic!"

Orson went on, "Berlioz symbolized her in the music by a melody, the *ideé fixe*, which acts as a motto theme, recurring in various guises in each of the five movements, almost like a Wagnerian leitmotif. Of course, Harriet was flattered. I suppose any woman would be. Anyway, she finally agreed to marry him."

At a traffic light, Orson squeezed my hand in a meaningful moment of silence.

Then he laughed grimly. "And that was their tragedy. In fact, the marriage was dreadful and ended in divorce. I'm afraid life isn't conducive to maintaining romance... but *what* Berlioz achieved by distilling his emotions into musical form!"

Our cab stopped in front of Avery Fisher Hall at Broadway. While Orson waited for his change, the driver said, "I should be paying you for the music lesson, Mr. Mahler."

"I'm glad you enjoyed it." Orson beamed and didn't wait for me to get out of the cab. He strode towards the stage entrance at his usual speed, forcing me to run to catch up with him.

At his side once again, I said, "Can I ask you a completely different question?"

He said impatiently, "No, you can't. All right, *what* is it?"

"Does Paula play poker?"

His face flushed with surprise. "Not that I know of. What an interesting idea. Paula playing poker..." He chuckled to himself as he walked even faster.

While he held the stage door open for me, I concluded that it had been a long time since he had paid a visit to his wife's bedroom.

34

"Good afternoon, Ladies and Gentlemen. I apologize for being late. I think we all know each other, and we are all familiar with the piece, so let's start right away at the beginning, bar one of the first movement, *Dreams, Passions*."

Seen from my seat in the darkness of the auditorium, Orson stood like a human tower on the podium. On the brightly lit stage he was surrounded by the large ensemble of the New York Philharmonic. He appeared much taller, exuding physical and mental authority as he raised both arms to indicate the downbeat.

Ah... how the bows rose and fell with the slow waves of his baton. Orson's hands conveyed communication as they led to creation. I closed my eyes and watched his hands conduct in the mirrors of my mind. I imagined them caressing me right at this moment, had he not picked up the phone.

The music stopped abruptly. I looked up. Orson had cut off the players in the middle of a phrase and shook his head. He crossed his arms as clear indication that he was about to make a speech.

"Ladies and Gentlemen, I'm fiercely determined to achieve the best. Therefore I suggest we seek to improve this passage. Please remember this is *romantic* music. This is *not* Mozart and I am *not* a metronome. Be more expressive, try to sweep the listener along. My tempo is going to be *unpredictable..."*

Some frowns ran across the musicians' faces, but there were nods too. When they resumed playing I wondered if Berlioz could have written such intense, emotional music without being driven by the inner turmoil of unrequited love. After all, the work had been composed *before* winning Harriet's hand.

From the back of the hall the sudden noise of a vacuum cleaner roared up. A janitor was just doing his job. In addition, a group of tourists was being ushered through the rows, and the harried voice of the guide warned them not to trip over the cord.

Alarmed by the commotion, Orson turned to the auditorium.

"That was *not* the kind of unpredictability I had in mind. I hope this noise doesn't constitute a permanent addition to the score."

The musicians grinned. Orson addressed them again.

"I cannot stress enough that this is less intellectual than sensual music. So let it breathe. There should be an exchange of give and take. Let's go back to letter 'N,' bar two twenty-seven."

But after thirty seconds Orson cut them off again. "No, no, no... may I ask you to be more alert. My indications are perfectly clear, but some of you are ignoring them. I'm fully aware that this rehearsal was called outside our regular schedule, and if some of you feel cheated of your nap, take comfort, so do I."

The ensuing laughter lightened the mood, and as they picked up their instruments, their spirits seemed to pick up too.

The tourists were asked to take seats and keep silent. Within minutes, they were either in rapt attention or peaceful slumber.

I was still holding Orson's Los Angeles Philharmonic program, but the light was too dim to read. I could barely make out the titles of the movements representing the *idée fixe,* the beloved one, set to sound.

She appears in a *Dream*, a *Ball*, *In the Meadows* and *Marching to the Scaffold*, where she falls under the guillotine as the music reaches a torrent of excitement to the point of hallucination. In the end, his beloved is nothing but an illusion, unreachable and lost forever in the *Dream of a Witches' Sabbath.*

Orson stopped the music in a repeated section of the fifth movement. He smiled. "Thank you, Ladies and Gentlemen. I think the rehearsal went beautifully. I'll see you all tomorrow night." And then he added jokingly with his eyes on his watch, "I'm letting you off eight minutes and twenty-three seconds early."

The musicians applauded lightly on their instruments and began to leave the stage. Orson, still on the podium, turned around, and his eyes darted through the darkness of the hall. "Isabella..? Are you still there?"

"Yes." I wasn't sure I had spoken loud enough, but I got up and walked down the aisle towards the stage. Orson was toweling his face. He looked tired but triumphant and glowed with perspiration. When he saw me he stepped to the edge of the stage and knelt down on one knee.

"Isabella, I'm glad you're still here. Just give me a moment to change my shirt." His eyes caressed my face. "Up there," he motioned to the podium, "I fantasized about you, how I could hold you in my arms instead of..." He shook his head and ran the towel through his disheveled hair. He whispered tenderly, "I'm sorry, Isabella... I'll make it up to you soon. Very soon."

I wondered if he knew how much he was capable of moving me and fought a rising tear. Or maybe it was just the lingering beauty of the music, or a combination of both. Against the empty stage I saw Orson through a thin veil of moisture.

He said softly, "Can you join me for dinner?" His hand reached out to touch my face but barely made itself felt. There was a fleeting moment between reality and dream.

I said, "I'm having dinner with my husband at the *Four Seasons*."

"Oh. I see." Orson cleared his throat. The dream was gone.

"What about tomorrow?" he asked with a new enterprising spirit. "Can you come to the concert? I'll have a ticket for you at the box office. We could meet around six-thirty for a light supper."

At last my head was clear again to think. Tomorrow morning James would fly to Cleveland and wouldn't return until late that night. My audition for the chorus was scheduled for five-thirty at CAMI Hall. The idea of celebrating my newly acquired membership with Orson couldn't suit me better.

"Fine," I winked at him. "By tomorrow I'll have a surprise for you."

35

As our car exited from Route 3 up the curve onto Valley Road, James rolled the window down. The saturation of summer was yielding to the first crispness of fall and we welcomed the cool night air on our faces.

By now my carefully chosen lace bustier was killing me.

James drove leisurely with his elbow resting on the open window. He sighed. "Man, am I full! Frankly, Isabella, I wish you wouldn't always make me eat half of your meal," and with a brief sideways glance, "You were unusually quiet tonight. Are you okay?"

I squared my shoulders and hastened to smile. "I'm fine, James, don't worry. The restaurant was an experience. At least now I know where Mr. Stringer takes his oh-so-efficient lady VP to lunch twice a week. It's a bit frustrating to always make reservations for someone else but never get to go there yourself."

James shrugged, "But you hardly touched your food."

I smoothed my blouse under the pressure of the seat belt.

"I just didn't want to overtax my stomach before the audition tomorrow. I'm afraid I already have butterflies."

"Aw," James waved his hand, "you'll breeze right through it. Just go ahead and do it, and don't worry so much."

How I wished he was right. But too much was racing through my head, and though it had been my wish to dine in the famous Pool Room of the *Four Seasons*, tonight the wish had turned into a waste. I had found it hard to concentrate on my salmon steak or James' elaboration about glycol esters and whether they could be used to make computer chips.

I had been too busy thinking about all the things I couldn't tell him. Yet the familiar timbre of his voice and the warmth of his brown eyes across the table had acted like a transfusion, cleansing my system with fresh oxygen and saving me from a feeling of suffocation. In James' reassuring presence, my visit to Orson's apartment seemed like an adventuresome farce from which the heroine had emerged unharmed, at least for now.

We passed Mount Hebron cemetery.

James broke the silence. "Anyway, I'm glad things are going a little smoother for you at work."

I yawned. "Mr. Stringer still thinks he's the best-looking man ever to grace the planet. But he's less demanding now, and he's finally resigned to the fact that his suggestive stare has no effect on me."

At a traffic light James grumbled, "If that bastard ever puts his hands on you..."

"I won't give him a chance."

"Good. It hasn't been an easy situation for you, but I know you can take care of yourself."

After a moment of silence, James's voice grew tender, almost tentative. "You know, even after all these years I still have this fantasy to elope with you, but then I realize all I have to do is take you home."

He pushed the button of the remote garage-door opener.

"And here we are. I'm a lucky man."

Every shade of James' feelings was etched on his face, and if hearts could break of confusion, mine would break now. In this moment nothing counted but the two of us. Together we felt something luminous and lofty, like an invisible ribbon encircling our souls and our skin.

James turned the headlights off. The wine was going to my head, and almost automatically my head sank against his shoulder. The garage door banged shut behind us.

James' hand raised my chin. "Hey, Beautiful."

Our lips met in a lush kiss. His fingers fumbled with the buttons of my blouse and ventured beneath it.

He said huskily, "Nice little lace thing you're wearing."

I kissed his earlobe. "You can take it off upstairs."

But his hand already groped for the hooks. "Why upstairs? Right here is just fine."

36

I sighed. This procedure was worse than applying for employment at the White House. The form I had to fill out was called "Personality Profile, Members of the Orson Mahler Oratorio Chorus," and my pen was inching through page three. Except for my voice part, what did my age, sex, parents, schools, colleges and countries visited have to do with the desire to sing? Would I be willing to participate in committees of fund-raising, reception planning or repertoire selection?

On the next line I reduced my seven years of piano lessons to four, just in case they would ask me to play, a notion that shook my carefully erected card-house of calm nerves.

During the day I hadn't allowed anything to get to me, including Mr. Stringer repeatedly banging his office door shut or requesting aspirin instead of cappuccino.

In fact, everything was quite nicely in place. I tried to visualize Orson's face when I told him over dinner that from now on he would see me every Wednesday night at rehearsal. Would the news delight or disturb him?

I had once asked him if he were ever present at the auditions for new chorus members.

"Very rarely." He had shrugged the idea off. "I have no time for it, except in emergencies, when Joan or Matthew can't be there, or I just feel like dropping in."

What a relief! Considering that he collaborated with the best voices of our times, singing for Orson would make me feel like a beggar asking for the crumbs of his acceptance. It would be less embarrassing to reveal my body than my voice to him, because I was less sure about the latter than the former. But Matthew had assured me that he would be there and I planned to give him a big hug and a box of *Mozartkugeln* from Austria once everything was over.

Back to the questions on the application form.

Other previous or present chorus associations? "None."

Foreign languages? "German, French, some Italian."

Through the thick door to the adjoining room, the sound of a soprano and a piano penetrated incoherently. At last I signed my name at the bottom of page four, as Joan leaned her slim ballerina figure through the door.

"Isabella? You're next. Bring your forms along."

The soprano who was leaving held the door open for me. After a few steps into the hall I was struck by lightning. Joan and Daisy were sitting behind a table and Orson was at the piano.

A lump formed, rock-like, in my throat.

Orson nodded politely with a straight, uninvolved face. Had he known about this all along? I stepped to the table, looking for a manhole.

"Isabella, are you all right?" Joan was gently asking.

"A little nervous." I turned my back to Orson and handed her the forms.

Joan leafed through them and nodded approvingly.

"So, you're an alto, Isabella."

Daisy, angel-faced as ever, smiled encouragingly. Her sneakered feet dangled like a child's, barely touching the floor.

She frowned prettily. "Matthew isn't here today, but you have the honor of Mr. Mahler accompanying you."

I briefly turned around but couldn't bring myself to look at him. Paradoxically I wondered if the box of *Mozartkugeln* was melting in my purse.

"Here is the material you'll be singing." Daisy handed me two pages of sheet music that smelled vaguely of lemon. I wondered which part of the Brahms Requiem it would be. My mind blanked at the title. It wasn't Brahms. It was Mozart. I was going to be auditioned on a fugue from the Mozart *Mass in C-Minor*.

I said with rising desperation, "I'm not prepared for this. I thought I was going to be auditioned on the *Brahms Requiem*."

Joan's charcoal-penciled eyelids didn't waver.

"We had a last-minute repertoire change for technical reasons. Besides, you're not supposed to know the music in advance. We want to see how well you can sight-read."

"I can't do this!" My voice screeched like the wagon wheels in Central Park, but it was already drowned by the opening chords from the piano. Orson was playing right past my entrance. How many bars had I missed? Tentatively, I began to form sounds, *Allegro comodo*, as Mozart had indicated, trying to connect the notes as if jumping over precipices. The black, running sixteenth notes spread along the staff lines like a wallpaper pattern before the eyes of a drunk. The words *in excelsis* made me squeeze my voice into ugly shrillness, and when it faltered at a repeated section, I heard Orson's voice from far away, "Go on" (I thought), but it was too late to think. I kept singing in spite of myself, and felt infinitely foolish in continuing my hopeless mission.

The piano ended on a "G," but my voice clearly didn't.

My cheeks flamed in a moment of uncertain silence. Peripherally I saw Orson's forehead knitted in a frown, as if he didn't want to slam the door of hope. A comment had to be made and there was no diplomatic way to make it.

Daisy cleared her throat. "Sorry, Isabella. Your voice was not quite on pitch, and you missed several entrances. I'm afraid we can't let you pass."

Joan tapped her sand-colored nails on the table.

"I'm sure you understand that we have to maintain our standards." Her tone contained an arrogance she took no trouble to conceal.

I nodded. At least it was over and I almost welcomed the sinking feeling in my stomach as a final act of defeat.

Orson whirled around on his swivel stool. His tone was a little forced. “Ladies, let me suggest bending the rules a bit...”

I dared to look at him for the first time.

He suppressed any expression in his face.

“Why don’t we let Isabella come to the rehearsals and have her repeat the audition at a later date.”

Joan’s delicate jaw moved uncompromisingly and, next to her, Daisy’s rosy cheeks grew ashen. They nodded with glacial grace, but would never forgive Orson for this. He had wounded their vanity by interfering with their administrative power.

I managed to say, “Thank you, Mr. Mahler,” and our eyes met for a piercing moment.

Orson forced his velvet voice into unsuspicious practicality.

“We’ll see you Wednesday night, Isabella.”

What could I do but pick up my courage, along with my purse, and leave? Joan dismissed me with a condescending look and Daisy’s voice sounded icily behind me.

“We have one more auditionee, Isabella. Could you ask Jess Samson to come in?”

Through a veil of mist and shame I perceived a good-looking young man in an impeccable three-piece suit.

“Good luck,” I muttered and let him pass in front of me.

From under a thick row of lashes he smiled at me warmly. The running mascara on my cheeks was comment enough on the outcome of my hearing.

On the street again, I felt like an asthmatic gulping for air. The winds of a distant storm made my skirt billow like a spinnaker sail.

What now? *Allegro furioso* and *accelerato*. The sky was dark and almost touchable. Under its pressure, I began to walk faster and faster, though my legs felt like lead.

We have to maintain our standards, echoed in my ears.

And now dinner with Orson! How I dreaded facing him. Would he tiptoe around the delicate situation or add fuel to the fire and make a complete fool of me?

Why don't we let Isabella come to our rehearsals and have her repeat the audition at a later date...? How belittled I felt by his attempt to compromise.

I swore by the dreary horses lining Central Park South that I would repay him for this. And then, angry with myself, I realized the injustice I was doing him by making him the scapegoat for my insufficient talents. With each step closer to Lincoln Center my mood worsened and the whole city turned into a witch's cauldron of menace and meanness.

In a daze of discouragement I began to walk in circles around the Lincoln Center fountain. The dreaded images of Orson's hands on the piano keyboard and Daisy handing me the sheet music seemed to be reflected on the water, sending a chill through my skin and making me homesick for my lake in Austria. In times of distress I had always surrendered to the elementary powers of water, cooling, cleansing and curative. Even if only temporarily, swimming had always freed me from the dry land of earthly troubles. To submerge myself in water meant reaching safety, and often I could hear my name in the whisper of waves splashing among the reeds before washing ashore.

"*Isa..bell..a..Isa..bell..a.*"

"Isabella!" A voice disrupted my reveries.

Orson was behind me.

37

I turned around and almost stumbled over him.

His "hello" was said in perfect equanimity.

"Hello," I hardly moved my lips, "how did you manage to get here so fast?"

"I took a cab. In fact I was here before you, but you didn't see me. I watched you walking around the fountain. You were miles away."

"Yes, I was."

Silence. For now, he skipped any reference to my lack of singing talent. For a split second I was about to dissolve in tears on his shirt-front, but the urge was counteracted by a sense of pride.

"I'm upset," I sniffled and wiped my cheek with the back of my hand. "Nothing's working out. *Nothing*. Not yesterday, not today."

He offered me his handkerchief like a doctor handing out a placebo. "I know, Isabella. Things could be better."

Under Orson's helpless glaze, I blew my nose resoundingly.

The flash of a thought crossed his face like a struck match.

"Do you want to hit me?"

"Hit you?"

"Sure, what's a friend for?" he shrugged. "If it makes you feel better..."

His suggestion triggered a wave of recklessness in me.

He insisted, "I want you to know that I'm not just a fair-weather friend."

I hesitated. But as he opened up his arms invitingly I gave in to an impulse I hadn't known before. My fists hammered against him, sending a hail of blows against his chest and shoulders.

"Try harder," he challenged me, and I complied, startled at my pleasure.

Orson didn't budge. He let it happen. In a deep, dark way he loved it. But for how long? I seemed to fall through spheres of violet clouds, until my energy subsided and I snapped out of my seizure.

Orson's face was white. My God, I thought, in less than two hours he had to conduct the New York Philharmonic and, of all places, we were in the middle of Lincoln Center Plaza, where the presence of the pre-theater crowd was already making itself felt. But I was pushing things from bad to worse. Filled with remorse, I collapsed against his chest and buried my face against his shoulder. Strong winds announced the storm, and my skirt fluttered around his legs.

His arms around me breathed new life into me.

I whispered, "I'm sorry, Orson. I didn't mean it."

He took me by the shoulders. "Oh yes, *you did.*" He laughed. "You don't have to lie to spare my feelings."

The truth was, I felt light-hearted enough to waltz around the fountain, whose lights were just being turned on for the night.

Carefully, I looked around, fearing a hundred gossip-hungry eyes on us, but miraculously nobody seemed to care about this non-descript man with dark glasses and a tall blonde engaged in a tantrum.

We took a step back from each other.

Orson grinned. "You're pretty strong, young lady."

I smiled. "I feel much better now. And I'm starved."

"I guess that means we're on for dinner." He checked his watch and took my arm. Wordlessly, we started walking. Our emotions had reached a healthy resolution, but there was a nakedness between our minds. Had we already become so close, or was our silence a failure to connect?

We passed the glass display cases for the coming concert season. Orson gestured with his head to one of the posters.

"I don't like that picture of me."

I protested, "Why not? It's a good picture of you."

"Yes, unfortunately, I'm afraid it is," he frowned. "I never liked my looks."

The first raindrops made me cling more tightly to his arm.

"Orson Mahler," I said solemnly, "your looks are not the most important thing about you."

He said, somewhat surprised, "What is it about me then... What do you want from me, Isabella?"

We passed Alice Tully Hall. I savored a little moment of suspense.

"I want your body and your mind."

Orson drew me closer. "Fine," he said, "that settles matters."

Despite the rain, our steps were free and easy. A moment later we pushed through the glass door of *Federico's* restaurant. It was Friday and the place was packed, but there was always room for Maestro Mahler.

We were given a table against a mirrored wall in the back room and under the stare of an attractive brunette seated at the table next to us. Her pink Chanel suit and tons of costume jewelry made her the most visible person in the room. From the moment we sat down she kept her gaze unerringly on Orson.

He and I sipped drinks and picked at red peppers and black olives. Heads turned and people smiled and whispered, making me terribly self-conscious.

Without his glasses, Orson's eyes were filled with stars.

"I'm elated."

"About what?" My fingers played with the vase of red carnations.

"That you *really* want me."

I gave a sentimental smile, "I guess I have the emotional flu and it's too late to fight it."

Under the table his legs braced mine from both sides.

"I'm not going to let you out of this again."

The pink brunette kept her antenna out for any scrap of information. I didn't think Orson was aware of her.

Halfway through our "Seafood Mediterranée," Orson put his fork down.

"You know, Isabella, 'being in love' is not a matter of the logical mind, it's more like an Act of God. I've often thought we have to deal with it in the same category as a fire, a flood or a storm. The survivors usually emerge healed or hurt. A love affair is like a hurricane of the heart, and there is not much that we can do to start or stop it. Or can we really?" He beamed with genuine delight.

I said, "That was a really nice speech."

We traded silent smiles. Outside it was raining and the flashing red light of an ambulance reflected on the faces of the people sitting by the window.

Orson said, "You look embarrassed."

"I'm not good at hiding it."

"Good. You look quite beautiful like that. Embarrassment is an important part of pleasure and it will heighten your excitement." Orson basked in his devilish advantage with an angelic smile.

I didn't dare look at the pink brunette. Was she still staring at us? Orson reached across the table. His fingers were eager to wrap themselves around mine.

"And something else, Isabella, I want to settle one thing."

"Yes?" I put my hand in his.

"I never sail under false colors."

I held my breath without knowing why.

There was no malice in his voice. "I can't promise fidelity."

I sat very still. His words fell like a bomb between us and the room went dead. My hand jerked away from his as if from a hot kettle and I moved back against the wall, repelled by the poison of his smile.

"Excuse me, maestro, for intruding on your meal." The voice with the French accent belonged to the pink brunette standing at our table. She presented her business card from a Paris concert agency. She didn't want to let this heaven-sent chance slip without talking to him. Of course she was coming to the concert tonight.

Orson, having endured this kind of talk for decades, showed no sign of impatience. How happy he was under the look of unknown eyes, bathing in anonymous adulation. He displayed his magic smile, of which I was no longer part or wished to be.

In my abrupt resolve to leave, I overturned the vase of red carnations.

"Excuse me." I avoided his eyes. "I'd better get in line at the box-office for my ticket."

"Come and see me in the Green Room after the concert," I heard Orson's unaffected voice, and I was not sure if he was talking to me or to her.

It didn't matter anymore. All I wanted was to get out of here before I suffocated.

What next? Outside it was pouring. My tightening stomach told me I was not going to the concert. Waiting up for James and bawling in his arms over my failed audition was now more appealing than watching Orson bow to waves of applause.

Under rolls of thunder I ran back to Avery Fisher Hall. It offered a dry place for the crisis to sink in. The lobby was jammed with concert-goers and dripping umbrellas.

A big poster of Orson made me want to punch it. How skillfully he had coaxed me into accepting something unacceptable, confident that the temporary absence of protest would lead to a slide in attitude, until it became his rule. Was I really desperate for what he had to offer?

First of all, I was desperate for an umbrella.

An usher announced that the concert was sold out, which left a line of long faces at the box office window. One of them looked strikingly familiar. It was Jess. Was it... Jess Samson?

The good-looking young man from the audition played undecidedly with his umbrella. He had obviously counted on attending the concert and now he was not sure what to do with the rest of the evening.

"Jess Samson?" I walked up to him. "I'm Isabella Barton. We met earlier at the auditions, at CAMI Hall."

His green eyes smiled under a row of lashes too perfect for a man. It took him a moment to make the connection. No wonder, I thought, I must look awful. I was soaked, in tears, and in the mood for murder.

Skipping the preliminaries, I said, "I'll make a deal with you. There's a ticket in my name at the box-office. You can have it in exchange for your umbrella."

The surprise on his face!

I added, "The storm will be over by the time the concert ends."

Jess revealed a row of perfect white teeth. I wondered if he was in modeling.

"Are you sure you don't want to use the ticket for yourself?"

"No. I have an emergency," I said importantly, feeling that my state of nerves qualified for the description. Anyway, the deal was done and the goods were traded.

Now home. On the street again, rain spattered everywhere around me. To catch my bus at the Port Authority I had to negotiate twenty-three blocks of puddles, but I decided that a brisk walk might help to lead me out of the twilight zone of uncertainty to the answer of a question. The question was whether to dump Orson or not.

His voice sounded in my ears as I crossed against a red light at Columbus Circle. *I can't promise fidelity.* It was hard to tell if his weapon of truth was easier to fight than a carefully concealed lie. They say that barking dogs don't bite. Maybe Orson needed to secure the idea rather than the reality of his emotional freedom. Gradually, with every block I walked, and every breath I took, I tried to convince myself not to worry about fixing something that wasn't broken yet.

I clutched Jess's umbrella and a crack of thunder made me shudder. At Forty-Second Street, before boarding my bus home, I found Orson's handkerchief in the pocket of my jacket and blew my nose and dried my tears.

All things considered, if I had known or even faintly suspected the course of today's events, I'd have rather stayed longer in the office and made new labels for the files.

38

The view from our bedroom window offered just the right frame for a painting of our backyard, with its cherry tree, shrubs and a small flower bed all connected by a pleasantly overgrown lawn. From upstairs, I waved to James and Barry sitting in jeans and T-shirts on wicker chairs on the deck. They were enjoying the setting sun, the suburban air, peanuts and root beer. A study in male bonding. In the decline of summer the colors were like photographs taken through a gold-filtered lens.

James got up to turn on the lawn sprinkler. My fascination with its mechanism had always been more aural than visual. It was less its proudly tossed fan of water moving from side to side that inspired my attention than the rustling sound of the water hitting the lilac bushes, alternating with the hushed silence of the leaves recovering from the shower.

Under the fragments of conversation that drifted through the open window, I slid out of my pumps and my suit to leave the day at work behind. In the bathroom I pulled my hair into a pony tail and slipped into an oversized T-shirt that expressed pretty much my state of mind.

I'd rather be hunting and fishing in Montana.

Downstairs in the kitchen I removed the pot of my home-made minestrone from the refrigerator and rattled some ice cubes into my glass of orange juice. I wondered about Angela. Where was she? She usually never let Barry out of her sight.

I stepped outside, and it looked as if a huge golden orange were floating between the lilac bushes and the driveway, with the lawn sprinkler flashing split seconds of a rainbow.

"Hi, guys." I greeted James and Barry with a fleeting kiss. It felt good to collapse on the wicker bench and put my feet up on a chair. James was explaining how to affix enzymes to bonded silica particles, and one look at Barry was enough to tell me he was lost. To James' distress, he could hardly ever move his audience beyond polite endurance.

Barry looked unkempt. He had deep lines between his bushy eyebrows, and there was no light in his blue eyes. His pipe sat, cold and abandoned, next to the root beer bottle, in an ashtray.

Except for the hiss of the sprinkler the air was unusually quiet. Even the birds seemed to hold their breath. The sound of James' steady voice was more soothing than its subject.

My eyes fell on my modest contribution to gardening. I had planted geraniums and begonias in the spring and they looked quite lovely. Barry furrowed his bushy eyebrows as he followed the focus of my eyes.

"Who planted this?" His voice bore an aggressive edge.

"I did. Why?" I stirred the straw in my glass.

James, having exhausted his silica particle soliloquy, nodded his head in my direction. "Isabella did a nice job, didn't she?"

Barry grimaced. "How can you plant geraniums with begonias, two shades of red that don't match?"

"All colors match in nature." I swung my legs to the floor, annoyed at his carping.

Barry gulped down a handful of peanuts and insisted. "You should have planted yellow marigolds and geraniums *or* begonias for color contrast."

My voice rose sourly. "Barry, sweetie, my bus got stuck in the Lincoln tunnel for twenty minutes, my boss's cappuccino-maker broke, and I lost the memory in the fax-machine. All I need is your advice on color contrast to make my day perfect."

Barry scratched his beard. “Isabella, sweetie, I guess along with the memory of your fax machine you lost your sense of humor too.”

Broodingly, I ran my fingernails along the lines of the wicker texture. The leaves moved in the breeze as if bewailing something unsaid. Barry cleared his throat and said in a conciliatory manner, “I really wanted to thank you for the great party, Isabella.”

I quipped, “Well, it’s about time you and Angela sent me a thank-you note.”

A tormented smile crossed Barry’s face. He untied one of his sneakers and emptied a piece of gravel out of it.

James’ eyes dashed helplessly from me to him.

“Isabella, give Barry a break. He’s upset.”

A few reddish clouds extended the twilight in which I tried to read in James’ face what he was *not* to telling me.

“What happened?” I asked into the silence.

James said, “Angela left Barry.”

The impact of his words was like a rock bouncing off water before sinking in.

I gave Barry an inquisitive look.

He shrugged. “Yup... she did.”

“But *why*?”

Hurt was written all over Barry’s face and speaking about it seemed harder than he was willing to admit. He hunched down in his chair. “I’m not sure. It just happened. Last Wednesday. A limousine pulled up and took her along with four suitcases to the airport. She’s back with her family in Rome now.”

James and I sat motionless.

Barry cleared his throat. “And just before she left she had the nerve to tell me, with her big laugh, that some months ago she had a fling with one of my colleagues at the hospital, but that he turned out to be an awkward lover.”

In a desperate effort to make Barry feel better I said, “I’m sure she meant to pay you an indirect compliment, as a parting gift, so to speak.”

But Barry exploded. "A parting gift? Telling me she cheated on me? You must be kidding, Isabella. I told her to get out of my house before I kicked her out."

His hands shook as he poured himself another glass of root beer. Surely his agitation made him oblivious to the sight of the first fireflies dotting the lawn like sprinkled stars.

Barry's voice was drained of life. "I felt it coming but I didn't want to face it. Maybe I couldn't take the guilt any longer for not responding to her *when-do-we-get-married* pleas, or maybe..," he paused, "maybe I just stopped being in love with her."

He took a tissue from his pocket and pressed it against his face. There was nothing James and I could do but listen.

"You know," Barry poured himself another glass, "our sex life was still good. But there are twenty-three other hours in a day, and when you run out of things to say to each other, it's a sure sign of trouble. Our feelings never reached the level of animosity. It was worse. Disillusionment turned into boredom."

James got up to move the sprinkler. Our silence grew like the long shadows on the lawn. It was not so much the loss of Angela that saddened Barry, but perhaps the loss of a part of himself that he had to let go along with her.

The dusk dissolved from gray to dark, clothing the backyard in a black disguise. I stood up and lit a candle in a storm light on the table.

Barry looked at James. "James, could you forgive Isabella if she told you about an affair, say... with your boss?"

James' mouth curved into a bemused smile.

"That would never happen."

Barry leaned forward and rested his elbows on his knees.

"Then what's the secret of your relationship?"

James ran his hand through his slightly too-long hair.

"Between Isabella and me?" He shrugged. "It's easy."

"*What's* easy?" Barry appeared terrified that he might have missed out on some magic formula.

James' laugh was that of a winner.

"It's really easy. I'm crazy about Isabella, and Isabella... is just plain crazy." He gave me a playful pat on the arm.

Barry's eyelids seemed heavy under the weight of confusion.

James went on. "Isabella is enchantingly crazy and often unpredictable, and yet she's so vulnerable at times that I want to shield her from the real world so she can live in her own. That's really it. That's why I love her."

His eyes, searching for mine, tore at my heart-strings. I knew that James' words would never leave me, even in Orson's arms, should they ever hold me.

Barry turned to me. "What about you, Isabella? What do you think the bond is between the two of you?"

"Mmm," I heard my voice as from a distance. "I truly love James. He is my refuge against loneliness and doubt. There's a natural chemistry between us, and I don't mean his enzymes or silica particles. James loves the person I am and not the one I *should* be. He doesn't care what I plant, be it marigolds, geraniums, begonias… or pumkins. He just lets me be *me.*"

"I see." A tiny smile crossed Barry's face but he wasn't satisfied. "Don't you ever fight about small stuff?"

I shrugged. "Could be. Sometimes. I can't think of anything right now."

James said, "What's so important about small stuff?"

Barry displayed a defeated smile. "You win. I guess the name of the game is finding the right person and not worrying about geraniums and marigolds."

I was about to bring up the subject of dinner when a car pulled into our driveway.

"It's Julia!" I got up and turned on the yard light. "She called me at the office today. She's cleaning out her apartment and wants to drop off some CDs she borrowed."

Her wooden sandals clicked on the deck and her ash-blonde hair shone silvery against the dark. James pulled up another chair but she refused with a wave of her hand. She and Barry nodded at each other with ill-concealed embarrassment, his blue eyes locked in her brown ones. Something that was almost tenderness replaced the tension in his face, as if a simple turn of the kaleidoscope of fate could change the pattern of a life forever.

But Julia shied away from Barry's searching stare and deposited my CDs on the table. She played nervously with her car keys, explaining that she had to go home to feed her dog.

"Nice seeing you," she whispered and left as promptly as she had arrived.

Unexpectedly, Barry called after her. "Julia, are we going to see you around some time?"

Her hair fluttered as she stopped and turned. Her face was hidden in the dark and her thin voice didn't carry well enough against the distant rattling of a passing truck. She left soundlessly, like the fade-out at the end of an old movie.

As the headlights of her car flared, Barry let out a high-strung laugh. What was it about Julia that pushed so many buttons in him?

The crickets had begun their song, and their monotony soothed our busy minds, buzzing with things said and unsaid. There was nothing else for the three of us to share. James and I knew that none of our efforts to be supportive would help ease Barry's unsettled state of mind. Now that he had shared his misery with us, he was erecting a silent wall around himself that we didn't dare cross.

My eyes followed the on-and-off dance of the fireflies. How they resembled human passions: They filled the night with glow and glitter, but faded into blandness at the awakening of dawn.

Barry started rubbing his eyes. James yawned.

I said, "How about some home-made minestrone, and some cheese, grapes and vanilla cookies?"

39

Unless there were an earthquake or a tidal wave, fate could no longer intervene. The pieces were finally falling into place for Orson and me. Today I hadn't bothered with my scratchy lace bustier, but I applied my mother's *Eau de Joy* to bolster my courage. At three-thirty in the afternoon the outbound Manhattan traffic was running a lot smoother than the blood in my veins.

Orson's fear of being recognized in a Manhattan hotel left no other choice than to take him across the state line to New Jersey. My fingers clamped tensely around the steering wheel while Orson, next to me, was completely at ease. At long last, at the edge of intimacy, our eyes met in the contract that would soon be signed by our bodies.

Orson smiled, "Excited?"

"Mmm." I hoped my stomach would unknot.

"Remember," Orson said, "I want you to be eager and not anxious."

"Yes, yes... I know the difference."

"Take a deep breath." His hand was unsettling on my shoulder.

By the time we came out of the Lincoln Tunnel it was drizzling. Where were we headed? Through the rhythm of the windshield wipers we began to look for signs, selectively and silently.

No turns. Headlights out. Turnpike Arcade. Exit. Tick Tock Diner. Quality Inn. Harmon Cove Exit. Hilton. Sports Complex. Howard Johnson's marquee, *Have your affair with us.*

To ease the uncertainty of the moment, I said, "Maybe someday we'll think back and laugh about this rainy Monday in September when we stole away like thieves..."

The way he beamed at me was *con amore* and a flash of mischief.

"You see, Isabella, for me the two most sublime things in life are making love to music by conducting, and, putting music into love-making. The first one is a lot of work. It's an intellectual and mechanical process to rehearse a piece to the point where it technically conveys the right emotion. And that happens only after a considerable amount of drudgery." He moved his beaten briefcase from his lap and braced it between his legs.

"Whereas the second," he continued, "putting music into love-making, can be achieved with much more ease. You only have to *feel,* to let go completely and surrender to your senses."

I nodded and changed lanes to pass a truck, only half listening to him.

Orson, whose concerts had taken him all over the world, had seldom been to New Jersey, and he looked right and left as if he were touring the planet Venus.

He smiled luxuriously. "Ah, there is no greater pleasure in the world than making love. Do you realize that it is the only art that involves all five senses?" He paused to space every word. "Touch, sight, hearing, taste and smell. And I also think in that order of importance."

I decided to think about this later and kept my concentration on the road.

However, when Orson whispered with a devilish grin, "I can't wait to find out how you smell and taste," I resented his ability to make me blush.

More signs flew by. Computerland. Bus lane closed. Days Inn. Bridge. Passaic River. Shell. Catering. Lounge.

By now it was raining hard.

We pulled into a place that, past the entrance, opened to an inner courtyard with a trickling fountain in the middle. My heartbeat went: *We-made-it.*

Orson nodded. I pulled into the parking lot. We looked at each other like two people who were about to begin to live.

Orson smiled but showed no sign of further action.

He cleared his throat. "In the interest of discretion, would you do me a favor and check in?"

"You can't be serious."

But Orson was. As he took out his wallet to hand me some bills a battle began to rage inside me. If I wanted to through with this I'd have to throw aside all notions of chivalry or convention.

Stupefied, I took Orson's money and Jess's umbrella and started jumping over puddles, past the trickling fountain and across the courtyard to the office.

This was far from my concept of a traditional beginning to overwhelming passion. On entering the lobby, I was convinced that I had fallen prey to some terrible force outside myself. At the desk another customer was still being helped. While waiting, I made sure I had my driver's license ready and an impenetrable expression on my face. Under the eyes of the man behind the desk I shrank into my raincoat like Alice after drinking the potion.

"Can I help you ma'am?"

The rain sliced against the huge glass windows behind me.

"I'd like a room for three hours."

This was no longer the good-mannered girl my mother had so carefully brought up.

The voice asked, "Do you want a room with whirlpool or rent movies?"

"No."

I wasn't receptive to any unexpected questions and filled out the registration slip in a handwriting that wasn't meant to be deciphered.

A key that read "44" was pushed across the counter. This was the point of no return and the pinnacle of my unease. At least, I inhaled deeply, it was over now. Again I opened Jess's umbrella, jumped over the puddles past the trickling fountain and across the courtyard and drove the car to No. 44.

"Would you go in," Orson said, devoid of romantic warmth, "and check whether the room is properly made up and the air-conditioning is working."

I couldn't believe he was putting me through this. But my thinking this would be the end of my tribulations proved to be delusive. Room 44 was *not* made up.

My first reaction, "Good thinking, Orson," was followed by a new realization. Obviously this was not his first experience of this kind. I got the notion that I was being punished for my sin before committing it. I had to open Jess's umbrella *again,* jump over the puddles, past the trickling fountain, across the courtyard and return the key. What a compromising prologue to the imminent engulfment of erotic pleasures! Momentarily, I fled into the thought of dropping everything, including Orson and the key, and driving off home. Although this was not the right time for feelings of hostility toward Maestro Mahler, I couldn't help thinking, To hell with his high-minded notion of the art of making love if he refuses to handle the basic courtesy of obtaining a room.

Surprisingly, the strain of inner combat made me more self-assured. This time I looked the man behind the desk straight in the eye.

"Room 44 is not made up."

"Sorry, ma'am."

Within three seconds I had another key. It was No. 23.

The rain didn't let up. With gritted teeth I opened Jess's goddamn umbrella, jumped over the goddamn puddles, past the goddamn trickling fountain, and across the courtyard to the car and drove it to No. 23.

This time I handed the key to Orson. "It's your turn, maestro. Could you also check if there is a mini-bar and enough towels?" Poison and pleasure mixed in my voice.

Behind his dark glasses, Orson made a face, as if someone had stolen his baton. But he got out.

With my arms crossed over the steering wheel I watched him step through the downpour and insert the key in the lock. For a moment I closed my eyes as if to convince myself that this was a wicked dream that would be gone when I opened them again.

When Orson returned to the doorway and gestured for me to come in, shouldn't I have felt excitement beyond words? What a pity not to be thrilled at a moment like this.

40

Inside the room, Orson made sure that the lock was firmly secured. I was standing in the middle of the earth-colored carpet and shivering in my raincoat. *So*. This was it. The consummation of our romantic promises was taking place in this ordinary room that could be on any highway between New York and San Francisco. I found it hard to convince myself that reaching the destination equaled the significance of all the moments leading up to it. The desert colors of the bedspread, the drapes and the prints on the walls reminded me of a room where James and I had once stayed in Santa Fe.

I said politely, "It's a nice room."

Orson displayed an enterprising smile. "We'll make it nice."

He crossed the room with bouncy strides, closed the curtains and turned off the lights, leaving us surrounded by colorless, dim shadows. When Orson put his watch and wallet on the dresser it seemed like the scene of an old movie which I was watching but in which I had no part.

My eyes followed the woman who threw her raincoat on a chair. I thought that she was never going to forget this day, not in her whole life… the rain, the puddles, the trickling fountain and the desert colors of the room. This was comparable to losing her virginity, only now she was crossing the threshold to adultery.

Orson looked at her from the bathroom door across the room.

His velvet voice said, "Nothing will happen against your will."

His arms threw long shadows on the wall as he opened them to catch her in a wave of warmth. Did she run to him because she felt anxiety or eagerness? His embrace created a different space, a secluding spell, another room within a room in which the woman became *me.*

Orson whispered. "This place only exists because we are here."

"We *are* here, Orson. We finally made it."

My life impulse rebounded with a sense of complicity for a team's victory over a difficult plan.

And here it was again, the gleam of joy in Orson's eyes, as if he had shut it away, sealed and held in readiness, for this moment. His kiss made me wish for a place outside of time and space. And then a slow, sweet sureness sang in my heart. *Yes... it was going to be wonderful.*

Orson put me on the bed and his command was soft, but firm.

"Don't move. Leave everything to me."

I felt his long arms around my shoulders and his velvet voice close to my ear. "If we had all the time in the world I'd spend hours just making love to your face."

I moved a little.

He said, "Lie still," and his lips started exploring every feature of my face the way a blind man tries to see by touch. But Orson moved with open eyes. He moved leisurely, like a violin player lingering over every phrase of his favorite sonata. Orson's kisses on my lips were spaced by unhurried pauses. Empty pauses. Empty with excitement. It was the excitement of the silence between lightning and thunder that carried the full impact of the storm.

He said, "This is a prelude to the pleasures of your body."

Ah, the tide of tenderness broke a wave over my head. How good it felt to drown. In the slow dawn of desire I responded with a soft moan of longing.

Orson beamed. "Can you hear yourself, Isabella? You make such lovely sounds. You become a soprano." His voice had the delight of discovery.

"Listen to yourself... With the sounds you make, you become more and more naked, and I haven't even started to undress you yet."

He begun to unbutton my blouse and his eyes followed each gesture of his hands.

"You probably want me to go faster, but there is so much beauty to appreciate along the way."

I felt my cheeks glow and my body stiffen.

"Easy Isabella... don't make me rush."

Every nerve I owned was on the edge of burning. I was grateful for the softness of his touch and the sureness of his lips and hands. He wanted to find out all about me, as if he had wondered about every curve and indentation or the feeling of my pulse in a narrow vein, and now he wanted to make sure that he had imagined right.

"Your body is a piece of art, but much more beautiful because it *lives.* Look at the lines and shadows of your breast," he smiled. "How did you manage to grow them this way?"

The hunger in his eyes made me feel like the first woman he had ever seen. He took off his clothes in record time and refused my offer to take part in the action. He insisted. "Not today. Today I don't want you to have any other responsibility than to lie back and accept pleasure."

To see him naked told me that the disciplined energy governing his mind also shaped his body. His lean, muscular torso was a curious contrast to his long, thin legs, a thinness that couldn't be guessed under the protection of his clothes.

As he lowered himself over me I inhaled the aroma of his skin.

His voice was tinged with hoarseness. "Isabella, your body is like a map of pleasure with instructions printed all over it, and there is no way to stop the trip."

At the first contact of his birthmark brushing against my thighs my longing soared into fire.

Orson raised his head. "Now I know that you are a *real* blonde.

I whispered, "Don't stop what you are doing."

He smiled. "That's exactly what I want to hear."

I felt my body open up, dissolving the limits between permission and pleasure, guilt and glory. And finally, as I was short of begging him, he came into me. It was effortless and easy.

While the shadows of our bodies danced in the pulse of pleasure, we were far away from falling in love. But rather we were rising. Not together, but each of us finding our own body's measure to arrive at the climax of desire.

Orson's voice floated with jubilation. "Oh, it's wonderful, it's glorious to make love to you, Isabella. And your squirms are thrilling... No music ever written can match the excitement of your sounds."

Excitement was followed by ease, and tension by tenderness. We came to a place we never knew existed. Or had we been here before? How many lifetimes had we been apart before finding each other again?

As if happiness were too much to bear, I closed my eyes. I had reached the center of the universe and knew all its powers. It had happened. I had committed adultery, and the fact could never be reversed. But the intense pleasure of the moment made me forget all my promises and problems, even James.

The world was perfect. There was nothing that needed to be changed. In a lingering hint of *Eau de Joy,* the desert colors of the room swam before my eyes.

Smiling his unique magic smile, Orson wrapped his arms around me. "Isabella, do you know what it means, to hold and to behold you?"

But oddly enough his words hardly reached my ears, because my mind was somewhere else.

Maybe there was nothing good or bad, but thinking made it so.

Part Two

- Andante –

(Experience)

Two loves I have –
of comfort and despair.

William Shakespeare

41

I returned home with my mind made up to feign passionate interest in today's *Art and Leisure* section of the *New York Times* and then to become overwhelmed by a sudden need for sleep. Would James notice that the weariness around my eyes was caused by something different than looking at a computer screen all day?

The sight of Barry's car in our driveway came as unexpected aid against the possibility that James could be in an amorous mood. Without Angela, Barry might find it convenient now to drop by after his office hours, a habit that I would have formerly called intrusive, but now was welcome.

I found the two of them glued to the TV-screen, watching a *Barney Miller* re-run. The newspaper was spread over the floor, and an empty bag of chips and two cans of root beer had been deposited on the glass table. Barry was leisurely puffing on his pipe. At any other time I would have dropped a remark about polluting my living room and blocking my driveway, but tonight I would have let him get away with indoor fireworks, anything to prevent James from paying too much attention to me.

Without turning his eyes from Captain Miller, James mumbled, his legs outstretched, "Glad you're back, Beautiful. We've been wondering if you got stuck in traffic."

I passed them, explaining that rain always seems to cause Route 3 to jam up and prayed for my words to ring true. Already on my way upstairs, I heard James' voice again. "I thought I'd order pizza for the three of us."

"Good idea." I looked back over my shoulder. "I'm starved. How about mushrooms, bacon and cheese?"

And then I closed the bathroom door behind me. *Alone.* It had been easier than I expected. Now I only had to turn on the bathtub faucet to signal my need for privacy.

I was somewhat surprised to see that everything was still the same. The seashells on the rim of the tub, my bottles of bath oil and my face in the mirror were all as faithful as ever to themselves. I watched myself inhale and exhale deeply. Any regrets? *No.* I had got what I wanted.

But then I became frightened. What if I uttered Orson's name during the night? What if a member of the chorus saw us together? What if he ended up breaking my heart? Whatever hell this might develop into, it had started out in heaven.

I sank into the tub in a bed of foaming bubbles, still alive with Orson's touch. But the next moment I felt as if it hadn't happened at all, because I could never tell anyone about it.

Driving back with Orson, I had wanted to turn time backwards, to make the raindrops ascend to the sky and be absorbed again by the clouds. Compared to the world we shared inside, the outside world seemed cold and hostile, and I fleetingly wondered where we had left the room key. Silently, we followed the swish of the windshield wipers.

A soft satisfaction spread on Orson's face.

"I'm still enveloped by your aura."

I turned my eyes to him. "Happy?"

"I call it *happimissimo*."

Orson played with a strand of my hair. Nothing else needed to be said. Our silence bore a sincerity outweighing all the lies of language. Before we said good-bye, we drowned for the last time in the warmth of our lips. But already the feeling was fading, giving priority to the demands of traffic and advancing time. Our intimacy was still fragile and I already wondered how long it would last. How long could I have my cake and eat it too? Still, I could finally stop wondering, my fantasy was no longer in need of fulfillment.

I let my body slide down in the tub and dipped my head under the water. In this submerged state, with my hair floating all around my head, I began to accept the woman that I had become.

A shadow moved above me. I heard James' impatient voice.

"When you get through with your whale impression, the pizza's here."

I sat up and flipped my hair back, reaching for a towel.

James' hand was on the doorknob as he looked at me with odd intensity.

"You get more gorgeous every day."

His words rang with the pride of ownership and filled me with a rising sense of misery. This was the kind of paradox my life would be from now on.

I started toweling my hair, unable to look at him.

"You and Barry go ahead and start eating. I'll join you in a little while."

42

The following day I sat at my desk with a kind of pleasurable anxiety. Would he call, or wouldn't he? My heartbeat alternated between wishful thinking that he would, and guarded self-protection if he wouldn't.

He did. He called, finally, around two.

"Isabella, how are you? Can I see you?"

I dropped my pen on Mr. Stringer's business expense report and, on the pretext of a late lunch, dashed out of the office. The thought of seeing Orson made the thirty-four-floor elevator ride seem endless, and never before was Park Avenue so slow to cross.

Moments later my feet carried me weightlessly along the burgundy-carpeted corridor of the Waldorf Astoria into the main lobby.

I saw him immediately. Orson was sitting in one of the green leather chairs at a small glass table to my left, in *Peacock Alley*. The quick and spontaneous way he rose was clearly due to something other than vitamins for breakfast.

When I stood before him his gray eyes shone like polished metal, and he pressed a chaste kiss on my cheek. Two glasses of orange juice were on the table.

He said, "I thought I'd go ahead and order drinks for us."

"That's fine."

We took a sip and held each other's gaze across the rim of our glasses, a look of enchantment and complicity.

Orson cleared his throat and asked with no preamble, "Would you do it again?"

I simply said, "Yes. It was wonderful."

His face lit up. "I'm glad. Isabella, I *had* to see you today to ask you this. In fact, I cut a rehearsal short to come here. You see, my love-making didn't stop yesterday when we left the room..."

Our attention was distracted by a noisy Italian family passing our table. And then I didn't see anything anymore, not the black marble columns of the lobby or the Japanese wallpaper facing us. All I saw was Orson's eyes, looking at me with the plea for staying locked in his.

He said, "Isabella, I want you to be aware of this. For me, love-making consists of three parts, each of which should be separately enjoyed. The anticipation, the actual act and the recollection. They are all part of the whole."

He reached for my hand and the mere touch of our fingers was enough to acknowledge the beast in our bodies.

I whispered, "Everything was fabulous."

Rapture radiated from every line on his face.

"Are you ready for a repeat?"

I said, "I am," and tried to ignore the thousand questions bubbling in my mind. What if this all turned out to be a mistake? Did anything as good as this really come for free?

Orson sat back and crossed his legs, looking vastly satisfied.

"Every time I see you from now on, I'll be making love to you. I'm doing it right now, just sitting at this table, because love-making takes place mostly in the mind."

I drank some juice and mulled this over. Out of the blue I wondered if he had told my mother the same thing. Now the idea caused me confusion.

Orson smiled playfully. "Any complaints about yesterday? Anything you *didn't* like?"

I shook my head. "No. No complaints."

After a moment's hesitation Orson said with quiet self-assurance. "I have one."

"One *what*?"

"A complaint."

My heart sank. But I lifted my head with a ready fighting-spirit. "I'm listening."

He straightened up. "Are you ready?"

"Shoot."

"Next time no perfume. I want to smell *you.* Nothing that comes out of a bottle can match the intoxication of your skin."

A beat of silence.

"I see," I said meekly and thought, This could have been worse.

Orson grinned. "Besides, I have a secret I want to share with you."

"What is it?"

"I once knew a woman who wore the same perfume, had the same defiant way of tossing her head and twenty some years ago must have looked exactly like you."

The hall around me was beginning to spin. It never occurred to me that he would remember my mother, and I was still not convinced.

Orson insisted. "Can you guess?"

"You once knew my mother."

Through the glass table my eyes followed the pattern of the pink blossoms on the green carpet, intertwined like the currents of my mind.

For a moment we didn't know where to begin, so much was popping to the surface. I was not sure whether the distant gleam in Orson's eyes was for my mother or for me.

He said, "And in the light of all your similarities, how could you both come from a small place like Pörtschach and not be related."

His revelation made me a little bit sarcastic.

"Congratulations, Mr. Romantic Detective."

After another moment Orson asked softly. "Did she ever tell you about me?"

For a split second I considered denying it, but then I nodded.

"Yes, she did. This summer. After all these years. She said there was never a good time to tell me before. You were a precious secret that would lose its power if it were revealed."

Orson's lips hardly moved. "When I met her backstage, after the concert, I knew immediately what was going to happen between us. I can see it in a woman's eyes, and I saw it in hers. I wanted to make those days as happy as possible for her, because I knew I'd never see her again. I couldn't change my life for her." He took a deep breath.

"You know, Isabella, regardless of how deeply you may feel at a certain moment, life requires you to move on. To get stuck would mean to stop growing, and I think your mother understood that..., and to this day I still remember her brilliant blue eyes, her quick *staccato* steps and her delightful sexual inexperience... *Elisabeth.*"

This wasn't easy to take in, not after what had happened yesterday. But I welcomed the truth as it surfaced from the past, so I could face it and then let it go. The only way to get through this conversation was not to make allowances for sentimentality. I told myself, *No tears.*

Orson rattled the ice cubes in his glass.

"What I need is freedom. In my heart I never quite forgot your mother, and subconsciously I may have kept searching for her, like a lost piece of music, a favorite song."

My mind flashed back to our carriage ride through Central Park. Orson had said to me, *You are like a lost song. And now that I've found it again, it's even more beautiful than I remembered.*

He said, "It's always easy to create ecstasy without commitment. In the long run I'm afraid I wouldn't have been good enough for her. Who knows?" A sigh mixed with his smile. "I'm afraid, Isabella, I'm not good enough for you either."

I made a wobbly attempt at humor. "I'm willing to find out."

He grinned boyishly. "Let me warn you." And then he attempted a more serious tone. "I remember when I first saw you, on the day of our lunch with Beverly. I waited on the steps leading to the restaurant and immediately picked you out in the crowd. I was so struck by your resemblance to your mother that I knew instinctively I had found that lost song again. The past few weeks I've been telling myself to proceed very carefully in order not to risk losing you again."

His carefree candor broke my world in half.

"That means you're with me only because I remind you of my mother."

Withholding my tears was no longer possible. I got up, intending to storm out of the lobby. But Orson caught my hand and held it firmly. "No, Isabella. *No.* Let me explain."

I sank back in the chair.

"Believe me, the big surprise for me was, that as I gradually got to know you better I discovered I had found much more than a song. I had found a symphony."

Despite his compliment I became aware of my gullibility as a newcomer to love affairs, someone who was unable to imagine that a cold shower could ever follow the feast of illusions.

I met Orson's gaze. The fire in his eyes said that a cold shower was hardly on his mind right now. He leaned forward and his lips almost brushed my ear.

"What's past is past, and we have only just begun. There is so much more to be explored. So far, our love-making is just a sketch, not a finished composition."

He smiled his magic smile. "I want you to think about that."

Still slightly defensive, I cut the conversation short. "Maybe I will, but certainly not *now.* It's almost three. I have to go."

While we waited for the check I felt his eyes on me, as if guarding my face in his thoughts so he could find it again when I was no longer with him.

He asked, "May I walk you back to your office?"

On the street, he declined the doorman's offer of a cab and took my arm. After today, crossing Park Avenue, with its centerpiece of flower beds, would never be the same.

Inside my building, Orson didn't leave me in the lobby. He followed me inside an elevator, and at this time of the day we were alone.

"I was hoping for this," he grinned and wrapped his arms around me.

I smiled. "You don't waste any time."

"I like to take what I can get." His lips let the sentence drift down the curve between my neck and shoulder.

I teased. "Shall we arrange to get stuck?"

He held me breathlessly close. Over his shoulder I followed the illuminated numbers above the door. We passed thirty, Beverly's floor. It was only four months ago since she had introduced me to Orson. If she only knew... Silently I mused, we all make mistakes. But this was a thought I didn't share with him.

At last the doors spun open at thirty-four.

Back at my desk, Orson's last words still sang in my ears.

"Beautiful, luscious female creature... Thank you for sharing yourself with me. Do you know what a lucky devil I am?"

43

Was Beverly aware that I would be attending chorus rehearsals as a guest listener? I was relieved that she didn't suggest we walk to CAMI Hall together, as we had done back in May. She might have told me about Orson's underwear again.

Everything between Orson and me was still too new, and I preferred to be spared her elaboration on her connection with the maestro. Or maybe her company had already moved to another location, as planned.

Anyway, the day after meeting with Orson at the Waldorf, I set out for the first chorus rehearsal of the fall season. Excitement had overridden the disappointment of my failed audition, which I kept concealed beneath a cool facade. I wondered if the electricity between Orson and me would be so intense that the whole group could feel it. I couldn't wait to spend a private moment with him, and if the opportunity didn't present itself during the intermission, I'd lag behind after the rehearsal.

In her role as chorus manager, Joan Hunter stood at the entrance of CAMI Hall to welcome everyone to the fall season. In her black knit dress she looked even slimmer than I had remembered, and she rolled her enormous ballerina eyes dramatically as she rattled her array of bracelets.

I was the one for whom Orson had "bent the rules," and when she saw me, her voice frosted over.

"Ah. So you've decided to come after all. The fact that Orson lets someone come to the rehearsals without passing the audition has made quite a splash. You're almost a celebrity." She smirked. "But without fans."

I made a huge effort at politeness.

"May I borrow a score for today?"

Lending me one of her precious copies of Mozart's *Mass in C-Minor* was clearly against her inclinations.

"For next week you'll have to buy your own."

I inhaled deeply. "I will."

One of her sand-colored nails pointed towards the back wall.

"You can take a seat in the last row behind the bass section. The chairs in the alto section are reserved for *members.*"

"That's what I'm aiming to become." I forced a smile and told myself not to argue with her unless I was ready for war.

Before sitting down, I took a look around. The rows were filling up quickly. Some singers were flipping through their music or affixing their name tags. Others were busily exchanging personal news from their summer months.

Matthew sat at the grand piano to the left of the podium and Orson stood behind him. Together they were going over some difficult passages of the Mozart mass. At the sight of Orson my heart contracted. They both looked up for a split second, but I couldn't tell if either of them saw me.

In the first row of the soprano section Beverly's curly red head bobbed up and she carried a steaming cup to Orson. Hot chocolate. He took it from her with a sunrise smile, which in turn made her rise far above the four inches of her heels.

At the opposite side of the hall, angel-faced Daisy was compiling an attendance list for the altos. At exactly seven-thirty, Matthew banged a few dissonant chords on the piano and within seconds everyone sat down

As Orson headed for the podium, Matthew stood up from behind the keyboard and behind Orson's back, and across the heads of thirty basses, smiled at me. With an elaborate pantomime he indicated that he would drive me home later on. As if on cue, thirty pairs of eyes from the bass section swiveled in my direction, acknowledging my presence with obvious curiosity.

From the podium, Orson's velvet voice rang through the hall.

"Ladies and Gentlemen, welcome back to our fall season..." But it trailed off uncharacteristically and became less velvety. "*Please,* I want *all* eyes on me at *all* times. I especially mean the basses, who seem resolved to sing Mozart with their heads turned."

Some sopranos and altos giggled. I forgot to breathe. Orson waited another mean moment to prolong the suspense.

"Basses, I give you one last chance to take a look at our guest, Isabella Barton, in the back row. Look at her, and then turn around and look at me again. I fully agree that it's more exciting to look at a lovely blonde, but I'm afraid you'll have to put up with me for the rest of the evening."

Between my hammering heartbeats, the room rotated and roared with laughter. In search of an ally, my eyes darted from Beverly to Daisy. But their stony faces betrayed no sympathy. Who would be my friend here?

While I tried to argue my fears away, Orson rolled up the sleeves of his white shirt.

"First of all, welcome to the new members. Old members, please make them feel at home. Talk to them in the intermission!"

And here I felt it for the first time, the gap that split Mahler the maestro and Orson, my friend and lover, into two separate personalities. Each of them held separate places in me, and the closer I got to know the private person, the more remote the public figure grew.

Orson explained, "Mozart's *Mass in C-Minor* had its origin in Mozart's vow that if his marriage to Constanze were to take place, he would write a mass in commemoration of the event. The *Mass in C-Minor* was the result. The first performance took place in Salzburg in 1783 under Mozart's direction, with his bride, Constanze, singing one of the difficult soprano solos."

As Orson's voice carried easily through the hall, I watched the singers watching him. He had their complete attention. His way of speaking to their heads *and* to their hearts never made them feel like underlings.

"The work is a mixture of many musical styles, which was a characteristic of Mozart's and Haydn's masses. However, as a chorus, you can look forward to some challenging music. The highly contrapuntal nature of the writing for the chorus was the result of Mozart's exposure to the music of Bach." Orson drew a deep breath like a runner before the start. "And *now,* let's go right to the difficult stuff, the fugue on page forty-nine, *Cum sancto spiritu.* But let me warn you, it's not an easy one..."

Everyone was sitting on the edge of his chair and holding the music up.

Orson raised his arm but remarked smilingly before giving the first cue to the basses, "If you get lost I'll meet you at the other end."

This got a chuckle out of everyone. Penetrating a human field of bodies, Orson's eyes darted across the bass section, and for a split second we held each other in our arms with our eyes. I was so proud of him. He was an example of excellence and encouragement to all singers to give their best. I glanced at Beverly's red head among the sopranos. Who cared that she bragged about knowing the color of his underwear?

Some sixty minutes later, at the beginning of the intermission, my intention to spend a moment with Orson was subverted by the number of people clustering around him. The women literally formed a line for a welcome hug after the summer break. How could he not be flattered by the way they made him feel younger and more handsome than fate had actually decreed?

I resigned to get in line for coffee instead, but not without keeping a close watch on the scene.

Daisy, who frowned prettily under her blonde curls, offered Orson a plate stacked with brownies, from which she helped herself generously, as well. Her ample bosom heaved in the vague promise of Orson's inescapable charm, which he used sparingly enough to keep her starved for more.

Beverly let her black T-shirt slide down her shoulder and tried her inexhaustible hot-chocolate-trick again. All Orson had to do was to accept and smile. I realized how Orson's smile, or the absence of it, could make women blossom or bleed. I took a deep breath and thought, Just don't pay attention to them. They only matter as much as I let them.

But how could anyone *not* pay attention to Joan? Her raunchy alto abruptly silenced the giggling voices around Orson. She swished through the hall with a don't-mess-with-me expression on her face.

"Orson...."

He continued to chew on one of Daisy's brownies.

"Oooorsooon....?"

His birthmark twitched. Beverly and Daisy exchanged knowing glances.

He brushed some crumbs off his hands and stepped down from the podium. At his obedience, Joan favored him with a slow, satisfied smile. As she took him aside, her bracelets rattled against his sleeve and her low murmur suggested mysteries to which no one else in the room had access. The only word from her burgundy lips that she made sure everybody understood was *darling*, which made me understand in turn that I still had much more to learn about Orson. I sighed. Romance with Orson would best be handled with the help of an enormous ego and the absence of imagination. Unfortunately, I possessed much more of the latter than the former.

This uneasy awareness made me turn away, and I stepped on someone's foot.

"Sorry!" I jumped and recognized Jess.

He said with a conquering smile, "Nice to see you again, Isabella. I'm glad I could help you with my umbrella the other night. The concert was truly spectacular."

Was I grateful for a friendly face!

I said, "I'm glad you enjoyed it. I see you passed the audition. You are a tenor, aren't you? Congratulations!"

Jess wore an impeccable three-piece-suit again, and when he handed me a cup of coffee the smell of his shampoo made me feel embarrassingly intimate with him. Through his long lashes he smiled at me as if he had just encountered a fairy-tale princess.

I sipped from my Styrofoam cup. "Well, I didn't pass, but I intend to one day."

"You will," he winked and gently took my elbow to lead me away from the table. Apparently I had passed the audition for his affections. We found a little niche next to the coat rack.

I asked, "What do you do besides sing?"

His green eyes glowingly pierced mine. "I just started a new job, I have a horse and I love to collect paperweights." As he told me proudly that he had just become a junior partner in a Manhattan law firm, I also imagined him sitting in a saddle. Yes, with his height and elegance, Jess would be perfect on horseback.

Before I could mention paperweights, Orson's bass cut through the chatter. "Let's resume everybody!"

Jess gave me a brief pat on the arm. "See you, Isabella."

At my "Take care, Jess," I felt his eyes rest on my lips. Just at that moment I saw Orson looking at us.

Matthew was back at the piano and the talking quickly died down. From the podium Orson smiled contentedly on his flock of singers.

"For a first reading it wasn't bad. But it wasn't good either. Let me assure you, the better you know it, the more thrilling it will become. Do you begin to see the manifestation of Mozart's mind? Imagine if this man had lived past the age of thirty-five, *where* would music be today?"

Shrugs and whispers went through the rows. Orson leafed through his score.

"Let's go to the fun piece, *Osanna,* on page one-fourteen. We'll sing through it first and then take the individual parts. Tenors, you have the most difficult part." He frowned teasingly. "Be assured of my total compassion."

Peripherally, I saw a grin rush across Jess's face. What was he thinking?

Orson nodded at Matthew and cued the basses, who had the first theme. I leaned back and let my mind drift off. Was Orson at all thinking of me?

My reveries stopped when Orson stopped the chorus.

"Ladies and Gentlemen, I'm asking for *expression* and *involvement...* This should move the heavens!"

Didn't it? I smiled to myself. Who could move *my* heavens better than Orson himself? Would I finally get my private moment with him after the rehearsal?

As it happened, however, I didn't. After Orson's last cut-off, Matthew packed his music and appeared beside me in a flash.

"Ready to go home, Isabella?" he asked cheerfully under his full mane of dark, curly hair. "I'm parked down at Tenth Avenue, but I know you don't mind walking."

"Absolutely not," I said and returned my score to Joan's desk.

In the flow of people leaving, Matthew placed his hand on the small of my back and maneuvered me towards the exit. I turned around to look at Orson. He was surrounded again by female fans, some of whom were fingering his shirt as if it were the Shroud of Turin. But for a sweet second his eyes swept across the hall and met mine.

Our brief bond repeated every shared touch and sensation. It said, *Yes, I'm thinking of you.*

44

Seen from the Hackensack River Bridge, the lights of New Jersey sprawled through the night like a glittering rug laid out to the west. Behind the wheel of his old VW beetle, Matthew apologized for the third time.

"I can't get over this goddamn Mozart Mass. It must have scared the hell out of you at the audition. Believe me, Isabella, I didn't know that my mother had talked Orson into changing the repertoire. You'd have passed if they had heard you on the Brahms."

I moved on the seat to avoid a protruding spring.

"I had it completely memorized. You wouldn't believe how hard I worked on that piece. But I don't want you to feel guilty, Matthew. It wasn't your fault. It just shows I can't sing well enough, or at least not sight-read."

Matthew had his foot down heavily, and I prayed that the police were on duty somewhere else.

He shook his curly mane. "How about this? I'll help you with the next audition, after Christmas. In the meantime we'll get together for some private voice lessons."

"Matthew… that would be *great!* Next time I really want to show them." I grimaced and thought, Especially Orson.

"I don't blame you," he giggled. "You must have been humiliated when they turned you down." Matthew's hand flew up to check the tiny earring in his earlobe.

"Actually," he went on, "my mother talked Orson out of the *Brahms Requiem* for financial reasons. The orchestra for the Mozart Mass requires only half the number of players, and that's a lot easier on the budget, at least for this season. When Orson saw the figures he went along with her proposal."

How strong was Joan's influence over Orson, anyway? I remembered the photo in the entrance hall of Orson's apartment, showing Matthew as a little boy between Orson and Joan. The three of them were holding a big bowl of popcorn between them.

A loud noise from the exhaust system jerked me back into the present.

I put my question carefully. "Matthew, how long have you known Orson?"

His fingers tightened on the wheel.

"I've known Orson all my life, but I've never really *known* him. And I'm not sure that I'd care to. A hot dog makes me feel more comfortable. Can't you see that he's constantly on stage? Figuratively speaking, he never steps down from the podium."

Mein Gott. How long had these feelings been festering?

I said softly, "If it upsets you, you don't have to talk about it."

He almost spoke to himself. "I wouldn't share this with anyone else in the chorus, but there's something about you that makes it easy for me to open up."

"Thanks," I whispered, but I wasn't sure he heard me.

His gaze floated far away, much farther than the horizon of Route 3. He sounded sad and strained. "I was only four when my father died. After that, Orson always came to see my mother. I felt he was an intruder who was trying to take my father's place. Today, of course, I realize he helped her a lot. Without him..."

"Yes?"

"Well, my mother needed a job and Orson hired her as the manager of his chorus. They met through my father's work. He was a professional photographer and used to take pictures of Orson for his record covers. After my mother was widowed, Orson had an office installed in her apartment and she still uses it. Back then, Orson was there so often that the doorman thought he lived in the building. Occasionally he used to buy me toys. I didn't know that he was married until I was six."

"How did you find out?"

"One night Paula called our place when Orson was with my mother. From my room, I could hear my mother's voice scream, *Don't ever let your wife call you here again.* I'll never forget the ugly sound in her voice. That night I stopped being a child."

In an instant of loaded silence the car's engine seemed to grow louder.

Was it only the day before yesterday that Orson and I had taken this highway together? The same signs flew by. Lounge. No turns. Motel. Daily and weekly rates.

When Matthew's voice returned, it sounded more resigned than angry. "My mother tolerated Paula like an Act of God that had to be endured, although Paula made it difficult for her to do her job. Paula made it clear to Orson that whenever she was with him, she didn't wish to have my mother around. Even in her capacity as chorus manager she wasn't permitted in Paula's box during concerts."

To sound compassionate I said, "That's mean," but underneath I had no trouble understanding Paula's feelings. A sudden flare of nervous energy made my hands twist my hair into a pony-tail.

I said, "Joan is very attractive. Why didn't she re-marry?"

Matthew shrugged. "Her love for Orson didn't leave her room for anyone else."

"I see." I rolled down the window for air.

Matthew sighed deeply. "I only wish my mother would recognize Orson's inability to love. He knows how to take, but he rarely gives. He never promised her anything, either. After all, he's a married man."

"Of course." I hoped to conceal my discomfort.

Matthew continued. "I consider him an emotional cripple, and I'll never understand why women run after him." And with a sudden sarcastic chuckle he added, "I just can't imagine him ever being truly in love. As a lover he must be extremely boring."

I began to feel claustrophobic.

"I never thought about Orson in those terms."

He giggled. "I didn't think you would. After all, you're married, aren't you?"

"Yes, very happily," I said and hastened to add, "in fact, James and I are celebrating our eleventh wedding anniversary tomorrow."

"Congratulations!" Matthew smiled warmly. "Well, forget Maestro Mahler. What would a pretty young woman like you see in him anyway?"

"Right," I mumbled through the lump in my throat.

Matthew laughed triumphantly. "Anyhow, at his age, who knows whether he can still get it up?"

I forced a giggle, feeling like a traitor.

I said, "Who knows..," and if anything spun faster than the car's axle, it was my mind in search of an exit from the subject. But silence seemed the only safe solution.

After a while Matthew shot me a side-ways glance.

"Why so quiet, Isabella?"

" I guess I'm just tired after a long day."

"I know," he smiled, his eyes squinting slightly against the diffused glow of the night.

All at once I was startled by his resemblance to someone I knew but couldn't place. In the distance towards the horizon the lights seemed strung in lines and loops, like entangled gold and silver beads, resembling my thoughts.

Matthew whispered. "You know, Isabella, you're really cute. I like you a lot."

I patted his arm. "I like you too, Matthew."

45

The card said on the front: *And they lived happily ever after...* I opened it and read the message aloud to James.

Who says fairy tales don't come true..? Happy Anniversary to both of you from Barry.

James smiled. "That Barry! What a guy."

Another card was from Julia. *Congratulations on your Wedding Anniversary! Keep up the good work.*

James unfolded his napkin and tried to catch the waiter's eye.

"I have to admit it's sweet of her to think of us. I suggest we take her advice and keep up the good work."

A waiter bowed politely and handed us the menus. But the small lampshade and the flickering candle on the table hardly shed enough light to read them. At this moment a thought struck me like a hammer. How could I forget?

I covered my face with my hands. "Oh, James..."

"What's wrong, Beautiful?"

"I don't have a card for you."

"Never mind," he laughed. "I don't need a card. I just want to enjoy the evening with you."

James looked like a little boy with a secret and did a bad job of hiding it. Or maybe the glint of mischief in his eyes meant nothing more than his contentment with the present moment, his life in general and his choice of restaurant.

Because of its rustic flavor, the *Saddle River Inn* had always been one of our favorite restaurants. During the time that James had been unemployed, we had restricted the use of our credit cards to basic survival purchases, but coming here to celebrate our eleventh anniversary meant linking the past to the future again.

This old barn, with its high-peaked ceiling and heavy beams, still smelled of hay and wood. James unwrapped our own bottle of *Chateau Neuf du Pape*, since the Inn didn't have a liquor license. A moment later the waiter poured a splash into his glass for tasting.

James nodded. "I guess we keep it. We can't send it back."

After we had both ordered *Tournedos aux fruits de mer*, I raised my glass and spaced my words as if they were a set of separately wrapped gifts.

"Happy anniversary, James. I love you." And I couldn't have meant it more.

"Here's to us," James toasted, and our glasses clinked.

Involuntarily, my eyes ran along the blue flower print of the wallpaper across the room to a distant table. *Surprise!* There was my boss, Mr. Stringer, with a woman who bore no resemblance to the framed picture on his desk. The brown mane of an artfully styled perm, next to him, belonged to his VP, Sandy Maxwell. She was dressed in black and purple, and her small pink tongue darted over her lips as she spoke. Mr. Stringer puffed on a cigar and smiled his white-toothed shark smile.

I discreetly pointed them out to James and then moved my chair to make sure they couldn't see my face. I chewed on a breadstick.

"I'll bet they're discussing the new expense account policy."

James grimaced. "By applying it."

His fingers twirled the stem of his glass.

"I assume your boss is one of those men who's in love with loving women."

I said, "That's the general consensus in the office," and thought, He'd like to get his hands on me too.

Two waiters arrived with our food. It looked fantastic, but before I could say so, James went on. "If you feel attracted to more than one person, you detract from the solitary splendor of the one relationship that counts. Look at you and me, Isabella. Don't we have the most beautiful love in the world?"

James' eyes were clear and level.

I nodded tensely.

He reached out to kiss my palm and then folded his fingers around it as if to seal the imprint of his kiss. A scallop seemed to swell in my mouth.

James leaned back and smiled philosophically. "Do you remember when I asked you to marry me?"

I managed to relax and pictured him again during that summer when we had first met. After his third visit to Pörtschach I saw him off at the airport when he left for Vienna. We had known each other only four months, but the short time we had spent together during his visits felt so right that we knew we had found what we wanted.

James' flight had just been announced when he turned to me and said, "I wanted this to take place in a more romantic setting, but I can't wait any longer. Will you marry me, Isabella?"

The departure lounge faded away and my knees began to buckle. Everything in me jubilated. *"Yes!"*

Falling into James's arms was like falling against a protective, sturdy tree. Our good-bye kiss was a sustained *legato* note, a promise at the beginning of a lovely melody.

When the last boarding announcement crackled over the speaker, we had to let each other go. Before he disappeared through the gate, James turned again and for the first time put my name together with his. "I love you, Isabella Barton." His call across a crowd of turning heads initiated my new identity as a woman who *belonged.* And James? How must he have felt? Though he was about to take off, he had really *landed.*

"I love you too, James Barton," I shouted at the top of my lungs, and with tears in my eyes.

And today, as I repeated those words over my tournedos, James reached into his pocket and pushed a small square box past the dish with the frozen butter cubes.

"Sorry, it's one year late. I wanted to give it to you for our tenth anniversary, but I didn't have a job."

"Oh, James..."

He watched me as I untied the white ribbon and opened the lid. Inside, rising out of black velvet, was the blaze of a diamond anniversary ring.

"James, this is..." I stopped in mid-sentence, overwhelmed.

"...exactly what you deserve," he finished. "Here, let me..." He lifted the ring out of the box and held it up to the candle. The diamonds formed a circle that shattered into primary colors and sparkled like fire and ice.

To steady myself I clutched the arms of my chair.

"It's so beautiful."

James slid the ring onto my finger and pressed my hand against his lips. "I hope this ring conveys the way I feel. It's as unbreakable as our love, even though it's, chemically speaking, only a lump of coal that knew how to withstand the pressure."

I swallowed hard and forced a smile. Maybe the reason James was so comfortable with chemistry was because it was an exact, reassuring science. No guessing. No mess. No paradoxes. Everything either worked or it didn't. To live with shades of "maybe" would be unthinkable for him. I looked at my ring and thought that perhaps one day I might have to ask him for a different kind of gift, the difficult gift of forgiveness.

"Isabella?"

I put down my fork. It clattered against the plate.

"You were far away." He shook his head and smiled. "Sometimes I wish I could follow you into your daydreams."

I didn't know what to say. But then James' voice was like music and caught me in its spell. For a glorious moment I was free of Orson. He moved into an indeterminable distance, leaving me with a sense of doubt and distaste. Yes, James was the man I loved, and I decided then and there to drop the furtive lure of secrecy and lies. A look of tenderness flickered in James' unsuspecting eyes. It was as if we were standing together on a sun-flooded landscape of the heart, with no clouds or shadows.

As the dessert menu was handed to us, Siegfried Stringer and Sandy Maxwell rose to leave. They bounded past our table and she was chuckling, "I found your missing sock under my kitchen table..."

Oops, I thought, Along with her brains for banking she also has a flair for finding stray socks.

James shook his head after them. "Is Sandy married too?"

I shook my head, dreading to elaborate.

The twin creases running from the corners of his mouth hardened. "Isabella, I think I could forgive you anything but infidelity," and in a softer voice, "but I know I'll never have a reason to."

The waiter materialized to take our dessert order. I felt a string tighten around my stomach and knew that I would have to force down my chocolate mousse.

Under the tablecloth I twisted the new ring on my finger, terrorized by the thought that James could not accept imperfection in our love. But his eyes showed no sign of trouble. He had ordered vanilla ice cream for himself.

James had fixed preferences in ice cream and in women. He could go into an ice-cream parlor that carried thirty different flavors and still come out with three scoops of vanilla. Of all the widely varied female flavors in the world, I was the one for him who tasted like vanilla.

The next scene could only happen in a sitcom, the scene where our waiter tripped and dropped three scoops of ice cream on James' jacket.

Before he could even apologize, James said dryly, "Never mind, I usually look good in what I eat."

We all laughed and the waiter was not the only one relieved at James' way of taking things so lightly. For the rest of the evening the incident allowed me to camouflage my rising tears with fits of chuckles and lots of fussing over James' jacket.

As we left the restaurant it was pouring and we had no umbrella. The car was parked about a hundred yards away and there was no way James could bring it around to this closed-off traffic area.

"C'mon, Beautiful. Let's run."

The way James took my hand, squeezing my fingers too tightly against the ring, pulling me through the downpour in the black, wet night, it became irrevocably clear to me that we would always be connected. Now, at least, it didn't matter if I cried. The rain was covering my tears.

In the car, soaked and out of breath, I watched the windshield wipers flap to and fro. A spark of fire translated through James' glance as we pulled out of the parking lot. His mind wanted me and soon his body would react, even with mascara running down my cheeks and my body shaking.

46

The red message light on my phone was blinking. It was always the same. The moment I left my desk to make copies or distribute a memo someone would invariably call. When leaving a message on my phone, Orson never identified himself by name, and today his unmistakable voice was hurried.

"Dammit, I don't like talking to that machine. Can you join me after work today? WQXR is hosting a party to celebrate the twenty-fifth anniversary of my association with the station. I had your name put on the guest list, so you shouldn't have a problem getting in. It's in the *Times Building.* Take the elevator to the ninth floor auditorium any time between five and seven-thirty for cocktails. I expect to see you."

Click.

I wasn't sorry I had missed him, because I was still pulled between regret and relief whether to end our relationship. At the sight of my sparkling anniversary ring my ears thundered. *I could forgive you anything but infidelity.*

Why shouldn't I be able to say *no* to a married man who would hardly ever tell me that he loved me and had told me squarely that he couldn't promise fidelity. Breaking up with Orson should be done fast and fearlessly, with the precision of a surgeon's knife. One cut, one phone call. Something like this: "Orson? This is Isabella. I've changed my mind. It's over."

He would simply answer, "Oh... I understand. You don't have to explain."

Orson would make it easy, knowing some other woman would always be waiting in the wings. And I? Would being without him free or freeze me?

It was Matthew who ruined my intention to avoid Orson. He called an hour later, and at my reluctance to go to the party, he said, "C'mon, Isabella, I'll meet you in front of the building and we can go up together. I mean, the old man has his quirks, but we shouldn't let him down on an occasion like this. Besides," he giggled, "I never turn down free food."

As he spoke I scribbled *O.M. - O.M. - O.M.* all over the pad in front of me. How simple. Matthew was right and my mind was too raveled. I dismissed my agonies and agreed to come along.

Three hours later an employee of WQXR checked our names off the guest list. She told Matthew and me that we had just missed the speech by George Jellinek to honor Maestro Mahler. Inside the auditorium, whose chairs had been removed for the event, we took in the milling crowd of about a hundred and fifty. There were representatives from the press, from his record company, his orchestra and chorus. Clusters of people were formed around the bar, the buffet and Orson.

A waiter hovered with a tray of champagne glasses. I took one.

"Oh. There she is." Matthew spotted his mother on Orson's left. Joan wore a leopard print dress and her brilliant ballerina smile. She glowed in the maestro's surrogate glamour.

At the sight of Orson's tight entourage, Matthew decided it was wiser to head for the buffet.

He said, "Isabella, I'll catch up with you later..."

I watched him fight his way through the crowd and then my eyes returned to Orson. *My* Orson? In the press of people and his squad of female bodyguards he was on a far-away continent.

Bodyguard Beverly was determined to monopolize Orson's attention. The way she twirled her red curls around her finger and rolled her eyes at him made her look irresistible...and common. But no, it was the sting of rivalry that caused me to be unfair. Beverly wore her slim green dress with a touch of ruthless verve that seemed to invite every male eye around her. But for her there was only one pair that counted.

Bodyguard Daisy hid her plump figure beneath a sky-blue floral tent-dress, and a pair of glittering stars dangled from her ears. She set aside her empty plate and flung her chubby arms around Orson's neck. He acknowledged her act of affection with a smile and a pat on her back. Both left her trembling with delight.

What amazed me was that Orson still needed the approval of a fresh audience. Shaking hands and exchanging smiles, he hung on every syllable from the lips of those he had never met before. Was this sort of flattery a coat of paint covering the cracks of some deep seated insecurity?

He had said to me in August, *We'll have a nice fall,* and now that fall was here it was turning out differently than I had imagined. I had basked in the naive illusion of having him almost to myself, but now with the beginning of the concert season, Orson became public property. I would have to share him with an orchestra, a chorus, a crowd of party guests, and worst of all, Beverly and Joan.

The two of them glanced at each other in fuming irritation. In this jungle of passions and possessiveness, where did I come in? What was I doing here?

In my plain navy suit and unresolved mood, I felt like an illegal alien. I sipped on my second glass of champagne and, curiously, the room began to dance in a pleasant rhythm. But I wasn't sure whether to flee the scene or fight the enemy. Should I turn on my heels or claim my territory on a man whom everyone wanted to keep away from me? A strategy formed in my mind. To realize it, all I needed was *three* seconds of Orson's attention.

I wound through the crowd, intent on catching Orson's eye. Miraculously, his arm went up to signal me over. Had he picked up on my SOS? For an insane moment I flushed with triumph.

Orson held out both hands. I felt the warmth of his palms in mine and he smiled his magic smile.

"Isabella, I'm glad you got my message. I've been watching you from the corner of my eye for quite some time. I thought I'd have to walk over to get you before you decided to leave."

Peripherally, I felt Joan's and Beverly's caustic looks.

I bent to Orson's ear and whispered my message with the sweet amorality of a child. *Three seconds.* My words struck fire on his face.

"Oh, that's lovely...," he exclaimed. "That's wonderful!"

Orson was still beaming as a guest stepped forward to congratulate him on a recent Gramophone Award.

Smugly pleased, I withdrew, but I couldn't get past Beverly. She pushed her glasses up on her nose and frowned.

"Bella, what did you tell him?"

I shrugged casually, "I want your body."

"*What?*"Beverly's soprano spiraled into dazzling heights. "That's the funniest line since Gracie Allen. If you'd really had the nerve to say that, he would have died laughing. He loves that kind of a joke."

I joined in her effervescent chuckle, unable to stop. How wicked, how satisfying it felt to claim my prize so qualmlessly. Now that I had drawn level with Beverly in my own way, it seemed better to join her than to fight her. We put our arms around each other. Tears came to our eyes as our laughter sprinkled like confetti across the seeds of jealousy and competition.

Suddenly I was convinced I couldn't be with a nicer group of people than Beverly, Joan, Daisy and Matthew. Joan showed real cleverness in answering questions on behalf of Orson about his future projects. And Beverly displayed admirable eloquence in supplementing his comments to the press with her own ideas. The room's slow, pleasant rhythm gathered speed.

Matthew sneaked a plate of brownies from the buffet, and he and I laughed uproariously as we took turns feeding them to Orson.

Orson munched blissfully.

"Ah... I can resist anything but temptation."

He had the whole group in stitches. How silly of me to have regarded them as rivals. After all, I was the newcomer and should feel honored for being accepted into their inspiring circle.

Then there was the first flash of a camera. Then another. Two photographers were snapping pictures. A woman next to me said, with her eyes fixed on Orson, "There's a kind of halo around him..."

I heard a female reporter mention something about "the man with the velvet voice," and Beverly declared importantly that she had found a professional author to co-write Orson's memoirs. Julia? I was alarmed. But I shrugged and continued sipping. Champagne had never tasted quite like this.

Orson spoke into a microphone that someone held up to him.

"Conducting is not a matter of beat or technique. It's carrying a vision from within you to the sound. You have to feel it with your heart, your hands, your eyes and ears."

Later, Orson came to stand beside me. Not hurriedly, but not losing any time either, he whispered in a soft, urgent voice without looking at me. "I want to make a date with you. You shall get what you want."

We tried to keep straight faces, but with little success.

A bald-headed PR man posed a question.

"Maestro Mahler, why do people join mixed choruses?"

Orson paused for the effect.

"Because it's less expensive than a dating service."

He grinned and handed me another glass.

Much later, the taste of champagne and the sound of Orson's voice were still with me as I let myself fall into the seat of the bus going home. By now the whole world around me was dancing to the same pleasant rhythm, only faster. Outside, the landscape was dipped in twilight and fell and rose in peculiar waves. In the reflection of the windows, signs appeared in mirrored letters. The wind tossed the branches of the willow trees along the river like the long flying hair of giggling girls. They seemed to whisper, *You shall get what you want.*

Somewhere from a radio in the bus, the *Wall Street Journal* Report crackled. Gently, I let my eyelids close and slumbered all the way to West Orange, the end of the bus line.

The bus driver's pat on my shoulder made me jump and within seconds I was sober. I looked around and realized I'd need a taxi to get home since James was in L.A. by now and couldn't pick me up.

I also realized I should stay away from careless champagne-drinking around Orson. If I decided to live my life on thin ice, I'd better make sure to keep my balance and a clear head.

47

The phone next to my bed rang late Thursday night when I had just put down my book and turned out the light. At first I thought it would be James calling from L.A. With the three-hour time difference he might just have finished eating dinner.

But it was Julia. Her voice was agitated.

"Isabella...? I'm glad I caught you. I have to tell you something…"

"What is it?" This could only be bad news.

"My sister's husband was killed in a car accident today, right in Harbour Town, where they live."

"Oh my God!"

"I'm flying down to Hilton Head early Saturday morning, and I'm probably going to stay with Hanna and the kids for a few weeks, maybe even months. She needs me now."

"Oh, Julia... all that sudden... I'm so sorry. How did it happen?"

"It was awful. Steve's car was hit by a truck. The driver was on drugs. Unfortunately, Steve wasn't wearing his seatbelt and was totally crushed. He died two hours later at the hospital, mainly from lack of oxygen, because his lungs were ripped apart."

"That's terrible," I whispered, at a loss to say anything else.

I had never met Steve or Hanna and feared that my condolences sounded more polite than personal. Of course I felt genuinely sorry for the widow and her three children, but at the same time an altogether different notion arose on the horizon of my selfish mind. This tragedy would miraculously put off, if not prevent, Julia's collaboration on Beverly's book about Orson. Enjoying my secret triumph should have made me feel monstrously ugly. But the fact was that it didn't.

Julia went on, "This means I have only tomorrow to pack, have my mail forwarded, stop the delivery of the *Times* and my car insurance suspended..."

"What about Ludwig?"

"I'm taking him along, naturally. He hates to spend hours in his travel carrier, but there's no other choice. I also feel he'll be a source of love and comfort for all of us."

It was only then that I realized that I was losing all my friends. First Angela, and now Julia.

I said sadly, "Oh, Julia, I'll miss you."

"I'll miss you too, Isabella and, well, I thought we could get together tomorrow night and have dinner. Didn't you say James was on the West Coast?"

My mouth went dry. I thought, *Not tomorrow.*

She added, "How about the Marlboro Inn?"

My anxiety rose.

"Uh... Julia, I'm afraid I'm not free."

"Why not?"

"I'm busy… uh... my boss asked me to play hostess for some European visitors." My voice sounded implausible even to my own ears.

She paused to think. "And there is nobody else in the company who could take care of these people?"

"Nobody who speaks German well enough." My lie came out with more authority now.

Julia still sounded doubtful. "Since when did your job include being a hostess for European visitors? I can't believe we can't see each other before I leave."

"I would see you, if I could, believe me, Julia," and thought, I *could* if I really wanted to, but I didn't. My ears rang. *I want to make a date with you.*

Julia cleared her throat. "Uh... Then I guess we won't see each other for a while."

I tried to be conciliatory. "We'll keep in touch. Please tell your sister I'm sorry. I'll send her flowers. It's all so sudden."

There was another pause, a silent struggle of our wills in which I knew she was biting her nails. I almost reconsidered. How could I be so cold-blooded with my best friend in need of my company?

I whispered, "Believe me, Julia, I'm really sorry."

Finally she said, resigned, "I guess it wasn't meant to be."

After we hung up I felt disconnected, not only from Julia, but from the old Isabella I had left behind. If this was the new person I had become, I didn't like her. Still, I had not surrendered the one thing I wanted most, my date with Orson.

I had said to him, *I want your body.*

And he had answered, *You shall get what you want.*

48

Orson put his watch on the bedside table. He smiled self-contentedly. "I gave you my word. Remember? And I'm keeping it. I said you shall get what you want."

His eyes shone with a mixture of challenge and excitement as his body stretched leisurely on the king-size bed next to me.

"I have this exquisite memory of you telling me *I want your body* in front of a hundred and fifty people."

Now, without the effect of champagne, I felt embarrassed, and it showed on my face. Bemused at my reaction, he raised himself on one elbow without moving closer.

"Well, here we are, and it's my intention to place my body fully at your service. I want you to take advantage of it in any way you choose. Move it anywhere you like and use it in any way you want to use it. Remember, you are my queen, and I delight in the idea of being your servant."

His gray-metallic eyes gleamed at me steadily.

I held his glance. "That's quite an offer, Orson Mahler."

"It's the best I can think of." Orson smiled a wide, wicked smile and turned off the bedside lamp.

In the soft half-darkness, I felt as if I were on a ship that had sunk to the bottom of an ocean where only fish and lovers live.

We had made it again through all the obstacles, and our room became a bubble that filtered out the world and our external lives. This time we had shrugged off the hustle of the highway and the awkwardness of obtaining a key as the necessary boarding-card to expectation.

Across the empty space between us, his eyes had long since begun to caress my mind, and I wondered how much longer we would be able to resist touching, lying side by side, fully dressed.

Was he able to read my thoughts? Orson reached and lifted a long strand of my hair, then ran it slowly through his fingers.

He said, "There's no need to rush. We have all evening. Rushing would ruin this precious moment when we can still say, *This is before.*"

Neither of us moved. I was convinced that this sweet fever in my blood would never die.

Although I hadn't told Orson about letting down my best friend for this date with him, I sensed that he probably had been forced to extricate himself from a similar domestic or social obligation. Because of the sparseness of our stolen time together, we would wring out its potential to the point of exhaustion, like a farmer cultivating a barren stretch of land, knowing it's the only one he has.

Orson's first touch unleashed enough electricity to light up Rockefeller Center.

His velvet voice said quietly, "From now on *it's during*," and he kissed my fingers, my forehead and my earlobes with soft deliberation. He took his time with buttons, hooks and zippers, handling each piece of clothing with maddening slowness before putting it away.

His eyes drank in each sight and his hands gradually molded me into a wonderful aura of surrender. His lips felt their way from my neck across my shoulders, sowing and reaping the first sighs and shudders from a body that was no longer mine.

"Ah, good," he whispered. "How you thrill me! That's what we came for, didn't we?"

Today he didn't stop me when I busied myself with his cuff-links and the buckle of his belt, but showed a slight smile of surprise at my impatience. At last, undressed, I drew him close to me. How eager I was for his warmth and the aroma of his body that acted like opium on me. And then, suddenly, he stopped holding me. Was something wrong?

"Isabella, this isn't right,"... he seemed to search for another word, "to me this feels *unequal.* I'm getting so much more out of this than you."

"But why?" The light from the bathroom cast a white glow on his face.

He shook his head. "I'm getting to hold this beautiful, young body of yours, to touch your smooth, white skin, your exquisitely curved hips and your lovely, delicate breasts... and what do you get in return?" Orson frowned at himself, "a past-middle-aged-man's body... bony, hairy and beginning to put on weight."

I let my head fall on the pillow and laughed.

"Orson, I think that's silly."

"I *don't* think it's silly at all." He searched my face. "*Why* are you here with me, Isabella? What are you able to get out of this?"

I said, quietly reflective, "I don't think of you as bony or hairy. I just take you as you are. I want the real Orson Mahler."

He shook his head with delighted disbelief.

"How you please me by the sheer sound of your words!"

His eyes held a universe of tenderness. His touch continued to whisper across my stomach, my hips, my thighs, my pubic hair. Its softness barely moved the air above my skin, preventing me from keeping any part of me to myself. Orson ravished my privacy like an insatiable youth.

Inadvertently, I felt myself drifting away. A hazy picture tried to take me from this bed, this room. Shouldn't I be with Julia right now, offering to take care of things while she was gone? And what if James called and I was out of touch?

But here I was with Orson, and I refused to condemn the magic of this moment, whether it was a blessing or a sin, or both. Orson's touch put the unique quality of our time together in perspective against the suspicious, rigid morals of eternity.

His breath brushed my cheek and his voice etched itself commandingly in my ear.

"Come back, Isabella, don't drift away. Don't allow your mind to stop you from enjoying what you feel. *Feel.* Just feel! Float and free yourself from everything else. I'm here to protect you and to give you pleasure. In fact," he grinned youthfully, "I have nothing better to do at the moment."

His words stopped my demons and his invasion of my body made me feel breathless and warm. Slowly, like the *Andante* movement of a symphony, we moved through a space that sparkled and seemed to vibrate at a fluent frequency. I understood now that maybe since the beginning of creation this space had been the source of inspiration for all the music ever written in the name of love.

How many heartbeats, minutes or hours did it take to turn our desire into the kind of heavenly exhaustion where touching in half-slumber and listening to each other's breathing was enough? The sound of stillness was like unplayed music that contained more than the sound of a full orchestra. Beneath my eyelids, the room blurred and bounced.

When I awoke Orson held out his hand across the bed and whispered, "Come here. Please."

His simple words spoke of a longing, as if I had moved miles away from him, instead of inches.

Time flew like the last grains in an hourglass, reminding us of the fleeting nature of our gestures.

I rolled over and looked this sexy stranger straight in the eye.

I said, "Is this *after?*"

Orson gave a lazy laugh. "Only if you say so..."

49

In the weeks that followed I found myself walking through a floating haze. In our backyard I listened to the rustling of leaves and marveled at the branches holding dots of blood and gold against a cloudless sky. The wind seeped through my sweater and the odor of smoke and burning leaves spoke of the inevitability of cycles and change.

Life appeared in the colors of fiction, not fact, and I didn't know how to dress my emotions for this fifth season of nature. A deep disquietude penetrated the pigment of my skin and emerged as *desire* like a glowing tan.

One morning on the Forty-Second Street cross-town bus, a man in a business suit winked at me and whispered, "You're gorgeous."

Rushing to hold the door open, a security guard in my office building said softly, "I had a dream about you," as I walked by him.

James rocked me in his arms. "You get prettier every day..."

I told Orson about all of them. He smiled without a hint of jealousy.

"I couldn't agree with them more."

Yet it was the devil's trick. He made me charismatic, while underneath, I was disturbed. My heart full of stars and my head full of sorrows didn't belong in the same body. Surely I had the best of everything, a devoted husband and a fascinating lover.

Torn by dual yearnings to be a good wife and to experience life to the fullest, I appointed logic as my jury. In the deliberation chamber of my mind the walls were white and empty. They made me apprehensive and I feared the first crack in the wall of my deception. How deep would it go? Soon I understood that there was nothing worse than a half-convinced jury.

Doubt and desire waxed and waned like the moon and became self-inflicted wounds. Desire caught me like an illness that doubt was not strong enough to fight. After the sweeping flood that Orson left within me, how could I possibly focus my attention on lesser issues? How important was the progress of nuclear disarmament, the exchange rate of the dollar or my broken toaster-oven?

When I felt the burn of unshed tears, I wondered if James were sensing something through the thin glass wall of estrangement. As I moved through the house, I felt his eyes on me. I gave him a fleeting kiss and the sweetest smile I could muster. Then I pretended to be absorbed in removing wax from the silver candle sticks or dead leaves from the Kentia palms. Later, I curled up on the couch under the ivory stares from the portraits of Austrian royalty, a book on my lap, but I hardly turned a page.

For weeks, sex just didn't happen between James and me, because it was either too late, or dinner was too rich, or one of us was on the verge of a cold, or I was purposely wearing some over-sized flannel nightgown that signaled I was not in a romantic mood.

Barry, settling into the comfortable I-come-and-go-as-I-please routine of a bachelor, often dropped by for dinner and the men stayed up talking while I went upstairs.

For the first time in my marriage I experienced a silence of my body when I was with James, and I wasn't sure whether it stemmed from guilt or exhaustion.

Rather than guilt, I decided, it was the loss of my safely-established identity of eleven years as a devoted wife. The morning after our wedding, when I woke up in James' arms in a castle, refurbished as a hotel, on my Austrian lake, I had established my identity as Mrs. Isabella Barton. I was fulfilled and happy to know who I was and who I was going to be. Now my identity was split, with half of me forced into secrecy and unable to connect with the half that I showed to the world.

I noticed a subtle change in my handwriting. My usually round, wide open lines turned into closed circles, fearful letters that hid something within them.

And I had other fears. What if I were involved in an accident when I was with Orson? What if, during the night, lying next to James, I cried out Orson's name?

Ironically, the opposite took place. Resting my head on Orson's shoulder, slumbering, I cried out for James.

A mildly accusatory *hush, hush* was all that came from Orson, and as a silent gesture of forgiveness for my lack of tact, he drew my face against his chest so I could say no more. In this moment I was frightened by my own emotions, that deep down inside I belonged to Orson and had made a pact with him against James. Yet as strongly as I felt that I belonged to Orson, I never felt that he was mine.

Besides turning into a dreamer, I also turned into a strategist. My calendar was divided into days with or without Orson, where James' business travels were coordinated with the time Orson was able to spend away from music.

Almost every Thursday, James had to go to Cleveland for the day, and on Thursday nights Paula took Lebanese cooking classes, Orson thought. But he wasn't quite sure. Orson didn't seem to know a lot about his wife's activities.

He remained blissfully at ease, while I felt the world was running out of time if we couldn't meet. A small East-side restaurant in the Sixties had become the breakwater between the stormy sea of our intimacy and the calm waters of our formal friendliness in public. I would have liked to disrupt Orson's perfect peace of mind by asking him if I occupied his dreams, if he thought of me while he was conducting, or, simply, if he loved me. But the right moment never seemed to occur for such questions, not even within the privacy of a high-walled booth in the backroom of our bistro.

Yet I thought it was a sign of passion to be impatient, to push for another date. But soon I concluded, painfully, that Orson's lack of urgency concealed a lack of passion. His excuse was always lack of time, and so I modified my behavior and buried the fire in my heart under a controlled cap of snow.

Or, I wondered, was Orson approaching our romance with the measured pace of a marathon runner? By withholding urgency, was he merely conserving energy for the long term? Eager to find out which was the case, I confronted him head-on.

"You are *not* the romantic-at-heart you claim to be."

"Oh yes. I *am,*" he protested. "How else can you explain the fact that, despite being born in New York City, I recently find myself getting lost in the streets?"

"Why?" I saw no connection.

"Here's *why..,*" Orson paused to give me an appraising look. "It's all because I'm thinking of your beautiful behind... Isabella, believe me, you have the most beautiful behind I've ever come across."

My feelings ran between self-consciousness and satisfaction.

"Seductive siren," Orson grinned while his hands formed a little tent under his chin. "Isabella, the process of making love is continuous and doesn't stop when we are no longer in bed. I'm doing it right now across the table or in my thoughts before I go to sleep. As long as it happens in our minds, it's *real.*"

His hand reached out for mine and our fingers interlaced on the white tablecloth between our plates of scrod and baked potatoes. A perfect moment. Our relationship would always be like this. Never temperate. We would either be too close or too distant, too ardent or too cool.

His hand tightened its grip. The diamonds of James' ring cut into my fingers.

Orson said softly, "You know, of course, that each of us experiences our feelings for the other from the vantage point of a different season. For you, it's still spring. For me, it's autumn… and still there is an impulse of nature between us that should not be suppressed, but rather sublimated."

"Are these the colors of our romance, Orson? Spring blossoms on an autumn tree?"

He nodded. "If you like..."

I motioned with my head towards the window. Outside, some trees planted in heavy concrete pots were stretching their branches with leftover leaves of rust and wine against the silver-steel frame of a building. Soon all the trees would be bare.

When the leaves fell again, a year from now, what would be? My birthday was coming soon. I was going to be thirty-four. Life's summer was here.

50

It is a misconception that birthdays are supposed to be happy days. They make us prone to expectations, and we shift the responsibility for our happiness into the hands of other people.

The morning of my birthday, a Wednesday in November, started out differently then I had wished for. There were no flowers from James (sometimes he hid them overnight in the garage). Instead, a steam cooker emerged from a gift-wrapped box, which he handed to me when I was still less neatly wrapped, in nothing but a towel.

James smiled, pleased at his choice, as I considered the statement behind his gift. So. A steam cooker. *A steam cooker.* Secretly I had hoped for another paperweight, *Eau de Joy,* or a seductive nightgown as a silent plea to see me in silk and lace again, rather than flannel and white cotton ruffles.

Trying hard not to show what I felt, I started reading through the forty-four pages of the recipe booklet that came with the pot. *Our guaranteed stainless-steel pressure cooker stews beef in 30 minutes, cooks chicken in as little as 6 and potatoes in 7....* The thought of chicken and potatoes at six-thirty in the morning made me nauseous. Some other time, I told myself and shoved the pot into the back of my mind and into the back of the kitchen cabinet.

Besides, I had to dry my hair and leave for work. To celebrate, I was going to wear the yellow silk dress I had brought back from Austria.

At the office, I was in charge of maintaining the birthday calendar for the other employees. As a result, my own went unnoticed. I remembered how Sandy Maxwell, on her birthday in October, had been careful to open Mr. Stringer's pink-ribboned box behind the closed door of his office. The empty champagne flutes that I cleared away later led me to believe that our boss's choice had *not* been a steam cooker.

And today, between two jangling phones and a stack of incoming mail, I smiled my brightest smile at my co-workers from behind my desk. I considered it a step in growing up not to feel upset over a forgotten birthday. Besides, the day was not over, and I was looking forward to the evening.

At six, James was waiting in the car outside my office. After my illustrious accounts of the Orson Mahler Oratorio Chorus rehearsals on Wednesday nights, his curiosity had grown to the point where he was ready to come along as a guest listener.

In the car, he dropped a package on my lap.

"From Barry for your birthday."

From the floral wrapping paper a cookbook materialized. Was this a hint for more variety in the meals Barry shared at our table? Was the female element always linked to food in the minds of men? As James navigated through the midtown rush hour, I wanted to punch both of them in their selfish stomachs, Barry for his cookbook and James for his steam cooker.

It was the worst possible moment to ask me if I wanted to have dinner at *La Grenouille* or *La Table des Rois* instead of going to the chorus. After his long day at work, James would most probably rather enjoy a filet mignon and a bottle of Bordeaux than music by Mozart. But I wasn't inclined to change my mind. The truth was, I couldn't wait to see if Orson remembered my special day.

When I had asked Orson's permission to bring James along, he was delighted at the opportunity to meet my husband. And later, when James and Orson smiled and shook hands, an immediate affinity was born from experienced diplomacy on one side and unsuspecting enthusiasm on the other.

Ah, to see them side by side, here in this hall of music, husband and lover, both loved and each liking the other. For an elusive moment their instant camaraderie made my world limitless and whole. An odd, mutual fascination turned them into sparkling conversationalists, and suddenly they laughed, roaring whoops of laughter that came straight from the heart.

I was several steps away and their words drowned in the general buzz of the choristers surrounding us, but I could hardly believe my ears when I heard the word *root beer*. And then I heard Orson say, "...there's nothing worse than a soprano throwing a temper tantrum...."

And then I picked up on the word *root beer* again. How odd.

There was a quick, natural closeness between them that no one dared intrude upon. Even Beverly and Daisy kept their distance and eyed them with perplexed curiosity.

As James signaled me to join them, Orson bowed, assuming a more formal pose. "It's nice seeing you tonight, Isabella."

James put his arm around my waist.

"You know, it's Isabella's birthday today."

Orson clicked his heels and said briskly, "Happy Birthday, Isabella," without giving me a hug. Had he really not remembered? How wooden he became when we were not alone. We stopped belonging to each other. Orson's eyes measured the length of my dress.

"Isabella, yellow is *not* a good color for you."

James nodded keenly. "I'm glad someone else thinks so too."

I couldn't believe my ears. The two of them teaming up against me. But perhaps they were right. With my tan long gone I suddenly felt unglowing and bland.

Before James and I took our seats behind the basses, a synchronized "Happy Birthday, Isabella," sounded from Beverly and Daisy. They had sneaked up on us and were all laughs and hugs. My face was momentarily buried in Beverly's wild curls and Daisy's chubby arms that smelled of lemon. Their spontaneous,"Isabella, what a stunning dress! You should *always* wear yellow...," left me wondering about the complexity of female friendships.

But they had already turned away from me and were showering James with the attention reserved for rare visitors. The thin lines running from the corners of his mouth revealed his pleasure at their admiration.

Standing with a group of tenors, Matthew spotted me. I waved at him to join us, and he placed a noisy kiss on my cheek. I smiled. "Matthew, I don't need a ride home tonight. My husband will take me. This is James."

"Oh, I'm sorry I didn't... ," Matthew looked at James, visibly intimidated. "I mean... uh... it's so nice to meet you." He shook James' hand as he nodded his head in my direction. "Everybody loves Isabella. There isn't enough of her to go around."

Thanks, Matthew, I thought. Here at least was someone who was not afraid to show his feelings.

But the call of duty forced him to rush to the piano, where he flexed his fingers and waited attentively for Orson's downbeat. Beverly and Daisy took their seats and all the chorus members were in their places, holding up their music, their eyes on Orson.

At his signal, Matthew began, and two bars later the altos entered, followed by the tenors. Orson gestured, pleaded and grimaced, while Mozart's music floated through the hall like a message straight from heaven. In the powerful *Qui tollis* Orson shouted, "More! More! and pointed to the soprano section. "Try to sound elated, but relax!"

Orson was his usual self on the podium, warm, witty and, if need be, intimidating. I saw James leaning forward in his chair, his interest rising. He laughed at Orson's warning, "Don't let your voices fade away because of a page turn. When I become dictator of the world, all choral music will be printed on toilet paper to eliminate the page turns."

I followed James' eyes watching Matthew's tireless fingers sweep across the keyboard with unfailing accuracy. He continued to play a particularly intricate passage with the greatest ease as he looked in our direction and winked at us. Unfortunately, he was unaware that Orson had just stopped conducting and the chorus had stopped singing. Matthew finally looked up, surprised. Orson was standing with his arms folded, tapping one foot and staring at him. Matthew sheepishly rolled his big eyes towards the ceiling and then began a serious examination of his fingernails.

James laughed, and so did the chorus. Orson had to chuckle, too.

When Matthew looked up apprehensively again, he was the mirror image of his mother. Joan had never been absent from a rehearsal, and just as I began to wonder where she was, she entered the hall with long, purposeful strides. She smiled at Orson like a crocodile, all jaws and appetite. She made a gesture with both hands, sharing a code with him that no one else could decipher.

Orson promptly stopped the music and stepped down from the podium to greet her with a kiss. Was this his capitulation in the balance of power between them? I thought of Matthew's revelation of their past relationship and couldn't help wondering *how much* was still going on between them. Joan did not seem the type to release her prey once it was in the trap. She pulled Orson aside as if they were alone in the hall or soon intended to be. In their respective voice sections I saw Beverly and Daisy throw optical daggers at her.

Joan turned to address the chorus.

"In the intermission I want everybody to fill out their forms for the seating arrangements on the stage at Carnegie Hall. Give them to Jess Samson. Jess is one of our new tenors, and he has volunteered to computerize the line-up." Her husky voice turned to Orson. "I have to speak to you, darling. Why not let them have their break now."

Orson nodded obediently, giving no sign of objection. He laughed and told the chorus, "As you all know, in this group Joan is the brain and I am the brawn... so get up and be unruly for fifteen minutes."

I felt it would be a good idea to leave now and take James up on his offer for dinner. My stomach began calling for food, but for

James food was forgotten, and now he was the one who was enjoying himself immensely.

I tugged at his sleeve. "There's Jess Samson. The tall young man in the blue suit. He's a lawyer. He also collects paperweights and has a horse called Melanie. Jess and I took the audition together. *He* passed, and I still have his umbrella in my car..."

As if picking up a telepathic message from across the hall, Jess gave me a long look through his thick lashes. His green eyes seemed to ask, Is this your husband?

James' swift inventory of Jess culminated in a sigh.

"With all these attractive young men around here, I'll have to keep an eye on you."

I turned a smile to James. "Don't worry. I'm not interested in attractive young men. I mean, except for you, of course."

With one finger, James mock-wiped imaginary sweat from his forehead. "Glad to hear that, Beautiful. You had me worried for a minute."

At that moment, I felt Orson's eyes on me. His look lasted a few seconds too long to be accidental. Joan, next to him, followed the direction of his glance. She scrutinized me from hair to hem-line and then her face took on the look of discovery. A question formed under her knitted brow and elaborately painted eyelids. Who was this handsome hunk of masculinity next to me? Her irises fastened on James, and when she had successfully established eye contact with him, she began to sway her hips towards us. James watched her as she floated through the crowd.

I said, "Joan, I'd like you to meet my husband, James."

Her bracelets clattered. "How exciting to meet you, James. I hope Mozart doesn't put you to sleep."

James bowed and I knew that he would try to kid her.

"Well, Joan, now that you mention it..."

Joan gave a controlled, passionless laugh.

"Well, let me know before it does... Maybe I can help you avoid it." Her laugh, like her power over Orson, had the raw edge of an emotional frost-bite. As she moved on I looked after her with mixed feelings, but James had already forgotten her. He scanned the crowd.

"Isabella, I'm really glad I came along. I'm having a heck of a time. And Orson's a great guy!" James's eyes followed Orson as he prepared the second half of the rehearsal, jotting down markings in his score and giving Matthew instructions for dynamic changes. I watched my husband in rapt attention, unable to take his eyes off the man he should despise.

James went on, "There's so much inside him that he has to give. It's obvious he's past any stage of experimentation. He knows exactly what he wants to convey to the public."

"I guess so," I replied with diminished enthusiasm.

James patted my arm. "C'mon, Isabella. From what you told me, I thought you had some kind of teenage crush on him."

I swallowed. "Maybe in the beginning. But I got over it," I said bravely. *Had he really not remembered my birthday?*

In a sudden need to hug James, I wrapped my arms around him. I whispered, "I'm glad you're here with me tonight."

"Isabella, why suddenly this face?"

I found a tissue and sniffed. "It's nothing. I'm fine."

But James didn't buy it. "Something is bothering you."

"I'm fine, James. I promise."

He put his arm around me. "Happy Birthday, Beautiful. I just want you to know, I'll *always* be there for you ."

The room resounded again with the splendor of Mozart. I closed my eyes and gradually was filled with a sense of peace and gratitude. A little later I felt James' hand on the yellow silk covering my thigh. It was a touch of comfort and complicity. We glanced at each other and his smile stopped the world.

I thought, Maybe his steam cooker is a nice gift after all.

51

The next day Orson called our home just before dinner, something he had never done before. It didn't feel real to hear his voice while standing at the stove stirring rice, and for a bewildered moment I thought he was calling James.

He asked urgently, "Isabella, can you talk for a moment?"

"Yes," I whispered and peeked out the window to make sure James was still jogging around the block.

I had come to my senses regarding my unrealistic expectations of the previous day. Had I really hoped to see Orson arrive with a dozen roses and a heart-shaped candy box under his arm? How could I have been so desperately foolish?

As if reading my mind, Orson asked. "Did you have a nice birthday?"

"Yes, very nice," I made an extra effort to sound calm and natural.

With the phone propped under my chin, I dropped some mint leaves into the boiling water for the green peppers.

Orson's voice smiled. "I was delighted to meet James. What a handsome man."

I said with a hint of arrogance, "I'm very proud of him."

Orson snickered. "With a husband like him, *why* do you need me?"

I decided to be daring. "Orson, *why* do you need me, with a flirt like Joan around?"

Orson laughed whole-heartedly and then became reflective.

"Ah, good old Joan... We've known each other for too long, and I'm afraid she knows me all *too* well..."

His tone bespoke more things unsaid than said. It occurred to me that he might think of me as his sanctuary, someone who believed he was flawless. I reached for the garlic salt on the kitchen counter.

Orson cleared his throat, "Isabella, the reason for my call is that I wanted you to know I'm leaving for Chicago tomorrow, for five days. I'm going to conduct three concerts with the Chicago Symphony. One of the works is Schubert's *Great Symphony in C.* I made a recording of the work two years ago. Do you have it?

"No."

"In that case I'll send you a copy, as a belated birthday gift. But I also wanted to invite you to come with me to a concert at Avery Fisher Hall next Friday, a week from tomorrow. Zubin Mehta will conduct the same work, and I'm interested to see what kind of approach he takes."

I took a look through the kitchen curtains. James was nowhere in sight.

Orson asked, "Can you come as my guest?"

"I'd love to. I'm sure I can."

The pendulum of my heart took a big swing in the upward direction. *Me!* Going to a concert with Maestro Mahler! Besides, this was something I could easily share with James, since he had to be at his usual corporate dinner on Long Island that Friday night.

Orson went on. "I'm glad you can make it. I'm very much involved with this symphony right now. You know, Isabella, some conductors like to pretend that they get their insights directly from the composer, but that's all bunk. Believe me, we all copy from each other."

"I see..." In view of James' impending return I kept my answers brief.

But Orson was like a wound-up music box.

"Especially with this symphony, there are so many ways of playing it. This is *not* one of those cut-and-dried pieces, like for instance...well, let's say, Handel's famous *Hallelujah Chorus*. I assume you're familiar with it?"

I placed four red peppers into the boiling water and told him about the *Messiah* concerts I had attended with my mother back in Austria. I sighed. With my rice and peppers boiling, it was not the time to analyze the intricacies of conducting. Besides, on the eve of his departure for Chicago I wished he would tell me he would miss me instead of elaborating on Handel and Schubert.

But Orson was blissfully unaware of my dismay.

He carried on, "Conducting the *Hallelujah Chorus* is *not* very challenging. Once it's started, it almost takes care of itself, and no matter how badly it's performed, the audience will always love it. It's the sort of piece that never fails."

Downstairs I heard the front door slam shut. James was back. He would spend a few moments taking off his socks and sneakers before coming up.

I whispered, "Orson, I have to go now..."

Yet Orson grew more single-minded. "In all seriousness, Isabella, holding you in my arms is much more exciting than conducting the *Hallelujah Chorus*. I want you to think of that every time you hear it."

Torn between triumph and the torment of James' anticipated footsteps, I struggled to cut the conversation short.

"It's a nice fantasy, Orson."

"*No...*," he protested, "it's a *fact.*"

I was desperate. "Orson... please..."

But he insisted. "It's a *very nice* fact indeed."

52

I was fully aware that Orson's presence in the auditorium of Avery Fisher Hall would not go unnoticed by the New York concert crowd. I envisioned hushed whispers behind our backs, as one voice said to another. "Over there, the gray-haired man in the striped suit, that's Orson Mahler, the *other* beloved New York maestro."

Someone else would say, "I remember his spectacular performance of the *Verdi Requiem*, back in May, shortly before Carnegie Hall closed for renovation..."

Some woman would make a vain attempt at whispering.

"He's much shorter than he appears on stage... and who's the tall blonde with him? Is she someone we should know? A singer? A friend? His.....?"

I realized Orson and I would be naturally friendly with each other and not be able to hold hands, except in our minds. But what an evening to look forward to! Schubert's symphony would become *my* secret symbol for our romance.

I had told James about Maestro Mahler's invitation, and James was glad I had something nice to do while he had to fulfill an obligation at a corporate function.

Orson had said, "Meet me at a quarter to eight at the box office."

At seven-forty, I was sitting on the rim of the Lincoln Center fountain, eating a hot dog from a street vendor. Why hadn't Orson invited me for dinner before the concert? The next moment I was worried about my looks. Was my hair a mess? Did I smell of mustard?

Nevertheless, at seven forty-five, in a surge of adrenaline, I climbed off the fountain rim. As I entered the Avery Fisher Hall lobby through one of the revolving doors I scanned the flock of concert-goers. The first thing that caught my eye was a large orchestral score pressed under someone's arm. It was Orson's. His head was partially hidden by another person. The next thing I saw was flashing red hair. *Red,* as in danger.

Orson was not alone. Beverly was with him. I stopped in my tracks.

Beverly's shrill soprano blurted out through the crowd, "Ah, there she is. Hi, Bella!" She waved dramatically.

I walked over, as in a trance.

Beverly smiled broadly, revealing a smear of pink lipstick on a tooth. "Orson and I were just talking about you over dinner. We're looking forward to having you as our guest tonight."

Dinner, I thought. They were having dinner together.

"Hello, Isabella," Orson bowed, pretending nerves of steel.

He smiled. "It's very nice of you to join us."

Us. He had said *us,* meaning him and her.

"It's my pleasure," I said weakly.

It was she, not he, who produced three tickets, and I followed them numbly past the usher onto the escalator to the orchestra level.

Moving up two steps ahead of me, one of Beverly's high heels became stuck on a metal strip, causing her to stumble. Instantly, Orson leaped to her side. He put his arm around her waist and left it there. Her red curls fell on his shoulder and their muted laughter fell on my ears like fragmented voices through a wall of questions. Orson held her with no attempt to hide his pleasure. Didn't he feel my eyes burning holes in his back? *Why are you putting me through this?*

We entered the auditorium and I forced a polite smile. It was still early and the hall seemed vast in its emptiness, though growing smaller with every person crowding in.

Orson sat between Beverly and me in the middle of row P.

He grinned. "Who could wish for more than to be surrounded by two beautiful women, and the sound of Schubert's music?"

As expected, heads turned, nodded, smiled and whispered. Orson, who was used to this kind of scrutiny, put on his magic smile and tried to find a comfortable position to balance the large orchestral score on his lap.

"You know, ladies," he avoided looking at either of us, "I'm always glad if I can experience an orchestra from the viewpoint of the audience, because acoustically, the worst place in any concert hall is the podium. You can't hear well from there at all. No dynamics, no balance between the instruments. You are drowned by the sound. The strings are always too close and the woodwinds are too far away, and you can never be completely sure of the ensemble. A listener in row twenty will hear much more precisely what's happening on stage."

Around us, the rows were filling up fast. The lights in the hall, resembling those of a make-up mirror's frame, glinted on Beverly's glasses as she fanned herself with the program. In her compulsion to monopolize Orson's attention, she launched into a description of the different kinds of pies she would serve for Thanksgiving. To her dismay and my delight, Orson showed no interest in her subject.

He immersed himself in program pages of *Stagebill* and mumbled, "There are two spelling errors in the text."

As the house lights dimmed and the applause began, it was obvious from the direction of Orson's gaze that Beverly's well-developed anatomy did not leave him unmoved. I detested her ability to make me feel insubstantial in her company. She looked at me triumphantly and her hair danced in the reddish glow of declared war.

Maestro Zubin Mehta stepped to the podium, and a little later, when I glanced at Orson I found that he was somewhat on edge.

Even Bach's *Brandenburg Concerto No. 6*, which constituted the first work of the concert, failed to relax him. He stopped himself several times from tapping his shoe on the parquet.

I looked around the auditorium and discovered Matthew in a First-Tier box. Next to him was a bald, wiry man in his early forties. Was this Tom, the man Matthew shared his life with? Tom, the pilot? Since our first ride together, Matthew hadn't mentioned him again, and now I wished for my mother's old-fashioned opera glasses for a better look at this seemingly ill-matched couple.

Did Orson or Beverly know Tom? I decided against asking them, and an inner voice advised me to avoid the two men during the intermission. I was relieved when Orson suggested in the pause that we stay in our seats, which would save him from having to shake a hundred hands.

Under the stare of passing people and in a well-played balance of divided attention between Beverly and me, Orson spoke of Schubert's *Great Symphony in C,* which we were about to hear.

Juggling his score on one knee and then the other, he looked at me. "Isabella, you have every reason to be proud of your Austrian compatriot." And then he added with a smile, "Your hair looks very nice today..."

"Oh, thanks," I showed him a well-mannered smile.

Beverly shot Orson a sour look, which he caught. He appeared to revel in his power to transfer victory from one of us to the other.

He kept his tone even. "To think that Schubert never heard this symphony himself! It was laughed off the stage by the musicians who first read it, because in 1825 it was too difficult to play. It's fifty-five minutes long, and Robert Schumann called it 'a symphony of heavenly length.' Of course, he didn't know that Bruckner and that *other* Mahler would come along with their mammoth creations. And Beethoven, who was completely deaf by then, read through Schubert's score and said, 'This man has the *spark*!'"

A deceptive truce had settled over us, mainly due to Orson's soothing voice. He opened the score on his lap and pointed at the opening of the work.

"Notice how he starts out, nothing but one French horn playing a noble theme, and then he has the oboes repeat the melody before going back to the traditional, slow introduction in the manner of Mozart and Haydn. And then later..," Orson flipped through the pages, "...see the plucked bass line, watch for it later, how lovely it sits on the ear."

Beverly took off her glasses to clean them and peered near-sightedly around the hall.

Orson choose not to look up and continued to point out various musical motifs in the score.

"Listen how Schubert uses and re-uses his themes. What he does is re-cycling, but it's magnificent re-cycling. He relates his melodies to everything else, varies them and uses them as a source of new development. By doing so he gives the greatest praise to Beethoven, because Beethoven was the first to compose this way."

"Speaking of Beethoven, that reminds me," Beverly exploded in a giggle, "how you spilled a cup of hot chocolate on your Beethoven score last year in Tanglewood. Remember? I had surprised you during the rehearsal in my belly-dancer costume."

At this shared memory Orson had to laugh too. With her foot now safely in the door, Beverly was in charge of the conversation. She spoke of people I had never met and parties I had not attended.

"And remember," she smiled suggestively, "how successful I was in that costume selling your autographs to raise money for the chorus? And that was the day Mary-Beth told me that she had fallen hopelessly in love with you."

Orson shook his head. "Mary-Beth? Who is Mary-Beth? I don't remember her."

Beverly had to take off her glasses again because she was laughing hysterically.

"And then, remember...? Donna fell into the pool in that skimpy little dress, and when you pulled her out you said that she had... uh... the most beautiful behind you'd ever come across..."

I did not make an effort to smile.

Suddenly Orson had a coughing fit and Beverly, efficient as ever, produced a lemon drop from her purse. Was coughing the only way Orson knew to shut her up? How did I get trapped with this malicious woman and this unfathomable man? How does a dolphin get trapped in a tuna net?

But I recognized the strategist in Orson. On the surface he allowed Beverly to bask in his undiminished favors, despite the arrival of an attractive newcomer. After all, she'd known him for many years. She had seniority.

On that rainy day of our first kiss in the streets of Manhattan Orson had said to me, *I'll be kind to your body but mean to your mind.* Now the ring of these words made me fear he would never stop saying them. Did he administer doubt and deprivation with the knowledge that they were stronger drugs than devotion?

People were pressing past our seats for the continuation of the concert.

Orson turned to me, "Would you like to follow the score with me, Isabella?"

I said, "No thank you," and thought, *Not even if it were written in Schubert's own hand.* I added with false generosity, "I'm sure Beverly would be delighted to."

But my last words were already drowned by the applause for Maestro Mehta as he appeared on stage with the musicians of the New York Philharmonic.

During the first movement Orson didn't seem at ease. Used to being the one on the podium, he had a hard time sitting still at concerts. He was conducting in his mind and nervously crossed and uncrossed his legs. At the *Allegro non troppo*, Beverly pulled Orson's score onto her knees and ran a perfect pink nail along the staff lines, nodding repeatedly to Orson, as if he needed help reading music.

I leaned back and tried to listen to the sound swell in my head. My eagerly-awaited concert had turned into a circus of rivalry and competition.

During a moment when Beverly had to blow her nose, Orson shifted the score onto my knees and pointed to some interesting triplet figurations. Under the large book his hand searched for mine and squeezed it. Did the gentle glow in his metallic eyes mean that he was really here with *me*? Funny, I thought, we ended up holding hands, after all.

Beverly's built-in alarm went off and sparks of lightning flashed from the reflection on her glasses. She tossed her head restlessly and the veins stood out in her temples.

At the conclusion of the symphony, the *Allegro vivace*, Orson was the first to rise for a standing ovation.

"A very successful rendition." He applauded vigorously. "It had the sweep and the lightness of a real Schubertian bounce."

To hear him better in the thundering ovation, Beverly and I stood up too.

In the stream of people leaving the hall, Beverly and I fell a few steps behind Orson. With one desperate leap, she cut through a group of people to draw abreast of him again. Orson turned to her, smiling, and with the briefest of gestures he tapped her lightly on the nose.

Going down the escalator they were far ahead of me, absorbed in whispered conversation. It was hard to suppress my impulse to aim my *Stagebill* at their billing and cooing heads, but instead I tossed it in a waste container when I reached the bottom.

They were waiting for me in the lobby.

Another surprise.

Beverly had her arms around a man whose casual but determined carriage was intimately familiar. *James*!

Standing on her toes, Beverly favored him with an elaborate hug, while over her shoulder his eyes followed me as I made my way towards them through the crowd. He had spotted me long before I had seen him.

Seconds later, James' lips met mine.

"Hi, Beautiful. I got here this very minute."

Eternally smiling, Beverly still showed a smudge of lipstick on her tooth. "James, you were lucky not to have missed us. Orson and I had such a wonderful time with Bella. She's so pleasant to have around."

Now that Beverly had achieved her most desired objective, to be left alone with Orson, she could afford to be gracious.

James glanced warmly at Orson. "My dinner ended early, and the Long Island Expressway moved better than I had expected, so I thought..."

"... that's what I call true conjugal love," Orson completed James' thought and the two men smiled at each other in perfect amiability.

"How was the concert?" James asked.

Orson showed his broadest grin.

"I suffered heroically through the evening's program. Of course, you realize what a horrible fate it is to sit squeezed in between two beautiful women."

James wrapped his arm around my shoulder.

"Your taste in women is impeccable."

Orson's birthmark twitched. "It's the best..."

They beamed contentedly, two men at ease, communicating good-naturedly.

"I know it's late," Orson said, "but I'd like to invite you all for a cup of hot chocolate somewhere."

James checked his watch. "Frankly, I had a long week, Orson, but thanks. Another time."

I nestled against James' raincoat and noticed the crowd thinning around us. A thought flashed through my mind. What a rare occurrence in the comedy of life! At this moment all four of us were *happy* for completely different reasons.

James was happy that he had found what he had come for, *me.*

I was not only happy to see James, but to have him see me in the irreproachable company of Orson *and* Beverly.

And Beverly? Beverly was thrilled to see me leave with James and have Orson to herself.

And what about Orson? What was the basis of his obvious contentment? Orson would be pleased whatever happened. He would be perfectly satisfied to enjoy some hot chocolate with Beverly, or with me, or both of us, or even as a foursome with James.

Anything, as long as he got hot chocolate.

53

On Thanksgiving the weather was cool, with a slight drizzle patting on the gutters and the bare branches of the shrubs. There was no better place to be than home for our turkey dinner. The fact that I could prepare a turkey without consulting a cookbook permitted me to think of myself as having become a *real* American. This acquired skill, however, did not prevent me from seeing James through the framework of my native Austrian mind. His flair for making pumpkin pie from scratch labeled him as an ultimate American. No European man I knew would know how to do it. And I loved James for it.

As he went through the ritual of kneading the dough and blending the spices for the filling, he was a man able to participate in the small pleasures of life. Unfortunately, I didn't care for the taste of pumpkin pie, probably because I had done splendidly without it for the first twenty-three years of my life. However, because of James' enthusiasm, I didn't have the heart to tell him about the singularity of my taste, or lack thereof.

The moment James took the pie out of the oven, his hands protected by the enormous strawberry-shaped oven-glove that I had brought back from Austria, we replaced it with the turkey. Now a few leisurely hours stretched ahead of us for preparing vegetables, laying the festive table and enjoying the warmth of the fireplace.

James and I agreed that preparing Thanksgiving dinner should be as much fun as consuming it, because the latter went so much faster than the former.

At the most inappropriate moment, though, when I was checking on our bird three and a half hours later, now surrounded by savagely sizzling juices, James came up with a suggestion that took me completely by surprise. He leaned leisurely against the refrigerator and asked, "What do you think of this idea? Instead of exchanging Christmas presents this year, we could donate some money to a worthy cause."

Undoubtedly his idea was not spontaneous, but stemmed from solid thought.

He went on, "What about the Cancer Society or the homeless people of New York? It would be a way to truly give thanks, now that we've escaped the perils of unemployment."

"Mmm..," I mumbled, bending down to read the meat thermometer.

Just browsing through the stores instead of buying, would not be much fun. I *always* had a list for Santa. I not only envisioned enlarging my paperweight collection, but had my eye on a cute Mickey-Mouse watch and a green velvet dress displayed on the third floor at *Saks Fifth Avenue.* The chance to wear it for the holidays was now slipping dangerously out of reach unless I could strengthen my case. It was a spectacular dress, velvety, sexy and outrageously green. So were the numbers on the price tag, green and outrageous, but justifiably so if it made me look half fairy-queen, half femme fatale.

"A contribution is a noble idea," I said, avoiding commitment while stabbing the turkey.

"I'm glad you agree, Beautiful." James seemed to have no problem with self-denial.

Kneeling side by side, we peered through the oven door at the bird as if it were our pet and we were about to name it.

"As far as I'm concerned," James kissed my earlobe, "*you*'re all I need."

In my mind he had just said one of the most romantic things a husband could say to his wife. He handed me the strawberry oven-glove, and with his words still lingering in my mind, I absentmindedly dropped it. On cue, the doorbell rang.

I looked up to make sure James would answer the door, and suddenly the oven-glove was gone. Where was the damned thing? It wasn't on the floor, it wasn't on top of the stove, it was nowhere. Well, never mind for now.

I hurried downstairs to find Barry with a boundless grin, a dripping umbrella and two bottles of *Chateau Larroque* under his arm. He handed the bottles to James and encased me in a bear hug, with his moist beard scratching my cheek. Except for this part of his anatomy, I liked Barry very much.

"Mmm... something smells good," he sniffed, following his nose up the stairs.

Barry had settled snugly into his bachelor routine, although he enjoyed complaining about it. In a way, he was comfortable with his broken heart and at the same time felt free to go on with his life. I gathered he didn't have a girlfriend yet, at least not one with whom he felt comfortable spending Thanksgiving.

James and I had decided not to inquire about Angela unless he volunteered something himself. But I couldn't hide the news that Julia had moved away. He appeared genuinely interested in my account of her brother-in-law's tragedy. But I couldn't answer any of his questions, because although I had explained myself to Julia in a long letter, she remained incommunicado.

James added more logs to the fire. Through the open flue the rhythm of the rain could be heard pounding on the roof. I wondered what had happened to the oven-glove.

"Hey, Barry." James patted him on the shoulder. "We're burning the old oak tree from the front of your house in our fireplace. Remember when you had that monster cut down?"

"I sure do." Barry pulled his thick sweater over his head. "My supply of logs will last me until I grow a new tree."

We laughed. The solid affection among us spread through the room. Barry leaned across the couch to scrutinize for the zillionth time my ivory portraits of Austrian royalty. "How many children did you say the Empress Maria Theresia had…?"

In the kitchen, James opened one of the bottles. He seemed to look for the oven-glove before removing the turkey from the oven. Where was it? Instead he used two kitchen towels to maneuver the heavy oven-pan onto the kitchen counter. I stepped next to him to get a good look at our bird, but James seemed mystified about something.

He whispered meaningfully, after making sure that Barry was still in the next room. "Hey, Isabella, did you intend to serve the oven-glove as a side-dish?"

He pointed at the disfigured brownish lump that had been simmering in the gravy for the last half hour. With one swift move James lifted it from the pan straight into the garbage.

"Oh my god, don't mention this to Barry," I pleaded. "After all, there's nothing we can do now… I just don't think I feel like eating any gravy tonight."

"I don't either," James grumbled under his breath and, addressing Barry, who had just stepped into the kitchen, "So, Dr. Schumann, how's the health business?"

"Not bad, not bad." Barry scratched his beard, admiring James' embroidered apron. "People have lots of colds and the flu is going around this time of the year, but fortunately I'm not on call today."

James sharpened an array of knives while the bird cooled off. With solemn respect, Barry and I watched him carve the turkey with the dedication of a first-rate chef. At the table, we lit candles, unfolded our napkins and raised our glasses.

"And how do you intend to handle this year's holiday hurdles?" Barry asked.

"Well," James said, passing the bowl of steaming yams, "for one thing, Isabella and I are going to save ourselves a lot of hassle. We've decided not to exchange Christmas presents. We're going to make a contribution to a worthy cause instead."

Barry arched his bushy eyebrows. Something seemed to tell him the idea was not mine.

"That's really very commendable of you." He smiled diplomatically and took a spoonful of cranberry sauce.

After helping himself to three slices of turkey, James handed Barry the gravy and declared proudly, "I'd like Isabella to make the final decision, though. I mean, about where the money should go."

James and I watched Barry pour rivulets of gravy on his meat and stuffing.

James said, "What do you think, Isabella? Should we give it to the Cancer Society or the homeless? Or do you have another charity we ought to consider?"

"Uh..," I hesitated, and Barry suggested innocently, "Take some gravy, Isabella, it's delicious."

I coughed and waved the bowl away with a weak smile.

It was no use. James was intent on charity, and so I said, "I think I'd like to give to the homeless people. There's so much poverty in New York, and maybe we can make a small difference."

"Fine. The homeless it shall be." James was always happy with a solution. He smiled, taking a forkful of beans and asked me to pass the pepper.

Secretly, I didn't really care if the money went to cancer, the homeless or under-privileged left-handers. I had inventoried my emotions and was ready to make a deal with fate. All right, I would forego gifts at Christmas. I no longer desired another paperweight, a Mickey-mouse watch or a green velvet dress. I would get up at six every morning, commute to Manhattan, work eight hours, come home, go food-shopping, cook dinner, do the laundry, take out the garbage, water the yard and help an elderly neighbor water hers. I'd write long and loving letters to my mother, clean the bathrooms, change the sheets and sew loose buttons on James' shirts while watching TV with him. A dutiful life entitled me to *one* frivolity: Orson.

On the runaway train of my dreams I envisioned Orson and me in a domestic setting instead of our scattered, strategically planned get-togethers. I could never imagine Orson cutting a turkey, changing a tire or trimming a Christmas tree. I doubted that he had ever taken out the garbage or knew how to use a tea bag. Domestic visions of Orson went only so far as having him undo the thirty seven buttons of my black dress with untiring patience. Orson was someone I adored but could not live with. Routine would turn us from allies into aliens, and the same gestures poisoned by limitless repetition would result in boredom and an end to desire. One day I'd wake up next to him to find his gray-metallic eyes belonged to a stranger. Where did the enchantment go?

"Romantic love," Orson once said, "is always doomed to die, either through neglect or abundance."

Love and time. Which was ultimately stronger? James and I liked to think that love could outlast time. For Orson and me love burned like a fire whose heat couldn't be maintained under the burden of abundant time.

Was it too much time that had killed Angela's and Barry's love, or only the prospect of it?

Barry glanced down at himself. He had spilled a considerable amount of gravy on his shirt and reached for his napkin to rub it off.

He frowned. "The shirt doesn't matter, but what a waste of good gravy!"

James grinned. Determined to see Barry's excellent red wine to the bottom of the bottle, he raised his glass.

"Here's to your wine, our friendship and to Isabella's gravy."

The three of us laughed happily, and my mind was washed clean of Orson. I left the table to open the window and put on some soft music, Albinoni's *Adagio*. The fire needed more logs.

"That's nice music," Barry smiled, reaching for his pipe.

Despite myself, I asked, "Have you heard from Angela?"

James glanced at me, raising his eyebrows.

Barry's blue eyes squinted. "No," he said with cold finality. "I can't bring myself to call her. It would be like trying to beat a dead horse into running again."

James cut the pumpkin pie as I sat down.

"It's really very lovely music," Barry insisted nostalgically. "It would be beautiful music to make love to."

I hid my surprise at his candor behind my glass of wine.

Barry whispered dreamily, "I miss Angela. I miss making love to he, to this kind of music... It reminds me of her, the softness, slowness and sensuality."

Barry's eyes flashed from James' face to mine.

"Do you ever, I mean… do you like making love to music? I think it can be wonderful."

"No," I shook my head conclusively, knowing that James disliked discussing the delicacies of intimacy, even with his best friend.

Barry's question had caused me to lower my eyes and re-arrange the stuffing on my plate. Only recently I had asked Orson the same question. What did he think of making love to music?

He had made a formidable face. "No, no, no...," he protested. "Never mix the two."

At first his reply had disappointed me. I had expected an occasional impulse on his part to combine the two activities he felt so strongly about, making love and making music.

"Never," he said sharply. "Don't you see what would be lost? Love-making produces its own kind of music, and nothing should detract from it. Music and love should be enjoyed separately at appropriate times, but they should not be mixed." There was a dream in his gray-metallic eyes as he said softly, "Isabella, aren't you aware of the thrilling sounds you make? It's a composition unlike any other…imagine, you become a natural composer."

Meanwhile, at the table, I looked wide-eyed at Barry without seeing him.

"Isabella, you're blushing," Barry declared between two bites of James' pie.

"What.... Barry? Sorry, I'm afraid I wasn't with you..."

"Why are you so embarrassed? Let's face it, there's nothing wrong with making love to music, is there?"

"Of course not." I let my words hang in mid-air.

Pleased with the product of his labors, James started on his second piece of pie.

Barry frowned at him. "Is she always like this... a little prudish?"

James assumed a respectful expression and winked at me across the table.

"Sometimes she has that absent air about her, and you can tell she's far away."

"I'm right here with you!" I snapped.

James searched my face. I took a plate with a piece of pie from him. Outside, the rain still patted on the gutters and the wind had swept the branches bare of birds. Barry puffed on his pipe and blew smoke in contemplative rings.

I still felt James' eyes on me. Their warmth made me feel the presence of our love, tender and tangible. Regardless of what I felt for Orson, my love for James was inextinguishable, like the sun, even if it was sometimes hidden behind the clouds.

The pumpkin pie lay untouched on my plate and I didn't feel like eating it. I thought of the green velvet dress that I would never own. I would be unselfish and renounce my gifts, but keep the one thing I wasn't yet able to let go of… yet.

Outside, the rain suddenly subsided. I swallowed and smiled and slowly began to eat James' pumpkin pie.

54

The only reason Orson had agreed to rent the Grand Ballroom of the Penta Hotel for his orchestra rehearsal was that every other hall or studio in Manhattan was booked in December, the busiest of all concert months. I had just arrived here after work and looked around. The place was huge.

Fifty players made the stage of Carnegie Hall look comfortably crowded, but they seemed like a lost flock in the vastness of this ballroom. Instead of on a podium, Orson stood on a bandstand against a backdrop of massive peach curtains. Instrument cases, coats and umbrellas were deposited all over dozens of empty chairs surrounding the musicians.

The sounds of Mozart's *Jupiter Symphony* greeted me as I took off my coat and shook the dampness out of my hair. I settled onto one of the chairs and a wave of fatigue encompassed me.

After a few hectic days at the office, with lots of overtime, Mr. Stringer and Sandy Maxwell were now on their way to the Bahamas for a professional conference, and I could leave the office early. Orson had been glad that I could make time to attend his rehearsal.

"At a rehearsal," he once told me, "you make beautiful music, and what a waste it is when no one is there to enjoy it."

People sat in scattered locations, some taking notes. Who were they? So far I didn't recognize anyone from the chorus. Not even Beverly or Joan were anywhere in sight, but I warned myself that they could turn up any moment.

Orson abruptly cut off the players. "Back to bar two-eighty, take the running sixteenth notes *non frantico,* please. Don't jump on a moving train... and *please* stay clean and clear! Mozart is not a Russian folk song!"

I caught myself yawning as the music resumed, tired from work, not Mozart. His *Jupiter Symphony*, the last before his death, was scheduled to be the curtain-raiser for Orson's concert with his chorus at Carnegie Hall next week. He had six more concerts this month, but he had told me that this one meant the most to him.

Orson was tense, his eyes full of worry. It was the looming prospect of having to cancel the whole concert in case Carnegie Hall didn't re-open on time. After a seven-month renovation period, the most famous concert hall in the world was scheduled to re-open its doors next Monday, and Orson was to conduct a Wagner overture at its Opening Gala.

The Orson Mahler Oratorio Chorus was scheduled only four days later, but there were rumors that for some technical reasons Carnegie Hall might not be ready in time.

"That would be an absolute financial disaster for the chorus," Orson had told me on the phone earlier today.

"But why?" I asked, sensing he needed someone to pour his heart out.

He sounded like a friend in need.

"Think of all the money that has already been spent on advertising, the flyers, the radio spots, the ads in the *New York Times*. Also, I'm honor-bound to pay the soloists. They might have turned down other engagements in favor of this performance. The programs and the posters have been printed, and today's rehearsal at the Penta Hotel costs a fortune. Consider the rent of the ballroom, and each of the fifty musicians is paid at an hourly rate."

"I see what you mean." I wanted to alleviate his worries, but didn't know how.

"Besides," Orson continued, "having to cancel the concert would be more than disheartening to the chorus. Think of all the hard work that went into studying the music."

"Orson," I pleaded, "you *must* trust that everything is going to work out. *It will.* Cheer up. Otherwise you'll make Mozart's *Jupiter Symphony* sound like a funeral march today."

"You're criminally optimistic, Isabella, but I love it. And I hope to see you there this afternoon."

And now Orson stood in front of his orchestra, energetic and in command as always, throwing shadows while conducting.

He cut off in the middle of the *Allegretto.*

"Ladies and Gentlemen, you are pushing ahead. Don't make it harder on yourselves. Play it as lightly as possible."

I was weary, and my eyes refused to focus, so I allowed myself to close them gently. It was as if some force were dissociating me from the surroundings, making everything unreal. In this profound flow of fatigue I felt a wave of tenderness going out to Orson, a warm feeling of giving and belonging. And strangely, it didn't feel wrong to think of James in the same terms, just as a mother could love more than one child, or a child could love more than one brother or sister. Love had a curious way of multiplying.

As I opened my eyes, Orson addressed the orchestra.

"Watch the intonation, please and *don't* underplay the dissonances. I want the audience to *hear* them."

Fighting to stay awake, I rocked back and forth on my chair, while from the distance, I saw Orson shoot me a short, intense look. The orchestra continued to play and the musicians peered at him with unbroken concentration.

Orson ended the first part of the rehearsal with a sweeping gesture. "Thank you everybody. We'll start with the most difficult part, the *Andante Cantabile* right after the break. We'll resume in exactly twenty minutes from now."

He turned his back to the orchestra, opened his beaten briefcase and shuffled through some papers. It took him a moment before he found what he had been looking for. Turning around, he held a cassette tape in one hand and with the other hand waved at me to join him. I drew every ounce of energy I could muster and got up from my chair.

"You look tired," he said as we stood face to face.

"I am, very."

"I noticed that far-away expression in your eyes and I feared that you'd fall off the chair."

Orson handed me the tape and dropped his voice to a confidential murmur. "Take this. Go upstairs and get some rest. Forget the second part of the rehearsal. I'll join you in an hour."

I noticed there was something other than a tape in the cassette case.

"My room access card...." Orson whispered. "It's a spare."

A faint blush warmed my cheeks.

"I can use a nap, gladly," I said under my breath.

In the corner of the hall, Joan appeared at the edge of my vision. She wiped the snow from the fur collar of her coat and her patent-leather boots. From across the room, her sharp eyes scrutinized Orson and me as if we were two insects under a microscope.

I pocketed the cassette case, picked up my coat and slipped out through one of the side doors, not wanting to submit to her interrogatory frowns.

From the mezzanine level I took an elevator to the seventeenth floor, fighting down the trepidation of entering a hotel room that was not mine. In my state of weariness, no sight was more welcome than the king-size bed. Hollow with fatigue, I drew the curtains and took off my shoes. On the bed at last, I felt lifted by a current, floating like a cork on water. In the dark, the radiator hissed and clanged. Suddenly unable to fall asleep, I watched the line of light under the door to the corridor. Outside the room footsteps came and went. Other steps approached and stopped in front of the door. Someone knocked. *Joan?* Alarm stabbed at me, and at loss for any strategic alternative, I leaped out of the bed and into the provisional shelter of the bathroom.

The doorknob clicks. The door opens and to my immense surprise I recognize Orson's footsteps and his voice. He enters, followed by a woman. The woman is not Joan. Curiously, they don't turn on the lights. Through the vague contours of the room and the small slit of the bathroom door, I peer out. My vision is blurred, as if someone has deprived me of glasses.

In my hair-trigger state of alertness, I feel my weight pressed against the tiled bathroom wall and my feet on the cool floor. Who is this woman? A vision of green. She is wearing my *green velvet dress, the one I had promised myself not to buy. This strange woman is snatching everything away from me, the dress as well as Orson. There must be some awful misunderstanding. I wonder if my senses are playing a trick on me, or are they?*

She stretches decoratively on the bed. Framed by a tumbling cloud of auburn hair, her face seems flat and lifeless, like a mask painted on paper. Leaning over her, Orson looks into her eyes.

"I've been expecting you. I'm glad you could come. You look absolutely beautiful."

She fingers her cheap pearls as her hair spills like blood across the pillows. "Oh, Orson. Finally. How long have we been waiting for this moment?"

With my eyes glued to the scene, my thoughts fly about like startled birds.

Orson measures his words. "I have one condition. I want you to be eager, but not anxious."

The woman's green dangling earrings dance to the inviting motions of her body. "Orson, I adore you."

"That's one thing I must be absolutely sure of." He smiles his magic smile. "Remember, a love affair is a hurricane of the heart."

Orson is about to lower his lips on hers but then he decides otherwise and straightens again to lift his head. He eyes her with dispassionate ease.

"And something else. Just for the record."

"Yes, Orson... anything you say."

"I can't promise fidelity."

In response to Orson's statement, the woman raises her head and blows a gigantic bubble of pink chewing gum from her mouth. It explodes noisily against Orson's face.

My eyes swim, trying to capture the instant before me like a photo. But the film is missing in the camera of my eyes and everything disappears and goes black.

The dream folded its wings and slipped away.

"Orson!" The room spun around my scream.

I heard his voice before I could see him.

"Hush, Isabella, hush. It's all right. You were dreaming. I'm here with you."

Orson was sitting in a chair by the table, his right leg crossed over his left one. He was reading the room-service menu. I sat up, bewildered.

Without looking up he said with an even voice, "Before I dedicate myself to your lovely body in the most ignoble way, how about ordering a Deluxe Hamburger with fries?"

Suddenly I felt famished and the thought of sharing a cozy meal seemed heaven-sent. But before I could express my approval, Orson's face lit up. Still seated, he had just turned the page of the menu.

"And wouldn't you know it, Isabella, they also serve hot chocolate."

55

A funny thing happened while I was doing the laundry. As I removed towels, shirts and socks from the dryer, I was suddenly holding a man's white cotton handkerchief that didn't belong to James. James preferred cotton handkerchiefs because he was slightly allergic to paper tissues. I would always fold James' hankies and put them in a drawer of the night-stand by his bed.

But here I was, holding a white hanky with three embroidered letters, *OMM.* I wondered what the middle "M" stood for? And then I remembered how it had come into my possession. It was in September after my failed chorus audition. Orson had handed it to me as consolation, when, in plain Lincoln Center Plaza, I had buried my head on this chest in tears.

Unknowingly, James must have taken Orson's hanky, along with some of his own, on his business trips. I realized how a small piece of evidence could bring down the fragile web of my divided heart and turn it into tragedy.

The next day Orson conveniently called me at the office, still concerned about whether or not Carnegie Hall would re-open on time for his concert. He seemed obsessed with worry and in the face of this unresolved issue, it was probably not a good idea to bring up a handkerchief that had gone astray.

I asked, "Orson, is your middle-name really *Magic*?"

"What do you mean?"

"You know, some people say, your middle name is *Magic*. Orson *Magic* Mahler."

"Of course it's *not.* That's nonsense created by the press."

"Maybe by the female press."

He began to sound somewhat impatient. "Maybe."

I insisted, "Then what *is* your middle name?"

His tone changed from agreeable to acid.

"It's Matthew. Orson Matthew Mahler."

My mind flashed to the picture gallery in Orson's apartment. On one of the photos he was sharing a bowl of popcorn with Joan and little Matthew.

I said, "So… Joan named Matthew after you?"

"No, no, she didn't. It's pure coincidence." His voice was like compressed air from the pressure of self-control. As if he hadn't explained himself well enough, he repeated, "I assure you, Joan didn't name Matthew after me."

How ironic, I thought, this accomplished maestro endeared himself to me for being an unaccomplished liar.

I said in a light and unsuspicious voice, "It's okay. I believe you, Orson, and I shouldn't keep you any longer..."

I was the better liar.

56

I pictured Orson closing his gray-metallic eyes and smiling to himself while heaving a huge sigh of relief. An enormous weight was lifted from his mind, and smiling along with him were all the members of the Orson Mahler Oratorio Chorus, including me.

Music lovers all over the world were turning their eyes and ears to New York. Carnegie Hall had re-opened as originally scheduled on Monday, December 15, 1986, and I couldn't wait for the *New York Times* to be delivered the next morning.

At five-thirty o'clock in the morning, before I even switched on the heat in the house or the coffee brewer in the kitchen, I rushed out into the cold morning in my robe and practically snatched the paper from the delivery van. On the front page, a picture of the hall's new interior immediately caught my eye, and its headline, *Carnegie at 95 reopens with several surprises,* promised to be revealing and informative.

Inside the house, I hesitated. Should I first take my shower or read the paper? Curiosity won over routine and I allowed myself the leisure of some extra minutes at the kitchen table. The sound of James' shower from upstairs mixed with the news from the radio announcing snow flurries and something about the United States having supplied Iraq with military intelligence about Iran. Not now, I thought, and turned the radio off and the coffee brewer on. Eagerly, I turned to the photographs and commentaries of the coverage that interested me most.

- *Horse-drawn carriages brought guests to the reopening of Carnegie Hall last night.*
- *Carnegie, renewed at ninety-five, is again the premier hall.*
- *Marilyn Horne performing with Isaac Stern, standing at left, and the New York Philharmonic last night at Carnegie Hall, Zubin Mehta, right, conducted.*
- *Orson Mahler acknowledging applause after conducting at the gala...*

I turned the page. Orson was also pictured in a box with Paula, Barbara and Frank Sinatra, Nancy Kissinger and Oscar de la Renta. The guest list, it seemed, included everyone who had ever appeared at a social or cultural occasion in the city.

Before embarking on Donal Henahan's article I got up to pour myself a cup of coffee.

Rest easy, Andrew Carnegie. Your great music hall has survived another crisis. Carnegie Hall's reopening last night, after a seven-month shutdown for a $50 million remodeling, contained several surprises, mostly pleasant. The 95-year-old auditorium began a new chapter in its existence last night, and the best news of all was that, in view of the extensive and ambitious refurbishing, the famous sound was so little changed.

There were, against all tradition at such gala events, no opening speeches or ceremonies of any sort. Music was the point of the evening, and everyone seemed to recognize that...

Vladimir Horowitz made an unprogrammed appearance to play a waltz and a polonaise by Chopin. Then, also unprogrammed , but not quite so unpredictably, Leonard Bernstein came on to lead the New York Philharmonic in the world premier of his "Opening Prayer."

A good preliminary test of the new sound came when Orson Mahler led the orchestra in the overture to "Die Meistersinger," in which Wagner builds the sort of sonorities that in the pre-remodeled Carnegie Hall used to rattle the listeners' bones and make the floor tremble under their feet.

The familiar creaking of the stairs announced James' arrival. The model of a morning person, he was humming a tune and looked marvelously alive in his brown striped suit, beige shirt and brown-and-yellow dotted silk tie.

"Morning, Beautiful." He bent down to kiss my temple. "Mmm… coffee smells good."

I said, "So do you. I like your aftershave."

"Why are you down here so early?" He helped himself to coffee and gave me an inquisitive smile.

I put the paper down and tried to sound important. "I have to keep abreast of the news from the world of classical music. You know, the re-opening of Carnegie Hall. Orson Mahler conducted at last night's gala."

James stirred lots of milk and sugar into his mug.

"I'm really glad for all you choristers, and Orson in particular, that everything fell into place for his concert. He seems like a really a great guy, at least from what I've seen of him. I wouldn't mind getting to know him better."

"Uh-huh," I said evasively and pointed to the page.

"I know you usually take the paper with you and you have to leave now, but I haven't finished reading it and I'd like to send the article to my mother. I'm afraid you'll have to get another copy for yourself."

He ran his hand through his freshly blow-dried hair. "Don't worry, kid. I think I can handle it. I'm good at solving problems in the morning." He placed his empty mug in the sink. "Should I pick up some Chinese food for dinner?"

"Great, that would avoid messing up the stove."

He put on his coat. "What do you want? Shrimp and snowpeas?"

"Good guess."

"See you later, Beautiful. There's a possibility of snow today. Be careful." He was already on his way out.

I called after him. "You too, James... I love you!"

At my words he turned around and came back.

"I love you too."

He kissed my lips and I abandoned the paper. A moment later I stood by the window, watching his car disappear, feeling the prick of tears.

After all these years, all the routine and repetition, all the happiness and problem-solving, there was still a magnetic force between us. Eleven years, I thought, and our feelings were still the same as at the beginning, only more solid. And suddenly I knew that my forbidden ways with Orson would always come second to protecting James' feelings of pride and dignity.

I remained standing at the kitchen window after his car was long gone, torn between the pull and pressure of two loves.

57

Joan Hunter stood at her desk in CAMI Hall, tapping her sand-colored fingernails on a choral score of Mozart's *Mass in C-Minor.* As I passed her she pretended not to see me, and vice versa. Because of today's special occasion, most chorus members had arrived well ahead of the usual rehearsal time. It was Orson's sixtieth birthday.

Orson stood beside the podium and his face was wreathed in smiles. Sopranos and altos assaulted him with affection, trying to plant kisses on his cheeks and teasing him unmercifully, with Daisy and Beverly leading the front rank. I forced a smile, trying to accept things as they were.

"*O-r-s-o-n,* darling...," Joan's voice penetrated the light-hearted laughter across the rows of chairs.

Today, Orson didn't look up, or didn't choose to. He was engaged in an inner struggle. In the face of such abundant female affection, his natural tendency was to indulge in complete surrender. On the other hand he knew all too well that ignoring Joan could lead to an undesirable aftermath, so he needed a fast way out.

He raised his arms in awkward self-defense.

"Stop, ladies, please....no more kisses or hugs. Please understand. A lot of colds are going around. I don't want to run the risk of catching some kind of bug before my concerts are over."

As they retreated he looked sorry, but couldn't suppress a grin. "But I encourage you to take rain checks. *After* the holidays I'll be all yours..."

Giggles rose.

If only my mother could see him like this, I thought as I hung up my coat. Would she laugh at Orson's indiscriminate need for admiration? Would I be able to laugh at it one day too? Perhaps the day it stopped bothering me.

Joan, still at her desk, was growing impatient. "Orsooon... just get over here. I need you to okay the press release for the concert."

Reluctantly, Orson excused himself from his fans.

Beverly pushed her glasses up on her nose, her eyes fixed on Joan. "That manipulative bitch."

Daisy's ample bosom heaved with resentment. "She only has to call his name and he follows her around like a puppy."

I joined them, and we stood together like the three veiled maidens in Mozart's *Magic Flute*, ready to defend the endangered prince from the deadly serpent.

Joan put her arms around Orson and cooed, "Happy Birthday, darling." Making sure that all eyes were on her, she favored him with a long exhibitionist kiss and added with a frosty smile.

"We can stand the gossip, Orson, *can't* we?"

The press release was happily forgotten.

Daisy wrinkled her nose with unusual effort. "For *her,* Orson would hang up on the President of the United States."

But Orson didn't seem particularly happy with Joan's romantic imposition. His face reflected the kind of resignation he had learned to live with, and something snapped in my mind. I suddenly *understood.*

I said, "I think Joan has something on Orson. Maybe it's a secret from the past, some emotional blackmail, as if there were a skeleton in his closet and she had the key."

Daisy's voice was compassionate. "I think of him as a trapped deer at the mercy of its hunter," and she added with disgust, "Joan Hunter."

My thoughts flashed to Orson's handkerchief with the initials *OMM,* and the poor job Orson had done denying that Joan had named Matthew after him. I glanced across the hall at Matthew who was warming up at the piano. I warned myself not to engage in dangerous speculations that could open a Pandora's box. Wasn't everything complicated enough already?

Orson stepped to the podium to open the rehearsal for Mozart's beloved mass. He adjusted the music stand and greeted the chorus, holding a section of the *New York Times* in the air.

"Good morning everybody," he said with a big grin. "I assume you all know by now that Carnegie Hall re-opened on Monday as scheduled," and pointing to the paper, "Has everyone seen this?"

Some "yeses," some "no's."

Orson went on. "I'll leave this on Joan's desk so you can look at it during the intermission. But let's begin now. We have a lot of work to cover. This is our last meeting before the dress rehearsal on Friday afternoon with the orchestra in Carnegie Hall. *Please* go over the music in the meantime. Needless to say, save your voices for the performance. No alcohol, and don't overload your stomachs."

I became envious. I hadn't passed the audition, so I couldn't be part of all of this myself. Being in the audience would be no consolation. I was fiercely determined that I'd be up there on the stage for the next concert. On several occasions, Matthew had come to my house and, with his bell-like giggles and the patience of a saint, practiced the alto part of the *Brahms Requiem* with me. This time it was certain that the Requiem would be sung during the spring season.

Orson's enthusiasm ran high and he rolled up his sleeves. He started with Mozart's magnificent fugue, *Osanna*, almost pleading with the singers. "Take advantage of Matthew's playing. *Listen* to him and *watch* me. Follow me... let me do the work for you."

Orson was wound up. "Bring out the *crescendo,* get *gradually* louder... You'll have to battle the full orchestra," and when Mozart says *attacca,* he means it."

The chorus was unusually tense. When things went well, Orson encouraged them. "Yes, yes, good... more of that elation," and I couldn't prevent myself from thinking, *This man has kissed my toes.*

When things went less perfectly, Orson stopped the music, grimacing. "Ladies and Gentlemen, I do *not* give up, so you might as well give in. I want *perfection!"*

At her desk, Joan took care of paperwork, and her bracelets clattered through the silent moments in the music. Orson shot her an irritated glance, but went on.

At the *Gloria* he shouted angrily, "No, no, no... your diction is not clear enough." And running a worried hand through his gray hair, he cut the singers off, discouraged.

"There must be an easier way to make a living. Maybe I should go back to managing those girls on the streets outside the Lincoln Tunnel..."

With Orson visibly upset, no one dared to laugh at his joke.

Unexpectedly, Daisy's heavy body rose from her chair, and in her own angelic manner she spilled out merriment to everyone.

"Orson," she suggested sweetly, "maybe this would be a good time to take a break."

Taking advantage of Orson's surprise, Beverly lifted her arms and, on cue, gave the downbeat. Everyone chorused. *"Happy birthday to you.... happy birthday to you... happy birthday, dear Orson...."*

Some of the women blew kisses from their fingertips. Orson folded his arms and his eyes danced with amusement. During the ensuing applause, Beverly produced a package wrapped in silver and with a golden ribbon, along with an enormous birthday card from under her seat. She rose to her feet.

"Orson, we're all proud to have you as our conductor. Stay as youthful and inspiring as you are for many years to come."

Orson couldn't suppress his pleasure. He opened the card and his eyes flew across the hundred wishes squeezed onto it. He laughed a musical laugh. "This will give me reading material for the next year."

Beverly placed the silver parcel at Orson's feet. Joan, determined not to let Beverly run the show, emerged in front of the podium.

"Orsooon..." She pointed to the box. "Open it *now.*"

Obediently, Orson pulled the ribbon open and a moment later held up an oversized red T-shirt. The golden lettering on it read, *Sixty and Still Sexy.*

The chorus sat in silent apprehension.

"Well, it's certainly *BIG,"* he stated shyly, holding it up for everyone to see against the background of subdued whispers. It was apparent that Orson was *not* a size XXL, and he eyed his new garment as a bull would eye a red cape.

A soprano suggested, "You can wear it as a night shirt."

Orson giggled helplessly. "For that purpose maybe someone would like to share it with me. It's large enough for two..."

General laughter.

Orson folded the T-shirt and tried to sound soul-stirring.

"Well, is anybody going to take me up on my offer? Any volunteers?"

Donald, a bass said, "Joan, here's your chance…"

A tenor shouted, "Joan, go for it!"

Now the whole group was in stitches. Joan's face ran scarlet. Our youngest tenor, still almost a boy, said innocently, "That shirt would look good on someone with great legs…"

Orson smiled at him warmly.

"I'm sure it would, thank you, Benjamin." He seemed to be relieved that the young tenor had unknowingly taken the sting out of this awkward situation.

Now everybody was glad to take a break.

To no one's surprise, Beverly handed Orson a cup of hot chocolate. Most of the female singers would have blissfully strangled her for this unfailing trick to secure his attention. I was itching to break into the sanctity of their hot chocolate idyll.

"Mind if I join you for a moment?" I asked cheerfully.

Orson's face lit up. "Please do, Isabella."

Beverly explained grandly, "I gave Orson a black cashmere sweater for his birthday. He modeled it for me this afternoon. He looks adorable in it."

I said, "Orson always looks adorable, with or without black sweaters."

Orson smiled his magic smile at me, and I knew exactly which memories were crossing his mind. This was probably a good moment to make my announcement.

"I would like to take another shot at the audition after the holidays."

Orson said without hesitation, "That's wonderful, Isabella. I'm glad to hear it. It's about time we got you out from behind the bass section."

Beverly laughed mockingly. "Well, Isabella, good luck. You'll need it."

Joan joined our group and put her arm around Orson's waist, smiling frostily.

"Really, Isabella, I'm surprised you want to re-audition. But if you want, I'll put your name down for the first week in January. I hope you'll do better this time."

Orson flashed an innocent grin from Beverly to Joan.

"Of course, Isabella will do better. Besides, she should sit in the first row anyway. She has great legs."

I managed to blush.

"That's a nice compliment. You deserve a birthday hug for that."

Orson beamed. "I insist on it."

Beverly exploded, "But he's afraid of germs!"

I copied Joan's frosty smile.

"We can stand the gossip, Orson, *can't* we?"

With deliberate slowness, Orson disengaged himself from Joan's arm and handed his cup of hot chocolate to Beverly. His arms pulled me close and enfolded me for a long moment. Over his shoulder I reveled in Beverly's and Joan's perplexed stares.

58

Despite Siegfried Stringer's frequently used motto, "We take pride in our professionalism," he was usually late for work. He would call me from home first thing in the morning, checking on the time of my arrival, hardly giving me a minute to settle in at my desk.

"We are people of instant action," he liked to say, starting to give me dictation and a list of things to do while riding his exercise bike.

I was beginning to tire of my job, or more specifically, of Mr. Stringer. I was tired of spending my time ordering and returning all kinds of golfing gear for him, tired of having to fiddle with his cappuccino-maker five times a day and tired of having to lie to his wife regarding his whereabouts. When he dictated from home while riding on his bike, his panting grew obscene, making it hard for me to understand him. But there were other background noises. Along with his poodle barking, one of his four daughters would invariably cry at the top of her lungs.

From the beginning I had sensed that he secretly desired me, but I gave him no encouragement. I could sometimes see a fiery flicker dying in his eyes, a turning point where passion switched to pride and desire was transformed into dictatorship.

Two days ago, Mr. Stringer and Sandy Maxwell had returned from the Bahamas with a deep, exotic tan. Everybody in the office itched to ask if their business meetings had been conducted on the beach. Mr. Stringer had lost his designer sunglasses and his silk robe *somewhere.* It was my job to contact the airlines and the hotels to track down his belongings. I thought, with James settled in his work, shouldn't there be another job for me in a city of ten million people?

The morning of Orson's concert at Carnegie Hall, on Friday, December 19, followed the same pattern, with Stringer dictating from home. Again there was his panting, his poodle barking and his daughter crying. As my pencil flew across the paper my hopes of leaving on time diminished in proportion to the number of pages that filled my pad.

I had to type and translate the general monthly report for our headquarters in Germany. Due to Mr. Stringer's absence from the office, it was precariously late. The last Board meeting of the year was to be held on the following Monday in Frankfurt, and the report had to be faxed that evening so it could be on the conference table for the meeting.

When Mr. Stringer showed up at eleven-thirty, the filter of his cappuccino-maker broke and his new stationery had to be returned because of a wrong initial.

Sandy swept through the office and dumped a folder labeled "urgent" in my in-box. She scrutinized my diamond anniversary ring.

"Well, Isabella, I'm afraid you'll have to stay tonight and finish the report. It has to be ready for the board meeting on Monday morning."

"That's what I gathered," I shrugged, sucking on a paper cut.

I sighed, wishing to hear the sound of James' voice, James who always saw a window where I saw a wall. As if picking up on my telepathic wave, James called from Cleveland airport a few minutes later to tell me his plane would arrive at La Guardia around ten P.M.

I said, "I have to work late, so I'm going to miss the concert."

"My poor Isabella." For a moment his voice dispelled my gloom. "Mahler will be devastated that one of his greatest fans is not in the audience. Just be sure to take a taxi home. I don't like the idea of you on the bus late at night."

Well aware that it would be impossible to reach Orson by phone, since he was already on his way to direct the dress rehearsal, I left a message on his tape. Orson regarded the phone as a personal extension of himself, so I was sure he would call in to listen to his answering machine.

Verdammt, I thought, today of all days this has to happen. By five I had reached page ten of nineteen, dealing with a contract commitment of six to seven million dollars. The investment was not related to the current business scope and had not yet been approved in the overall plan.

At six, Sandy and Mr. Stringer explained grandly that they had tickets for a Mozart concert at the newly-renovated Carnegie Hall and left the office together for a bite to eat. With my head buried between the dictionary and the synonym finder, I shot them an irritated glance and shoved another diskette into the computer.

They dedicated their lives to earning money and not much else. Doubtlessly, they preferred money over Mozart, and I chose not to tell them about the concert ticket in my purse that would go unused. I tried to imagine their faces if I told them the truth about me and the man on the podium whom they were about to applaud.

Left alone, the empty office looked larger, even peaceful. The lights of the Christmas tree by the receptionist's desk had been turned off and it was wonderfully quiet without the constant sound of ringing phones. The paintings came to life against the white walls and the charts, with their exchange-rate curves of the dollar versus other currencies, turned into imaginative webs.

The cleaning lady arrived at seven, and at seven-thirty I reached for my package of "emergency cookies" in the bottom drawer of my desk. I was at page fourteen, dealing with transactions and/or agreements that affected the company as a single legal unit.

At eight I closed my eyes. I imagined the applause of the full concert hall. This was the moment when Orson would bow to the audience, then turn to the orchestra and wait for complete silence before lifting his baton.

Mozart's *Jupiter Symphony* would be video-taped by CBS to be broadcast nationwide as part of this year's Christmas Concert. After the intermission, the Orson Mahler Oratorio Chorus would file up onto the risers to perform Mozart's *Mass in C-Minor*.

Had Orson got my message? I took my earrings off and yawned. I planned to work myself into a state of numbing exhaustion and not think further about the concert.

When the cleaning lady left at eight-thirty, my back started to feel stiff. I was chewing on my last cookie when the phone rang at eight-forty-five.

"Hello, Isabella?"

My heart flew from frost to fire. It was Orson.

"It's the intermission. I got your message," and in a more confidential tone as if he were not alone, "I'm sorry you can't be here. The *Jupiter Symphony* went beautifully."

After a brief hesitation his voice was hardly above a whisper.

"I just wanted to let you know that I was thinking of you while I was on the podium," and much louder again, "Is there any chance you can join us for the post-concert party at Café Carnegie?"

"Thanks for inviting me, but I'll be too tired to go anywhere but home."

"I understand, of course. I just wanted to see your lovely face again tonight."

In this moment I loved him more than at any other time. I pictured him standing in his dressing room, surrounded by Paula, Beverly and Daisy (Joan was not allowed in Paula's presence). Regardless of how busily they moved about to help the maestro change his shirt, Daisy handing him a towel, Paula rubbing his back and Beverly serving him hot chocolate, *I was the one moving him.*

Orson's call raised my energy level to carry me past ten-thirty, when I typed page nineteen of nineteen. As an addendum to the financial outlook, Mr. Stringer usually selected a topic of general interest. Today it was an excerpt from a newsletter published by the

Equal Employment Opportunity Commission. Mr. Stringer's report ended with the following remarks: "I require our employees to meet their obligations in accordance with the stated guidelines. Discriminatory or unethical conduct of any nature will not be tolerated. We take pride in our professionalism."

By eleven, the complete report was translated, typed and printed. Weary-eyed, I proof-read it before faxing it to our German offices. I rotated my shoulders to relax while waiting for the transmission print-out on the fax machine. It indicated that all nineteen pages had safely arrived at five-thirty on Saturday morning, German time. I put the originals on Mr. Stringer's desk, a copy in Sandy's in-basket and another copy in the files. I shut down the computer and the printer, locked my desk, switched off the copier and the lights and locked the office door. Maybe James and I would arrive at home around the same time.

As I left the building, I exchanged a friendly nod with the security guard. He helped me find a taxi and I settled in the back seat. The lights of Park Avenue flew by and I thought, There must be a better job for me somewhere, and a new boss for whom the words "We take pride in our professionalism" were not just an empty formula.

59

On Christmas Eve the company closed at noon, and ten minutes later I was on my way to meet Orson for lunch. For the last couple of days my employment situation had been almost obsessively on my mind. It would feel good to share my thoughts with Orson. He would take my hand across the table and listen, and surely he would agree that one year was enough in a job where I wasn't happy.

As I waited in one of the high-backed leather booths of *our* bistro in the east sixties, I nervously checked my watch. The waiter had just brought my second glass of orange juice and I wondered why today of all days, on Christmas Eve, Orson hadn't arrived yet. He was usually on time or even a few minutes early.

The moment I decided to pay the check forty minutes later, Orson came striding in, carrying his beaten briefcase, breathless. The tense expression in his face told me that he was here by default, rather than desire. He hung his coat next to mine and said, "I'm sorry," without looking it.

He didn't smile at me, he didn't ask "How are you?" and my happiness to see him faded. He slid onto the opposite bench.

"Paula and I just got home from a delightful breakfast with our old friends, the Horowitzes. You know, of course," he explained grandly, "Vladimir Horowitz and his wife, Wanda. She's Arturo Toscanini's daughter. They live just a few blocks down from us in a charming brownstone. Paula and I have been friends with them for years, and oh, what memories we share!"

The waiter bowed and handed us two menus that we already knew by heart.

Orson continued to elaborate with pride on the friendship connecting him with Horowitz and Toscanini, one that could be considered a lasting imprint on the history of classical music.

"In the early 1950s, you were hardly even born," he interjected with a belittling smile, "there was a studio recording of Tchaikovsky's *First Piano Concerto.* I considered myself the luckiest twenty-five year-old conductor in the world to witness Arturo Toscanini conducting the NBC Symphony Orchestra with Vladimir Horowitz at the piano. I never dared to hope that one day I'd work with Vladimir under my baton."

Pretending to be fascinated by the menu and Orson's memories, I sat still, but sighed inwardly, *Aren't you going to listen to me?*

Irritated by the sound of Christmas music from a speaker, Orson made a face. "Back in the early fifties there was no editing. The music was split into small segments to fit on the old 78 records. They just recorded different takes of the individual segments until they felt it was acceptable. It was never as perfect in the technical sense as it is today, with all the editing and cutting, but what exciting music-making it was!"

He sighed, sipping from his juice, his gray eyes miles away.

"Now, with all this modern technology, they sometimes lose the music in the process."

I felt intimidated. In the face of such music history, everything I had meant to tell him was strangled in my throat. I thought, while tasting the first spoonful of my lobster bisque, How could my little crisis on the job compete with Horowitz's genius?

While Orson continued with remembrances of Horowitz and Toscanini, my thoughts flew to the future. All at once, the reality of what awaited me in January became relentlessly clear. I would have to update my resumé, contact employment agencies, and prepare for interviews. All this stretched before me like the twelve labors of Hercules. My confidence faltered and I felt as fragile as the glass ornaments on the snow-sprayed Christmas tree in the restaurant doorway.

For seemingly no reason Orson cast nervous glances around the room. Next to the Christmas tree, a man with a beard was talking to our waiter. He handed the waiter a tip along with a small envelope. The waiter nodded and crossed the room towards us.

"Maestro Mahler?" He bowed and shot me a curious glance.

"Yes?" Orson turned and took the envelope from him.

He extracted a note and his eyes flew across the lines. A moment later he got up.

"Excuse me, Isabella, I have to see someone." And he disappeared into the main dining room. When he returned to the table, I had finished my lobster bisque and Orson's was cold. Preoccupied, he sat down.

"That was a journalist who wants to do a feature article on me for *Stereo Review*."

"Did you agree to give him an interview?"

"Yes, I've known him for several years. He was going to call me after the holidays, but he spotted me here by chance."

With an air of distraction Orson began to pick at the black olives in his Salade Niçoise, and I knew that the occasion had passed to tell him about Mr. Stringer. He made a tent of his fingertips, an indication that he had something up his sleeve.

"Isabella, I have to discuss something with you."

"Yes?"

"You know, people are used to seeing me in public. I often meet with reporters or musicians. I don't believe in locking myself up at home just because someone might recognize me or come to my table to exchange a few words. In fact, I love it."

He hesitated.

I said, "But?"

"But... when you and I are together in public, we have to be extremely cautious."

I understood instantly. The white tablecloth between us began to stretch like the arctic ice.

I said calmly, "You're afraid to see your name in the gossip columns."

"Exactly." He put down his fork.

I took a deep breath. For the first time I envisioned a future when his voice would no longer sound like velvet and I would no longer know his phone number by heart.

"Don't worry," I rubbed my palms against the napkin on my lap. "I promise *not* to throw a glass of water in your face in public."

"So," he grinned cautiously, "I see you know the story of the flautist from the New York Philharmonic. That was several years ago."

"But no secret. How did Paula react to it?"

Orson fiddled with the stem of his glass and didn't comment. Despite our closeness there was still a line that couldn't be crossed.

He mumbled, "I just don't want to be crucified on the altar of trash journalism. I also hope, Isabella," his voice was clipped now, "that you are extremely discreet about us. A careless slip of the tongue can never be taken back, and I don't want to be on the cover of the *National Inquirer* instead of *Stereo Review*. I prefer to have my ideas about music featured, rather than my sex life."

He cleared his throat. "You know, I'm a romantic in my genes, but if there would be the slightest hint of scandal, that would be the end of us. I hope you realize that we could never be seen with each other again."

A chill passed through me. A romantic in his genes? I had never seen him in such a cutting mood! *Of course.* On his list of priorities, his public image ranked ahead of any feelings he might have for me. I had no place in his heart other than the one I had invented in my dreams.

I said, "Do you think you would be the only one in trouble if our affair were discovered?"

He looked at me as if I had just delivered some news from another planet.

I said, "I'm not a stupid little girl who needs to be warned about gossip. If our relationship constitutes a risk to your reputation, why don't we break it off? I'm not possessive. And I'm not *that* desperate for sex."

Orson's face turned as white as the snow-sprayed Christmas tree behind him.

I assumed the voice of a surgeon, disguising my knife with roses.

"Breaking up would be easy, Orson. If you want, we can do it right now. We don't need to fight. We just have to get up and go separate ways and stop struggling against all the obstacles of finding time together."

In suspense between love and loss, Orson looked at me defensively. My pale prince. Suddenly he was nothing but a stranger sitting opposite me on a train, while through the windows of my eyes the film of our romance flew by like a frozen landscape in the sun. But hadn't I said *yes* to this stranger, *yes* to an instinct that was bigger than life itself? Now every *yes* seemed to be used up.

I took a thirsty gulp of water.

The stranger opposite me on the train reached across to take my hand. His touch forced my gaze back into his eyes.

"Don't go on, Isabella, please."

I didn't move.

Intent on smoothing my ruffled feathers, he leaned over.

"Have I told you that you look absolutely lovely today?"

"Not that I can remember," I said without enthusiasm.

Orson fidgeted with his fork but didn't eat.

I said, "I've never seen you in such a rotten mood. Have you forgotten? It's Christmas Eve. We're sitting here, like two strangers, trying to make each other feel miserable."

Orson took a slow sip from his glass.

"Celebrating Christmas was never important to me."

I had said everything I had to say. How heavenly it would be to spend Christmas Eve with James even if there was no prospect of presents.

I blew my nose. "Orson, I want to leave. I want to go home. And I'd like to catch the two-thirty bus from the Port Authority."

"All right. As you wish." He raised his shoulders in a sheepish shrug.

Outside, the wind had quickened and I twisted my hair into a woolen hat, wishing for spring. Orson put on his dark glasses. We exchanged uncertain glances, testing each other's signals. I assumed he'd take a cab home and said, "Thanks for lunch. I have to hurry."

"Wait a minute. You can't run off like this, Isabella." And after a brief hesitation, "I'll walk you to the Port Authority."

"Orson, it's *quite* a walk. The Port Authority is twenty blocks away. I'll have to walk very fast to make it."

"Have I ever given you the impression that I'm not a fast walker?"

I made an effort to change emotional gears. "No, of course not. I still remember our walk through Central Park in the spring."

"See?" He grinned. "So, may I have the pleasure, madam?"

"All right, sir," I said and we started moving, our minds circling around each other. Orson took my elbow and guided me across Madison Avenue, and for a brief moment he put his arm around my shoulders.

"Orson, I thought you were concerned about your public reputation."

"I made certain no one was looking."

"Liar."

Suddenly my hand was in his, though I wasn't sure who had made the first move.

Fifth Avenue was alive with the glitter of the holiday season and packed with tons of tourists. A sharp cutting wind made last minute shoppers clutch their packages against their coats.

As we passed the skating rink and the Christmas tree at Rockefeller Center, we began to talk, as lovers do, about the places we had been together: Central Park, the subway, the art gallery in Soho, Avery Fisher Hall, the Waldorf Astoria, the Penta...

If Beverly and I hadn't got stuck in the elevator together... If he hadn't been able to come to our first lunch...

Orson smiled reflectively. "Sometimes the gods can be kind."

My eyes ran along the lights of Radio City Music Hall. In my high-heeled boots I had a hard time keeping up with Orson's strides, but I didn't admit it. I sensed that he was aware of my predicament and enjoyed it a little, just enough to keep him smiling.

As we crossed Times Square, the moment felt right to tell him about my concerns in the office. I saw no reason to omit anything what bothered me about Mr. Stringer, including his inviting glances. When I had finished, Orson shook his head.

"I don't understand, Isabella. *Why* didn't you tell me earlier, in the restaurant? Anything that worries you is important to me too." He pulled me closer by my sleeve.

"Orson," I reminded him, "you were busy talking about Arturo Toscanini, your public reputation and the insignificance of Christmas."

"You should have interrupted me and said, *Goddammit, Orson, will you listen to me now?*"

He thought it was a good idea for me to look for another job, and from that moment, Siegfried Stringer became an insignificant person.

"I know a lot of people in the music business. I'll keep my eyes open for you. Someone might just have an opening for an efficient, multi-lingual person like you."

"Thanks for offering your help. I can use it."

He squeezed my hand. "I'll do what I can. It's a promise."

I felt my cheeks blush against the winter wind. Salvation Army Santas were ringing their bells, undauntedly penetrating the noise of the traffic. Orson grimaced at the jazzy sounds of *Joy to the World* from an open shop on Broadway. But I felt that everything was perfect as it was. Along with the sounds of bells, music, horns and traffic, hope was in the air. The Christmas spirit was finally growing in my heart, just as I had felt it when I was a little girl. I started to laugh for the sole reason of being alive and in love with life itself, and after a moment Orson laughed with me.

At the Port Authority Bus Terminal Orson took the crowded elevator with me to the fourth level and we got in line for my bus to

Montclair. I doubted that he had ever set foot in this place before. Already, long lines of commuters, eager to get home early, had formed at each gate.

Orson took off his glasses and his gray-metallic eyes searched for mine. Mindful of his public reputation, I was about to wave good-bye to him. But here, in one of the most public places in the city, in the middle of the Port Authority Bus Terminal, Orson took me in his arms and kissed me. Releasing me from his embrace, he said gently, "Merry Christmas, Sweetheart."

That was the only time, *ever,* that Orson Mahler called me *Sweetheart.*

60

James and I could never agree whether to have a real Christmas tree or an artificial one. James favored artificial trees because they were efficient and clean. In his eyes, the advantages of symmetry and freedom from maintenance could never be matched by Mother Nature's crooked messiness. Besides, he disliked having to empty needles from the vacuum cleaner in July.

I loved the life and aroma of real trees and couldn't care less about needles in the vacuum cleaner, nor the month in which they might be found. So we took turns, and this year it was James' turn.

On Sunday we had maneuvered the huge box labeled "Xmas Tree" from its storage place in the garage into our living room. James helped me untangle and string the lights, unwrap the ornaments and affix the hooks to them. With the treetop porcelain angel in place, the crocheted snowflakes, the glass balls in red and gold, and the gilded cherubs from Austria, the eye was sufficiently distracted from the vinyl branches. The beast had turned into a beauty after all.

I couldn't fail to notice the empty space under the tree. Fleetingly, I thought of all the earrings, robes, books, boots, candies and paperweights I would *not* get this year. But instead of gifts, I discovered a new feeling, the weightlessness of being able to do without, and it felt good. Even the idea of owning the stunning green dress had lost its thrill. My old red one would do just fine.

And this evening, Christmas Eve 1986, as we enjoyed our dinner and a bottle of *Château Renard*, our laughter filled the room.

Candles flickered in the silver candlesticks my mother had given us for our wedding, throwing a warm light on our festive meal: a traditional roast, yams, carrots and mashed potatoes. The three hundred lights on our tree sparkled against the black night beyond the window. A stack of logs crackled in the fireplace, and the smell of burning rosin filled the house. The flames, from a distance, danced in James' dark-brown eyes, exuding a quiet glow. In a soft, slow tone I heard my name. "My Isabella," and with an upbeat bounce, "I've always liked you in red."

James' words were tinged with the music of ease and contentment. This, I thought, was all that mattered. Not the choice between an artificial tree or a real one, or the presents beneath it. The real prize was the message of peace and joy, timeless as the security of belonging together.

James rarely opened up, but tonight he volunteered memories of his childhood back in St. Louis. He spoke about the hand-carved wooden railing of the stairs in the house where he had grown up. He remembered the yellow tiffany lamp over the dining room table and the smell of chamomile tea in the kitchen. He seldom mentioned his parents, who were no longer alive, and of whom he curiously had no pictures. There was a loving shine in his eyes when he spoke of his mother, who had been forty-two when he was born. Later she had suffered from arthritis and from the undesirable ways her husband spent his time and money.

"What ways?" I asked.

"Women..," James replied with contempt. "And when I saw my mother's distress, I made a vow never to cheat on my wife, or else never get married at all. You can trust me, Isabella, and I trust you. Trust is the major component of commitment. You can learn to trust another human being, and I believe that you can learn it as an adult, without having to be hopelessly damaged by the failure of your parents to set a good example. We all have the power to change our lives."

"Of course," I said in a clipped manner that hid my nerves.

The twin creases at the corners of his mouth deepened.

"You know I never dwell on the past. The future is the only thing we can change for the better. It's just that I despised my father for making my mother's life miserable. Besides," he made an effort to lighten up the atmosphere, "he never let me eat popcorn when I was a kid. He said it would stick to my teeth."

James let out a sarcastic little laugh.

"Imagine, a childhood without popcorn!"

I shook my head. "*Poor* James."

We smiled, both absorbed in private thoughts.

James was right. He was able to let go of the past, and I couldn't think of a single time when he had ever confided his hurting heart to me, his hurt over a relationship or the loss of one. It was not that James was inarticulate or out of touch with his feelings. But for him, once released, feelings could undergo the dangerous conversion from control to chaos. Released feelings were a lot like dead needles falling from a Christmas tree. They got out of hand, implied the loss of power and damaged the image. They were no longer orderly. James' remedy was simple. To avoid the messiness of needles or emotions, one only had to acquire the perfection of a smile, the willpower to leave the past behind, or an artificial tree.

James helped himself to a big piece of pineapple tart and said, "Well, that's enough emotional junk for today."

I piled a heap of whipped cream on his tart and said encouragingly, "All the food we eat on Christmas Eve has zero calories."

He raised his eyebrows.

"Where is that written in the nativity story?"

The phone rang. James grimaced and moved without hurry to pick it up. He listened for a moment, then signaled for me to come over. I got up from the table. "Who is it?"

Holding his hand over the receiver, he grumbled, "It's Julia."

"*Julia!*" I screamed with delight. My god, Julia! This was the first sign of life from her since her swift departure for Hilton

Head three months ago. Time and separation were wiped out in a matter of seconds.

"Isabella, Merry Christmas..."

Her voice was spiced with a new, happier bounce. To hear from her was a present I hadn't dared to dream of. She poured out the pieces of her life, with one item of bad news. Poor Ludwig had died a week ago. He had been an old gentleman, and the Southern climate hadn't agreed with him.

And no, I wasn't angry with her for not answering my letter, and yes, James and I were enjoying Christmas Eve. After Steve's death, her sister had needed her and, following her own divorce, she had needed to burn all her bridges and draw a line between past and future.

And now, by a careful process of regeneration, a new Julia had been born. She was ready to face life again, maybe even lift the dust-cover off her typewriter and start writing again. The crisp South Carolina sea-breeze had done wonders for her appetite and nerves. She would skip the New Jersey winter and come back in the spring to her apartment in Montclair.

James had settled, with a second piece of pineapple tart, on the couch in front of the TV and was flipping channels. I jumped when a cookie commercial was followed by the second movement of Mozart's *Jupiter Symphony*. Listening to Julia with one ear, I stretched the phone cord to its limits in order to peek around the corner into the living room. I jumped. *Orson.* His smile filled the screen. Orson in his tails. Orson in Carnegie Hall, conducting the concert I had missed when I was working late in the office. Of course, this was the Christmas Special Orson had told me about: *Mozart in Manhattan.*

"Julia," I explained hastily, "I have to go now. Orson Mahler is on TV. I'm going to be a member of his chorus soon."

She was surprised at the importance I attached to a TV show.

I cut the conversation short.

"I promise to write you a letter soon."

Once I hung up, I felt that I had abandoned her again for Orson, just as on the day in October when she had asked me to spend a last evening with her.

James called from the living room, "You might want to watch this. Your friend Orson is on TV. How's that for a surprise?"

I nestled next to him, my legs curled under me, my eyes glued to this absurd, luminous box that projected the illusion of a man who had called me *Sweetheart* in the middle of the Port Authority Bus Terminal.

The sweeping movements of Orson's baton were artfully superimposed on Manhattan Christmas scenes, the window displays of *Saks Fifth Avenue* and the Empire State Building lit up in red and green. The giant Nutcracker parade in front of the Paine Webber building seemed petite compared to Orson's long, sensitive hands. Ah, his hands, I thought.

James shifted restlessly. "So how's Julia?"

With no interest to elaborate, I replied laconically. "She's coming back in the spring."

The music had stopped, and the skaters at Rockefeller Center could be seen circling the rink. Towering above it was the enormous Christmas tree, the same tree that Orson and I had passed earlier today.

A reporter explained that this tree, with its twenty thousand seven-and-a-half-watt colored bulbs, reached as high as seventy feet. A scaffold had served as the workplace on which electricians spliced five miles of wiring that fed current to the lights. Heat lamps had helped to keep their fingers nimble. It took twenty-two men six days to trim the tree, with each man tying close to a thousand lights. One electrician was heard to say, "After a while you can do it in your sleep."

And finally, with all the bulbs in place, the signal had been given for the traditional lighting ceremony that had begun in 1936. How many people had had their pictures taken in front of this famous backdrop since then?

The camera swung around to focus on the exquisite soprano voice singing Mozart's *Laudate Dominum*. The soprano was wrapped in a Canadian fox coat and I recognized Mirella Freni from the Metropolitan Opera. Next to her, dressed in a stunning lynx coat, was her counterpart, soprano Kiri Te Kanawa, joining Mirella in the duet *Exultate Jubilate*. Their breath was visible in the cold winter air against the golden statue of Prometheus behind the skating rink.

A pair of hands applauded, hands that I knew so well. Orson stepped in front of the camera and was greeted by the two divas with hugs and kisses.

On cue, they chorused, "Here he is, the man with the velvet voice."

Orson smiled, a little bit embarrassed. "That's a *real* compliment coming from you ladies."

The TV crew had made Orson wear a red woolen hat that made him look like Santa's helper. A reporter moved into the picture with a microphone.

"Orson Mahler must be one of the busiest people in town these days. The only person who's busier is probably Santa himself. As the holiday season reaches its peak, Maestro Mahler will conduct an exceptional array of special events."

Now he turned to Orson, and the cameraman pointed his lens at both of them.

"Maestro, you will be conducting five concerts between now and the New Year, sometimes two a day. How do you manage the stamina for a schedule like that?"

Orson gave a musical laugh. "First of all, Jim, you and I have known each other for quite a few years now, so please don't refer to me as 'Maestro.' It's Orson. And second, as far as my stamina is concerned, it's very easy." He winked into the camera. "All you have to do is put the right score in front of me. My energy level has a way of rising in proportion to the number of concerts on my schedule, and I love it."

I glanced sideways at James. His eyes gleamed, picking up on the stimulation that flowed from Orson's magnetism. For me,

Orson had receded into an unattainable vision, which made it hard to put him in context as the private man I knew so well.

Now Orson turned the tables, leading the interview, instead of being led.

"Jim, I wish you would ask me what advice I'd give to those listeners who are newcomers to classical music."

The other man laughed good-naturedly and cleared his throat elaborately. "Orson, I've always wanted to ask you what advice you would give to those listeners and concert-goers who are newcomers to classical music."

Orson grinned contentedly. "I'm so glad you asked that question, Jim. First of all, I'd like to put everyone at ease. No one should think, 'Oh, I don't know anything about classical music, so I won't be able to enjoy it.' That's nonsense, trust me. You will enjoy it, under one condition. *Relax.* Sit back. Let the music wash over you. Just *listen.* Let go of any attempt to intellectualize. After all, music is created first and foremost to be listened to and not to be read about. Just say to the music *Here I am. Take me. See what you can do for me.* Always remember that it is the composer's job to get you excited."

I remembered that he had told me almost the identical words during our walk through Central Park. Was that only last spring, or lifetimes ago?

The camera was blending details of the Christmas tree. Orson blew his breath into the hollow of his bare hands before tucking them away in the pockets of his coat. His eyes shifted to the tree.

"What a job it must have been to wire it," he smiled, admiring the finished product. "Those are the people who deserve to be interviewed on your show. At least I, as a conductor, don't have to stand on the scaffold in the cold and battle with the bulbs and branches."

A playful sparkle appeared in his eyes. "You know, as a conductor, I'm the only one on stage who doesn't make a sound. All I do is stand on the podium and turn the pages of the score, and I've made it my firm rule to always stop conducting the moment the orchestra stops playing."

Orson's joke put Jim away. He could hardly catch his breath.

"Orson, one last question. What makes you tick?"

Sincere again, Orson smiled gently. "It's easy. I love music and I love people, and I love to bring the two together."

The camera had frozen Orson's smiling face as Jim thanked the audience.

James, still with his arm around me, said, "I'm impressed by this guy Mahler. You can feel a great artistic mind paired with a genuine sense for humanity."

I struggled free of James' arms. Suddenly, I felt a hint of suffocation and turned off the TV by remote control. The room felt crowded. There was too much of Orson here with us.

I said, "Why not sit in front of the fire and look at an old photo-album, maybe when we were in Austria together, two years ago."

James said, "Let's do that. And I'll get more logs for the fire."

He stood up, stretching his tall, athletic body, as if unsure what to do with all his limbs. He disappeared for a curiously long time in the garage. When he came up the stairs again, he was smiling like the proverbial cat that had eaten the canary. Along with a stack of logs, he carried a gift-wrapped box.

"I thought..." he coughed, not sure how to begin, and put the parcel in my lap.

"I thought... uh, Isabella...you'd like...." He looked at once helpless and thrilled.

"But James," I protested, "we had a deal not to give each other presents. It's not fair, because I have nothing for you."

"I know," he smiled happily. "I don't need any presents as long as I have you."

"Oh, James! When did you buy this?"

"Remember that Saturday when I pretended I had to catch up on work in the office?'

"Yes, and you left your reading glasses at home on the breakfast table."

"You didn't suspect me of anything, did you?" He burst out laughing.

I looked at the box in my lap. It was wrapped in silver with a red ribbon.

"Aren't you curious to see what's inside?"

"I hate to destroy the fancy paper." The cubic shape of its box and its considerable weight was revealing enough.

"Is it a paperweight?"

"Right! It's one from the new *Caithness* edition. It's called *Moonflower*."

When it emerged from the box I marveled, "Wow, it's stunning. Thank you so much, James," and I felt the excitement of a child visited by Santa.

Outside, it had started snowing. This was the first Christmas Eve in years with snow on the ground. Glowing against the black night outside the window, our tree blinked and glittered. James touched my face and his eyes took on a special shine, telling me "I want you" in a thousand small ways.

I said, "I'll go upstairs and get the album."

James grinned boyishly. "All right, but first things first. How about a big bowl of popcorn?"

I wondered if there would ever be a moment when I would love him more.

61

When writing a letter to Julia I always felt at a disadvantage expressing myself on paper. My writing skills could hardly compare to her flair for language, and her ability to wring out pages of brilliant eloquence on *any* subject always amazed me.

Contrary to Julia, who dreamed of writing a bcstseller but had no story, I was experiencing all the fret and frenzy she could use for a plot. But my writing resembled that of a composer who had too many conflicting melodies wheeling through his head, making it impossible to shape them into the disciplined form of a sonata or a symphony.

And here I was writing to Julia, and the longer my letter became the more of a mess it turned out to be. I wrote about James' idea of a charitable contribution instead of gifts, but omitted the paperweight he had given me. I told her how nervous I was about the upcoming chorus audition, but didn't admit that I had failed it the first time. I wrote about my decision to go job-hunting, but left out Mr. Stringer's unprofessional behavior or inviting glances.

After reading my letter over, I found it meaningless and hollow, because more things were unsaid than said. I yearned to share the one thing I kept locked away in my heart, but the pages of my story had already been turned too far to make sense on paper. How could I share my inner *knowing* of having reached the zenith of my romance with Orson and wondered, if, on my way down, I'd dance, run or fall.

My decision to tear up my letter was a signpost in the stream of my mind, alerting me to change direction. Could it be that I was moving toward the dead-end of my integrity? How high was the price of secrecy?

I was seized with a longing to connect with Julia again. Maybe she would help me face my blurred priorities. And then I thought, *Why wait?* It would be easier to talk than to commit myself on paper. Sometimes a phone call, like a confessional, can best bring out hidden sins. Hadn't she always been the one I trusted? And so, with my letter torn into pieces, I dialed 803 for Hilton Head.

The phone rang five times. Her sister Hanna answered and we exchanged a few polite words about how she was facing life as a widow and how grateful she was that Julia could be with her during this difficult time. Then one of her children came on and told me how poor Ludwig had fallen sick and how they all missed him, and about the heavy rains they had last night.

By the time Julia arrived from the porch, where she had just scraped her hand cleaning up broken branches from the storm, the moment felt no longer right to talk about Orson. Instead I resolved to listen to *her* and enfolded my secret in my heart again.

62

I was still holding my breath when Matthew stopped playing the piano. A second of silence followed that contained all possibilities. Finally, I dared to look up from my score and tried to read from Joan's and Daisy's expression if I had passed or failed the audition.

"Okay, Isabella," Joan smiled the warmest smile she was capable of, "your tone is thin, but it's pitched correctly and it's clear enough to carry the part. You've passed. You are now an official member of the chorus. Congratulations."

Her benevolent nod was seconded by Daisy in her function as audition committee assistant. Daisy rose from her chair and leaned her clumsy body across the desk, extending her arms in an awkward hug. "Welcome to the Orson Mahler Oratorio Chorus, Isabella," she chirped, smelling of lemon.

"Thank you all," I stammered, still glued to the spot, hardly able to believe the unbelievable. Here I was in CAMI Hall, where I had attended so many rehearsals, but always sitting in exile behind the basses, feeling like an intruder. Now, at long last, I was one of them! I could take a seat among the altos and participate in the concerts. I would be on-stage in Carnegie Hall. *Me...* in Carnegie Hall!

Solemnly, I accepted the official name-tag I would wear at rehearsals. I handed Joan the borrowed score and felt something soft and leathery against my shoulder. It was Matthew's jacket. He had got up from the piano and enfolded me in his arms.

"I knew you'd do it, Isabella! Didn't I tell you? I knew you'd do it!"

On the street, darkness had fallen and the temperature along with it. Matthew landed a kiss on my cheek and kept his arm around my shoulder as we walked along in the Fifty-Seventh Street rush-hour crowd. A broad grin was on his face. My success was his too, and rightfully so.

He said, "Remember how I made you practice those difficult intervals of the fugue in the sixth movement? You did beautifully, Isabella. I'm so proud of you, and I know you'll make a real contribution to the chorus."

And tonight, at the first rehearsal of the New Year, it was my first chance to prove it. After my audition, Matthew's services as pianist were no longer needed. Orson had given him the night off. In his place, a young prodigy would be there to accompany the chorus's first reading of the *Brahms Requiem*. The boy's mother, eager to get her offspring into the Manhattan School of Music, had continually pressured Orson for a letter of recommendation. Orson had repeatedly refused to grant the boy a private audition, with no interest in his talent, but had come up with the idea of having him play the *Brahms Requiem* at sight. With this challenge Orson hoped to get rid of both of them.

Matthew and I stopped for a red light at Sixth Avenue.

He sighed, "What mother in her right mind would want her son to become a pianist anyway? Take me, for instance. With all the jobs I have to take to make a living, coaching opera singers, giving piano lessons and playing at corporate functions... But anyway," he brightened up, "I'm off for the rest of the evening. Let's celebrate!"

I said, "What did you have in mind?"

"Well... shall we write graffiti length-wise on the Empire State Building?" he giggled.

"Any chance you can you make it less complicated?"

"Or…go ice-skating at Rockefeller Center. Yes, let's go *ice-skating*!"

Before I had a chance to consider it, he picked me up and whirled me around in the middle of Sixth Avenue, afire in the cold with the joy of living.

"Only," he admitted, putting me down, "I haven't skated in a while."

"Welcome to the club," I said, still undecided. I told him about my winters in Austria, where as a child I had practically lived on skates. When the lake froze over, the two miles from the north shore, where I lived, to the south shore, where Gustav Mahler had his villa at the beginning of the century, could be crossed on skates or sleighs. As soon as the local authorities declared the ice safe, the whole population would be there, skating, cheering, taking pictures, with sandwiches and hot tea…or bandages.

Matthew smiled. "What memories you have. You're so lucky."

"Lucky, if you consider how many times I fell on the ice and never broke a bone."

We had been walking fast and were now approaching the flood-lit skating rink with its many-colored flags flying in the wind. I stood spellbound at the scene, and yet my thoughts returned to Orson and the chorus.

I said, "Matthew, I don't think it's a good idea if I miss my first official rehearsal tonight, Orson will wonder where I am, after learning I've passed the audition."

"I wouldn't worry about Orson. He won't even notice if you're not there, and you know the music so well already."

Pleased with the last part of his statement, but not the first, I allowed Matthew to convince me. How tempting it felt to be on skates once again. I said, "Let's do it then." In the wind, the hollow clicking sounds of metal from the flagpoles mixed with Tchaikovsky's *Nutcracker Suite* from the speakers.

Matthew frowned. "I hope this isn't going to be the 'Bone-Cracker-Suite'."

"If we stand here much longer, we're going to get cold feet in more ways than one," I said and pulled Matthew by the sleeve down the steps to the skate rental office at the end of the Promenade. We stood in line to check our coats and afterwards squeezed onto the wooden bench in front of a row of lockers to lace up our skates.

"All set?" I asked. We laughed at our first cautious attempt to stand up.

On the ice, we moved tentatively at first, then with growing ease, chasing our flood-lit shadows or running away from them as we glided around corners. I felt the thrill of speed and laughed at Matthew.

"This is so much fun!"

We clasped our gloved hands and were encircled by a group of youngsters, chasing each other to the sounds of the *Blue Danube Waltz*.

Matthew remarked dryly, "Imagine if people had three legs, armies would be waltzing to war instead of marching."

Desperate for balance, he grabbed me from behind. I let out a scream, and we slammed into the fence under the golden statue of Prometheus. Oddly, the flame in the giant's palm brought back a burning question in my mind. Here and now, at the risk of turning the skating rink into a minefield, I needed to solve a mystery.

"Matthew, did your mother name you after Orson's middle name?"

I held my breath.

He made a face. "Orson's middle name is Matthew? I didn't know he had a middle name. Where did you get that idea?"

What should I say? I couldn't tell him that I had seen the initials *OMM* on a handkerchief Orson had handed me when I was crying on his shirtfront.

I shrugged. "One of the chorus members mentioned it to me." Then I rummaged for a tissue and purposely changed the subject.

"Your mother was exceptionally friendly at the audition today. I hope she doesn't consider me an intruder any longer."

A couple was cutting a figure eight in front of us. In the multi-colored crowd, we raced around the rink in silence, the chilly air rushing against our faces and the ice receding under our skates with the dull tone of etching blades. Only a few inches separated us, but Matthew seemed far away.

He said reflectively. "My mother is a very misunderstood person. I just wish she could find a life away from Orson and the chorus."

I could see the bitterness in his eyes. "I don't know what whim of fate kept her around him all these years. And when my father died... uh... tragically, twenty years ago, Orson offered her this job and assured a living for both of us."

"Tragically?" My mind trailed behind his words. I couldn't tell if the tears in Matthew's eyes were from the wind or nightmare images of the past.

"Matthew... I'm so sorry."

But instead of offering me an explanation, he bit his lip. He looked as if he were trying to avoid a crack on a slippery secret of the past that could make him fall.

He sniffled noisily. "I wonder if my mother will ever be able to start a new life of her own. Frankly, I've wanted to quit my job with the chorus many times and move someplace else with Tom, maybe. But then, I might as well stick around and keep an eye on her."

Poor Joan, I thought for the first time. The desperate Mrs. Hunter of Orson's distant heart.

Matthew made no effort to hide his disapproval.

"Women are like glue around Orson. He uses them to keep his life together. He has Paula to run the house, answer the mail and bake brownies for him. And my mother takes the chorus administration off his shoulders."

He sighed, and it was clear whom he would mention next.

We chorused in unison, "and *Beverly!*"

"Yes, look at Beverly." He was more relaxed now. "Some people in the chorus wonder if her services go beyond investing his money and supplying him with hot chocolate at rehearsals."

I said, "She once mentioned to me that she calls him several times a day."

"And she's not kidding."

"I can't understand why Paula wouldn't put her foot down."

Matthew tightened his scarf around his neck. "Paula? Let me tell you what I think about Paula. When Beverly first appeared in Orson's life, Paula had very mixed feelings about her. But Beverly handled it cleverly. She helped Paula with her paperwork, told her all the gossip from the chorus and joined Paula in her dislike of my mother. Paula realized that, because of Beverly, Orson spent less time with my mother. That qualified Beverly for Paula's friendship."

I nodded. "The antagonism between your mother and Beverly is obvious."

"Yeah, Beverly seems so harmless with her flirtatious smile under her thick glasses, but watch out, Isabella. Don't ever get too close to Orson or she'll be out for your blood."

I moved ahead of him but Matthew clutched my arm.

"Hey, stay with me! Don't run away!"

In the blue light of the night, the buildings surrounding the rink stood like ghost towers against the clear, black sky. The stars spanned the rooftops like bridges. We skated hand in hand, finding comfort in the same subjects for different motives.

I veered to miss a small, tentative boy with mittens dangling from his sleeves.

"No doubt Beverly would go over Niagara Falls in a barrel for Orson," I shrugged.

Matthew said, "She's always flaunting her femininity, her tax breaks and her thermos bottle. She's always the pursuer, never the pursued."

His candor made me daring. "Matthew, do you think Orson is romantically interested in Beverly?"

There was no surprise on his face.

"A few years ago there was a little rumor or two..."

"And *now?* What about Orson and Beverly now?"

"I recently heard him say that Beverly can be too pushy and that it's impossible to get rid of her. But I think it's too late. He's trapped. She'd never let up on him, and he's too dependent on her to change the status quo. So he's caught between three fires. Beverly has become another useful gadget, just like my mother and Paula. But none of them is clever enough to know it."

Plumes of frost flew from Matthew's mouth into the cold night. We tried for longer glides now, flapping our arms in exaggerated gestures.

A smile curled on his lips.

"Do you want to know what I think, Isabella?"

"What?" I wiped my nose with the back of my glove.

"Orson really likes *you.*"

"*Me?* What makes you think that?"

"I know him all too well. I can read the emotions in his face, and I see the way he smiles at other people and how he smiles at *you.*"

I didn't dare to look up. "Am I supposed to feel flattered?"

"That's up to you. I know you're happily married, and I'm very glad of that."

"Why?"

"Because there are still some things in life and some women on earth that even Orson Mahler can't have."

"I get the impression you don't like him very much, do you Matthew?" Peripherally, I looked at his face, not sure I cared to hear the confession I might have triggered. But it was too late.

Instead of moving on the ice, the ice moved under us. The shock of falling was a hammer blow to our behinds. I don't remember if I pulled Matthew down or if he made me fall. Maybe one of our skates had got caught in a grove in the ice.

After the first rush of surprise I looked at him.

"Matthew, are you all right?"

"Yeah, I guess so... How about you?"

"I'm fine." I forced a grin, trying to ignore the piercing buzz in my tailbone.

A skating attendant came to a spraying stop in front of us, covering us with snow. "Are you okay, folks?"

"Uh... yes." I accepted his outstretched hand and he pulled me to my feet.

Matthew and I brushed off our clothes and looked at each other like two children caught at the cookie jar.

I asked, "Ready to give it another try?"

But Matthew hadn't heard my question. Again, he had this far-away look on his face.

"You're absolutely right, Isabella."

"About what?"

"I don't like Orson Mahler very much."

63

The next day, when Orson called me at the office, he was all maestro, used to giving orders and seeing them executed. Instead of asking "Are you free to see me?" he said, "I want you to have lunch with me," and gave me the name of a Chinese Restaurant on Times Square.

Due to a conference call to the West Coast which I had to co-ordinate, I arrived late for our date. Orson's impatience hung in the air between us, his face was tense.

"Hello, Orson, I'm sorry for being late," I smiled, sitting down. "How well you contain your enthusiasm to see me."

Orson, dressed in one of his conservatively tailored suits, drew doodles on a placemat showing the twelve signs of the Chinese zodiac. We sat in silence and I waited while he connected the rabbit and the snake with baroque curves and flying dots.

There was an edge of defiance in his voice.

"Well, congratulations, Isabella. Joan told me you passed the audition."

"Th... thanks," I sputtered and resented his ability to intimidate me by the sheer power of his presence.

His birthmark twitched. "Isabella, *where* were you last night?"

"Matthew and I went skating."

"You did *what?"*

I reached for the glass of water on the table. "We went ice-skating at Rockefeller Center to celebrate my audition."

We measured each other's perplexity. Then he started doodling again, dotting lines around the horse.

I said lightheartedly into the silence, "Matthew and I had a lot of fun," and my thoughts strayed to my aching backside.

"I'm glad to hear it." His sarcasm could chill the steaming teapot on the table.

Trying to ignore his air of arrogance, I bubbled along. "I hadn't bought the new edition of the Brahms score yet, and you know how cheap Joan can be if she has to give out one of her own. Besides," I hastened to defend myself, "I don't need your permission to go skating."

Orson tore the paper cover off his chopsticks and the silence between us magnified every sound around us. The waiter bowed, and Orson ordered sweet and sour pork for both of us. I never cared for sweet and sour pork, but before I could object the waiter was gone and Orson was embarking on a speech.

"Isabella, now that you are an official member of my chorus, it's not a good idea to skip rehearsals. The *Brahms Requiem* is a difficult piece, and we only have two months until the concert on March seventh. Plus, during that time I'll be away for three weeks on a concert tour through Europe, as you know. I have to appoint a substitute conductor for those three weeks, and that bothers me considerably. So please try to be there every Wednesday. Moreover, I was worried when you didn't show up." His tone was velvet now. "I kept looking at the door all evening and I almost called you at home."

His sincerity sent an arrow into my heart.

I nodded, trying to smooth things over.

"And how did the piano prodigy work out?"

Orson sighed. "The kid never showed up. Nor did his mother. I guess the prospect of having to play a piece of that caliber at sight scared them off. She called me this morning while I was still asleep. I told her to break the boy's arms and have him go into the candy business. This country is flooded with aspiring pianists, and there are no jobs for them. You know how concerned I am for Matthew, realizing all too well that he's not destined for greatness."

"But if Matthew wasn't there, who played last night?"

"Guess who? I had to bang out the damned Requiem myself. What a killer of a piece it is when you're out of practice. All those thick chords that never breathe. It's so intricate, you could use twenty fingers instead of ten. Isabella, I'm afraid I loused up deplorably in front of the chorus."

I thought that an expression of empathy would be in order but had to suppress a malicious grin.

"You gave Matthew the night off, didn't you?"

"Hell, yes. I mean, no. I told him he didn't have to play, but I didn't mean he didn't have to show up at all."

I was enjoying this. Just for once, Orson didn't have the upper hand.

I said, "It seems that I missed an interesting rehearsal..."

Orson looked vulnerable, but I sensed he'd soon turn our talk around in his favor.

"Isabella, I'd like to make a suggestion for Wednesdays in the future."

"Yes?"

Our sweet and sour pork was served.

"From now on I want you to sit in the front row of the alto section."

I fidgeted with my chopsticks.

"I feel too new for such a prominent position."

Orson began to eat with a boyish grin. "From now on no more hiding behind the basses. I insist that you sit in the front row, and you know why?"

"Why?"

"Because I want to get a better look at you."

"You mean *keep an eye on me*?"

"No, just to *look* at you. Believe me, Isabella, from now on I have much more reason to look forward to the Wednesday night rehearsals."

He reached for my hand and held it firmly.

"Congratulations again. I'm proud of you. Besides," he whispered meaningfully, "I want to make another date with you."

But I pulled my hand away and said with an impenetrable air, "That's all very nice, but there's one more thing I'd like to straighten out."

"What's that?"

"How come you're ordering my food for me?"

"Uh... I thought you liked sweet and sour pork."

"No, I don't, and I would like to have shrimp and snow peas instead."

"Oh..," his voice grew timid. "I'm sorry. We'll order what you want."

I cleared my throat.

"Orson, please don't tell me what to eat or where to sit." I tried to sound unemotional. "Sometimes you need a reminder to step down from the podium."

There was a small but significant pause during which color rushed to his face, but he recovered in a second.

"You're wrong, Isabella. I can't wait to get up there on the podium again." His clear, simple tone held no hint of teasing.

"Isabella, I'm asking you again, very respectfully, to sit in the front row. Because from now on you have my permission to disrupt my concentration with your beautiful legs."

I thought, maybe this was the maestro's variation on the music in his heart.

64

The untouched emptiness of our hotel room was charged with a delicious thrall, like empty staff lines on white paper, waiting to be filled with our song. Wasn't this the same room we had stayed in the very first time? The desert-colored pattern of the drapes and bedspread was registered only by my eyes, not my mind. My mind held its breath, connecting to a reality beyond colors or patterns, a reality that took place in a different orbit.

Across the semi-darkness Orson warned me, "Watch out for that step in the bathroom. I don't understand what these damned architects get paid for."

Orson put his watch and wallet on the dresser. I placed my earrings and my diamond anniversary ring at a little distance.

Our relationship was stripped of that special mystique it held in the beginning. The gates of candor and closeness were now forever open, like a line of mirrors in their own reflection. Finally we could unleash the excitement we had been forced too long to repress, slowly releasing our urgency like a punctured sandbag, and by looking at each other, we looked into the same mirror.

Orson's eyes were an invitation. They said, *Hand me your wishes, your unknown self, your fears and fantasies. Tell me the truth of the moment. I'm reaching for the music in your body. Let me in.*

And knowing that he would master the instrument of my body and make beautiful music, I shut out the gamut of ordinary life and surrendered to the promise of what was about to be.

Today was Martin Luther King's birthday, and most people were off from work. That was why Beverly thought it was a good day to have a party at her home later in the afternoon. She planned to serve Chinese food, knowing Orson loved it. Orson, of course, would be the guest of honor. Along with a group of other chorus members, I was invited too. James was on his way to Houston in the corporate jet.

I had never been to Beverly's apartment in Manhattan. Orson and I would drive there together in my car, but discreetly arrange to arrive separately. Officially, I'd come from New Jersey and he from his apartment on Park Avenue, and no one would be the wiser.

But all this would be later, lifetimes later, after *this.* This moment felt timeless, releasing the past and rejecting the future. It moved us out of the sphere of society and judgment back into the realm of instincts, with our bodies freed from the bondage of our intellect.

I turned around from the rack where I had hung my coat and saw Orson turning back the spread of the king-size bed.

"The culprit is said to always return to the scene of the crime."

I had to smile to see him use his fingers to count the times we had been here together.

"It's the tenth time, Isabella. Happy anniversary."

"Your arithmetic is impeccable, Orson. I came up with the same total."

I took off my boots and pulled the barrette from my hair, allowing it to flow free. On the thick, sand-colored carpet we took a step towards each other, smiling a slow, soft smile.

"Ten times," Orson repeated, somewhat pensively, as if for a moment he would consider the transitory fate of passion.

Orson's first kiss created a moment where touch loses its innocence and turns into a pledge. He savored the first sensation of my skin, not afraid to share his hunger.

Orson's voice was velvet. "I want you to think, Isabella, that my arms protect you from everything in the outside world. I want you to enjoy and be enjoyed. Let yourself fall. I'm here to catch you and to attend to your every whim."

I relished the moment of falling on the bed, like falling to the bottom of the sea. Orson's desire was devoid of haste. Lying side by side with our bodies bare, he brushed my skin with nothing but a gentle breath. Its stimulation created ripples in a still pond, soft, floating ripples, culminating in a wave of wanting, making me beg for his hands and lips.

He said, "Easy, Isabella, easy. We don't have to catch a plane. It's my greatest pleasure to see you excited."

But desire had become too powerful for words. Propelled by our held-in need, our bodies intertwined, saying things by touch that no words could express. Everything that happened, happened because there was no way we could make it stop, our skin cringing with sensations, our fingers opening up closed places, our bodies demanding and enduring, drawing new maps of desire with all roads leading to the sweetest pain there is.

"You feel wonderful," Orson reveled, "so soft, so sweet, so womanly. My god, what must it feel like to *be* a woman..."

I couldn't help but feel amazed at how perfectly his body fit mine, how right it felt, this chemistry between us, this magic whose formula didn't always work when we were no longer in bed. There was no logic in the law of love. The whole universe was reduced to the limits of this bed. We rocked together, flesh entering flesh with the need to identify, yet to be different. I could no longer repress the pulse preceding the pinnacle of passion. Its tremor rendered me helpless, spellbound and ecstatic.

"Good, Isabella! Yes....ah...here it is..." A thousand stars danced in his eyes.

We were whole now, we were everything at once. He was me and I was him. At his peak, he groaned with madness, with tones so high that no one would believe his deep voice capable of reaching them. He clung to my body with despair and tenderness, combining the fiery fierceness of youth with the gentleness of age.

"Isabella," he sighed breathlessly, "Do you know what is the most wonderful part of my pleasure? It is the thought of holding you in my arms. Did you notice how I tightened my grip on you?"

How touching to see him so young, so vulnerable, so genuinely taken. The ghost traces of all the bodies of the women of his past seemed to be erased from the memory of his skin. In this unique moment I was the only woman he had ever loved.

Orson pushed some pillows off the bed. He turned over and rested my face against his chest. Drunk with the taste of skin, we felt languid, timeless, in a pool of bliss. In this ordinary room, the longing of our souls and sexualities was satisfied. Our bodies felt hot against the sheets and we fell into a restorative slumber.

And yet I fought the lure to succumb to the luxury of sleep or the drunken state of dreams. Secretly we were both listening to each other's breathing, afraid to miss a single moment of awareness.

In the stillness of the room, the world outside now seemed to move in on me. How heavy will the traffic be going to Manhattan? Was it snowing? I couldn't help thinking of the party that would force us to behave like strangers. Orson had told me that Paula would also be there. For the first time I would shake hands with Orson's wife.

Would I be able to look her in the eye? I thought back to when I had seen Paula once before, in Carnegie Hall after the *Verdi Requiem* concert. Her matronly form, short silver hair and the lively expression of her blue eyes was all I could recall. Paula, who had joined forces with Beverly to keep their eyes on Orson, in public and in private.

Beverly's features began to swim before my eyes. I depict her in the kitchen. Is she peeling shrimp, chopping beef and pork? Is she fidgeting over bamboo shoots, Chinese cabbage and snow peas?

I see a pot of won-ton soup simmering on her stove, exuding the spices of water chestnuts, scallions and ginger root.

I can't resist lifting the lid. I lower my head over the hot steam and to my surprise see Orson's face mirrored on the surface of the soup. So that's where he is! He smiles conspiratorially, his voice grotesquely begging, "Don't give me away. I found a hiding place." I laugh back at him and can't stop laughing. "Orson, you look so funny. You have no business being in this pot. Paula and Beverly are looking all over for you. Do you think they can't find you in here? Well, I found you. So get out. You look like the man in the moon."

Startled, I opened my eyes. Everything was reversed. Orson's face was now bent over mine. For a moment I didn't know where I was.

He said, "You were laughing."

"Was I asleep?"

"Yes, for quite a while. And then you started to laugh."

Now I recalled my dream. Should I tell him about it? No, I decided, not yet. Maybe later in the car. I laughed again.

I said, "I'm hungry. I'm beginning to look forward to Beverly's Chinese food."

Orson placed a long, lingering kiss on my temple. "You must have dreamed something funny. I was watching you, and you were laughing in your sleep. You looked lovely. You radiated the essence of a happy woman."

His eyes gleamed, as if he were about to give a signal.

Was he going to ask me, *Let's skip Beverly's party. Let's go somewhere else, another planet, where we can stay together around the clock and not go out except for walks at night under the stars...*

What would my reaction be? I shivered, frightened by the recklessness of my response and relieved by the knowledge that he would never ask. Instead, shifting on his sheets, Orson asked with soft probing eyes.

"Isabella, what is it like to be a woman?"

I looked at him and shrugged, knowing that he wasn't referring to nail polish or high heels. "I don't know what to say. It just feels natural to me."

His unhurried hand ran from my neck across my shoulders down along the curve between my breasts.

"Are you aware of the beauty that you carry around with you? I'm allowed to share your beauty only for a short time, but you will still have it when I'm no longer with you, at the party later on, at work, or even when you're asleep."

I felt oddly frightened, reading my power in his eyes, the power he bestowed on me. I held my breath. I didn't move.

"I don't know of anything," he continued thoughtfully, "not even music, that equals the sensuous softness of a woman's body such as yours. If I could only change places with you, just for *one* day, to feel what it's like to be *you.*"

I could sense the deep longing in him to recognize the stranger in me, to be me, to identify, to merge. Was this his quest for his own definition of the meaning of love?

What had Orson done to me by asking, *What is it like to be a woman?* Had he exalted me? Or enslaved me? Still suspended by my inability to supply a satisfactory answer to his question, Orson played with a strand of my hair and put it back in place. Time had run through our fingers like a precious liquid, fugitive, too swiftly. Hours had passed in the brief gesture of a single act of love.

I sat up on the edge of the bed.

"I'd better take a shower if I'm going to be presentable at the party. I hope there's a hair-dryer in the bathroom."

Orson, still stretched out, stayed me with his hand.

"Don't. Not yet. Don't shower. Stay just as you are. Stay in my arms. Just a little longer. Come here."

And I did. And nothing in the whole world could make me feel more like a woman than his long, enfolding arms and the brief illusion that he would never let me go. But how could I make him understand? He, the interrogator, for whom I had no explanation, supplied me with the answer to his own question with the ease of his embrace.

Yes, *this* is what it felt like to be a woman.

65

Outside the hotel room the daylight blinded our eyes despite the gray-hung sky. The fountain in the middle of the courtyard had been turned off for the winter. In the car I switched on the headlights and the heat as Orson rubbed his hands briskly together.

"Some music?" I shot Orson a quick sideways glance and fiddled with the knob of the radio, trying to find WQXR. It took Orson just two bars to recognize the piece.

"It's Rachmaninoff's *Second Piano Concerto in C-Minor*, Opus 18," he explained. "Very popular. Very romantic, very performance-effective."

To turn onto Route 3 East I had to fully concentrate on the traffic. I was also somewhat irritated at Orson's ability to change mental gears so quickly. Suddenly he was all professor.

"Rachmaninoff was born in 1873 in Russia. He was one of the supreme virtuoso pianists of all time, but continued to compose highly romantic music well into the 20th century as if the modern age had never happened." He sighed a little. "I guess you could call it both his limitation and his strength. But what a spell he exerted on the popular audiences in this century!"

Forced to keep my eyes on the road, I only half-listened as Orson leaned back and indulged in the luxury of closing his eyes. It had started to snow, and a truck shot past us in a whine of sleet. For an eerie moment it threw a shadow, like a monster leading the way.

Flurries danced around the windshield wipers and my fingers flexed tensely around the steering wheel.

Earlier, before leaving the room, we had decided, capriciously, *not* to take a shower. We secretly wished to hold on a little longer to the memory of our skins. Did Orson still smell like me and I like him? Did intimacy still cling to us like powder burns, giving us away?

Orson had watched me in the bathroom brushing my hair and dry-rubbing my body with a towel. Standing behind me, he glanced at me in the mirror, softly smiling, before pulling on his black sweater, Beverly's birthday present, over his head.

Dressed again, we turned around for a last time to take in the rumpled sheets, the scattered pillows and the towels on the floor. A sudden sadness settled over me. Orson was about to leave for this three-week concert tour of Europe. When would we see each other again?

With his hand on the doorknob, Orson asked with a glint in his gray-metallic eyes, "Shall we take this room with us? Shall we have it taken down and put up somewhere else, just for the two of us?"

And now, as the *Allegro scherzando* of Rachmaninoff's piano concerto competed with the noise of the traffic, the memory of our room receded more and more, not only in terms of time or distance.

I was careful to keep the car in the middle of the lane. Because of the falling snow, the stripes were hardly visible and I fumbled in my coat pocket for the Lincoln Tunnel toll money.

Usually, when Orson was not with me, I was frightened by the idea that we could be seen together in the car. What if we were hit by a motorcycle or slid into a truck? Each harmless noise would cause me alarm and I would feverishly check the controls. Did I have enough gas? Was the car overheating? If someone saw us, how could I explain his presence?

But, strangely, now that Orson was actually sitting by my side, there was nothing that caused me to be afraid. His hand on my shoulder seemed to change the world around me. Nothing was that serious or dangerous anymore.

In the streets of Manhattan, with their clouds of exhaust fumes and steaming subway shafts, the snow was turning into rain. Beverly and Rudolph Honeycup's apartment was on West Seventy-Ninth Street, and I let Orson out of the car two blocks away.

"I'm starved," I said as he started to get out. "I can't wait to taste Beverly's Chinese cuisine."

He shrugged and put up the collar of his coat, and I noticed a smudge of lipstick on his cheek. I reached over and rubbed it away. From this moment we had to leave the blind world of two lovers to enter the casual state of mere acquaintances.

Orson smiled meaningfully. "*Auf Wiedersehen.*"

I snickered, "I promise to behave, but it won't be easy."

He laughed lazily. "I know you will, and I know it won't."

I watched him disappear and felt him take part of me along with him, making him stronger and leaving me weaker.

I had to drive around the block four times to find a parking spot. In the morning I had stopped to buy roses for the hostess. In the open trunk they looked exactly as I felt, thirsty and listless. The rain was whipping in cold gusts that slapped and stung. Head down, I hurried along the puddled sidewalk, glad to reach the shelter of the lobby of Beverly's apartment building.

A white cardboard sign caught my eye.

We're sorry. Elevator temporarily out of order.

Considering my heavy purse, dripping umbrella, damp feet and dying roses, I would have much rather turned around and driven home than embark on an eight-flight climb on a steep staircase.

66

It was Daisy, not Beverly, who opened the door. "Sorry about the elevator," she frowned prettily. "I'm glad you made it through the storm."

Her small chubby hand clutched a wine glass, which, in order to take my coat and umbrella, she put down on a small side table next to the phone. Still out of breath from climbing the stairs, I gave her a brief hug, noticing her ever-present scent of lemon.

"It's so nice to see you, Daisy. You smell wonderful, like spring."

She blushed and, following the trail of party laughter, steered me across the hall. "Orson just got here a few minutes ago. Paula will come a little later."

With my pink roses clutched against my angora sweater of the same color, I stopped in the doorway. About twenty chorus members were milling around the large living room. Under the bright spotlights in the ceiling, the party moved around a large oval table covered with a white tablecloth. A dozen chairs were lined up against the windows opposite a wall of built-in bookcases. Faces and smiles flooded me. With the chatting crowd the room seemed to breathe to its limit of comfort.

Beverly, all charming hostess, sat on the armrest of the sofa, talking to Orson. She wore a short, black woolen dress that revealed plenty of her white, freckled skin and advertised that she was bra-less. Her red curls were artfully tamed in a French braid. Spotting mc, she waved vividly through the moving maze of bodies.

"Hi, Bella. Good to see you," she exclaimed without leaving her post next to her guest of honor. Her reason for inviting me was only a polite return for my own party back in August, an accommodating social lie which she tried to cover up with hollow amiability. Orson nodded politely in my direction.

How could I get rid of the flowers? I looked for the kitchen and, finding it, I stopped, surprised. The stove sparkled, unused. There was no casserole simmering with Won-Ton soup, no pots filled with shrimp or chopped beef and pork. Instead of the fragrance of water-chestnuts, scallions and ginger-root, all I smelled was Lysol. Baffled, I put the flowers beside the spotless sink. Footsteps and a male voice were suddenly behind me.

"How thoughtful of you to bring flowers."

Rudy was carrying a tray with empty champagne flutes and instantly made them disappear into the dishwasher. He looked nice in his navy corduroy jeans and white shirt. His big brown eyes smiled at me shyly.

"I haven't seen you since the summer. Welcome, Isabella. I'm sorry James couldn't make it. Can I offer you a glass of champagne?"

He took a new bottle out of the refrigerator.

"I'd love one, Rudy, yes. But only *one.* I still have to drive home tonight."

Freed from my flowers, I returned to the living room, exchanging glances, nodding brief hello's. I moved aimlessly among the others, and though I knew everyone's name, nobody seemed real. Jess, Daisy, Lynn, Mark, Judy, Christine, Dick, Susan, Richard, Carol, Mary, Chris and Barbara were like holographs that could be seen from all sides but lacked solidity. The moment I reached out for them there was nothing but illusion. Caught in the middle of their specters, an empty white wicker chair in the corner by the window seemed to call me. *Come here, relax.*

Sitting down and taking an invigorating sip of champagne made me realize that I had reached a mark beyond happiness and that my fulfillment didn't need anything added to it. I let my eyes wander across the room and told myself, *Hold onto to this feeling. Don't let go of it too soon.*

I had lost an earring in the hotel room, but shrugged off the loss, grateful that it wasn't my diamond anniversary ring. I refused to imagine the nightmarish consequences if *that* had happened.

A rumble of laughter rose from the group clustered around Beverly and Orson. Someone was snapping pictures. The flash of the camera irritated Orson and with a sudden gesture to protect his eyes he caused Beverly's champagne flute to spill on Jess's impeccable three piece suit. In an instant, Daisy, deeply blushing, was all over Jess in an effort to rub his vest dry. I thought, How is it possible that this good-looking young man doesn't know the effect he has on women? At times his green eyes, framed by a thick row of dark lashes, bespoke a far-away sadness, as if they were chasing a dream as unattainable as a glass flower encased in a crystal paperweight. On several occasions during rehearsals we had discussed our respective paperweight collections and exchanged catalogues and reference books.

My thoughts about Jess were cut off as Rudy passed by my wicker chair. He handed me a pencil and the menu from a Chinese take-out place.

"We're ready to order the food. Mark your choice on the margin with your initials."

Surprised at Beverly's mode of entertaining, I obliged. Rudy assumed the duties of the host because she was too busy with our maestro. And Daisy, balancing her heavy form on heels that were too high, followed Beverly like a devoted second lieutenant, content to pick at the crumbs of Orson's attention.

Orson whispered something in Beverly's ear and seemed charmed by her silvery, shrill laughter. Her eyes returned his glance with unmistakable suggestiveness.

"Don't be a spoil-sport, Orson. I remember when your participation was more... imaginative."

A group of guests momentarily blocked my view, but I could make out Orson's voice.

"Beverly, you deserve to be spanked for this." Orson's laugh could be heard a block away. His eyes still on her cleavage, he slowly disentangled himself from her grasp, gently leading her back within the limits of propriety.

Outside, a freezing rain was coming down. For a while I felt lost in time. Rudy drew the curtains and lit a dozen tea lights on the empty table in the middle of the room. At the sound of the doorbell Daisy announced, "The food is here!" A mixed chorus of "ooh's" and "ah's" rose and roared.

The group around Orson and Beverly dissolved, and Orson carved a path through the crowd, suddenly materializing in front of my chair. Our eyes met and for a second all barriers dropped away.

He said in a full voice, "I haven't had a chance to say hello yet. How are you, Isabella?"

On an impulse he bent down, letting his fingers slip into my hair. His eyes exuded gentleness and so did his voice. "How are you holding up? You still have the most incredible bedroom eyes."

I didn't dare breathe until he had straightened up again and stood smiling down at me. I kept my voice down to a whisper.

"Orson, I'm exhausted. How about you?"

"Me?" He gave a boyish grin. "Don't you know, stamina is a conductor's stock in trade. For me it was pure relaxation." He laughed leisurely before adding, "...*glorious* relaxation."

I noticed that from a distance Beverly witnessed the scene with considerable disapproval. At the sight of Orson whispering to me, her mask of amiability crumbled into ugly pieces. Beverly, I thought, if you knew what I know, you'd go positively crazy. Next to the couch, she and Daisy stood motionless side by side, like handmaidens in a frieze, watching us.

Rudy was busy arranging containers of Chinese food on the table. And a moment later Beverly was at Orson's side, cooing like a tropical bird. "The food's ready, Orson. Help yourself." And side-glancing at me, "I'm sorry James is out of town. Are you O.K., Bella? You don't look too well."

"Isabella looks perfectly fine to me," Orson rushed to my defense too quickly and I thought, C*areful, Orson, careful.*

In the soft glow of the candles, a colorful assortment of dishes invited everyone to line up for the buffet. Daisy, eternally engaged in a war with weight, tugged at my elbow.

"I can't decide what to eat first. Moo Shu Pork, sliced beef with scallions, dried chicken with cashew nuts, or sweet-and-sour pork..."

"It all looks delicious," I agreed and resolutely filled my plate with duck and sautéed vegetables.

Struck by my decisiveness, Daisy brushed aside her bangs, along with her guilt, and loaded up her plate.

"I'll go on my egg diet tomorrow."

Seeing that my white wicker chair was taken, I decided to join Jess. He had positioned himself on the fringe of the festivities, in front of the bookcases. Rolling a brandy snifter in one hand and holding his plate with the other, he looked somewhat distant. I detected a slight blush on his cheeks as I got to stand beside him.

"Hi, Jess," I smiled between two mouthfuls of duck.

"How's the justice business these days?"

His polite bow was in contrast to his dreamy eyes.

"Fine, Isabella. How are you? I've been meaning to say hello to you from the moment you walked in."

The Chinese noodles refused to stay on his fork. We laughed. Being tall myself, I found Jess was one of the few of his species I had to look up to, and I enjoyed doing so. Together we let our eyes run along the spines on the book shelves behind us. Jess's green eyes looked at me with pronounced seriousness.

"Isabella, do you like to read?"

"Yes, very much. My parents owned a bookstore back in Austria. And my mother once told me that books were her best friends. So I guess it runs in the family."

He placed his plate on top of the TV set and picked up his brandy snifter. His tone was full of purpose. "I love to read too, I love to immerse myself in a world of imagination, but uh... I think that imagination should also serve as inspiration to concrete experience, and if the goal is worthwhile there's nothing wrong with taking a risk."

The way he searched my face told me that he somehow connected me with the process of taking a risk. I asked, alarmed, "What are you getting at?" Or had he found out about Orson and me?

Jess finished his brandy in one gulp. "I just mean, uh... as an example, look at our maestro. I have the feeling that he has mastered the secret of turning imagination into experience."

Relieved, I scraped the last sauce off my plate and answered casually. "He seems to be an idol to a lot of people."

My eyes flew across the room to Orson. In the midst of the party guests he was larger than life, and today he seemed to exceed himself, laughing, joking, sparking all kinds of emotions. There was one thing, however, that set him apart from everybody else in the room. Orson did not eat or drink, despite Beverly's repeated reminders to help himself from the buffet.

"No, no food for me." There was a commanding edge to his voice, bordering on defensiveness.

Beverly gave him an indignant look. "I thought you liked Chinese food."

"Oh, I do. Believe me, I do," Orson reassured her.

"Then why don't you eat any?" Her voice became impatient. "I planned all this especially for you."

"No, no food for me, please." Orson held up a hand.

Daisy frowned until her brows disappeared under her bangs.

"You didn't have anything to drink either. Are you sick?"

Orson raised both his hands, as if washing himself clean of an accusation. "Ladies, let me assure you. I am fine."

Daisy's bosom heaved in disbelief. Beverly pushed her glasses up on her nose and then banged her fork down on her empty plate.

Rudy, who had so far resisted conversation but had done all the work, made an attempt to protect Orson. He rolled his big brown eyes shyly. "Maybe our maestro is on a secret diet..."

He reaped an exasperated glance from his wife. Orson stayed firm and refused any further comment.

Suddenly Jess was gone. Had he left without saying good-bye?

The party wore on. Daisy, gazing at Orson with love-sick eyes, ended up sitting on his lap, almost cheerfully breaking his legs with her weight. Over her shoulder and with the instinct of an animal, his eyes found mine and a look was exchanged.

From the moment Orson had appeared at the party, Beverly had demonstrated how thrilled she was that he was wearing the black cashmere sweater she had given him for his birthday. Over the span of two hours she had declared repeatedly, "Doesn't he look adorable in it?" to make sure everybody knew the sweater's origin. During it all Rudy's earnest brown eyes had silently followed his wife's compulsive conduct.

With Jess gone, I thought of leaving myself, wondering about the road conditions in New Jersey. But… did I hear a Mozart piano sonata? I wasn't imagining it. It was Mozart and someone was playing it across the hall. With Matthew not here, who could the pianist be? Drawn by the sound, I moved to the door across the living room and tip-toed inside the other room.

Jess was sitting at a grand piano that took up almost the entire space. Three enormous corn plants towered over his head. The walls were covered with dozens of posters and pictures of Orson.

When he saw me, Jess stopped playing and improvised a *glissando* that was surely not from Mozart's pen.

"Sorry for the interruption." I stepped closer. "It sounds lovely. I thought you had left. Do you need a page-turner?"

"I'll gladly accept your offer."

"Jess, I had no idea you possessed such accomplished piano skills." I walked around the piano and took in the Baldwin sign above the keyboard.

He moved over. “Sit down here,” his hand patted the spot on the bench to his right.

“My mother started teaching me at the age of six. I used to hate it as a child, but now solitary practice very often makes me happier than the swirl of a party.”

“I know what you mean. All right then.” I seated myself next to him. “Which sonata are you playing?”

He pointed to the score. “It’s the *K331*. Let’s begin at the *Andante grazioso*.”

How beautifully he captured Mozart’s spirit with his crisp, clear touch, and I noticed that, except for some difficult spots, he hardly needed to look at the music. I also noticed that his eyes strayed, taking in the contours of my body with explicit slowness. The thought of his wandering eyes made me lose my concentration, and halfway through the third variation I got lost in the maze of running sixteenth-notes and missed the page-turn.

Jess promptly stopped playing. This was all my fault. But before I could apologize, I felt his arms around me and his lips on mine. His decisive grip and the shock of my surprise incapacitated me completely.

For an instant, his warm, moist flavor was devastatingly male and a soft wave began spreading through my body. Or was it just the residual taste of brandy on his lips? I fought for air and pushed him away.

“No, Jess. No!”

He let go of me abruptly, as if the touch of me had burned his hands. “My God, Isabella.”

His green eyes were still only inches away from my face. Hardly grasping the inner turmoil we had triggered in each other, I sprang to my feet. What had we become, allies or adversaries? I knew the decision would be mine to make.

In the quiet room his voice trembled.

“I’m sorry, Isabella. I was so attracted to you. There was such a glow of sensuality about you.”

Jess rose from behind the piano and angrily tossed the music on the floor. “I don’t know what came over me.”

Pushing the leaves of the corn plants out of his way, he moved towards the window, his back turned to me. He loosened his collar.

“I just had to let you know how I felt.”

He spoke with the certainty of someone who had thought about his words for a long time.

Gradually my nerves settled and I managed a smile.

“It’s all right. Let’s just forget it happened and be friends.”

As he turned around, a cautious smile reappeared at the corners of his mouth. He was clearly relieved that instead of slapping his face, I had acknowledged his slip for what it was, a compliment.

I opened the door. “Come on, pick up the music and let’s join the others.”

Outside in the hall, a noise made us jump like two children who had been caught playing hooky. Rudy was rattling along the corridor with a tray of dirty dishes.

“I heard your recital. Who was playing?” he asked.

I pointed to Jess, praying that I wouldn’t blush.

“Pretty good. Pretty good.” Rudy turned on a light switch with his elbow. “That’s a hard piece, at least at the level I’m at.”

In the kitchen, Rudy put the tray down with considerable clatter. Almost like an echo, the doorbell rang. Jess and I sneaked back into the living room, trying to look innocent.

Whispers flew around and a name was spoken with great reverence. *Paula.* Mrs. Orson Mahler had arrived. The moment she stood in the doorway, every head turned and the sudden silence underlined the significance of her appearance. Orson’s entourage parted from him like the Red Sea, giving way for him to greet his wife. He walked towards her like a magnanimous monarch and they exchanged abstract kisses on their cheeks.

His simple “hello” was returned by her soulful “My Orson.”

Paula was panting heavily from the eight-floor climb and clung to him as if he were a life-preserver in a stormy sea. Her deep voice had a pleasant timbre, and I noticed that in contrast to her husband she was wearing a wedding band.

I instantly liked this woman's friendly face, surrounded by short, stylish silver hair. A simple turquoise dress covered her heavy form without any attempt to make less visible how generously nature had endowed her. Despite her age, she was two years older than Orson, her face revealed no struggle. Her blue eyes mirrored the clear and alert mind that Orson claimed she possessed. She probably belonged to that admirable category of wives who saw much but said little, content to witness her husband's life. How long ago had she learned to accept other women as part of her life with Orson?

Regardless of Paula's heavy stature, over-powering Orson's slender frame in more than the physical aspect, they gave the impression of a close couple. As they stood together it seemed as if they couldn't draw a breath without each other. Whatever grand passion might temporarily have had a grip on Orson, the thought of such a thoroughly cemented marriage being dissolved was impossible. My thoughts flew back to my first visit to their apartment in September, when Orson was called away to fill in to conduct a rehearsal with the New York Philharmonic. I remembered Paula's bedroom, her pink bed, pillows and curtains, the perfume bottles on her dressing table, as well as the book on her bed-side table. *The Complete Guide to Winning Poker*.

Beverly was the first in line to greet her. What a spectacle of hugs and kisses!

"I'm so happy to see you, Paula!"

"You look fabulous, dear!"

"Well, you look spectacular! Have you lost weight?"

"Where did you have your hair done?"

"Where did you get that stunning dress?"

Only women could assault each other with endearments. It was sickening. Daisy had taken off her high heels and waddled clumsily into Paula's embrace. Besides their plumpness and their love for Orson, Paula and Daisy shared diet plans and recipes for chocolate mousse.

Suddenly my palms were moist. I wished I had left the scene before Paula's grand entrance. It was inevitable that we would be introduced. If only I could still find a way to escape. A faint ringing noise began to sound in my ears. Was she already moving towards me? Where was Jess? I closed and reopened my eyes. Paula and Orson stood in front of me.

He said gallantly, "Isabella, I'd like you to meet my wife, Paula." A curious smile broke across his face.

Mrs. Mahler's assertive eyes were friendly, her handshake firm. "I've heard a lot about you, Isabella. My Orson told me that for quite some time you were the only non-singing member of the chorus. You made history. I found it very strange."

She looked at me expectantly. I didn't flinch.

"Naturally," I swallowed, "I've heard about you too. I'm so pleased to meet you, Mrs. Mahler."

"It's Paula, dear."

"Thank you, Paula." I smiled politely, trying to dismiss the stress within me.

She turned her eyes to Orson. "How is the food, my pet? Why don't you go over there and get me something from whatever's left? I haven't eaten all day."

Orson had been holding his breath and he was glad to be charged with some practical chore, ridding him of the strain of psychological ambivalence.

Hardly the kind of person who enjoyed standing for any length of time, Paula invited me to sit down with her on the sofa. I waited for her to lower herself onto the beige cushions and then took my seat a foot away. Her heavy frame prevented her from crossing her legs. Rudy circulated with more champagne. Paula took a glass, and in view of my precarious situation I allowed myself to have a second one.

Orson arrived with a full plate of Mo Shu vegetables, shrimp with snow peas and sweet-and-sour pork. Elaborately, Paula spread a napkin across her spacious lap, took the plate and asked if I would mind holding her champagne glass. She leveled her blue eyes at Orson.

"I'm sure you've tasted this already, my pet. You gave me an awful lot." She speared a piece of sweet-and-sour pork and held it up to Orson, offering him a bite.

"No, Paula. Thank you. Nothing for me," he refused with obvious impatience.

Beverly materialized. Seeing her, Paula frowned. "Beverly, dear, did you go through the ordeal of cooking all of this?"

Avoiding a direct answer, Beverly began to whine.

"Imagine, Paula. Orson didn't touch my food at all!"

Paula shook her head at Orson. "That's funny. I thought I saw you taste something on your lips," and turning to Beverly, "Well, my dear, I must say that's very inconsiderate of my Orson."

Without looking at him I could sense Orson's blood boil under the punishing glances of the two women. Why didn't he eat? Wasn't he feeling well? The ultimately troublesome question sprang up in my mind. Had he over-exerted himself earlier in the day?

Paula's deep voice and starry-blue eyes brought me back to the present. "Isabella, I hear you come from a very interesting part of Austria."

"Yes, I come from Pörtschach. It's a small town on Lake Wörth…" and mindful not to drink from the wrong glass of champagne, I went on. "Johannes Brahms wrote his *Second Symphony* in Pörtschach, less than half a mile from where I was born, as well as his *Violin Concerto*."

Paula's eyes brightened. Orson nodded, happy to move onto safe ground and encouraging me to go on.

I explained, "Brahms described Pörtschach as an exquisite spot, so stimulating that he felt the air was full of melodies. He said, *One has to be careful not to tread on them.*

"How absolutely charming." Paula handed her empty plate to Beverly, asking for seconds.

Orson's eyes sparkled at me.

"Tell Paula what you told me about Gustav Mahler."

Still juggling two glasses of champagne, I continued. "At the turn of the century, when Gustav Mahler was director of the Vienna Philharmonic, he had his summer residence on the south side of the lake, in Maiernigg, just across from where I grew up. He lived there with his wife, Alma, and his two daughters. When his elder daughter died, they sold the house because it was haunted by too many memories."

To cover my nervousness I fled even deeper into the safety of facts. "What I remember most was that high up in the woods above the villa he had a little composition cottage where he wrote his last four symphonies. I was there many times as a child, mostly to collect pine cones to color them as Christmas ornaments."

Beverly came back with Paula's plate. She took it absent-mindedly and began eating at a steady pace. Paula seemed spell-bound, but I wondered how much longer I could hold her attention. Orson settled on the armrest behind her, facing me.

"Also," I continued, as if by continuing to talk I could assure universal peace, "a few miles east of Mahler's villa, Alban Berg owned a house in Auen. He called it his beloved *Berghaus*, his house on the mountain. It was here that he composed his twelve-tone opera *Lulu* between 1928 and 1935. He died four months after its completion from blood poisoning resulting from an insect bite."

"You know, Paula," Orson interjected, pulling Beverly's black sweater off over his head, "Isabella used to work for the local tourist office there. I just wish we could visit all those places."

"I'm afraid it's impossible," Paula said, "although I have no doubt that it must be a very inspiring area."

"Indeed," Orson beamed imprudently, "just look at Isabella. I consider her a perfect product of that area. She can be quite inspiring herself."

Paula's glance sharpened and descended on me like a dark crow. I began to feel dampness on my forehead. *Orson. Be careful.*

"Paula," Orson went on to suggest, "I wish we could go there just for a weekend. We could do it at the end of my concert tour, which happens to be in Vienna."

"Pörtschach is only three hours from Vienna by car," I hastened to add. "I could take care of your hotel reservations from this end."

But Paula, now unencumbered by her plate, glass or appetite, had made up her mind. "My pet, you know as well as I that there is never time for detours, inspiring as they might be. You know your rehearsals always start the day after we get back to the U.S."

"I'm afraid you're right." Orson looked a fraction less happy.

He glanced respectfully at his wife, as if she were something fixed and inevitable, like the federal government.

The party was slowly thinning out and I wanted to go home. I rose and offered a polite hand to the Mahlers.

"It was very nice to meet you, Paula."

Turning to Beverly, I asked, "Could I have my coat, please?"

"Sure, Bella." She was obviously relieved at the prospect of my departure. "I'll meet you at the door outside."

In the hall a big yawn crept up on me.

"Are you sure you don't want to stay for the chocolate cheese cake?" Beverly's voice asked behind me.

I shook my head. "No, thank you, Beverly. Everything was so nice. Thanks for inviting me."

"In that case," she deposited my coat and umbrella on a small chair, "your share of the food comes to eleven dollars and fifty cents."

I shot her a surprised look.

She explained further. "I subtracted your share of the chocolate cheese cake."

"It's okay," I assured her, silently amazed at her money-geared mind. If she handled Orson's investments as wisely as she had shouldered her guests with the buffet bill, his finances were probably in excellent shape.

Would she also collect money from Orson, her guest of honor, who had yet to do her the honor of eating? I'd never know. Nor would I know the reason for Orson's insistent abstinence.

The living room door swung open and Orson appeared in the doorframe.

"I'll see Isabella out, Beverly." His voice was an indication that she was no longer needed. Her eyes widened under her glasses. Somewhat bewildered, her hand clutched my money, and I was glad to see her disappear.

Orson looked at me intently. At last I could ask him.

"Orson, are you feeling well?"

"I couldn't feel better. Why?"

"You haven't eaten at all. You should be starved." I kept my voice low, "…after all we've been through together."

Holding my coat open for me, he whispered intimately.

"I haven't forgotten it. It was wonderful, Isabella."

"Yes, it was," I smiled, "but..."

"Why *but...*? Are you sorry about anything that happened?"

"No, no... of course not, Orson. But *why* aren't you eating anything?"

In a wordless, instinctive way his eyes spoke of images we both knew as he bent over to my ear.

"All right, I'll tell you why I'm not eating. I still have the taste of your skin on my lips. What better flavor could I wish for?"

I felt my jaw drop. After a beat of silence he concluded with a broad, happy grin, "Do you think I'd be dumb enough to replace it with a piece of sweet-and-sour pork?"

67

Before Orson left for Europe I met him once again. It was two days after Beverly's party and two days before he was to leave for Paris, his first stop. I picked him up from an orchestra rehearsal at Avery Fisher Hall, where he was putting the finishing touches on the repertoire for his tour. We had two hours to kill before his last rehearsal with the chorus, where he was to introduce the young conductor who would substitute for him during his absence.

The knowledge that this was our last time together heightened my susceptibility and blocked out the surroundings. Was the sky clear or cloudy? The air humid or dry? Except for Orson's face, bare of his usual dark glasses which he removed at nightfall, I didn't recall the color of his coat or whether he was wearing gloves or a hat. The only thing that stood out in my mind was his velvet voice and his breath condensing in the air next to mine. He took my arm to help me over a pile of snow.

"I wouldn't mind having a bite to eat. How about you, Isabella?"

A small cafe on Broadway advertising broccoli quiche and New England apple cider looked inviting. Under the bright bulb of a tiffany lamp we settled into a wooden booth with a red-and-white checkered tablecloth. Orson snapped his beaten briefcase open and handed me his twenty-three page itinerary. He and Paula would visit thirteen European cities in twenty-two days, together with his orchestra, the tour director, the managing director of the orchestra, an administrative assistant and a librarian.

"Why a librarian?"

"The librarian of an orchestra has to take care of all the sheet music, the orchestral parts for all one hundred and ten players, different, of course, for each instrument and each piece being performed. It's a big job."

My hands were warming up on the steaming mug of apple cider. "Who takes care of all the instruments?"

"Watch out, Isabella, it's hot!" Orson shrieked and pointed to his quiche, his mouth on fire. Gulping for air, he finally swallowed.

"Fortunately, we don't have to take the grand piano along, but all the other instruments have to go." Deep lines appeared on his high forehead. "The insurance premiums are horrendous, and they're going up each year. Some day we won't be able to afford insurance at all."

How odd, I thought, chewing carefully on a hot bite of quiche. With Beverly not there to fuss over his finances, they seem to cause him a disproportionate amount of frustration. I leafed through the itinerary. There would be a total of sixteen concerts, and in Paris, London and Vienna two concerts were scheduled on consecutive days.

The main section of the stapled folder contained the dates of the concerts, the times, the pieces being played, the length of the works in minutes and seconds, the location of the concert halls, hotels, telephone and fax numbers, names of the tour staff, press representatives, receptions, interviews, rehearsal times, plane and train departures and customs regulations.

The tiffany lamp shone on our meal like a large, yellow tulip. Orson pushed his plate away, leaving the crust of the quiche untouched. "I'll try to call you now and then, Isabella. You realize, of course, my time will be extremely tight."

He rummaged through his briefcase and produced a press release about the tour, in which he was quoted as taking special pride in presenting an all-American program to European audiences. The flyer had a most becoming picture of the maestro, waving his baton, the stylish tool of his trade. The picture, as well as the real man in front of me, exuded a patriotic gleam, poised to step onto planes and podiums.

Orson smiled. "It's going to be a great tour. I want the Europeans to become aware of American composers. With the vast array of their own music and their superb Bachs, Beethovens and Brahmses, they easily forget to cast their eyes and ears to the new continent in the west."

In the press release, reference was made to Orson's concert tour of last year through Japan, where he had pursued the same concept. His notion of a fully American repertoire raised excitement and intrigue with the oriental audiences. The *Mainichi Shimbun* had called Orson *a star on the symphonic heavens*. It read on: *In every piece, Maestro Mahler created phrases that drew one in, and which animated these insightful performances. His way of blending lustrous strings and bright winds created a body of sound that emphasized one unified musical culture... the American Symphonic Sound.*

The repertoire Orson had chosen to take to Europe consisted of Aaron Copland's *Third Symphony*, Gershwin's *Piano Concerto in F* and Bernstein's overture to *Candide.*

"It's a symphony of many moods," Orson explained the Copland work dreamily. "It's sprawling, surprising, unsettling... and at times deceivingly soothing over an immense inner tension."

While he spoke, my thoughts wandered off. Would everything be the same when he returned? Would we be able to pick up where we left off? I resorted to a joke. "Why don't I drop everything and come along with you?"

His birthmark twitched as he waved at a fly above his head.

"Do you know, Isabella, who actually *is* coming?"

"*Who?*" I sensed thunder in the air.

"Beverly decided to join us at the last minute. She plans to attend all the concerts and take Paula on sightseeing tours while I'm rehearsing. Rudy couldn't get away from work."

Oh, I thought and said flatly, "What a surprise."

Orson laughed diplomatically. "It was for me too. I can always use an extra pair of hands and Paula is delighted to have company during her free time."

I couldn't tell whether he was pleased or bothered at the prospect of having Beverly around for three weeks.

After a restorative gulp of apple cider I concluded, "I can't help wondering if hearing the same concert sixteen times would be an overwhelming thrill."

"Honestly," Orson snickered, "it wouldn't be for me." He reached out for both my hands.

An eerie silence began to envelop us. I knew that this was our good-bye, *this* moment, and not later, when after the chorus rehearsal Orson would be surrounded by fifty female fans dying to steal a farewell kiss from him.

Orson's eyes drew mine like magnets. They said, *Take good care of yourself, Isabella. I'll miss you.*

Or was I just projecting my mind onto his when he was really thinking about paying the bill or the expiration date in his passport? His magic smile started a fire in my heart, burning away my unshed tears before they could reach my eyes.

Forty-eight hours later, Orson was on an Air France flight to Paris. His absence triggered an unexpected energy within me. On one hand it allowed me to devote my time to job-hunting and on the other it propelled me to do things I'd put off for months. Or was my first-time visit with James to the planetarium and my guided tour through the U.N. just a subconscious safety net against sadness? Were my separate lunches with Matthew, Jess and Daisy only an excuse to be in the presence of someone who was linked to Orson, or did they represent a feeling of freedom from the grip of an unsettling love?

Under the sparkling crystal chandeliers of *Johnnie's Restaurant*, Matthew and I had plenty of laughs. Over pasta *fra diavolo* we recalled our fall on the ice and palavered mercilessly about the quirks of Orson's substitute conductor, who had a strange way of letting himself be guided by the chorus instead of leading it. Halfway through our espressos, Matthew placed a small book on the tablecloth next to our gravy stains.

"A selection of American poetry," he smiled proudly. "I want you to have this, Isabella."

"Why, Matthew?"

"No special reason." He let his long fingers dance on the cover of the book. "Just to tell you *you're* special."

For my lunch with Jess we went to a small Chinese place. He said in a somewhat formal voice that it was to atone his *faux-pas* at Beverly's party. He was impeccably dressed, as usual. He squeezed four packets of soy sauce over his rice and showed me a picture of his horse Melanie that he stabled in Connecticut. We compared notes on the early editions of *Caithness* paperweights from Scotland, and after we had read our fortune cookies to each other, he produced a small packet from his pocket.

He made me open it. It held a tiny crystal vial on a black silk cord. Blushing a little, he bent across the table to put it around my neck and followed it with a devastating smile from his green eyes.

I stammered, "I'm not sure I can accept this, Jess."

He said, "Please do," and looked at me as though shielding his thoughts behind his inordinately long lashes.

I removed the stopper from the vial and pulled out a minuscule spool.

Jess said, "You have to blow in it," and a moment later we were surrounded by a cloud of soap bubbles that danced and drifted upwards. How could I not be charmed?

It was only appropriate that Daisy and I would lunch at a vegetarian coffee shop. Frowning prettily, she played with the fringes of the yellow shawl over her black sweater. Her short, round body almost disappeared behind the mountain of spinach leaves on her plate.

Daisy was loaded with love-sick remarks about Orson, little secrets about other chorus members and inquisitive tricks in order to extract from me every detail about my reaction to our maestro. How well did I know him? Had I ever met him outside regular rehearsals?

She reached for another roll with butter. Had Beverly appointed her as a spy? Was cross-examination, wrapped in smiles and sweetness, the reason for this lunch?

Fidgeting in the depths of her huge tote bag, Daisy produced a cubic box and pushed it to my side of the table.

"I found this for you, Isabella."

"For me?"

It was a white coffee mug with *Isabella* written on it in raised, blue letters with a bleeding glaze.

"Daisy... how thoughtful of you. I'll use it in the office for my morning coffee."

"When I saw it, I just had to get it for you," she giggled harmlessly, making me feel guilty at suspecting espionage when there was nothing but warm friendship.

Sadly, I realized that Orson, the man for whom I had abandoned all the rules, had never given me the smallest present, nothing to tell me "you are special in my life."

It triggered another question. Wasn't it time I saw him objectively, rather than through the veil of mindless admiration? Contrary to expectation, Orson's physical presence was less important than I had anticipated. How powerful I felt in the knowledge that if someday everything were over, I would emerge unharmed.

I even considered taking his absence as an opportunity to put an elegant end to our relationship. On his return I could tell him in a triumph of self-control, "It's over, Orson. It was just a fling, a venture in romance. I'm choosing this moment because being apart for three weeks was a good way to facilitate estrangement. It's the moment of minimal hurt. My body is healing of you."

So there. A perfect theory. But in the middle of pretending not to miss him, each time the crackling of static on the phone alerted me to an overseas call, I experienced a surge of heat.

When he called me from Paris, his voice came through like a reminder of a past paradise, but his tone was business-like and rushed. Was he calling while Paula took a shower before leaving for the concert?

He didn't ask, "Have you found another job? How are you spending your time?" Nor did he say, "I miss you."

Instead, he complained about piano rentals and how one flute player jeopardized the first concert with his sudden vagaries of dynamics and phrasing. He talked about non-available rehearsal space, difficulties with instrument transport and something about parts for the violas being lost.

The acoustics of the concert hall in Cardiff produced too much echo, and he grumbled about the lack of privacy and being the chief trouble-shooter of his traveling circus. Full of praise about the sound in the new Barbican Hall in London and the resulting concert there, he laughed tensely.

"Paula and I can't figure out what to do with all the fruit baskets we find in our room each time we check into a hotel."

He talked about receptions, the reactions of the press and a terrific review in the *London Times*. On his visit to Westminster Abbey he thought he remembered that they had moved George Friedrich Handel's grave to another location. But then he admitted that he may have just come in through a different door than the last time he was there.

Through Copenhagen and Hamburg his messages remained unchanged, dealing strictly with the technicalities of the tour. Apart from his opening greetings, "How are you, Isabella?" to which he expected no elaborate reply, his words remained factual and safe. How difficult could it have been to simply add, "I miss you."

Now that he was on German-speaking territory, he added with a tinge of despair, "I could certainly use your language skills. Trying to use the vocabulary of Wagner's *Tristan und Isolde* or Bach's *Weihnachtsoratorium* doesn't get me very far."

And instead of mentioning just once that "Europe is empty without your lovely face," he fretted about inconsistencies in the orchestral parts and the fact that one of the sponsors of the tour, a large American food company, had withdrawn its financial support for economic reasons.

The tour was scheduled to take a flight from Berlin to Frankfurt, but Orson's morning rehearsal session was broken up by the news of a security alert at the Frankfurt Airport. A bomb scare called for an immediate emergency meeting of the entire orchestra and staff. After lengthy consultations with an international security specialist, it was decided to send the players to Frankfurt by train, thereby losing one whole day in the itinerary. The physical and emotional toll that these conditions took on everyone made him wish for good that he had become a chemist instead of a conductor.

I religiously followed Orson's route on the map. How often had he called me? The remaining concerts in Stuttgart, Salzburg and Vienna were free of stress. Overall, ticket sales were more than satisfactory. Yes, Paula and Beverly were well. Beverly was taking tons of pictures.

I chose not to tell him that my mother would be in the audience in Vienna. I felt too distant from him now that he was gone. How much more distant must she feel from him, or he from her?

But finally Orson admitted that he was satisfied with the way the tour was turning out. Of course, everyone was ready to come home, despite the old-world splendor of Vienna's concert hall, Der Musikverein, a taste of the well-known *Sachertorte, Mozartkugeln* and a performance of Mozart's *Cosí fan tutte* at the State Opera.

Orson didn't say, "I can't wait to see you again." His mere "So long" made me wonder if I had ever made a difference in his heart. With the defiance of a spoiled, self-centered child I refused to acknowledge his good will to find the time to get in touch with me at all. All I saw was that he was losing sight of the *one* thing I wanted to hear most. *I miss you.*

Out of the bulk of so many calls, where was the bonus?

68

When Orson finally called me at work on the fourth day after his return, he caught me with my head buried in a translation of "Primary Market Trends."

"Isabella?" His voice had a boyish bounce. "I'm back from Europe. How are you? Can I see you today at five for a quick cup of hot chocolate?"

He mentioned a coffee shop around the corner from my office, and added meaningfully, but not in the romantic tone appropriate for his request, "Would you be free on Friday for a *date?*"

Time, the great healer, had healed nothing in his absence, and his voice broke down the fragile barrier I had built against him. Orson's last words were followed by Mr. Stringer's squawk through the intercom.

"Isabella, I'd like to have another cup of cappuccino."

I said to Orson, "I have to go."

He smiled, "I'll see you soon," and suddenly we laughed in a wave of happiness. Effortlessly, we were able to pick up where we had left off. Everything was perfect, almost frighteningly perfect. On the wall, the portraits of the distinguished members of the board of directors seemed to sing the *Hallelujah Chorus* from their frames.

Unexpectedly, Orson called again later. A single violin was playing in the background.

"A meeting has come up. I have to cancel our five o'clock today."

"What kind of meeting?" I asked.

"Isabella, I'm not accountable to you about my whereabouts."

"Oh."

"You know me," he tried to make a joke about it, "I can't stand to be asked too many questions."

I felt mystified and, yes, a little miserable. It was less by his cancellation than by the manner of his defense, as if he had something to hide. It was almost from a far-away distance that I heard him say, "Well, I'll see you tonight at chorus rehearsal, and we'll keep Friday open."

69

My uneasy feeling was fueled by a call from Beverly. Her soprano shrilled with familiar exuberance.

"Hi, Bella. Everybody's back from Europe. I just got my pictures back this morning. Orson and I had such a wonderful time. Why don't you get yourself a sandwich and come down to my office for lunch so we can look at them together?"

I reluctantly abandoned my plans to attend a mid-day concert at St. Bartholomew's and agreed. A cold feeling of purpose settled in my chest.

"But I have to warn you," she said, "our offices are moving to a new location on Madison Avenue. Remember, I've been telling you about it. The move was always put off. Some lawsuit with the realtor. Anyhow, we're in the middle of it *now.* If you don't mind the mess..."

"Don't worry." I said, and thought, Let's see what Beverly has to say about the trip.

"I'll be down at twelve-thirty. How's that?"

The receptionist at Beverly's investment firm, a voluptuous blonde, indicated a long corridor where Beverly's office was located. Beverly had been right. The place was a disaster area. Movers were emptying the contents of file cabinets into boxes piled upon each other, forming towers of cartons. Some wrapped plants stuck oddly out of shopping bags. In front of Beverly's office a friendly secretary was emptying the drawers of her desk.

Beverly appeared. "Come in, Bella. What a mess. Since I was away so long my office is the last one to be moved."

She turned to her secretary. "Lisa, I'm not taking any calls, except..." Beverly's sentence trailed off and was completed by Lisa's dutiful smile. "Mr. Mahler, I know..."

Beverly's freckled skin went from pale to ruby in a second, but I pretended not to notice. I followed her inside her office and she closed the door. Suddenly there was a tenseness about her, an eagerness to be of service as she pulled up a chair opposite her desk.

"Take a seat, Bella."

Lisa's involuntary remark hung still between us and Beverly desperately tried to cover it up with an altogether different subject.

"Have you found a new job yet, Bella?"

Sickened by the way she called me "Bella," I shrugged with a helpless smile. "Not yet." This was not the moment to tell her about my unsuccessful pilgrimage through six Manhattan employment agencies, with application forms, typing tests and math problems that a parakeet could figure out.

Except for Beverly's desk and her credenza, the office was almost bare. Its emptiness made me feel that I was in one of those modern plays where, in order to enhance the drama, the stage is stripped of scenery.

Beverly ran her hands through the flurry of her titan curls.

"What can I get for you? Coffee, tea or hot chocolate?"

"Black coffee would be fine, thanks."

As she left the room, my eyes traveled across her walls. They were covered with rows of white documents, all framed under glass. At first glance they all looked alike, but on closer inspection they turned out to be Orson's concert programs from *Stagebill.* How many were there? Fifty? Sixty? I shivered. This office was the shrine of an Orson Mahler addict, with the looks of a concert agency rather than an investment firm.

Beverly returned with two steaming mugs and kicked the door shut with one of her high heels.

"I never drink coffee. Orson doesn't either. It makes us both feel jittery. Orson always says one cup of coffee before a concert and the audience will witness the first one-hour performance of Bach's complete *Brandenburg Concertos.*

Our contrived laughter rang out as we sat face to face.

Beverly opened a container of cottage cheese with fruit. I noticed that she wasn't wearing any make-up, and for the first time I considered that she was not beautiful. Most likely I had placed too much stock in her charms all along. Maybe I ascribed so much power to her because I was unable to imagine my own.

Between spurts of small talk I sipped my coffee and Beverly fished for strawberries with her fingers. "Bella, the trip was marvelous. Orson and I had such wonderful times together."

"What about Paula? She was along, wasn't she?" I chewed on my sandwich.

"Paula and I got along beautifully."

Presently, her empty cottage cheese container sailed into the waste basket and from her drawer a stack of envelopes materialized. She spread them elaborately across her desk and put them in separate piles.

"Twelve rolls," she explained grandly.

I had anticipated shots of Paula looking at the Eiffel Tower, of Orson on a walk through Hyde Park or outside the British Museum. I had expected to see Orson and his players at the stage entrance of the Concertgebouw in Amsterdam or Beverly sitting on a rock, imitating the posture of the Copenhagen Mermaid. Instead, the four hundred thirty-two photos spread out on the desk seemed all the same. Rehearsal scenes. Nothing but snapshots of Orson and his orchestra.

Reading my thoughts, Beverly pushed her glasses up on her nose. "I decided not to do any sightseeing. It would have meant spending too much time away from Orson. Paula did some touring with some of the orchestra members who weren't required to rehearse on that day."

"But Beverly," I gasped, "you took the same picture four hundred times. I thought I'd see the Gran' Place in Brussels, the Berlin Wall or the State Opera in Vienna..."

"Sorry to disappoint you," her vowels rose. "We were *not* tourists. The trip was an important contribution to American culture, and I think my pictures showing Orson at work are an excellent documentation."

"No doubt the maestro will be pleased," I admitted.

"I'm hoping that one or two of the close-ups might lend themselves as cover photos for the booklets of Orson's upcoming CD releases."

Typically money-minded, Beverly showed her broadest grin.

"Wouldn't it be great if I could sell them to his record company?"

"Good luck. I hope it works out."

Suddenly she leaned forward. "Except... uh... I haven't shown you this one yet," she eyed a single print, face down, under her desk lamp. She turned it over but I couldn't see it yet.

"I caught Orson off guard in his hotel room in London," and handing it to me, she giggled, "Doesn't he look cute in his pajama bottoms?"

And there he was. Orson in black silk pajama bottoms and bare chest, standing, or better, about to run away from something, most likely the photographer.

"Isn't it a darling shot," Beverly's voice rose to its highest register. "It's a voyeuristic joke. I can't deny that there's a streak in me that loves to pry. But don't we all?"

My jacket felt too warm.

"How did you manage to sneak into his room and have your camera along? Where was Paula?"

She spilled her words in an excited rush.

"It was one of the rare nights without a performance. After dinner, Orson wanted to retire early and left Paula partying with some of the orchestra guys in the bar downstairs. I think they went to some other room later for a round of poker. She sent Orson ahead to hit the sack. So I knocked on his door."

"Under what pretext?"

"I said it was an emergency and that I needed his help right away. So he let me in before putting on a robe."

"What kind of emergency did you have?"

"None, of course, but by then he had already opened the door and I snapped the picture."

"How did you know you'd find him in his pajamas?"

"That was pure guess-work. I hoped I'd find him wearing... uh, even less..." She laughed, and her fingers reached under her glasses to wipe her eyes dry.

"Bella, you should have seen the sour look on his face. *Was he upset!* I thought he was going to throw me out of his room. Isn't that hilarious?"

"And... did he?"

"Uh... yes and no... kind of..." She rummaged through her purse for a tissue and added triumphantly, "I surely have something to hold over him," she snickered, "Imagine if I would pass the picture around during chorus rehearsal tonight."

"Orson would be thrilled." My words had never sounded more grotesque.

And then we started laughing, because nothing that might have been said would have made sense, and because I would have loved to do something horrible to her. While the prized picture exchanged hands, we both jumped at the ringing phone. As she picked up, a forbidding feeling arose in me.

"Oh.... Oooorson, I'm fine." Instantly she was at her flirtatious best. "I just got back the pictures from the tour. They came out super. Bella and I are looking at them this very minute." Her hand played with her earring.

"Yes, I mean 'Isabella,' she's here. We had lunch together."

I got up and stood in the empty office like a forgotten child whom grown-ups talk about as if she weren't there. As she listened to his lengthy speech, she curled and uncurled the cord with her fingers and said after a while, “Orson, I told you before, you’re lost without me.” She raised her chin. “I love it when you say that.” She went on, her voice heavy with satisfaction, “and yes, I’ll meet you later at five for a cup of hot chocolate. I’ll bring the pictures. “

Finally, they finished the call.

In a wave of antagonism I stepped to the window. It was drizzling. On the street, people came streaming out through the heavy doors of St. Bartholomew Church after the mid-day concert. Their dancing umbrellas spilled like colorful glass marbles down the steps of the church and across the sidewalks of Park Avenue. Why wasn’t I down there with them? Why was I in this awful office with this awful woman whose mere proximity was draining my strength? I had to leave before I broke one of her legs.

“I have to get back to work,” I strained to keep my voice casual.

“Well, thanks for stopping by. I assume I’ll see you at the rehearsal tonight?”

I nodded flatly as I crossed the office.

She held the door open for me and gave a secretive laugh.

“I can’t wait to show Orson that... uh... you know...”

Lisa still sat dutifully at her desk and handed two pink message slips to Beverly. I moved along the corridor and decided to nurture my grudge by ignoring Orson during the rehearsal that night.

The men from the moving company had laid down wooden planks to protect the floor from the hand trucks and heavy boxes they were hauling. One of the planks stuck out from beneath another, forming a dangerous trap. As I headed along the corridor I heard Beverly’s shrill warning, just barely in time.

“Watch out for the step, *Bella*,” and after I had caught my balance she let out a sigh. “Thank God. I don’t want you to break a leg.”

I turned around and nodded thanks. It was because of her warning, not because of my stumbling, that I felt woozy. I steadied myself, disturbed by a question:

Would I have done the same for her?

70

Two days later the air was heavy with the smell of snow and I thought how odd it felt that everything with Orson had ended in such a quiet way. The radio forecasted a snowstorm. It started coming down as I rode the bus from Manhattan to Montclair, a mixed whirlwind of white precipitation and dark human passions, outdoors as well as in my heart. James was at his usual business dinner on Long Island, and I was worried about the road conditions for his return.

Inside the house I took off my suit and slipped into my old cuddly robe. It was a garment of considerable age and non-distinct color (once it had been pink), and I wouldn't have wanted the neighbor's cat to see me in it. Through the window I could make out the surrounding houses covered with a confectioner's sugar coating, and the scene reminded me of a black-and-white photo from the turn of the century.

A gusty wind pummeled the house, drawing creaks and groans from everywhere around me. I closed the curtains, shutting out the storm and welcoming my solitude. I switched on the floor lamp and brought a few logs from the garage to start a fire. The faces of my ivory portraits of Austrian royalty looked out sternly from their frames, still imprisoned by the dark riddles of their past.

Too lazy to cook dinner and not hungry enough, I poured myself a glass of burgundy and settled on the rug in front of the fireplace. I always enjoyed holding the first match under the crumpled newspaper, watching paper and wood catch fire. And soon the flames roared and crackled, sending sparks flying up the chimney. Their warmth crept into the pores of my skin as the wine spread to my head. It felt good to let go, to enjoy a dreamy emptiness, to be free of the feelings from a love that had lost its clarity and grace. With my knees pulled up under my chin, my thoughts returned to the chorus rehearsal two days earlier.

I had arrived at CAMI Hall in the general flow of choristers, laughing and chatting right and left. Once seated, I stayed glued to my chair, pretending to study the score on my lap, while Orson watched his troops assemble. So this was our first meeting after his return. Avoidance.

Had he been searching for my eyes? If so, I had returned his glance with a blank stare, though fully attentive to his directions concerning Brahms' music. It was not difficult to stay out of Orson's way during the intermission. Glad to see him back from Europe, everyone flocked around him, eager for handshakes or hugs. My moments spent with Jess, Daisy and Matthew were filled sharing our excitement for our upcoming concert in Carnegie Hall. *Damn Orson.*

After my visit to Beverly's office I hadn't called him again, nor had he called me. Not yesterday. Not today. How odd, how weightless it felt to know that suddenly there was nothing left between us.

Besides the spitting and crackling of the logs, another sound pierced the silence and made me sit up. Was it a car in the driveway stopping and starting again? And a little later, was that the doorbell? Angry that someone should interrupt my precious peace, I tip-toed downstairs, ready to lower James' old baseball bat on any unwelcome visitor's head.

After a moment of hesitation I opened the door. A man emerged from the darkness. Behind him, snow was still coming down, white and quiet like a dream. Under our entrance lamp he looked like a soon-to-be snowman with his collar turned up. Being alone, I feared he might be an intruder and I was both soothed and startled to see who he was.

Orson!

The shock of seeing him must have registered on my face. But, oddly, his first words were, "Your face looks lovely, backlit like that by the chandelier in the hall."

I pulled the belt of my robe tighter.

"How did you know I was alone?"

His voice was low, his phrasing measured, "Remember, Isabella, you told me once that James was in Long Island Friday nights."

A rush of cold air swept into the house and made me shiver.

"How did you know I wasn't going out?" I asked, still glued to the spot.

"That was a chance I had to take," Orson said evenly, "but... aren't you going to ask me in?"

He bowed in a wooden, impersonal manner, and as I withdrew he moved toward me. Regardless of how uneasy Orson looked, in no way could his discomfort equal mine. Entering the house, he brushed the snow off his coat and a calm smile carved half-circles into his cheeks.

"Or," he took in the surroundings, "would you feel better if I left? You wouldn't have to explain, Isabella. I'd understand."

But I had already closed the door behind him.

"Of course not," I assured him, contrary to my conviction, and asked, "How did you manage to get out here all the way from Manhattan?"

He opened the buttons of his coat.

"I took a taxi. I always wanted to see where you live. And here I am." He laughed smugly. "I've never been a man to waste an opportunity."

I took his coat, careful to avoid the coldness of his hands.

A sheepish grin curled at the corners of his mouth.

"Just imagine, Johann Sebastian Bach once traveled two hundred miles on foot to attend a concert by Dietrich Buxtehude. He was a well-known composer of the time. And, personally, I find my destination equally promising, to say the least."

I couldn't do better than a half-hearted grin and gestured at the stairs leading to the living room. "Let's go upstairs," I said.

Leading the way, I tried to dismiss my uneasiness, looming like a monster under the bed of a child's nightmare. I had occasionally fantasized about Orson coming here, but now that the moment was upon me, all I felt was terror.

I could still tell him, *Leave.* Leave now. But everything that sprang to my mind stalled at my lips. My whole being was at a loss whether to tremble, talk or touch. But after all, this was my home and Orson had to accept whatever role I assigned him as my guest.

Upstairs, Orson stopped and looked around.

"Ah, this is beautiful. Your living room. The fireplace, the fire. Here's where you live..."

Then silence grew between us. No reference was made to the rehearsal, no mention of my avoiding him. His purposeful self-confidence unsettled me.

"Orson, you shouldn't have come here."

"Why not, Isabella? Give me a dozen good reasons for not coming to see you."

He looked at me expectantly and I told him all the reasons I didn't mean. "It's snowing. You might have a problem with the roads going back. You might have to spend the night here."

"That's exactly why I'm here," he smiled meaningfully.

"Orson, don't look at me. I look awful in this robe, like a scarecrow."

"I don't mind seeing you like this at all, because I know exactly what's hidden underneath."

Orson slowly took off his jacket. His eyes darted across the room, from James' favorite chair by the window to the couch, the round glass table and the bookcases. Beads of sweat were beginning to gather under my arms. I offered him a seat.

"Would you care for a drink? Maybe a cup of hot chocolate?"

"Nothing to drink, thank you, and nothing to eat. I didn't come here to be nourished. At least," his mouth formed a coy smile, "not that kind of nourishment."

Orson began pacing up and down as though to acquaint himself with the dimensions of the room, carrying himself with the dignity of a general. We stepped around each other as if dancing a gavotte… approaching, turning, retreating, all with utter courtesy, but charged with an underlying, grinding tension.

He glanced at me with frankness. "I thought we had a date tonight, Isabella. I asked you to keep Friday night open, and since nothing was called off, I assumed our agreement held."

The cracking flames seemed to dance with laughter while Orson watched me in a bemused silence from a distance.

"Besides," he touched a branch of my Kentia palm, "I haven't had a chance to see you since my return from Europe, and my calendar has been filling up like crazy."

I grabbed the back of a chair and for a second the diamonds of James' anniversary ring picked up the sparkle of the flames.

I said, "I don't want to interfere with your busy schedule."

Orson laughed, "I *love* to have you interfere with my busy schedule."

In the dim room Orson walked to the fireplace, gazing at the flames, one hand touching the mantelpiece.

He explained, "Yesterday I started rehearsing a new repertoire and had a meeting with some union representatives regarding the new contract for the orchestra players... Allow me?"

Orson picked up a huge piece of wood from the log carrier and threw it on the fire, obviously enjoying the gesture. The heat of the fire grew oppressive. I took a deep breath and plunged into my speech.

"Did Beverly show you the pictures of the tour?"

"Oh, yes. She did indeed."

He snickered to himself. "They all look the same to me. I wish she'd gone sightseeing and taken some shots of the cities we visited, so at least I'd have some idea of where we were...."

"Did she show you the picture she took of you in your hotel room in London?"

"Oh... that...? Certainly." His face formed into an angry frown. "I know she had the poor taste to show it to you. I told her if she passed it on to anyone else, I'd have enough reason to dismiss her from the chorus."

That settled it, I thought. Though everything began to feel less tense, my nerves still jangled as Orson took slow, deliberate steps in my direction. My restraint was still stronger than my readiness for reaching out. I didn't like Orson being here with me. I didn't like him looking at my paperweights, my portraits of Austrian royalty or my potted palms. They revealed things to him about me that I cared about, but he didn't. Orson was such a stranger in this room that he made the shadows of its objects hold hands in defense against him.

He stopped in front of me, his eyes pleading. As we exchanged empty superficialities, his presence pressed hard on my emotions. I had to get rid of him before James returned.

Yet so far, Orson had carefully observed all the rules of a first-time visitor and continued to ask polite questions about my paperweights and CD collection. I fled into the idea of playing one of the Mozart piano concertos for him, which I knew he loved. But no. I found myself reacting in exactly the opposite way by telling him squarely that his intellectual inquiries sounded insufficiently convincing. How glad he was. He sighed with relief and drowned me in the deep sea of his arms.

It was only an instant, yet it felt forever, before I broke away from him. I thought, Not here. *Not here!*

What if I heard footsteps on the stairs coming up from the garage? Would James attack one of us? And whom? The intruder or the traitor? How I feared James' fury. But most of all, I feared he might not fight at all, just turn and leave.

I had to explain this to Orson and ask him to leave. I opened my mouth, frightened, but Orson placed a finger on my lips. His hands curled around my arms and suddenly he looked at me with untypical sadness, as if fearing loss. Under his metallic eyes my resistance swam and sank just for a moment, like rose petals in a wineglass.

Orson's voice was powerful and persuasive, disarming my tentative objections with silent handcuffs.

"You're not going to fight me, Isabella, are you?"

As if holding their breath in solidarity with me, the potted palms began curling their leaves. In this instant I found the strength to block out Orson's presence.

I said, "I want you to sit with me in front of the fire, just sit."

He followed my command and we sat on the rug, gazing at the flames, like refugees from passion.

"You see, Isabella, I resent you. You take away my control over my body without even touching me. The thought of you disrupts my concentration on the podium and at night I lie awake and fantasize about your beauty. I have dozens of phone calls to return and stacks of mail to read, and what do I do? On this chilly night I come out to New Jersey when I'm not even sure you're at home. And do you know why?"

"Why?"

"Because my need to see you is stronger than my reason. You torture me with your beauty and your innocence and there is nothing I can do to stop this madness." His voice bore a detached conviction that stemmed from a lifetime of anguished affairs and lost loves.

He reached over to play with my hair in a gesture of possessive tenderness. For moments we sat still. The first smoke was beginning to curl from the ashes. I could no longer endure the pressure of time and James' imminent return. Seconds seemed to stretch into minutes, and minutes into hours, making me feel as if I were a captive in my own house.

"You must leave now, Orson. Please!"

He said flatly, "Indeed, Isabella, I understand. Can you call me a cab?"

In the kitchen my fingers moved feverishly through the yellow pages in search of a local taxi company. The voice at the other end gave me a confirmation number for the car and said it would come in ten minutes. How late was it? I wasn't wearing a watch.

"It's twelve to ten now," Orson was standing behind me.

While we waited, he agreed to have a quick hot drink. His shoes shuffled uncomfortably on the kitchen tiles as I fiddled with a bag of instant hot chocolate. It had stopped snowing and the road conditions shouldn't be a problem. I was glad. Miraculously, Orson's cab came within five minutes. He gulped down his hot chocolate and I saw him downstairs.

"Thank you for your hospitality. It was a pleasure." He bowed stiffly, as if the reason for his visit had been nothing else than to enjoy a hot drink.

We exchanged a silent glance.

Before closing the door I watched his footprints in the snow as he walked to the car. I watched him talk to the driver and climb into the back seat, and I watched the car recede to a miniature toy, soon to be swallowed by the darkness. It left a smoke trail behind that, like the sound of Orson's voice, softly curled into the past. I wanted to laugh and cry, but most of all I wanted to be by myself.

With Orson gone, the living room reasserted itself, as if regaining consciousness after a coma. Gradually, reason and reality returned. I needed air. I opened the windows despite the cold winter air. I turned out the lights, closed the glass doors of the fireplace and fell into bed. James' bed and mine. The bed untouched by Orson.

I felt delighted at the feel of warm flannel sheets and the sweet repossession of a part of me that had been lost. Under the cover of darkness I fought off hollow echoes that followed me, and finally, from a far-away corner of my mind, I heard the sound of the garage-door opener. James was back. I listened to the footsteps on the stairs, confirming his presence, and at long last allowed myself to fall asleep.

71

Sunday, March 1, 1987

Dear Julia,

In my dreams, why do I keep diving into pools without water? I dive, but I never hit the bottom. At the crucial moment, instead of waking up, I pass through a mirror into a large room. Several fans rotate lazily on the ceiling and empty chairs form circles around tables set with silverware and glasses. The day is dawning. No one has arrived for breakfast, but there is a smell of coffee from the kitchen. Is someone throwing gravel against the window? Outside, a dull gray sky broods over a bluish seascape that melts into a blurred horizon.

I sit at one of the tables with a book of blank pages, feeling forced to fill them. I want to connect things, put visions of pools without water, rotating fans, seascapes and silverware into context. I want to convert objects into symbols and symbols into a narration. But the wings of my mind are clipped and my wrists weigh a ton. A vague terror seizes me at the crackling of the wooden floor behind me. Footsteps. An intruder? I turn around and look into his face. A gray-haired man in a gray suit looks at me with a purposeful smile. He says with a velvet voice, "Just relax. Enjoy. I want to go swimming with you." I close my eyes and lean against his body as he stands behind my chair. I whisper, "There is no water in the pool..."

I know, Julia, it's silly of me to drag you through the subconscious layers of my mind. But a quiet melancholy has taken possession of me, maybe it's nothing but fatigue. Or is it madness? I've come to believe that anything is possible. Yes, anything, because nothing is ever quite definite... least of all the future.

Ah, the future! Since the start of my job-hunting I've been through nine interviews and hated every minute of it. Either the job was uninspiring, the office too cramped and without a window, or the boss's smile too inviting. (One actually promised me the job if I would always look as pretty as on the day of the interview.)

Frankly, I'm discouraged. My interviewing smarts, as well as my high heels...they're worn down from running around. James and Barry laugh at me good-heartedly. According to them, the right job will pop up as surely as the blossoms on our cherry tree.

Anyway, I had one more job interview, for a classical record company. The very company Orson Mahler has been recording with for thirty years. Mr. Mahler arranged for me to have the interview with the Artist & Repertoire Director, who is looking for an assistant.

I suspect I got the interview mainly for my language skills. German, French and some Italian would come in handy if I had to deal with La Scala, the Vienna State Opera or some artist management agency in Paris. Besides, which A & R Director wouldn't want to do Maestro Mahler a favor?

So, anyway, Dan Maddox was willing to see me last Thursday after work. Do I have a solid knowledge of classical music, he asked me over his silver-rimmed glasses behind a full, clean-shaven face. He had a hearty laugh and a heavy stature as he got up to greet me from a desk covered with files and piles of demo tapes.

Dan Maddox is about my age, forty pounds overweight and a head shorter than I. I see him as proud, dictatorial and kind, a little Napoleon. I liked him. Did he like me?

"In our business," he reclined in his chair, pushing his glasses into place, "we have to say 'no' more often than 'yes.' We have a dozen different form letters for returning unsolicited demo tapes and," he sipped from his Styrofoam cup, "I don't mind telling you, Mrs. Barton... uh... may I call you Isabella? Uh... Isabella, so... I don't mind telling you, that I have a dozen applicants for this job.

This means I have to turn down eleven people," he shrugged, trying to find a point of focus on his chaotic desk.

"I really need someone to organize my stuff," his eyes swept apologetically across his disorderly office. Obviously he doesn't think much of filing cabinets.

I handed him my resumé. He didn't even look at it, but asked, "What can you tell me in your favor, Isabella. Why do you think you would be good for this job?"

After my helpless hesitation he insisted, "Level with me."

I rattled off my education and the list of my qualifications, including my sense of punctuality and order. But it wasn't enough. Feeling menaced by a squad of eleven rivals, I had to tell him something special, something that no one else could come up with. Because suddenly I wanted this job, and suddenly I didn't mind being confronted with his monstrous mess and the prospect of having to spend my working hours without a window. Suddenly I felt that this little man, this little Napoleon, was striking a match in my heart. How could I strike one in his?

Meanwhile he told me he started out in a classical record store, barely making enough money to buy all the records he wanted. He tapped his fingers on a pile of CD-booklets.

"In the A & R business you'll meet a lot of artists ...pianists, violinists, opera stars, world-famous conductors... And some of them can be difficult to deal with."

I swallowed, feeling my irises grow rounder and still feverishly searching for something special to tell him about me.

He coughed. "But I have to warn you. Some artists, of course, transmit a certain charisma, and one of our iron rules is never to let your feelings for an artist carry over into your private life. Don't confuse the music with the musician. You have to divorce yourself from the impact of their personalities and the beautiful music they create. It's all art, and it's all business. There's no place for romance."

My cheeks burned, I was impressed. How could I impress him in return? And then I thought that the best solution was simply to tell the truth.

I pressed my hands into my lap. "I was born and raised in Pörtschach. It's the village where Johannes Brahms wrote his Second Symphony as well as his Violin Concerto. Right across the lake from my parents' house Gustav Mahler had a villa at the beginning of the century. According to his own designs he had a little composition cottage built high up in the woods, and he composed his last four symphonies there. And a few miles to the west Alban Berg wrote 'Lulu.' I think the music is in my blood."

Dan's face lit up. "Oh really? How interesting."

There was a warm, awkward silence, like one that occurs during a first date that's going well. Dan continued to explain recording schedules, release planning, copyright registration and production follow-up.

Julia, HELP! Did he like me or didn't he? Will I get this job? He told me I'd hear from him. Meaning WHAT? It's like having to wait for your lottery ticket to be drawn. So far, I haven't seen my name in the winner's column.

But soon I'll see my name printed in Stagebill, albeit along with one hundred singers of the Orson Mahler Oratorio Chorus. We're performing the Brahms Requiem and I'm positively ecstatic about it. Imagine, ME in Carnegie Hall! Don't you hate not being able to witness it?

No doubt the maestro will grind us through some tough rehearsals in the week ahead. He is known for not being easily pleased, but for producing pleasing results. Orson Mahler, again that name. Is HE the man in my dream?

Julia, we HAVE to talk. I'm struggling with myself trying to fight off a secret that pushes out and longs to be shared. But it can't. My secret wrestles like a weakened monster in the seascape of my dream. What, if I hit the bottom of the empty pool?

Julia, I can't wait for your return. Please try to understand. Try to read my words in more ways than one. I know you can. And you know I love you.

Your Soul Sister. Still?

Isabella

72

Tears are not predictable. They can't be produced at will, on time, or when another person expects you to shed them. My mother has never forgiven me for not crying at my own wedding. And James still has some difficulty accepting that I went through the ceremony of being sworn in as an American citizen with dry eyes. Would it be wise to share with them that the moment when I sensed something wet rolling down my cheek was on the brightly-lit stage of Carnegie Hall?

How appropriate for me to sing my first concert with a work of Johannes Brahms, a composer I grew up with, not just as a matter of formal education, but as an element of daily life.

"In this work," Orson had explained to the chorus, "Brahms comforts the living instead of mourning for the dead. While attaining the heights of expressiveness, this piece is a deeply moving combination of hope and grief. It's considered Brahms's most personal musical statement. To him, it was not only a means of rising above the grief that he felt over the loss of his mother, but also a kind of musical 'coming of age.' Each of the seven sections of the work ends on a note of hope. Brahms's warmly romantic style and rich orchestration enable him to achieve his aim with notable success. The Requiem starts softly and ends softly."

As Orson shared his musical convictions with us, his voice grew intimate, as if he were spilling a secret.

"I've always thought it a sign of maturity when a composer ends a work softly. It means that he is forsaking a powerful ending, because the work is sufficiently exciting in itself."

Another time Orson had explained, "When you think of the *Brahms Requiem,* I suggest you banish from your mind the mental image that most of us have of Brahms as an elderly, portly man with a long white beard. He was a slender, clean-shaven young man in his early thirties when he wrote this work. In fact, it marked his first big success as a composer."

For over two months the chorus had rehearsed without orchestra and soloists, and there was great anticipation before the dress rehearsal on the afternoon of the performance, when all the elements would finally be put together. The uniform for the rehearsal was jeans and sneakers. Later, for the performance, the women would be in white blouses and long, black skirts and the men in tuxedos.

And at two sharp, Orson commanded from the podium of Carnegie Hall, "Ladies and Gentlemen, no more talking or gum-chewing, please. With the whole orchestra and all the soloists here, every minute of rehearsal costs a thousand dollars, so let's not waste any time!"

Orson exhibited an unusual tenseness and repeated some trouble spots with no mercy on the singers' voices or the players' concentration.

He shouted, waving his baton, "Bar one sixty-five is *subito piano,* so don't drag the previous beat! I'll let you know where the cut-off is! Pencil in a pair of eye-glasses, meaning *look up!* Keep your eyes on *me,* please!"

Orson shook his head. "I'm not doing this for my ego. I'd *love* to conduct by just twiddling my thumbs and have the audience wonder how the hell I'm getting you to perform. Believe me, the greatest compliment you can pay a conductor is to make him feel unnecessary."

A short time later he rolled up his sleeves and demanded, "Sopranos, *float* that beautiful line, show the audience that you're singing *romantic* music... If you have any feelings for this work, now is the time to let them out!"

Under the bright stage lights, his face shone with moisture as he tried to impose his will on one hundred and eighty people.

"The acoustics are different here from our usual rehearsal space. You'll have to adjust to it!"

True, in this grand hall the carrying-power of our sound seemed disturbingly diminished.

Orson sighed, "This is an oratorio, Ladies and Gentlemen, so please *orate!* Open your mouths. I want clear articulation!"

Turning a page of this score and running a weary hand through his gray hair, he pointed at himself. "Look at this hair of mine. Don't make me lose any more of it..." His patient tone was beginning to wear thin.

Three hours later, when every throat was dry and everyone's feet hurt from standing, Orson's enthusiasm was beginning to build. He opened his arms wide, his face shining with perspiration and excitement. "*Yes, yes,* we're getting there," he nodded victoriously. "Can you bottle it until tonight?"

His glance swept over his beaten flock and he put down his baton.

"All right, get some rest everybody. Have something to eat before the concert, but don't overload your stomachs. Don't drink any alcohol, only water or tea. But not too much, so you won't have a bathroom problem."

The chorus began to file off the risers with Orson still busy over his music stand, mopping his forehead with his arm. During the rehearsal, Paula had been sitting in the hall. Now she hurried down the aisle and handed him a towel. He took it from her absent-mindedly and called after the chorus a last time, pointing at the three-thousand seats behind him.

"Please think of all the people who come here tonight from all over the city and from miles around. They battle the mid-town traffic, pay a lot of money for the tickets, the baby-sitter and a parking space in order to listen to this Requiem. So please, don't let them down. I have every confidence in you. It's going to be beautiful. See you at eight."

An hour before the concert the backstage area sizzled with excitement and last-minute preparations. Even after Carnegie Hall's seven-month renovation, the dressing-room facilities were still not adequate. The women's dressing room was officially five floors above the stage, normally used as a rehearsal room. The men shared a large dressing room with the orchestra on the ground level. But there was lively traffic between the two rooms. Chorus members needed to borrow a red music cover, a roll of cough drops or a safety pin. Or they just wanted to exhibit the color of their underwear. Beverly tried to look innocent as she displayed a purple bra with matching panties. As she changed, she saw no problem mingling with tenors and basses, determined to inspire male minds with something to fantasize about.

Among clothes racks, tote bags, thermos bottles, soft-drink cans, stray sneakers and the occasional hum of a hairdryer, most choristers were trying to find a comfortable place to sit down. A few had their feet up on tables, on radiators along the walls or in each other's laps. They were reading newspapers, peeling oranges, munching on sandwiches, applying blush or joining the lines to the bathrooms.

I edged my way through the crowd to a long mirror where Daisy was having difficulty closing the zipper of her skirt.

She frowned desperately, "It must have shrunk at the cleaner's. It fit me fine at the last concert..."

Presently, Joan, like a mother hen, entered the dressing room to make sure her troops were geared to do battle. Her chestnut hair was pulled back in a ballerina-style chignon, adding years to her worried face. She raised a hand. "Listen carefully, everyone, especially new members. For the stage line-up, find the people with the numbers before and after you and then give the number slip back to Jess at the door before you go onstage. And *please* don't wave to your uncle Max and your aunt Mary in the audience. Carry your score in your right hand and remain standing until Jess gives you the signal to be seated."

For a moment Joan closed her eyes and leaned her head against the wall before deciding to sit on the radiator, slipping off her shoes, obviously tired. No one paid attention to her, and I felt a wave of compassion for her.

"Somebody should thank her for all her work. A paycheck isn't everything," I said to Daisy and bit into an apple.

She popped her chewing gum and shrugged.

"You mean send her a dozen roses, or what?"

"Yes, something like that," I replied. "She deserves it. But I'm afraid Orson is not the kind of man who sends roses to a woman."

Surprised by the sarcasm in my own voice, I became aware that Orson had never given me a single flower. Even a cactus would have been nice. I checked my watch. Twenty minutes before eight.

"We should start to get in line," I hastened to add, eager to change the subject.

My line-up number was six in row five, the last row. Several minutes later, and careful not to step on the long skirt of the person in front of me, I moved onstage and along the risers, hoping they were stronger than they looked. I clutched my score in my right hand and didn't dare to look up before reaching my assigned chair.

Ah, Carnegie Hall seen from the stage! A warm, yellow light enveloped the plush red seats, the pillars and walls, richly ornamented in gold relief. The audience seemed to wrap around me, and I felt like a tiny element in a jewel box.

Carnegie Hall means to musicians what the White House means to politicians. Each institution, respectively, has become the maker of musical and political destinies. Carnegie Hall is locked into a glorious musical history of almost one hundred years, with memories of musical giants such as Tchaikovsky, *the other* Mahler, Toscanini and Stravinsky on the podium. And today, Orson Mahler would carry the torch of a tradition of golden-age performers.

"There is something in this hall," Orson had said to me, "that makes it possible to attain every human musical aspect."

I looked at the rows of people stretching a full city block from the stage and wondered how they would all like the music. James and Barry sat in one of the First Tier boxes. They were trying to catch my eye, and I nodded discreetly to let them know I had seen them.

The chorus was now in place and Jess gave a silent signal to sit. It was seven fifty-five. From the orchestra rose the discordant sound of tuning instruments.

To my left, Barbara gestured to the First Tier Center box, where a heavy woman wearing a bright red dress was ushered to her seat. It was Paula, looking a little like a fire engine. She wanted Orson to be able to spot her. But her signal was not aimed only at him. It was a signal to all the women in this hall. *I am Mrs. Orson Mahler. However strongly the storms of Orson's secret passions may blow, I remain married to him. No other woman can reduce my status.*

And now the moment had arrived. The dimming of the house-lights left the stage in a blaze of illumination. The last fragments of conversation died and applause rose. Should I pinch myself?

The chorus members cleared their throats for the last time, and some took off their shoes. Someone whispered, "The maestro approacheth..." Following the three soloists, Orson strode onstage. To my left, Barbara crunched a cough-drop between her teeth and whispered, "Orson looks so elegant in his tails. Really adorable. I mean, he's no Robert Redford, but I could fall for him..."

Presently our maestro stepped onto the podium, acknowledged the applause, smiled and turned around to face the orchestra and the chorus, waiting for complete silence. His eyes spoke to us. *Is everyone ready? If you are, so am I.*

After a second of quiet electricity, he lifted his baton and with a purposeful motion gave the first cue. The work started softly with the bases, cellos and violas. At bar fifteen the chorus entered.

Selig sind, die da Leid tragen, denn sie sollen getröstet werden (Blessed are they that mourn, for they shall be comforted).

The concert started off well. Every eye followed Orson as the focal point and when he smiled the whole chorus smiled with him. Yet his expression of controlled ease hid a strong force of concentration.

Because of her shortness, Daisy stood five rows in front of me, behind the trumpets. Beverly was in the middle of the soprano section on the opposite side of the stage. One of the spotlights caught her red hair and turned it into liquid fire. She showered Orson with looks that Cleopatra would have loved to master. Compulsively, she tried to catch his busy eyes for a second, like a miner panning for gold.

I wondered if Orson ever singled out a face in the waving field of singing heads. Did his mind ever wander, apart from wishing for a glass of water? Did he ever think of making love while he conducted? During the act of love, did he ever think of conducting?

He had told me once that conducting was like making love… because for him, it *was* making love to music. Making love to music meant bringing out the spark and spirit of what the composer had written for the instruments and voices. In Orson's mind, making love to a woman meant exactly the same thing. It meant bringing out the best in her through the instrument of her body.

But something happened down on the stage, pulling me from my trance. There was a sharp bounce on the floor that Brahms had not intended. Quickly Orson turned his head, raised an eyebrow, and brushed his right cuff with his left hand. Something rolled across the stage.

"One of his cuff-links came off," Barbara murmured under her breath.

A cellist reached down and scooped it up. Orson gave her a nod of thanks while the concert continued. The audience had probably not noticed it. Breathless, they absorbed the magic of the music, the lush sounds of the strings, wind instruments and drums.

It felt strange now, to think that Orson's hands, now shaping the music, knew every inch of my skin. Seen from the fifth row of the risers, he was galaxies away. I recalled his voice from the rehearsals, as well as moments of intimacy. *Easy, easy, don't rush ahead of me. Stay with me. Trust me. I'm here to guide you. Feel it!*

The intense heat from the stage lights above produced a film of moisture on my hairline, making me float into a soft fever.

The sound of Orson's voice reached me again, inadvertently, from another recollection. *You see, Isabella, I resent you. You take away my control over my body without even touching me.*

I turned the page to the most popular section of the work, the fourth movement, *Oh, how lovely are thy dwellings*. Right now, I couldn't imagine any other sound, not even Orson's voice, more soothing than this romantic melody we were singing.

The movement ended softly, and it was then that I sensed a slow tear rolling down my cheek. Much later the hall reverberated with a standing ovation. When Orson bowed, elated and relieved, sharing the applause with the orchestra, the soloists and the chorus, he exemplified an accomplished leader in control.

At that moment I recognized his need to balance his responsibility of being in control by surrendering himself to a woman. *Me?*

73

"Isabella, congratulations on your first concert in Carnegie Hall!"

I sank against James' chest as he closed his arms around me. His lips touched my earlobe.

"I was so proud of you. It was wonderful. Everything went well and the audience loved it."

Exhausted and exhilarated, I felt at home in James' arms and for a moment oblivious to the masses of people surrounding us at the post-performance party.

A hundred chorus members, plus their friends and spouses, had turned Café Carnegie into a box of upright toothpicks, where no one was able to move unless someone else did. With the adrenaline still pumping through everyone's veins, the air was alive with chatter, the clicking of glasses and the clattering of dishes.

"Where's Barry?" I asked.

"Barry left. He has to be on duty at the hospital in the morning at six. He's going to call you to tell you how much he liked the concert." James' eyes wandered in the direction of the buffet.

"Poor Barry. Always so dutiful." I took James' hand. "Let's fight our way through to get something to eat. Joan promised us a special treat."

A buffet was set up in the middle of the room. Calls like "What a spread!" and "Wooow..." could be heard at the sight of the artistically arranged hors d'oeuvres. Two matching mermaids, sculpted in ice, balanced a platter of oysters and clams. People around us were filling their plates with smoked salmon, avocado rounds and mousse of duck. One of the tenors dropped an olive on the sleeve of my favorite silk blouse.

My eyes searched for Orson, but he hadn't arrived yet.

James handed me a glass of wine and made a goofy face at Daisy who pushed into the line between us. Recognizing James, she smiled but preferred to give her attention to piling up her plate with melon balls wrapped in prosciutto.

When we had fought our way back to the bar, a silvery soprano voice rose. "Hi, there! What a surprise!" Beverly enveloped James in a lengthy hug. She had changed into a bright, floral dress that rustled when she moved.

"James, it's been so long... I saw you in one of the First Tier boxes and I was hoping to see you here..." She laughed between two bites of mini-pizza, ignoring me completely.

Alarmed by a general commotion behind her, she swallowed too quickly and came close to choking. From one second to the next the whole room fell silent and then there was a burst of applause. Orson had appeared in the doorway, bowing, basking in a hundred looks of admiration.

Instantly, Beverly disposed of James and her plate to elbow her way through the flock of fans. Flashbulbs went off. Orson raised his hands to ask for silence.

"Thank you for your warm reception."

A reporter asked, "How do you feel after such a successful performance?"

Orson accepted a glass of wine from the waiter.

"I can't say it often enough, I did the least of all. I was the only one on stage who didn't make a sound."

Laughter rose. Every eye in the room was on him. Orson wore his tails with utter ease. In a way, they were his work clothes.

"Fifteen years ago," he mused, "it took me seventy-one minutes to conduct the *Brahms Requiem*... now I take eighty. Paula says it's age and exhaustion. I say it's conviction. I now find that the music asks for time and broadness... and by the way, where is she, Paula... uh... my wife?"

On cue, two red sleeves appeared from behind a golden column and were flung around Orson's shoulders from behind him.

"My Orson." Paula carried her words like two pieces of luggage that had been sanctified by time and habit. He didn't do a good job of hiding a tiny look of inconvenience.

Other hands claimed him, and he was carried by a flow of bodies, yet fully in tune with the tide of their pulls in non-specific directions. Beverly stayed close enough to secure his knowledge of her presence, but never close enough to touch him. She was like a bodyguard, ready to act, but not allowed to make contact with her object of love.

Daisy, her food forgotten, fastened her clumsy arms around Orson's neck and sniffed noisily.

"Thank you Orson...you know we all love you."

Orson disentangled himself from her grip.

"Please... no, don't thank me. Remember *you* did all the work."

From the middle of the crowd, his eyes turned and found mine in a flash of recognition. Between us the air was filled with the tension of attraction and avoidance. Awkwardly, we looked away.

James touched my arm and asked, "More smoked salmon?"

I shook my head. "No thanks, I've had enough."

Impassively I watched one female admirer grab Orson tightly around his shoulders. But our maestro showed no sign of displeasure. Orson's inclination to accept female advances could understandably have driven poor Paula into the consolation of bourbon, the bible, or both. But where was Paula? She was no longer near her husband...

"Isabella?"

Her voice. Paula's pleasant timbre. I jumped and swung around. She carried a plate with meatballs and curried shrimp in her left hand.

"Isabella... is *this* your husband?" Paula looked at James with quick approval. "Why, he's gorgeous..."

James bowed, and the creases along his mouth deepened in a gentle smile.

"It's an honor to meet you, Mrs. Mahler."

"The pleasure is undoubtedly mine." Her blue eyes shone with unhurried ease.

While James was visibly impressed by the grandeur of her personality, she winked at me and smiled wisely.

"Isabella, at a party like this you are *not* supposed to hang around with your husband all the time. As for me, I always try to stay away from my Orson as much as possible..."

"Paula, you have a point," I laughed and disengaged myself from James. "I leave him to you. You two have fun."

On my own, I pushed towards the bar for a re-fill and listened to some of the comments around me, hoping to pick up bits of gospel and gossip. My first target was a group of five ladies fingering the stems of their empty glasses.

The youngest of them, still a teenager, frowned. "...at his age, I'd think he'd be beyond chasing women."

Another said, "Years ago he had quite a reputation, but his name hasn't appeared in the society columns lately for reasons other than conducting."

My next eavesdropping exercise presented itself behind Daisy and Jess, who had their backs turned to me. Daisy stood on her toes to speak into Jess's ear.

"All my life I wanted things I couldn't have, like a twenty-eight inch waist and ... uh.... Orson..."

Through his long lashes Jess smiled at her with gentleness. He leaned against a golden column and displayed the forlorn look I had seen on him before.

"I know how it feels if a special person is unattainable."

Wondering who that person could be, I retreated around the column in the opposite direction. Since his attempt at romance, Jess and I had kept our conversations safely sealed around paperweights and singing.

At the buffet the crowd was slowly thinning out, and the sculpted ice mermaids had started to melt. Sipping my wine, I watched James and Paula from a distance. An animated expression flickered across her round, rosy face. They had found some kind of common ground and I doubted it was bourbon, the bible, or even Brahms. Behind the protection of a golden column, I inched close enough to hear James' voice.

"... a good poker player will win in the long run, provided he's able to forget there's money involved. It's all mathematics and psychology..."

"But the real excitement lies in luck," Paula cut into James' sentence, spearing a meatball with her fork.

"Of course, if you have a poor hand, you have to fall back on bluffing," James replied.

I studied my husband. He smiled at Paula patiently as she spoke and ate. The scene took place at the edge of my consciousness. A bell of memory rang in my mind. *My first visit to Orson's apartment. Paula's room and the book on the table next to her bed. "The Complete Guide to Winning Poker." Later I had asked Orson, "Does Paula play poker?" and he had said, "What an interesting idea. Not that I know of..."*

How well did Orson know his wife? How well did I know my husband? In eleven years of marriage, James and I never had a conversation about poker, and now I heard him say, "I think evaluating a poker hand is a form of art."

He seemed to inspire confidence in Paula. Her passion would be safe with him.

Her hand touched his sleeve. "When the cards are finally put away at the end of the night, or rather at dawn, there's no other thrill to match it. Even if you've lost and you know you'll wake up at noon with a reduced bank account, there's this dark folly that frees you from ordinary life."

I stepped forward.

"I think of it as a deal with fate," she continued, but my appearance made her jump. We seemed to have that effect on each other.

Meanwhile, Orson had come full circle from the other side of the room. How much had he heard? James and Paula had been engrossed to such an extent that they looked lost at the sudden sight of us.

Paula avoided Orson's gaze. The maestro looked grotesque. His face was smeared with lipstick from too many kisses.

His eyes settled on me dreamily. "Isabella, how does it feel to sing in Carnegie Hall? It was nice having you on the stage with me."

I blushed a little and felt James' arm slide around my waist.

Our glasses were refilled and I proposed a toast. "To Maestro Mahler. And continued music-making."

Everyone took a sip.

Orson, recognizing James, punched him playfully on the arm. It was a gesture so unlike Orson, so totally out of character.

"James, I'm glad you could come tonight."

James raised his glass. "The pleasure was all mine."

He and Orson exchanged the easy glance of natural allies.

We all drank again, too eagerly. Paula was the first one to make a face. Three seconds later, Orson and James grimaced simultaneously. The wine tasted ... peculiar.

James raised an eyebrow.

"Well, a wine is only as good as the wine-maker."

Paula gasped for air.

Orson asked, "*What* is this?"

I said, "The wine smells like rotten eggs."

James, still holding my waist, diagnosed with expertise, "There's nothing to worry about. If there are impurities in the bottle, the wine can combine with something like copper sulfate to produce hydrogen sulfide. And when there's too much of it... you get this." He frowned. "You get the smell of rotten eggs."

Paula shot James a look of admiration.

Orson said, "How interesting."

James held his glass up against the dim light of one of the chandeliers trying to confirm his conclusion.

Beverly and Daisy joined our group, uncharacteristically quiet.

Paula took Orson's glass from his hand and her lips quivered in awe. "Orson, my pet, what James is saying is so fascinating. Maybe you should have become a chemist instead of a conductor after all."

Paula's attempt at humor failed to put anyone at ease. Immediately, Beverly and Daisy started a storm of defense on Orson's behalf, but he silenced them with a gesture.

"It's just, well...," Paula insisted, "chemists have such an enviable way of grasping the facts of life."

"Yes, Paula, indeed," Orson hesitated, and his gray-metallic eyes brushed James and then turned to rest on me. The moment seemed eternal. No one breathed. When he continued, there was a paced calmness in his words.

"*Maybe* I should have become a chemist. Chemists have such an enviable way of grasping the waists of their pretty wives."

74

To an outsider it looked as if Beverly and I were standing in line with all the other women to get an autograph from Orson. We could have done so, just for the fun of it. Pretending to be strangers, we could have asked him for his signature for our cousin Cathy or our uncle George. Orson would, as always, meticulously write his name and reply with his velvet voice, "It was nice meeting you." Then the three of us would burst out laughing. If we had done it, maybe the day would have ended on a happier note.

Actually, Beverly and I were just waiting for Orson until the last of his fans got his autograph, written on one of the *Mahler on Mahler* flyers. That was the title of a series of six lectures that Orson was giving at the Metropolitan Museum of Art. Each lecture focused on one or two symphonies by Gustav Mahler. Tonight had been the opening lecture, and Orson had started with the *First Symphony*, subtitled *The Titan*.

From the stage, after reassuring the audience that he was not in any way related to *the* great Gustav Mahler, his voice took increasing possession of the auditorium.

With the slow movement of the *First Symphony* playing in the background, Orson explained, "There is nothing rushed about Mahler. He takes his time... His music sprawls. Listen, here is the well-known 'Frère-Jacques Canon' in a minor key with timpani, double-bass and bassoon. My namesake Mahler was a magnificent orchestrator. And here the oboe comes in high... and now ... the tenderness of the solo strings! But watch what happens! Mahler distorts these lovely melodies and creates a dark mood. Innocent beauty is turned into grotesqueness. What happened to the idyllic quality? It's gone..."

Beverly, next to me in the front row, filled page after page of her spiral note-book. Words, written or spoken, meant the world to her. I enjoyed just sitting there, letting the lecture wash over me, as Orson had suggested.

As excerpts from the symphony sounded from the large speakers, and Orson commented on them, I listened with closed eyes to the two distinct levels of sound. How appropriately Orson Mahler's words blended with Gustav Mahler's music. Orson's presence on the stage went beyond physical space. It didn't seem to matter *what* he said, his voice would be considered magical if he had read from the Manhattan Telephone Directory.

And now, at the conclusion of the lecture, Orson seemed to be infinitely surrounded by admirers. Beverly leaned back in her seat and pushed her glasses up on her nose.

"What a shame Orson didn't use his own recording to demonstrate the music."

"I'm sure he had a reason." I rummaged in my purse, checking the schedule for my next bus home. "Maybe he chose someone else's interpretation so the lecture wouldn't look like a promotional campaign for himself."

She gave a condescending shrug, applying lipstick. Our wait for Orson was a cat-and-mouse game. If either of us left, she would grant the other the privilege of Orson's exclusive company.

Beverly said, "Look, Bella, you don't have to wait for *us*. We wouldn't want you to miss your bus back to New Jersey. It's much easier for me, since I live in Manhattan. Orson and I can hop in a cab together."

I checked my watch.

"That's very considerate, but I have plenty of time."

Orson interrupted the ensuing silence. "How lovely of you to wait for me, ladies. May I offer you a ride home?"

We left the auditorium, Orson in the middle. I buttoned my coat as the three of us walked down the steps of the museum. Though spring was just around the corner, there was a cold breeze in the air. I shivered. Beverly didn't seem to mind the chill. Her coat hung from her shoulders and blew flamboyantly around her figure. The grandeur of her manner caused people to make way for her. Orson hailed a cab.

Beverly asked him, "Did you notice that gorgeous blonde who was sitting in the row behind us?"

Orson seemed surprised and a trifle absentminded.

"Oh? I thought the gorgeous blonde was sitting next to you."

Beverly's smile froze. Had she ever considered herself not first in line for Orson's favors?

In the cab we kept Orson in the middle.

I said, "Orson, I hope you don't mind being squeezed in from both sides."

He beamed, placing his beaten briefcase on his lap.

"Not at all. I *love* it."

Orson directed the driver to go first to West Seventy-Ninth Street, to drop Beverly off at her apartment. This meant that in the end she would have to leave Orson to me. Her jaw dropped, indicating disappointment.

As the taxi weaved its way down Fifth Avenue, Beverly fought to cover her defeat with a torrent of words, and anything that came to mind was worthy of articulation.

"Orson, do you like to have breakfast in bed?"

He moved cozily between us.

"My preferences in bed do not include breakfast."

I almost said I didn't think so, but remained silent. The cab turned west into Central Park.

Beverly met Orson's eyes boldly.

"And would you give a sexy waitress a bigger tip than a plain one?"

His dry, "I tip service, not seduction," didn't deter her from the basic topic she was aiming for.

Right then I summoned the determination to change the subject from seduction to the music we had just been familiarized with.

I said, "Orson, what meaning do you think Gustav Mahler intended to attribute to his symphony?"

Before Orson could answer, Beverly rushed in.

"Orson and I agree that music has no other meaning than music itself, it's a skillful organization of sound."

Orson began to move uncomfortably between us, as if he knew exactly what Beverly would say next, but he had no means to stop her.

She took a luxurious sigh.

"And the same applies for sex, of course, doesn't it, Orson?" Without waiting for his reply, she went on, "The act of sex has no other meaning than sex itself, and like music, should be explored in every conceivable variation."

She shot Orson a side-ways glance through her thick glasses that bespoke volumes of experience.

When he didn't respond, she insisted, "Don't you agree, Orson?"

The driver glanced back in the mirror, and his eyes opened up like wagon wheels, searching for Beverly's face, and then, catching my eyes, hastily averted his gaze. Nobody spoke. Unable to bear the silence, Beverly continued her need to provoke.

"Why complicate the pleasures of sex with the burden of emotional promises?"

To my surprise, Orson declared his solidarity.

"Beverly, I know exactly how you feel. I can't bring myself to say *I love you* to a single person, and I never expect to be nominated for sainthood."

I felt a slow stab at my heart.

Satisfied with Orson's reaction, Beverly made an effort to sound harmless, turning her face to me.

"Of course, Bella, Orson and I agree that both music and sex can be sublime."

Her line *Orson and I agree* was obviously her lifeline. Deliberately, she had let the hemline of her skirt ride up to the middle of her thighs as she twirled a curl of her red hair. I leaned my head against the window and turned my head to look outside. What I saw against the darkness of nightfall was a face with tired lines. My own.

Finally, the cab stopped in front of Beverly's building. As she stepped out of the car she let her coat fall open to reveal her legs. She looked back, her eyes curiously magnified by her glasses.

"Orson, I'll call you later tonight."

He nodded, "Yes, please do."

She threw him a kiss. The gesture needed no decoding. I looked at her and hoped the venom of my eyes could reach her heart. But she had no heart. Beverly could not be hurt.

Without her, the car suddenly seemed un-peopled, its air clearer and lighter.

Orson told the driver, "Our next stop is the Port Authority Bus Terminal, and with a side-ways glance, "Isabella, you're awfully quiet tonight. Why?"

I looked down at my hands and said, "With Beverly around I would have to mail in my share of the conversation," realizing that my reply was anything but an invitation for further talk.

Orson searched for my hand, but I withdrew it instantly. I refused to look at him. Spots of light circled around us in the darkness. For the first time I understood the flautist of the New York Philharmonic who had, years ago, thrown a glass of water in his face. She had committed an act of retaliation for all the women whose feelings he had hurt. I had the sudden revelation that, by treating women carelessly, Orson would assure that they eventually left. That way he created room for new conquests.

Around us, cars honked angrily. The neon lights of Broadway made Orson's skin look green and purple, like a visitor from outer space. Times Square. With its thirst for life after dark, this city never slept. I felt the vibrations of its vitality, but I was out of step with them. Instead, I became more withdrawn with every block we passed.

Orson made another attempt to hold my hand. His touch seemed apologetic, desperately so. The silent tension seemed to open up a telepathic flow between us. His hand appeared to be saying, *Look, I'm glorifying the pleasures of the body like a form of art, because that's all I'm capable of knowing. I don't know what to do with the word "love." For me, it's just a word and it frightens me. I wouldn't be good at it, even if I tried.*

His wordless desperation made his hand an iron trap clutching my fingers. I sighed, watching the street lights whizzing past.

Orson asked, "Did you say something?"

"Huh-uh..." I withdrew my hand again.

Orson decided to return to safe ground. "Have you had any reaction to your interview with Dan Maddox?"

"No," I said flatly, "I didn't. I guess they haven't made a decision yet."

"Let me know as soon as you hear from them. I'll try to give Dan a call tomorrow."

Forty-First Street. Our cab turned West. At the intersection of Eighth Avenue we stopped at a red light. I leaned forward and said to the driver, "You can let me off here," and to Orson, "Thank you for dropping me off."

By now the traffic had started moving again. Some cars behind us were already blowing their horns. The driver asked, "Do you still want to get off here, Miss?"

"Yes," I answered. I tried to push the handle, but the door didn't open. Orson put his arm around my shoulders, pulling me into the opposite direction, close to him.

He instructed the driver, "Pull ahead and let her off past the intersection."

"Okay." The driver shrugged and the cab rolled through the green light. The siren of an ambulance sounded in the distance, coming closer. Several horns blasted at the same time. We came to a stop on the West side of Eighth Avenue. At this moment I felt

Orson's lips touch my ear. Through an interval in the earsplitting siren, now right behind us, Orson said, "*I l.... you.*"

The air seemed to tremble from the fear on his lips. Brakes squealed and cars opened a lane to let the ambulance through. I thought, No, Orson, you're not good at it. And the fact that he fell back against the seat, helpless, substantiated my assessment.

I opened the door and stepped onto the pavement without turning around, afraid of rewarding him with a look of pity.

Yet, as I disappeared into the crowded terminal, there was a small place inside me that grew warm. And slowly his words began burning like a brand that would forever be tattooed on my heart.

Part Three

- Rondo –

(Untying the knot, The meaning of love)

Against ill chances men are ever merry,
but heaviness foreruns the good event.

William Shakespeare

75

When I arrived home, I found James and Barry in the process of cleaning out our garage. Both wore jeans and sweaters. James lowered a box containing old books. He planted a fleeting kiss on my cheek and gave a bemused frown.

"You look a little frazzled around the edges, how was the lecture at the museum?"

Barry puffed on his pipe and carried an old footstool to his car. He asked between his teeth, "Yeah, I saw the ad in the *New York Times* about Mahler's lecture on Mahler. Was it any good?"

I said, "Very inspiring."

But both men seemed to have something else on their minds than being educated about Gustav Mahler's soul-searching music: *Food.*

James led the way back into the house and said, "Are you ready to go out for a bite to eat? Barry and I are starved. Hey, let's all go to that little Italian place on Bellevue Avenue. I have a craving for sea food lasagna."

I nodded, ready for a dish of pasta myself.

"Oh, and something else, Beautiful," James was saying with a big grin, "before we leave, you should listen to the message Dan Maddox left for you on the phone."

With a leap, I reached the blinking phone and pressed the button.

This is Dan Maddox from RCA Records. (He audibly cleared his throat.) *Isabella, I'm pleased to offer you the position as my assistant in the A&R department. Please call me back to arrange for a time when you can come back to my office to discuss further details, such as starting date, and uh... I'd like you to meet the president of our division.* (He gave a hearty laugh and said), *Congratulations, Isabella, I'm looking forward to working with you.* (After a moment's hesitation he added), *uh, and just to let you know, the personnel department has already mailed some forms to your home regarding health coverage, savings plans and tax deductions.* Click.

I exploded with a scream, "I did it, I did it!"

Next thing, I embraced James with a bone-crushing hug and a sigh that released a dam of doubts, hopes and expectations. The next moment Barry received the same treatment, never mind his fuzzy beard.

I said, "I am so excited, so relieved, so grateful. I have to call Orson tomorrow, I owe him the job." After making a pirouette in the middle of the carpet, I continued, "James, we have to celebrate! Let's have dinner at the *Tavern on the Green* and see a Broadway show… or… do you know it's been years since we went dancing?" and without giving him a chance to answer, "let's go dancing this Saturday… it's been ages since we've been out on a real romantic date…" I couldn't stop. It all came out on a tide of suppressed emotions.

James ran his hand through his slightly too-long hair and a muscle grew taut in his cheek. "Not this week or the next, I'm afraid," he said defensively. "Of course I'm happy for you, Beautiful. Very happy. But I have to spend the rest of the week compiling a huge report, and that means I'll have to stay in the office late. I'm sorry, Isabella… and on Saturday," he shot a meaningful glance at Barry, "Barry and I are signed up for a tennis tournament at the club. It's the first of the season. Remember, I mentioned it to you? I'll be too tired at the end of the day to go dancing."

Suddenly sober, I nodded. Hadn't I heard something like this before? Why should I be surprised now ?

James went on, "and on Sunday... Oh, I didn't tell you...? On Sunday afternoon I'm flying to Cleveland to visit a division of Wexton Laboratories early Monday morning. I'll be there for four days. I'll be home Thursday...and on Friday I'll be out in Long Island for the usual corporate dinner."

I was still standing on the same spot, rooted. Something didn't sound right. From the corner of my eyes I saw Barry with his pipe heading for the ash tray on the glass table.

James said, as if defending himself, "Maybe the following week, Isabella, remind me, when I'm back from Cleveland."

I bit my lip. It wasn't only romantic dinners or dances that had been missing during the last months. Everything had become so efficient and rushed. When had we last taken time for *ourselves?* James was always traveling, perched over reports, playing tennis or reading novels. He was always nurturing something other than our love: our bank account, his tennis muscles, his love for Tolstoy. Wasn't celebrating my new job more important than a tennis match? And for his trip to Cleveland, couldn't he take an early flight on Monday morning?

While we drove to the restaurant together, Barry brought us up to date on his mother's travels. When Louise came home from Hong Kong, the airline had lost two of her six suitcases and a bird cage. After innumerable phone calls to airports and lost-luggage personnel, her stray bags, including the birdcage, were traced via Lima and Miami to JFK airport.

While sitting in the back of the car with James driving and Barry next to him, all this information hardly registered with me. But yes, I remembered, Louise had spent five months with her brother in the Far East. Now she was looking forward to return to her East-side apartment, tea at the Plaza and matinees at the Met. She had hardly been back a week and had taken up volunteer work and an evening class in origami.

I had to force myself to be present. James' self-absorption had put a damper on my feelings of success. His manner made me wonder if a crack had sprung up in the cement of our marriage. I felt a hedge of ice flowers growing around my heart, frightening and menacing. It seemed to warn me that I might have to worry about something more important than Orson's refusal to attribute meaning to music or sex. Inadvertently, I had the absurd vision that I might lie in Orson's arms, longing for James. The hedge of ice flowers around my heart began to hurt.

Before we entered the restaurant, I decided I would make three calls the next day in my lunch hour. And I did.

The first call was to return Dan Maddox's message. He was happy to hear from me and we agreed I would come to his office the next day.

My second call was to Louise, welcoming her back after her long stay in Hong Kong. Because she was in a hurry to leave for her volunteer work, she bubbled much faster than she would have in a more leisurely conversation.

"I'll tell you about my trip another time, love, I just wanted to let you know I spoke to Orson and I'm so glad you are in his life at this difficult time…"

"What kind of difficulties?"

"Well, you know, uh… Paula is giving him reason for concern, and I'm so glad I can be here for her, to help her in a personal as well as a professional way."

"Louise, I had no idea…"

"Please understand, Isabella, I can't say any more at this point, but Orson is under a lot of pressure with his upcoming concerts, and he spends every free minute of his time studying the score of Beethoven's *Missa Solemnis,* which he'll perform at Carnegie Hall in May. On top of all of this he has meetings with the orchestra board, fund raising committees and union representatives. Right now you are his escape and his inspiration. I would like to talk to you longer, love, but I'm afraid I can't." She sounded very short. "I have to go."

After hanging up I thought, This was more information than I could have wished for.

My third call was to Orson. It was a courtesy call to thank him for his help with my new job and I wasn't concerned should Paula answer the phone. Luckily, he picked up himself.

I blurted out, "Orson, imagine, Dan Maddox got back to me! I got the job! I'm so happy! Thank you so, so very much."

His smile sounded through the phone.

"Isabella, believe me, I couldn't be happier for you. But please don't thank me. I just arranged for the interview, you were the one who impressed them."

Impulsively, and without thinking about his busy schedule or any difficulties he might have with Paula, I said, "We'll have to celebrate!"

"We'll certainly celebrate, Isabella. We'll do something nice, anything your heart desires. It's a promise." He hesitated for a moment. "Only next week I'm guest-conducting the Cleveland Orchestra in three performances of Beethoven's *Seventh Symphony* and the Prokofiev's *Second Violin Concerto*. Although both works are considered repertoire pieces for a seasoned conductor, I need some time to familiarize myself with the scores again. I want to be certain how to shape the music before I meet the orchestra. And then, oh, did I tell you about the *Missa Solemnis* yet?"

"No, you didn't. But of course, I understand about your busy schedule, Orson." I said it without resentment.

Right then I realized that Orson and James were both very busy professionals, each in their own field of expertise. They had important commitments. If I could accept Orson's demanding schedule, I should think about James' work in the same way. This awareness lifted some pressure from my troubled feelings about my husband.

Before hanging up, Orson said, "Maybe the following week, Isabella. Remind me, when I'm back from Cleveland."

I thought, *Cleveland?*

76

James blew me a kiss without taking his hands off the steering wheel. Our car was inching around the last bend before the in-bound entrance to the Lincoln Tunnel. It was the usual Saturday night traffic.

"Do you happen to have some singles?" James asked.

A little irritated at his habit of always asking me for the toll money, I protested, "I never carry any money when you take me out, especially when you make such a secret out of it... A surprise night in Manhattan! We're practically there, and I still don't know where we're going."

James shrugged and fumbled in his pockets for the bills.

"Besides," I pointed to the tiny black object on my lap, "my purse is too small to hold anything but a lipstick."

James lowered the window and handed four bills to the toll booth attendant. After entering the tunnel I couldn't resist describing Siegfried Stringer's face for the third time when I had handed in my resignation. He ended his speech about how sorry he was to see me leave with, "Isabella, if you'd change your mind, I could make you a much better offer."

I shared my news with Sandy Maxwell when we were standing by the coffee/cappuccino maker. She said, "It's funny, Isabella, I handed in *my* resignation two days ago. I found a better position too. Siegfried was going to make an announcement later today. I guess it's going to be a double announcement."

We looked at each other and snickered, almost spilling the coffee in our mugs. Our expressions bespoke volumes of victory over a villain brought down from his high horse.

James, next to me, gave a leisurely sigh.

"It's nice to see you so happy..."

"I am. I would be even happier if I knew where you were taking me tonight."

"I thought you wanted to celebrate. Want to guess?"

"No idea. Are we going to *Windows on the World*, or did you get tickets for *Cats* or *42nd Street*?"

We passed beneath the seemingly endless lights along the tunnel below the Hudson River. If I had a choice, I'd have traded any restaurant or Broadway show for Orson's concert tonight at Avery Fisher Hall. He was conducting the Philharmonic in a program of Rossini, Schubert and Strauss. I hadn't mentioned it to James for fear of appearing too eager to attend every Orson Mahler event in town. Besides, Orson's concerts, especially on a Saturday night, were invariably sold out, and when James had returned from his trip to Cleveland two nights before he had spontaneously announced that he was going to take me out on a surprise date tonight. This had left me with no say in the matter.

James didn't turn south after the tunnel, so it was clear that we were not going downtown to *Windows on the World.* He headed north, up Tenth Avenue, so we weren't going to the theater district either.

"I'm taking you to a concert at Avery Fisher Hall. Your friend Orson Mahler is conducting," James said casually, changing lanes to avoid a double-parked car.

"Oh, James!" Blood rushed to my cheeks. "What a surprise! How did you manage to get tickets?'

"I don't have them yet, physically, but they'll be at the box office in our name, as a courtesy of Maestro Mahler himself."

I gasped for air. "But how?"

We came to a red light. James took a maddeningly long moment to answer. "Orson and I ran into each other in the Cleveland airport on Thursday, and we came back on the same flight."

"You mean, you traveled all the way from Cleveland to New York with Orson Mahler and you waited two days to tell me about it?"

"But I'm telling you *now*... I wanted to surprise you. Orson told me about the concert today and said he'd be honored if we could come as his guests."

It took me a moment to grasp the situation.

"Any idea why Orson had to go to Cleveland?" I asked, cautious not to volunteer what I already knew.

"He was guest-conducting the Cleveland Symphony. Three concerts, he told me."

James made a right turn into the Lincoln Center parking garage. At the entrance he took a ticket from the machine and we parked the car. As we walked across the garage I took James' arm.

"So you and Orson just ran into each other?"

"That's right. It was around three when we met. I had just dropped off my rental car and was checking in for the flight to New York when I heard a voice behind me say 'I think I know this face.' I turned around and there was this man wearing dark glasses. It took me a second to see that it was Orson. How's that for a coincidence? Actually, he was on a different flight, one that left two hours later. But he said he'd like to spend some time talking to me, especially since he loved the fact that I'm a chemist and his secret interest had always been to know more about chemistry."

I said, "He flattered you."

James grinned. "So we changed his ticket to my flight. Fortunately, he only had carry-on luggage, so he didn't have anything checked in already. He told me he usually gets to the airport too early and always runs into people he doesn't care to meet. Apparently there's no airport in the world where he isn't recognized by people he's supposed to know but has no clue to who they are." James straightened up, visibly proud. "But he said meeting me was a pleasant surprise."

We entered the lobby of Avery Fisher Hall and joined the line at the advance sale window. I was still in a semi-state of shock.

"And then what happened?"

It was James' turn at the window. He gave our name and received an envelope containing two tickets, as promised.

James checked the location of our seats.

"We have to go upstairs, door 4."

"So you changed Orson's flight," I pressed on, careful not to lose the thread.

"We didn't have much trouble getting two seats together," James said on the elevator going up. "And then as we were walking to the gate, something funny happened. Orson suddenly turned his face away. He said, 'Speaking of the devil, here comes the kind of person I spoke about earlier, the kind I don't seem to be able to avoid at airports.' "

"Who was it?"

"I looked around and saw a woman dripping with jewels and wearing a Dior creation with a big white floppy hat, about to jump out of her skin at the sight of Orson. She came running toward us in high heels, carrying a pink overnight case and a white poodle. You should have heard her gushing in an Italian accent.

'Orsooon, Orsooon! Ciao, caro mio!'

"When she saw me, she became more formal. 'Ah, Maestro Mahler, I have been looking for you all over the world. E'bellissimo...molto bene.. to see you.'

"By this time she had deposited her overnight case and her poodle at our feet and was hugging Orson with what I would call true Italian passion."

"How did Orson react?"

"As politely as possible."

"What did she look like?"

James snickered. "She was quite elegant, really, but as she continued to cling to Orson, that awful hat kept falling off."

I gave a hearty laugh.

James went on. "As it turned out, she was the head of an arts committee in Italy and had once collaborated with Orson organizing a concert in Venice. She was headed to New York too, but on Orson's original flight. Naturally, she regretted that fact immensely. Meanwhile, her poodle was taking an active interest in Orson's socks. She explained proudly that *Bacio* was a full-fare passenger."

"And after that," I laughed at James, "Orson couldn't thank you enough for saving him from two hours of advances, Italian style, and a poodle in love with his socks."

We entered the auditorium and showed the tickets to the usher. The concert didn't start for another ten minutes, but instead of reading the *Stagebill*, I kept James talking.

"And then, on the plane, what else did you talk about?"

James crossed his legs and looked around.

"Nice seats, right in the middle of the hall."

I repeated, "Come on, what else did you talk about?"

James leaned over and removed a long blonde hair from my burgundy dress.

"Orson showed a lot of interest in my work, and I kept him entertained with enzymes and hydrocarbons for about an hour, which is longer than I could ever hold *your* attention on the subject."

I smiled. "I'm truly glad you finally found a fan for your carbohydrates. No one else seems to be crazy about them."

"We also talked about Beverly," James volunteered.

"Beverly? Beverly Honeycup?"

"Yeah, Beverly. The lioness with the red hair."

"What about her?" I began to feel uncomfortable, like a black dog on a hot day.

"Orson told me that Beverly is his investment broker, and he thinks she's very capable. Maybe we should consult her about an investment plan for ourselves, now that our savings are recovering."

My hands rolled the program into a tight tube.

"I'm not convinced that Beverly is the one to ask for financial advice."

"Okay, it was only a suggestion. I thought you and Beverly were friends. Don't you two have lunch together sometimes?"

"Not anymore." My mouth felt dry. I forced a ring of joviality into my voice and tested the waters a little farther.

"Did Orson mention anything about Paula? How is she?"

James ran his hand through his slightly too-long hair.

"I guess she's fine. They're both having dinner with us a week from tonight."

"You mean we're going out for dinner with them?"

"No, I invited them to our place."

"You did *what!!*?"

"I invited them for next Saturday."

"... to our home?" I thought I was dreaming.

James laughed lightheartedly. "Sure. Maybe you could cook a real Austrian dish. You know, something like *Gulasch* or *Tafelspitz* with *Beschamelkartoffeln* and horseradish sauce. You haven't made horseradish sauce in years. And you could bake some *Apfelstrudel* or a *Linzer Torte*, or even some *Salzburger Nockerln* if you still know the recipe. This is your chance to show the Mahlers that Austria has more to offer than Mozart, Haydn and the Schönbrunn castle."

"But James... uh, couldn't you have checked with me first, before you actually, uh...invited them?" My stutter sounded like Morse-code signals.

"It all happened on the spur of the moment. What's the big deal? I thought you'd be elated."

I swallowed. "Did Orson agree to come?"

James nodded. "In fact, I was surprised myself that he accepted so readily, but he said it's one of the rare Saturdays he's not conducting somewhere and that he hadn't had a real home-cooked meal in quite a while." James cleared his throat. "That makes me wonder. Didn't you tell me Paula was taking cooking classes? That doesn't make sense, does it?"

"No, it doesn't," I said, paralyzed, and thought, Why doesn't Paula cook for him? What's the matter with her?

I shivered. I knew it was too late to prevent the two men from becoming friends. There was nothing I could do to avoid this dinner unless I broke my wrist or came down with shingles. How could I possibly reverse the invitation?

My self-esteem took on a fluid quality. Would I be good enough as a cook, a hostess, a conversationalist? What should I wear? Should I look like Mary Poppins or the Virgin Queen?

I jabbed James with my elbow. "I hate you for this."

James stood his ground. "I don't get it, Isabella. It'll be fun, you'll see. I'll help you with the cooking and I'll pick out the wine. Just think, you can get Orson to autograph all your records. We could even take some pictures that you can send to your mother. Didn't you tell me she used to have a crush on him twenty years ago?"

"That's not the point. In two weeks I'll be working for the same company that Orson has been recording with for thirty years. They don't like employees to socialize with artists on a non-professional basis. It's a matter of principle."

James loosened his tie. "Who says you have to tell anybody about this. Our personal life is nobody else's business."

In the meantime, the musicians had taken their seats onstage and were tuning their instruments. I heard a woman behind me say, "The hall is sold-out. We're so lucky Edward got sick so we could use his tickets."

James' hand brushed mine.

"Do you want to go backstage after the performance and say hello to Orson? You could look at it as your first official function as a representative of your record label."

"Sure, why not?" I surrendered to the situation. Any protest would have been drowned out anyway by the rising applause for the orchestra. When Orson appeared and took his bow from the podium, I asked myself if I would have preferred if James had bought tickets for *Cats* or *42nd Street* instead? But frankly, no. Everything had fallen quite nicely into place. I allowed myself to sit back with a relaxed smile.

77

April 1987

Dear Julia,

You should have seen the superintendent's smile when I told him you're ready to move back here. You say you've lost the key to your place. Well, I have the one you left with the super. Instead of sending it, I'll have it delivered by personal messenger. Guess who? It's Barry Schumann, our family doc. You met him once at Carnegie Hall and at our summer party last August before your precipitous departure for Hilton Head.

Barry happens to be going to Hilton Head next Thursday for a medical convention. He'll stay at the Hyatt Regency for four days and may add a day or two of vacation time, depending on how long his colleague is able to cover his practice. I gave Barry your phone number along with your key. How's that for service?

Since Barry's break-up with Angela, it appears that no woman has been allowed near his home except the cleaning lady. Coming to Hilton Head as a first-time visitor, he'd appreciate some local company (you) and some recommendations for where to go for the biggest lobsters.

I have to end. James and Barry are playing tennis and will soon be home for dinner. I'm still so excited about starting my new job. Wish me luck, Julia, as I wish you.

Isabella

P.S. Did I ever make Tafelspitz *for you? James wants me to cook it for some friends of ours, and I can't find the recipe any more.*

78

As much as I tried, I couldn't get my spirits up at the thought of having Paula and Orson over for dinner. Unlike the impersonal terrain of Café Carnegie, where people could mingle or disappear at will, the intimate setting of a foursome at my home provided no escape.

But Saturday night came, with the table laid and the food simmering sedately. I happened to look out of the window when the headlights of a yellow New York cab stopped in our driveway. The first surprise was that Orson got out of the car alone. Where was Paula?

James and I rushed to the door. The second surprise was that Orson and James greeted each other with a spontaneous bear hug.

Orson didn't hug me. We didn't even shake hands, too anxious to conceal something that lay hidden behind our cautious smiles.

In the hall, James took Orson's coat and said, somewhat intimidated, "I'm really happy you could come." Assuming Orson had never set foot in our house before, he led the way upstairs.

"First of all," Orson explained, "I have to apologize to the hostess for Paula's absence. Unfortunately, she wasn't able to come along."

"Isn't she well?" I asked, piqued by curiosity.

"Considering the circumstances, she's doing fine."

"What circumstances?" James and I chorused.

We had reached the top of the stairs. Orson's voice was low but firm. "I'd prefer to tell you about Paula later."

James nodded. "Of course, we understand."

Orson's eyes swept the fireplace, James' armchair, my ivory portraits of Austrian royalty above the couch. Looking around, he showed the face of an accomplished liar, hiding the images that this room must bring to mind.

"What a charming place you have here, James, and so spacious," Orson said.

"I'm glad you like it, Orson."

How strange it sounded to hear James' name pronounced by Orson and Orson's name by James.

I wanted to show Orson my paperweights, but James was already steering him outside, and they proceeded to walk around the backyard. Under the spotlights from the deck, the white cherry blossoms stood out against the dark sky. Was it a twist of fate that had caused them to run into each other in Cleveland? Besides chemistry and conducting, what else had they talked about during their flight to New York? In this friendship of theirs, was I an obstacle or a link?

As we took our seats to begin with the meal, Orson's eyes took in the dining table.

"You've gone through a lot of trouble, Isabella. Everything is so beautifully color-coordinated, the tablecloth, the napkins, the candles, all in yellow."

"Thank you."

I passed around a plate with stuffed mushrooms, James' favorite appetizer. Orson helped himself generously.

With my attention divided between the conversation at the dining table and the simmering pots on the kitchen stove, I said, a bit concerned, "I hope my *Tafelspitz* came out all right."

Orson smiled, "The stuffed mushrooms were a great success. But what is *Tafelspitz?*" Orson nearly sprained his tongue trying to duplicate the pronunciation.

"It's beef boiled in bouillon and served with vegetables, potatoes and horseradish sauce," I said and got up to collect the used appetizer plates.

James looked expectant. "I love *Tafelspitz*, but Isabella hasn't made it in a long time. I had to wait for your distinguished visit."

"I'm glad I came."

After our first glass of wine, the men agreed that they would rather drink root beer for the rest of the meal. I was left with almost a full bottle of vintage burgundy.

"Your *Tafelspitz* tastes wonderful, very tender," Orson chewed savoringly, "I have new respect for you."

"Specialty of the house," I ventured, watching James happily pour root beer.

"How did your second meeting with Dan Maddox go?" Orson helped himself to more horseradish sauce.

"It went very well." I looked straight into his metallic eyes.

"Did you know there's a life-size poster of you behind the rubber plant in the sales manager's office?"

"I've never seen it." It was obvious Orson was flattered. "And what did you talk about?"

"Dan Maddox is going to keep me busy setting up files for artists, recording dates, venues, producers and sound engineers. It's going to be a bit confusing at the beginning."

"That's only normal." Orson displayed his reassuring smile.

"In a few weeks she'll manage the job just fine." James scraped at some candle wax that had dripped on the tablecloth.

"How do you like Dan Maddox?" Orson asked.

"I'm confident we'll make a good team. I admire his professional knowledge. He's kind, regal and unorganized. I'm going to organize him, and he'll teach me all about royalty payments and repertoire decisions. Thanks to you, Orson, he hired me."

"I'm sure he won't ever regret it."

James and Orson nodded and exchanged smiles.

I shot a triumphant look at Orson. "I'll have access to all your files, press coverage, concert tours and sales figures."

Orson frowned, "I assume that means I have to be nice to you from now on."

With staged formality, I said, "I'd hoped you would be nice to me anyway."

James snickered and asked Orson, "Can you pass the peppermill, please?"

Orson turned the gesture of handing it to him into a ritual of politeness. But it was much more than politeness that rallied the men through the meal. Regardless of what they talked about, James' hydrocarbons or Orson's mode of memorizing music, they were so engrossed that I felt an urge to kick them to remind them of my presence. My peripheral vision swept Orson's face. Suddenly a strange kind of strain showed on his face. Strain? Or Sadness?

He began tentatively. "I feel I should let you know what happened with Paula."

Paula. Finally, he mentioned her.

James looked concerned. "I hope it's nothing serious."

I finished my second glass of wine.

"Paula..," Orson hesitated, "Paula is sick, at least in a broader sense..." Orson spoke softly. "Paula has a gambling problem. She plays poker, and I was the last to know. Louise and Beverly have known for a while."

"Why Beverly?" I asked, immediately defensive at the mention of her name.

Orson looked down at this plate in helpless contemplation.

"It was Beverly who had to break the news to me. She takes care of my finances. I trust her completely. She does a great job, but there came the point when she could no longer hide the fact that Paula had lost close to thirty-thousand dollars over the past year. And that's a conservative estimate. Despite Paula's begging, Beverly could no longer keep the loss from showing in our accounts. My god, I'm paying Beverly a small fortune to manage my money. I might as well burn hundred-dollar bills in the fireplace."

James looked baffled. Our eyes were on Orson, waiting. His sigh implied relief at being able to unburden himself.

"I found out that Paula was going to an illegal gambling club on the East Side every Thursday. Last month alone she lost about five thousand dollars. That's when she finally confessed and promised to stop. She *never* took those Lebanese cooking classes on Thursday nights."

Thursday nights, I thought, and looked at Orson. Our *jour fixe.*

Orson continued with the voice of an invalid. Who knows what went wrong in Paula's mind, maybe years ago? When I asked her why she'd done it she said the desire to defeat the opponent or beat the system touches off a killer instinct in her. She said nothing else in life brings out more intense feelings in her."

"Nothing else?" I exclaimed. "Not even music?" And to myself, Not even Orson.

Was Paula's passion a balance for not daring to show anything but a smiling face as the devoted wife of Maestro Mahler? Was this her revenge, because her husband took her for granted and looked upon her as an object of convenience? Could a long night at the poker table soothe the wounds of worthlessness and a lack of love?

James refilled their glasses with root beer. Orson drank quickly.

"Where's Paula now?" I asked.

"Paula requires intensive psychiatric care. On Louise's recommendation, she's going to spend several months at the Institute of Living in Connecticut. It has a supportive environment, with beautiful English Tudor buildings on thirty-five acres. The hospital offers special in-patient programs for all kinds of dependencies and addictions, including gambling. Louise assured me that Paula would be under the care of the most skilled specialists."

Orson's face lapsed into a distant darkness.

James said, "I'm sorry to hear all this. But in time, Paula will get over it, and in the end she'll emerge a stronger person."

Orson forced a bitter smile. "She may get through it all right, but I'm not so sure I can handle it."

James passed empty dishes to my end of the table and said philosophically, "A crisis occurs in our lives so we can find a way to overcome it. It might hurt, but we can't avoid the reality of having to deal with it." James' arm brushed Orson's and he smiled warmly. "With your support, Orson, Paula will be all right. The money isn't important. The important thing is that Paula is a strong woman."

"... but perhaps neglected by her husband," I whispered and immediately bit my lip.

Yet my sarcasm held little currency against the value of James' consolation. Orson's hand on James' shoulder was a pat of brotherhood. A brotherhood powerful and vital, a brotherhood bred into mankind for millions of years. How could anyone argue with such comradeship?

Their communication continued to flow effortlessly and was only the surface of their well-attuned minds. To lighten the atmosphere, James told a joke and Orson wiped tears of laughter from his eyes. Soon Paula and I were left light-years behind, on another planet. I seemed to be sitting at an enormous distance from them, like a space-walker watching the world.

After a while James looked at me. "What about serving coffee and dessert, Beautiful? The horseradish sauce was a little too strong, wasn't it?" He made a funny face and got up. With James' back to the table, Orson reached for my hand, just for a second.

Orson said, "Blue is a good color for you. It matches your eyes. You look very pretty in that blouse."

Unexpectedly, James turned in the doorway.

"Yes, she's a cutie, isn't she?"

The two men smiled at each other in perfect solidarity. Shouldn't I feel an intense pleasure about James and Orson becoming friends? What more could I wish for? From now on, I wouldn't have to worry about being seen with Orson. But instead of pleasure, I felt emptiness. Something was wrong, terribly wrong, and I couldn't face the thought of spelling it out.

"I'm going to put on the coffee," I stood up. "I baked an Austrian *Linzer Torte* for the occasion. After all, Mozart wrote a *Linzer Symphony,* didn't he?"

"Indeed he did," Orson said. "It's number 36 in C, K. 425. He wrote it in 1783 in Linz."

"No arguing with that kind of expertise," James laughed, returning to the table. Still standing, he put his arm around my waist and kissed my cheek. "I can't wait to have a piece of your *Torte*."

I smiled, "I get the message. Dessert will be served in a minute."

"Shouldn't we help her?" Orson made an attempt to get up, but James gestured for him to remain seated.

"No need. Isabella has excellent organizational talents."

I felt myself under observation.

Orson nodded, sipping root beer.

"The lady leaves nothing to be desired, does she?"

I swung around. "Are you two making fun of me?"

"I meant it as an honest compliment," said Orson.

"Would I ever kid you?" asked James.

Their smiles broadened. I was glad to get out of their way for a while. Alone in the kitchen, I discovered that James had already eaten a piece of my cake, thereby making it impossible to serve it whole. So I had to cut it into single slices. I intended to tease James for giving in to his unruly appetite, but when I returned to the dining room balancing a tray with cups, saucers and the cake, my jaw dropped.

James was leaning back and looking down at the front of his shirt. "Orson, you've been studying my shirt for the last five minutes. Did I spill something on myself?"

Orson snickered. "Not at all. I'm sorry I was staring. What really intrigues me is your tie. The knot is so full and symmetrical. How do you do it?"

"I learned to tie it like this back in high school. It's a tight Windsor knot."

I put the tray down on the table and passed out the plates.

Orson leaned closer to James. "My tie always looks too thin, and the knot is usually high on one side. Yours is much more elegant. You don't just loop it around, do you?"

"No, it's a double knot. Let me see. I'm trying to visualize it without looking in the mirror. I do it so automatically that it's hard for me to figure out how it goes."

They laughed. I poured the coffee and put a silver spoon into the bowl of whipped cream.

James began tying an imaginary tie in the air.

"I think you have to cross the large end over, and then you go half-way and pull it through from the back."

Orson leaned forward, lost in James' demonstration. "Now you wrap it around, is that it?"

"No not quite. Then it goes back behind the small section, and then...," James tried to picture the geometry involved, "yeah... then you pull it through from the front to the back again."

I watched them with a rising sense of the ridiculous. Their behavior resembled that of roommates trading life experiences, with the next possible step resulting in giving each other a haircut. Still laughing, Orson took off his tie and looked at it helplessly.

James said, "I may have to give you my tie so you can have it analyzed." His face brightened. "Wait, I've got it now." He drew a whole choreography of movements in the air. "Did you follow that, Orson?"

"Frankly, no," Orson grinned.

"Look, Orson, why don't you just call me whenever you get dressed and I'll come over and tie your tie for you?"

Orson clapped James on the back and they roared with laughter. In the company of the two men I loved, I had landed on a lonely island. There was a magnetism that pulled them to each other and away from me.

Instead of coffee, they continued to drink root beer and at last tasted my cake. Their eyes came to rest on me. In perfect synchronicity they each took one of my hands across the table and held it.

"Your *Linzer Torte* is divine, Isabella. I'll have another piece," said Orson, and James seconded, "So will I."

"I'm glad there's an Isabella in my life," said James.

"I'm glad there's an Isabella in my life, too." Orson smiled almost wickedly. He looked at James, not at me.

Then he added, more formally, "She's a fine addition to my chorus, and soon will be to my recording company."

They let go of my hands at the same moment.

My alarm was total. What did all this imply, their complicity, their smiling, their sharing?

Sharing. I felt terror at the notion of sharing. Had they secretly agreed to share me? Did James know about Orson and me? And did he, liking Orson, silently agree? Which camp was James in, anyway? How many camps can there be in a group of three? Who was the solid leg in our triangle, who the prize? Who was competing for whom? James and I for Orson? Orson and I for James? Or James and Orson for me?

I finished my second glass of wine and the dimensions of the room seemed to shift.

I looked at James, resenting him for unbalancing the established nature of the relationship between Orson and me. And then I looked at Orson, resenting him for doing the same thing to James and me. When would I stop looking for self-approval in the reflection of these two men? Or was all this just the wine whispering to me?

James got up and returned with a chemistry book for the layman. "Here, Orson, I picked this out for you."

"Oh, thank you..." he drew a long breath and flipped through its pages with genuine appreciation.

A tea spoon fell to the floor, but I didn't pick it up. I was tired of being the perfect hostess. It was two-fifteen, and I doubted if I would be able to sit gracefully through James' explanation of the glucose conversion to glycogen to an end phase that produces a phosphate radical.

James must have seen me check my watch. He cleared his throat. "Isabella, why don't we ask Orson to stay overnight? It's late already, and this way we could spend some more time with him tomorrow."

Without meaning it I smiled enthusiastically.

"Of course, what a wonderful idea. Orson, you are most welcome to stay overnight."

Orson bowed politely. "Thank you for your hospitality. No one is waiting for me at home anyway, and I usually never turn down an invitation for breakfast."

"Wise thinking," James smiled, turning a few pages in his book.

I got up. "Excuse me, I'm very tired. I'm going to bed. You may stay up as long as you please. Additional toothbrushes are in the cabinet under the sink. Sheets and pillow cases for the guest room are in the second drawer next to the mirror. Orson can use a pair of your pajamas, James. I take it you'll find everything. I'm glad you liked my food. Good night, gentlemen. You may also clean up the dishes."

Their perplexed eyes followed me through the room.

I laughed over my shoulder. "You may also talk about me while I'm asleep."

79

Even though I felt part of me was running away from Orson, he still owned the territory under my feet. With Paula gone for several months, it was easy to meet in Orson's apartment. Without having to find a neutral place, our meetings required less planning and resulted in less passion. Our romance became less daring, less stressful, and less exciting.

On my arrival at Orson's apartment the entrance hall was filled with the sounds of Beethoven's *Missa Solemnis*. He greeted me with a warm hug and we took a leisurely look at some of the photographs in the entrance gallery.

"Here," Orson explained, "is Paula with JFK at a party in Washington in 1962. She had such a crush on him. And here... in Hollywood with Marilyn Monroe and Arthur Miller. He had come to some of my concerts and asked me in all seriousness if I could give Marilyn private music lessons."

"Did you do it?"

"I had to turn it down because of other obligations, but of course I regretted the fact immensely." His smile told a tale of what might have been.

There was one empty frame without a picture. I pointed at it.

"For this space, I'm going to have the picture blown up that I took of you and James cooking breakfast in our kitchen."

Orson didn't look convinced.

Our eyes swept across photos of a young Joan holding Matthew as a baby and of a younger Orson holding Matthew as boy.

Two frames to the left was Matthew playing Orson's grand piano. Matthew, Matthew. I burned to know why there were so many photographs of Matthew, but then I remembered how defensive Orson had become when I had asked him if Matthew's name had been chosen from his middle name.

I noticed that Orson was not standing behind me anymore. Suddenly, he switched off the lights of the hall and the people in the pictures disappeared, like ghosts, into the darkness.

I felt Orson's arm around my waist, leading me away, but the people in the pictures slipped out from under their glass frames, flocking around us. Joan, Matthew, Marilyn, Paula and John Fitzgerald followed us into the kitchen. Orson wanted to show me his new cappuccino maker, a gift from his Artists agency.

We didn't talk about Paula. We didn't talk about James. Yet they were both here with us, like the ghosts from the pictures. Paula and James were powerful in their absence.

He said, "That was quite a breakfast we had at your place last Sunday. I can't remember having so much fun eating pancakes since I was a child."

In my mind I re-ran Sunday. The three of us had met at noon for breakfast. While I made coffee and cut fresh melon slices, James and Orson each balanced a frying pan, cheering each other on across the hissing oil. Soon pancakes were being flipped through the air, and *most* of them were caught in the pan on their way down. The stacks that were kept warm in the microwave seemed sufficient to feed the New York Philharmonic.

That's when I took a photograph to make sure I wasn't dreaming it all. At the breakfast table, cheerfully passing the syrup bottle, James sat listening as Orson gave a lecture on music.

"Music cannot tell a story." Orson's voice was all benevolent professor. "Music by itself is not able to make a simple statement unless it's accompanied by words. Music alone is not able to say 'Can you pass me the sugar' or 'the coffee is too hot.' Music, seen as a succession of organized sounds, can only convey a mood that is appropriate for the text that it is set to. But by itself, unaccompanied by words, the same music may express sadness, loss, or just a quiet landscape."

James was fascinated and put down his fork.

Orson went on. "Many composers, above all Bach, used the same melody for completely different texts on different occasions. Handel did too. He used an Italian love aria in one section of the *Messiah.* That's why the words sometimes don't fit the notes very well."

At last James remembered to pass the pancakes and Orson helped himself.

James said, "I didn't realize that."

Orson continued between bites, "Therefore, unless it's stipulated by the composer himself, you are free to imagine whatever you wish. What you feel about music is very subjective, and the nice thing about it is that, *whatever* you feel, you are never wrong. The experience is strictly between you and Mozart or you and Beethoven. Don't let anyone tell you what to feel in music."

Hadn't I heard a similar lecture from Orson before? But now the man who was sprinkling sugar on his pancakes was a different Orson. This was no longer the same Orson who had walked with me through Central Park and said, *Relax, Isabella, just listen. Let the music wash over you and say 'Here I am. Take me. See what you can do for me.'*

This was no longer the same man who had taken me on my first subway ride and joked *Do you want to marry me?* or the same man who had told me through a mouthful of black olives *I can't promise fidelity.*

This Orson, spilling maple syrup on my placemats, was a man separated from his character, like Romeo inserted into the play of another writer. Without Shakespeare's lines, Romeo was lost and out of place. So was Maestro Mahler at our breakfast table, wearing James' bathrobe. This Romeo had stepped into a comedy and, freed from drama, was enjoying himself immensely. Was he aware that his Juliet began to see him in a different light?

It was the bright light of the morning that stripped the maestro of his magic. Ironically, it was the power of James' presence that enabled me to see myself at a distance from Orson. And though my heart had not yet crossed this distance, the idea was planted in my head. So why had I returned to this famous man's apartment? Was routine still stronger than the subtle call of reason?

When Orson and I stood in the kitchen, admiring the brand-new, yet unused cappuccino-maker, there was a lack of playfulness between us. We were no longer flirting with the forbidden.

He said, "Shall we try to make it work?"

I said, "Have you filled the water tank? You know, you have to press down the ground coffee in the filter holder, and you have to make sure the water softener cartridge is in place.

"Orson," I began to laugh, "You *do* realize you need milk for this, don't you? Where is it?"

"Oh," he waved, obviously confused. "Here… here in the fridge. I completely forgot." He handed me the milk carton, unopened, of course.

He frowned. "I hate to deal with the nitty-gritty of daily life. I hate it when people ask me practical questions, except when to start or end a *crescendo* or how fast an *allegro* should be taken. I don't like to deal with union regulations or payroll computerization…"

"…or," I cut into his speech, "the operation of a cappuccino-maker."

"Right," he smiled, fascinated by the bubbling sound of boiling water and the thermostat pump system.

"I need two cups, please, Orson, *fast!* It's working!"

His reaction was that of a blind man who didn't know his way around. I opened the first cabinet and found the cups we needed. Together we watched the cups being topped with a thick foam of milk, and I found a small tray to carry them to the kitchen table. Holding the tray, I felt Orson behind me, placing a kiss behind my ear.

I said, "This is not a good moment to jeopardize my balance."

The music of Beethoven's *Missa Solemnis* stopped *suddenly.*

Orson explained, "That's exactly the way Beethoven intended it."

Sitting across from each other, sipping foam and waiting for the coffee to cool down, Orson said, "What now, Isabella? I assume you didn't just come here to help me with my cappuccino maker."

I took another sip and recognized the invitation in his gray-metallic eyes. He smiled. "Should you decide to offer me your honor, I'd be delighted to honor your offer."

Across the rims of our cups we looked at each other for a long moment.

Finally I said, "Remember, when we made love for the very first time, you said that if we had all the time in the world, you'd spend hours just to make love to my face."

"I remember it well." He put down his cup. "Then why don't we imagine we have all the time in the world right now…"

He reached out to take my hand across the table.

A sense of premonition, just for the duration of a second, told me that everything between Orson and me would end in exactly the same way as it had begun, taking my hand across the table and wishing for a place outside of time and space. I realized this place was nowhere but inside of us, somewhere inside of him, and somewhere inside of me. The place began to feel invaded, slowly, by the seeds of doubt and reason.

80

On Easter Sunday the New Jersey sky was so bright, so promising, so shamelessly blue. The chimneys and gables of Ringwood Manor stood out against it like a collage pasted on a blue base. The forsythia bushes competed in their most indecent shades of yellow, and at the bottom of the hill beneath the mansion the pond lay like a rippled mirror.

In the parking lot Beverly took the large picnic basket that James handed her from the open trunk of the car.

She looked at Orson and sighed. "What a pity Paula can't be with us today. Look at the blue sky. We couldn't have wished for a better day. Paula was so enthusiastic when the idea of this picnic first came up, and now..." She cut her words off in mid-air.

Daisy, next to her, concluded, "...and now on Easter Sunday she can't even join us." She frowned prettily at Orson and took a folding chair from James.

The picnic had been Beverly's idea, and I had been looking forward to it. But now, with my feelings for Orson in a landslide, I'd have much rather spent the day alone with James.

Beverly, fighting a cold, pushed her red curls out of her face and sneezed. She turned to Orson. "When did you last speak to Paula?"

While Orson made every effort to stay away from Beverly's cold, I sensed that his eyes scanned the outlines of my white cotton dress against the light. His face was hidden behind his usual dark glasses, and his glib tone implied that he didn't want to discuss Paula's condition.

"I talked to her this morning. She's fine. My two nieces from Connecticut are spending the day with her."

He had told me that Paula was upset with Beverly for divulging her poker passion, and Orson was upset with her for not having divulged it sooner.

Blissfully unaware of the tension between Orson and Beverly, James unloaded two more chairs and asked, "How does Paula like her therapy?"

Orson assumed a milder voice. "She's convinced she's in the best hands."

"I'm glad to hear that," James said, still bent over the open trunk. "Do you want to carry the blankets, Isabella? I'll take the other chairs and the cooler."

"I can carry something else," Daisy said and tripped over the open shoelaces of her sneakers, falling with her whole weight against James.

He caught her, laughing. "I think you should tie your laces first, kid. Mmm, you smell good. Like lemon. I like it." He winked at her and her face ran from pink to purple.

James closed the trunk. "Now let's find a place to picnic."

I suggested, "We could try to find a spot down by the pond and feed the ducks."

James locked the car. "Sounds good to me. I know Isabella is always happiest near the water."

Orson frowned. "I think we should look for a place closer to the mansion. The ground is more even there for sitting down, and there's hardly any shade by the pond."

I shook my head at Orson. "I know you can't stand the bright daylight. If it were up to you, you'd probably move our party to some dark room in the basement of the mansion with one weak light bulb dangling from the ceiling."

Orson grinned. "Bravo. You've got me figured out exactly, Isabella."

There was an underlying discomfort between us that went beyond the choice of sun or shade. It was my obvious emotional reserve. It perplexed Orson, though he concealed it well.

Always geared for battle, Beverly shot me a victorious glance. "Orson is right. Ultra-violet rays aren't good for your skin."

I hissed under my breath. "What's wrong with a little sun?"

James' eyes signaled me that he understood my feelings. After two weeks of working in an office without windows, the sight of the sun in a blue sky was as desirable as a midday nap, both of which I was looking forward to today.

We made our camp on the lawn behind the mansion, between two lonely Greek columns and under the protective shade of a magnolia tree in full bloom. As we spread out the blankets and set up the chairs, six curious Canada geese came wobbling by.

I unfolded an old wicker chair and placed it in the shade.

"You can sit here, Orson," I said, "It's my favorite chair. I brought it all the way from Austria."

"Yes, I remember," said James, trying to find a spot for the ice-bucket, "and the air freight was about ten times its value."

"I'm honored," said Orson and sat down. "Ooops... this chair is low..." he laughed, surprised.

I said, "I know. I like it because it stretches my thigh muscles in a certain way."

James said dryly, "Isabella, I can stretch your thigh muscles in a certain way any time you want..."

Daisy giggled. Beverly sneezed and laughed hysterically.

My skirt billowed in the breeze. I felt Orson's eyes travel along my legs, and I said, slightly uncomfortably, "Let's unwrap the food."

I was glad that he and I were not alone.

I passed out napkins and put the sandwiches, olives, cheese, grapes and apples in the center. I asked Beverly, "Where are the glasses?"

Her watering eyes became round. "Oh my god!" She sneezed again, covering her face with her hands. "I forgot to bring them."

"At least I have a cork-screw," I said and held it up.

"I guess we'll have to pass the bottle around," James said and took a bite from a turkey sandwich. Orson snickered and we all joined in.

A moment later the root beer bottle was being shared between Orson and James in complete contentment, and Beverly and Daisy drank hot tea from the thermos. It was my fate again to be stuck with a bottle of burgundy by myself. Apparently no one, including me, had thought of bringing water.

Beverly produced a camera and began snapping pictures of the group. The wind blew through the branches and the magnolia petals drifted down on us like blown snow.

I asked, "Weren't Matthew and his friend Tom supposed to come along with us?"

I purposefully mentioned Tom's name, that mysterious live-in friend of Matthew's whom no one had ever met. Tom's job as a corporate pilot had always given Matthew a convenient excuse for not bringing him to any social gathering. Why was Matthew so careful to hide him?

Orson explained, "According to Matthew, Tom hasn't been feeling well lately. He's in the hospital to have some tests done. When I spoke to Matthew I could hear from his voice that he was worried about Tom."

"Oh...," we all sighed, the kind of polite sigh for someone we had never met.

More geese came promenading by, stretching their black necks.

James licked some cheese off his fingers. "Beverly, that Camembert is delicious. Where did you get it?"

Beverly searched for another tissue. "There's a French deli around the corner from where I live. I buy all my cheeses there. I got some for Orson too and put it in his fridge." She smiled grandly. "Now that Paula's away, I'm looking after Orson."

Under his dark glasses, Orson didn't move a muscle. Daisy's face fell in surprise. James raised an eyebrow. My crunching bite into an apple pierced the momentary silence.

Having sufficiently milked her moment of triumph, Beverly smiled at me, holding up a piece of cheese with the top of a kitchen knife. "Here, Bella. Try some. Orson adores it."

I said tightly. "No thank you. I don't care for Camembert," and thought smugly, I don't need to supply Orson with a care package to get into his apartment.

Beverly lowered her knife and, in a wave of nervous energy, gathered her red curls into a pony tail.

Daisy suggested, "Why don't we all go inside and take the tour of the mansion? Maybe we can buy a postcard and send it to Paula."

"As I understand it," James was munching some grapes, "Ringwood Manor was originally owned by two New Jersey families in the iron and steel industry. Sometime in the middle of the eighteenth century, the Ringwood Company was sold to the American Iron Company that operated out of Ringwood. About a hundred years later, the Cooper Hewitt Corporation bought it and it became the private estate of the Hewitt family."

Daisy wiped her hands on a napkin. "That's right. I read in the brochure that it became a state park in 1939."

"Now that you two have told us everything, I don't need to take the tour anymore." Orson sounded pleasantly satisfied and cut himself another slice of Beverly's damned cheese. I avoided looking at him.

Beverly, momentarily tired from practicing her charms on Orson, stood up. "I'd like to take the tour. It starts in a few minutes, at two."

Daisy said, "I'm coming too," and applied some lip-gloss on her mouth. "James and Isabella, what about you?"

James said, "Isabella and I took the tour last year. You two go ahead. We'll stay here and watch the store."

James and Orson elaborately waved good-bye to the ladies, but as soon as they were out of sight, Orson murmured in a confidential tone, "After what happened with Paula, I mean her losing all that money playing poker and Beverly knowing about it, I'm not sure I'm willing to trust her with the management of my finances any longer."

James said, "You have to understand, she was torn between her professional duty to you and her friendship to Paula."

"But how can she expect me to trust her again as a professional?"

Orson looked lost and James seemed at a loss to give further advice. I thought with satisfaction, See, Beverly, putting Camembert in someone's refrigerator is not everything.

Silently, the root beer bottle was passed between the two men like a peace pipe. The issue of whether or not to trust Beverly in the future remained unresolved.

After two sandwiches, an apple, some grapes, and a good part of the bottle of burgundy, a welcome somnolence began to steal over me. It was time for a nap. As I stretched out on the blanket, I listened to the men's voices.

Orson spoke of his upcoming concert of Beethoven's *Missa Solemnis* at Carnegie Hall. James took a conscious look around and picked up Orson's thought.

"Wouldn't a place like this, a beautiful mansion with a terrace, a pond and well-kept grounds, be an ideal setting for an outdoor concert?"

Orson shook his head in quick denial. "Not at all. There is nothing ideal about an outdoor concert."

"Why?" I lifted my head to show them I was not yet asleep.

"Because it's better to conduct in an acoustically closed hall without the interference of birds, bugs and crying babies."

James pointed appropriately to the sky, "... and passing airplanes."

"Right," Orson agreed, "they're the worst of all."

James told Orson about his company plane, a Cessna Citation jet, and I let myself drift off. I cautiously wrapped the skirt of my white dress around my legs. James described the cruising altitude and the plush interior of the cabin. I shut my eyes, drinking in the moment.

Above my head, the white, blossom-covered branches of the magnolia tree whispered in my ears and soon my body no longer seemed to touch the ground.

In a whispered, unsettled call, the wind is blowing under my dress, causing it to billow like a balloon. I am flying up into the sky. As I lift off, the gusts tear my dress apart into a fluttering pair of white birds. But instead of being free, the birds are caught prisoner in the design of white silk scarves, creating lines and circles in the air. I realize that I am naked, or am I? Against my will, I am pulled into the no-man's land between two scarves, two birds, two loves. Two pairs of eyes are resting on me like a pair of open wings. They cover my skin with a tenderness that teases and tortures.

James smiles. "Lie back. Put your head on my shoulder."

Orson's whisper sounds close to my ear. "You have no other responsibility than to accept pleasure."

But in their eagerness to bestow attention on me, they pull my hair in opposite directions and twist my arms. They tear my heart in two, as the wind has torn my dress. My heart is high up with the birds, white and fluttering, afraid of the loneliness in the sky as well as the fear of being lost on the ground. Between heaven and earth, where do I belong?

Tired of being torn between sanctified and secret loves, I see at last: I need to let go, and balance will return. I need to re-possess my heart.

The blue sky above me, with flowering magnolia branches painted on it, is like a new continent, offering peace. I let myself fall from a great height. There is darkness and a chill, and then again there is ground under my body. A shrieking goose startles me and I stumble through the black curtain of my eyes.

"Halloo, there..." James' voice reached me from mysterious horizons. I looked up and saw Orson and James, their positions unchanged, the empty root beer bottle between their chairs. All the food has been cleared away.

Orson adjusted his dark glasses.

"We thought you'd never wake up. You were asleep for more than an hour."

I sat up, fighting the stiffness in my bones. Behind me, Beverly sneezed. Daisy handed her the tissue box and frowned at me.

"At one point the wind blew under your dress. It looked awesome. We thought you'd fly up to the sky at any moment."

I rubbed my eyes. "I *was* flying, across the most amazing landscapes. But I decided to come down and stay on solid ground."

Daisy said, "What a pleasant dream that must have been."

She handed me a postcard and a pen.

"For Paula. You're the only one who hasn't signed it yet."

I asked, "Is there any food left? I'm hungry, and I'm exhausted, like coming home after running a long race."

Unaware of my philosophical metaphor, Daisy peered into the open wicker basket. "Egg salad or ham?"

I tucked my skirt under my knees. "I haven't had any of Beverly's Camembert yet. I've changed my mind. I'm ready to try some of it now."

81

I walked up the steps to the entrance of the Manhattan Recording Center on Thirty-Fourth Street and closed my umbrella. This was the first time since I had started my job that the guard in the lobby didn't ask for my company identification.

I checked the board to make sure the recording session had not been moved to a different studio.

"For Maestro Mahler and the Empire Chamber Ensemble, is it still the seventh floor?"

He said, "Yes, but they haven't finished recording, so it's better to go to the sixth floor and walk up one flight."

"Okay," I nodded. After three weeks on the job, I understood. In this magnificent old building, dating from 1906 and originally built as the Manhattan Opera House, and in whose studios hundreds of recordings had been made over the decades, the faint noise of the elevator had more than once ruined a take. Orson had told me that the previous summer a whole day's recording with the New York Philharmonic had to be done over because one of the thirty-six microphones suspended above the orchestra had picked up the hum in b-flat from an air-conditioner two floors up.

In the elevator, I clamped my briefcase under my arm to free one hand so I could open the belt of my raincoat. My mind ran over the paperwork I had brought along. There were the completed forms for the musicians' payments according to union scale, the contract for the hall and a typed list of all the players for Jack Mace, the producer, and Orson. The list, showing each musician's name and instrument, made the job of the producer and the conductor a lot easier. They wouldn't have to call the players by their instruments, such as "third first violin," or "second cello."

Orson had never worked with the Empire Chamber Ensemble before, and recording Angelo Corelli's *Concerti grossi, Op.6,* was a first-time experience for him.

On the sixth floor, I removed my shoes and tip-toed to the seventh and then across the large, red-carpeted studio, past Orson and the musicians, upstairs to the gallery where the control room was located. Every cubic inch of space reverberated with the floating strings of Angelo Corelli's music.

As I entered the control room, Jack Mace and the two engineers gestured a friendly hello. They sat at the control panels, their eyes moving from the score to the flickering lights at the huge console that took up the width of the room. On the monitor, Orson could be seen from above conducting the sixteen musicians in the studio against the red background of the rug.

The three men at the controls followed the score, sometimes circling a note or a bar. When the music stopped, Jack spoke through the microphone.

"Orson, that sounded better than the previous take, but I think we should do it again from bar fifty-one through seventy-four. The balance of the strings was better, but I prefer the intonation from the first time."

Orson looked up. "Yes, Jack, I agree. And the attack at bar thirty-six wasn't quite together."

Jack said, "I noticed that too. Don't worry about it. We can fix it in the editing studio."

Orson sighed wistfully. "This is what technology has brought us to. The players come out on the record better than they actually play."

He leafed back in his score and raised his baton. The musicians followed his lead through the repetition.

I sat down in a black leather chair next to the exit sign, fascinated by the flickering lights that indicated the sound frequencies of the music. The clock on the wall showed 3:46.

Orson had told me that this collection of Corelli's twelve concertos was considered the quintessence of Italian musical development around the middle of the seventeenth century.

Watching Orson on the monitor, an immense feeling of relief came over me. My admiration for him as maestro and mentor had finally surpassed my private passion, and to prove to myself that this was true, I swore by Angelo Corelli's ghost that he would never again be able to hurt my feelings.

The music stopped, and Jack's voice broke the silence.

"We got it right that time, Orson. What do you want to do now? We've recorded all day. If you want to go on, it's fine with me. Or we can continue on Monday. I'm confident we have all the takes we need for numbers one, two and six."

Orson put his baton down and ran a tired hand through his gray hair.

"I think the players deserve to go home," and, addressing the ensemble, displayed an appreciative smile.

"Thank you, Ladies and Gentlemen. I'll see you Monday at ten-thirty sharp. Enjoy your week-end."

To Jack he said, "I'd like to come up and listen to the takes for a while, if you don't mind. After dealing with the same piece all day, I'm afraid I may have been a little tired. I hope it didn't come through in my beat."

Jack laughed reassuringly, "Not at all, Orson. You can hear for yourself."

A moment later Orson came through the door next to my chair. He was wearing a black T-shirt, with a pink towel draped around his neck.

"Hello, Isabella. What a lovely surprise to see you here."

I smiled back. "It's nice to see you too." In front of Jack and the two engineers I avoided addressing him by name and rummaged through my briefcase.

I said, "I brought you a list of the players, arranged by instrument. I apologize that it's too late for today. I only got it this afternoon by fax from their management company, but at least it will come in handy for the remaining sessions."

"Thank you. That's very helpful. I'll take it home with me tonight." He took it from me and bowed stiffly.

"Jack," he said, "I believe this young lady has settled admirably into her new job. What do you think?'

Poor Jack had no choice but to agree. "If she can put up with guys like you and me, she'll probably be stuck with the job for a long time."

"Why?" I asked naively.

Orson smiled good-heatedly. "Because no one else is able to do it any better than you."

Jack's grin accentuated the lines in his face, a face not much younger than Orson's but marked by a multitude of pleasures other than music. Orson sat down next to him and opened his score. The two sound engineers took their coats and left. In their profession, spending time with Maestro Mahler had long since lost its thrill, and going home was more important.

However for me, everything was still new and exciting.

I asked, "Do you mind if I stay?"

Orson turned around in his swivel-chair.

"Not at all, Isabella. Here's an extra score for you."

I took it from him, but didn't use it. I just wanted to sit back and listen to the music, along with Orson's and Jack's comments on the takes.

Orson had explained to me that the conductor's job is to create the musical "values" of a composition, and the producer's job to properly capture his performance on record. Sometimes the slow tempos have to be played just a little faster, and the fast ones just a little slower in order to shape the recording into a well rounded piece.

"Now, here, this *fermata* at bar thirty-nine," Jack said, "where the *Allegro* goes into an *Adagio*... I think we're having difficulties in agreeing what an *Adagio* is supposed to mean here. What do you think, Orson?"

Orson said, full of vitality, "It sounds fine to me. The attack of the ensemble is perfectly together, and I believe the sudden, dramatic slowing down is justified for the sake of creating a contrast."

Jack shrugged. "Whatever you say. The conductor has the last word."

After a long week at the office, Corelli's baroque music transported me into a welcome state of relaxation. For about an hour the two men went over the takes of the day, content to have "canned" a lot of good material.

Finally satisfied, Orson suggested that we call it a day. As I slipped into my coat, Orson and Jack not only shook hands, but gave each other hearty pats on the shoulders. They even hugged each other and spontaneously chorused in perfect synchronicity, "*Hasta mañana, amigo… y Viva Mexico!*" There was no doubt that they had done this many times before.

Alone with Orson in the elevator, I wanted to inquire about the meaning of their Hispanic interlude, but Orson was faster in articulating what was on his mind.

"May I take you out for dinner?"

"I'm sorry, but James and I want to pick out new curtains for the kitchen tonight. I'm already a little late. Here, can you hold my umbrella for a moment while I button my coat?"

"Mmm," he mumbled, taking the umbrella, "what about lunch on Monday?"

"On Monday, Dan Maddox is taking me to a luncheon in honor of some outstanding producers at the New York Chapter of the Recording Academy. He feels that the sooner I get to know everybody in the business, the better."

"I'm impressed, young lady. Here's your umbrella. Dan Maddox certainly didn't invite me."

"There's very limited seating," I said with mock-arrogance, but secretly welcoming my excuse.

As we crossed the lobby, he said shyly, "Does this mean that I'll have to take a number in order to have lunch with you?"

The eyes of the security guard followed us. Not sure whether he had overheard Orson's words, I chose not to answer until we were on the street.

"You may have to, Maestro," I smiled vaguely and opened the green-and-yellow golf umbrella that I had once borrowed from Mr. Stringer and never returned.

The rain was coming down in a rhythmic pitter-patter, washing Manhattan clean. There was not a taxi to be found on Thirty-Forth Street.

Pressed for time, I said, "I have to go to the bus terminal. It's only seven blocks away. I can walk."

Orson took my arm. "I'll walk you to the bus."

"If you promise not to take such long strides," I urged him. "Let's go, then."

We fell into a bouncy step and in innocent familiarity Orson took my arm and huddled closer under my umbrella. It occurred to me that he was blissfully unaware that I was drawing away from him. I thought, I'll have to tell him. *Soon.* But not here. Not here in the middle of the rush hour traffic and the thousand faces of Eighth Avenue, among colliding umbrellas and the rain impinging on the street like fine, dancing needles. Not here. *Tomorrow.* I'd tell him tomorrow. I shuddered at the prospect, but said in an even tone, "You and Jack seem to work well together."

"Yes, we've been a good team for many years."

Orson turned up the collar of his coat and I belted mine more tightly.

I asked, "Orson, what was that all about *Viva Mexico?* You two were so perfectly synchronized."

He laughed. "It's a standing joke between us that goes back some fifteen years or so. Do you know the story? Of course, you don't. In fact, few people do. Maybe I'd better not tell you..."

"Oh, come on, Orson, tell me..."

We were crossing Thirty-Ninth Street and for the first time I welcomed a story that would prevent us from becoming personal. At the corner, a man was selling umbrellas for three dollars.

Orson fell into a near-monologue. “Okay, Isabella, here’s what happened...”

There was something in his tone that caused me alarm, making me feel like a cat sensing an impending earthquake.

“It was, as I said, about fifteen years ago, when Paula and I went to Mexico on vacation. We had just survived a major marriage crisis and hoped the trip would be helpful to ...uh... patch up things between us. However, by the end of the first week we were hardly on speaking terms anymore. We were ready to fly home separately and meet again in a divorce lawyer’s office. But the next day, right in the middle of Zocalo Square in Mexico City, we ran into Jack and his wife, Elaine. What a surprise! The four of us immediately agreed to meet for dinner.”

We were waiting at a red light to cross Eight Avenue now.

“Believe me, Paula and I were glad for their company. That night, over enchiladas, Jack and Elaine told us they were celebrating, if you could call it that. That very day they had obtained a divorce. In Mexico you can get a divorce fast, inexpensively and discreetly, and that was the reason for their trip. Why pay horrendous fees to American lawyers? After all, mature people can come to a personal financial agreement that satisfies both parties.

“Paula and I just looked at each other. We asked Jack and Elaine about the procedure, and the next day we followed their example. Two days later, the divorce papers came through, and we decided to enjoy the remaining five days of our vacation. On the plane back to New York we weren’t so sure anymore that we had done the right thing and we agreed to burn the papers ceremoniously in our never-used fireplace. But it was in the beginning of summer, and it would have been ridiculous to use the fireplace.

“Back in our apartment, we got into another fight and decided to keep the papers in our safety deposit box at the bank, just in case. They’re still there. Somehow, Paula and I managed to stay together. Somehow there was never a right time to announce that we were officially divorced, and somehow neither of us made the first move to look for a separate place to live.

"Routine took over again and when our next anniversary came around, we found it quite exciting that after years of marriage we were now living together in sin. So we stayed together, but I have always considered myself... uh... unattached. I think I enjoy the best of two worlds, being married, and at the same time free."

I stopped and disengaged myself from his arm. I was stunned. The rain, my bus and the kitchen curtains were forgotten. I could only stare at Orson.

Still in the momentum of his long speech, he added, "Legally speaking, Isabella, I've never cheated on Paula. Between you and me, you are the one who committed adultery."

The pavement moved dangerously beneath my feet.

I gasped, "Who are you to judge me!!? And you think it's funny!"

"Yes, it is, it's very funny." His birthmark twitched.

To add to my annoyance, Orson's face shone with boyish bliss. "Listen, Isabella, life within the rules of society is only an illusion of order. As you get older, you'll learn that it's easier to adjust to it, rather than to wrestle against it."

Orson smiled with the ease of a free man.

I swallowed hard. Now, I thought, now would be the time to tell him off, and not tomorrow. But if I told him now, I'd end up out of control and lower Mr. Stringer's heavy umbrella on his head until I'd see him hit the ground.

Some protecting force, like a hand pressing against my forehead, held me back, reminding me of my professional association with this esteemed conductor.

Hadn't I just sworn by Angelo Corelli's ghost that Orson would never again be able to hurt my feelings?

I swallowed hard and said in a perfectly controlled voice, "Orson, did you remember to bring the list of the musicians I gave you? You said you wanted to go over it at home."

He shot me a perplexed side-ways glance.

"What's the matter with you, Isabella? Why are you suddenly so formal?"

I said tightly, "Please, Orson, from now on let's always be formal."

The rain was coming down harder. Its silent veil merged with the fading colors of the city. And with the rain, the sky was falling down on me. I couldn't endure his presence any longer. Without a word, I leaped across a large puddle and stormed away into the crowd, leaving him behind without an umbrella.

82

The month of May. The month in which this story started was here again, only a year later. *Only a year?*

As I awoke the next morning, Saturday, May second, the day James would fly to Denver for a week, I sensed uneasiness. Destiny seemed to be moving in on me, like the sound of crunching gravel under the footsteps of disaster. How could I keep it from moving closer? The reality of James lying next to me diminished the demons in my mind, yet still leaving me with the question of how to get rid of Orson.

James stirred and stretched lazily, like a big jungle cat. In a warm, lulling daze I looked at his features, as handsome in sleep as in wakefulness. With his facial muscles relaxed, he looked like a younger brother of himself, and I felt a deep tenderness for him. This would last forever now. I was free of Orson, as though a long infection was finally conquered by my body's fever. Everything was in its proper place again, my husband, my heart and my vision of the future. How fortunate that James had been unaware of the danger that existed, or that it would end today.

As the rays of the sun squeezed between the blinds, I stretched and pulled the blanket over my shoulders. If only I hadn't promised to meet Orson today. But then, I had to tell him.

I rolled over and did something I hadn't done in a long time. I reached up and brushed back James' slightly too long hair. My fingers twined in his hair for a long, tender moment.

"James... pssst...James... are you awake?"

James rolled over and I slipped into his arms, content beyond words.

He sighed sleepily, "I suppose I'm awake *now.* What time is it?"

"Around seven." I snuggled against the length of his body.

"Why do you have to wake me so early?"

Instead of answering I brushed my nose against the abrasive morning stubble of his chin and, moving upwards in playful circles, my lips landed on his. His arms tightened around me and his kiss was sweet and sensuous. I wanted to stay in this moment forever. Slowly, at the edge of my awareness, I felt his invitation under the covers, promising and passionate. One of his hands caused the strap of my nightgown to fall across my shoulder, while the other hand peeled the gown from my body until there was nothing separating his flesh from mine…not a thread, not a breath, not a thought.

I sighed, "Invitation accepted."

He whispered huskily, "We're in this together, and it's too late to turn back."

Tentatively, our bodies curved and stretched in and out of the shadows of the morning, like doves opening their wings without yet flying. With our arms around each other we were pulled together by a force that held our bodies down, but lifted our souls like feathers in a breeze.

James' hands and lips moved with natural assurance, beyond petty violence, beyond wildness, with the ease of instinct and experience.

When I whispered, "Come to me, come to me now," he navigated our bodies with slow, deep, rousing strokes, tying the act of making love with love itself into a self-sustaining cycle.

Hadn't we always flown up high like this together, today, yesterday, or in a different life? Wouldn't we always do so in the future?

Eventually, the same power that made us soar also made us fall. And when we fell at last, at the perfect moment, it was from a glorious height. When we landed, James cried out my name as he flowed into me. I was finally home. Home for good with James. And James was home for good with me.

Out of the ashes of lies, secrecy and disillusionment our marriage was born again into a new spring. This time the spring blossoms would reveal themselves in their brightest pink, yellow and white, like the colors of a painter who had discovered a new way of mixing shades.

With my head on James' shoulder and his breath brushing my eyelashes, we drifted off into a post-orgasmic doze, and I felt pampered and protected from all the perils of the planet.

When I woke again, it was from the approaching sound of rattling dishes as James came up the stairs. He walked cautiously into the bedroom, balancing a tray heaped with plates, mugs and silverware, the coffee pot, the sugar bowl and the milk pitcher. He had placed the cover of a frying pan on the plates to keep the eggs and toast warm.

I reached for my robe beside the bed and sat up, cross-legged.

"James, I can't believe this. In eleven years of marriage we *never* had breakfast in bed."

He grinned. "So maybe it's time we give it a try."

"But you always said that you hate crumbs between the covers and vitamin pills getting lost under the pillows."

"For once we should think beyond the petty considerations of messiness and concentrate on the elevated quality of life that breakfast in bed promises."

James smiled and put the tray down beside me.

I shook my head, highly amused.

"*Wunderbar*. I'm open for surprises."

He slipped next to me under the covers and propped our pillows up behind our backs, then moved the tray onto our laps.

"Everything looks so good," I beamed, "but... it's a little awkward sitting up, trying to balance the tray... I need more pillows."

"There are no more pillows. Try to make up for it with poise. Here, this is yours. I burned your share of the toast the way you like it."

"This is fun. I may hire your services permanently."

"Just do me a favor. Your elbow is in my ribs."

"I'm only trying to reach the jam. This set-up was your idea, remember?"

James tried to pour coffee, but his hands shook and the tray started to slide.

He sounded irritated. "It's just hard for me to balance this tray on my knees and keep the milk from spilling and hold the coffee pot at the same time. Maybe you'd better do it."

I eased the pot out of his hands and filled our mugs.

"What are you going to do while I'm away this week, besides working?" James asked after his first sip. But before I could reply, he cried, "*Nuts*!"

"What's wrong?" I asked.

"I'm getting a cramp in my leg!"

"Do you want me to pull on your toes?"

"No! *Ooouch!* I have to stand up!"

He almost overturned the tray, but I leaned over and rescued it. James jumped up and hopped around the room, changing feet as though he were dancing on hot coals.

"*Uhhhh!*" He grimaced and asked through clenched teeth, "Do I remind you of Fred Astaire?"

I couldn't help laughing. He looked so comical, and after two more weaving circles, he stopped and exhaled audibly. "*Whew!* That's better. Maybe breakfast in bed wasn't such a good idea after all."

"Why not? I wouldn't have been able to see you perform those steps you just invented."

I pushed the breakfast tray out of the way.

"You know what? Why don't we take the tray downstairs and sit at the table. It's our last breakfast together for a whole week. I already miss you."

James smiled sweetly, "I'll miss you too," and he picked up the tray.

As soon as he was on his way downstairs, I stood up and raised the blinds. Outside, the unblemished blue sky had never seemed clearer or more promising. With my disorderly life back in good order, today the ordinary seemed extraordinary. Beneath the surface of my rapture, though, I felt pressured by the question of how to handle Orson. Maybe it would be easier just to call him and tell him straight out *It's over.*

Orson. Suddenly, I pitied him for being left a loser and a loner. From my new position of inner harmony and balance, I understood that I had to see him one last time, not because of desire, but because of decency. I owed him an explanation face to face, because putting an end to it over the phone meant handing him a *finale* that was unworthy of the story it concluded. Yes, I'd make the trip to his apartment one more time, and seeing him would be the evidence to my emotions that I had left him long ago.

83

Five hours later, when I arrived at Orson's apartment, he became everything I ever wanted him to be. I stepped from the elevator and he was waiting for me in the doorway, dressed in a beige sweater and corduroy pants. Despite my passiveness, he enfolded me in his arms and held me with a need that was raw and almost frighteningly intense.

"Isabella... if you knew how I've been looking forward to this moment! I thought of you all night. I'm sorry about yesterday. I acted inconsiderately. Please forgive me."

He had never sounded more convincing.

As my lack of responsiveness became apparent, he held me at a little distance, searching my face.

"I hope your feelings haven't changed."

His expression of love had finally reached me when I no longer desired it. The old sparkle in his eyes reached out to me, but the fire didn't catch.

Yet there was a moment of unburdened stillness. It was like a dreamy breeze that touched us, and at some instant in the future I might remember this as the most complete moment of our romance. The graph lines of our emotions had reached the intersection, the awesome point where past and future are joined in a second of togetherness, a second of sadness and salvation.

I broke the spell. "Orson, I need to use your bathroom. Look at my hands... all smeared black with who-knows-what. It's some kind of grease or tar."

"How did that happen?"

"I decided to take my car today instead of coming by bus, and after I'd found a parking space and got out, I suddenly had it all over my hands. It's all over the fender too. I suppose a passing truck must have thrown it on the car."

Orson led me through the photo gallery.

"I was wondering about your lack of response. I'm glad it's only some grease that can be washed off."

"I'll join you in the kitchen after I've scrubbed my hands."

"Why the kitchen?"

"How about some cappuccino? I assume you've practiced since we last used the machine."

Orson grinned. "So you only came for my cappuccino?"

"Right," I laughed as he opened the bathroom door for me.

"Need any help?"

"Thanks, no. If I do, I'll let you know."

It wasn't easy, even with the help of a brush, to get the grease off. It had settled into the lines of my palms and between the single stones of my diamond anniversary ring. I took the ring off and let it soak in a small bowl with soap and warm water. I remembered how Orson asked me to take it off when during the act of love because it had scratched his back. Today when I took it off for a non-romantic reason, I experienced a voice of warning but dismissed it.

When I entered the kitchen, Orson was leaning against the refrigerator, reading the *New York Times*. He looked up.

I said, "I don't smell any cappuccino."

"I thought I'd wait until you came back." He put the paper on the kitchen counter and smiled sheepishly.

"You remember, making cappuccino is not my forte."

"Sorry, Maestro, no marks for effort. James made coffee for me this morning, and he made toast and eggs, cut a grapefruit, put everything on a tray and served me breakfast in bed. Doesn't this inspire you to improve your domestic skills?"

At his discomfort, I experienced satisfaction, a cold sunlight replacing the fire in my heart. It was finally true. I had fallen out of love with Orson.

"How's my friend James?" he asked, avoiding the domestic issue.

"Just fine, thank you." I began to fill the water tank of the cappuccino maker. "James is sorry he won't be able to attend your *Missa Solemnis* concert on Saturday. He's flying to Denver this afternoon. In fact, he should be in the air soon. He and his boss are taking the company jet, the Cessna Citation. Remember? He mentioned it at the picnic. He says it's like flying in your own living room."

I was glad for a neutral subject and babbled on. "No more waiting time at airport gates. And his boss thinks eight million dollars is a great price, considering it's one of the new jets than can be flown by a single qualified pilot, instead of having to pay a crew of two or more."

Orson watched me pour coffee powder into the filter cups.

"What is James doing in Denver?"

"Attending a convention, with seminars and promotional lectures for the drug companies. He'll fly back on the jet again Saturday night. He'll be in the air at the same time you'll be conducting Beethoven in Carnegie Hall."

Orson opened the refrigerator door and handed me the milk.

"But you'll be at the performance, I hope?"

"Yes, I have my ticket."

His arm touched my shoulders.

"If you aren't in the audience, the concert won't mean the same to me."

"Do you have two cups?" I asked.

"Here."

With a gallant gesture he invited me to sit down at the kitchen table, but he didn't look his usual, confident self. Seeing him no longer through the eyes of love made him look older, paler. He placed our cups on the table and we sat facing each other.

"What else is new?" He wiped some foam from his lips and looked fatigued.

I said, "James and I have been talking this morning at breakfast about taking a vacation this summer, maybe Hawaii. As you know, during the summer the recording industry is slow, and it would be the best time to be away for two weeks."

He seemed vulnerable, almost at the point of admitting his need for intimacy.

"The only thing I see, Isabella, is that you're looking forward to being away from me for two weeks."

"Since when are you so sensitive?"

"You're right. I'm normally not like this. But with everything else going on right now, I admit I might be a bit touchy."

I became aware of a dripping faucet, but it was not the right moment to get up and turn it off.

"Isabella... I hardly know how to begin." He took a deep, desperate breath. "I'm worried to death about Matthew. He's in the hospital with a serious nervous breakdown."

"Matthew..?" I gasped, "but *why?*"

Orson's face hardened. "Has he ever talked to you about Tom?"

"Tom, the man he lives with?"

"Yes, Tom, the pilot."

"What about him?"

"Tom has tested positive for the HIV virus."

His words took a moment to sink in. The faucet continued to drip.

"*Mein Gott!* I hope Matthew doesn't get infected too."

"Fortunately, Matthew's tests have been negative so far. But he's in love with Tom and at a total loss to deal with the situation. Matthew says that when they moved in together, four years ago, they made a vow, *Til death do us part.* Neither would leave the other, no matter what happened."

I shook my head, at a loss for words.

Orson looked miserable. “Matthew’s afraid, not of catching the virus, but of Tom taking his own life. As a matter of fact, Tom has apparently threatened to do so, and to Matthew it didn’t sound like an empty threat.”

“Where’s Tom now?”

“Who knows, somewhere flying people around. So far, he has refused to tell his employer.”

Distracted for a moment, I gazed at Orson’s hands, thinking that I had seen them before on another person.

I said, “I’m sure Matthew will come to his senses and deal with the situation in an appropriate way.”

Orson said grimly, “I’m afraid he won’t. He’s vowed to stick with him. He says Tom’s illness should be seen as a challenge and not as the end of their relationship.”

There was a silence, filled with helplessness and hurt, and water drops bouncing in the sink.

Orson lowered his eyes. “I’m afraid I’m not handling this too well...” His face showed dark rings under his eyes.

I asked, “What is it Orson? Why are you so afraid?”

“I’m afraid I’ve fouled up my life.”

“I don’t get it. What has your life to do with Tom catching AIDS?”

“It’s not Tom, it’s Matthew. If anything should happen to Matthew, I wouldn’t consider my own life worth living any longer.”

In the passage of a few moments Orson had grown old, drained of energy and enthusiasm. His profile stood out, ghost-like, against the white kitchen cabinets. For a moment it didn’t seem to be his profile, but a copy of someone else’s, someone I knew all too well.

I tried to catch his eye. “Orson, you can’t let yourself be affected by the life or death of Matthew’s lover. You have to keep a healthy perspective. Matthew is Joan’s son and the pianist for your chorus. You have other responsibilities, to your music and to the public, and right now you need all your strength. You’re conducting an important concert a week from today. The Brighton Festival Chorus will be here for rehearsals on Wednesday. You still have to find a replacement for the soprano soloist and, in your own words, the *Missa Solemnis* is one of the most difficult works ever written. You can't squander your energies on something you have no power to change. The critics expect nothing short of a sensation from Orson Mahler."

He nodded and stared at his hands, hands that were powerful enough to lead a stage-full of musicians, but were now incapable of holding a cup of cappuccino.

"Orson?"

"Yes?"

"Matthew is your son, isn't he?"

Except for the dripping faucet, the kitchen was still.

Orson's voice was barely above a whisper.

"Yes, he is. How did you know?"

"It's been at the edge of my mind, but it wasn't my business. In this light you look like him. Your hands are the same. I remember the initials on your handkerchief. *OMM.* Joan named him after you."

"Yes, she did. Without asking my permission."

"Asking your permission! That's not the question any more. The question is, does Matthew know you're his father?"

"No."

"You have to tell him, Orson. *Now.* Maybe knowing he's your son will give him a new reference point in his life. Maybe you can help him to find a new direction. He needs you now. He has a right to know."

Orson shrugged and remained silent. I felt sorry for the frightened boy inside the man of worldwide acclaim.

"But *why*, Orson? Why did you withhold the truth from him?"

"To protect Paula, and Joan's marriage. When Matthew was born she was married to Lawrence. He died when Matthew was four."

"And later?"

"Later, there never seemed to be a good time to talk."

"Did Joan's husband ever know the truth, or did he think Matthew was his son?"

Orson shrugged with an air of capitulation.

"He knew from the beginning, because as a baby Matthew was a spitting image of me. The fact was obvious to him. And Lawrence was a completely different type. People said he resembled Clark Gable a great deal, which flattered him immensely."

"What happened when he discovered that his baby son looked like you?"

Orson's face lit up unexpectedly.

"He was very generous. For seven years, Lawrence had wanted a son, and he loved the boy so much that he forgave Joan. He always referred to Matthew as his little angel. He played with him for hours and gave him his bottle and bath. He overlooked the flaw that had produced the blessing. And he assumed that since he had forgiven Joan and accepted Matthew as his own, our affair was naturally over."

"And it wasn't." I didn't bother to employ the intonation of a question mark.

"No, it wasn't. Joan and I continued to see each other. Nothing changed between us." A smile eradicated the weariness in his face. "Joan is quite a mistress, you know? She's a woman who knows her way around a man's body."

The faucet kept dripping.

I laughed sarcastically into the stillness between the splashes.

"I admire your tactfulness, Orson. Besides, I'm aware that you're using the present tense. But never mind. I assume Lawrence found out that Joan was still warming your bed. What happened?"

Orson's eyes darkened. "Something very tragic. Lawrence couldn't take it, not a second time. It was too much for him to handle. He took a hotel room and swallowed a bottle of sleeping pills."

"What a tragedy!" I jumped up and began to pace across the black and white kitchen tiles. "I don't know what to say, Orson..."

And then my memory recalled an instant I had never really forgotten.

I said, "I remember now, when Matthew and I went ice-skating in Rockefeller Center, he made an implication.... *And when my father died... uh... tragically, twenty years ago..* I recall he had tears in his eyes, but I wasn't sure if they were from the wind or a painful memory."

Orson sat, petrified, on his chair.

I came around the table and said, "Orson... How could you have lived with this all these years?"

"I'm sorry, Isabella, I..."

"And Matthew?" I shook my head and cut into his sentence.

"Matthew doesn't know to this day that I'm his father, because legally, I'm not."

"And you think because it's not on his birth certificate that he doesn't have the right to know? It's the same as keeping your divorce papers in a safe and considering yourself a free man."

"Don't get so upset, Isabella. I've never heard you raise your voice before. I shouldn't have told you all this."

I had to do something, move my hands. I picked up the empty cups from the table and put them in the sink with considerable clatter.

"I think Matthew has a pretty good idea of what's going on between you and his mother. Joan isn't blessed with the good taste to hide it in public."

Orson frowned naively. "Is it that obvious?"

I sighed loudly and thought, My god, I have to get away from this man. Our relationship had reached the state where, rather than wanting to bottle the moment of togetherness, I was looking at my watch.

Orson said, "You're not going to leave me now, are you?"

I nodded. "I'm afraid so."

"Why?" He moved closer. "Stay with me tonight. Look, I didn't even have a chance to hold you. I'm sorry I spoiled the mood.

I didn't mean to. I shouldn't have burdened you with my problems. I'm afraid I'm not very entertaining."

"Ironically, you were very entertaining, Orson. The fact is that I'm afraid of you and the way you play with other people's lives. I'm leaving."

He tried to touch me, but I moved away.

Still refusing to believe me, he reasoned. "You said James would be in the air by now. I can understand if you don't want to stay the night. James might call later and you should be there to answer the phone. But it's a long flight to Denver. We could still... I mean, we could still spend some time together. We wouldn't have to talk. We've done too much of it already. I just want to hold you, Isabella. You could comfort me by just letting me touch you."

"I think you should comfort Matthew and tell him he's your son."

Orson smiled, the shadow of a smile.

I said, "Orson, when do you finally stop playing games? I'm sorry. I can't comfort you, I just can't."

"All right. I respect your momentary mood. But promise to come back soon?"

"Promises were never part of our agreement, remember?"

I stopped at the kitchen door. We looked at each other like awkward kids. He followed me across the hall and helped me into my jacket.

He asked, "Does this mean you won't come back?"

I said, "I wouldn't know what to do for an *encore*."

His face didn't move. The tension between us had given way to emptiness, and we had taken the first step into the ugly state of disenchantment.

I pressed the button for the elevator. Orson held the door open and nodded with an air of resignation.

But knowing him, he would refuse to understand.

84

My hands were firmly clamped around the steering wheel, as buildings, traffic lights and people flew past my car. On the flower beds of Park Avenue, the proud heads of red and yellow tulips were moving in the breeze.

If only I had someone to talk to. If only Julia could be at my side right now. Would there ever be a time when I could tell her the whole story?

It was over. What a strange realization. If I had the choice, would I do it all over again? Would I do it differently? If I had acted in a different way, could I have created a different Orson?

A cold calm settled over me. This must be the feeling after surgery: pain, and relief that it was finished. Exhausted from a year of emotional turmoil, I was ready for the fast that follows the feast.

In the sunset of disillusion, the past was already colored by an aura of nostalgia. I remembered how, last May, Orson had said to me during our carriage ride through Central Park. *To me, true romanticism is to hold and behold a woman in the natural flow of love-making.*

His words had been thunder in my ears, trailing into an echo of the rhythmic clapping of the horse's hooves.

At *Federico's,* over the bitter taste of black olives, he had shocked me with his honesty. *I can't promise fidelity.* From today's perspective it was easy to see why. *Joan's quite a mistress, you know?*

How willfully he had planted the seed of jealously in my mind, knowing that we often suffer more from our imagination than from reality.

Reality. Where was I? Had I gone too far south? Shouldn't I have turned west for the Lincoln Tunnel? For a second I let go of the steering wheel before grasping it again tightly. I realized the screeching tires were my own. I awoke from my reverie to the sight of a swerving cab that had caused me to jump on my brakes.

My seatbelt had snapped tight. That was a close call! Luckily, nothing was shattered but my nerves. I pulled into a parking space that miraculously materialized. I had to collect myself. I crossed my arms over the steering wheel and let my head sink down on them. Still under the shock of a missed collision, more memories drifted around my head, like petals in the wind.

I recalled once sharing a hamburger with Orson. It had been in a coffee shop after my return from Austria.

He had explained, *Conducting is merely making love to music. No detail should be left unattended to bring out the best in music or in a woman. If a piece of music is worth playing and a woman worth being made love to, it's worth giving it your best.*

My head swung up. Someone was knocking against the window of my car. Through the glass I was separated only by inches from what appeared to be the oversized head of a police officer. I rolled down the window.

"Are you all right, miss?"

"Yes, yes... I'm fine." I pushed my bangs back.

"You're sure you're not sick or somethin'...?"

"No, no, I was just feeling tired."

His eyes took inventory of my overall appearance. He paused before clearing his throat.

"Can I see your license? You're in a no-parking zone."

"I'm sorry, I had no idea." I took my purse from the passenger seat, opened it and handed him my driver's license. He studied it with mind-boggling slowness.

"Okay, Isabella," he smiled. "That's a nice name, by the way. You're not from around here, are you?"

I shook my head and forced a smile. "No, I'm from Austria."

"You have a real cute accent."

He handed my license back.

"Just move along. And don't park here again."

"I promise I won't. Thank you, officer."

He glanced at my license plate and waved.

No more daydreaming, I decided. From now on I'd better keep my mind on the road ahead.

Once out of the Lincoln Tunnel, I turned on the radio to WQXR. Lloyd Moss's voice was praising a new production at the New York City Opera. The next announcement started with the powerful choral sounds of Beethoven's *Missa Solemnis,* over which a deep, velvet voice was heard.

This is Orson Mahler. On Saturday, May ninth, I'll be conducting Beethoven's towering masterpiece, the Missa Solemnis, with the Brighton Festival Chorus at Carnegie Hall. Beethoven himself considered this mass his most accomplished work. And in my opinion, Beethoven was right. Some tickets are still available at the Carnegie Hall box office. You may also call Carnegie Charge. Come and join us.

The announcement concluded with several bars of the *Allegro vivace* from the *Gloria* section.

Orson had already moved far away. Even the sound of his voice had become impersonal. I had changed my universe by changing my mind. Didn't philosophers agree that it was possible?

Orson had once said, *I admire a composer who has the poise to end a powerful composition quietly. I admire his courage to forego the trumpets and drums in the final measures of a concerto or a symphony. Because, if the piece has said enough, it can afford to just softly fade away.*

That's exactly how it was with our romance. No trumpets or drums. I forced my mind back to the traffic. Now back in New Jersey, the sun was a red ball dancing between fluffy clouds on the horizon. In the golden light of the afternoon the telephone wires stretched like spider webs from pole to pole. Ah, the might and misery of love! In rational terms, the only phenomenon that could compare to the feeling of *falling in love* was the opposite, *falling out of love*.

Fortunately, the timing was good. By now, James would be on his way to Denver and would be back in a week. On his return I would have fully regained my emotional balance and would start a new life with him.

In less than ten minutes I would be at home. I could take a bath in gardenia bubbles, or just give myself a scrub with good, old-fashioned soap. My hands weren't quite clean yet from the tar I had picked up. *Wait a minute.* My hands tightened around the wheel and something felt wrong. Something crucial was missing from my finger. *My diamond anniversary ring!*

I had left it in Orson's bathroom when I had washed my hands. *Verdammt!* I would have to call and ask him to see that the ring didn't get lost. *Verdammt! Verdammt!* I just hoped he wouldn't pressure me into any discussion beyond the subject of the ring. *Verdammt!* I would have to go back to his apartment during the week to pick it up before James returned. What a nuisance!

I turned onto Valley Road. As I drew close to our house something else was wrong. Under the blooming lilac bushes I saw James' car standing in the driveway. He should have left for Teterboro airport hours ago. If he had been picked up by a limousine he would have parked his car in the garage. But James didn't like taking a limousine because he preferred to have his car handy when he landed.

My first thought was not about the reasons for James' presence, but that I wouldn't be able to immediately call Orson about my ring. I would have to wait until James had left or was safely out of earshot. If only he wouldn't notice that it was missing. Still, there was no reason for panic. Everything would work out all right. A forgotten ring wasn't such a big deal after all.

85

The instant I turned the key to get into the house, James opened the door from the inside.

"That's funny," he laughed. "I heard your car. I just got back thirty seconds before you."

He was wearing his brown suede jacket, and three shopping bags stood next to him on the floor. Except for Christmas, James never went shopping unless I sent him off with an itemized list.

In the first shock of surprise, I asked, "Why did you go shopping?" and added quickly, "I thought you would be on the way to Denver by now."

He picked up the bags and went upstairs.

He said, "After I put my luggage in the car, I came back into the house to get my jacket. At that moment I got a call from Tom, our pilot saying that we wouldn't leave until tomorrow. The boss had to change his plans. For some reason he has to be in New Jersey tonight. He said it didn't make sense for me to go on ahead on a commercial flight. Anyway, we wanted to go over a few things together during the flight, and we can do that tomorrow."

We had reached the top of the stairs. He turned and winked at me. "Actually, it's fine with me. You and I can spend the evening together after all. I bought a bottle of your favorite champagne, and... uh..." He motioned to another bag which he had deposited on the kitchen table.

"What's in there?" I took off my blazer.

"Why don't you see for yourself?" James grinned and threw his jacket over the back of a kitchen chair.

I peeked inside the bag. "A cake?"

"I stopped by the Village Bakery and got a cherry-chocolate cake for us."

"That's very sweet of you, in more ways than one, but what's in the other bag?"

"Oh, I picked up a few books at the mall. I thought it wouldn't hurt to read James Michener's novel in preparation for our trip to Hawaii. I also bought two travel guides, and guess what?"

"What?" I sat down on the opposite side of the table.

"I found a book on turbojet aircraft. Since I've flown on the company plane, I've really become fascinated by it. It's a completely different flying experience from a commercial jet."

"And now you want to read up on corporate jets?"

"That's right. Listen, how about having a piece of that sinful cake right now?"

"Sure, if you want..." I got up to take the cake out of the box, wondering if I could still find a way to call Orson about my ring today.

James turned around on his chair. "I have to admit there's another reason for buying this book. I want to impress the pilot with my knowledge about planes."

"Why? What kind of person is he?" I asked, placing a piece of cake in front of him.

"Oh, I thought I told you about him before. Tom's okay, a little on the sarcastic side."

"*Tom...*," I repeated, feeling alarmed.

Unaware of my hesitation, James reeled on, "You know, I'd really like to show Tom I know something about planes. It's not that I don't get along with him, but there's a strange tension between us, like some sort of competition. I find him somewhat arrogant. But Mr. Harte thinks the world of him."

I got up to pour myself a glass of juice.

James explained between two mouthfuls of cake, "The thing is, the old man is saving the company big bucks by not having to employ a regular co-pilot."

I picked up some dead leaves from the hanging plant over the telephone table.

"According to federal air regulations, all aircraft referred to as 'Transport Category' usually require a minimum flight crew of two licensed commercial pilots. Regulations also require that the Pilot-In-Command be 'Type Rated' in the particular aircraft."

"I think you explained this to Orson at the picnic." I sat down again, carefully hiding my hand with the missing ring under the table. "In other words, a single pilot can fly a corporate jet after all..."

"Yes, but apparently it's not easy to find one who meets all the requirements, and Tom does. That's why Mr. Harte thinks he's so valuable."

"That's interesting. What are the requirements compared to a regular two-crew pilot?"

James reached into the third shopping bag while chewing his last bite of cake. He took out the book on turbo-jet planes and leafed through some of the middle pages.

"I scanned through it in the store. There's an interesting passage... I wish I could find it... You know, that cake is delicious. Why don't you have a piece too?"

"I just don't feel like eating cake right now."

Secretly, I blessed James' sudden fascination with aviation. It had prevented him from wondering where I had been, though I was prepared to mention a visit to the museum, if necessary. I vowed that this would be the last time I had to extricate myself from such a predicament. I longed for a life without lies.

James' face brightened. "Ah, here it is. Listen. It says, to qualify, 'a single pilot must possess at least a Class II Medical Certificate, have a U.A. Commercial License, have at least 1000 hours of flight time logged, possess a Type Rating for that particular aircraft, have logged at least 75 hours of Instrument Time, logged at least 50 hours of night flight and logged 500 hours as Pilot-In-Command in Turbojet Aircraft.'"

He looked up. "Impressive, isn't it?"

Restlessly, I wiggled my toes under the table.

"Yes, very impressive. At least I know you're in good hands with Tom."

James' eyes swept past my shoulder to the telephone table behind me.

"The message light's blinking. I turned the answering machine on before I left the house, just in case of another change in plans. You never know with the old man."

"James," I said with sudden urgency, "what do you know about Tom? Where does he live? Does he have an apartment in Montclair?"

"Why do you ask?"

"It may be a strange coincidence, but Matthew, the pianist of our chorus, has a room-mate named Tom. And he's a pilot too..."

James rose to play back the message on the answering machine.

I pressed again, "What do you think? Could it be the same Tom?"

"No idea, Beautiful," he shrugged and hit the *play* button for the message.

Someone had called from the New School of Social Research asking for the renewal of our annual contribution.

I sneered, "These guys always call on Saturday afternoon when people want to take a nap or paint their toenails."

I smiled grimly before I noticed that there was a second message. I recognized the voice within a fraction of a second, and my blood ran cold.

Hello, Isabella, this is Orson. I know James is on his way to Denver, so I feel safe leaving this message. You probably haven't made it home yet. Anyway, I enjoyed seeing you and I wanted to ease your mind about your ring. I found it and I'll keep it under lock and key until you pick it up, which will be soon, I hope.

Orson's voice hesitated as if weighing whether or not to go on. I sensed James' eyes on me and felt the pounding of my heart in my throat.

Orson continued. *I'm sorry you decided to leave so suddenly. And I'm sorry I burdened you with all my problems. I feel like a fool, Isabella. I should have taken you in my arms and made love to you, as I have so many times before. I ruined my chance for today, but I trust you'll return. I look forward to having you pick up your ring sometime this week. I suggest you delete this message immediately.*

For a few seconds, James and I stared at each other in thunderous silence. A few seconds, and life was changed forever. From now on, everything would be divided into two categories, *before and after*.

James was the first to stir. He chuckled nervously.

"He's quite a character, our friend Orson. Not bad for a joke," and staring at my ringless finger, he still willed himself to prevent the seeds of suspicion from taking root.

"He's making all this up, isn't he?"

The way I felt my face running scarlet, I might just as well have signed a confession. In the dawn of doubt, James stood transfixed, an ashen statue.

"Answer me, Isabella. Orson is just kidding, isn't he?"

I decided against lying. My chances of white-washing the facts wouldn't hold up.

"No, James. Orson isn't kidding. I was at his apartment and took my ring off in the bathroom. I had gotten my hands dirty from the car."

James took a deep breath. His chest rose, and with it, the volume of his voice.

"That's not the point of my question, and you know it."

At my refusal to defend myself with a story that would explain everything and put all the elements of error back into their original places, the light died in James' eyes, James' gentle, brown eyes that were not made for pain. Yet it would make no sense playing the little girl caught in a naughty act, because it was more, so much more.

I got up and James took a step in my direction.

"I want an explanation, Isabella. Why did you go to Orson's place today?"

I stepped back. My hip hit the telephone table.

"I wanted to see Orson today in order to tell him... to tell him that everything is over between him and me."

"I seem to be missing some important details here. What exactly do you mean by *everything is over.*"

The kitchen spun before my eyes.

"Orson and I had an affair."

"James pinned me with his eyes, still not certain that this wasn't a dream. Fate seemed to hesitate.

After a moment of deceptive silence, he railed at me. "*An affair...!* I can't believe this! My wife and Orson Mahler...!"

I had to turn away from his accusing stare and took several steps across the kitchen floor.

"It's over, James, I assure you. It's over."

"No kidding! According to the message we just heard, Orson doesn't seem to think so!" His chest rose and fell convulsively. He threw his words like stones at me.

"Look at me, for Christ's sake!" He planted himself in my path. "I think you owe me an answer to my questions!"

The flush of his face looked painful, like new-grown skin after a burn. His grip on my arm was excruciating. There was no mercy in his eyes.

"Let go of me, please, James. There's no sense in hurting me."

He stepped back. "You violated my trust in you, Isabella! How long has this affair of yours been going on?"

"A few months," I said softly, hugging my hurting elbow.

"And where did your romantic meetings take place? In his apartment?"

"Yes, while Paula was away in Connecticut."

"And before that?"

I hesitated. I would tell him the truth if he insisted, but didn't want to punish him with any further revelations.

"I wish I could explain to you..."

"*No,* goddammit, spare me your fucking details...!" His rage was monumental and could be heard a block down the street. James ran a desperate hand through his hair and began pacing.

"I'm hurt, I'm disappointed, and I would love to beat both of you to a pulp! I'd love to see the great maestro conduct his next concert from a wheelchair."

He stood with his back to me.

"And you, Isabella... I always adored you. I can't remember a time when I didn't love you. I've never loved anyone the way I loved you. You were without blemish. You belonged to me, entirely. And now..."

He swung around, and we stared at each other like two fighters wondering who would be the winner, who the loser in this race of errors and emotions. His hands were clenched tightly, his knuckles shining white, as he hung onto his self-possession with masterful control. He was afraid to let go and do me bodily harm.

"Where did I fail you, Isabella? Tell me, for Heaven's sake! Where did I fail you?"

I hit the refrigerator with my shoulder and one of the magnets, holding the photo of James and Orson making pancakes, fell to the floor.

I tried to keep my voice from trembling.

"You never failed me, James, never. And I never stopped loving you. Not for a moment. Please believe me."

"Believe you? Give me one good reason why I should believe you?"

James came to a stop at the window, his eyes ablaze with a terrifying knowledge. Then, looking out, he suddenly seemed distant, as if switching gears. Turning around, he glanced at me differently, with the face of a man stripped to the bones of an emotion I'd not known he possessed. Hadn't I lived through this in my worst dreams a thousand times before? But reality needs no rehearsal. It just happens.

I took a step in his direction.

"James, I love you. You must know that I love you. You must feel it. You have to believe me."

His face was carved in stone. "Then *why* did you do it?"

"It was like a drug that I had to take in order not to need it anymore."

He lowered his head like a bull before the charge, and his eyes squinted to fiery slits. We stood at opposite ends of the kitchen, separated by much more than space. The sudden softness of his voice scared me.

"I'm leaving."

I tried to close my eyes, but the echo of his words bounced back from the walls.

Groping for the keys to his car, James picked up his suede jacket.

He repeated, "I'm leaving. I'll be at the Sheraton near Teterboro Airport, in case I get a message. I assume you'll be more comfortable alone, unless you have different plans." He laughed with a sarcastic bite.

I stood rooted to the spot, wishing for the floor tiles to open up and devour me. It had all happened too quickly. I heard James running down the stairs and leaped after him.

"James... komm' zurück! Please come back! *Please!"*

My throat was tight with the ache of unshed tears. At the door he spun around. Happiness and blood was drained out of him. He looked at me. Though his glance was steely and sad, it opened a second of possibility. Heedlessly, he banged into the door behind him, but the impact didn't appear to bother him, for his inner struggle seemed to increase in intensity. And then the door slammed shut and he was gone.

He had done it. He had delivered the *coup de grâce* to our love. He would no longer love me. The world he faced was altered. Where would he go with his pain? Where would I go with mine? I had caused something that I was unable to undo, I had driven my husband out of our life together. The thought struck me that I might not see him again. I ran outside. His car was already out of sight and the scales of destiny froze in the emptiness of his absence.

86

I hadn't thought of taking an umbrella with me and got caught in the rain after work. But then, since James had left, I hadn't thought of a lot of things because the only thing I could think about was him. Crossing Fifth Avenue, I was about to get soaked, so I decided to roam around in *Saks* until it let up.

I had been putting off buying a gift for Julia's upcoming birthday long enough and might as well do it now. In the crowd, I let myself sweep past the counters of the store that was considered the Mecca of many a shopper. But the scarves, bags and hats blurred before my eyes. My thoughts went out to James. *Always James.* My head hurt from the windmills that my thoughts had become, windmills that never let me go.

The week didn't seem to move. Today was Wednesday, four days since he had left and three more days before he was scheduled to return. The three days ahead seemed to stretch like infinities of suspense and worry.

I had not heard from James. I imagined him fighting his pain, fighting for an answer, but his answer eluded me too. He had not called, and the anguish of his leaving me for good grew like a cancer in my mind. Was his present already running away from our past?

If only he would call me, even if he were angry, call me names, shout and scream. But he was not ready to talk. He had not yet worked things out for himself. Not yet. Maybe I still had a chance, maybe only a slight one. Compared to *what?*

A day again with James seemed like an unearned bonus, the best gift of life imaginable. If I could only explain to him that a valuable lesson had been crafted through this struggle. The truth always had a price, but this was a costly realization that divided loyalties and loves are destructive companions to live with.

The decision about our future was out of my hands, and I could only concentrate on waiting. I should say a prayer, but I was out of practice and I feared that my plea might not please the heavens.

I couldn't fall asleep. I lay on James' side of the bed and wondered if he would ever again tease me about my flannel nightgowns or my refusal to drink root beer. In the long hours of the night, the open question of my fate hung over me like the Sword of Damocles, exhausting me by the pull between hurt and hope.

In this uncertainty I had no one to count on but myself. The one time I needed Barry as a friend, he was on vacation. The nurse at his office told me had taken the week off after his convention to go to Marco Island and would return Saturday. I had also tried to call Julia at Hilton Head. Her sister told me she had gone to Marco Island for a week. To collect shells. Despite my dilemma, I smiled, putting two and two together.

Whichever gift I bought for Julia today, introducing her to Barry was the gift that mattered. And if there was still any doubt in her mind about moving back to Montclair, Barry had now become the prize. In the middle of my hurt there was a niche of happiness for her, and I decided that, once she had returned, I would encourage her to write her long-dreamed-of bestseller. Good fortune, like misfortune, often comes in pairs.

If I only knew what to buy her now. What kind of scarf would she like? My fingers ran through the silken materials spread out on the counter. This was not my day to choose between polka dots and poppy blossoms. I had to disappoint the sales lady. No scarf for Julia. Maybe Barry would buy her one with a shell pattern on Marco Island. I pictured them together, on the beach, at the bar, in bed. Had Barry told his mother?

I had tried to call Louise, but she was in Connecticut visiting Paula at the Institute of Living.

I had also tried to call Matthew at the hospital but was told that he was not accepting calls. He was fighting the scream in his soul over Tom contracting AIDS. Matthew's lover, Tom. And James's pilot, Tom... I didn't know the last name of either of them. Were they the same person? What was either of them doing now, and where were they? Flying airplanes while harboring thoughts of suicide? Was one of them flying *my* husband? Was James at Tom's mercy without knowing it?

My head ached. I was imagining things. I was feeding self-pity by adding far-fetched facts to the horror in my heart. I was trying to escape my marital mess by substituting another kind of plight, like apples for oranges. Maybe I should call James' office and ask about Tom, who he was and where he was. Maybe I should try talking to James about Tom, about *us,* even if it meant arguing. After all, James had argued and shouted. He had cared. One has to care in order to argue. But my energies were paralyzed and I couldn't bring myself to call his office. Similarly, I couldn't bring myself to settle on a gift for Julia.

I was looking at pins now. Would she like a small golden safety-pin with a tiny diamond? Or would she prefer a bracelet of faux-pearls or a Mickey-Mouse watch?

A patient saleswoman had spread out a dozen watches on the counter, giving me advice on interchangeable watch-straps and frames. I had to decide at last. I realized that following someone's advice meant not trying hard enough myself.

As for Orson, disaster had replaced the dream. I had called Orson yesterday. Of all the people I knew, he seemed to be the only one who was not out of town or in the hospital. He sounded rushed and told me that he was in the middle of a voice rehearsal in his living room.

I said, "Orson, we have to talk."

"Isabella, if it's about your ring, don't worry. It's safe with me."

"It's not about my ring, but I can't talk about it over the phone like this."

His impatience rose. "I'm sorry, it has to wait until after the concert."

"It can't wait that long. It's an emergency. I have to talk to you before James returns."

He gave a startled sigh. "You're not sick, are you?"

"*No,* I'm *not* sick..."

"Thank God." He gave a sigh. "In that case it'll have to wait. Please try to see things from my perspective. Every minute of my time is needed to make the *Missa* a success. I promise to be there for you after the concert. Will you come to the reception after the performance? Please come. I'm looking forward to seeing your lovely face again...."

I gave up. So much for starting with a clean slate on James' return. *James...* my thoughts went out to him again.

"Can I show you anything else?" The voice of the saleswoman returned me to the busy ground floor of *Saks Fifth Avenue*.

I said, "I'm afraid I've been staring at these watches without seeing them. I'll take two of the Mickey-Mouse watches. One in yellow and one in red. Can you gift-wrap the red one please?"

I would give the red one to Julia, and treating myself to the yellow one would temporarily lift my spirits. As I was signing the credit card slip, the buzz of voices around me fell silent save for one.

"Bella!"

A head of red curls emerged from the blur of unknown faces.

"Beverly!"

We hugged each other briefly.

She laughed. "Where have you been hiding? I haven't seen you since the picnic at Ringwood Manor."

Her olive eyes danced with undiluted friendliness, and something funny happened. My heart opened. In a world where everyone seemed to draw away from me or was temporarily unavailable, Beverly struck me as a part of the past where everything was still in order. All at once I remembered how we had met in the elevator, how we had got stuck, how she had arranged for me to meet Orson. In fact, my first lunch with Orson had been exactly one year ago today.

I smiled. "Beverly, I'm so glad to see you," and couldn't have meant it more.

She looked at me for a long moment. "Is everything all right with you? Your eyes look as if you've done some crying."

"I'm quite well," I said as steadily as possible. "I'm having a tough time at work, though. I practically never have time to eat lunch. You know, there are times like that..."

"Don't push yourself too hard, Bella. You look tired."

"It's just lack of sleep. But thank you for your concern. It's really sweet of you. Now tell me about yourself."

For once she didn't laugh, but scratched her chin awkwardly with one of her dark, purple nails.

"I've got news. Rudy and I separated. I moved out."

"Oh... I'm sorry Beverly." I touched her arm consolingly.

"Don't be. I was the one who suggested it. We are just too different. We're still on speaking terms, of course. It's all very amicable. In the meantime I moved to a studio apartment two blocks down from Orson. This way I can be more of help to him."

I gasped at her news. But nothing was new, really.

She rattled on in her usual shrill voice.

"Believe me, Orson keeps me on my toes. He's so busy with the preparations for his concert, and with Paula away I try to make life a little easier for him."

I tried to sound innocent. "You're so good to him."

"Well, I'm helping him with all kinds of practical things and he needs it."

A demo girl sprayed us with one of the latest designer fragrances. Beverly pointed to the *Chanel* counter.

"If you buy their body lotion you get a free make-up consultation," and in the same breath, "Have you spoken to Orson lately?"

"No," I lied.

"Well, I just talked to him." The old triumph was back in her voice. "The poor man is under so much pressure. I feel there's something he doesn't want to talk about, though. Maybe he misses Paula more than he lets on. He says the rehearsals for the *Missa* aren't going too well. He spent the last two days auditioning sopranos to replace the one who's in bed with jaundice. Additional choral scores were supposed to be sent from Brighton and haven't got here yet. But hey... don't we know Orson? He always knows how to turn initial failure into success."

She laughed her grand, flamboyant laugh and climbed onto a tall chair in front of the cosmetics counter. A make-up artist, a blue-eyed young man who needed a shave, launched into a dissertation about suitable shades for her foundation, eye-shadow and lipstick.

I asked, "So how do you like your new apartment?"

She crossed her legs, showing a lot of them.

"It's small, but adorable. They just haven't delivered the bed yet. I'm tired of sleeping on the couch. I thought I'd ask Orson if I could use Paula's bedroom for the time being."

I said dryly, "Good luck," and thought, Beverly, no doubt your mind is set on something other than Paula's pink pillows. But my sarcasm had no bite and reverted into pity. Would Beverly end up like Joan, chasing a heart that never stopped running?

As the young man busied himself cleaning her face with a milky lotion, she closed her eyes and asked unexpectedly, "How's James?"

I almost panicked and said quickly, "James is fine. He's in Denver on business. Have you heard anything from Matthew?"

"Now, that's a strange case. Orson tells me he's in the hospital with a nervous breakdown. But the worst is over and he's expected to be released by the end of the week. Of course, Joan is worried to death. She's at his bedside around the clock."

"Why a nervous breakdown?" I pretended not to know.

"Orson keeps beating around the bush. He implied something about Matthew's friend, that mysterious Tom. I think they're breaking up. Frankly, who cares?"

The unshaven young man stopped applying mascara to her half-closed eyes.

I said, "You look very pretty, Beverly. Are you going out tonight?"

"Orson is taking me to dinner."

She paused for effect. With her head still turned to the make-up artist, she rolled her eyes in my direction in order not to miss my reaction. Her triumph left me with blissful indifference.

She checked her watch. "I'm meeting him right after this, but I'm afraid he won't be in the best of moods."

"I trust your glamorous looks will do wonders for his spirits."

As the consultant plucked her eyebrows, she tried not to move her face.

"Orson has asked me to do him a favor. Has he ever told you about his commission from the Lincoln Center *Stagebill* to write a series of program notes?"

"Yes, I remember, now that you mention it. That was a long time ago. Almost a year."

"Right. Well, he finally finished writing the series. He missed the deadline by a few months, but what could they do?"

She chuckled and climbed from the chair, happily inspecting her face in the mirror. I had no wish to face my own reflection.

Beverly smiled proudly. "Anyway, Orson is going to give me the pages of his hand-written manuscript tonight. I promised to type them for him. This way I'll also get my foot in the door for his permission to let me start the research on his biography. You know, I'd *love* to write it. Wouldn't that be exciting?"

Disregarding her question, I said, "That's very generous of you. I mean, your offer to type the manuscript. For that, he owes you much more than a dinner."

"I can't wait to do it. It'll be a real musical education for me. It'll only be fifty or sixty pages, double-spaced. I'll have it done in a week. And I have the privilege of being the first to read them."

Beverly bought her body-lotion and we started towards the exit.

I said, "I remember Orson was having a hard time finding a title for the series. Has he finally come up with one?"

"Yes, he has." Her tone became strangely secretive.

"As a matter of fact, I find his choice somewhat... unusual, if not perplexing. And I have a feeling that some people will find it... uh... out of line."

Although the subject no longer interested me that much, I asked anyway, "What is it? Is it a secret?"

She smiled mysteriously, as if no force could make her say it. We had reached the exit. I held the door open for her and didn't expect her to reply.

On the street again, I said, "The rain has stopped. Please tell Orson I said hello."

She touched my elbow. "I'd like your opinion, Bella."

"About what?"

"The series. About the title of Orson's series..."

"Oh. What is it then?"

We were still standing at the entrance, barring other people's way in and out. To my utter surprise, Beverly blushed deeply.

"Orson wants to call his series *Making Love to Music.*"

She coughed importantly.

"He calls it a metaphor for conducting and says it reminds him of a very special person in his life."

At my silence, a look of bewilderment crossed her face and her shrill voice sank into a confidential whisper. "Any idea *who* it could be?"

What could I possibly say? It didn't matter any longer what Orson called his series or whom the title might remind him of. Before my eyes and in my ears the sounds and colors of the Fifth Avenue rush hour traffic swam in a song of sadness and despair. I felt the grotesque drip of tears on my cheeks and my thoughts went out to James. Since he had left, I could think of little else.

87

The sound of instruments being tuned had never irritated me before. But tonight, sitting in Box 55 in Carnegie Hall a few minutes before Orson's concert, I perceived them as threatening and squeaking voices from the underworld of my troubled mind.

With still no sign of life from James, Saturday had come at last. The timing was hardly favorable to fully appreciate my first experience with Beethoven's masterpiece, the *Missa Solemnis*. I adjusted my chair to face the stage and picked a piece of lint from my navy dress.

Any moment, Maestro Mahler would begin to conduct Beethoven's glorious and gruesomely demanding mass for the first time in his life. When a reporter had asked Orson why he had waited four decades of public life to perform the piece, he answered proudly, "The score is so difficult, there's a pitfall a minute. Besides, I just followed Toscanini's example. He conducted the *Missa* for the first time when he was in his middle sixties, even older than I am."

"Perhaps," he further explained, "he felt that he wasn't ready for it earlier in his career. At least, that's the way I felt about it, but I was always convinced that one day I'd close the gap in my repertoire. As an ardent Beethoven admirer, conducting the *Missa* signifies the most important concert of my life, because I believe that great interpretations come only after a lifetime of experience. I wanted to do it with conviction and maturity, like a modest servant, in order not to let myself down. Or Beethoven."

And now the event was eagerly awaited by an apprehensive audience in a sold-out Carnegie Hall. Ushers handed out programs as the last seats were taken. On the stage, all the musicians were in their seats, and an alert Brighton Festival Chorus sat on five rows of risers behind the orchestra. My eyes swept the half-circle of First Tier boxes. To my surprise, Joan sat in the center box usually reserved for Paula. Paula had not made the trip for the most important concert of her husband's career.

Joan, in Paula's seat, wore a simple black dress and was without jewelry or make-up. Surely her mind was geared less to Beethoven than to her (and Orson's) son. By drawing a parallel between her fears about Matthew, and mine about James, I felt a deep empathy with her.

I looked down from my box, and Beverly's red hair was easy to pick out among the parquet seats. She and Daisy were giggling like teenagers, each holding a single red rose on their laps, no doubt intended for the maestro. Maybe Beverly was telling Daisy about the unusual title Orson had chosen for his series of program notes. Or they might be trying to guess who the mysterious person behind the metaphor could be.

Making Love to Music. I thought, Perhaps art and life should never mingle, and all that was able to survive, at best, was a series of program notes.

An insert from the program fell to my feet. It was the last-minute announcement about the change of the soprano part. I leafed through the *Stagebill,* chasing an errant fly from the print of Beethoven's words in an 1819 letter to Archduke Rudolph.

The day on which a High Mass composed by me will be performed during the ceremonies solemnized for Your Imperial Highness will be the most glorious day of my life. God will enlighten me so that my poor talents may contribute to the glorification of that solemn day...

The lights dimmed and the details of the hall vanished into darkness. For me, Carnegie Hall seemed to have lost some of its grandeur, exuding a muted atmosphere, like a room of someone who had died. At Orson's appearance, applause covered the last murmur of voices as he stepped onto the podium. In a moment of silence the hall held its breath.

Orson lifted his baton and the first bars of the *Kyrie,* marked *Assai sostenuto,* floated through the strings. The chorus entered, followed by the soloists. Orson led them as a monarch rules, with absolute control, steering them into a state in which they felt the work's mystery and could convey it to the public.

In this moment, Orson combined his public and his personal appeal. He was himself and at the same time he was something outside himself. He became the incorporation of Beethoven's music itself.

Who could resist such an enticement of the senses? For a short moment the experiences of the last year fell away, and I re-experienced the unspoiled magic that Orson had first cast on me. Whoever had coined Orson's nickname must have felt the same emotion. *Magic. Orson Magic Mahler.* How could I not have fallen for it myself? Hadn't I voluntarily walked into his trap? And if I had avoided it would I still be wondering what might have been? Leaving behind a piece of reality is much easier than letting go of an unlived dream. Here and now, I needed to forgive myself for the crime of my heart, my venture in romance. Maybe if I forgave myself, others would follow.

I released Orson from my heart and sent him off on his lonely quest for a heart he couldn't break. I returned him, like a library book, to the public, the press and Paula.

The hall felt hot. I shouldn't have worn this long-sleeved velvet dress. During the joyful opening choral section of the *Gloria*, my hands kept rolling the program into an ever-tighter tube and later, after the intermission, the soul-piercing violin solo of the *Benedictus* hardly penetrated the reeling of my mind.

Again, my thoughts returned to James. He had not called. Not once during the whole week. Such frightening silence, a silence that no music, not even Beethoven's, could fill.

How frightening to leave my old life behind, how frightening to envision a life without James. Would he ever understand that Orson had been as unavoidable as a hurricane passing through my life? Right or wrong had hardly mattered, and the only manual I had ever consulted were my inner demons, just as my mother had done many years ago.

Only yesterday, I had asked her on the phone if she still thought about Orson. She gave a little laugh. "That was long ago. In the meantime I've found that happiness is less complicated and much easier to come by. Isabella, imagine...," she sounded almost shy, "I wanted to tell you something. I'm going to get married again."

"Mutti, ich gratuliere dir!"

After endless questions and good wishes, she promised to send pictures of Dieter, and we discussed the possibility of meeting them on their honeymoon in Hawaii.

I couldn't bring myself to tell her of my fear that I might be getting divorced at the same time she was getting married. She might be going to Hawaii and I might not. It was for James to decide. Where was he right now? Was he in the air, on his way back from Denver, as scheduled? Would I see him tonight after the concert, or ever again?

The concert dragged. I checked my watch. Had any composer ever written a longer *Agnus Dei? Dona nobis pacem.* God grant us peace.

And then suddenly there was silence followed by thunderous applause. The hall rose to its feet. Orson stood before the audience, bowing, admired and adored.

I remembered Orson's comment about the conclusion of the work which ends so suddenly that it leaves the listener hanging in the air. It now seemed an appropriate analogy to our affair. It too had ended suddenly, followed by the feeling of being left hanging in the air…

88

Downstairs in the milling crowd of Café Carnegie, I stood like a statue in the midst of dancers. I got in line to buy a glass of wine and looked around. Beverly and Daisy were nowhere to be seen. Nor was Joan. They were probably backstage with Orson, helping him change his shirt and feeding him hot chocolate, while everyone down here eagerly awaited his appearance.

Still, the lingering glow of Orson's grand performance outweighed the oppressiveness of the narrow room. Everyone was gathered here with the hope of securing a small part of the maestro, to take home a tiny treasure after a momentous concert: a smile, a word, a handshake, or the privilege of a hug or kiss. I wanted none of these.

Why was I still here? Shouldn't I be rushing home to James? Going home was what I wished for the most, but also feared the greatest. I had vowed to myself not to face James until I had told Orson in person that everything was *over.*

It's over, Orson would suffice to break with everything that had ever been. But how could I hope to say anything to him without dozens of ears sharing the message? *It's over, Orson.* I kept the words like a letter in my pocket, to be read at a later time. The letter in my pocket burned.

Again, my thoughts went out to James, and I recognized that the tears pushing up in my eyes were clearly unsuitable amidst the lighthearted party chatter all around me. Clutching my glass, I headed for a hiding-place behind one of the golden columns and bumped into Julia and Barry exchanging a kiss.

They jumped apart, and a small scream escaped her lips. "Isabella!"

And then her arms were around me. Her wonderful arms. How I had missed her all these months, my friend, my soul-sister. Now she was back.

"Julia, Barry! What a surprise!" I disengaged myself from her. "I didn't expect you two to be here tonight. I thought you were still on Marco Island."

Barry put his arm around Julia and laughed. "We came back yesterday and decided spontaneously to take a room at the Plaza for the weekend before starting life again in New Jersey. We were hoping to see you here tonight. In fact, we were lucky to get tickets. We had to buy them from a scalper on Seventh Avenue and we still wound up in the balcony."

"You both look wonderful." I marveled at their tans. They were radiant, and no longer the same people who had once crashed on the rocks of heartbreak.

"I called your nurse, Barry, and your sister, Julia. It wasn't difficult to guess that you two had taken off together."

They looked at each other and laughed self-consciously, like first-time lovers, not certain if their new union needed to be explained.

Barry kissed Julia's forehead. "We had a great time."

Julia smiled and closed her eyes. "The best ever."

Behind her closed lids, she was holding hopes like a candle.

Then she asked, "But where's James?"

The dreaded question.

I bonded my voice into bars of self-control.

"James is on his way back from a convention in Denver. He should be in the air as we speak."

Barry asked. "So late? Which airline is he flying?"

I took a sip of wine. "He's coming back on the company jet."

"Ah, yes," he said, "I remember him telling me about it. It's one of those Cessna things, right? A Citation?"

A waiter offered us a tray with cheese puffs and foie gras. Barry took two of each. Julia borrowed a sip from my glass. The surprise of meeting each other was still fresh. The distraction of food was welcome to get used to the new feeling, the new order of relationships. Barry stuffed a cheese puff in Julia's mouth.

He asked, "Are you and James free a week from tonight? We want to celebrate Julia's birthday."

Julia's green blouse contrasted with the blush crossing her face. "It's going to be a very special birthday. But it wouldn't be the same without you and James."

"We may also have a little announcement to break to our friends." Barry looked at her with the proud eyes of a new owner.

Her whisper, "Barry nervously proposed marriage, and I said *yes,*" was followed by hugs, kisses and tears.

"Congratulations, I'm so happy for both of you."

At last. At last I was free to cry.

Julia said, "... Isabella...you're so sweet... but you look changed. Are you all right?"

"Julia's right." Barry exhibited a professional frown between his bushy eyebrows. "You don't look well, Isabella. Was there a special reason why you called my office?"

With tears running down my cheeks, I forced a smile of steel.

"I'm fine, really. I'm just so happy for you. I've been going through a rough time at work, though. It's all still so new and we have problems compiling the recording schedule. It's a global manhunt to get specific artists to commit to three or four days of recording time."

Julia said, "It sounds so interesting. You'll have to tell us all about your new job soon."

Suddenly there was a turning of heads, a collective gasp and then the room exploded with applause. Maestro Mahler was making his appearance.

He bowed. He smiled, and light danced in his eyes.

Two photographers buzzed around him.

Orson raised a hand to request silence.

"Thank you. Thank you all. As I've said so often, the *Missa Solemnis* is so impossibly difficult to perform that the best one can hope to do is to fail honorably. But I think we succeeded honorably this evening. And Beethoven along with us."

Applause again. Behind him, Joan looked protective and pale, her ballerina-eyes filled with worry about Matthew. Yet, with Paula absent, her place was at long last at his side.

A tall, white-haired man separated himself from the crowd and stepped into the half-circle that had formed around Orson. It was the president of my recording company. With him was my boss, Dan Maddox, the Director of Artists and Repertoire.

Both men were smiling, content with the positive publicity that this concert would produce for one of their top recording stars.

Orson shook hands with each of them as they muttered words of gold. They proposed recording a new Beethoven cycle, including the *Missa*, and suggested some symphonic works by Bernstein after that. Orson nodded happily and turned his immediate attention to a glass of orange juice.

How could I hope to have a private word with him tonight? I stepped back to hide behind the golden column, determined not to be seen by Dan Maddox. The prospect of having to engage in small-talk with my boss surpassed my strength. I needed to concentrate on the letter burning in my pocket. Every other deterrent had to be avoided. Regardless of how many other people were claiming Orson's time, I had to talk to him alone.

Julia and Barry had joined the line at the bar. I leaned my head against the column, wishing to take off my heels. A stranger next to me tried to get my attention. He smiled, hoping for a chat.

"If you can perform the *Missa Solemnis*, you can do anything in the repertoire."

I nodded absently. My eyes swept to a distant place across the room. There was Jess, with his arm in a sling. I had heard he had fallen off his horse. He was by himself, as usual. Miraculously, across the sea of heads, his emerald eyes caught mine. We smiled at each other, but a moment later he was surrounded by a group of chorus members.

Orson was still besieged by an army of admirers. After all this triumph, how would he stomach the words of someone who wanted to break with him for good?

Barry's face re-emerged from the crowd. He was carrying two drinks. Julia, beside him, moved like a swan. Everything in her world was in the right place. She spoke of their future, giving up her apartment to move into Barry's house, and plunging into the wilderness of free-lance writing again. She hesitated, searching Barry's face. And after the wedding, they might start a family...

Barry played with a strand of Julia's hair, never taking his eyes off her as she spoke. She spoke slowly, using large spaces, as in a dream drawn out of proportion, and with only James on my mind, I feared I would fall between the spaces of her words.

Beverly materialized from nowhere, flamboyant as ever. With no warning, she was all over Julia and exploded in her usual shrillness.

"Hi, there! You're just the person I've been looking for. I was afraid I'd never see you again. Remember how we once discussed writing Orson Mahler's memoirs as a joint project?"

Julia and I exchanged quick glances.

Beverly reeled on, "Now that Orson has finally finished his essays for the Lincoln Center *Stagebill,* I got him to agree to spend some time with me and tell me... uh, some things about his life. But I need a professional writer to help me."

Barry, who had never heard of this idea, scratched his beard.

Julia smiled politely. "I'm flattered by your offer. But I'm afraid that all my time is taken up, at least in the near future."

I put a protective arm around her shoulder.

"Julia will be very busy becoming Mrs. Barry Schumann." I tilted my head in Barry's direction.

Beverly's eyes flew from Julia to Barry.

"Oh, you're getting married! I had no idea. That's awesome. Congratulations!"

Julia acknowledged Beverly's high-volume declaration with a silent nod, indicating the subject was closed. When Beverly disappeared into the crowd again Julia turned her eyes to me.

"There's no way I could ever work with that woman. She's just too much."

Despite my troubled state of mind, I couldn't have been more pleased about my friend's reaction.

Julia's fingers curled around the stem of her wine glass and she suddenly asked, "How long does it take to walk from here to the Plaza Hotel?"

I said, "It's not far from here. Maybe ten minutes."

She looked at Barry, and without the need to explain, the two excused themselves.

An hour later I was still waiting for Orson. When would the weight of this day be lifted from my shoulders? Tomorrow? *Ever?*

After the reception at Café Carnegie, a number of people accompanied Orson to his dressing room. I followed them at a distance and was now waiting outside the room, feeling like a spy. When I was certain Orson couldn't see me, I peered in briefly as the door opened for a moment.

He had thrown his tails on top of the grand piano. Surrounded by black and white photographs of dead conductors on the wall and a dying fig-leaf tree behind the sitting area, Orson looked tired. He was listening to a music critic prying for information, a photographer looking for a job and a soprano hoping for an audition.

I stepped back and took off my earrings. My head whirled. *It's over Orson. It's over.* This was my dance of death with him. A few more turns and everything would end.

The door of the dressing room opened and closed. The soprano left. So did the photographer and the critic. To my great surprise, Joan left too. She rushed past me, her face marked by fatigue. The door was closed from the inside again. Orson was alone now. Finally alone.

I knocked and turned the knob. But Orson was not the only one in the room. The scene was like a symbolic snapshot. Orson as the eternal prey of women...and enjoying it. Beverly held a measuring tape to his outstretched arm, and Daisy wrote down the numbers on a pad.

As I entered, their faces fell in surprise, along with Orson's arm. They leaped apart.

Daisy hastened to explain, "I want to knit a sweater for Orson's birthday and I want to get started in plenty of time for December."

"I'm sorry to burst in on you like this," I said. Free from the shackles of passion, I felt powerful at last. The room was mine.

Finally I saw a lot of things in a clear light. The Beverlys and Daisys of this world would always be around a man like Orson. It was wasted energy to be jealous of their efforts to reach his heart, because all they could do was surround him with measuring tapes, thermos bottles and typed manuscript pages. They knew how to make themselves useful, but not loved. I had judged Beverly too harshly all along and was on the verge of telling her that I was sorry for my feelings of rivalry and competition. Possibly her pursuit of the maestro was all bark and no bite, as a substitute for fulfillment. True fulfillment was discreet, it needed no flamboyancy. But perhaps our rivalry had shown me some traits I refused to acknowledge in myself: possessiveness and the need to be noticed.

It was liberating to see that I was neither Beverly's nor Daisy's rival. We were rather allies around a much-loved figure. I had invaded their territory even more than they had infringed on mine. Looking back, it had never been a matter of Orson choosing Beverly or Daisy over me, or me over them. For him it was a case of making room for someone else, with them... and with me.

A smile broke on Orson's face and he held out his arms.

"Ah, I'm so glad to see you. Come in, Isabella. I've been wondering all night where you were."

Witnessing his demonstrative welcome for me, Beverly's and Daisy's cheeks turned red, like the heads of their roses, dangling sadly over the edge of the piano bench.

I didn't walk towards him, but said, "Orson, may I have a word with you alone?" and gestured to him to follow me out of the room. I began moving along the hallway towards the winding stairwell.

I heard Orson's footsteps following me without delay. At the top of the stairs I swung around, my hand grasping the railing, my voice in control. "Orson, listen carefully. It's over between us. There's no way to continue our relationship. I'm scared. James found out about us, and I don't know what he's going to do."

"What happened?"

"It was your damned message about my ring! James was still there when I got home and he heard it."

"Oh my god! I'm sorry, Isabella."

We looked at each other for a helpless moment.

I spoke quickly. "James is scheduled to come back tonight. In the company jet from Denver. Remember, I told you about it? He's supposed to land at Teterboro Airport. He hasn't called me since he left. This week was sheer hell for me, and you were too busy to talk to me. Orson, I love James and I want to spend the rest of my life with him!"

Relieved by the delivery of my speech, I mustered a smile from somewhere in my crumbling heart. "Besides, Maestro, I'm tired of being the fifth wheel in your life."

Orson's face didn't move. "Sometimes, Isabella, the fifth wheel is the important one, because all the others have gone flat."

Our eyes locked for several seconds, like magnifying glasses on our hearts.

"This is good-bye, Orson. I want to catch the midnight bus home."

Without looking at him, I ran down the stairs, out the stage entrance and hailed a cab.

89

At midnight there was little traffic on Route 3, but the bus ride home was the longest ever. The night was black, and God had switched off the stars. Only three people and the driver were aboard, and the bus bounced in the wind, struggling not to be blown away, a struggle many of the spring blossoms would not survive.

We struck a pothole, and my purse slipped from my lap and bounced under the seat in front of me. I retrieved it and held onto it like a life-preserver.

My life was between acts and something broke in me. I wondered if a mind could break in pieces, like a heart. I recalled how I had met Orson a year ago and wondered how I would feel a year from now. Would the memory of him still haunt me, or would I laugh at my ease of shedding him like a winter coat at the beginning of spring?

It was futile now to consider the things I was powerless to do or undo. I had followed my stumbling story along a road of secrecy and sin to reach a milestone of maturity. Maybe something good came of this after all. My year with Orson had taught me to expand my mind, to make it as large as the universe, so it could hold everything in existence, including paradoxes.

My thoughts went back to James. This was the defining test of love. Seen from a place beyond right and wrong or good and bad, the ultimate expression of love was to grant someone the right to fall short of expectations.

The wine burned in my empty stomach. My eyes tried to penetrate the darkness outside the bus. Somewhere in the far distance to the right were the lights of Teterboro Airport. Had James landed? Would we face each other through a silence, like a forest of shining swords?

But as the bus stopped on Valley Road, my anxiety turned into joy, immaculate joy that was free of fear or guilt, and I ran towards our house. If I had fallen off the bus and broken both legs I still would have run home. The lilac bushes had been trimmed on our block and offered their aroma to the wind. On another night I might have stopped to smell it, but this was not the time for such demure delights. My heels flew across the asphalt of the street, too impatient to follow the flagstone path along the lawn.

The wind had overturned one of the garbage cans. There was no light in the windows of the house facing the street. Nor was the entrance lamp lit. I looked through the garage window. James' car was not there. James was not home.

90

The house didn't feel like mine, and from the outside it incited a feeling of claustrophobia that made me want to turn away at first. Inside, the familiar shadows of the hall whispered in the dark with the voices of a ticking clock and a quiet hum, the distant murmuring of the refrigerator. My fingers found the light switch, and the sudden brightness suppressed all the voices into startling silence.

James! My inner cry was lost in a void. Why wasn't he home? A lump grew in my throat and the only thing that could have released it was the rattle of the garage door opener announcing his car.

In the hall I hung my jacket on one of the coat hooks next to the Venetian mirror and took off my high heels. I made my way upstairs and turned on the floor lamp in the living room and the lights in the kitchen. The blinking light on the answering machine made me shift into overdrive. *James?* Had James called? I pressed the button and listened, but it was someone who had hung up without leaving a message. I felt as if James' eyes were watching me, but from where? Where was he?

At the kitchen table, I tried to concentrate on tonight's *Stagebill* and recapture the evening's concert. I ate every brownie in the cookie jar, hoping with each one that, before I had finished the next, James would call or come home. But he didn't. Fidgety and sick to my stomach, I got up and filled the watering can on the kitchen counter, but didn't bother to water the plants.

The clock next to the spice rack showed five minutes before one. James' absence was gathering weight by the minute. A sharp draft from the vent above the stove made me spin around and I spilled some orange juice on my dress. I covered the vent and wiped the juice off my dress and the floor tiles, convinced that James' plane was delayed by the storm. The pilot had probably been forced to avoid the strong winds or fly around them. Maybe the plane had been diverted to Baltimore or Boston, or was still circling, waiting for permission to land. Or maybe James was in a hotel somewhere.

The sickening feeling that had gripped my stomach slowly receded. I had eaten too many brownies and was overreacting. Everything would have an explanation.

Too alert to go to bed and too tired to take off my orange-juice-stained dress, I curled up on the living room couch and switched on the news. I bargained with my tired eyes for the arrest of time, then for its acceleration.

The anchor man said, "The latest news of a mysterious plane crash…after this."

For a second the room was eerily quiet. Then, slowly, the beat of drums began to haunt my head and became louder, its pulse overriding the commercials for cereal, cars and pain-relievers. God, I prayed, not him. Not James. Not *my* James. God, please. *Please!* But my prayer died under the drums in my head.

The anchor man returned.

In our top story this morning, authorities in Ohio are still trying to determine the cause of an airplane crash earlier in the evening. At approximately eight-forty p.m., local time, a Cessna Citation plummeted into Lake Erie about twenty-five miles east of Toledo. The private jet was on its way from Denver, Colorado to Teterboro, New Jersey. A spokesman for the Federal Aviation Administration said that the plane had been reported to be in perfect condition before take-off. The pilot had not complained of mechanical difficulties in flight or transmitted any emergency signals to air traffic control. No bodies have yet been recovered, but it is believed that everyone on board perished when the plane hit the water. Investigators do not rule out the possibility of sabotage. No explanation is known as to the cause of the crash, but the plane is said to have been off course to be flying over the water.

I felt encased in a vacuum of light and glass, with everything in it and around it translucent and distinct, and with every question elucidated and explained. My god, hadn't my intuition warned me that something like this would happen? Why hadn't I acted on my premonition? Instead of indulging in guilt and self-pity, why hadn't I stopped James from taking this plane? Now I had myself to blame for my husband's death.

But wait, no. It wasn't true. It wasn't true that I would never see James again, that I would never hear his voice or feel his arms around me. It wasn't true. I tucked my legs still tighter under my skirt, convinced that it couldn't be James who was dead, but someone else, and that James would walk in any minute, whole, well and laughing.

I switched off the TV, wondering how long the dam of my refusal would be able to hold back the tide of terror.

Still in the awesome state before pain, I perceived the contours of the room falling prey to the illusions of a fun-house mirror. I clutched the armrest of the couch and pictured James' last seconds of horror.

As reality began to hit, I knew I would never again see the deep creases of his face breaking into a smile, nor see him run his hand through his slightly too-long hair. I would never see his face covered with shaving cream or watch him separate his black socks from his brown ones. I would never hear him complain about my using the last of his aspirins. Now I only had memories to assure me that those times had existed.

Was this the bitter taste of widowhood? The terror seemed too bottomless to face, the shock too new to act upon. Shouldn't I get up, move, call the police, friends, neighbors, my mother? I couldn't. Eventually the police would call me with details and questions, and their way of fitting tragedy into a case for the files. Separation from James was like being amputated from the world and all its systems.

I sat motionless, fighting off the urge to breathe and the thought of a future without sharing. The absoluteness of death is the deprivation of sharing. To share a bed, a book, a bathtub, a checking account. To share memories.

Now James had left them all with me, freed from them forever. He would never be anywhere but away, extinguished. Death as the extinguisher leaves everything without importance... possessions, passions, pain.

How much time would elapse before I could grieve? When would I begin to feel the itch of tears?

My portraits of Austrian royalty leaned forward from their frames, their painted faces laughing and alive, trying to take away my innocence, trying to harden my heart in the face of loneliness, trying to make me join in their laughter in order not to cry.

But no, the reason for my laughter was not their sardonic smiles, it was the time bomb rattling in my head, the time bomb of pain. The rattle was everywhere. It came from inside me and around me, shaking my head, my heart and the garage door opener downstairs. The rattle was someone using the garage door opener. *The time bomb of my pain. The rattle. My mindless laughter.* What sort of trance had I managed to laugh myself into?

I listened.

James? Was James here?

For the first time I felt my legs and arms again. James? Only James had the remote device to open the garage door. But it was impossible, because James was dead, the remnants of his body floating in Lake Erie. The thought made me freeze.

But a second later I was racing down the stairs to the garage. I flung the door open to the headlights of James' car, with James sitting behind the wheel, his face lit from the dashboard lights!

But it couldn't be. I knew then that I was hallucinating, because Orson was sitting next to James. My mind and my eyes were deluding me, while my body was still sitting on the couch, motionless, with my legs tucked under my stained dress, or were they? James and Orson were only a vision that would vanish at the next blinking of my eyes, lulling me now for a last blissful second into an illusion of the past.

James brought the car to stop a yard from the pile of firewood. He shut the engine off, extinguished the headlights. The garage door slammed shut behind the car, and the inside garage lights went on. James was the first to open the car door. He had on the same suede jacket he had worn when he left a week ago. The other door opened and Orson got out from the passenger seat. He was still wearing the tails in which he had conducted Beethoven.

The scene was too much to believe. My need for physical proof was stronger than my need to faint.

"*James!*" I ran past Orson into my husband's arms. "You're alive!"

I felt his energy, the warmth of his breath, the aroma of his suede jacket, and at long last, I heard his voice.

"*Isabella.* My Isabella."

91

Of all the luggage of United Flight # 302 from Denver to Newark, James' bag showed up on the conveyor belt first. No doubt it must have been put on the plane last, because James had just barely made the flight and he considered it a miracle that his bag had made it too.

He was tired from the long trip, the long week at the convention and the status of his marriage. In his world of neat formulas and chemical reactions, he had never known that unsettled emotions could be more draining than a fourteen-hour workday on a scientific project.

At this hour of the night, the plane had landed at 1:00 A.M. after a one-hour delay, he didn't have to wait long for a cab. There were only four people in front of him at the taxi stand.

James' driver was heavy, his gray hair bundled in a ponytail, and his glasses were so thick that James wondered if this guy could make out a procession of white elephants crossing the road, let alone the tail lights of another car.

Inside the cab James had to bang the door twice to get it shut and then pushed his briefcase onto the seat beside him.

"I'm going to Teterboro Airport, please."

The cabby pulled out into the traffic and barely missed a passing station wagon. He looked back at James over his shoulder, driving by pure instinct.

"Are ya gonna take another flight from Teterboro?"

"No, I was supposed to come in to Teterboro on a private jet, but my plans were changed and I wound up taking a commercial flight instead. I have to go to Teterboro to pick up my car." James kept looking behind him, hoping the man at the wheel would take the hint and watch where he was going.

"Ya know, I nevah been on a plane in my life. I'm scared-a dose tings. My wife always wants ta fly someplace, but I ain't about ta get on a plane at my age. I figure it's a lot safer on the ground."

He glanced back at James again and pulled the wheel to the right, taking the fork towards the New Jersey Turnpike at the last moment. James realized that he was holding his breath.

The cabby continued. "Now, ya take that plane crash tonight. That's exactly what I mean. They don't make them planes safe enough. I hear they cut a lotta corners when they build 'em. A buddy o'mine worked in a plane plant a long time ago, an' he tol' me they was always cuttin'corners."

He looked in the mirror to get James' reaction as he cut off another car and barreled into the toll-booth at the turnpike entrance.

James asked, "Was there a plane crash tonight? I didn't know that. Where was it?"

"Yeah, the guys was talkin' about it while we was waitin' in line at the airport. One of them private jets crashed in the lake. I think it was Ohio. Lake Erie, they said it was. Man, I know I ain't ever gettin' on a plane."

He darted across five lanes, on the tail of a speeding semi, while craning his neck to look at James. "Hey, I think that plane was headed to Teterboro too. Ain't that a coincidence?"

James stiffened in his seat. "Do you know where the plane was coming from?"

They were speeding down the long incline of the turnpike overpass. James was vaguely aware of the lights of the Manhattan skyline to this right.

"Yeah, it was someplace out West. Let's see, was it Denver? Yeah, that's it. Harry said it was Denver. He's got a brother livin' out there. Says it's cold as hell in the winter. Man, I wouldn't wanna live there. I get enough winter right here. Drivin' in snow is a pain in the ass, if ya know what I mean. So I don't miss it, ya know?"

James felt moisture forming on his forehead. He thought, *Tom, what the hell did you know that I didn't? If the plane was defective, why did you fly it? I could be dead too. My god, I could be dead!*

The realization paralyzed his mind and his body. The outline of Giants Stadium came into view farther north.

"Man, I'd hate ta be in a plane like that one t'night. If I saw the water comin' up at me, I'd have a heart attack before we hit. Nope, I ain't never gettin' on a plane. Even if ya put a gun ta my head."

The cab left the turnpike at exit 16. James no longer noticed when they rounded the curve to Route 3 West much faster than they should, or that he had to fight to stay upright in his seat. *I could be dead!*

His thoughts went back to his dinner conversation with Randolph Harte about Tom, and to Tom's insistence earlier today on flying the plane back alone.

James knew that his voice would tremble, but he could no longer contain his thoughts.

"*Jesus Almighty!* I think the plane that crashed was the one I was going to take. I was supposed to come home from Denver on our company jet. The pilot said he was concerned about a minor problem in the electrical system and told us he was going to fly back by himself. So I had to re-book on a commercial flight at the last minute."

They were on Route 17 now, heading north. Teterboro Airport was just a few minutes away. James had sounded so anguished that the cabby was quiet for the first time since leaving Newark. He felt intimidated by James' account and didn't know what to say. He drove up the exit ramp much more slowly and turned left into the parking lot at Teterboro Airport.

Finally alone with his bag and his briefcase on this windy, starless night, James fumbled for his car keys. Under normal circumstances he might have gone for a five-minute walk to stretch his legs, but it was late, the wind was blowing too hard and shock had overtaken his fatigue.

I could be dead!

Inside his car, he turned on WABC and listened to a brief recitation of the crash. He felt his whole being fall apart at the thought of what had happened, and worse, what could have happened to him. He had to force himself to re-assemble his separate parts into one human being again, a new human being, terrified and thankful to be alive.

Mr. Harte had told him Friday night, over Steak Diane, that he was arranging a surprise party in New York in three weeks to celebrate Tom's tenth anniversary as the corporate pilot. Tom had been an exemplary employee, and the company was going to show him how much he was valued. He wanted James and Isabella to attend, along with management personnel and their families. Besides, Mr. Harte had added, he had never met the man Tom lived with, some kind of piano player, he'd heard…

That night at the hotel in Denver, with ten people sitting around the table, the conversation soon turned to the highlights of the convention. James' private thoughts went back to his lingering confusion about Isabella, the issue of marital infidelity and the distracting cleavage of the conference coordinator sitting to his left. The subject of Tom's surprise party quickly drifted to the back of his mind, unfinished, like the steak Diane that he didn't care for anymore.

"Aren't you hungry tonight?" Athena, the conference-coordinator was asking him with a dimpled smile.

James tried to focus his eyes above her cleavage.

"No, I guess I'm not."

A little later he thought that Athena was really a cute little thing with her lively dark eyes, quick mind and cherry colored lips. It turned out they shared the same home town, St. Louis, and it was nice to talk about places they both knew.

An hour later they sat on high stools at the bar and Athena sipped on the straw of her second cocktail while rolling her eyes at James. For the first time James felt able to let go of the tension that had drained his energy all week long, but maybe it was only due to the bourbon re-fills in his glass. They chatted about Technicon, St. Louis, and James' designer suede jacket. For a moment, when Athena reached and brushed her fingers against James' lips, his forty-four-year-old heart jumped as if electrified. He didn't dare to return the gesture. It might trigger the unstoppable. There was a silence in which both digested the awareness of the chemistry between them.

James had never before felt so confused and torn. Athena's dark eyes and dimpled smile were all willingness and invitation. *Should he... or shouldn't he?* It was one of those difficult moments when the scales of virtue versus sin trembled at a 49 versus 51 percent balance. For him, it had almost came down to flipping a coin.

The next morning James was relieved to find himself alone in his bed, his room. He had slept like a stone and his thoughts turned to the night before. Now, with an (almost) clear head, and somewhat conscious-stricken, he blessed his narrow escape from temptation. For him, Athena meant unfinished business and he intended to leave it that way. They were employees of the same company and he wanted to avoid further complications at all cost.

In the clear light of the morning he refused to admit that it was really his deep fatigue which had ultimately balanced the scales in favor of virtue versus sin. In his mind, however, his willpower, his power to make a choice, and his sense of right and wrong had served him well again, as so often before. He was just glad the week was over and he got up to shower, shave and pack.

And now, sitting behind the wheel of his car, his recollection of earlier today at the hotel took on an alarming meaning. James and Tom had found themselves in the same elevator going down to the lobby with their luggage, all set to leave. Tom was usually open and friendly, but today he seemed withdrawn. James had made a crack about the conference coordinator's inefficiency. This little woman, with her dynamic ideas and her low-cut blouses, had not managed to have the hundred and fifty give-aways for the convention participants delivered on time. While he was talking, James noticed the unusual dark rings under Tom's eyes. The pilot apparently couldn't care less about sweatshirts or pens with the corporate logo printed on them.

This was the moment when Tom suddenly insisted on flying back alone because of some "minor defect" in the plane's electrical system.

James' first reaction was one of frustration. Dammit, what an inconvenience it was to have to change to a commercial flight on such short notice. On a commercial plane he couldn't work as efficiently and would get home hours later than originally scheduled. He didn't need anything added to the stressed state of his nerves. There were the pressing evaluation of the meetings that he had to finish, his conflict with Isabella, and the hardest of all, facing the test of his own values.

And now this.

James drove south on Route 17. He was automatically headed home, but was that where he really wanted to go? His hands were clenched around the wheel, and he occasionally took his eyes off the road to check the time. It was one thirty-five. In another fifteen minutes he would be home.

I could be dead!

He wondered if Isabella was waiting up for him or if she had heard about the accident and was worrying herself to pieces. Now he regretted that he hadn't called her all week, but he had been too devastated by her affair with Orson.

When he had first found out about their relationship, his fury had fueled his fantasies. They had run the gamut from hiring someone to plant a bomb under Orson's podium in Carnegie Hall to sending a box of poisoned brownies to his home.

And what about Isabella? His desire to wring her neck had grown into dangerous proportions. Should he pardon or poison her? Does infidelity justify murder? He realized it made sense in the novels of the nineteenth century, but no longer in our times. But then as now, betrayal triggered excruciating anger and disappointment, and he had to decide whether to let go of the pain or the person who inflicted it.

In the first stage of anger and hurt, he had felt his enormous love for her draining out of his body, his mind, his soul, leaving him so desperately empty, empty with pain, empty with a life that wasn't worth living. And yet to his surprise, his hurt was counterbalanced by a deep longing for her, a longing that bit like acid into his soul.

James sighed. He slowed down, then accelerated again, and as he gazed ahead through the night, the car seemed to eat the road. But no matter how his thoughts roamed in confusing circles, the same images kept returning.

I could be dead!

What should he do with Isabella? Love her or leave her? He thought of her soft body with its smooth skin, her delicate breasts and her secret warm places. He thought of her dreamy blue eyes with the look that bespoke a separate world within her, a world whose threshold he had never crossed, nor had he ever tried to share those dreams behind her eyes. There was a part of her that he had never understood. Did anyone? Did Orson?

Imagining her womanhood explored and shared by another man, imagining her thinking forbidden thoughts, thoughts that she withheld from him, imagining her tasting forbidden pleasures other than the ones he was able to give her, stabbed at his heart like a hot knife. Would he ever be able to free himself from these haunting images? By experiencing his pain in the form of a knife he had an awesome revelation: He could let the knife cut him or serve him, depending on how he grasped it...by the blade or by the handle.

Suddenly, despite all the evidence, James still found it hard to picture himself as the defeated husband in the triangle of a dark romance. Wasn't he, the outsider, the one who was least involved, the one who had all the power? He had the power of choice, the power of madness or mercy. Only he wasn't yet sure how to use it.

It was a matter of his ego versus his love, a decision between love and pride. Was the airplane crash an omen? Was love too precious to be thrown away on revenge?

I could be dead!

Witnessing the infidelities of his father, James had learned early to suppress any pleasures that threatened the carefully established order of his life. Whenever he had toyed with the idea of pursuing another woman, he had clung to his promise to Isabella like a flag, an emblem of righteousness, even if at times the flag seemed rigid and heavy, as it had felt last night. Why had it never occurred to him that there could also be a moment when the same flag might become too heavy for Isabella?

He turned onto the ramp to Route 3 and rummaged in the glove compartment for a tissue. Reminding himself to keep his eyes on the road, his thoughts flashed to a future without Isabella. A month ahead. A year ahead. Ten years. Twenty.

Without Isabella? *Dammit*, he thought, why should he stay with a woman who had made him so miserable?

Without Isabella, he would never be hurt again. For the next twenty years he would try to forget her, perhaps in the arms of the Athenas, Carols or Kathryns of this world, whose bodies he would use as a pretense for the one that counted. Life without Isabella might be amusing or boring, but he knew that he would find no rest in it, because they had rested in each other.

He would wear armor to protect himself against all the gentle approaches of other women and he would have limitless time to feel sorry for himself. But one day he might regret that he had not put his hurt behind him when it still could have made a difference.

James pictured Isabella living alone. Who would do all the things for her that she couldn't do? Replace the screen doors in the spring, change the filters of the air-conditioner, remove a spider from the wall... or salvage her burning oven-glove at Thanksgiving?

His emotions see-sawed.

But how could he avoid having his hurt turn into scars that ulcerated his heart? It was easy, in theory, to speak of liberal ideas, generosity of the heart and forgiveness, but in reality infidelity meant agony. He had never before cared enough for a woman to learn how to forgive. *Love is as love does.*

How had Orson managed to seduce her, his wife, his Isabella, his love? Or maybe she wasn't as sweet and demure as he believed her to be? Perhaps his perception of her was unrealistic. Maybe she was much more independent, more eager for excitement than her serene shell of routine and reason made her seem.

James thought, *Orson, that miserable bastard. I will not grant him the power to pollute the most beautiful thing between my wife and me. Maybe he succeeded in intruding in our marriage, but our marriage is still ours alone.*

In truth, Isabella hadn't chosen Orson over him, she had made room for a lover along with her husband. Now it was in his hands to destroy or rebuild the hand-made treasure of their marriage, so rich in its texture and trust.

Hadn't he always told Isabella that a crisis occurred in life so we could find a way to overcome it? It might hurt, but we couldn't avoid the reality of having to deal with it. Hadn't he told her during the months of his job-hunting that the stage of life kept turning and you had to turn along with it? No one could jump off the platform except cowards.

Was this *his* test, *his* challenge?

James recalled the nineteenth century heroines of the novels he had read. People like Anna Karenina and Madame Bovary always died as a result of their conflicts, enabling the author to conveniently bring the story to a seemingly judicious end. But, unlike fiction, life had to continue, challenging us to define our priorities, to compromise, to forgive and to move on. *Forgiveness is an act of will and not emotion.*

Deep down, James knew that every pain contained a lesson. What was his lesson? Forgiveness? Willpower? The power to make a choice?

James left Route 3 and turned onto Valley Road. The last commuter bus from Manhattan was in the distance ahead of him. He didn't realize that they ran this late.

A few more blocks and he would be home. He rolled down the window. The fragrance of the lilacs came to him through the spring night, and he realized that in the middle of each night a new morning was beginning.

The bus in front of him pulled over and stopped. A single passenger got off and the bus drove on. The man in tails standing somewhat lost at the curb looked alarmingly familiar.

James was shocked. *Am I seeing things? It's Orson Mahler, the very man who caused me all this misery. Look at the bastard!*

The feelings of pain exploded again. How the devil could Isabella lose her head over an unimpressive man like him?

James slowed down, but his thoughts shot through him with the speed of light. There was still enough time to speed up again, run him over and let the bastard die in the street.

James grimaced. *Ah, sweet revenge!* The idea bore irresistible appeal. But what was Orson doing out here, anyway? Determining the reason for his nocturnal visit might be wiser than harboring thoughts of homicide. There had been enough tragedy tonight. Tom's death shouldn't necessarily be followed by Orson's murder. Why not ask him what the hell he was doing here? James shook his head and stopped the car.

Obviously, the story was a long way from over.

92

Upstairs, before the bathroom mirror, I wiped the tear-smudged mascara from under my eyes, though I couldn't recall having cried. This still didn't seem real, because everything after James' and Orson's arrival had happened in a trance-like flow and nobody yet knew how it would all end. The feel of cold water on my face wasn't strong enough evidence that I wasn't merely dreaming.

How could ecstasy and terror mix so qualmlessly, burning every cell of my being? The moment had come when I had to confront the hurt I had inflicted on James. I had broken his heart and wondered if after this night of chaos and catharsis there was hope for the recovery of our marriage.

I scanned my nail polish bottles on the shelf, feeling the absurd urge to paint my nails, as if watching them turn red could switch my mind from trance to truth. While fantasizing over *volcano red* and *frosty pink* I recalled the bright vision of James' car entering the garage, a brightness lasting only for a moment, but long enough to light the darkness of a lifetime. How long had I clung to James, afraid he might disappear the moment I let go of him? How long had I stared at Orson? The three of us had looked at each other, sharing the silent embarrassment of actors with too many lines but no cues to begin them. When the automatic timer switched off the garage lights, we were forced to go inside.

With a grand, flowing gesture James motioned to the stairs.

"After you, maestro. Make yourself at home. I believe you know your way around."

James' smile bespoke controlled pride and repressed sarcasm, and I feared the latter might erupt in fury.

We went upstairs, and each of us must have experienced this awkward moment as differently as the way we looked: Orson in his starched shirt and tails, James in a polo shirt and suede jacket and I in my juice-stained velvet dress and stockinged feet. The one thing we had in common was that we were clueless. But once at the kitchen table, our awkwardness gave way to an unexpected sense of camaraderie, the kind that develops between people in a crisis, where the demands of the present supersede the problems of the past.

I seemed to be the only one who didn't understand what was going on and, like a blind person, repeatedly touched James' sleeve. Seeing him was not enough to believe he was there.

"James," my voice was agitated, "did you know that a Cessna Citation went down over Lake Erie? My god, I thought you were dead..." and looking from James to Orson, "And *how* did you two end up in the car together?"

James leaned back in his chair. To my amazement, he appeared inconceivably relaxed and in control.

"Go ahead, Orson. Tell Isabella your part of the story."

Orson put his elbows on the table and folded his fingers into a tent. He looked at me intently.

"Isabella, I heard the news in the taxi on my way home after the concert. From the description, I concluded that the plane was the one James was on. I was deeply shocked by the thought of what you must be going through. So I decided to come out to New Jersey to be with you, to help you through this horrible experience."

"But how did you end up on the bus?"

"When I told the cab driver after the concert not to go to my apartment and turn around and take the Lincoln Tunnel, he said that his shift ended after this trip and he wanted to go home to the Bronx. I offered him a hundred dollars extra, but he said he didn't know his way around New Jersey and was afraid of getting lost. I insisted it was an emergency, but he would take me no farther than the Port Authority. There was no other taxi that would take me to New Jersey at that time of the night, but someone helped me to find the gate for the last bus. Believe me, my thoughts were with you the whole time. I wondered if the police had already contacted you or if anyone was with you. Anyway, when I got off the bus at Valley Road, there was James in his car."

Orson caught his breath and looked at James.

"Honestly, *that* was the most surprising moment of my life."

And mine too, I thought, assessing my reflection in the bathroom mirror, while applying a trace of lipstick.

When James explained why he had been on a commercial flight, it seemed the most precious gift of fate, but I still couldn't be sure of *his* most precious gift, his choice of love over pride. Although James had not yet shown any negative emotion, he might still reserve his revenge of rejecting me.

At the kitchen table, at long last, the three of us had gotten through sorting out the facts. Orson had had no idea, that Tom Davis, the HIV-positive-infected lover of his son Matthew, was the same man as James' pilot. And James had no idea that the young pianist he had once met at a chorus rehearsal was Orson's son, who lived together with the pilot whom he knew as Tom Davis. And now Tom had carried out his threat of suicide.

Would there be any more surprises before the night was over?

Through the open bathroom door I could hear the voices of the two men downstairs. They sounded loud and heated, and I wondered what had snow-balled the debate. My knees shook, and I held on to the banister on my way down, fearing that they had begun to argue. *The* dreaded argument.

What I saw downstairs was a picture of cozy domesticity of two men sitting at the kitchen table. Orson had taken off his tails and James his suede jacket. They sat facing each other, their facial expressions alert and tense.

I stopped halfway in the door and heard James' laughter. His joviality sounded unreal and strangely out of place. But then, he had just escaped death. Life had been given to him all over again, and it was natural for him to feel uninhibited and alive.

Orson's voice held a hint of defiance. "Well, if conducting hadn't been my calling, it would have been chemistry, but now I wouldn't want to trade my podium for your pollution..."

At my entrance, they both stared at my stockinged feet.

James turned to Orson. "What the dickens makes you think that music is so superior? After all, science is the driving force behind the advancement of civilization. The ability to perform research is what sets man apart from the monkey."

"Yes," Orson mused, "that, and the use of underwear."

Troubled by the undercurrents of this debate I decided not to sit down with them, but leaned against the kitchen counter, watching from a safe distance.

James grinned provocatively. "If you ask me, music could be done away with, because it's science that's responsible for the standard of living we enjoy today. If it weren't for scientific innovation your orchestra would still be playing stone violins and we'd be watching soap operas on kerosene television sets."

Orson shook his head and laughed. "James, you shouldn't be overly proud of a generation whose major accomplishment is the production of polystyrene and carbon monoxide."

"Aha," James leaned forward, "but the same materials you attack are used to make records and compact discs. Don't you owe your world-wide fame to the sale of records?"

Orson grinned. "If you're interested in my records, they're available at the Manhattan District courthouse."

James made a face. "I'm sure there'd be enough evidence to lock you away. The world would do just fine without your music."

From my observation post across the kitchen, I wondered how much longer this war of the ridiculous could last.

Orson grinned, "James, I'm afraid you haven't got the slightest sense of what music can do for the fulfillment of the human soul."

James leaned back and ran his hand through his definitely too-long hair. "But did you know that I tried playing the violin when I was a kid?"

"You probably thought you had to blow into it for the first six months, didn't you?"

James cleared his throat. "I admit I detested it. But my neighbors liked it so much that they broke my windows so they could hear better."

Orson began clapping, but the applause was mocking.

James' voice rose. "At least I tried making music myself. I guess if you can't do that, you have to settle for conducting."

"Oh, oh, I detect another insult coming." Orson tried to look stern but couldn't suppress a chuckle.

James leveled. "How difficult can it be? It seems to me that anyone can be a conductor. My father was a conductor, for instance."

"You mean he worked on a streetcar?"

"No, he was struck by lightning." James kept a straight face.

It occurred to me that a hundred years ago they would have challenged each other to a duel. Thank God for modern times, where a contest of bad jokes could substitute for the use of bullets.

Orson said, sounding sober again, "I guess that's it. So much for conducting versus chemistry." He was ready to put the insanity to rest.

But James shot Orson a defiant glance. "Wait a minute, who says we're through yet? Orson, I bet you can't tell me what's warm and brown and sits on a piano bench?"

Orson rubbed his chin. "No. What?"

"Beethoven's last movement."

Abruptly, I cut in. "Stop it, James... it's *sickening...*"

But the two men laughed again.

Orson said, "I'm amazed, James, at how long you were able to keep your low taste in jokes a secret."

An aggressive glint appeared in James' eyes.

"I'm an advocate of free speech, but I'm warning you: I'm easily pissed off with anybody who says something I don't like..."

I intervened, "*Jaaaames...* That's enough!"

Orson forced a grotesque grin . "Isabella is right. I think it's time to cool off your genius for insults."

I said, "James, I agree with Orson, you're overheating."

James balled one of his fists and punched it into the palm of the other hand. His face ran red.

"Isabella, how dare you tell me that I'm overheating? *How dare you!* I think I can see now that you and Orson make perfect allies against me. It proves that practice makes great partners in betrayal."

Betrayal. I thought, *Now he wants to discuss betrayal.*

In a second of uncertain silence the tension tightened like a spring. This airless kitchen had become a microcosm of our intertwined lives, where we had gone beyond wise-cracking and had arrived at being truthful. *What next?*

I felt spurred into frantic action and stepped in front of them. I needed a miracle to break this awful spell. And I needed it *right now.* I had no idea where it could come from, maybe from an invisible hole in the ceiling from where it could drop on my head. Wasn't there *one* thing they had always agreed upon?

And then I simply said, "Would either of you care for a glass of root beer?"

Heavy with the potential of all possibilities, the room held its breath.

The eyes of the two men widened. "Root beer? *Yes!*" Their unison was perfect.

I didn't dare to move, not yet sure of what would follow.

Swiftly James got up and moved towards the refrigerator. "Isabella, you're a genius."

But the moment he opened the refrigerator door his face fell. "But where *is* the root beer?"

I stepped next to him to check for myself and suddenly remembered. "Uhhh, I'm afraid I didn't buy any this week. I'm sorry..."

Not ready to give up yet, James opened the door of the freezer. As we stood against the backdrop of frozen peas and pizza we came to fully look at each other for the first time. James' dark brown eyes held mine and it seemed that he was waiting for me to say something.

I looked at him pleadingly. Only the truth could safe me now.

"James, I'm sorry. I'm sorry for not having any root beer and I'm sorry for *everything.* How can I ask your forgiveness... for not being a perfect wife?"

With the door of the freezer still open, I felt an eerie chill hit my chest. The touch of his hand on my shoulder was the lightest imaginable and something was different in his eyes. There was a resolution, a firmness of intention, as if he had landed on a calm shore after a thunderous voyage. The deep creases running from the corners of his mouth broke into a soft smile, making me want to merge with it and stay there forever.

"Isabella, I didn't want you to be my wife because I expected you to be perfect. I can do without root beer, and I can do without a lot of things. What matters is that we're alive and that we believe that there is nothing you and I can't do..." With a quick, playful gesture he tapped my nose with a finger and closed the door of the freezer.

My heart threatened to explode. "And you really mean it?"

He caught my chin in his hand. "Don't you know I love you?"

And then suddenly he put his arms around me and kissed me, and I clung to the softness of his lips with a passion born of the fear of loss and loneliness. It was a long, blissful kiss, and I felt as if we had just crossed a minefield of blame without being blown apart. We had reached solid ground again.

The elaborate sound of Orson clearing his throat caused us to turn around, and we were somewhat surprised that he was still there.

The maestro began searching through his pockets.

"I have something with me that I meant to give back to you. In fact, I had it with me during the concert, but there was never an appropriate moment to return your diamond ring, Isabella."

"My ring!" I exclaimed, as Orson put it on the table.

My god, I thought, my forgotten ring, James' anniversary ring, fate's tool for revealing my betrayal.

Still spellbound, James and I let go of each other and sat down at the table again. I reached for the ring, but James stopped me before I could pick it up.

"Let me do this," he smiled with a certain solemnity.

"James... what are you doing?"

He took my hand against his lips and kissed each finger one by one. When he slipped the ring on my finger his voice had the tenderness of a caress.

"I'd marry you all over again, Isabella..."

Still holding my hand in his, the fire of the diamonds mirrored in his eyes.

He whispered, "For better or for worse, in sickness and in health..."

I said, "Til death do us part..."

James smiled. "Is that a promise?"

"It is..."

In this moment I knew that the old Isabella had shed her skin and the new woman was one of self-reliance and gratitude for the things life had so abundantly in store.

Orson nodded importantly. "And you even have a witness for the renewal of your vows."

James motioned with his head towards Orson. "What do you think, Isabella? Can we trust him to be our witness?"

I said, "I'm afraid he'll have to do. There's no one else around at three in the morning."

We laughed. It was a laughter of immense relief.

A new door in our marriage had opened and we stood before it, determined to pass through it hand in hand. How safe we felt in our home, our castle. It was safe and strong because the door had remained unlocked and the hallways open to visitors, welcoming the storms and the excitement of the change of seasons. Together we would see them come and go, and we would stay.

Orson was a visitor who had come and was about to leave.

Still here with us, though, he suggested, "After this impressive ceremony, I could still use something to drink."

"Ooops..." James got up instantly and took another look into the refrigerator.

He turned to Orson. "Sorry, maestro, no more root beer, but how about some orange juice for all of us."

Orson and I nodded eagerly and James began to fill the glasses.

In the meantime Orson had reached across the table and peeked into the empty brownie jar that I had left there earlier.

He mumbled, "... and no brownies either. Isabella, what kind of a hostess are you? No root beer, no brownies..."

I said, "Frankly, I ate them all before you came. They're still lying in my stomach like a rock." I shrugged apologetically. "But Orson, speaking of brownies reminds me of Paula. How is she? I heard through the chorus grapevine that she's looking forward to coming home."

Orson said, "Well, the chorus grapevine is wrong."

He faltered, at a loss for further words.

James put the glasses of orange-juice on the table and sat down again. "How's her therapy coming along?"

Orson gave a sigh. "Too well, I'm afraid. Paula told me that she's not coming back. She's leaving me. She has discovered a new side of herself, I guess you could call it a new fighting spirit. Her addiction to poker was a refuge from her life with me. She says she's tired of living in my shadow and wants to look for a house in Hartford, close to my two nieces. She's going to take up vegetarian cooking and pottery classes, and she insists on digging out those Mexican divorce papers which have been sitting in the safe deposit box for years..."

Blissfully unaware of the Mahlers' Mexican divorce episode, James said, "Wait a minute. What divorce papers?"

I said, "That's another story, James. Let's keep it for a rainy day..."

Orson managed a defeated smile. "Anyway, Paula says she's through with having to deal with concert agencies, the management of Carnegie Hall, Joan and my, uh... my insistence on considering myself a free man. She says living alone will not be easy, but it will be less difficult than living with me."

I took a deep breath. "Good for Paula. I'm glad she found the courage for a new beginning. Orson, you ruled her life and now she wants to be free."

Surprised by my support for Paula, Orson showed a trifle air of annoyance. But I no longer needed to please him and said, "In a funny, round-about way, Paula found her salvation through her poker vice. Without her therapy she'd still be stuck with you."

Orson moved uncomfortably. "I realize that Paula is right. Our marriage was nothing but a catalogue of guilt feelings."

James shook his head. "I had no idea..."

Orson's expression darkened and he seemed to look beyond and through us.

"Besides Paula, I realize I hurt a lot of people over the years..." He lowered his eyes. Neither James nor I knew what to say in an instant that might be considered a turning point in the great maestro's life.

When Orson looked up again, it was with an older, haunted face. "I suppose it's my turn to say to both of you *I'm sorry.*"

His gray-metallic eyes shot a glance at me and then came to rest on James. In the absence of words, the two men looked at each other in a moment of powerful communication. James' tiny nod was an indication of his huge decision to no longer dwell on Orson's regrets, even if they included an apology to him and me.

But maybe I misread my husband's thoughts, because an unaccustomed shadow crossed his face. He squirmed restlessly on his seat. Apparently there was still something on his mind that asked to be acknowledged.

James said, "Well… uh, as long as we're talking about Paula and poker, I've something to confess, too."

Orson and I looked at him in perplexed anticipation.

What now?

I felt an uncertain heartache threaten my re-found happiness.

James cleared his throat. "To tell the truth, my business dinners on Long Island on Friday nights weren't quite as frequent as I let on. In fact, they took place only once a month."

I asked, "And?" sensing the seeds of shock taking root within me.

"Well," James continued, "on the other Friday nights I got together with some poker buddies at a West side apartment and we had a heck of a time playing some hands."

After a long moment of silence I swallowed hard and realized it was my turn to say something, anything…

"That's why sometimes your clothes smelled of smoke and sometimes not."

James made a funny little nod with his head.

"There you go."

The muscles in my chest tightened, but then relaxed in the absence of a greater anguish and I simply said, "James, it's okay…it's all okay." I was glad to forgive and grateful that he was granting me the same in return.

With a sweet and tired smile James took my hand and squeezed it in a gesture of relief.

I thought, *It's going to be okay. We might talk about it at a later time, or we might not. It's all okay.*

The kitchen clock over the sink showed three-thirty-five. At this hour of the night, what else could possibly be in store?

Pressed by curiosity, I asked Orson, "Has Beverly already moved into Paula's bedroom?"

Orson's birthmark twitched and he looked embarrassed.

"*No, no!* I turned her down. I don't want her living with me in my apartment. But how did you know?"

"Beverly told me that she left her husband and wanted to move in with you."

"Well, that's not going to happen." Orson finally took off his white bow-tie and loosened his collar.

He continued, "I'm going to visit Matthew in the hospital tomorrow, uh... it's more like today. Physically, he seems to be fine and he's supposed to be released on Monday. I'll finally tell him that I'm his father and ask him to come and live with me. If he agrees, he can become my artistic assistant and still continue with his piano coaching jobs."

James asked, "Do you think Matthew knows about the plane crash?"

Orson shrugged, "He might not know until later in the day. I want to be there when the news reaches him. Living with Matthew would be quite different. It would be a challenge for both of us." He tried a smile. "But I'll miss Paula's home-baked brownies…"

I said, "No doubt Beverly will gladly organize a baking-contest among the chorus members for you. In the meantime, why not try eating cream-puffs?"

This caused an unexpected, diminutive smile between the two men.

On cue, James said, "Speaking of food, I don't know about you folks but I'm starving."

Propelled by the call of his empty stomach he got up and took a pizza from the freezer. Standing with his back to the table he searched for scissors in a drawer, removed the pizza from the carton and read the instructions. Orson and I looked at each other, like strangers thrown together in a storm. We accepted our discomfort as a condition for survival, exchanging smiles and feeling our recollections already receding into the past.

I looked at Orson with an objective heart. What kind of story had we created? Was ours a love-story? Yes, I thought, it was. We had created our own music.

The music of an unequal love.

His velvet voice whispered almost inaudibly, "Isabella..."

And suddenly I perceived him as I had in the beginning. There was the old familiar sparkle in his gray-metallic eyes, their lure, their invitation. I thought, *Don't look at me like that, Orson. Not anymore.* I wanted to avert my eyes from his, but they held me with their gentle power of suggestion, saying, *Time has been running out so fast. Hadn't we just begun? You know, Isabella, in music "da capo" means to start all over... I always thought it a wonderful idea to take everything right from the beginning...*

I shot him a determined glance. *No, Orson, I'm not going to start all over with you. Things only happen once.*

Meanwhile the microwave was buzzing and James looked through the window to check on the status of the cheese melting on the pizza.

Then suddenly, at the edge of past and future, I changed my mind. Maybe our story was worth resuming after all, but not in a physical sense. Perhaps this was the story Julia had been looking for to write her best-seller. My own writing skills wouldn't do it justice, but at least I would be able to help her with the first sentence.

I caught my first glimpse of Orson Mahler when he was not wearing his dark glasses.

A Musical and Culinary Glossary

This glossary is a tool to better understand some of the musical and culinary language used in this book and to enhance your reading pleasure. To all newcomers to classical music, please don't feel intimidated by the musical vocabulary. It's just a way of distinguishing certain musical meanings – like a cookbook – when you are directed to steam, broil or sauté your vegetables.

Bon appétit – happy reading and "listening."

Adagio	*Italian.* Indication for a movement of any composition to be played at a slow measured tempo.
Agnus Dei	*Latin.* Lamb of God. Section of the mass. Set to music by many different composers.
Allegro	*Italian.* Indication for a movement to be played fast, or, according to its meaning, "happily."
Alto	Lowest female singing voice.
Andante	*Italian.* Indication for a movement to be played at a slow, "walking" tempo.

Apfelstrudel — *Austrian/German.* Puff pastry filled with cooked apple slices.

Aria — *Italian.* A piece written for solo voice, usually composed for an opera or oratorio (with orchestra) – or as a song, accompanied by piano.

Arpeggio — *Italian.* The notes of a chord played in succession.

Bar — A musical measure, a group of beats.

Bass — The lowest male singing part.

Beschamelkartoffeln — *Austrian dish.* Similar to scalloped potatoes.

Cadence — A harmonic closing progression for a section or a composition.

Cadenza — *Italian.* A solo passage in a concerto, played by the soloist, unaccompanied by the orchestra. This is often used to show off the skill and virtuosity of a violinist, pianist, cellist, etc..

Carnegie Hall — New York's most famous and traditional concert hall, seats approx. 3,000. It first opened in May 1891, and in 1986 underwent a seven-month renovation – just as described in this book.

Chamber Music — Music written for small ensembles, where each musical voice (or part) is played by one instrument only.

	Examples: String quartet or piano quintet.
Chord	Three or more notes played together to create a harmonious sound.
Coda	The final part of an instrumental piece.
Con amore	*Italian.* Indication to sing or play "with love."
Concerto	*Italian.* A multi-movement composition for orchestra and soloist (i.e. piano, violin, cello, harpsichord, oboe). There are also double and triple concertos, i.e. Mozart's "Concerto for flute and harp."
Crescendo	*Italian.* Musical indication to play gradually louder.
Da Capo	*Italian.* ("from the head") To play or sing from the beginning again.
Diminuendo	*Italian.* A musical indication to play gradually softer.
Dies Irae	*Latin.* Day of Wrath. A section of the Requiem Mass.
Dirndl	Rustic Austrian/Bavarian dress, often worn with an apron.
Dissonance	One or more notes that are not in harmony. The listener may experience dissonances (which are part of all major compositions) as

	"wrong," "disturbing," or even "exciting."
Dynamics	The gradations and shades of volume of the music (becoming softer or louder).
Fermata	*Italian.* A pause mark.
Fortissimo	*Italian.* An indication to play loudly and forcefully.
Fugue	A composition comparable to a canon, i.e. "Three blind mice." A short melody or a theme is imitated and enters repeatedly.
Genre	A category of music, i.e. symphony, concerto, chamber music, opera, oratorio or song.
Germknödel	*Austrian dish.* A sweet dumpling with a jam (fruit) filling, served as dessert.
Glissando	*Italian.* A musical "trick" to slide up or down the keys on a piano with a finger, or on a violin sliding along a string.
Gulasch	*Austrian/Hungarian dish.* Beef cubes are first sautéed in oil, then simmered in a sauce with onions, peppers and different spices.
Key	A succession of seven notes in a major or minor key, also called "scale," and marked on the pages of the sheet

	music as the "key signature," a pattern of flats or sharps.
Lacrimosa	*Latin*. Lamentation. Section of a Requiem. Set to music by various composers.
Legato	*Italian*. Musical indication to play broadly and smoothly, connecting the notes.
Leitmotif	A recognizable, short melody line or phrase that recurs throughout a composition in the same or varied form. The "motif" often represents an idea (love, danger), a person (the beloved), or an object (a sword).
Libera me	*Latin*. Deliver me. Section of a Mass or Requiem.
Libretto	*Italian*. Text of an opera or an oratorio.
Lincoln Center	New York's Center for the Performing Arts, consisting of The Metropolitan Opera, City Opera, Avery Fisher Hall (home of the New York Philharmonic), and Alice Tully Hall.
Linzer Torte	*Austrian Dish*. A dark, sweet cake named after the Austrian town of Linz. Served as dessert.
Major	The happier, brighter of the two modes (keys) of a composition, written in a "major scale," in a succession of whole and half steps.

ma non troppo — *Italian.* Musical indication for: not too much.

Mass — Traditional liturgical service of the Roman Catholic Church, always consisting of the same sections (also called the "Ordinary"): *Kyrie, Gloria, Credo, Sanctus, Agnus Dei.*

Over the centuries many composers have written masses, following the sequence of the "ordinary" sections and using their Latin text. Yet the results are vastly different, since each composer (among them Bach, Haydn, Mozart, Beethoven, Schubert) expressed their own musical style and vision through the "matrix" of the mass.

For the composer, writing a mass also increased the possibility of the music actually being performed (in a church).

Melody — A succession of notes organized into a musical line. In Western music the "melody" is one of the three basic components of music – the other two being "harmony" and "rhythm."

Minor — The darker or more "mysterious-sounding" of the two modes or keys (see: major) of a composition.

Minuet	A graceful, elegant three-beat dance which originated in the sixteenth century from popular folk songs.
Missa Solemnis	*Latin.* Solemn Mass (see: Oratorio). Large-scale work for orchestra, chorus and soloists, composed by Ludwig van Beethoven between 1818 and 1823. It is considered Beethoven's greatest composition.
Moderato	*Italian.* Indication to use a moderate tempo.
Movement	A musical component or part of a sonata, symphony, orchestral suite, mass, oratorio or chamber music. It is a smaller composition within the composition, like an act within a play.
Mozartkugeln	*Austrian.* Ball-shaped chocolates, filled with green almond paste, named after Wolfgang Amadeus Mozart.
Musikverein	Concert Hall in Vienna, Austria
Oratorio	A large and usually long work for chorus, soloists and orchestra. It is performed on stage or in a church, but without scenery. It consists of an overture, choruses, arias and recitatives, often based on sacred texts. Masses, Requiems and Passions fall under the musical genre (or category)

	of an Oratorio. Some of the greatest oratorios ever written include: *Handel's Messiah, Bach's Mass in B-minor, the Mozart Requiem, the Verdi Requiem, the Brahms Requiem and the Requiem Mass by Fauré.*
Overtones	Sounds generated by sympathetic vibrations with other fundamental sounds.
Overture	Opening movement for a longer work (i.e. opera, oratorio or orchestral suite.)
Piano	*Italian.* Musical indication to play softly.
Polyrhythm	Two different rhythmic patterns going on simultaneously.
Requiem	A mass for the dead (see Oratorio). The most well-known and beloved Requiem is probably the *Mozart Requiem.* Mozart died before he could finish it and it was completed by one of his students, Süssmayr.
Rhythm	Long and short notes form specific rhythmic figures of specific durations. Rhythm can also be considered the flow of the beat.
Rondo	A dance or section in which the first musical theme intermittently recurs. It is often used as the last movement of a concerto or a sonata.

Salva Me	*Latin.* Save me.
Salzburger Nockerln	*Austrian dish.* A soufflé of eggs and sugar, served as dessert.
Sanctus	*Latin.* Holy. Section of the Mass. Set to music by innumerable composers.
Score	A conductor's orchestral score is a large book, containing all the parts (or voices) of a composition, aligned vertically. Whereas the players in the orchestra only use the part for the instrument they are playing (i.e. violins, cellos, flutes, etc.), printed horizontally, the conductor sees the parts of all the instruments vertically at a glance. It is his responsibility to keep the players aligned and to "conduct" the different "parts" and "voices" in the appropriate tempo, beat and rhythm.
Sonata	*Italian.* A composition of several movements for one or more solo instruments, i.e. a "cello sonata," or a "sonata for piano and violin."
Soprano	Highest female singing voice.
Sotto voce	*Italian.* Indication to speak or play in a soft voice.
Staccato	*Italian.* Musical indication to play notes very short and separated from each other.

Stagebill	Name of program publication for all performances at New York's Lincoln Center and Carnegie Hall.
Staff lines	The lines (five) on which music is written or printed.
String(s)	String instruments produce sounds by vibrations of thin strands of wire or gut, i.e. violin, cello, bass (by bowing), harp, guitar (by plucking), piano (by hammering).
String Quartet	A chamber music ensemble consisting of two violins, viola and cello. The term also refers to a composition for four parts or players.
Subito piano	*Italian.* Indication to play suddenly softer.
Symphony	A multi-movement work for a large orchestra. The "classical" and "romantic" symphony typically has four movements, i.e. *Allegro Andante, Menuetto (or Allegretto), Rondo (or Finale).* In 20-century music a symphony might have any number of movements or might be in one movement only, i.e. *Sibelius' 7th*, or might be in any other form.
Tafelspitz	*Austrian dish.* Beef is cooked in a broth with added spices and veggies, served with horseradish sauce.

Tempo	The speed (pulse) in which the music is played, indicated by the terms for a single movement, such as, *Allegro (happy, fast), Andante (slow) or Moderato (moderately).*
Tenor	Highest male singing voice (except for a boy's castrato voice.)
Unison	Two or more voices singing a melody together in identical pitch (unless one or more octaves apart).
Voice	1.) A speaking or singing voice. 2.) In any ensemble, a "voice" may also be called a "part." This may refer to a human solo voice or a choral section (soprano, alto, tenor, bass), or to the "parts" of the different instruments.
Weihnachtsoratorium	*German.* Christmas Oratorio, written by Johann Sebastian Bach. Large work in six parts, for chorus, orchestra and soloists.
Wiener Walzer	*Austian/German.* Vienna Waltz.

To order copies of this book
and learn more about the creation of
The Music of an Unequal Love,
or to write your own review,
or obtain an autographed copy with a
personal dedication,
please visit:

www.gigistybr.com

Gigi is also a Certified Angel Therapy Practitioner®

She is available for 60-minute
intuitive counseling sessions
in person or over the phone.
For more information please visit her angelic website at:

www.angelreadingbygigi.com

Notes:

Notes:

Made in the USA
Charleston, SC
18 January 2011